PRIS
TOMORROW

Books by James P. Hogan

PRISONERS OF
TOMORROW

※ ※ ※

JAMES P. HOGAN

PRISONERS OF TOMORROW

This is a work of fiction. All the characters and events portrayed
in this book are fictional, and any resemblance to real people or incidents is
purely coincidental.

A Baen Books Original

Baen Publishing Enterprises
P.O. Box 1403
Riverdale, NY 10471
www.baen.com

ISBN: 978-1-4767-8065-8

Cover art by Kurt Miller

First Baen paperback printing, July 2015

Distributed by Simon & Schuster
1230 Avenue of the Americas
New York, NY 10020

Library of Congress Cataloging-in-Publication Data

Hogan, James P.
 Prisoners of tomorrow / by James P. Hogan.
    pages ; cm
 ISBN 978-1-4767-8065-8 (omni trade pb)
 I. Title.
 PR6058.O348P69 2015
 823'.914--dc23
                                    2015013073
Printed in the United States of America

10 9 8 7 6 5 4 3 2 1

❀ CONTENTS ❀

ENDGAME ENIGMA

Acknowledgments

❂   ❂   ❂

I would like to express my gratitude to the following people for their help and advice in writing this book:

Brent Warner of NASA's Goddard Space Center, Maryland, who spent many hours thinking about pendulums, gyroscopes, vortexes, and rotating geometries, and gallantly placed his sanity at risk by sharing for a while the weird kind of world that science-fiction writers inhabit. Jim Waligora of NASA's Johnson Space Center, Houston, for information on the physiology of low pressures and spacesuit design. Steve Fairchild of Moaning Cavern, Murphys, California, for thoughts on just about everything and his invaluable penchant for devil's advocacy. Lynx Crowe of Berkeley, California, for suggestions on security methods. David Robb of Applied Perception Technologies, Minneapolis, for lots of data on space colonies. Cheryl Robinson, who helped hatch Lewis and his companions from a pile of barren notes. Owen Lock of Ballantine Books, for sharing some of his immense knowledge of the world of military intelligence. Kathy Sobansky, for her assistance with Russian language translations. And Takumi Shibano, for his guidance in penetrating Oriental inscrutability.

And then there was Jackie, who doubled as electrician, plumber, handyman, auto mechanic, gardener, chauffeur, and carpenter, as well as being a mother to three small, rowdy boys—and never once complained about the hours a writer works. She made the book possible; they made it necessary.

Dedication

❧ ❧ ❧

*To EDWARD JOSEPH, my third son in a row, who,
after three daughters in a row, restored my faith in mathematics
by proving that the law of averages does work in the end,
provided one gives it long enough.*

◎ PREFACE ◎
TO BAEN BOOKS EDITION

The original Bantam "Spectra" hardcover edition of *Endgame Enigma* was published in August 1987. When I conceived and wrote the book, which would have been in 1985 through 1986, neither I nor very many others—if any—guessed that the Soviet empire, which had withstood through the best part of a century so many predictions of imminent demise, was indeed tottering into its final few years, and by 1991 would be in the process of becoming history.

The speed with which these events overtook the astonished world may be gauged from my own experience as a guest of the annual European science-fiction convention, which was held that year, 1991, in Volgograd (the former Stalingrad), in the USSR. A few days before I was due to leave on an Aeroflot flight from Dublin, an agitated travel agent called me to ask if I still wanted to make the trip.

"Well, of course I do," I replied, surprised. "Why shouldn't I?"

"Because of everything that's going on there?"

"How do you mean? What's going on?" I should explain that I haven't owned a TV for longer than I can remember, and seldom open a newspaper—and then usually just to do the "Crossaire" cryptic crossword in the *Irish Times*. I regularly have to call the phone operator to check what day it is, and I've gone a week past the summertime clock adjustment without being aware of it.

"There's a civil war going on," she told me, astounded. "Tanks in the streets, people getting shot."

"And the planes are still flying?"

"Well, yes. . . . I suppose so."

I was thrilled. It was happening—ordinary people actually standing up to one of the most brutal regimes of modern times. "Well, if they can face tanks, the least I can do is be there," I said. "Sure, I still want to go."

But so swift were the events that by the time I got there it was all over. When I checked in for the flight, the board behind the desk said DUBLIN-LENINGRAD-MOSCOW. By the time I returned, the flight announcement read MOSCOW-ST. PETERSBURG-DUBLIN. There were already pictures of the former Czar in windows and adorning souvenirs and gifts. There's something reassuring in looking at the march of history and noting how consistently it seems that the oppressors end up being buried by their intended victims. Nero's Rome has crumbled, but Christianity flourishes worldwide. The Nazis are gone, but the Jewish people prosper. And now Stalinism and the horrors of the gulag are no more, and Russia is again becoming a part of European culture.

So what's the point of reissuing a book set in circumstances that will never, now, come to pass? Well, for one thing, obviously, the story is still the same, and as the whole realm of science-fiction, fantasy, myth, and legend attests, the setting doesn't have to be factual or even plausible for a story to do its job and be enjoyable. But beyond that, this is a story involving political realities that remain constant beneath the superficial ebbs and flows of the particular power rivalries that happen to constitute the present, and which it pays to remain mindful of precisely because they are no longer reiterated in every other morning's headlines.

The prime reason for forming government has always been to protect individuals from the violence they inflict on each other when each is left to face the prospect of survival as a law unto himself. Today's democratic nation state—which appears, from the struggles witnessed in the twentieth century to be the most successful form of social organization to have emerged so far—seeks to achieve this through the establishment of one system of law before which all are judged equally, to which each individual forf the right to make and execute his own law privately. However such arbitration applies to affairs between governments, and that of war that was once the lot of tribal groups everywhere reemerges periodically as collisions between nations. The authority God is no longer compelling as a restraining influence—and was ver all that notably effective, anyway—and those of us raised the tradition of individualism and freedom are suspicious moves toward an international order with all its socialist derpinnings and ramifications.

What, then, will contain passions and excess on the global scale? I have no glib formula to offer. Some place the faith in reason (is there not a certain attendant irony in such a plse?), others in the spread of better understanding as modern comminications dissolve barriers of prejudice and misunderstanding, whisome have hope in the ability of technology and industry to eradice the differences in wealth that they believe are the causes of strife. B the question needs to be asked, especially in these comparatively tnquil times, for it can never be repeated too often that those who forget the past are doomed to repeat it.

As half a century of ferocity has shown, ideologies in conflict will stop at nothing. In *Endgame Enigma*, it is Lew McCain's grasp of human nature and the constancies of political reaty that enable him to see through deceptions that others would hav followed them to disaster. What deceptions? Well . . . that would be giving away too much. But as a gentle hint let's just say for now hat in keeping with any spy thriller that involves political intrigue and some out-at-the-edge technological ingenuity, nothing is quite what it seems.

James P. Hogan
Bray, County Wicklow
Ireland
April 1997

❀ PROLOGUE ❀

The Mig-55E fighter-bomber, code-named "Grouse" in Western military parlance, was rugged, easy to maintain, and equipped for a variety of ground-attack roles, making it popular for counterinsurgency operations among rulers of the Third World's teetering Marxist regimes. Western military intelligence was interested in it, too, because it carried the first production version of the Soviet OC-27/K target-designating and -tracking computer, which the countermeasures experts were anxious to learn more about.

Like most Soviet aircraft, ships, and ground units, the MIG carried a black box that could compute its position accurate to a few feet anywhere on the Earth's surface with respect to an electronic navigation grid laid down by Soviet satellites. What Pilot Officer Abel Mungabo didn't know when he took off on a training flight from Ziganda, one of the two Madagascar states into which the former Malagasy Republic had fragmented, was that aboard the Australian destroyer cruising fifty miles offshore was a group of professional mischiefmakers with some highly classified equipment, which in conjunction with transmissions from the USAF high-altitude bomber that just happened to be passing over at the time, was causing Mungabo's black box to come up with wrong numbers. He turned back after becoming hopelessly lost over the ocean, but missed the tip of Madagascar completely and ended up off the coast of the South African mainland. There he ran out of fuel and bailed out.

What happened after that was never cleared up officially. Mungabo swore upon his return that he saw the plane go down in the sea. The South Africans said he must have been mistaken: the plane crashed on the shore and exploded. They even produced pieces of twisted wreckage to prove it. But the Soviet engineers who arrived in Ziganda to examine the remains were suspicious. The damage, they said, was more consistent with demolition by explosives than with a crash. And it seemed strange that not one piece of the more sensitive electronics devices aboard the aircraft had been recovered. The South Africans shrugged and said that was the way it was, and the ensuing diplomatic accusations and denials continued for a while longer.

But by that time, specialists in several Western military laboratories were already acquiring some interesting new toys to occupy them. The OC-27/K target-designating and -tracking computer found its way to the US Air Force Systems Command's Cambridge Research Labs at Hanscom Field, near Bedford, Massachusetts.

◉ CHAPTER ONE ◉

Dr. Paula Bryce brushed a curl of blond hair from her forehead and studied the waveforms on one of the display screens surrounding her desk. She tapped a code into a touchpad, noted the changes in one of the pulse patterns and the numbers that appeared alongside it, and commanded a reconfiguration of the circuit diagram showing on another screen. "That's better," she said. "D-three has to be the synch. E-six is coupled capacitively to the second-stage gate."

On a bench a few feet away, the Russian computer had been stripped down into an assortment of frames and subassemblies that were now lying spread out amid tangles of interconnecting wires and test leads. Ed Sutton, another Air Force communications scientist, peered through a microscope at a detail of one of the boards and repositioned a miniature probe clipped to it. "That's it again with the input on both," he said. "Anything now?"

Paula looked at the waveforms again. "Aha!"

"Bingo?"

"It's triggering. . . . Threshold's about point two of a volt."

"So it is differential?"

"Come and look."

"But not for noise rejection?"

"Uh-uh. That wouldn't figure."

Sutton straightened up from the microscope and sat down on the stool behind him. He pivoted himself to look across in Paula's direction. "It's starting to look the way you guessed," he said. "Initialization for a smart missile with its own inertial reference, updating from the aircraft's grid-fix."

Paula nodded. "Air-to-ground fire-and-forget."

"That was a pretty good hunch you had."

"Not really. It's a modification of something I've seen before. This version would permit tighter evasive maneuvers while attacking." Paula shifted her gaze to a screen displaying text, and began updating her notes. As she tapped deftly at the pad, glancing intermittently at the display of the reconstructed circuit and the data alongside, she was aware of Sutton staring over the cubicle between them. Almost thirty, she was slimly built—bony almost—beneath her lab coat and jersey, with fair, wavy hair, which although cut to neck-length and battened down with a clip, broke free into unruly wisps wherever it got the chance. Her features were clear, but somewhat sharp with a prominent bone structure, and her nose a shade too large and her chin too jutting to qualify her as glamorous. Nevertheless, men found her candid, light-gray eyes and the pert set of her mouth attractive in a way that derived from her poise and the self-assurance that it radiated, rather than from looks. "Challenging," was how many of them said they found her. She didn't find that especially complimentary. If they meant formidable as an object of conquest, it wasn't exactly flattering, while if it referred to something ego-related in themselves that they saw her as potentially instrumental in resolving, well, that wasn't her mission in life or reason for existing. The real challenge was to recognize that the challenge was to avoid being placed in either of those categories. It was too subtle to be articulated, for the whole purpose of the game was to divine its rules, but the few who could pass—those were the really interesting ones.

"Good reason to celebrate, maybe," Sutton ventured after a while.

"Really?" Paula continued entering her notes. Typically, he was waiting for her to put the proposition. Just for once, why couldn't he simply say straight out what was on his mind?

He skidded off along the tangent. "Cher's away this week—gone to the Catskills. We've got relatives and a vacation lodge up there, you know. Good skiing area in winter. Ever get up that way?"

"No, I never did." Paula sighed inwardly with exasperation. The stupid thing was that Sutton wasn't too bad a guy. His being the man had nothing to do with her refusing to help him out, or with any hangup about who was supposed to make a first move to whom. It was simply that the matter seemed important to him, while it wasn't especially important to her. Therefore the game required him to do something about it. That was what the challenge was all about.

"Did you ever try skiing?" he asked. Before Paula could reply, a call-tone sounded from the flatscreen terminal on the desk. She touched a key to accept, and as she swung the unit toward her, a picture appeared of a pinkish, heavy-jawed face with crinkly yellow hair combed back from its forehead. It was Colonel Raymond, who headed the section. He was framed against a background that included part of a picture hanging in a conference room two floors up from the lab.

"Paula, I'm with some people here in G-eighteen. We've, ah, got something we'd like you in on. Can you get up here right away?"

"Sure thing. . . . Oh, will you want the latest on Squid?" "Squid" was the code word for the OC-27/K computer.

"No, it's nothing to do with that. But how's it going?"

"We're progressing."

"That's good." The screen blanked out.

Paula closed the log on the other screen, got up from her chair, and tidied together the papers she had been using. "I've updated the log for Charley and Bob when they get back from lunch," she called back from the door as she left. "And yes, skiing's okay."

Sutton shook his head and looked back at the disemboweled Soviet computer. He wasn't sure why he persisted in making a fool of himself from time to time like this. It made him uncomfortable, and he was always secretly relieved inside when she turned him down or the subject changed. But somehow he felt better for going through the motions of having tried. God alone knew what he'd do if she ever took him up on it.

❊   ❊   ❊

The picture showing on the large wallscreen facing one end of the conference table was a prototype habitat designed to test ideas and technologies for living in space. It housed over twelve thousand people, in an immense torus more than a mile in diameter. Six spokes—three thick, major ones alternating with three thinner ones—connected the torus to a central hub structure. Part of the image was shown in a cutaway to reveal miniature cityscapes and residential areas alternating with multilevel agricultural sectors and parks. At intervals around its exterior, the colony carried the Red Star emblem of the Soviet Union. The Soviets had named it *Valentina Tereshkova*—after the first woman to go into space, more than fifty years previously. They claimed that it symbolized the peaceful goals of their space program and would stand as a showpiece to the world of what a Marxist economic system could achieve. Completion of "Mermaid," as the structure was code-named by the Western intelligence community, was targeted for the following year, to coincide with the centenary celebration of the Russian Revolution.

Gerald Kehrn, from the staff of the assistant secretary of defense for international security, was more concerned about the colony's suspected hidden function, however. He was an intense, restless man with a bald head and a heavy black mustache, who radiated nervous energy and paced agitatedly below the screen as he spoke. "Then, about a year ago, an East German defector appeared in Austria, who claimed to have worked on construction of *Tereshkova* from 2013 to 2014. He was brought back to the States, and in the course of further interrogations described some of the hardware that he'd seen, and in some cases helped install."

Dr. Jonathan Watts, a civilian adviser with the decade-old US Space Force, who had come with Kehrn from the Pentagon, interjected for Paula's benefit, "Big-mother X-ray lasers. Nuclear-driven microwave pulses strong enough to melt metal. A giant accelerator track buried inside the main ring—what you'd use to feed batteries of matter-zappers." He tossed up his hands and shrugged. His face was constantly mobile, changing expression with each thought progression behind black, heavy-rimmed spectacles. "Other parts of the place seemed to be for launching ejectable modules, probably fission-pumped eggbuster lasers. And according to other reports, certain key parts of the structure are double-shelled and hardened against incoming beams."

"Yet nobody else has seen a hint of all this," Paula remarked. "Enough visitors have been through the place, haven't they?"

"Just on the standard tour," Colonel Raymond said from his seat opposite Watts. "They only see what they're allowed to see. The place is over three miles around, not counting the hub. There'd be enough room backstage to hide the kinds of things we're talking about."

Paula nodded and looked again at the image on the screen. Except for its inner surface—the "roof" facing the hub—the main torus was not visible directly; it moved inside a tire-like outer shield of sintered lunar rock which, to avoid needless structural loading, didn't rotate with the rest of the colony. The shield was to exclude cosmic rays. Supposedly. Or was that another part of the defensive hardening? The question had doubtless occurred to other people too, so she didn't bother raising it.

In the center of the group, informally chairing the proceedings, was a broad-framed, craggy-featured man with a dark chin, moody eyes, and gray, wiry, short-cropped hair. He was Bernard Foleda, deputy director of the Pentagon's Unified Defense Intelligence Agency, and had arranged the meeting. The UDIA was essentially an expanded version of the former Defense Intelligence Agency, now serving the intelligence needs of the Space Force in addition to those of the traditional services. He had said little since Paula's arrival, tending instead to sit back for most of the time, watching and listening impassively. At this point, however, he leaned forward to take charge of the proceedings again.

"Obviously this was something we had to check out." Foleda spoke in a low-pitched, throaty voice that carried without having to be raised. "We put a lot of people on it. To cut a long story short, we succeeded in recruiting one of the people who worked on *Tereshkova*—a Russian, who was code-named 'Magician.'"

Paula's eyebrows lifted. "As a source? You mean you actually got yourselves an inside man up there?"

Foleda nodded. "Luck played a part in it. He was someone we'd had connections with for a while. The details don't matter. Magician was an electrical maintenance supervisor, which meant he moved about a lot—exactly what we wanted. He worked there for almost six months. But as you can imagine, it wasn't the easiest place to extract information from. The snippets he did get out to us were tantalizing. He indicated that he'd collected a whole package together, but he couldn't get it down to us. The security checks on everybody who came back for leave or whatever were too strict. He wouldn't risk it. But what he said he had up there sounded like dynamite. We christened it the 'Tangerine' file."

"Dynamite," Jonathan Watts repeated, tossing up his hands again. "Weapons specs, pictures, firepowers, ranges, configuration data, parts lists, blueprints, test data, installation dates . . . the works."

Foleda resumed, "Then somebody had an idea." He stopped and then looked at Colonel Raymond. "It might be better if you explain the technicalities," he suggested.

Raymond turned his head toward Paula. "It involved the packet-header and checksum protocols used in the Soviet communications link down from Mermaid." Paula nodded. The terms related to data-communications networks.

In many ways, communications networks are like road systems: their purpose is to move traffic quickly from one place to another with minimum congestion. They therefore present similar problems to their designers. Speed is important, of course, and so is safety, which means essentially the same in communications as it does on highways: what arrives at a destination should bear as close a resemblance as possible to whatever left the departure point.

Also important in both fields is using system resources efficiently, which means avoiding situations in which some channels become choked while others are not being used at all. Thus, morning commuters seek out alternative routes for getting to work, which spreads traffic out over all the available roads, to come together at a common destination. A standard technique for sending large files of information from one computer to another through a communications network works the same way. The sending computer breaks the file up into data "packets," which follow different routes through the network to the destination, with different computers along the way deciding from moment to moment which way to route any given packet, depending on the conditions at the time.

To guard against errors due to interference, equipment faults, or other causes, the computer at the sending end uses the data content of a packet to compute a mathematical function known as a "checksum," which it sends along with the message. The receiving computer performs the same calculation on what should be the same data and compares its checksum with the one that has been sent. If they match, then the message is clear; or more precisely, the chances against it are astronomically remote.

Raymond went on, "We figured out a way to transmit Magician's Tangerine file down, using the Russians' own Earthlink. Basically the idea was very simple: rig the packets to carry a bad checksum, which means that the receiving Soviet groundstation throws them out as garbage. But NSA is watchlisting the mismatches. Get it?"

Paula was already nodding and smiling faintly. It was neat. When the checksums failed to match, the receiving computer would simply assume that the message it had assembled was corrupted, disregard it, and signal for a repeat transmission. What Colonel Raymond was saying was that the checksums for the packets containing the Tangerine file would be *deliberately* miscalculated. Therefore they would, in effect, be invisible to the message-processing computers at the Soviet groundstation. But the computers in the US National Security Agency's receiving posts in Japan, Australia, Britain, and elsewhere, which eavesdropped on the Soviets' communications all the time—and just about everyone else's, too, for that matter—would be programmed to look for just those mismatches. Thus they would be able to intercept the information that the Soviet system ignored. (It went without saying that it would be a simple matter to abort the retransmission attempts for each packet after a couple of tries, to avoid getting the system into a loop that would otherwise go on forever.)

"Tricky, though," Paula said. "Magician would have to get inside the communications center up there."

"He was a maintenance supervisor," Raymond reminded her. "That part was okay."

"Yes, but it would involve actually getting into the system software somehow, and tampering with it. Was that really Magician's field?"

Foleda gave a heavy sigh. "You've hit it, right on the nail."

Paula glanced around quickly. "I take it from the way we're talking that this didn't work out."

"We worked with what we had," Foleda said. "Magician wasn't an expert on Soviet software. But we got the job down to what seemed like a straightforward procedure, and he was confident he could hack it. . . . But something went wrong. He got caught. The last we heard he was back in Moscow—in the Lubyanka jail."

"The Tangerine file wasn't transmitted?" Paula said.

Foleda shook his head. "Nothing ever came through."

"Presumably they got him first," Kehrn said, still below the wallscreen. He came back to the table and sat down at last.

Paula looked away and gazed at the image of *Valentina Tereshkova* again while she thought over what had been said. So, if it was a disguised battle platform, in combination with the other weaponry that the Soviets were known to have deployed in space, it would outgun everything the West had been putting up for the past decade. But why did that call for the meeting in progress now, and in particular her presence at it? Then it came to her suddenly what the meeting was all about. She jerked her head away from the screen to look at Raymond and Foleda. "That file is still up there," she said.

"Right on the nail, again," Foleda confirmed. "Magician managed to get a message through to us after he was arrested—it doesn't matter how—saying that as a precaution, he created a backup copy of the file. Apparently the Soviets never found out about it." Foleda gestured at the screen. "It's up there right now, inside a section of Mermaid's databank, stored invisibly under a special access code. We have that code. What we don't have is somebody up there who would know how to break into a Russian computer system and use it."

Paula stared hard at him as the meaning of it all became clear. They had risked using a nonspecialist, and the gamble had failed. But by a small miracle, the prize was still waiting to be claimed. This time they wanted an expert.

She swallowed and shifted her gaze from one to another of the faces staring back at her questioningly. "Now wait a minute . . ." she began.

⚙ CHAPTER TWO ⚙

"Now wait a minute," Paula had repeated in the privacy of Colonel Raymond's office an hour after the meeting ended. "My degrees are in electronics and computer communications. I'm a scientist. If I wanted to get mixed up in this kind of business I'd have joined Foleda's outfit or the CIA, not the Air Force."

"But this job needs your kind of expertise," Raymond had said. "And the way they've got it figured out, it wouldn't really be that risky."

"Tell that to the last guy who tried. He's in Lubyanka prison."

"This approach would be different. You wouldn't have to get inside the computer center—or anywhere that'd be all that difficult."

"Except a Soviet space station nearly two hundred thousand miles out."

"Kehrn explained how that could be arranged. . . . Paula, just promise that you'll take a few minutes to think over how important this is, would you, please? It's not only the potential military value of getting detailed intelligence on those weapons. The political implications are monumental. The unaligned great powers that we've seen emerging in this century—Japan, China, Brazil, the Southeast Asian alliance—have tended to regard both us and the Russians as equally crooked in the long run, and played us off against each other. But *this* would prove to the world, irrefutably and finally, that all the assurances we've been hearing about how the Soviets have changed but nobody understands them are just as much horseshit as everything else they've told us over the years. It would show that we are not victims of paranoia . . . that our suspicions all along have been grounded in reality, and their aim is still to spread their system worldwide, by force or otherwise, as much as it ever was. But against the lineup of global power that this could generate, they'd be powerless—ruined politically. This 'Pedestal' operation that Foleda's people are talking about could do it, Paula, the end of the line for them—*kaputski*. That's what this job could mean."

That was when she had made her first mistake, she decided: she'd agreed to think about it.

A male voice that incongruously blended an American twang with a guttural Russian accent spoke from a loudspeaker somewhere overhead and interrupted her reverie. "Ladies and gentlemen, we are now approaching *Valentina Tereshkova* and should be docking in approximately twenty minutes. Arrival formalities will be minimal, and there will be refreshments while we hear a short address in the hub reception lounge before commencing our tour. The Soviet Ministry of Space Sciences hopes that despite the limited space aboard the transporter craft, your journey has been comfortable. Thank you."

On the viewscreen at the front of the cabin, *Tereshkova* was almost a full circle, highlighted as two brilliant crescents slashed in the black background by the Sun off to one side. Around Paula, the other passengers were stirring and becoming talkative again, and those who had been asleep were stretching, yawning, patting hair back into shape, and refastening ties and shirtcuffs. There were a hundred or so altogether—mainly political and military figures, scientists, and reporters from Western and Asian nations—invited on a special visit to the colony to commemorate the Soviets' centennial May Day. The voyage from the low-Earth-orbiting transfer platform where they had boarded the transporter from surface shuttles had taken over fifteen hours. Although this was probably the first spaceflight for most of them, the initial excitement had lasted only so long, even with receding views of Earth coming through on the screen periodically to relieve the unchanging starfield. Now there was something new to see.

"Time to wake up," she murmured to the man sprawled in the seat next to her, a still-open magazine resting loosely between his fingers. "We're here. Welcome to Orbitskigrad."

The man whom she still knew only as Lewis Earnshaw stretched against his restraining belt, held the pose for a few seconds, while emitting a long-drawn mixture of a yawn and a groan, and relaxed. Then he rubbed his eyes, sat up in his seat, and looked around. "Home, home at Lagrange?" he murmured.

He was in his late thirties, solid but athletically built, and had straight dark hair parted conventionally, brown eyes that were alert and humorous most of the time but could be reflective when the occasion demanded, and a clean-cut, square-jawed face with a tight, upturned mouth. This kind of thing was his business. He was a civilian agent from a department that Bernard Foleda ran somewhere in the murkier depths of the UDIA, known nebulously as the "Operations Section." Like Paula, he was wearing a badge that identified him as representing Pacific News Services of California, USA.

"Quite an experience, eh, General?" someone inquired in the row behind them.

"More boring than driving across Texas," another voice drawled loudly in reply.

"The people don't seem exactly wild with excitement," Earnshaw said, closing the magazine and slipping it back in the pouch in front of him. "That's what you get when a generation raised on electronics grows up. Gotta have new stimulation all the time."

"Reality can be a good substitute," Paula answered dryly.

"So long as you don't get hooked on it."

She had met him before their first briefing together by some of Foleda's spooks from the Pentagon underworld. After Colonel Raymond finally talked her round, transfer orders had come through with amazing rapidity, assigning her to temporary duty with the UDIA. She had moved from Massachusetts to Washington within a week, and after a crash course in regulations and procedures for offplanet duties, she found herself in orbit aboard a USSF manned platform as one of a dozen trainees undergoing practical familiarization with a space environment. Talk about personal backgrounds had been discouraged, so she had learned little about her classmates, including Earnshaw. At that time, before their cover identities had been invented, she had known him only by his class pseudonym of "George," and had herself been known to the rest simply as "Joyce." It only occurred to her later that the entire class had probably consisted of final candidates for the same mission. She wondered how many people that last dozen had been selected from. Foleda certainly wasn't taking any chances this time.

Earnshaw had struck her as capable and self-assured, which she respected, and the two of them had worked well together on group tasks, despite her stubborn independent streak and his perennial skepticism and refusal or inability to trust anyone, which at times exasperated her. On the other hand, he didn't talk when he had nothing to say, and he wasn't especially bothered about maintaining an image and having to be popular all the time. It was a pity he was in a profession that bred such cynicism and suspicion, she remembered thinking. He might have made a good scientist.

"What attracted me into science as a career?" she had answered once to a question he'd asked her. It was something they'd talked about during time off and breaks between classes aboard the space platform. "I guess because the challenges were demanding intellectually. It doesn't leave room for pretentiousness or self-delusion, as you get in a lot of other areas—I've never been able to stand phoniness. It deals in facts and truth, its conclusions are unambiguous, and it tests them against reality."

"The rest of the world has a lot to learn, eh?" he'd said, in the way he had of talking absolutely neutrally when he wanted to—usually when they drifted into something controversial—with no discernible expression or intonation, neither approving nor disapproving, agreeing nor disagreeing, encouraging nor discouraging. Somehow it always had the effect of opening her up more. She'd wondered if it was a result of gumshoe training.

"The rest of the world runs on deception and manipulation—what else can you say?" she'd answered. "It's what people perceive and believe that matters. Whether or not the perceptions and beliefs happen to be true has nothing to do with it. What matters is that everyone buys the product, votes the right way, and behaves themselves. I don't know who I blame most—cynical leaders, or the gullible people who listen to them. The irony of it all is that I should end up here, working for this outfit." Yet, here she was.

On another occasion, while they were having lunch together in one of the Pentagon's cafeterias during the three-week preparation period after they were selected, she had said, "You see, the whole problem with the world is that fools and fanatics are always so certain of themselves, but wiser people so full of doubts."

"Who said that?" Earnshaw had asked.

"Bertrand Russell." She'd waited a moment while he thought it over. "A philosopher."

"Philosopher, eh?"

"Sometime back in the last century."

"Just like that?"

"What do you mean, 'just like that'?"

"That's how he said it, just like that?"

"I guess so."

Earnshaw had eyed her skeptically, then asked, "So how come he didn't put 'I think' at the end of it?"

The pressure of the seat against her back increased as the transporter came round and decelerated into its stern-first final approach. The image on the screen had enlarged noticeably. Then the view cut to a close-up of the central part of the hub structure with its array of communications antennas, and the docking port's outer doors swinging open to admit the ship. The sight of the bay inside loomed larger, ablaze with arc lamps, provoking a twinge of nervousness inside her. Her second mistake, she decided, had been to go ahead and think about it after she'd promised to.

A quarter of an hour later, the passengers collected their coats, bags, and other belongings, and exited through the forward door, moving awkwardly and using handrails for assistance in the low-gravity conditions near *Tereshkova*'s axis. They emerged onto a carpeted ramp, where smiling attendants in gray uniforms were waiting to usher them through to the reception lounge.

❀ CHAPTER THREE ❀

"Dobro pozalovat v Valentinu Tereshkovu," the Russian official said when they came to the front of the short line at one of the reception booths. There had been a baggage check when they transferred from the surface shuttle in Earth orbit. He peered at their badges and switched to English. "Welcome to *Valentina Tereshkova.*" Earnshaw handed him their two document holders. The Russian extracted a plastic card from Paula's, passed it through a reader, checked the information and picture that appeared on a screen in front of him, and entered a code into a keyboard. Then he repeated the process with the other folder. "Ms. Shelmer and Mr. Earnshaw, both from Pacific News Services, Los Angeles, California." He studied the screen again for a moment. "Yes, these are correct. What is the purpose of your visit?" His tone was one of personal curiosity rather than of officialdom.

"Special coverage for a consortium of West Coast agencies," Paula replied. "We've scheduled a number of special-feature items on this for the next few weeks."

"I see. Well, we must be sure to take good care of you. Can't afford any bad publicity, eh? I'm sure that Americans know all about that." The Russian passed across two preprepared ID badges in red frames. "Wear these at all times for your own convenience and safety, and remain within the designated visitor zones, which are clearly indicated. The stewards wearing red armbands are at your service if you have questions or need assistance." He indicated the camera and other equipment that Earnshaw was holding. "Pictures are permitted anywhere within the visitor zones. Thank you, and enjoy your stay with us. Next, please."

Still loping in bounds more than walking—because of their negligible weight near the spin axis—they followed a short ramp to a gate that led from the arrival area into the reception lounge. Groups of people were already forming around tables set, cocktail-party style, with assorted hors d'oeuvres, breads, meats, and cheeses. Earnshaw's wrist unit, which looked like an ordinary computer-communicator, beeped almost inaudibly as they passed through the gate. He stopped a few feet into the lounge to press something on it and consult the readout.

"That Russian was quite civilized," Paula said as she stopped along side him. "Are you sure we're in the right place? I thought they were all supposed to be monsters."

"Today, they're all on their best behavior," Earnshaw said. "Shop window to the world. Come on, let's get a drink and eat." They began moving toward the bar that had been set up by one wall. "Oh, incidentally"—he made it sound like an afterthought—"you've just been X-rayed." Fortunately the special equipment they were carrying had been designed with that kind of possibility in mind, and would have shown nothing unusual.

For the next half hour or so, the guests munched on snacks and stretched their legs as guests of the Soviet press agency *Novosti,* while two speakers delivered a double act that alternated welcoming remarks and a preview of the coming tour with a lament for misunderstood Marxism. Then the party moved on out of the reception lounge into a large, brightly lit gallery with corridors leading off in all directions, railed catwalks above, machinery bays below, doorways everywhere, and a confusing geometry in which verticals converged overhead and the floor was visibly curved.

As they waited to board elevators for the half-mile "descent" to the rim, Paula looked around to reconcile the surroundings with the published construction plans that she and Earnshaw had spent hours memorizing. She wondered if it was significant that the tour didn't take in any part of the hub system. The same thought seemed to have occurred also to a woman behind them, who was wearing a European Space Agency badge. "Excuse me," the ESA woman said to the red-armbanded steward by the door as the group began shuffling forward into the elevator.

"Madam?"

"Are we going straight down to the ring now? We're not going to see anything up here first?"

"There is really nothing of special interest to see up here."

"Nothing? That's surprising. What's behind that far bulkhead, and the pipes back there, for instance—between here, where we're standing, and the next spoke?"

"Only storage tanks—fuel for the Earth and lunar transporters, various agricultural and industrial chemicals, and water."

"You must store an enormous amount of everything. There's nothing else?"

"Just storage tanks, madam."

Earnshaw glanced at Paula and raised an eyebrow. That was where the launchers for some of the ejectable modules that Jonathan Watts had talked about were supposed to be located.

After the long flight up from Earth orbit, the return to normal bodyweight as the elevator moved out to the rim felt like a debilitating heaviness creeping through their bodies; but in another respect, it was reassuring to emerge walking naturally again.

Valentina Tereshkova contained three built-up urban zones inside its main torus, which in the official bureaucratese of the predistributed literature were designated, mind-bogglingly, "high-density residential-occupational social units." The bureaucrats didn't have to live there, however, and the Russian guides who accompanied the visitors down from the hub referred to them simply as "towns." Each was clustered around the base of one of the major spokes, which formed a central tower disappearing through the roof to connect to the hub. Alternating with the three major spokes were three slimmer ones, which terminated in the middle of the agricultural zones between the towns at built-up transportation and processing complexes known simply as Agricultural Stations 1, 2, and 3.

The town that the party arrived in was called Turgenev, and constituted the administrative and social center. The tour began with a stop high up on the central tower above the main square, where the guides led the visitors through from the elevators onto an outside terrace for a general view of the colony. Paula judged the roof to be fifty to a hundred feet above where they were standing. The cross-section of the rim was not circular as in a true torus, but flattened like a wide automobile tire, with the roof stretching away horizontally for a distance on either side before it curved over and down to become the sides. Illumination came from two rows of what looked like immense, golden-glowing, venetian-blind slats receding upward and out of sight with the sweep of the roof—louvered reflectors that admitted light from an external mirror system. Power for the colony's industries came from nuclear reactors located at the hub.

Below the terrace, a ribbonlike miniworld curved away and upward between enclosing walls a little under a sixth of a mile apart. The nearer buildings were higher, merging into a monolith of tiered plazas, ramps, pedestrian ways, and bridges around the tower to form the town's center. Architectural styles were varied and followed light, airy, clean designs incorporating plenty of color and glass, intermixed with screens of natural greenery. The strangest thing was the geometry, or lack of it—for everywhere and on all levels, walls met at odd, asymmetrical angles, passages branched between buildings, roadways curved beneath underpasses to emerge in a different direction, and nothing seemed to run square to anything else, anywhere. Presumably the intention was to break up the underlying continuity and dissolve the sense of living inside a tube. If so, it worked.

"The architect who designed this must have had a fetish about rhomboids," Paula remarked as they looked out from the terrace.

There were many figures moving about; below, a vehicle emerged from behind a building, moving along some kind of track. Farther away, the townscape gave way to a more open composition of public buildings and residential units, trees, and parks, with glints of water in several places. The terrain climbed on either side to form a roughly U-shaped valley about a central strip, with buildings giving way to terraces of crops and pasture strips for animals farther away in the agricultural zone. Due to unanticipated difficulties with maintaining the ecological balance, which the Russians freely admitted, the general scene was not as idyllic as their public-relations releases had enthusiastically promised when construction commenced. In some places the metal shoring walls stood bare between tiers of barren, grayish-looking soil formed from processed moondust, and in others the vegetation was yellowy and limp. Their official line now was that this was only the first phase, and aesthetics would be attended to later; and most reactions were to concede that that was what experimentation was all about. This was a prototype colony, after all.

"Conventional enclosed dwellings are not functionally necessary, of course, since the climate can be controlled at all times," the Russian guide was saying. "As you can see, however, familiar styles and arrangements into neighborhood groupings are used, to give a feeling of normality as far as is practicable. The designers of *Valentina Tereshkova* took the view that the forms of houses which people have evolved on Earth over long periods of time best reflect the kinds of surroundings they prefer to live in. There seemed no reason to change it—at least, until much more is known about how people adapt to living in space."

"What materials are used for construction?" somebody asked.

"Of the buildings? Mainly aluminum, titanium, and other light metals processed from lunar ores. Currently the ore is catapulted magnetically up from the lunar surface, but we are constructing an experimental facility on Mare Cognitum to test high-power lasers as a launch mechanism. The Moon is not rich in hydrogen or carbon. You will find many things fabricated from ceramics and metals here, but few plastics. That will change, of course, when technologies for transmutation of elements are developed on an industrial scale."

"What's outside the town?" someone else wanted to know.

"A recreation area that includes sports fields and a lake. Beyond that is the region called Ukraine: one of the agricultural sectors where we raise food and livestock to feed the colony. We will be taking a look at it when we leave Turgenev. Past Ukraine, at the bottom of the next major spoke, is the town of Landausk, *Valentina Tereshkova*'s scientific and industrial center. We will have dinner in Landausk, and accommodation will be provided there tonight before we tour the town in the morning. Now let me point out some of the more interesting things that are visible from where we are now . . ."

Paula tried to take her mind off the mission that had brought her here. She found herself envying the other people around her, wishing that she, like them, could enjoy the experience without apprehension. She went through the mission plan once again in her mind, mentally rehearsing every step as she had a hundred times, like a nervous, first-time actress muttering her lines while waiting backstage for her entry cue. She thought of the crew back in the lab in Massachusetts, secure in their familiar day-to-day routine. Her third mistake, she decided, had been rationalizing to herself that she could use a little more excitement in her life. If she ever got out of this, an occasional dabble in sin with the likes of Ed Sutton would be just about all the excitement she'd need.

"The six-sided building behind, with the glass frontage, is the university gymnasium, with courts for squash, tennis, and volleyball, a swimming pool, a weight-training room, and a general arena with seating for fifteen hundred people. The students come from . . ." The guide's voice droned on interminably. Wouldn't they ever get on with it?

She glanced at Earnshaw, who at that moment was doing a convincing job of panning slowly sideways to record the view with his camera. He lowered the instrument from his face to let the shoulder strap take the weight, and looked around casually, if anything seeming slightly bored, like someone passing a slow Sunday afternoon at the city museum. But as always, his eyes were constantly mobile, missing nothing, checking everything. She tried to tell herself that if there had been anything unsound about this mission, someone like him would never have let himself be talked into coming on it.

". . . transportation around the ring, as we shall see later. Good. Well, if there are no further questions for the time being, we will board the elevators again and complete our descent to the central concourse, and from there come out into the central square of Turgenev. Actually it's not square really, but an irregular polygon, as you'll see. I suppose we call it that through convention. So, if you would follow the stewards at the back, ladies and gentlemen . . ."

And then they were all moving back inside the tower. One of the voices around her commented that the place was artistic as well as functional, showing spontaneity and individualism. Surprising. Not at all the staid, crushing conformity you came to expect from Russian bureaucracies. Another voice explained it was because the Russians had copied it from a Japanese design.

Despite her resolve, Paula found her chest thumping. Now it would be only a matter of minutes.

◎ CHAPTER FOUR ◎

Russians had been mistrusting and spying on each other for centuries, long before the abdication of the czar in March 1917 and the subsequent seizure of power by Lenin in November. Largely as a result of this kind of tradition, their officials worried about anything they couldn't predict. They worried especially about behavior by their subordinates that they couldn't explain to their superiors. Hence, all the way down the lines of command, the overriding formula for survival came to be: follow orders, don't ask questions, never volunteer, and always behave predictably. One consequence was the stifling of innovation and creativity. Another was that they never—well, hardly ever—deviated from precedent. The operations analysts in Bernard Foleda's covert section of the UDIA had established from records of previous tours of *Valentina Tereshkova* that the schedule, the route, and the procedures followed were always the same. This fact had been of great help in drawing up the mission plan.

As the party of a hundred or so visitors assembled from the elevators in the main central concourse at ground level, the guides divided it into a number of special-interest groups according to preferences which had been indicated in advance. Thus, all the visitors would be able to see what they wanted to without being wearied by overload and without taxing any one location unduly. Furthermore, in a way that was uncharacteristically flexible for

Russians, people were allowed to change their minds and switch groups at the last moment. Invariably some did. On this particular tour it was certain that quite a few would, because they had been asked to. They didn't have to know why.

Hence, for a while the compositions and sizes of the various groups would be uncertain. The Russians could have kept track precisely if they wanted to, of course, but not without subjecting the visitors to a lot of cattle-like herding and head-counting, which on previous occasions they had refrained from doing. It was certain, however, that the total would be verified when the whole party came together again for lunch two hours later. Thus, Paula and Earnshaw would have somewhere in the region of an hour and three quarters to complete their task and reappear by the time the groups reassembled in the central concourse before proceeding through to the restaurant.

The plan required them to leave the zone that visitors were free to move in, and the first problem was with the badges they had been given on arrival. As anyone conversant with security practices would have assumed—and checking with various intelligence sources had confirmed—the badges contained electronic microchips, which when triggered by a particular infrared transmission would transmit back a code uniquely allocated to the wearer. When sensors detected somebody about to pass through a doorway, say, the badge would be interrogated and its response forwarded to a computer that knew who was authorized to go where, and which would raise an alarm if it detected a violation.

Earnshaw and Paula drifted to the side of the central concourse. For the moment conditions were disorderly, with people milling around between the various groups, some splitting away into the short corridor nearby that led to the rest rooms, and others coming back out. Earnshaw looked around, saw nothing to arouse suspicion, and nodded. They moved on into the corridor. It was fairly broad, with the entrance to the men's facilities lying to the right, the women's to the left, and some doors to storage closets on both sides. Facing them at the far end was a second exit, which they knew from their briefings led to a foyer interconnecting various machinery rooms, technical workshops, and offices. A large sign above the far exit announced in several languages, no visitors past this point. There were no physical guards—shipping people from Earth was too expensive a business for them to stand around all day doing nothing—but it was clear that anyone setting off the alarm wouldn't get very much farther before being apprehended. That was the way Earnshaw and Paula needed to go.

Earnshaw entered the men's room and unslung his camera and satchel of accessories. A half dozen or so other men were inside, and some of the cubicles were occupied. To one side of the entrance was the white, louvered door of a janitor and maintenance technician's closet. He looked around and overhead but could detect no sign of surveillance. According to a CIA report that he'd seen, the Soviets resorted to such extremes of snooping as concealing lenses in rest rooms only in top-security locations. This was hardly a top-security part of *Valentina Tereshkova*—indeed, according to the Soviet claims, the whole place was just a civilian experiment in space colonization. But on the other hand, if it really was a disguised battle platform . . . But there had to be some risks.

"Long way to come to see Disneyland, huh?" the ruddy-faced man wiping his hands by the mirror said.

"I guess this has to be the real Space Mountain," Earnshaw answered. The ruddy-faced man laughed and left.

Earnshaw locked himself in one of the cubicles and commenced his transformation. A touch of facial cream to dull his skin, some shadow to enhance wrinkles, a graying, ragged, Stalinesque mustache, and a modest application of hair whitener added a dozen years to his age. His vest, turned back-to-front, became a worn crewneck sweater; his suit reversed into a dark green, grease-stained work uniform; and a pair of false uppers changed his shoes into crumpled boots. The satchel that he was carrying wasn't as rigid as it appeared. With its stiffening frame removed it could be turned inside out, and when the frame was put back again it became a toolbox of the kind issued to mechanics all over the colony, large enough to hold the dismantled "camera." Finally, he rubbed a trace of grime into the creases of his hands and under his nails, added a streak to his forehead, and pulled on a cap.

When the Russian steward stuck his head in the door of the rest room to check, all the visitors had left. "No stray sheep left in here?" he said to the maintenance engineer in the green uniform, who was rummaging in the closet near the door.

"They're all gone," Earnshaw mumbled in Russian without looking round.

"It's chaos out there this time. You know, I swear our schoolchildren make less fuss than some of those people."

"No discipline. That's what it is."

"You're right. Although, mind you, I wouldn't say no to some of those American women out there. How do they afford such clothes?"

"Well, if they don't do anything that's worth enough to pay for them, then somebody else must pay for them. That's capitalism."

"Give me a break. You sound like a Party hack."

Earnshaw finished putting tools into his box and turned from the closet, holding a reel of electrical wire. He had hidden his red-framed visitor's badge in the closet and had exchanged it for an imitation blue-framed one, as worn by general workers and inhabitants of the colony. "I don't know you," he said to the steward. "You might be KGB."

"Do me a favor! I transferred here from Landausk a few days ago."

"I see. Landausk, eh?" Earnshaw lifted a stepladder out from the closet. "I suppose we'll be seeing more of you around here, then."

"Yes, I suppose so. Well, I'd better be getting back. See you around."

"Sure."

The steward disappeared. Earnshaw waited for a few seconds, and then carried the ladder out into the corridor. He positioned it in the center of the floor underneath the translucent panel covering the light, climbed up, and had just begun undoing the fastenings when Paula emerged from the ladies' room. She was wearing a maintenance engineer's uniform, too, now. Her face had shed its makeup, and she had acquired dark hair.

When a tubby man in a blue shirt came through from the off-limits direction a minute or so later they were hard at work, with several of the lighting tubes removed and wires trailing down from the opened panel in the ceiling. They said nothing, and the tubby man went through into the rest room. Earnshaw reached into his toolbox and handed down one of the subassemblies that the camera had come apart into. Superficially it looked like an electrician's test meter. Recessed into it at one end, however, was a tiny lens sensitive to infrared. When the tubby man came out again and went back through the doorway, Paula aimed the unit to read the interrogation signal emitted by the transmitter above the door. It also read the response code from the tubby man's badge, which reflected invisibly off the surrounding wall. A moment later, a sign appeared in the unit's readout, confirming that the computer inside was set to mimic the tubby man's code. Paula glanced up at Earnshaw and nodded.

Earnshaw came back down the ladder, and Paula plugged a lead from the unit into another meter to program it from the first. Then she disconnected it and handed it to Earnshaw. Now they each had a device that would mimic a valid response signal. Earnshaw picked up his toolbox and approached the doorway. A light on his unit flickered as he went through, indicating that it had been interrogated and had responded. Paula came after him, and hers did the same. Now they were committed. They followed the wall on the far side of the doorway for a short distance and stopped at a switch panel, where they set down their equipment and tools. Paula removed the coverplate and began loosening connections inside, while Earnshaw squatted down and made a play of searching in the toolbox while he checked the layout of the surroundings against what they had been led to expect. Two men walked by, talking, then turned a corner and disappeared. A woman came out of a door and went off in the other direction.

Paula fought to keep her hands steady and look as if she were working normally. The method they had used was far from foolproof, and it was possible, even now, that they had triggered an alarm, although there were no whooping sirens or flashing lights to indicate the fact. If the computer that the badge-readers talked to was programmed to check each individual's movements from place to place, for example—which it possessed all the information to do—it would just have deduced that the same person had passed through the same point three times without going back again. Or perhaps the system used a one-time code for every badge, where the response changed according to a predetermined formula every time it was used. In a top-security environment, precautions like that would be routine. But the whole essence of the new plan was to avoid having to penetrate into such areas, and this location had been selected for the operation precisely because nothing of other-than-domestic significance went on there. In those circumstances, the Washington experts had pronounced—probably keeping their crossed fingers out of sight behind their backs, Paula had come to suspect only when it was too late—automatic tracking would be unlikely. As long as there was nothing to indicate that anyone had gone where they weren't supposed to, and that no visitors were about to wander off and get lost, the computer would be happy.

Earnshaw seemed satisfied after surveying the surroundings. "Let's go," he whispered. They had an hour and fifteen minutes.

Leaving a sign saying, in Russian, danger—high voltage, below the opened switch panel, they picked up their things again and followed a corridor out of the foyer to a metal-railed staircase. A flight down brought them to a landing overlooking a machinery bay, with a catwalk leading off and running along above it on one side. They went on down to where a narrow passage led the other way at the bottom of the stairs. A man in a white coat appeared out of the passage, stood aside and nodded perfunctorily as they passed, then went on up without giving them a second glance.

They entered the passage. After a short distance, one side opened into a gallery full of ducts, piping, structural members, and cable runs, with a bank of electrical cabinets standing in a line along one wall. The passage continued on, but they left it and picked their way through the gallery to a set of steps leading down into a shallow bay, partly screened from the corridor by the clutter of machinery they had climbed through. Three sides of the bay consisted of banks of plain metal boxes containing environmental monitoring and control computers, along with conduits bringing in signals from sensors and instruments in thousands of different locations. Although the place was normally unmanned, it contained a bench for use by service engineers when they came to perform checks or repairs. At one end of the bench was an instrument panel containing test meters, switches, a keyboard and display screen, and fitted with various supply sockets. One of these sockets was a standard type provided for the engineers to plug portable computers into to access the maintenance department's database for reference data—with the complexity of modern systems, carrying the requisite manuals around would have required a wheelbarrow. And it was inside the maintenance department's section of the databank that Magician had hidden the backup copy of Tangerine—the file that the whole operation was aimed at recovering.

Earnshaw took out the final section of the "camera" from his toolbox. It was, in fact, a specially designed microcomputer, with a plug that matched the standard Russian data socket. Paula pulled a stool from under the bench and sat down. She plugged in the set, connected the power lead, and activated a search routine to begin testing access routes into the system. She worked quickly, nervously, pausing to study a response on the set's miniature screen, thinking for a second, entering a command—wanting to get it over with. Earnshaw stood behind, silent, watching the approach into the bay. There were maintenance points like this all over *Tereshkova*, but this one was more secluded than most. That was why they had picked it.

Paula bit her lip with suppressed tension as a hunch yielded a positive response. The maintenance department's system used a fairly straightforward method of access codes, which was to be expected, since it contained relatively insensitive information. As another line of code appeared, opening the executive level of the file manager, she breathed a silent prayer of gratitude for Magician's presence of mind in choosing *this* system to hide the file in. Or had it been simply because he worked in the maintenance department? Breaking into one of the higher-security systems, such as the research department's, or the information bank kept by *Tereshkova*'s branch of the KGB, would have been impossible in the time available.

She attempted a direct request for the file. It failed. The initiating address pointer had been erased to make it invisible. She obtained a sector table, located the header she wanted, and commanded a forced read. The system acknowledged that it had the file, but demanded an access validation to release it. She supplied the code she had been given. There was a pause. Then a new line appeared, requesting an output-destination spec. "I think we're getting there!" Paula hissed up at Earnshaw.

He turned and hunched down to peer over her shoulder. She entered another line and sat watching the screen tensely. A delay of perhaps two seconds dragged by. Then a confirmation appeared. In the same instant a line in English appeared below:

gp700 "tangerine"; stat ok: ready to read. mem des? file des? read acc?

Paula shifted the keyboard from Cyrillic alphabet to English and complete the dialogue. A final, single-word line confirmed:

copying

She sat back, closed her eyes, and exhaled a long, silent breath of relief. Earnshaw's fingers closed around her arm and squeezed reassuringly. She blinked and peered at the screen again, as if to make sure. The word was still there, glowing solid and jubilant. It meant that Magician's file was being copied through to create a duplicate inside the high-density memory-crystal arrays contained in their portable device. The copying would take just a matter of seconds, and then the original inside the maintenance department's databank would be destroyed. All that would be left then would be to get the copy home.

copying completed and verified

confirm source erasure?

Paula leaned forward to enter a reply . . .

She wasn't sure what it was that registered—a sound, something glimpsed from the corner of her eye, an unconsciously perceived sense of movement? Earnshaw was still down next to her, watching the screen. She turned her head suddenly to look up past him . . . and gasped out loud in sudden dismay.

"Remain as you are!" the Russian officer snapped, pointing his pistol. Earnshaw's head jerked around. Paula could do nothing but stare up numbly.

There were four more uniformed guards behind, two of them

holding leveled submachine guns. The officer moved a pace forward to the edge of the bay, and looked down. He had a Tartar face beneath the peaked cap, olive-skinned, with narrow eyes and high cheekbones. "Keep your hands in sight," he instructed. "Now, back slowly against the far wall. Make no sudden moves."

◉ CHAPTER FIVE ◉

The night's rain had freshened the air after a week of early summer heat that had become oppressive, and the scattered clouds left over Washington, D.C., by morning promised a spell of cool relief. Bernard Foleda let the drape fall back across the bedroom window with a satisfied "pom, pom, pom, pom, pom-pom-pom-pom-pom" to the tune of Mozart's overture to *The Impresario*, and finished knotting his tie. He took the jacket of his suit from the closet, and, draping it over an arm, pom-pommed his way in a gravelly bass-baritone downstairs to breakfast. There was no reason for him to be humming to himself, considering the disaster that had befallen the department in the past week—it was simply a habit born of years. And besides, he had learned a long time ago that when people in his profession started letting the job get to them personally, they tended not to last very much longer.

Myra was sitting at the kitchen table with a cup of coffee in her hand, studying selected items from the morning's news offerings on a flatscreen pivoted to face her from the worktop opposite. Like him in her fifties, she was a tall, normally full-bodied woman, with a face that had managed to retain its composure and humorous set despite eyes and cheeks still sunken from a five-month illness that had lasted through winter. The skin on the backs of her hands was still loose from her not having fully regained her weight yet, and her dark, neatly trimmed hair showed gray streaks which she hadn't attempted to disguise by tinting. They had been married for almost thirty years, and unlike the mysterious, withdrawn spy chiefs of the popular movies, Foleda discussed his work with her regularly. He didn't understand how scriptwriters could expect people like him, on top of everything else, to carry on being furtive and secretive after they got home. Maybe they did it to give themselves an excuse for introducing beautiful women into their plots—usually Chinese, for some obscure reason—who made their livings by coaxing secrets out of semicomatose government officials in between bouts of frenzied lovemaking. If so, Foleda had no objection—the image was good for recruiting.

"The rain's stopped," Myra said as Bernard came in and hung his jacket over the back of one of the kitchen chairs. "It looks as if it's going to be cloudy today. Nice and cool for a change."

"Yes, I already looked. We could use it." Bernard walked over to the chef, took out two plates of scrambled eggs, ham, and a hotcake, and pressed a button to start the toaster. His wife poured the coffee while he sat down. The item on the screen was about a Japanese astronaut who had scored a first by achieving escape velocity under his own power with a series of hops and a leap off the surface of Deimos, the smaller of the two moons of Mars. "So maybe the old nursery rhyme isn't so silly after all, if we just change it slightly," the commentator babbled cheerfully in a way that Bernard found indistinguishable from banal at that time of morning. "The cow jumped *off* the moon, ho-ho!"

Foleda snorted. "What else do we have?"

Myra touched a button on the handpad lying beside the coffeepot, and a yellow light on the wallpanel by the stove came on to indicate that the house-manager was active. "Cancel," she said in a slightly raised voice. The picture vanished and was replaced by a selection of options. "Five-three," Myra instructed, and a new list appeared. "Poland," she said. A headline replaced the list: more warsaw demonstrations. Myra glanced at Bernard. He nodded. "Yes," she said at the panel. Then, "X-out, out." The yellow light went off.

The item concerned Soviet responses to the latest round of

protests and strikes in Poland and East Germany. As usual the media were emphasizing the military aspect, with dramatically narrated scenes of troops confronting crowds, NATO units being put on alert—Foleda recognized one shot of rolling tanks as being months old, with no connection to current events at all—and snippets of military and political spokesmen being questioned about the risk of a general European escalation. That was the kind of material that delivered audiences to advertisers, and was only to be expected. Western intelligence had been following the developments behind the present situation since long before the public became aware of them, however, and opinions were that the likelihood of any real shooting was remote.

The Soviets had accelerated their military buildup in the final decades of the previous century. Their intention had not been so much to provoke war, for they had no more desire than anyone else to be devastated again if they could avoid it, but, taking their cue from the woeful performance of the democracies at Munich in response to Hitler's aggressions, to gamble that, as before, their adversaries would back down without a fight from the *threat* of force. And for a time, as Western pacifists howled for appeasement and rediscovered moral outrage with the realization that every pulpit, podium, lectern, and armchair was just twenty minutes from somebody's launch site, it had seemed to work. But in the crucial early years of the twenty-first century, the Soviets had wavered when they found themselves faced by the prospect of having to take on not only the West's military technology, but the larger part of the numerically overwhelming population of Asia as well. Originally the Bomb had redressed the balance between sides whose different political systems resulted in unequal commitments to conventional forces. The irony was that when both sides drew even in terms of Bomb-power, *people* should become the deciding factor to tip the scales. And as Marxism's original appeal waned in the face of Asia's rising affluence, the Soviets fell farther behind in the competition for minds and souls. Their moment had gone.

Paradoxically, it was just this that made the present situation so precarious in a different kind of way. At one time, before Khrushchev, communist dogma had held that the capitalists would launch a last, suicidal war rather than submit to the final triumph of Marx's immutable laws. Now it seemed more likely to happen the other way around: that in desperation, an irrational element in the Soviet leadership might decide to take everyone else down with them if they perceived all to be lost anyway. It was Asia's armies that stabilized the situation; in turn, their protection was the West's "Starshield" orbital defensive system. If that shield were destroyed, the entire system of deterrence and containment around the Soviet bloc would disintegrate and set the stage for exactly the kind of last-ditch gamble that the West's strategic analysts feared most. That was what made knowing the true nature of *Valentina Tereshkova* was so important.

That something big was in the wind, the various intelligence agencies of the US, Western Europe, and Eastern Asia were agreed. Also, it would happen some time within the current year. But what or exactly when, nobody knew. In the eyes of many, the game was nearing its end. But endgames have a perplexing tendency to suddenly go either way. At this stage of this particular endgame, there was no latitude for error.

"I'll take a copy to read when I get a chance," Bernard said. Myra activated the audio again and directed the text to be hardcopied in the den. Bernard washed down the last of his toast with some coffee, and rose from his chair. "How are we for time?" he asked.

Myra went to the window and looked down over the tree-lined avenue outside, normally peaceful but busier at this time of the morning with people leaving for work. There was a black Chevrolet parked halfway along the next block. "They're here," she said matter-of-factly.

"Damn," Bernard muttered as Myra helped him on with his jacket. That meant he was running late. The two KGB agents from the Soviet embassy who tailed him every morning always arrived punctually and circled the block three times before parking. He bustled through to the den, picked up the sheets of hardcopied text, and slipped them into his briefcase. When he came back out, Myra was waiting in the hallway with his raincoat.

"You'd better take this," she said. "It might start raining again later."

"Thanks, I will." Bernard took his hat from the stand.

"Oh, and if nothing pressing comes up, remember that Ella and Johnny are coming this evening. I know you wouldn't want to miss your grandson's birthday if you can help it."

"I'll try not to. What have we bought him?"

"A junior spy kit, of course. It has invisible ink, false beards and mustaches, a codebook and some software to go with it, and a miniature camera. You see, just like the real thing."

"You mean they haven't got something for kids to tap into phone lines?"

"Give them time, dear."

"Okay, I'll see you later tonight."

"You too. Have fun today." Myra kissed him lightly on the cheek and watched from the door at the top of the stairs leading down into the garage as he descended and climbed into his maroon Cadillac. The outside door opened, and he backed out.

Minutes later in the thick of morning traffic streaming toward the Beltway, he caught sight of the KGB car, sitting solidly four places behind him as he swung right off an overpass to take the ramp down to the freeway. Several cars farther back still, just coming across the overpass, was the blue FBI Ford that tailed the KGB every morning. Foleda shook his head as he turned on a piano concerto to relax himself before the working day started. It was all sure as hell a crazy way to run a planet.

Gerald Kehrn was a born worrier. When he was younger he had worried about the things he read that said resources were about to run out. And then when they didn't run out and scientists began convincing the world that the whole problem had been exaggerated, he had worried that too many resources would produce too many people. When right-wing administrations were in power he worried about conservative fascists and fundamentalists, and with left-wing administrations he worried about liberal fascists and regulators. And of course, he had always worried about a war breaking out; the more time that went by without there being one, the more he worried that because weapons were constantly getting bigger and deadlier, it would be so much the worse when it did. He worried especially about things he didn't know about, and so tried to keep himself informed about everything. That made him good with details and a useful person to have around, which helped explain how he had made it to a senior position on the staff of the defense secretary. And the position suited him, for if worse did come to worst, he would prefer to be right there in the center of the action—not able to influence the course of events very much, perhaps, but at least knowing what was going on.

As he drove toward the Potomac on his way to the Pentagon on the morning of May 4, an inner foreboding told him that this was the beginning. He wasn't sure why, for there had been enough diplomatic goofs and intelligence screwups before, and this was hardly the first time the Soviets had nailed a couple of agents. Maybe it was the involvement of Mermaid, which had been taking on such big proportions in everyone's thinking lately. But something about the situation filled him with the dull, cold certainty that this was the first tripping over the edge into the scrambling, steepening tumble that would take them all the way to the Big One.

Because he worried about being late whenever he had an appointment, he always left early. Hence, none of the others had arrived yet when he got to Foleda's office. He found Foleda's operations assistant, Barbara Haynes, a tall, graying but elegant woman in her late forties whom he knew well, and Rose, Foleda's personal secretary, discussing something being displayed on a screen in the outer room. The strains of some piece of classical music coming through the open door at the rear—Kehrn had no idea what it was; he preferred jazz himself—indicated that Foleda was already ensconced within.

"We heard there was a snarl-up on the George Mason Bridge," Rose said. "Didn't think you'd make it so soon."

"A vegetable truck decided to unload itself there," Kehrn said. "But I left in good time. It wasn't so bad."

"Well, at least the rain's stopped."

"I'm glad I came in the other way this morning," Barbara said.

"Who's out there?" Foleda's voice called from inside.

"Gerry Kehrn," Barbara called back.

"Tell him to come on in. And you might as well come too, Barb. Let's get our thoughts together before the others start showing up. And now Volst"—who was the secretary of state—"has just been on the line saying he wants a report on the whole thing personally over lunch before the big meeting starts this afternoon. I've got the feeling this is gonna be a long day."

Kehrn went on through, and Barbara followed after exchanging a few final words with Rose. Foleda touched a button below his desk to cut the music and pushed aside some papers he had been reading. "Hi, Gerry."

"Good morning, Bern. Or is that the wrong thing to say today?"

"Why should it be?—It's stopped raining. Sit down. Relax. You look worried."

Kehrn pulled out one of the chairs at the meeting table set at a tee against Foleda's desk and sat down, placing his briefcase in front of him. Barbara shut the door. "Who wouldn't be worried?" Kehrn said. "What a goddamn mess."

"A million years from now it won't matter," Foleda assured him.

"Who else have we got coming this morning?" Kehrn asked.

"Pearce and somebody else from State. Zolansky from Operations. Do you know him?"

"We've met."

"Uh-huh. And Uncle Phil will be coming in at around eleven to see where we're at." Philip Borden was the UDIA director. Foleda sent an inquiring glance at Barbara.

"Zolansky's deputy will probably be coming too," she said, sitting down at the far end of the table.

"But keep your party-joke book in your pocket, Gerry," Foleda advised. "They won't be in the mood."

Kehrn fiddled with the lock of his briefcase and began taking out notebook, compad, and several files. "So what do we have?" he asked. "Anything new?"

Foleda shook his head. "Nothing."

"What's the story with Pacific News Services?"

"Forget them. They're out of it. PNS agreed to being used as cover for a government operation. If our operatives haven't come back, it's our problem. The Soviets haven't lodged any protest with PNS, and PNS isn't going to go out of its way to pick a quarrel with the Soviets."

"The Soviets know they were our people, and they're letting us sweat for a while," Barbara said. In other words, the Soviet reaction would come via the official channels.

"And there's been nothing so far through State?" Kehrn checked.

"As Barb says, they're letting us sweat," Foleda said. "In fact, I wouldn't be surprised if they let us stew for a lot longer and don't do anything."

"You mean, like waiting until we bring the matter up with them."

"Sure. Let us come crawling. We have to do something. Two of our citizens have disappeared, who were last heard of heading for a Soviet transfer station. Presumably they were caught red-handed committing espionage. Why should the Soviets be in any hurry to come to us?"

"How much trouble are we in with the Air Force?" Kehrn asked Foleda.

"None yet. Bryce was assigned to us for the duration. So far they don't know bout it."

Kehrn shuffled some papers aimlessly for a few seconds and fidgeted in his chair. "What, er . . . what about the two people up there?" he asked at last. "Do we know what to expect?"

"I imagine they're still up there, and possibly will be for a while. Is that what you meant?"

"I was wondering more, how much are they likely to give away?"

"You're worried?"

"I'm worried."

"Well, Lew McCain's an old hand. You needn't worry about him," Foleda said. "He's worked for me for years. He won't tell them anything. Even if it's something that's obvious and undeniable, he won't confirm it. That's the way he is. That's the way they're trained." Foleda's brow creased and his expression became more serious. "I wish I could say the same about the girl, though. This kind of thing isn't her specialty. She's from a different world. I don't know what to expect there."

"It's one of the things we'll try and get an opinion on from Colonel Raymond up at Hanscom when we've figured out how to break the news," Barbara said.

Kehrn nodded and looked uncomfortable while he wrestled with some new thought. Finally he said, "What are the chances of the Soviets using . . . well, let's say, 'extreme methods' of interrogation?"

"I can't see it," Foleda said. "This whole business has big propaganda potential if the Soviets decide to go public, and they know it. This one they'll want to play clean for the world to see. They wouldn't jeopardize their advantage by risking bad counterpublicity."

"But threats, maybe," Barbara said.

"That's something else," Foleda agreed, nodding. "Threats, implications of nasty things . . . McCain would read the situation and not be intimidated. But again, with the girl . . . who knows?"

"We shouldn't have used her," Kehrn said. "There had to have been someone else, with the right background as well as the technical know-how. It was a bad decision from the start."

"Maybe," Foleda conceded with a sigh. "Somehow I think we're gonna hear that said a lot of times today."

A tone sounded from the screen by the desk and Rose's face appeared. "They're arriving," she announced. "Zolansky and his partner are on their way up, and Pearce has checked into the building."

Foleda glanced at the other two and raised his eyebrows. "Okay, Rose," he said resignedly to the screen. "You'd better start breaking out the paper hats and squeakers."

❂ CHAPTER SIX ❂

There was a subdued humming sound, and buried within it a periodic resonance that came and went. Lewis McCain lay listening to it with his eyes closed, allowing the preoccupation to keep other thoughts from entering his mind for a few moments longer. He was aware that he had just woken up. The hum, with its rising and falling undertone, was not something familiar. He was not in a place that he was accustomed to waking up in.

He opened his eyes and saw a white ceiling with an air-conditioner vent off to one side of his field of vision. He moved his head to look at it. His head felt muzzy; the image was blurred, and swam. An ache shot between his temples and down the back of his neck as he strained to rise. He abandoned the effort, letting his head fall back on the pillow, and lay for a while until he could breathe more easily. Then he rolled over onto his side and opened his eyes again.

The cot was in a small, windowless, sparsely furnished room containing a plain table and a single upright chair with his clothes draped over them. Above the table was a shelf with some books and a few other oddments. The walls were dark blue up to a black strip running at half height, and cream from there to the ceiling. Slowly his head cleared, and the surroundings registered as the cell he'd been occupying for—how long had it been? three days? four days?—inside the KGB Internal Security Headquarters at Turgenev. The door was solid, with a small grille and sliding panel on the outside, and led out to the corridor. In the opposite corner was a partition screening a tiny washbasin and toilet.

Moving slowly and cautiously, he raised himself onto an elbow. Pain stabbed through his head once more. He held the position this time, and after a few seconds the pain eased. He sat up, pushed the single blanket aside, and lowered his legs over the side of the cot. A wave of dizziness swept over him, then nausea. He braced himself for the effort of having to make a sudden dash to the toilet, but the feeling passed. He pulled on the baggy, beltless pants and canvas shoes he'd been given in place of his own clothes, stood up gingerly, and moved to the table. One of the books on the shelf above was a travelogue about nineteenth-century life among the Yakut hunters. McCain took it down and opened the back cover to reveal three small notches cut into the edge, about an eighth of an inch apart near the top. He pressed a fourth notch with his thumbnail, replaced the book, and went behind the partition to the washbasin to rinse his face. He felt unusually lead-limbed and sluggish when he walked.

He had seen nothing of Paula since their arrest. The interrogations had been constant and relentless, but so far he hadn't been treated improperly. That wasn't necessarily grounds for comfort, however. No doubt the Soviets intended to exploit the propaganda opportunities of the situation to their fullest, and had no intention of compromising their advantage by laying themselves open to counteraccusations. But how long that political condition might persist was another matter, he reflected as he wiped cold water from his eyes and peered at his reflection in the polished-metal mirror cemented to the wall. Certainly the Russians would be in no hurry to ease the pressure on the US, which probably had something to do with his not being permitted to communicate with his own authorities back on Earth. In fact, he had been told nothing to indicate even if the incident was public knowledge yet.

He had just emerged from the washroom and was about to put on his shirt, when the panel behind the grille on the door slid aside and voices sounded outside. A pair of eyes scrutinized him for a moment, and then came the sound of the door being unlocked. It opened, and a tall, lean man with gray hair and a pointed beard entered, followed by a younger, darker-skinned companion. Both were wearing white, hip-length physician's smocks and gray-white check pants. There were also two uniformed guards, who remained outside in the corridor when the bearded man swung the door shut. McCain tensed, but the manner of the two was not threatening.

"Well, how do you feel this morning?" the bearded man inquired. His tone was intermediate between genial and matter-of-fact, as if he presumed that McCain knew what he was talking about. McCain looked at him and said nothing. "Fatigued? Not quite coordinated? A little hazy in the head, eh?" He sat back against the edge of the table and folded his arms to look McCain up and down. The younger man put down a black medical bag that he had been holding. "Well, come on," the bearded man said after a short pause. "The patient can hardly help us look after his interests if he won't say anything, can he?"

"What interests?" McCain asked. "What are you talking about?"

The bearded man regarded him curiously. "You don't know who I am, do you?" he said.

A pause. "No."

"Oh, dear." The bearded man glanced aside at his colleague. "I think we may have a complete block here." Then, back at McCain, "My name is Dr. Kazhakin. We have met before, I assure you—several times, in fact. You've been a little sick, you understand." He gestured nonchalantly. "It's not uncommon among people unaccustomed to an offplanet environment. Space-acclimatization sickness. The weightlessness during the trip up plays a part, and so does the excess of cosmic rays, but primarily it's an upset of the balance mechanism caused by adapting to a rotating structure. The effects can be quite disruptive until the nervous system learns to compensate."

"Really?" McCain sounded unconvinced. "And that causes amnesia?"

"We put you under a rather strong sedative," Kazhakin explained. "You've been out for a couple of days. What you're feeling is the aftereffect. Sometimes the memory can be impaired slightly—rather like a bump on the head."

Although McCain's expression didn't change, inwardly he felt alarmed. Kazhakin was trying to justify memory loss and symptoms of the aftereffects of drugs. As McCain knew well, some extremely potent substances were available to psychological researchers and therapists, and to military and police interrogators. Although there was no truly reliable "truth drug" of the kind beloved in fiction, combined chemical assaults of different stimulants and depressants affected different individuals in different ways, and in general anything was possible. Suddenly he had the worried feeling that perhaps his interrogation mightn't have been so gentlemanly after all.

"Let's have a look, then," Kazhakin said. He motioned for McCain to sit on the edge of the cot, then inspected both his eyes, his tongue and mouth, and dabbed around on his chest and back with a stethoscope while the assistant prepared a blood-pressure gauge. "And we'll want sample bottles for some blood and urine," Kazhakin told him.

Tattered remnants of recollections were beginning to float back. He saw the image of a man in a Russian major general's uniform, with black, crinkly hair showing gray streaks, bright, penetrating eyes beneath puffy lids, and a craggy, heavy-jowled face. "Of course it's obvious you're not a journalist . . . Did you know what the file contained? . . . Which organization sent you? . . ." There was another Russian there, too, inseparable from the general as part of the image swimming in McCain's memory, but the details remained obscure.

Kazhakin was watching McCain's face as he inflated the bulb of the sphygmomanometer. "Brain starting to function again now, is it? Some things coming back?"

"What day is this?" McCain asked.

"May fourth. You abused your guest privileges on the first, you fell sick the day after, and you've been out for two days, as I said."

If that were so, there ought to have been one notch in the book, not three, McCain thought. It was strange that he had woken up remembering to update his tally of days—or at least awakenings—and yet had no recollection of having done it before. It pointed to his having been out of control of his faculties for longer than Kazhakin was claiming. That would have been consistent with potent drugs, which was not exactly a reassuring thought.

"You probably feel a bit heavy and weak, but in fact you've lost a little weight," Kazhakin said. "I'll give you some pills to pick you up—no tricks, I promise—and we'll put you on an enrichment diet to build up your strength. I'm sure that General Protbornov wouldn't want you thinking of us as inconsiderate hosts." He saw an involuntary flicker in McCain's eyes. "Ah, so you remember the name, eh? That's good." Kazhakin unwound the bandage from McCain's arm and smirked at him with undisguised sarcasm. "Yes, we'll soon have you back to normal, *Mr. Earnshaw* of Pacific News Services, California. I do hope your readers won't be too upset if they have to put up with your being out of circulation for a while."

McCain watched expressionlessly as Kazhakin handed the sphygmomanometer back to the assistant and wrote some numbers onto a chart. It was obvious from the circumstances of his and Paula's capture that the cover story had capsized immediately. He wondered how much more—that he didn't even know about—might have started taking water since, or already have foundered completely to join it.

◉ CHAPTER SEVEN ◉

"You were apprehended in a place you had no right to be, in the act of obtaining misinformation fabricated to discredit the Soviet Union—and not trivially, but on a scale that would have had the gravest international repercussions. You were in possession of specialized espionage equipment, and you came here under assumed names, carrying false papers." Major General Protbornov paused to allow the gravity of his words to sink in. The action was for effect— this was hardly the first time he'd been through this. He continued, "We can all admire loyalty—indeed, we take justifiable pride in our own—but there is a point beyond which it turns into unreasonable stubbornness. At least tell us who you are and the name of the organization that sent you. You must agree that we are entitled to know that much."

Paula Bryce squinted against the light at the vague form outlined on the far side of the desk. At least they had turned the brightness down from the blinding level it had been at all through yesterday. And Protbornov's restraint was a relief after the shouting and impatience of the other general who had interrogated her initially, before she'd gotten sick a few days earlier. It was all part of a game they played, she told herself. The problem was trying—against fear, fatigue, and a numbing lack of sleep—to tell which of the roles and threats that she had been exposed to were for effect, which were real, and which, depending on expediency, might be interchangeable.

The bruises on her body still ached from the roughing up she'd been given on arrival at Internal Security Headquarters by two female Russian guards with sow faces and the physiques of weight lifters—a ritual doubtless intended to set roles and establish for future reference whose place was whose. Then had come the ordeal of hour after hour of demands, threats, and the same questions repeated over and over, always with the implication of further possibilities that her treatment by the two guards had represented a first taste of.

But she hadn't given away anything. That was the most important thing that she'd forced herself to recite in her mind, as had been drummed into her by Foleda's people. "Clam up, deny everything, never admit or confirm anything, even if it's obvious to everyone and staring you in the face," one of the UDIA men in the Pentagon had told her. "Because one thing leads to another. The first admission is a step onto a slope that gets slipperier all the way to the bottom. It's like after quitting cigarettes: the only way to stay off is to stay off completely. You don't fool with even one, because there's a whole world of difference between *no* cigarette and *some* cigarettes. But there isn't a lot of difference between one and two, or between four and five, or nineteen and twenty. Okay? It's the same with revealing information: once you make that first slip, there's no place to dig your heels in and stop."

Or could she have given away a lot more than she thought, without knowing it? She had fallen ill for a couple of days—so they'd told her—with an acclimatization problem that affected some people on going into space. She couldn't remember much about it, but from the way she'd felt when she started seeing things coherently again, she concluded that she'd been under some kind of drug. The doctor told her it was a sedative. But she had been told something about drugs, too, before leaving on the mission . . . she couldn't remember what. She didn't have clear recollections of anything right now. All she wanted to do was rest and sleep . . . Everything was too muddled and took too much effort to think about.

"This is getting nowhere," the figure next to Protbornov complained—a colonel, younger, businesslike, projecting the image of being ambitious and unprincipled. His name was Buvatsky. "Give us just half a day. I guarantee everything you want to know." Bluff, Paula told herself. Nice guy-bad guy. Part of the act.

"Let us hope that extremes won't be necessary," Protbornov rumbled. "You agree that you came here to *Valentina Tereshkova* under a false identity, and with the intention of committing acts of espionage?" His voice was louder this time, evidently directed at Paula.

She shook her head, feigning even greater fatigue than she felt. "What?"

"You agree that you came here under a false identity, intending to commit espionage?"

"I don't agree anything."

"But that much is obvious."

"I wish to communicate with a representative of the United Sates government."

"You know very well that there is no such person for you to talk to here."

"I didn't say talk to. I said communicate with. That can be arranged."

"That is impossible."

"Why?"

"For now, it is impossible. And besides, you are hardly in a position to be making demands. I ask you again, Do you not agree that you came here under a false identity?"

"I agree with nothing."

"What is your name?"

"I wish to communicate with a representative of my government."

"Do you still claim to be this person, Paula Shelmer?"

"That's what my papers say."

"Do you still claim to be an employee of Pacific News Services, California?"

"I'm not claiming anything. You'll believe what you choose to, anyway." Wrong, a part of her mind groaned. She was starting to talk back to them. Whether or not she revealed anything that mattered wasn't the point: it was just as much a first step.

"Common sense dictates that such is not the case. The equipment that you had with you was purpose-designed—hardly the kind of gadgetry that a news agency issues its staff, you have to admit." Protbornov's tone was casual now, almost chatty. He turned down the lamp, as if making a symbolic gesture to stop all this unnecessary unpleasantness. She needed to talk, it seemed to acknowledge. "It's clear you were employed by the American government. That much is true, at least, isn't it?" His voice held a note of regret that sounded almost genuine. Or was she projecting into it something that a part of her deep down needed to hear? There was a short pause. Her head nodded down onto her chest, and her thoughts swam. "It is true, isn't it? You are not with Pacific News Services, are you?"

"No," she heard herself whisper, even as another voice inside her head woke up, shouting too late in protest.

"But you are with the American government. Is that not correct?"

From somewhere long in the past she remembered hearing about the way salesmen were taught to begin their closing pitch with a series of statements that the prospect could do nothing but agree with. Once begun, the pattern was difficult to break out of and made it easier to go along with the salesman's proposal than refuse it. She had just made her first slip, not by telling Protbornov something he already knew, but by agreeing with him. She shook her head and said nothing.

"Which department of the American government are you with?" A pause. "The CIA?" Another pause. "The UDIA?" Silence. Then, "I should remind you that it is possible to ask these questions again, but utilizing physiological monitoring instruments that will make concealment of the truth impossible. . . . Very well, we've established that you are not Paula Shelmer of Pacific News Services, and that you are employed by the American government. Now, purely for our records and to enable us to furnish information to your own people and to the various human-rights organizations who concern themselves with the welfare of those in your kind of predicament, what is your name?"

"I wish to contact a representative of the United States government."

Buvatsky got up with a snort and paced impatiently away to the side of the room, outside her field of vision. Protbornov raised a hand to massage his brow with his fingers, and leaned back with a heavy sigh. "Look," he said, "it is clear from the contents of the computer file you were in the process of copying that your mission was to obtain misinformation created to support the propaganda campaign which your government has been waging concerning the true nature of *Valentina Tereshkova*." Protbornov looked up and shot at her with sudden sharpness, "Have you ever heard the name 'Magician'?" Even before the word registered consciously, Paula knew with a sinking feeling that her face had supplied the answer. Protbornov went on, as if the fact were too evident to be worthy of mention, "Magician was a traitor, who was uncovered by our counterintelligence operations, as you well know. He has recanted and gone on record voluntarily to confirm that the information he planted in the file was false. He was working in league with American propagandists as part of a plan to mislead world opinion at a time when the newly emerging great powers remain unaligned. We can show you a video recording of his admission. It was made quite freely, I assure you." Paula looked skeptical. "We could arrange for Magician to be brought here from Earth to tell you to your face, if that would convince you," Protbornov offered.

Paula frowned down at her knees. The significance escaped her. Or was she just confused? She looked up wearily. "Why do you care whether I believe it or not?"

Protbornov sat forward, and Paula sensed Buvatsky turning in a corner of the room. Too late, she realized that she'd said the wrong thing again.

"Don't you understand? That is what this whole issue revolves around," Protbornov said. "Your people told you that this colony is a disguised war platform, is that not so? They described various weapons that they claimed were concealed here, yes? And their proof was to be in the package that Magician had compiled. Oh, don't look so horrified—it was an elementary deduction from the facts that we possess. . . . But what matters is that you understand they were lying to you . . . lying, just as they have been lying to the world. As I said a few minutes ago, I admire your loyalty, but don't allow it to blind you to the possibility that the United States can be less than perfect sometimes, and that perhaps we of the Soviet Union are not always wrong." He allowed a moment for her to reflect on that, then continued, "You see, where Colonel Buvatsky and I differ is that I believe all of us are basically the same beneath the surface—all unfortunate victims of the mistakes of history and our own, unnecessary, mutual suspicions.

"I don't have to spell out the tragedy that could result from this paranoia. . . ." Protbornov raised a hand as if to forestall her reply. "Yes, on our side as well as yours. The world has been trembling for over half a century. But don't you see what an opportunity this represents? For once, the delusions that the paranoia is based on can be exposed for what they really are. It wouldn't put an instant end to all the tensions that have plagued our two nations for so long, of course, but it would be a solid step in the direction of defusing them. Every withdrawal from a brink has to begin with a first step somewhere. Don't you owe the peoples of that world down there that much—a chance to hope?"

Paula had been blinking her eyes, trying to follow. "I'm not sure I understand," she said. Her voice was dry and cracked. Protbornov poured water from a pitcher in front of him into a glass and set it down across the desk. Paula stared at it. Whether it was the wrong thing to do or not, she suddenly didn't care. She picked up the glass and gulped down the water gratefully.

"We are prepared to take you, in person, to all the places in *Tereshkova* where you were told these weapons were supposed to exist, and let you see for yourself that the accusations are simply not true." Protbornov threw up his hands. "What could be fairer than that? We want the truth to be known."

Paula replaced the glass on the edge of the desk, noticing as she did so that her hand was shaking. "Why not open the whole place to international inspection, if that's what you want?" she asked. "Let everyone come and see for themselves."

Protbornov tossed up his hands again. "I agree! And if I were First Secretary of the Party, that is precisely what I would do. But I am not Comrade Petrokhov. And for reasons which I do not make it my business to criticize, our policy is that we will not strip ourselves naked before the world on demand, just to prove our good intentions."

"You've already demonstrated your good intentions," Paula said, massaging her stomach tenderly.

"I apologize for that incident. It was an accident. The guards responsible were transferred only recently from one of our military punishment units, where procedures are different. They have been reprimanded and removed."

Having served their purpose, Paula thought. "I'm still not sure what you're saying. . . ." Despite her resolve, she heard herself getting talkative. . . . But, dammit, stuck out here, two hundred thousand miles away from everything, she needed somebody to talk to, even a Russian general. That sounded a little like the beginnings of self-pity, she reflected idly. It wasn't like her at all to feel that way, but she found that the thought didn't really bother her very much. She had reason to feel sorry for herself—oh God, had there been something in the water?

"All we want you to do, after you've satisfied yourself that what I've said is true, is simply to make a public statement confirming what you've seen with your own eyes. If we can show you that our country has been slandered before the world, is it unreasonable that we should ask this? It is, after all, the truth which is supposed to matter, isn't it, even when it inconveniently fails to support preconceived notions? Isn't that what you were trained to think as a scientist?"

"Yes," Paula answered automatically, even as she saw the mistake.

Protbornov gave a satisfied nod. "So, we have established that you are a scientist. With whom? A private corporation, perhaps? But then, how would you come to know so much about Russian equipment? It was you who was operating the device. More likely one of the services, then, yes? . . . Yes. Very well, which one? Army, maybe? . . . Navy? . . . US Air Force, perhaps? We can run physiological tests, you know."

It was all being recorded by concealed cameras, Paula guessed. Afterward, Protbornov and his specialists would play the recordings over and over, studying her every response. Probably other hidden devices were measuring changes in her skin temperature and reflectivity, muscular tensions, eye movements, and other giveaways, at the very moment. Suddenly she found herself weary of it all, helpless against forces that she didn't comprehend and didn't know how to resist. It was all pointless. In the end they were bound to win. And in spite of herself, what Protbornov was saying *did* sound only fair and reasonable.

"Maybe," she said. She wasn't sure what she had said it in response to. Every thought that started to take shape dissolved away again.

"You will agree to consider making a statement, if we can show you that the allegations concerning weapons are false? This would not have to be a public declaration. It need only be for the information of certain Western and Asian governments. In fact, we could arrange for the recording to be vetted by your own people before it was shown to anyone else. That would relieve you of any personal responsibility, and it would cause no unnecessary embarrassment in international circles. You see, our aims are quite honorable. A wrong has been committed, and we simply wish to put it right." Protbornov paused and looked across the desk.

Paula rubbed her eyes. All she had to do was agree to a request that sounded reasonable, and she would be able to sleep. How could she be wrong for simply telling the truth about what she saw? God alone knew how much trouble throughout history had been caused by people refusing to. Protbornov waited a few seconds longer, then added, "It goes without saying that your cooperation in this small matter could make a big difference to eventual agreement between our governments concerning your future. We understand the regrettable necessity for the kind of work you were drawn into. Given a suitable incentive, we can find it very easy to let bygones be bygones over such things. Otherwise . . ." He shrugged.

Paula stared at the glass on the desk. A distorted, inverted image of Protbornov's face peered back at her out of the thick curve of its base. As she stared, it took on the appearance of a grotesque parody of a spider, watching from the center of its web for its prey's struggles to die away before it moved. She shook herself out of the stupor that had been creeping over her. Then it came to her that the Russians would have known far more than they seemed to if Earnshaw had given away anything to them at all. She wondered suddenly what he might be going through at that moment.

And gradually a feeling of self-disgust overcame her at the thought of what had almost happened. She drew in a determined breath and shivered as she fought back visions of what she might be letting herself in for. She looked up, clasped her hands together between her knees to prevent them from shaking visibly, and steadied her gaze across the desk.

"I wish to communicate with a representative of the United States government," she said.

✹ CHAPTER EIGHT ✹

The air conditioner hummed, and the resonating undertone came and went. Lewis McCain lay on the cot, staring up at the ceiling. Now that his head was clearer, isolated recollections from the hazy period following his arrest would appear suddenly in his mind in a seemingly patternless fashion. Lying here, staring up at the air-conditioner grille, was one of them. It had a gray-painted metal escutcheon surrounding it, with a scratch by one of the corner screws where a screwdriver had slipped. The sound hadn't contained that distinctive resonance then. Something must have loosened itself in the ducting fairly recently, he thought idly.

McCain didn't trust Russians. In his experience, whenever they started behaving reasonably, they were up to something. They'd been giving him too easy a time. Why? What were they after? From what he knew of Soviet interrogation practices, it was likely on two counts that Paula was having a tougher time: one, she was a woman, and therefore more easily intimidated, according to standard KGB thinking; and two, she would quickly have been identified as a technician rather than an intelligence professional, and hence more vulnerable through knowing less of what to expect.

So why were they playing a restrained game with him? Probably because they anticipated international ramifications and had no intention of compromising their own position by showing less-than-spotless hands. If they saw the affair as eventually being made public, they'd probably be putting pressure on Paula to make a signed statement. In his case, seeing there would be little chance of getting anywhere with a similar demand, they might simply have decided to work on convincing him that they weren't such bad people after all, and see what accrued benefits they might be able to squeeze from the results later. Yes, he thought, nodding up at the air-conditioner grille, that would be consistent with the way they had been acting.

He thought about how he had come to find himself here at the age of thirty-six, a prisoner in a Soviet space habitat hundreds of thousands of miles from Earth.

When people asked what had induced him to make a career in military intelligence, he usually told them it was ideological: that he believed the Western way of life was worth defending. Despite its faults, a democracy based on free enterprise allowed him to be himself, to believe and say what he chose, and, apart from a few not-unreasonable constraints, made how he preferred to lead his life none of anyone else's business. That suited him just fine. So, the answer was true as far as it went; it was the kind that people expected, and they accepted it. But there was another side to it, too, which involved more personal things.

McCain had been born in Iowa, but his mother, Julia, was Czechoslovakian. She had escaped during the anti-Russian uprising of 1968. He remembered her telling of the Czechs' disgust over the sellout by the British and French to Hitler at Munich in 1938 of the nation which they themselves had created a mere twenty years previously and pledged solemnly to defend. Instead, at the very moment when Czechoslovakia was mobilizing to defend itself, they had surrendered it to six years of Nazi barbarism. The story had made a deep impression on the developing mind of young Lewis McCain. It had convinced him that tyrants and dictators could not be appeased. The lure of easy pickings merely excited them on to greater excesses. As with people, nations able to defend themselves, and prepared to do so if they had to, were left alone.

Julia retold stories that her parents had told her of listening around an illegal radio to reports of Hitler's armies storming eastward, apparently overwhelming the Russians as effortlessly as they had overwhelmed the Poles. Czechoslovakia, left hundreds of miles behind the front, had surely been consumed in a nightmare that would lie across Europe for generations to come. But then the news began to change. The Russians counterattacked from the very gates of Moscow. They held at Leningrad. They stopped, then encircled and annihilated the Germans at Stalingrad. In the years that followed, the Germans were driven back remorselessly, until eventually the Red Army entered Czechoslovakia. On the day their T-34 tanks rumbled into Prague, Lewis's grandfather had strode into the house and announced in a voice shaking with pride and emotion, "I am a Communist!" And for a while Czechoslovakia became perhaps the most faithful of the Soviets' allies.

But the elation was short-lived. Ironically the Russians, like the Nazis before them, became oppressors of the people who had welcomed them as liberators. Instead of the independence they had promised, they imposed a Moscow-controlled puppet regime and brought in the familiar Bolshevik apparatus of ruthless persecution, midnight arrests, trumped-up charges, brutally extracted confessions, deportations, and executions to eliminate potential opposition. And, fanatically pursuing their socialist ideals, they seized land, property, and all small businesses, which henceforth were to be owned by the state.

The foundry and engineering shop that Lewis's grandfather had worked strenuously to build up through the worst years of the thirties was taken from the family and handed over to be managed by a Party bureaucrat who had never seen a lathe or a grinding machine, had no comprehension of taking pride in excellence, and who was incapable of thinking in any terms other than of quotas. Within six months the business was ruined, and Lewis's grandfather lost his income, which was replaced by a subsistence wage. Later, when years of anger at corruption, incompetence, and lies finally boiled over into open rebellion in the streets, he was shot in the fighting when the Red Army's tanks returned to Prague. That was the last thing that Julia remembered seeing before she and her companions fled for the border. She ended up in Holland, where she met her first husband, an

American marketing executive. They moved to the US, but the marriage didn't work out, and Julia spent some years raising a son, Ralph, on her own before she remarried, this time to a widowed Iowa farmer of Scottish descent: Lewis's father, Malcolm. That was in 1981, during the latter years of what had been a confused period for America.

After emerging as the most powerful among the war's victors, the nation had gone on to enjoy two decades of growth and prosperity unprecedented by any society in history. Uninterested in the creeds and passions responsible for turning half the rest of the world into rubble, the generation that had grown up through the lean and threadbare years of the Depression turned to Sears, General Electric, General Motors, and the loan officer at the local bank for fulfillment. In their own eyes they were overcoming the problems of poverty, disease, hunger, and ignorance which had devastated human populations for as long as humanity had existed. They were proud of their achievement and of the society that had made it possible. They assumed their children would be grateful. They tried to export their system to other peoples and assumed they would be grateful, too.

Pendulums swing, however.

The next generation, watching the rest of the world's problems on color TV over refrigerator-fresh steaks after driving home from school in air-conditioned automobiles, instead of feeling grateful, felt guilty. By some curious twist of logic it became America's fault that the rest of the world still had problems at all. Through a sweeping extension of the "Eat-up-your-potatoes-because-the-children-in-China-are-starving" syndrome—as if, by some natural law of protein parity, every uneaten potato on a plate in Minnesota mysteriously induced the symmetric disappearance of rice from a bowl in Peking—America's enterprise in putting its own house in order was to blame for the disorder that persisted everywhere else.

The result was a moral crusade against the American system and the institutions that gave it substance: capitalism and the business corporations, the technological industries that supported them, the science that made technology possible, and ultimately the faculty of reason itself, which was the foundation of science. The weapon was fear. Wreathed in clouds of acid rain, radiation, and carcinogens, buried under indestructible plastics, deluged with genetically mutated microbes, and stripped of its ozone, the planet would ferment in swamps of its own garbage—if the Bomb didn't get it first or bring on a Nuclear Winter. And America had provoked the Soviets by refusing to disarm unilaterally and thereby ensure world peace—as the European democracies had ensured peace by disarming *them*selves unilaterally in the 1930's.

The greater the contribution to the success of the system, the greater the guilt. It followed that, along with the chemist, the auto maker, the pharmacist, and the nuclear engineer, one of the most persecuted victims of the process should be the American farmer. He had, after all, raised productivity to a point where three percent of the population could not only feed the country better than seventy percent had been able to a century earlier, but could also export a hefty surplus—freeing lots of intellectuals to write in comfort on the evils of production and to campaign for the civil rights of the malaria virus while treating people as pollution.

Consequently, after putting up with years of harassment from inquisitorial regulators and political activists seeking to ban everything from fertilizers to farm mechanization, Malcolm sold the farm and moved the family to California, where he invested the proceeds in an agricultural-machinery business that provided a reasonable living. Throughout Lewis's teenage years, Malcolm had continued to rage about "corporate socialism"—by which he meant the agribusiness giant that had bought the land in Iowa—as much as Julia warned against collectivism. It no more represented the spirit of America, he used to fume, than the liberal-socialist element in Washington, and had played as great a part in bringing about the economic mess and cultural negativism of the seventies.

Thus, one of Lewis's parents was a refugee from a tyranny that had destroyed the worth of a lifetime's labor; the other had been a victim of legalized witch-hunting in the name of ideology. Reflection on these things produced a deep sense of resentment and injustice in Lewis as a youth. He concluded that there were no such things as inalienable "natural" rights. The only rights that meant anything were those that could be defended—by custom, by law, and, if necessary, by force.

McCain graduated from UCLA at twenty-two with BA degrees in Political History and Modern Languages. These qualifications, along with his innate skepticism and desire to preserve his individuality, added up to a good grounding for work in the intelligence community. Hence, when, desperate to escape from the tedium of California farm-country life, he attended on-campus interviews for entry into the armed services, a recruiter from another department of the government pounced on him instead. So, he'd ended up back at school, this time with the UDIA at its training center in Maryland. Upon completion of the course he went to its headquarters to work as an administrative assistant, which he fondly assumed would be a cover title for more exciting and glamorous things. But the job turned out to be just what it said—clerk—and for two boring years he proved his loyalty by shuffling papers, filling in forms, sorting incoming material, and checking facts . . . and checking them again, and then rechecking them. The experience turned out to be vital to becoming an effective agent.

Since then he'd spent some years in Europe with NATO intelligence, which was followed by six months back in the US for intensive training on such things as codes and communications, observation, security, concealment and evasion, weapons and self-defense, breaking and entering, lock picking, safe cracking, wiretaps, bugs, and other noble arts. After that he'd gone back to Europe to be introduced to counterintelligence directed against Soviet espionage into NATO weaponry, and then back to the States for courses in Eastern languages and advanced Russian—he'd spoken Czech and German, which Julia and Ralph had often conversed in, since he was a boy. From there he'd been sent on a series of assignments in the Far East, beginning with a position at the US embassy in Tokyo. His last job before being recalled to Washington for the Pedestal mission was developing a network of intelligence contacts and sources in Peking. And through all of it, everything he'd seen reinforced his original conviction that the Western way wasn't such a bad way to live. Yet there were lots of people out there who for one reason for another, real or imagined, were ready to bring the West down if they got the chance.

The key sounded in the door, and McCain sat up. It was too early for lunch. Protbornov entered, accompanied by a major called Uskayev. Behind them was a guard carrying a canvas bag. Protbornov looked around, his dark eyes moving casually beneath their heavy lids. He took a blue pack of Russian cigarettes from one of the pockets in his tunic, selected one, and almost as if it were an afterthought offered the pack to McCain. McCain shook his head. "You must be feeling almost at home here by now," Protbornov rumbled. "Well, how would you say we have treated you? Not unfairly, I trust?"

"It could be worse," McCain agreed neutrally.

Protbornov lit his cigarette and lifted one of the books from the shelf to inspect its title. "A pity that it requires so much to convince you that we really are not so uncivilized. You do have an extraordinarily suspicious nature, you know, Mr. Earnshaw—an impediment for a journalist, I would have thought. Your female companion thinks so, too. I'd imagine that many people you've met in life have said the same. Have you ever thought about that? Is it possible, do you think, that you could be wrong on some things, and that the consensus of others might have some merit?" He flipped casually through the pages of the book, and then, either accidentally or making the motion appear so, ran a finger down the edge of the back cover. From the corner of an eye McCain saw Uskayev watching him closely, and forced himself to suppress any flicker of reaction.

"I don't think it's a good idea to be too influenced by other people's opinions," McCain said.

"Your Air Force scientist friend would agree with you on that," Protbornov replied, searching McCain's face as he spoke. "A most obstinate woman. But be that as it may, she recognizes the importance of the present situation and its relevance to world security, and she has agreed to cooperate responsibly by making a public statement of the kind we have requested." Protbornov gestured in the air with his cigarette and shrugged indifferently. "So now you don't matter to us so much. The only issue you need concern yourself with is your own fate. If you adopted a more reasonable attitude than the one you've been showing, well, anything is possible. If not . . ." he shrugged again, "what happens then will be up to the Kremlin. But as I said, it is no longer of primary importance to us."

McCain looked at him almost contemptuously. "I expected something better than that. Don't tell me you're slipping."

Protbornov seemed to have been prepared for as much. "Policy decisions are not my concern," he said. "My job is simply to carry them out. For whatever reason, orders have come through for you to be moved to another location. You should find it more congenial— at least you will have company . . . and the opportunity for more stimulating conversations than ours tend to be." He indicated the bag that the guard had placed on the table. "Collect your belongings. You are to be transferred immediately."

McCain began gathering together the clothes and personal effects that he had been given. "With a personal sendoff by the general? Why so honored?"

"Why not? I feel we have come to know one another a little in the course of the past three weeks, even if your attitude has been less than candid. A common courtesy from the host to a departing guest, maybe? Or simply a way to indicate that we desire no hard feelings?"

McCain went around the partition to retrieve his toilet articles. So far the whole thing had been an exercise in testing and probing for weaknesses, to be exploited later—and probably the same with Paula, too. What for? he wondered. There was a lot more behind it all than he had unraveled so far.

"So, where to?" he asked as he came back out, closing the bag. "Earthside?"

"Nothing so exciting, I'm afraid," Protbornov replied. The guard was holding the door open. "It's expensive to ship people between here and Earth. Why should we pay the bill for returning one of the United States' spies to them? They can come and collect you when the time comes—assuming, of course, that Moscow decides to let them have you back. Until then, you remain here on *Tereshkova*, at a place called Zamork." A guard went ahead. Protbornov walked by McCain, with the major a pace behind, while the guard who had held the door brought up the rear.

"Oh, you mean the gulag that you've got up here," McCain said. Zamork was on the edge of the town known as Novyi Kazan, and was labeled vaguely on the maps as a detention facility. "I always admired how faithful a copy this is of the Mother County."

"Oh, don't think of Zamork as a gulag," Protbornov said breezily. "Times are changing. Even your Christian heaven needed somewhere to keep its dissidents."

"I take it that means we're unlikely to be seeing the last of each other."

"I'm sure the Fates have it in store for us to meet again."

"What about Paula Shelmer? Will she be moving too?"

"We have received no orders concerning her." There was a short silence. Then Protbornov added, "However, she is in good health and spirits. I thought you might like to know."

"Thanks."

Ten minutes later, McCain, accompanied by two armed guards, boarded a magdrive car at a monorail terminal underneath the Security Headquarters. Soon afterward, they departed around *Tereshkova*'s peripheral ring, bound for the town of Novyi Kazan.

❂ CHAPTER NINE ❂

According to the Soviet publicity material, Novyi Kazan was a center for arts, sports, and education, intended to provide rest, relaxation, and a contrast to Turgenev's administrative bustle and the scientific-industrial concentration at Landausk. The travel guides made little mention of its including a prison. Maybe, McCain thought as he looked out of the speeding monorail car, that was what the Russian interpretation of rest and relaxation meant.

The car seemed to be a standard model containing three pairs of double seats facing each other on either side of a central aisle, but its only other occupants besides McCain were two armed guards.

Evidently this one was not for public use. It had left the jumble of Turgenev's high-rise core and moved out along the valley that he and Paula had viewed from the terrace high over the town's square on the day of their arrival. On one side, the central strip was an irregular ribbon of green, wandering among grassy mounds, clumps of shrubs, and occasional trees, with a stream threading its way from pool to pool between rocky banks as it collected cataracts tumbling in from the valley sides. Farther away beyond the green strip, wheeled vehicles vanished and reappeared at intervals on a hidden roadway roughly matching the monorail's route. There were plenty of people, alone, in pairs, and in groups, talking, walking, or just sitting and watching the water; a woman was feeding ducks, and two boys were sailing a boat.

Above it all, the twin ribbon-suns curved away out of sight in their artificial sky.

In an earlier century, the Russian empress Catherine the Great had decided to tour the countryside to observe the living conditions of the people for herself. Her chief adviser, Grigory Potemkin, sent advance parties ahead of the royal entourage to erect a whole make-believe world of fake villages with gaily painted facades to conceal the poverty and misery that the peasants had to endure. The people were forced to put on new clothes, loaned for the occasion, and dance, wave, strew flowers, and cheer to maintain the illusion. Afterward, scores of Western observers who had traveled with the royal party returned home filled with enthusiasm and admiration by the scenes they had witnessed. As McCain stared out of the window of the monorail car, he thought back to the reports he'd read by excited visitors to *Valentina Tereshkova*, bringing to the world their revelation of the changed face of communism. Just as others had come back with glowing accounts of Hitler's Germany in the 1930's.

Halfway along the agricultural zone outside Turgenev, the line passed through the clutter of processing plant, freight elevators, storage silos, and handling machinery piled around the base of the minor spoke, which was known as Agricultural Station 3 and possessed a geometry every bit as irregular and disorienting as that of the town. The roof here was clear for some distance on either side of where the spoke passed through, giving a breathtaking glimpse of the spoke's entire length, soaring away to the hub structure a half mile overhead. Another half mile above that was the far side of the ring, and beyond, an endlessness of space and stars. The sight made the enclosing walls of *Valentina Tereshkova* suddenly seem very thin and fragile. For a while, McCain had almost forgotten he was in space at all.

Beyond the spoke, the car passed through more of the agricultural zone, all pretty much as before, and finally entered the outskirts of Novyi Kazan. Houses and apartments appeared strewn down the valley sides as at Turgenev, but with more greenery and water; a sports field came and went, with figures playing soccer, and the view ahead became one of buildings merging and rising toward another chaotic downtown center. Then the track entered a tunnel. The car slowed, and McCain watched through the front window as it lurched to follow a branch tunnel off the through-route.

One of the guards moved forward to the console under the window, which appeared to be the driver's position when the car was being operated manually, and the car halted before a sturdy-looking metal door closing off the track ahead. A tone sounded, and an officer's face appeared on the console screen. "Prisoner two-seven-one-zero-six for admission," the guard said. The officer consulted something off-screen, then leaned forward to operate a control. A camera mounted inside the car pivoted slowly to survey the interior, pausing for a few seconds when it came to McCain's face. Then the door ahead slid open. The car moved through and stopped beside a platform. The guards motioned to McCain to get out. When they emerged, the door across the track behind had already closed.

They were in what looked like a loading and unloading bay, with the track branching into two lines that ran parallel between service platforms for a distance and then merged again before disappearing through another door at the far end, also closed. More guards were standing on the platform that McCain and his escorts had stepped out onto. With them was a group of a dozen or so men in plain gray jackets and matching pants with scarlet stripes, who began filing into the car. They were of various colors and races, and McCain guessed them to be from the place that he was on his way to. Several of them glanced curiously at him as he passed. They seemed healthy enough and alert. At least it didn't look as if he were about to join a house of zombies, he reflected as he walked between the guards toward the door opening off the platform.

Behind the door was a guardpost, inside which McCain saw the officer who had appeared on the screen within the car. A short corridor brought them to a stairway and elevator. They took the stairs up a level and crossed a hall containing rows of seats to enter a room with a counter running along one side, where the senior of the two escorts from Turgenev produced papers for the duty sergeant to sign. Then a captain came out of a room at the back to take charge, and the escorts departed. The captain asked the routine questions, and

McCain gave his routine fictitious answers, which the sergeant duly entered into a terminal on the counter. Then McCain was conducted through to an examination room, where he waited forty minutes for the doctor to be found to perform a physical check. At last, after being fingerprinted, voiceprinted, blood-sampled, facially scanned for computerized mug-shotting, typed, tested, measured, and weighed all over again, he was given an outfit like the ones he had just seen in the monorail terminal. The captain handed back the bag he had brought with him, along with another containing a spare change of clothes. Finally he told McCain to hold out his left arm.

"Why?"

"You are not here to ask questions."

McCain raised his arm. The captain pulled back the sleeve of his jacket, and the sergeant clipped an electronic unit on a red, plastic-coated band around his wrist, and then crimped and sealed it with a special tool. The captain pressed a button, and two more guards appeared from a door at the back of the room.

"This is your key to the areas which you are authorized to enter," the captain told McCain, indicating the wristband. "Security is mostly electronic at Zamork. Guards are too valuable here to stand around doing nothing, and the same applies to prisoners. Therefore you will be required to work a minimum-forty-eight-hour week. Your duties will be assigned by the foreman of the billet you're put in. Enforcement of discipline is firm, but not unfair. After an initial probationary period, a sensible attitude can earn privileges. Movement outside quarters after curfew, and attempts to cross the compound perimeter or to leave designated work areas in other parts of the colony are strictly forbidden—although escape from *Valentina Tereshkova* is, of course, quite impossible. Do you have any immediate questions?"

"What about communications with my government and messages home?"

"That does not fall within my area of authority."

"Whose area of authority does it fall in?"

"Such matters are questions of policy, decided in Moscow."

"So who's in charge of this whole place?"

"The governor is Lieutenant General Fedorov."

"So, how do I talk to him?"

"When *he* decides he wishes to talk to you. You will be interviewed by your block commandant later. Bring the matter up with him. In the meantime, you report to the foreman in billet B-three. The guards will take you there."

The guards took McCain back through the door that they had come from, and along a corridor to some stairs which led down to another door. A red light above the door came on as McCain approached, and a moment later went out again, accompanied by a beep. On the far side was a wide thoroughfare running crossways, with lime-green walls that were featureless except for welding seams and bundles of piping. There were large doorways opening off at intervals. It suggested, if anything, an enclosed street. Figures in gray tunics, singly and in pairs and groups, were walking on both sides, while in the center an electric tractor was hauling a trailer loaded with boxes. Just two guards were visible, pacing slowly together some distance away and looking more like street cops. McCain and his two escorts followed the road right to a corner, where it went left and continued, looking much the same as before. They passed an opening flanked on either side by sections of fixed bars, with a center section consisting of a sliding barred gate, which was open. A sign above read BLOCK A. Farther on they came to a similar gate, this time labeled BLOCK B. A red light came on as McCain followed the first guard through, then went out with a beep. McCain had the feeling that he could get really tired of red lights and beeps before very much longer.

They were at one end of a more-or-less square hall, with two rows of doors facing each other across a broad center space. On a higher level above, two more rows of identical doors looked down from behind railed walkways reached by metal stairs. Footbridges at both ends of the hall connected the walkways to complete a gallery overlooking the central floor area from all four sides. At the near end of the hall were several long tables with benches, at which men were loosely scattered, some in groups, others sitting alone. As with the group that McCain had seen boarding the monorail car, they were a mix of races and types. Some were reading, one writing, others playing cards, while many just sat. In the open area beyond the tables, more were standing talking, and others were gathered in a circle around some kind of game that involved tossing coins.

As he and his escorts moved on across the hall, McCain caught babbles of different languages. The voices dropped for a moment as he passed by the tables, and curious eyes followed him. They came to one of the doors on the right, which carried a large "3" painted in yellow. One of the guards gestured toward it. McCain stepped forward; the red light lit and the beeper beeped. He tried the door, and it opened. Without a word the two guards turned and left. McCain pushed the door wide and stepped through. The light was dimmer than in the area outside, and he paused for his eyes to adjust. Then he moved on inside, letting the door close behind him.

The room had an open area running all the way down the center, containing several tables with chairs pulled up on both sides. He moved forward and deposited the two bags he was carrying on the table nearest the door. To left and right, the space along the sides of the room was partitioned into a series of five or six bays, each of which contained two double-tier bunks, one alongside the partition on each side, separated by a narrow aisle containing kit lockers. There were pictures adorning the walls in places, some mugs and eating utensils on shelves, books, a long, carved wooden pipe resting in a bowl, and an unfinished game of chess on one of the tables. The place looked reasonably clean, but had a distinct odor of too many bodies living in too confined a space. Whoever the bodies were, they were absent for the moment.

There was an open door at the far end of the room, and as McCain's hearing adapted to the quiet after the hubbub outside, he discerned sounds of movement. A moment later a figure appeared framed in the far doorway, holding a broom. McCain waited. The man shuffled out and approached around the farmost table. He was of Oriental appearance, lithely built, and wearing a black skullcap in addition to the regulation gray tunic. As he came closer, McCain found that he had an abstruse face that managed to both reinforce and contradict at the same time the impression of years conveyed by his physique. It was furrowed and wizened about the eyes, yet surprisingly smooth everywhere else. His chin sprouted a short beard that was turning gray, but his stare was bright and alert like that of a curious child.

"You must be the American," he said. "My name is Nakajima-Lin Kohmei-Tso-Liang." His voice and expression were neutral, carrying neither undue warmth nor hostility. McCain was instantly confused. The construction was typically Asiatic with the family name coming first, but the double name itself was a composite of Japanese and Chinese; the first of the given names following sounded Japanese, but the other two were Chinese. He watched McCain curiously, and McCain had the feeling that he was able to read if the contradiction meant anything to McCain or not. "Generally I am called Koh."

"Lewis Earnshaw," McCain responded. "Most people call me Lew."

Koh came to where McCain was standing and indicated the lower tier of the bunk by the first partition to the left. "Your place will be there," he said. He nodded toward the corner bunk behind McCain's right. As McCain had noticed with some of the other bunks, its upper cot was hinged upright out of the way. It suggested that the place was not occupied to full capacity at present. "I live across there. It seems, therefore, that for a while we are to be neighbors." Koh spoke English well, with slow and careful articulation.

McCain picked up his bags from the table and moved across. "Well, I guess that's fine with me. Does your name make you Japanese or Chinese?"

"A mixture of the two, which goes back many generations. Appropriate to this century."

"I've spent some time in both countries. It sounds as if you were expecting me."

"The billet foreman is usually notified when a new arrival is due."

"What exactly is a foreman?"

"You are not familiar with the system?"

"How could I be?"

"Aren't you transferring from another part of Zamork?"

"No, I only just arrived."

Koh nodded. "I see. Every billet has a foreman. It's a trusted category of inmates who are responsible for discipline, take complaints to the right quarters, and hand out work assignments. Ours is called Luchenko, a Russian." He gestured vaguely in the direction of the far end of the room with his free hand. "His place is back there. He'll talk to you when he gets back."

"So, what's he like?"

"Oh, some days good, some days not so good. Most times okay."

McCain looked down at his cot, which held just a bare mattress. "What do we do about getting blankets and stuff?"

"You pick up a kit at OI—dishes, eating implements, and so on."

"What's OI?"

"The Official Issue store, in the Core complex across Gorky Street."

"Gorky Street?"

"Outside the block mess area—where you just came along. If you wish, I will show you the way when I'm finished."

"Are you here all the time, Koh?"

"One half day each week is for cleaning. This week it's my turn. It provides a welcome opportunity to think in peace and quiet. One seldom gets time to be alone in Zamork."

"How long have you been here now?"

"A year, roughly."

McCain nodded absently and stepped back to survey the bunk above his, trying to gauge something about the person who would be his closest neighbor. There were several raunchily explicit pinups attached to the head end of the partition, a rock magazine cover showing a pop group in action behind a star-spangled logo in the shape of the letters "USA," and, folded on the pillow below, an Ohio State University T-shirt. "What are you in here for?" he inquired.

"*Vy govorite po-Russki?*" Koh asked suddenly from behind him— *Do you speak Russian?*

McCain turned and studied his face for a second, then nodded. "*Da.*"

"Where are you from in America?" Koh went on, still in Russian. "Have you been on *Tereshkova* long? What was *your* offense?"

McCain saw the point and nodded resignedly. "I don't know you," he agreed, switching back to English.

"Nor I, you. As you obviously already understand, one learns not to ask such questions of strangers."

"Would I have admitted to speaking Russian if I'd been planted here?" McCain asked.

"Unlikely," Koh conceded. "But then again you might, if you were being very clever."

"Are they often very clever?"

"No. But when they are, that's when they're at their most dangerous."

McCain sighed. There was nothing he could say to alleviate all suspicions instantly. It would take time and patience. He sat down on his bunk and turned his attention to transferring the contents of his bags into his locker. "Who's the guy upstairs?" he asked, changing the subject. "Looks like another American."

Koh gave a short laugh. "No, not an American. An Americophile. His name is Mungabo. He's Zigandan. The Russians have strange impressions of American life, especially with regard to racial tensions, which their propagandists exaggerate. They also have a strange sense of humor. Luchenko thought it would be funny to put the American under the black man." He turned and began walking back toward the far end of the room. "Toilets and washing facilities are through there. I'll take you over to OI when I'm through."

"So, what did this Zigandan guy do for America that caused him to wind up here . . . or is that something we don't ask about, too?" McCain called after him.

"Oh no, everybody knows about that. He gave them a top-secret Russian plane—a MIG-55. At least, that was what the court-martial decided. Mungabo claimed that his electronic navigation system malfunctioned, but the KGB refused to believe that the whole thing wasn't a put-up job."

"What made them so sure?" McCain asked.

"It was elementary. Equipment produced under a Marxist economy, they pointed out, cannot malfunction."

❀ CHAPTER TEN ❀

Dr. Philip Kress, from the Brookhaven National Laboratory on Long Island, stared out unhappily from behind the table of panel members at the rows of delegates to the Third Conference on Communications Physics, sponsored by the Japanese Science Council and being held at the "university city" of Tsukuba.

"There are no doubt several reasons why the underwater neutrino-detection experiments have given ambiguous results," he said. "The biggest problem all along has been statistical. We're talking about trying to separate out a very few real events from an enormous background noise. Whichever way you approach it, you end up subtracting one big number from another big number, neither of them guaranteed absolutely, to yield a very small number, which is the answer you're looking for. It's a tricky problem, and we're working on it. What else can I say?" He tossed up a hand to indicate that he was through and sat back in his chair to light his pipe.

The panel moderator, Jules Dupalme, from the French telecommunications corporation CIT Alcatel, looked from side to side for further comment from the others. "Okay? Any more questions from the floor? No? Good. Well, there is one announcement before we end the session for lunch. Would all those who—"

"One question." A Japanese about halfway back near one of the aisles stood up. In the fifth row, Dr. Melvin Bowers, from the Plasma

Physics Institute at Livermore, California, sighed and looked at his watch. He was getting hungry, and speculations about communicating via neutrinos beamed through the solid Earth weren't his field. He shifted in his seat and tried to recall the name of the bar in the city that Sam and Max said they'd found the night before—the one with the underwearless hostesses that sat on the customers' knees. From behind him, the voice of the Japanese continued, "I see a difficulty with the data that have been selected as candidates. There is nothing that positively excludes every one of them from being an atmospheric muon, and not a neutrino-induced muon at all. For example, if the detected muon came from below, it would *have* to be neutrino-induced. But that is not so in a single case. All the ones we have seen came from above. Even with a small sample, this asymmetry bothers me."

"Phil?" Dupalme invited.

Kress shook the match between his fingers to extinguish it and dropped it into an ashtray. "I agree, it's strange . . . not what you'd expect . . ." The answer wasn't satisfactory even to himself. He sighed. "But we have pushed the detectability threshold back an order of magnitude. Maybe we need to reexamine the sensitivity of the detectors. . . . It's difficult to say without further analysis."

"Thank you." Unenlightened, the Japanese bowed and sat down again. Dupalme glanced down to read the announcement he had been about to make.

Then, Professor Masaki Kurishoda from Osaka University, who had been curiously reticent throughout most of the proceedings, pulled a microphone across the table. Bowers in the fifth row groaned inwardly. Kurishoda had a pudgy, humorous face and shot a genial smile at the audience through his heavy-rimmed spectacles before he spoke. "Of course," he said, "another reason why you gentlemen are not getting unambiguous evidence for the existence of neutrinos might be that they don't exist." Somebody near the front started to laugh, then stopped abruptly with the realization that Kurishoda was serious. The professor regarded the audience calmly, shifting his eyes until sure that he had everyone's attention. Even Bowers had forgotten lunch for the moment. Kurishoda spread his hands expressively. "Explaining the unknown by means of the unobservable is always a perilous business. The neutrino was postulated by Pauli simply as a book-balancing device to preserve the conservation laws of momentum and spin in the beta decay of a neutron into a proton and an electron. Every subsequent interpretation since has merely extended that convention. We scientists, you see . . . we think we construct objective views as dictated by facts, but really we do not. Sometimes we seek solutions within a framework of ruling academic opinion." He paused and sent a broad smile around the room. Nobody interrupted.

He continued, "If we extend the conservation laws to include the *negative* energy states proposed by Dirac—and why should we restrict it to positive states only, except to satisfy convention?—then pair-production is explained without the need for a photon to mysteriously 'turn into' an electron-positron pair: the positron becomes simply the 'hole' left in the Dirac sea by the electron that has been promoted to a positive state as a result of absorbing the photon. The notion of a hole behaving like a particle might have been strange in Dirac's time, but today, in our world full of semiconductor electronics, we take it for granted. Now, neutron decay becomes such a simple pair-production event, with the electron escaping and the positron being captured. We no longer need a neutrino to carry away the missing energy, since the electron was raised from a negative energy level to begin with. And since three particles are involved in the process, spin conservation is also satisfied."

Kress was already spluttering farther along the table. "But . . . now wait a minute, I mean, what does that do to the weak nuclear force? You've just pulled the rug out from saying there is a weak force at all. I mean . . ."

Kurishoda shrugged. "I agree. And you are about to remind me of the theoretical work that has unified the weak and the electromagnetic forces since the 1980's. But I suggest that the 'weak' interactions are nothing more than electromagnetic forces acting between the dipoles of elementary particles and those of electrons in negative energy states. So, if the two forces were actually only one to begin with, then the whole thing will have to be reexamined."

A lot of muttering and head shaking was going on in the audience. "But it's been verified, hasn't it?" someone objected. "I mean, neutrinos are *detected* routinely. They have been, ever since the fifties."

"Cowan and Reines," another voice supplied. "Neutrino-induced transmutation of chlorine into argon."

"*Presumed* to be neutrino-induced," Kurishoda threw back, beaming, as if he had been waiting for just that. "The mechanism I have just described accounts for it equally well."

"Experiments have been conducted which suggest they not only exist, but possess mass," another member of the panel pointed out. "It's been measured."

"How else do you account for the missing mass in the universe?" somebody else in the audience called out.

"And other experimenters have found no indication of mass," Kurishoda replied. "Some experimenters have reported that neutrinos oscillate among three forms, while others say they don't. As for the missing mass, well, maybe we just have to look for another kind of galaxy-glue." He half-turned, and motioned with his head. "Phil Kress himself has told us about the difficulty in observing anything, and then the ambiguity in deciding what it is. In short, it all relies on statistical methods that are questionable. There is nothing *conclusive* that proves neutrinos have mass, that the oscillate among three types, or that they exist at all. I contend that everything attributed to them can be explained more simply in terms that are already familiar. William of Occam would have approved."

The audience was clearly all set for a showdown on this. Dupalme raised a hand before anyone else could respond. "Ladies and gentlemen, lunch *is* waiting. Perhaps we could arrange a special session this evening to explore this subject further?" He looked down inquiringly to someone in the front row, who leaned forward to mutter something up at the dais. "Yes, we'll post details later this afternoon. . . ." He searched for something with which to wrap the topic up for the moment. "Maybe our speculations on neutrino-beam communications through the planet were a little premature, then, eh?"

Some of the panelists grinned, while others shook their heads. The atmosphere relaxed.

"Well, there's always tachyons to think about," someone quipped from the audience.

"How about that, Professor Kurishoda?" another called. "Do tachyons exist?"

The professor beamed back over the top of his spectacles. "But of course," he replied. "A tachyon is a quantum of bad taste."

Five minutes later, the attendees were spilling through into the central dining hall and dispersing among the tables, already set with a fish appetizer, fruit juices, and tea. Melvin Bowers headed for a quiet spot in a far corner of the room. Jenny Hampden, a research manager from Bell Labs, joined him. They'd met the previous day at breakfast in the hotel, and talked briefly during some of the breaks between sessions. She liked caving, classical music, and cats.

"Well, there goes my favorite theory," Bowers said as they sat down.

"What theory?"

"My neutrino-bomb theory."

"*Neutrino* bomb? That's a new one."

"Think about it," Bowers said. "It meets all the requirements for the perfect strategic weapon. It keeps defense contractors profitable and employs people. It justifies the jobs of Pentagon generals and defense analysts. And it gives the media a new scare-word and the peaceniks something to howl about." He smoothed his napkin across his knees and turned up his palms. "*But,* it has no undesirable side effects: it doesn't damage property or kill people. The perfect bomb!"

Jenny laughed. "Maybe we could have neutrino-power reactors, too—something to divert the oppositionists away from fusion. Then maybe it could all come on-line, and they mightn't even notice."

"Hm, there might be something in that, too. I wish somebody'd thought of it back in the seventies."

Jenny put down her fork suddenly. "Oh, Mel, there's something I forgot. Look, I have to see Takuji right now. I promised him some slides for the talk he's giving this afternoon. Would you excuse me? I'll be back in five minutes."

"Sure. I'll have them hold the entree."

"Thanks." Jenny got up and disappeared in the direction of the door.

Bowers carried on eating alone. Was it called the Yellow Dragon? Red Dragon? . . . No, not Dragon, but Red something . . . He didn't notice the tall, elegantly groomed figure approaching from among the bodies still milling about to find places in the middle of the room. "Ah, Dr. Bowers, good day to you."

Bowers looked up. "Igor Lukich," he said, using the Russian familiar patronymic.

"Do you mind if I join you?"

"Not at all. Sit down, please. Oh, not there. That side's taken."

It was Professor Dyashkin, the director of a Soviet communications-research establishment in Siberia. Dyashkin's name was known internationally, and he and Bowers were friends from previous professional gatherings in Moscow and Bombay. They had both been involved in an informal spontaneous discussion that had taken place the night before among a group of scientists at one of the hotels in which the conference attendees were staying.

"An interesting notion of Kurishoda's," Bowers said after Dyashkin had sat down. "I was just saying to the friend I'm with— Jenny Hampden of Bell, I don't know if you've met; she'll be back in a few minutes—neutrinos would make the perfect bomb. Then all of you and all of us could stop worrying, eh?"

Dyashkin smiled automatically, but he didn't ask Bowers to elaborate and was evidently not in the mood for small talk. He scanned the surroundings constantly with his eyes, and seemed nervous. Bowers became serious and looked at the Russian inquiringly as he continued eating. "We know each other from several years now, yes, Dr. Bowers?" Dyashkin said. He spoke guardedly, with an elbow resting on the table and a hand covering his mouth.

Bowers nodded. "I guess so—in a formal kind of way, anyhow."

"Even so, sometimes we must take risks and trust our judgment. I judge you as someone who can be trusted."

Bowers wiped his mouth with a corner of his napkin and resumed chewing slowly. When he spoke, his voice had dropped to match Dyashkin's. "What are you driving at?"

"When are you due to go back to the USA?" Dyashkin asked.

"Well, I'm on a one-year exchange here in Osaka. But I was planning to go home for a vacation right after this conference is over. Why?"

"Anyone might join us at the table, so I come straight to the point while we are alone." Bowers waited. Dyashkin drew a long, shaky breath. "Look, Dr. Bowers, it is possible that I might be interested in coming over, if the conditions were right. You understand?"

It took Bowers a moment. "To us, you mean? Over to our side?"

Dyashkin nodded almost imperceptibly. "Yes. Personal reasons—too much to go into now. But what I want to know from you is, would you be willing to convey my proposition to the appropriate authorities?"

"Proposition? But I don't know anything about what it is. How would—"

"I can arrange that. What I have to know now is, would you be willing to help me?"

Bowers chewed in silence for a while. "I'll have to think about it," he said finally.

"How long will you need? Please understand that we constantly risk being under observation when we travel abroad. The KGB even infiltrate their people into conferences such as this."

"Give me until tonight. I'll meet you in the bar of our hotel at, say, eight. Do you think it would be safe to talk there?"

Dyashkin shook his head. "I don't want to talk. All I need at this stage is a yes or a no answer."

"Okay, I won't say anything. If I offer to stand the first round of drinks, the answer's yes. Okay?"

"As you say, a deal."

Two more figures materialized at the table. "Gustav and Sandy," Bowers greeted. "It's about time—we were starting to get lonely here. Say, did I ever tell you my theory about the perfect bomb? . . ."

That afternoon, Bowers called the US embassy in Tokyo for advice. Later, back at the hotel, he went through into the bar for an after-dinner drink. Precisely at eight o'clock, Dyashkin appeared and joined him. "Hi," Bowers said. "Quite a day today, eh? What are you having, Igor? The first one's on me." The Russian asked for a vodka and soda.

Later, while they were talking, Dyashkin pointed to the orange document folder that Bowers had placed on the seat beside him. It was one of the packages issued to each attendee, and contained the conference agenda, copies of the papers being presented, and other information. "Obtain another package from the registration desk," he said. "Tomorrow there is a paper on laser solitons scheduled for three o'clock. Be there, and place the folder on the floor by your chair. I will exchange it for one I'll be carrying, which will contain details of the proposal that I wish you to carry to the American authorities."

❂ CHAPTER ELEVEN ❂

"The fractional Fourier-Brown-Wierner series with independent Gaussian coefficients converges to a sum for all H greater than zero, you see. But above H-equals-one, the sum becomes differentiable . . ."

The end of the day was approaching. McCain lay on his bunk in the billet and listened to Rashazzi expounding vigorously to Haber over a pile of books and papers strewn across the table in the center aisle. They had introduced themselves to McCain earlier, when they returned from the day work-shift. Rashazzi, or "Razz," as everyone called him, was an Israeli, young, handsome, dark-eyed, and of boundless energy and enthusiasm. Haber was a West German, with a pink, crinkled, bespectacled face and thinning white hair, who was getting on somewhat in years and gave the impression of belonging more in a sanatorium than a prison camp, although McCain already half-suspected this could be an act. They were both scientists of some kind, obviously. Rashazzi said he was a biologist from the University of Tel Aviv. Maybe, McCain had conceded. Maybe not.

Each pair of bays facing each other across the central aisle along the length of the billet constituted an eight-man "section"—two double bunks in each bay. The front section—i.e., the one immediately inside the door—housed Rashazzi, Haber, and Koh in the bay on the far side, and on the near side, McCain, with Mungabo the Zigandan above, and opposite them, occupying a single bunk by the end wall like Koh, an Irishman called Scanlon. Koh and Scanlon were elsewhere for the moment.

"Where did you get that from, you pig!"

"It was a fair play, you-who-were-not-born-but produced-by-farting!"

"And your father was a pig, and your mother was a pig! . . ."

More voices filtered through from the next section beyond the partition. They sounded like Siberian dialects from Soviet Central Asia. The gambling had begun immediately after the evening meal, the squabbling soon thereafter, and the aroma of strange substances being smoked was wafting around the partition. Rashazzi had warned McCain that this went on all the time, but not to worry about it. From others who had crossed through on their way between the rear of the billet and the mess area outside, McCain had caught snatches of Czechoslovakian and recognized several Russians. The bunk above creaked as Mungabo shifted his weight. McCain stared up at it. Escape was surely out of the question. Finding something purposeful to focus on in this place could get to be a problem, he decided.

A figure came along the center aisle from the far end of the billet and stopped near the bottom of the bunk. "No, we don't want none today," Mungabo's voice said from above. The figure ignored him. McCain looked out when he realized that the figure was staring at him. He was tall and lean, thirtyish, perhaps, with waves of blond hair flowing to the base of his neck, a yellow mustache, and clear, penetrating eyes set in a hawkish face. The addition of a beard would have made him a natural for the lead role in any Bible movie. "Hello," he said. "I guess we should get acquainted." He spoke in even, measured tones, with what sounded like a Midwest accent. McCain swung his legs off the bunk and sat up. The other stretched out a hand. "Paul Nolan, Springfield, Illinois."

"Lew Earnshaw, just about everywhere, but Iowa originally."

Nolan sat down on the edge of Scanlon's vacant bunk opposite. "So, how did you manage to get yourself in here?" he asked lightly. When McCain didn't reply immediately, he went on, "I heard a rumor going around that a couple of American journalists were arrested a while back, during the May Day tour. Were you one of those?"

McCain's eyes narrowed. "I'm not sure I want to start answering questions like that," he said.

Nolan smiled condescendingly, as if he had been expecting as much. McCain didn't like people who smiled too easily. "That's wise. I started out training to be a lawyer, you know. It's not all the way people think. It's vicious and competitive, like going back to the jungle. There's no sense of decency or ethics left anymore. Just money. They all sell their souls to the corporations. So I got out. Ended up in government, with the IPA in Washington—on their legal staff."

"The Industrial Policy Agency was scrapped years ago," McCain said.

"Yes, well, that was a while ago . . ." Nolan seemed to be about to say something further, then changed his mind. "Anyway, what I came to tell you was that Luchenko wants to talk to you. He's down at the other end."

McCain raised his eyebrows, wondering momentarily what the American was doing running errands for the Russian foreman. Then he dismissed the thought with a shrug and stood up. "Okay. Let's go."

They walked past the torrent of varied suidian insults still flying prolifically from the game in progress on one side, and through into the section beyond that. A bearded man at the center table was making tea from a hot-water pot that seemed to have a permanent place there, while another talked as he watched: "She never believed anything anyone said. She'd call on the phone and ask if her daughter was there. I'd tell her, 'No, she's out.' And then five minutes later the woman would call again and ask the same thing. She'd try to disguise her voice, but I could tell it was her because . . ." The next section contained more Asiatics on one side and empty bunks on the other, except one in which a pink-faced man with a high forehead was lying reading.

Passing through the next section, McCain caught snatches of a man who sounded Polish talking to a group. "They stopped short of Warsaw and sat there for two months to let the Germans wipe out the Polish Resistance for them. It was deliberate."

"That's a lot of rubbish," someone replied. "They couldn't go any farther. Look how far they'd advanced all through July."

The first voice dropped to a murmur. "Hey, Smovak, who's he?"

"New arrival today—in the front section."

An older man sitting with them threw in, "My father was there, you know—with Konev's army. . . ."

"An American," Smovak said.

There was a man lying on a bunk, staring morosely at a photograph of a woman on the locker beside him. . . . Finally they arrived at the end section. Five sections, eight men per section. Space for forty in the whole billet.

Two men were waiting at the last table. The one at the end was roundly built and on the heavyish side, with thinning hair combed straight back from the forehead in typical Russian style, and a fleshy moon-face amply provided with chins. McCain's first thought was that he'd have looked more in place in crumpled clothes at the front of a schoolroom, or fussing with rosebushes outside a house in the suburbs. The younger man sitting across the corner from him was his opposite: solidly muscled, with a mat of short, curly black hair, a chin of blue-shadowed battleship armor, and scowling eyes that were already weighing McCain as a potential adversary. The moon-face motioned for McCain to sit down. McCain did so, across the bouncer. Neither of them proffered a handshake, and McCain didn't volunteer. Nolan, whom McCain had mentally dubbed "Creeping Jesus," sat down two chairs away on the same side.

The moon-face had a buff-colored cardboard folder open on the table in front of him, containing papers. A clipboard with a chart of some kind lay next to it. "You are the new American, Mr. Earnshaw, two-seven-one-zero-six," he said, glancing down. "From Pacific News, California."

"That's right."

"It says here you are a journalist."

"Uh-huh."

"My name is Luchenko. I am the foreman of this billet. This is Josip Maiskevik." McCain gave a curt nod. Maiskevik continued staring at him without moving. "You know how things work here?"

"They told me a little about it at the front desk when I checked in."

"Do not think of Zamork as a punishment institution. Its purpose is to encourage socially desirable attitudes and behavior. It operates by incentives and privileges, not by coercion. But the privileges have to be earned. I am responsible for seeing that the rules are followed in this billet. If you wish to initiate any communication with the authorities or lodge any complaint, you do so through me. Also, I pass out the work allocations. You will be working in one of the machine shops in the Core, commencing tomorrow morning."

Luchenko went on to explain about working hours, rules, and procedures. Next in line beyond him was a "block supervisor," who was also an inmate. The supervisor was the means of access to the commandant in charge of the block, whom the captain had mentioned when McCain was admitted. In the case of Block B, the commandant was a Colonel Bachayvin. Then there was the governor, Fedorov, who reigned above the block commandants. But it appeared that he dwelt on a higher existential plane, from which he seldom descended to deal with prisoners in person. Incorrigibles who were unimpressed by the incentive process could expect a harsher time and solitary detention. The penalty system was more or less standardized, and everyone soon got to know how much time various infractions could be expected to bring. Failing to be back in one's block an hour before lights-out was good for three days, and being insolent to a guard who was in a bad mood that day, a week. Fighting with other prisoners or sabotaging the work output put you in the month-plus class. Attacking a guard was worth three days at most—

"Before they shoot you," Nolan interjected, smiling.

"I believe in being reasonable," Luchenko concluded. "You will find I deal fairly with those who deal fairly with me. Nolan can fill you in on other details. Do you have any questions for now?"

There was something about Luchenko's manner that didn't quite fit, McCain had been thinking as he listened. The Russian was trying to affect an air of brusqueness, but it wasn't him. He was like a salesman trying to put into practice what he'd read on assertiveness, but without the force of character to pull it off. The appeal to reasonableness was for his own protection more than anyone else's,

McCain guessed. And what was the reason for Maiskevik's brooding, silent presence at the table? A hint, maybe, of how the power structure really worked for anyone who didn't buy the reasonableness line? That added up. Luchenko's style would require a strong-arm man behind the throne.

"One thing," McCain said. "When I was arrested, I was with a colleague, also from PNS. Her name is Paula Shelmer. I haven't been told anything of her whereabouts or her condition. I want to talk to the block commandant or whoever I need to talk to for some news."

Luchenko pursed his lips for a second, then leaned forward to scribble a note on one of the papers in his folder. "I can't promise anything," he said. "The request will be passed on."

"I'd appreciate it."

"Anything else?"

"I guess that's it."

"Very well. As I said, follow the rules, and you will find that life can improve rapidly. Play fair with me, and I will play fair with you. That is all I have to say for now."

McCain walked back to the front section of the billet and sat down at the far end of the table from Rashazzi and Haber, who were still in the throes of their animated mathematical discussion. Nolan, who McCain hadn't realized had followed him, pulled up the next chair. "It'll be a change to have another American in here," Nolan said.

"Are there many around?"

"Only a couple, in other billets. I don't have a lot to do with them—too brash and loudmouthed." Nolan had a habit of smiling all the time, as if he were anxious to avoid being annoying. McCain found it overplacating and as annoying as hell. But this was only McCain's first day, after all. The onus was on him to show some willingness to fit in.

"Illinois, eh?" McCain said. "I knew a girl from Chicago once . . ."

"Women know nothing about politics."

"She wasn't into politics."

"All they're interested in is clothes, painting themselves up, and other people's money. They're not intellectual."

"This one happened to be a doctor of recombinant engineering. She ran a company that remodeled plant DNA."

"Mutating nature for profits."

"It sounds like you disapprove. Have you got something against feeding people?"

"No, against greed and criminal corporate vandalism."

McCain nodded. Suddenly he was losing interest in trying to be accommodating. "Now I'm beginning to see what kind of government lawyer you were. Or did you flunk that, too?" he said.

"I told you, I got out of the whole rotten system. I emigrated—to the Soviet Union."

McCain regarded him distastefully. "You mean you defected."

Nolan sighed, conveying the understanding tolerance of one who had heard this a thousand times, but whose eyes see farther. "I betrayed none of my principles," he said calmly. "Americans are forever preaching about freedom and the right to choose. Well, I exercised my right and chose. Why is the choice wrong just because you happen to disagree with it?" He leaned closer. "None of you understand. It's because of the brainwashing that you—all of us— went through. The USSR is a rich, strong nation. The people are happy with their leaders, and together they are building the world of tomorrow—a world based on equality and justice for everyone. Oppression and exploitation will end. It will be what mankind has been struggling toward for thousands of years."

"And you're calling *me* brainwashed?"

"I simply know what's true."

McCain waved a hand to indicate the billet around them, and by implication the rest of Zamork outside it. "Well, your faith's been rewarded. Why did they put you in here? Was it what you wanted, too? Okay, good. Have fun." He made to rise to go back to his bunk, but Nolan caught his sleeve.

"That was another story. I thought I understood the philosophy of socialism, but it wasn't true. I was brought to realize that I, too, had flaws which I'd never suspected. But they are curable. Being here is part of the process, you see. As Luchenko said, it's not a punishment. I don't think of it as imprisonment at all."

"What, then—a vacation resort?"

"A process of guided enlightenment, as in a monastery, I guess. Purification."

"So why the gulag and the KGB? Why do you need land mines and barbed wire to keep the workers in Paradise?"

"That's only temporary. When world revolution is achieved, it will change."

"Bullshit."

Nolan nodded as if he had been expecting it. "It's possible that you may come to change your outlook while you are here," he said, rising from the chair. "I just wanted you to know that I'd be happy to talk, whenever you feel like it."

McCain watched as Nolan returned to the far end of the billet. Then he got up and went back to his bunk. Mungabo was beaming at him from the top tier. "I knew all Americans couldn't be like him. It looks like maybe you and me might get along." He thrust out a pink-palmed hand. "Name's Abel."

"Lew."

"From Iowa—I heard you earlier."

"That's right."

"D'you ever see the New York Bears play?"

"It's the Chicago Bears. Or do you mean the New York Yankees?"

"Just testin'. You passed."

"That doesn't prove anything, Abel. A KGB plant would know things like that."

Mungabo grinned. "True, but that wasn't the test. You'd never imagine the horseshit those people believe. A real Russian, trying to pretend he's American, wouldn't have shaken hands."

McCain grinned back. Actually, a real KGB man would have known that the horseshit was horseshit. The popular view of American racism expounded by Tass was purely for Russian domestic consumption. That told him that Mungabo was probably straight, too.

❂ CHAPTER TWELVE ❂

Metal shrieked on metal as whirling sawteeth bit into toughened aluminum alloy. The note dropped while the motor labored under the load, and then soared again as the blade broke through and the end of the length of L-section girder dropped onto the pile in the scrap bin. McCain released the vise and transferred the piece to the stack waiting behind him for Scanlon to drill and deburr. Then he lifted another uncut length from the rack and laid it on the bench to be marked and center-punched against the standard jig. If he ever got out of Zamork and back to normality, he decided, he'd buy himself a waterbed. He'd never want to see another metal bedframe. What the powers that ran *Tereshkova* thought they were going to do with so many bedframes, he couldn't imagine. Did they plan on turning the whole place into a prison?

Kevin Scanlon was the Irishman who occupied the single bunk opposite McCain and Mungabo in B-3, enjoying a measure of extra space that afforded one of the minor but worthwhile comforts of life. He had become mixed up with espionage and the GRU—the Soviet military-intelligence organization, which in many ways paralleled the KGB—in the course of his former IRA activities and connections through them to the Cubans and Palestinians, until one day he found himself on the wrong side of one of Moscow's eternal comradely vendettas. He had sparse hair, with a lean build and gaunt, hollowed face that made his eyes seem protrusive, especially when he was in one of his intense moods, which usually produced either passionate discourses on Irish history or invective harangues about the "Brits." McCain had worked with the British when he was with NATO in Europe, and he'd found them likable enough despite their occasional stuffiness. But he kept his opinions to himself, and on the whole he and Scanlon got along, which was as well since Luchenko had assigned them as regular working partners.

"What I'd give to be able to walk out and down the street for a pint o' the porter now," Scanlon called across from the drilling table, lifting a gloved hand and wiping his brow with his sleeve.

"Something else to think about for when you get back, I guess."

"Or the Guinness. Pure Liffey water the Guinness is made from in Dublin. Nowhere else in the world does it have the same taste."

"If anyone ever gets back."

"Cream. The head on it is as smooth as tasting pure cream."

A horn somewhere overhead gave two raucous blasts to indicate the midday break for lunch. McCain thumbed a red button, and the saw freewheeled to a stop. The din in the rest of the workshop subsided as other machines were turned off and the figures attending them stripped off their greasy coveralls before joining the general movement toward the main door. Scanlon came round the bench, wiping his hands with a piece of rag. "Now, isn't it nice to think of all the Ivans and Vladimirs who'll sleep comfortable in their beds for the charitable work we're doing here today? And wouldn't Father O'Halloran from Ballingarry be proud of me for that?"

McCain hung his coverall on the end of a storage rack. "Is that where you're from?"

"Ah, many years ago now, it was. That was when I met my first Americans. There was a development estate set up not three miles from the village—light industry, they said, electronics and the like. An American company came first and built a computer factory there. Then the Germans and the Japanese came, I recall. We weren't exactly wild about being invaded by all the foreigners, but the money they paid was good."

They came out of the workshops and began walking along a wide corridor of grimy, battle-scarred, lime-green walls. Meals were brought to each block and eaten in the common mess area. "How did the Americans fit in?" McCain asked.

"They were always chasing around after the girls, which didn't please the local lads at all. There were fights sometimes. The Germans preferred their beer, but they liked ordering people around too much. Me, I had more time for the Japanese than any of them. Very polite people—always bow and smile sort of apologetically before they knock anyone's teeth in."

"I thought it was the Irish who were supposed to be famous for all those things."

"Is that a fact, now?"

"Great lovers, drinkers, and always good for a fight, isn't that what they say?"

"You don't strike me as the sort of man who pays much attention to what people say. How about yourself? Are you blessed with any Irish in the family?"

"I'm not sure," McCain replied, with deliberate vagueness.

"Surprising. I thought all Americans were obsessed with genealogy."

"I guess what I'm trying to say is that Earnshaw sounds more English to me, if anything."

"Hmm, yes, now. Kind o' what I was thinkin' meself. . . . But you're not so bad a fella for that."

They came out of the Core and turned south onto Gorky Street.

Compass directions in *Tereshkova* were the same as on Earth. The spin axis through the hub defined north-south, with the direction that the hub docking ports faced being arbitrarily taken as north. Following the convention of a normal, spherical, inside-in and outside-out planet, the equatorial plane was perpendicular to the axis and midway between its poles, dividing the entire wheel of *Tereshkova* into a north zone and a south zone—like a tire cut in two along a line running around the middle of the tread. The equator itself was the circle where this plane intersected "ground" level in the ring—i.e., the midline of the central valley floor. It followed that a person walking along the equator—or parallel to it at any level from the rim to the hub—would be moving east or west. Once more the familiar convention applied: when facing north, east was to the right and west was to the left. Which way the colony happened to be rotating had nothing to do with it.

Zamork lay off-center against the colony's south wall, on the eastern side of Novyi Kazan. The front, which consisted of administrative offices and guard quarters, faced the roadway and monorail tracks, with the road running above the monorail at that part of the ring and entering Zamork on a higher level. The rear of the administrative section opened onto the main thoroughfare known as Gorky Street, which closed on itself to form a square dividing the inner Core complex from the surrounding blocks that formed the rest of the facility. The Core, which was also on two levels, contained the kitchens, laundry, stores, a library, and workshops for such activities as machining, tailoring, and shoemaking. Outside the Core were six prisoner blocks, two on each of Gorky Street's remaining three sides. A walled exercise compound open to the "sky" lay on the east side, behind A and B Blocks. Blocks C and D were segregated for women prisoners, who wore light blue tunics instead of gray and had their own, fenced-off portion of the east compound. Segregation was not total, and the male and female inmates sometimes found themselves working alongside each other in the Core and on some of the outside labor details. This made communication between them routine, and for a moderate outlay in ingenuity afforded ample opportunities for amorous diversions. None of the women whom McCain got a chance to exchange a few words with knew of an American fitting Paula's description, however.

As Luchenko had said on McCain's first day, a high emphasis was placed on incentives. Prisoners could earn "points" for above-quota job performance, and there was a store at which points could be converted into additional comforts such as tobacco, candy, games, and materials for hobbies. Accrued points could also be traded for bonus time off work. So, when a prisoner spent his savings on the basics for a new pastime, he then found that he needed to behave himself for the extra time that he now needed to enjoy it. Prisoners could even debit and credit points among themselves by voucher, using individual accounts maintained in the administrative computer system and known collectively as "the Exchange." This could be useful for things like buying illicitly distilled vodka—for which a thriving underground market existed, acquiring goods to barter on the colony's black market when on outside work details, and settling gambling debts. None of it fitted with what McCain knew of the way the Russians ran their prisons. Why, in fact, would the Russians bring prisoners this far at all? He found it difficult to believe that it was just to provide cheap labor for the mundane work. There had to be more to it.

As McCain and Scanlon entered B Block from Gorky Street, Oskar Smovak and Leo Vorghas, who were also from B-3 billet, caught up with them. "Two points, I'll lay you two points!" Oskar Smovak exclaimed to Vorghas as they joined the line inside the mess area and began shuffling forward with their metal messtins. At the table in front, a kitchen orderly in a smock that looked greasier than the machine-shop coveralls was ladling stew out of a hatch in a rubber-tired, stainless-steel trolley, covered in flaps and lids, that looked like a scaled-down armored car. "No trotter ever timed a mile in under a minute fifty. Three points!" Smovak was Czechoslovakian, a stocky, solidly built cannonball of a man, with black hair, a ruddy face, and dark eyes looking out over a Fidel Castro beard. He had a voice that was loud and cutting, but most of the time it was because he was being jovial rather than pugnacious, McCain had learned. He claimed to have been arrested because of a relative of his who was caught photographing missiles being loaded into a Russian submarine at Murmansk.

Leo Vorghas was a Lithuanian, in his early forties, perhaps, with an open, high-browed face, thin, sandy hair, light-colored rounded eyes, and a pinkish complexion. The breast pocket of his jacket always bulged with spectacle case, ruler, and an assortment of more pens than anyone could ever know what to do with. His claim to notoriety was that as a government statistician he had made extra money on the side by selling details of the Soviet economic disasters to Western journalists: they'd paid better money than Western intelligence agencies had offered.

"One forty-eight point something." Vorghas insisted. "I remember reading it. No, wait a minute, the Ukrainian over in F-ten—he showed it to me in a book. You ask him. He'll tell you."

"Ah!" Smovak roared. "That was a *pacer*, not a trotter. No trotter has ever beaten one fifty. Check it out, Leo. You lose."

"Bah. Well, it's the same thing."

"It most certainly is *not*. Trotters move the diagonally opposite legs together. Pacers move the ones on the same side."

"But the carriages are the same, aren't they? I say that makes it the same thing. Nobody wins."

"Oh, nonsense."

They each collected two ladles of a tolerable concoction containing potatoes, cabbage, and a few scraps of mutton, a plate with two pieces of dark bread smeared with margarine, a slice of sausage, an apple, and a mug of black tea, and carried them over to one of the tables.

"What do you say, Mr. American?" Smovak asked, giving McCain an unusually keen look. "Know anything about racing?"

"Not really. . . . It's not my scene," McCain answered.

"That's surprising," Smovak said. "I thought it was popular there. Russia and America have had a common interest in trotting since long before the Revolution."

"I didn't know that."

"Oh yes. They're both large countries, you see—with bad roads that couldn't take heavy stagecoaches, before there were any trains. So they both bred horses for pulling light carriages over long distances. You mean you didn't know?" McCain shrugged and carried on eating. "Does the name Sam Caton mean anything?" Smovak asked him.

"Never heard of it," McCain said.

"Oh, why don't you come straight out with it, Oskar? Tell him you're wondering if he's really an American at all," Vorghas said irritably.

"Well, I've never heard of the fella either," Scanlon threw in. "Oskar, will ye lay off giving Lew a hard time. The man's only after hanging up his hat, for heaven's sake. What kind of Czechoslovakian welcome do you call that?"

"Kevin is right," Vorghas agreed. "This place breeds mistrust. Prudence is all very well, but it can go too far."

"And how will you ever become a priv if you don't trust people?" Scanlon asked. Vorghas laughed.

McCain had heard the expression before. It was a saying of Luchenko's and seemed to be a joke of some kind among the inmates. "What's a priv?" he asked, looking at the others.

"Hasn't anyone told you about them yet?" Vorghas asked. McCain shook his head.

"Privileged-category prisoners," Smovak said. "You're only regular category, see."

"They live up on surface level," Vorghas said.

Clearly that hadn't conveyed much to McCain, either. Scanlon explained, "There's an upper level to Zamork, out on the surface, above the part that we're in down here. They live in huts with grass around them, and trees—not packed into smelly billets as is good for the likes of us. There's less work for them to do, of course, and more frills—just like in the real world. *And,*" he added with a wink, "the women and the men are mixed together. Now, there's a carrot for you if ever there was one. Mungabo, the poor fella, drives himself wild thinking about it."

"They've even got a beach up there," Vorghas said.

"A beach!" Smovak repeated, as if daring McCain to challenge it. McCain stared at them in astonishment.

"You see, there's a high-level reservoir next to this place, between Zamork and the town," Vorghas said. "It feeds the water system that drains down through the recreation area between Novyi Kazan and the ag zone. Well, the privs have got a beach on it up there."

"What kind of people are these privs?" McCain asked, growing more curious.

"The professional class of the classless society," Smovak told him.

Vorghas nodded. "Scientists, teachers, and such—dissidents that the Party wants to keep out of the way for a while, but without upsetting them too much. They're worried about the risk of bad publicity later."

"Frightened of changes in the winds that swirl through the Kremlin's blustery halls," Scanlon recited lyrically.

McCain smiled faintly as he chewed his bread. It was heavy and grainy in texture. "And people from down here can get promoted?" he said.

"It happens," Scanlon replied. "But 'tis a rare thing when it does. Many a Luchenko lives in hope, but few are chosen."

McCain nodded distantly. So the foremen and the block supervisors had their incentives, too. It fitted with the general scheme of things, but that still didn't shed any light on the reasons why. "So what's it all for?" he asked the others. "Why is this place here, and why is it the way it is?" There was a quick exchange of glances among the others, and a pause of a second or two. McCain obviously wasn't the first to have wondered about such questions.

"Progressive psychology," Vorghas declared. "I think it's an experiment that the KGB psychologists dreamed up—a new approach to behavior modification." He leaned forward and let his voice fall a fraction. "Look around. You haven't got any of your ordinary criminals and riffraff here. These are all potentially useful people. Think of the advantages if you can find out how to rehabilitate people like these and save their skills for the state." He gestured vaguely around and overhead with the spoon he was holding. "It's the isolation. Everything is supposed to take on a new perspective from this oasis of humanity out in space—the vastness of the universe and the puniness of Man, and that kind of thing. We're supposed to come to see that we're all alike underneath and have to work together. . . ." He shrugged and resumed eating. "That's what I think, anyway." McCain listened but wasn't convinced. That might have explained the privs with their huts and beach upstairs, but what about the rest? That was a fat lot of vastness of the universe to be seen from a bottom bunk in the lower level of B-3.

"Why make a complicated issue out of it?" Smovak asked. "The Russians are a century behind the times. They're only just finding out about methods the rest of the world has been using for years, and they don't want to admit it. So they've set their experiment up nice and quietly, away from where it would get attention, so they can fold it all up and forget it without any embarrassment if they make a mess of it. That's Russians all over."

"Ah, is that so, now?" Scanlon challenged. "That's every bit as involved as what Leo said, I'm sitting here thinkin'. Why couldn't they simply be doing the same as the rest, and shipping the troublemakers as far away as they can from where they might do damage? Didn't the Brits have to send half o' themselves all over the world because there wasn't a decent one of them? I can't agree with what either of ye is saying, now. Jet planes and telephones have moved Siberia a lot closer to Moscow than it used to be, and that's all there is to it."

McCain looked down and carried on eating his stew in silence. He'd listened to the answers, and he didn't believe any of them. The curious thing was that he'd watched the people giving the answers, and he didn't think they believed them any more than he did. But they were safe answers. The simple fact was that nobody in the place trusted anybody.

Maybe that was the whole idea.

❀ CHAPTER THIRTEEN ❀

McCain sat at one end of the center-aisle table in the front section of the billet, contemplating the diagram that he had been sketching. On the top bunk behind him, Mungabo was admiring a new addition to his collection of lascivious pinups. Mungabo's passion for Americana—an attitude that had done little to improve his credibility with the KGB at his court-martial—it turned out, derived from his dream of the kind of life he'd seen blacks living in American porno movies, which he took to be representative of the typical New England suburban social scene.

"Hey, Lew, waddya say to this for a piece of pink-shot?" he called down dreamily. "Isn't that the horniest thing you've ever seen in your life? Did you ever make it with a chick like that back in the States?"

"All the time," McCain drawled over his shoulder. "They come as extras with the hotel rooms. Hell, I did better'n that while I was at college." Mungabo sighed and stared agonizedly at the picture. He'd never understood why the Russians wanted to take over the West if they got the chance. Now it was all starting to make much more sense.

McCain's sketch was of the system of mirrors by which sunlight illuminated the interior of the colony. It had begun with an idea that Scanlon had mentioned first in the machine shop. Scanlon had tried drawing it but didn't have enough knowledge of the details, whereas

McCain had the benefit of the information he'd memorized for the mission.

The first component of the system was a large, annular, primary mirror that hung detached in space a mile away along the colony's axis, looking like an enormous version of an ophthalmoscope, which old-time eye doctors wore on their foreheads. It produced a ring-section beam of reflected sunlight—a tube, like a hollow tree-trunk—and according to the relative motions of the Earth-Moon-Sun system could be steered by thrusters to keep the beam trained down on the axis, onto the hub. Here the beam encountered a ring of plane secondary mirrors around the hub, which relayed the light radially outward to the roof of the outer torus, where an arrangement of louvered reflecting slats admitted visible light and heat, but blocked cosmic rays. The secondary mirrors could be tilted independently to illuminate or darken different parts of the torus as required.

The path that a ray of light followed was thus from the Sun to the primary mirror, from there down the axis to a secondary mirror, and after a couple more reflections in the chevron-section roof slats, down to a point somewhere on the "ground" inside. Scanlon's thought was that if a laser were aimed at the roof from the ground inside, its beam ought to trace the same optical path, but in the opposite direction. In other words, it might offer a means of communicating information out. The problem, of course, was that whoever the information was intended for would have to be looking for it, which presupposed that some other way of talking to them existed in the first place. Besides, Scanlon wasn't even sure if the idea was feasible, and McCain didn't know either. This would be more in Paula's line.

He sat back, chewing his pencil while he watched Haber and Rashazzi over by the bunk on the far side, fiddling with an improvised contraption of lenses and mirrors. They seemed to have access to an inexhaustible number of sources of components and materials for the Rube Goldberg gadgets that they made to demonstrate the incomprehensible things they talked about. Those two would know if the idea was feasible, McCain thought. But how was he to broach the subject? His instincts told him that they, if any in the billet, were clean; the problem would be convincing them that he was.

He was certain now in his own mind that Rashazzi was no biologist, although the Israeli kept cages of mice in the washroom at the back of the billet, which he told Luchenko were for breeding experiments. But on one or two occasions he had used figures of speech that were straight from the specialist jargon that McCain was used to hearing around the Pentagon—such as "eggbuster," for an X-ray battle laser tuned to vaporize the hardened shells of warhead reentry vehicles. He was pretty sure that Razz was a defense scientist of some kind.

He hadn't formed any clear impression of what Haber was. All Haber had told him was that he'd been apprehended in Moscow and accused of receiving Soviet military secrets during an exchange visit. From his varied topics of conversation, he seemed to be one of those all-rounders from the grand old classical school of scientists.

The problem was the universal mistrust. Fostering mutual suspicion among enemies and subjects was the traditional Russian way of making organized opposition all but impossible. And it was also part of the traditional Russian character to submit, which was one reason why totalitarianism had survived there for a century. But McCain was not a Russian, and it wasn't in his nature to conform to other people's ideas of how he should behave. He *needed* some way— even if just a token—of defying the system. But how? Escape, the usual outlet for such urges in this kind of situation, was surely impossible. Blind rage and destruction was hardly his style. What else was there? Whatever he came up with, he'd have to start finding out pretty soon who his friends were.

"If Americans designed a space colony, it wouldn't be like this one, would it, Lew?" Mungabo said from the bunk behind. "It wouldn't be all antiseptic."

The question caught McCain far away in his reverie. "What? . . . I don't know. What do you mean, antiseptic?"

"Look around at the towns and places. Everybody lives in nice, clean, respectable boxes, and does nice, clean, respectable jobs, and they play healthy games in the parks, and the kids sit in lines in nice schools. . . . You see, it's all the perfect picture of an academic professor's or some social-work counselor's idea of how other people oughta live. Except nobody asked the people. It's like living in a museum. . . . How can anyone have fun being a respectable social statistic?"

McCain half-turned and rested an elbow on the back of the chair. "How would you change it if it were up to you?"

"Hell, I'd add a bit of nightlife to them squeaky-clean towns they've got out there—a few bars, maybe some strip joints, the things that make *real cities* cities. Give people a chance to be honest-to-God, flesh-and-blood people, know what I mean? That's how Americans would have done it, right?"

"Maybe," McCain said. "It goes to extremes both ways, I guess."

"I remember when I was a kid growing up in Ziganda, we had this preacher came all the way from Boston to save us from hell," Mungabo said. "He told us that America was God's second chosen nation. And do you know how he figured that?"

"How?"

"He said it was a revelation because 'USA' was right there inside 'Jer*usa*lem.' Ain't that something?"

McCain blinked, looked back over his shoulder, and thought for a moment. "Was that the same God that put the ass in Massachusetts?"

Mungabo threw back his head and laughed. "Can't say I know about that. But you know, Lew, that whole business that guys like him talk about—it always struck me as the neatest con operation that anyone ever dreamed up. I mean, they're selling eternity, and your payoff in some hereafter, right? Well, that keeps 'em all pretty safe from complaints by dissatisfied customers, don't it—or from being sued because they didn't deliver? When did the last person come back and tell everyone it ain't the way they were told it is?"

"Well, I guess it's not my problem," McCain said. "It's not something I ever did buy any stock in."

Razz, Haber, Mungabo, and Scanlon were probably okay, McCain had decided. What about Koh? . . . He still wasn't sure. As proverbially impenetrable as the Chinese side of him, Koh was a philosophical observer of life—and hence of everybody and everything—with innumerable ancestors, and living relatives seemingly everywhere on Earth. Nobody knew how he had come to be in Zamork. McCain had heard some say he was an obvious plant; and others that no plant would be that obvious.

What about the rest? McCain turned in his chair and surveyed the billet. Nolan was too transparent. He had to be the decoy. So who was the real one? Luchenko, of course, was excluded from the list of potential allies. Along with Luchenko, McCain eliminated the rest of the group that seemed to form a constellation around him at the far end, which apart from Nolan and the Bulgarian Maiskevik, included Borowski, a Pole, and a morose Frenchman called Taugin.

And yet, for all that watching and listening was part of the foremen's job, McCain was discovering that they could, usually for a price, be surprisingly ready to turn a blind eye to some of the things that went on. The underground distillery trade and black market with the towns, for example, couldn't have existed without their knowing; and he'd heard of one instance where the foreman of another billet had cooperated in covering a prisoner's absence from work. Why would a foreman put his own privileges at risk when there was nothing to gain? It wouldn't make sense. So in reality it had to be a covert part of their job. If that were true, then the security precautions and detention-style discipline were to a large degree a superficiality carried out for effect—a charade to satisfy expectations. What did that mean?

"Uh-uh. Shouldn't have taken the name in vain," Mungabo's voice murmured behind him. Nolan was approaching through the next section, where Smovak and Vorghas were engrossed over a game of chess. He sat down at the end of the table a couple of places from McCain. McCain folded the papers he had been drawing on and tucked them into his jacket pocket.

"How are you finding things?" Nolan inquired casually.

"I've seen better."

"The place isn't so bad?"

"On the whole, I'll take Manhattan. You never give up, do you?"

Smovak looked up from the next table and groaned. "Oh God, you two aren't starting all that again, are you? Look, I'll tell you what the difference between capitalism and communism is. With capitalism, man exploits man; with communism it's the other way round. See? Ha-ha-ha!"

"I just want you to see that it isn't all black and white," Nolan said.

"I never said it was," McCain answered. "But I do know that where I come from, you live how you want, you go where you want, and you say what you want, without needing a permit from any commissar. And US soldiers don't shoot US citizens in the back for trying to leave the country. That mightn't be black and white to you, but it's getting pretty close for me."

"But what about the inequities, the injustice . . ."

"Unlike in the classless society? Oh sure. Everyone in Moscow drives a Cadillac?"

"Crass materialism. The cravings of greed. Can't you see that it's competition and rivalry that lead to conflict? Such things can't be permitted in today's world. We must impose harmony, which can only come through serving the collective good. Peace must be objective, at any price. If we fail in that, then everything else is lost anyway. You must agree with that."

"No objective is worth *any* price," McCain said.

"Not even preventing a global nuclear war?"

McCain shook his head. "No."

Nolan stared disbelievingly. "What price could conceivably be too high to pay for that?"

"Submitting to the kinds of things that some people have had inflicted on them in recent times," McCain said. "If it meant seeing kids being put into gas chambers by thugs, I'd rather fight and risk the consequences. If it meant having innocent people dragged from their homes to be worked to death as slave labor, I'd rather fight. If it meant giving up the right to be me, I'd rather fight." He sat back in his chair and regarded Nolan oddly for a couple of seconds. "I don't understand what it is with people like you. You come from the best-fed, best-educated, healthiest country, that gives you more opportunity than anywhere, anytime in history, and you want to tear it down. . . . Where d'you come from, out of curiosity? Want me to guess? Pretty-well-off family, was it? Was that the problem—you felt guilty because you were rich in a world where not everyone was rich?"

McCain saw a flicker of discomfort cross Nolan's countenance. He nodded. "Well, you could always have made yourself feel better by giving it away. But that wasn't good enough, was it? Everybody else had to be made to give theirs away, too, so *you* could be equal." Smovak and Vorghas were watching from the next table; Rashazzi and Haber were listening, also. At that moment the door opened and Scanlon came in. He stopped when he saw them all watching McCain. McCain went on, "It was rage and envy against a world that didn't *need* people like you. You didn't have anything to offer that people wanted freely, by choice. So get rid of freedom, eh? We'll *make* them take notice of us. Pull down the system, paint everybody gray, and we can all be happy nobodies together." He got up and turned away to go back to his bunk. "Fuck you, Nolan. We'll keep our bombs. If you think you can take what we've built, come on and try. But don't try selling me a guilt trip that says it's my duty to give it away."

Nolan stood up flushed and tight-lipped, and marched toward the door without saying anything. The light above came on, the beeper beeped, and he was gone. The two scientists stared for a moment longer and returned to what they had been doing.

"Hear, hear," Smovak murmured barely above his breath, and looked back at the chess game. Mungabo was cackling delightedly in the top bunk by McCain. Scanlon moved over to his own bunk opposite and sat down. "I see ye've been getting a piece o' the indoctrination," he said to McCain.

"Doesn't he ever quit?" McCain asked.

"He's worse with the new fellas," Scanlon said. "Either he makes a friend, or he shuts up . . ." he nodded at McCain, "and sometimes somebody shuts him up. It's a little peace we'll all be having for a while now, I'm thinkin'." Scanlon watched until McCain turned his head toward him, then pulled the top of his jacket aside to reveal the top of a metal flask. He winked, and his voice fell to a whisper. "From a little still that somebody's got running in a place I won't mention. As good as poteen, but I can't vouch for how well it compares to your own mountain dew. Maybe a drop or two later, eh?"

"Sure. Is there a price?"

"Oh, let's say it's on credit. When I need a favor, I'll let you know." Scanlon scratched the side of his nose pensively. "But then again, from the tail end of what I just heard, I'd say you've already earned it."

"Well, I never argue with a guy who's buying."

Scanlon gave McCain a long, curious look, as if weighing him up. "And it's not as if that system of theirs is anything for himself to be getting so excited about."

McCain looked uncertain. "What system? You mean Nolan? The Russian system?"

"Ah, sure, and what else would I be talking about?" McCain frowned, wondering what this had to do with anything. Scanlon rolled his eyes pointedly, indicating that walls had ears.

"They don't trust anyone, either," McCain replied, nodding to show that he understood. "It's kind of a conditioned reflex. Did you know that Tolstoy's serfs didn't want him to free them when he tried? They thought it was a trick. They wouldn't have a school either. They said the only reason he wanted to educate the kids was to sell them to the czar as foot soldiers."

Scanlon shook his head solemnly. "That's terrible, now."

"I wonder what does it."

"Centuries of living under rapacious rulers," Scanlon said. "A system that did nothing to discourage exploitation."

"You mean like the Brits?"

Scanlon stared back fixedly for a moment. "Let's go for a walk outside," he suggested.

"It seems to me that you're already well on your way to understanding the way things are in Zamork, Lew," Scanlon said. "I've a feeling you're from some kind of background that hasn't exactly made you a newcomer to such things, but what it might be I'll leave as your business." They had come out through the door at the rear of the B Block mess area into the general compound, which contained its usual evening crowd of gray-clad figures standing, walking, talking, watching. "What do you make of the place so far?"

"Strange kind of a prison," McCain answered.

"It is that. And have ye had any thoughts as to why that might be?"

McCain could see nothing to lose by being frank. "It's an information mine," he said.

"Now there's an interesting thought," Scanlon answered.

"Mines have miners in them. Also, there has to be something to dig. But in this mine it's hard to tell the difference."

For McCain's conclusion was that the whole place was set up for the gathering of sensitive information—the practice of which had always been a Russian passion. From foreign intelligence operatives like himself to Russian domestic dissidents, Zamork was full of people who knew a lot about the enemies of the regime at home and abroad, and their intentions—a priceless trove of information to be gathered. It followed that the place would also be full of others put there to do the gathering. He was unlikely to be the first to have arrived at such a conclusion, and no doubt that was why nobody trusted anybody. The theory fitted, too, with the laxness in discipline beneath the superficial pretense: the authorities *wanted* the inmates to mix, talk, and go through the motions of defying the system—and the looser their tongues became in the process, the better.

They passed a group practicing gymnastics on homemade equipment, and Scanlon steered McCain toward a gathering in the center, where an improvised choir a dozen or so strong was delivering a hearty rendering of a Romanian folk song. "Well, Mr. Earnshaw or whoever you really are, I've decided to take a chance on ye." He had to lean close to McCain and shout into his ear to be heard. McCain noticed that most of the others around them were behaving similarly and taking no notice of the singing whatever. He smiled faintly as the meaning of the choir dawned on him.

He turned his head toward Scanlon. "Why?"

"Three things ye did that stoolies don't do."

"Such as what?"

"It doesn't matter," Scanlon said. McCain thought he already knew, anyway. He hadn't posed as a transfer from elsewhere in Zamork, which would have provided a reason for being familiar with anything a new arrival wouldn't know about; he hadn't denied that he spoke Russian; and he hadn't shown any eagerness to tell a cover story and get it accepted. Scanlon went on, "And besides, I pride meself on being a sound judge of people."

"Okay, Kev, I'm glad to hear it. So what do you want?"

"To buy your soul. What else would you expect from the devil himself?"

"Who said it was for sale? In all the stories I've read, it never turns out to be a good deal."

Scanlon clapped him on the back. "Aha, always the cautious one, eh! That's good. Now, I'm thinking that there's some of us as might be able to be of a little help to ye."

"I'm interested. Go on."

"My understanding is that you've been trying to obtain certain information through the official channels via Luchenko."

"I asked him for an interview with the commandant," McCain agreed. "I brought it up the day I arrived, and again three days after that."

"And what was the result?" Scanlon asked.

"Nothing. I think they're jerking me around."

"What was it that ye wanted to know—in general, if you take my meaning? You don't have to be specific."

"I was with a colleague when I was arrested. I just want to get some news."

Scanlon nodded and watched the singers for a while, who had switched to a song that McCain recognized as the melody of part of a Brahms violin concerto. Then, as if abandoning that line of conversation suddenly, Scanlon said, "It's not that Russians are incapable, you understand. But their system doesn't give them sensible goals to aim at. They're not rewarded for being efficient. They're rewarded for achieving the Plan, even if the Plan makes no sense." He paused, and added absently, "It leads to a lot of corruption—endemic to the society, you might say. . . . A man will get nothing done without paying the right price to the right person. And then again, if you look at it the other way round, there isn't anything that can't be done, provided you know who to ask."

"If Luchenko needs greasing, he should find a way to say so," McCain said. "I don't read minds."

"Ah well, it's his way to let people stew until they get anxious. It raises the price. But then, on the other hand, maybe it isn't Luchenko that ye need to be dealing with at all." Scanlon paused, giving McCain a sidelong glance, and moved his head closer as he came to the point. "Some of us have a little understanding with one of the guard officers, who has access to central record information. I can put you in contact with him. He'll be able to find out if there's any news of your friend."

"And what will he want out of it?" McCain asked.

"What does anyone want out of anything? Money, drink, sex, a good time. A new coat for the wife, if he has one, or bikes for the kids. Asian and Western goods still fetch fabulous prices on the Soviet black market."

"Look, this may come as a surprise, but I didn't come here stocked up for a long stay. And I don't think of myself as all that pretty."

Scanlon went off on one of his apparent tangents again. "Tell me something, Lew, is it a fact that ye've been something of a Russian scholar in your time? You seem to know a lot about them."

"I majored in modern history and languages. That's not uncommon for a journalist," McCain said. Both statements were true. It was best if cover identities drew as much from reality as was practicable.

"Did you ever read Dostoyevsky?"

"Sure."

"Then ye'll have heard of the secret society of thieves who as good as ran the Russian criminal underworld back in the times of the czars. They penetrated the prison system, too, got themselves special treatment, and sometimes intimidated the authorities. Also, they had a communications network that bordered on being uncanny." McCain nodded. And as Solzhenitsyn had described a century later, they were still around and doing a thriving business long after the Revolution. Scanlon drew on McCain's sleeve and they began walking slowly across the compound, keeping their distance from the walls. "It works like this," he said. "Today it's turned into a sophisticated operation called 'the Cooperative,' and survives through having connections into all the state bureaucracies, even the KGB. And it exists here, too."

"In Zamork, you mean?"

Scanlon waved a hand vaguely. "Around *Tereshkova*, generally."

"Do we know who?"

"Not unless they want you to. But there are account numbers in the Exchange that you can voucher points to, which through processes that we needn't concern ourselves with will end up as rubles in a Moscow bank. Through a code system, you authorize your creditor—in this case the guard officer that I mentioned—to draw it out. So whether he wants a blonde for himself or a bike for the kids, he'll find the wherewithal waiting for him when he goes back on his next Earthside leave. Then, when you finally get out, you settle your accumulated account with the Cooperative in US dollars, yuan, or yen—plus interest, naturally."

"In other words they're offering a loan service for bribing the guards."

"Exactly."

"How much does this cost?"

"Well, it's not cheap, I'll admit. But then again, we're not talking about the world's most secure line of investment either."

"Suppose a guy doesn't get out."

"Bad debts are factored into every business. So you can see why it wouldn't be cheap—the losses have to be recovered somehow."

"Suppose somebody forgets to settle up when he does get out?"

"I'd advise strongly against it."

McCain fell silent as they turned at the tripwire five feet inside the wall and began retracing their steps. With the ability to put guards, officers, and possibly even some of the senior officials in their pocket, a termite operation like that could undermine the whole system. The fact that it extended into Zamork suggested that somebody influential somewhere had been persuaded that he'd serve his own interests better by not interfering. If this typified what was going on beneath the surface everywhere, then maybe the whole Soviet Potemkin illusion was on the verge of caving in.

He thrust his hands into his pockets and considered the

implications and risks. If the officer failed to deliver, all McCain would have lost would be a few points of Monopoly money, and the Cooperative would have forsaken any opportunity of doing repeat business. If he got what he wanted but rubles failed to materialize in the Moscow bank, that would be the officer's problem, not McCain's. What was Scanlon's angle on it? he wondered. The Irishman made no secret of having worked with terrorist groups, and McCain had already categorized him, beneath his superficial bonhomie and calculated loquaciousness, as capable of acting with utter ruthlessness if a situation called for it: a killer. Not somebody who was disposed to handing out favors just to be nice to people.

They came back to the group standing in front of the choir, and stopped. "So, what's in it for you?" McCain asked. "Are you on a percent of the take or something?"

Scanlon continued staring ahead impassively and shrugged. "A man has to make a living," he said. It was as much of a concession as anyone could have asked for.

McCain drew a long breath and sighed. "Okay, deal me in," he agreed. "Where do I sign?"

"Leave it with me," Scanlon told him. "You'll be hearing."

◎ CHAPTER FOURTEEN ◎

The next morning, four of the Siberians in the central part of the billet went on strike. Although from different nations and sects, they shared a religious taboo about pigs, and were protesting at being assigned to a work detail that involved cleaning out animal pens in one of the agricultural sectors. It was McCain's turn for cleaning the billet that day, which meant that somebody from one of the other billets would be working the shift in the machine shop with Scanlon.

Some of the cleaning materials kept in a closet in the washroom area at the rear of the billet were getting low. McCain made a list of the items he needed and picked up an empty cardboard box to take to the OI store to collect them. When he came out into the billet, the Siberians were still sitting impassively on their bunks, as they had been when he passed through. Luchenko was standing in the center space, remonstrating with them. "Let us discuss this reasonably. You be fair with me, and I'll be fair with you . . ." He directed his words mainly at a tall, clear-skinned Uzbek called Irzan, who seemed to be the strike organizer. Maiskevik, as always, was standing a few paces back, arms folded across his chest, scowling and silent.

News of the strike had spread, and when McCain emerged into the mess area he found a crowd of inmates from B-3 and other billets gathering outside the door to demonstrate their solidarity with the Siberians. A guard officer was facing them with several guards, urging them to disperse and leave the matter with the authorities. McCain left the mess area and went out onto Gorky Street. He crossed to the other side and began walking in the direction of the next corridor leading into the Core.

"Settling in?" a voice called from behind him. McCain turned and saw he was being followed by Peter Sargent, an Englishman from B-12, one of the upper-level billets. He was in his late thirties, with light hair and somewhat boyish features which he attempted to disguise, McCain suspected, with his ragged, sandy-colored mustache. McCain found him cheerful and amiable, reminiscent of some of the British he had worked with in Europe.

McCain waited for Sargent to catch up, and they resumed walking together. "I'll get used to it, I guess—even all these crazy Asian gambling games. Why doesn't someone teach 'em to play decent football or something?"

"Do you mean soccer?"

"No, our kind, you know . . . NFL, super Bowl?"

"Oh, *that!*" Sargent sniffed. "I can't imagine why you call it 'football' at all."

"How come?"

"Well, for one thing it's not a *ball*, is it? If you're going to be logical, it ought to be foot-prolate-spheroid. And then, why 'foot,' when they spend most of their time running around throwing it?"

"What part of England are you from?"

"Cheltenham, over towards the west. Ever been there?"

"Not to that part. I was in England a couple of times, though. I like the cities that you can still walk around in. Too many of ours got turned into airports with streets on them."

"You have to walk," Sargent said. "It's the only bloody way to move."

Just then, they heard the sound of feet crashing in unison and growing louder, and a moment later a squad of guards led by a captain and moving at the double appeared from around the corner and passed, heading in the opposite direction. McCain turned his head and stared after them uneasily. "Something's up somewhere," Sargent said. Obviously he had been elsewhere and wasn't aware of the latest developments in B Block. McCain spent a few minutes updating him, then left Sargent at the intersection and followed the corridor from Gorky Street into the Core.

He made his way past several workshops and the laundry to the OI store, where he passed his box over the issue counter along with the list he'd compiled. Two women were there also. McCain realized that they were watching him intently while he waited. After a while he turned his head and acknowledged them with a quick upturn of his mouth. "Hi."

The taller of the two, who had black hair tied high, looked him up and down with shameless approval. Her face wasn't bad looking, but it had a hardened edge to it. "I haven't seen you around."

"Do you know everybody?"

"No, but I remember faces."

"What accent is that?" the other one asked. She was dumpy, with a rounded face, snub nose, and reddish hair. They both sounded Russian.

"American."

"An American!" The tall one looked impressed. "That's a rarity. We don't see many of them. You are new here, yes?"

"Fairly."

She pouted and stretched out a finger to toy suggestively with the top button of McCain's shirt. "Are you making many friends—I mean *close* friends? There are ways, you know. Interested?"

"Who knows? How do I call? They haven't installed my phone yet," he said. The small, dumpy woman giggled.

The taller one gestured across the counter as a mountain of a woman dumped McCain's box down on the counter. "Just leave a message with Hannah anytime. Only fifty points on the Exchange. For eighty you can have two girls and a really good time."

"I'll think about it."

"What do we call you?"

"Lew. But for now, I gotta go."

"Lew. I'll remember. I'm Zena."

McCain walked away carrying his box and wondering what the West imagined it could teach the Russians about the profit motive.

When he got back, it was obvious that there had been trouble. The prisoners in the mess area were standing back behind a cordon of guards with weapons at ready, and in the cleared area around the door of B-3 more guards were hauling out three of the Siberians. Luchenko was to one side of the door, gesticulating to the guard captain and Major Bachayvin, the block commandant. As McCain drew nearer, Maiskevik appeared in the billet doorway. He paused to send a strangely challenging look out across the faces of the prisoners watching from a distance, then moved over to Luchenko. Seconds later, four more guards came out, supporting the sagging form of Irzan between them. His mouth was puffed and swollen on one side, his face bruised, and there was blood on his chin and down the front of his shirt and jacket. It seemed the strike was over.

A squad of guards formed around the four Siberians. The captain rejoined them, and the group began moving toward the exit out onto Gorky Street. Major Bachayvin remained behind with two aides and the rest of the guards. "Well, what are you all staring at?" he said to the watching prisoners. "The mess area of this block is to be cleared, and movement outside restricted for the rest of today. Everyone will return to their billets immediately." Murmuring angrily among themselves, the prisoners dispersed under the threatening muzzles of the guards' weapons, after which the guards closed the barred gate onto Gorky Street that McCain had just returned through.

McCain went into B-3 and found Smovak, Borowski, and another Asiatic Siberian, whose name was unpronounceable and whom everyone referred to as Charlie Chan, straightening out the furniture in the center section of the billet. Evidently McCain's first cleaning day wasn't going to bring him much of the solitude and contemplation that Koh valued so highly. He went on through to the washroom at the back and found a pool of blood on the floor, with stains on the back of the door and down one wall. Rashazzi's mice scrabbled about in their cage indifferent to it all. He stood looking at the pattern and could almost reconstruct the events. Had the guards delayed coming into the billet until Maiskevik had finished with Irzan, or had they left the two of them alone for a few minutes after they took the other three Siberians out? McCain wondered. He was still staring at the scene when the door opened wider and Luchenko looked in and gazed around casually with no show of surprise. Then he looked at McCain curiously with his expressionless moon-face. "You'd better get busy," he suggested.

Scanlon came back with the rest when it was time for the midday meal. With the Gorky Street gate closed, guards posted there to admit only B Block inmates, and the mess area cleared except for those eating, he didn't have to be told what had happened. "So that's how the system works, eh?" McCain said. "I see now where Maiskevik fits in."

"He's a nasty piece of work, right enough," Scanlon agreed He looked at McCain curiously. "Do you think you can handle him?"

"Why should I think about that?"

"Because you're going to have to, if you're to do what you're wanting to," Scanlon said. McCain forced a questioning frown, but Scanlon's insight was so close to the mark that he didn't reply. There was nobody else nearby and Scanlon went on, "I don't know exactly what kind of mischief it is ye've in mind, but there's something. And you're fly enough to know that there isn't a lot that a man can do on his own. The rest o' the fellas in here are all waiting for the right man, and the man they'll follow will be the first who can take the Bulgarian. It might not be exactly what you'd call sensible, but it's the way the world is, and the way that everyone kings to scoundrels has always had to deal with it—as if there was any difference."

McCain reflected on the prospect. He was fairly sure he'd never take Maiskevik in an even fight if it came to that. . . . But on the other hand, he wasn't from a school that had placed too much stress on fair play and giving the other guy an even break, either.

The next day, back in the machine shop, Scanlon told McCain to go to the library on the upper level in the Core later that evening, and to open an interactive file at one of the reference computer terminals under the label ARCHITECTURE, BYZANTINE. Scanlon also conveyed the hardly illuminating, and highly questionable observation that "Cabbages dance in Kamchatka."

"What the hell's that supposed to mean?" McCain asked him.

"Just remember it."

McCain did as instructed, and at 19:10 hours that evening was seated before one of the reference screens in the library, when without warning the text he had been reading vanished, and in its place there appeared the question, *Where do cabbages dance?*

McCain entered in reply, *Kamchatka.*

The screen cleared, and then presented, *Understand you are in need of certain information. Can possibly assist. Require details.*

McCain composed a brief message explaining about Paula Shelmer and asking for news. The screen cleared once more, and the invisible correspondent stated a price. McCain rejected it. *Must appreciate market realities,* the screen advised, and repeated its offer. Again McCain refused. They haggled, and eventually struck a deal. McCain was told he would hear more in the next day or two, and then he was staring at his original material again, with no trace that the conversation had ever taken place.

He calculated on the basis of the going conversion rates of points into rubles and rubles into dollars that the exercise had cost him almost a quarter of a day's worth of his Washington salary. He dreaded to think what the total might be by the time he got out if much more of this went on. If UDIA's Accounts Section didn't accept it as legitimate, reimbursable business expense, he reflected, he'd be in real trouble.

❀ CHAPTER FIFTEEN ❀

The road surface was loose and gravelly because of the repairs in progress, and there was a break in the line of traffic going the other way. A short distance behind, the black KGB Chevrolet had been stopped by a delivery van pulling out ahead of it. And there were no police cars around.

"Watch this," Bernard Foleda said. He accelerated suddenly when the oncoming gap was just ahead, then braked and spun the wheel to send the car slewing round in a one-hundred-eighty-degree turn to point back the way it had come. He throttled off for a moment to regain grip, then accelerated again and slipped smoothly into the stream, heedless of the indignant toots and blares from the startled drivers behind, and sending a cheerful wave at the faces staring helplessly from the stranded Chevrolet.

"Bernard, what in God's name are you doing?" Barbara asked in amazement from the seat next to him.

"Keeping my hand in. It's nice to know you can still do it." Foleda lifted a hand from the wheel to make a throwing-away gesture. "Anyhow, every once in a while I get tired of it. It can get to you—having those creeps behind you everywhere you go."

"Do you do this kind of thing when Myra's with you, too?"

"Would you believe me if I told you that she showed me how to do it?"

Barbara gave him a curious look. "You know, I would. Why, is it true?"

"Yes. Her brother used to do stunts for movies when she was a kid."

"Didn't they cover it when you took field training?"

"Oh sure, but Myra's way is better."

They left the road to cut across the parking lot of a shopping mall, and exited into a lane at the back. "Are we still going to make it on time?" Barbara asked, glancing at the clock in the dashboard.

"Probably sooner than we would have it we'd gone the other way, from the look of how they had that road dug up," Foleda said. "This leads to another route to Langley. It's worth knowing." They were en route for the CIA's headquarters. A man by the name of Robert Litherland had called from there to say that the CIA had picked up something that would be of interest to Foleda's department, but didn't elect to go into further detail. However, since Gerald Kehrn from Defense was also going to be there, Foleda guessed it had something to do with *Tereshkova.*

"Anyhow," Barbara prompted, "before this sudden urge seized you to recapture lost youth, you were saying . . ."

"Oh yes, about Lew McCain and the Air Force woman. The impression I got when Uncle Phil and I talked to Volst was that State and the Soviets are playing a cat-and-mouse game over the whole thing. It took us long enough to even come clean and admit we're missing two people. We want communications contact, and until the Soviets give it to us, our people will only refer to the cover identities. But the Soviets are rejecting that as ludicrous. They want the real names and positions, and an admission that it was all official and we goofed."

"But they're not going public?"

"Not so far, anyway. That's something they can afford to keep in reserve. Meanwhile, we don't know what's happening with our two people. We don't even know for sure where they are."

Barbara sighed and stared out at the procession of well-kept, older-style clapboard homes with screened porches, bright-painted shutters, and glimpses of lawns sheltered in privacy behind barricades of flowering shrubbery. "Lew can take care of himself, I don't doubt," she said distantly after a while. "I feel more for that Air Force woman, Bryce. It's a sorry way to wind up when all she wanted was a little adventure." Foleda grunted—either noncommittally or in sympathy; it was difficult to tell. Barbara looked across at him. "What kind of a person is she? Did you find out much when you talked to Colonel Raymond up at Hanscom?"

"Some. She's from a family with something of a military tradition, mainly Navy. Born over in Tacoma, Washington State. Her father was an engineering officer on nuclear subs, and her mother was a Navy brat, too—raised around bases from Scotland to Japan even before she married Bryce's father. So the mother was used to getting along without a man around. Raymond figures that was what gave Bryce her stubborn streak."

"Stubborn, eh? That might not be too bad a thing in this situation."

"Maybe so, maybe not," Foleda said. "Raymond and I couldn't make our minds up. Apparently she's good as a scientist, but defensive about it to the verge of fanaticism—you know, the ethical purity of science, objectivity, honesty, that kind of stuff."

"Uh-huh. So?"

"It makes her more than a little disdainful toward things like politics and the reasons why this kind of job needs to be done. Raymond says it can make her difficult enough to work with sometimes, even when she's on the same side. In other words, she won't take easily to the idea of knuckling under to people she feels inwardly are her intellectual inferiors. That sounds like good news. But if she came up against an interrogator from the same mold, and it turned into a battle of will, it could backfire. Let's just hope it isn't getting her a harder time than is necessary."

The story at the CIA was that a prominent Russian scientist, director of a major research and communications establishment, wanted to defect. He had approached an American called Melvin Bowers at a scientific conference in Japan, and Bowers had initially contacted the embassy in Tokyo. Now Bowers was back in the US.

Foleda sat back and tapped absently at his tooth with a thumbnail while he stared at the map of the Soviet Union being presented on a wallscreen. His brow creased beneath his wiry, short-cropped hair. "Where's this place, again?" he asked after a thoughtful silence.

Gerald Kehrn operated a control on a panel inset below the edge of the table. For once, to Foleda's relief, he was managing to keep reasonably still this morning. On the map, a light-cursor moved to seek out a point located in the Vilyuisk Mountain region, in a desolate part of Siberia between the Olenek and Lena rivers. A moment later, one of the auxiliary screens beside the main one showed an enlarged satellite picture of a fenced-in cluster of buildings and other constructions scattered among a forest of communications antennas. A pattern of rectangular buildings arrayed in monotonous, barrack-like lines was partly visible outside the fence on one side, while an open expanse of wet-looking terrain broken by patches of scrub and an occasional tree rose toward a ridge of hills on the other.

"It's called Sokhotsk," Kehrn said. "Located on the Central Siberian Plateau about two hundred miles southwest of a city called Zhigansk. We know it's a major node in the Soviet military- and emergency-communications network; also, it's one of their primary space-operations groundlink stations."

Litherland, a solidly built CIA man in his late thirties, with collar-length blond hair and broad, linebacker shoulders, was sprawled casually in his chair in the center in a way that contrasted with Kehrn's tense, upright posture. He tossed up a hand loosely to interject, "There's more going on at that place than we've figured—something very big and very classified. That's why Cabman could be extremely useful." In the eternal double-talk that pervaded the intelligence world, "Cabman" was the code name that had been given to Professor Dyashkin.

"Is that the nearest town—the one two hundred miles away?" Foleda asked, still studying the display.

"There's a small industrial town called Nizhni Zaliski about ten miles north," Kehrn replied. "About five thousand people. But it doesn't have much connection with Sokhotsk. It was built for the workers of a new mining and construction project over the mountains from Sokhotsk."

"How far from Sokhotsk is this project?"

"Aw, six to ten miles, I'd guess." Kehrn glanced at Litherland. Litherland confirmed with a nod.

"Over the mountains," Foleda said.

"Yes." Kehrn looked puzzled. "Is it important?"

Foleda shrugged. "Who knows? Just trying to get the picture." He looked at Barbara. "Did you have any other points, Barb?"

She glanced at her notes. "Is Bowers okay?"

"Yes, how about this Professor Bowers from California?" Foleda asked. "Are we happy he's clean?"

Litherland nodded. "First-rate record. He's had top clearance for government work for six years. Stable, married, no personal problems, and a history of everything okay in the family. We're running a check on anything that may have changed since his last review."

"Is he available if we need to talk to him?" Foleda asked.

"He's staying in the area, for the time being," Litherland confirmed. "Fifteen minutes from here."

Foleda nodded, satisfied. He glanced first at Kehrn, then at Barbara for possible further questions or comments, then looked back at Litherland. "Okay. So, Robert, what can you tell us about Comrade Professor Igor Lukich Dyashkin, alias Cabman?"

Litherland called a databank record onto the tabletop screenpad that everyone had before them. A heading CABMAN: SUMMARY PERSONAL PROFILE appeared at the top, and below the name. Underneath, a picture appeared in the upper left corner of a man in his late forties, fresh-faced with a straight mouth, candid stare, and boyishly cut hair parted conventionally on the left. Beside the picture was a summary of height, weight, and other personal statistics. After a couple of seconds, a synthetic voice began reciting details of Dyashkin's history, which appeared as text in the space below, line by lie, as each was narrated.

Born April 6, 1964, Tula, USSR.

Father: Anton Konstantinovitch, b. Leningrad, 1935, production engineer.

Mother: Natasha Pavlovich, nee Sepirov, b. Odessa, 1939, civil servant.

1973 Moved with family to Orel.

1979 Joined Komsomol, Young Communist League, @ high school.

1982 Admitted Kharkov University. Graduated 1987, electrical/electronic engineering.

1987-1994 Soviet Navy. Two years postgraduate studies, Naval Technical Institute, Leningrad. One year posting to satellite tracking station, Archangel. Two years Pacific Fleet communications, based Vladivostok. Discharged with honor, second lieutenant.

1994 Naval Underwater Research laboratory, Sevastopol, work on submarine communications. Awarded doctorate in communications systems, 1996.

2003 Married Anita Leonidovich Penkev, administrator with Aeroflot. Marriage subsequently dissolved, 2011.

2005 Professor of Communications Engineering, Moscow State University. Also, permanent consultant to Ministry of Space Sciences on strategic military command networks. Admitted to Soviet Academy of Sciences, 2010.

2015 to present, Director of Operations at Sokhotsk facility.

Foleda continued studying the text for a while after the voice had stopped speaking. Then he looked up and gazed at the far wall. "Seems pretty solid," he murmured. "Do we have any leads on why he might want to come over?"

"We're not sure," Litherland said frankly. "He does have something of a reputation as a ladies' man—it seems that screwing around too much was what got him divorced. He could have upset some of the prudes among the high-ups—but that hardly sufficient. Obviously it's something to go into when we start talking to him."

"Yes, exactly," Barbara said, as if she had been waiting for them to get to that. "How are we going to do that? Where is he now?"

"Back in Siberia, as far as we know," Litherland said.

"So, how do we talk to him?" Foleda asked.

Kehrn answered. "That was part of what was inside the folder that he slipped to Melvin Bowers in Japan. It contained a number code that he's proposing to use to communicate to us directly, via the NSA system."

"You mean straight into our communications net?" Barbara checked. "None of the usual things like drops for our embassy in Moscow?"

"He's three thousand miles away from Moscow," Kehrn reminded her. "And besides, what does he need melodrama methods for? He's got a billion rubles' worth of some of the most sophisticated communications equipment in the world sitting right there."

"Okay . . . so how is he proposing to use it?" Foleda was beginning to look uncomfortable.

"He's in a position to initiate all kinds of transmissions worldwide that NSA listens in on all the time," Kehrn said, shrugging. "Now that we know what code he's proposing to use, we just wait for anything that comes in addressed to us."

"And can we reply the same way?" Barbara asked.

"Sure, why not?"

"How hard is this code of his?" Foleda asked.

"Grade-school," Kehrn admitted. "He's a professor, not a spy."

"So we know their codebreakers will read it."

"So, they fish it out of the air," Kehrn agreed. "But even if they know what we say, it doesn't follow that they understand what it means. And on top of that, they won't have any way of knowing who we're saying it to."

Foleda looked more uncomfortable. "It's another technical gimmick," he said. "We've seen enough already. First we had a 'foolproof' way of getting the Tangerine file down from Mermaid. But we never got any file, and Magician wound up in Lubyanka prison. Then we sent two people up after it with another gizmo that was the wonder of the age. We still don't have the file, they never came back, and this time we don't even know where they are. Now you want me to buy into this."

Kehrn tugged at his mustache, then leaped to his feet and paced across the floor. He turned in front of the large screen still showing the map. "But this time, believe me, Bernard, it really is different," he insisted. "I've been through the details personally, and I'm satisfied.

This time we don't have to send anyone anywhere. All the guy wants to do is talk. We just listen. And when we want to say something back, all we have to do is squirt it out through one of the computers at Fort Meade on a regular beam that we transmit all the time, anyway. All the risks are on the other side this time."

"It sounds like too many things I've listened to before," Foleda answered.

"But Cabman's out where the reindeer are, in the middle of Siberia," Kehrn said. "What else are we supposed do?"

"Hmph." Foleda began tapping his tooth again, and stared moodily at the pad in front of him, studying the face of Dyashkin once more and then shifting his gaze back to the satellite picture of the Sokhotsk groundstation. Finally he looked away again and asked Litherland, "Why are you people involving UDIA, anyway? This kind of thing is routine for the CIA. You must figure we have some stake in it."

Kehrn moved forward from the screen and rubbed his palms together agitatedly. "You're right. Where it involves UDIA, Bernard, is that Sokhotsk is the groundstation that handles the main communications beam up to Mermaid, where our two people might still be."

Litherland added, "And if Cabman is looking for favors, he'll be expecting us to ask for some evidence that he's genuine. Maybe we can persuade him to try and find out something about what happened to your people. It seems worth a shot."

Foleda was looking more interested already. "So what's this?" he said. "The CIA handing out freebies?"

Litherland returned a faint grin. "I guess we've decided that maybe we're on the same side after all," he said.

Foleda looked at Barbara. She inclined her head in a way that said she couldn't find any snags. "Okay," he announced resignedly. "Let's suppose I'm sold. But it's obvious that Cabman can only serve our purpose for as long as he stays at Sokhotsk. Therefore we should react encouragingly, but keep stalling him."

"That's what we were hoping you'd say." Kehrn came back to his chair and sat down.

Litherland nodded. "Fine."

"Callous, calculated exploitation of another human being," Barbara remarked.

"It's that kind of business, Barb," Foleda agreed with a sigh.

❖ CHAPTER SIXTEEN ❖

Back in the days when she was an engineering student, Paula Bryce had had a poster among the pictures, astronomical charts, and assorted samples of encapsulated philosophy cluttering the wall of her apartment, which read:

He who knows not, and knows not that he knows not, is a fool. Avoid him.

He who knows not, and knows that he knows not, is ignorant. Teach him.

He who knows, and knows not that he knows, is asleep. Waken him.

But he who knows, and knows that he knows, is a wise man. Follow him.

At the bottom, in a fit of exasperation one day, she had scrawled, *He who knows not whether he knows or knows not anything at all is a politician. Get rid of him!* Paula had never been exactly enamored with politics.

After growing up in a Navy family with an independent-minded mother whom she admired, she had found most of the girls she met in her teenage years silly and boring, and the boys either crude and immature or despairingly wimpish, rarely somewhere in between. So she tended to spend her time in solitary occupations, usually at a computer keyboard or behind a book. She read Ayn Rand, Kant, and Nietzsche when she was in a serious mood, hard science-fiction to relax, and books that debunked UFO's, psychic powers, quack medical fads, ancient astronauts, and the like, for amusement. She experimented with drugs, which she didn't like, alcohol, which was okay, and sex, which great. In her studies she found the challenge and rigor of the sciences stimulating, but kept liberal arts and the humanities to a minimum; they struck her as wishy-washy, too subjective in their conventional wisdoms, and they invariably attracted in droves precisely the kinds of people she couldn't stand.

On one occasion during the campus period of her life, she found herself representing the opposition to a group of sociology students who claimed to have obtained positive results in a series of ESP card-guessing tests, which they challenged the science fraternity to debate. Paula showed how a comparable score could be derived by matching the results to a selected portion of a random-number string, thus proving once again to the world that sometimes people have lucky streaks, sometimes unlucky, and most of the time they muddle along somewhere in between. The revelation would not have surprised any experienced gambler, but her efforts made little impression on the judges and the editors of the college magazine, who awarded the verdict to the paranormalists on the grounds that "the influence of ESP has not been disproved." And neither had the existence of Santa Claus ever been disproved, Paula pointed out in disgust, but to no avail.

Deciding on a career in science or engineering but unable to face the prospect of more years in academia, she followed the family tradition by opting for the services, and joined the Air Force in 2000 at age eighteen. After basic training she entered the USAF electronics school at Keesler AFB, Missouri, qualified there for a grant scholarship, transferred to Communications Command, and went on to complete her doctorate under Air Force sponsorship at the University of Chicago. After that she moved to the Pentagon to work on the performance evaluation of special-purpose military hardware, which involved stints at NASA, Goddard, and the USAF research center at Langley. Life settled down to a fairly humdrum routine in these years, and she relieved the boredom through a protracted affair that she rather enjoyed with a married officer twenty years her senior, called Mike. He was the kind of nonconformist who attracted her, and had earned his promotions through competence rather than the kind of social image-building that was typical in any nation's peacetime officer corps. But after two years Mike was posted to the Mediterranean, and for a change of scene Paula applied for a posting to Systems Command. She was accepted, and eventually became a specialist in analyzing purloined Russian and East European hardware.

In all this time her disdain for politics and economics persisted. In her view, for anybody with the brains to see it, breeder reactors and fusion, spaceflight, computers, and genetic engineering had laid Thomas Malthus firmly to rest. There was no longer any necessary reason for people anywhere to starve, or anything logical for them to continue fighting each other over. In fact, wars squandered the resources that could have solved the problems that the wars were supposed to be about. Scientists had been saying for over fifty years that there was plenty of energy and everything else, that the planet wasn't overcrowded and would never come close, and that modern-day lifestyles were incomparably healthier, safer, more prosperous, and more varied in opportunities than "natural" living had ever been. But nobody told the public. It wasn't news, and what the media didn't talk about didn't exist. Politicians couldn't see it, or perhaps they pretended not to because it wasn't the kind of talk that generated fears and attracted funding, and in the course of it all they had created the cultural pessimism that was handing the twenty-first century to Asia. That labeled them in Paula's book as just about the worst class of people to be running the world.

And ineptitude seemed to be just as much a mark of whoever was responsible for running the place she was in now, she thought wearily as she sat with her back to the wall on the thinly padded cot and surveyed the austere cell that she'd been cooped up in for she didn't know how long. The single unshaded bulb in the ceiling was turned down sometimes but was never out, the intervals varying erratically so that she had lost all track of time. They had moved her here from a double cell, where the series of cellmates who had come and gone had been so transparently planted that, on the one occasion since her capture, she had actually laughed out loud. If that was an example of the Russian fiendishness that had kept the West paralyzed for a century, then the West deserved to be eclipsed by Asia, she concluded.

First there had been Hilda, the East German, with her smile, blond fringe, and baby-doll blue eyes. "I am your friend. It is a mistake that I am here in this place. I know some important people outside, and I can help you after I am released. But first I must know more about you. What is your name? Where are you from? . . ."

Then there had been Luba, supposedly arrested for spreading subversive propaganda among students in Rostov. Her line had been scare tactics: "They tell the world that they've changed their ways, but they haven't. Nothing has changed. They're still as bad. They will keep you from sleeping for a week or more, leave you for days in a cell below freezing, and starve you until you can't stand up. By the time you meet your own people again there will be no marks. But you'll tell them what they want to know eventually. I like you. I don't like to think of you doing something like that to yourself. Why not make it easy?"

But the effect had been the opposite of that intended. Paula's initial fear had given way to a resolve that stemmed from a growing feeling of contempt. As the interminable interrogations went on without change of tune, and the facade had peeled away from Protbornov and his troupe to reveal them as played-out actors in roles that had become mechanical and stylized. The monotony was not, after all, a deliberate ploy to wear her down, as she'd first thought. In fact it wasn't anything clever at all. She had vague, incoherent recollections of her interrogators rambling on about religion, social sciences, things that had nothing to do with the present situation—anything to take up time, it seemed. The simple fact was that they had nothing else to say, nowhere left to go, and they were waiting for somebody else to figure out what to do.

She leaned forward on the cot to pull the blanket up around her shoulders and tuck the edges under her knees. That was another thing: the room was always either too chilly or too hot, but never comfortable. She snorted beneath her breath. Was this really a measure of the opposition she was up against? If so, it wasn't just mediocre, but infantile. People could do themselves a disservice by overestimating their opponents, she reflected. Maybe the West had been doing just that for a hundred years.

During the days, weeks, months—however long she'd been shut up—she had occupied herself by going through old debates again in her head. She remembered reading tales of calculating prodigies, and tried devising methods for performing calculations rapidly in her head. There had been a woman in India who could mentally multiply two thirteen-digit numbers in the astounding time of twenty-eight seconds. Paula found the best way was to work from left to right, adding the part sums progressively, rather than from right to left as taught in schools. She wondered if schools taught it that way because it used less paper. She had passed the time playing word games in her head (how many palindromes could she think of?), compiling lists of useless facts (how many place-names start with G?), playing with scientific speculations (what would the world look like if Planck's constant were a millions times larger?), and reminiscing over events in her life.

From the time she had spent in Massachusetts, she remembered warm summer Saturday evenings in the waterfront marketplace of downtown Boston, where she went with her occasional dates to walk among the crowds and the sidewalk restaurants, maybe visiting a bar or two before deciding where to have dinner. The hearty locker-room types who made opening gambits by cracking off-color jokes had never lasted long. The ones with something worthwhile to say, and an interest in what she thought, did better. Earnshaw had refused to oblige by fitting into any of her categories. She often wondered what had happened to him since the first of May. Perhaps he was no longer even on *Tereshkova*.

The sound of the door being unlocked interrupted her thoughts. It swung inward, and a blank-faced guard with Oriental features stepped through while a second waited outside. "You come now." Paula sighed, pulled the blanket aside, and stood up. She did her best to smooth her crumpled shirt and slacks, and instinctively brushed the ever-recalcitrant curl of hair from her forehead. The guard moved a step nearer and reached out as if to jostle her elbow to hurry her. She moved her arm out of the way and glared. The guard hesitated, then stood aside. Paula walked by him, out into the familiar corridor of gray walls and numbered doors.

They went up a flight of stairs, around a corner, and along another corridor to a narrow hallway with benches by the walls on either side. The doorway into the room that General Protbornov used was open, and Paula could see him already seated behind the desk inside, smoking a cigarette. The guard who had been leading motioned her forward, but before she had moved more than a step a telephone rang inside the room, and another officer appeared in the doorway with his hand raised for her to wait. He closed the door, and Paula drew back. The two guards had reverted to zombie mode and were standing a few yards away, one in each direction along the hall, apparently without much idea of what was supposed to happen next. She sat down on one of the benches to see what they would do. They didn't do anything.

Then she became aware of a commotion of raised voices coming from behind one of the other doors. She looked up curiously, and as she did so the door opened partly and a Russian lieutenant started to come out. A woman's voice called from behind him, unmistakably sarcastic in tone, but Paula could catch only a few of the phrases since her Russian was not fluent. "That's right, run and call a guard . . . afraid I'll bite? . . . and *we* expect *you* to protect us!"

"Please sit down," another man's voice pleaded from inside.

The lieutenant turned to talk back into the room. "Look, you said you wanted to talk to somebody with the appropriate qualifications. Well, I'm going to fetch somebody now, all right? As you say, we do not have the qualifications."

"You don't have the sense, you mean," the woman's voice retorted. "What do you take me for, a common criminal or something—a pickpocket or a whore? Look, I am a senior scientist from Novosibirsk." Paula raised her eyebrows. Novosibirsk was one of the major Soviet scientific centers, especially for advanced physics.

"Does that mean anything to either of you? I have been brought here because of political protest, which I claim is my right, and I object to the way this is being dealt with. I demand to speak to whoever is in charge of this entire establishment. Don't you realize this could get you shipped back to Earth and ten years in a camp?"

"Be patient, if you are capable. I will seek instructions." The lieutenant turned back from the doorway into the hall. The two guards straightened themselves up. "It's all right, at ease," the lieutenant muttered. "See that the bitch in there doesn't leave." He saw Paula sitting on the bench. "Oh God, another one." She watched him walk away along the corridor, shaking his head.

The lieutenant had left the door open, and through it Paula could hear the voice of the other man who had spoken earlier. "Yes, this is Colonel Tulenshev. I want to know if Sergei Gennadevitch is there. Have you seen him recently? . . . We have a small problem here. See if you can find him and put him on the line, would you? . . . No, it's not serious, but I would like . . ."

Then Paula realized that the woman who had been doing the shouting was standing in the doorway. She looked at Paula for a moment, and then, tossing an indifferent glance at the two guards, came out and sat down next to her on the bench. The guards had been told not to let her leave. She wasn't leaving. So they remained where they were and didn't intervene.

The woman was somewhere in her mid-forties, Paula guessed. She had fiery hair, almost orange, tumbling to her shoulders in waves, a firm face with high cheeks, a sharply defined brown, an outthrust determined chin, and clear, unwavering eyes. Her body was full and rounded beneath a tan sweater and brown skirt, and her breast heaved visibly as she recovered her breath. She studied Paula's face for a few seconds, then muttered something quickly in Russian. Although Paula didn't catch the words, the tone was sympathetic and curious. A wave of eagerness surged up involuntarily inside Paula, something from deep down, reaching instinctively for the promise of a first true contact with another human being since the day she and Earnshaw were captured. She shook her head and explained that she was a foreigner and hadn't understood.

The woman stared at her. "*Anglicanka?*"

Paula shook her head again. "*Nyet. Amerikanka.*"

"Ah." The woman nodded slowly and spoke in English, keeping her voice to little more than a whisper. "I heard a rumor of two American spies being arrested a while ago. You were one of them?" Paula shrugged and said nothing. The woman smiled faintly. She leaned closer and rested a hand lightly but reassuringly on Paula's arm. "Listen to someone who knows them. They will try to frighten you. Don't let them—it's just bluff. Stalin has been gone a long time. The fossils in charge of things today are not made of the same stuff. Their whole rotten system is about to fall apart, and they know it. Face up to them. Admit nothing. When they see they can get nowhere, they will give up."

Before Paula could reply, the colonel who had been speaking on the telephone inside came out. "What is this?" he thundered at the two guards. "The American woman is under solitary detention. She is not permitted to talk with anyone! Anyone!—Is that clear!" He looked at the Russian woman. "And you, high and mighty as you may think you are, you have not been dismissed to go walking about the building. The general is on his way here now." He held open the door. The Russian woman rose and went back in, carrying herself proudly and without haste. Just before she disappeared, she turned her head and sent Paula a faint nod of reassurance, as if to stress her words. It had been just a matter of seconds, but, maybe because she needed to so desperately, when Protbornov finally called her into the other room, Paula felt as if some part of the indomitable strength that the Russian woman seemed to radiate had rubbed off on her. She admitted nothing. They threatened; she defied them. It was the same the next time, and the next.

And finally, as the Russian woman had predicted, the interrogators gave up. They informed Paula one day that she would be going elsewhere, pending further directions from Moscow. She was to be moved, they told her, to a place called Zamork.

☸ CHAPTER SEVENTEEN ☸

With smoke billowing around them from a German tank burning in the street below, two Red Army infantrymen with tommy guns slung across their backs clambered to the rooftop of the shell-scarred Reichstag building in Berlin and unfurled a Soviet flag. The theme music rose to a triumphant crescendo, and the camera closed in on the hammer-and-sickle emblem flying proudly on red against a background of three Stormoviks crossing the sky in formation.

Applause spattered from the more appreciative among the audience as the lights brightened. The Saturday night movie in B Block mess area was over. It had been about a Russian James Bond figure from the days of the "Great Patriotic War," called Stirlitz, who infiltrated the Nazi SS and sabotaged an attempt by Heinrich Himmler and Allen Dulles, then the head of American intelligence in Europe, to make a separate peace in the West in early 1945. Such an arrangement would have allowed the Nazis to concentrate their remaining forces against the Soviet Union—and after Hitler was removed, the film implied, would have prepared the way for the Americans, British, and Germans to join forces against Russia in a typically treacherous bid to protect their capitalist interests.

The rows in front of the screen dissolved into groups of prisoners dispersing to carry their chairs back to their various billets, and the guards who had been watching from the back returned to their duties. McCain was walking alongside Peter Sargent, when Oskar Smovak caught up with them. "So, there you are," Smovak told them. "Now you've seen it for yourselves—how Stirlitz saved us from you scheming Americans and British. We don't know how much we have to thank our leaders and the Party for, eh?" McCain never knew whether or not to take Smovak seriously. Stirlitz was obviously fictitious, and the story as depicted bore only a remote connection to the events that had actually taken place.

"You don't really believe all that, do you?" Sargent said incredulously. From their conversations, McCain had come to suspect that he was connected with Western intelligence, too.

"Stirlitz has become legendary among the Russians," Smovak said. "A lot of them accept him as real, without any question."

"Yes, and everything else that it said, by association," Sargent replied.

"How do you know it wasn't so?" Smovak challenged. "The Russians get their brand of bullshit. You get your own bullshit. How do you know which is right. How do know any of it is?"

"When the Moscow Film Studio can make a movie that doesn't have to be passed by Party censors before you can see it, then come and talk about it," Sargent said. He upended the chair he was carrying and turned toward the stairway leading to the upper level. The others continued walking to the door of B-3 and entered the billet to a frenzied accompaniment of red flashes and beeps. In the mess area behind them, a deeper note sounded from a klaxon to signal five minutes to go before in-billets—the time for the mess area to be cleared and everyone inside. Lights-out would be one hour later. There was little of the roll-calling that had characterized earlier prison environments. Counting and checking that people were in the right places was performed automatically by remote computers monitoring the electronic bracelets that everyone wore.

Inside the billet, Koh, propped upright at the end of his bunk with an open book, watched silently as the moviegoers trooped in. Rashazzi and Haber were taking turns to scribble on symbol-packed papers littering the front table. "Now we need a way of relating v-prime to theta, and eliminating x-bar," Rashazzi was saying.

"Use the expression for the work integral," Haber suggested, rummaging. "Where was it? . . . Yes, here."

"Why don't you two learn a language that other people can understand?" Smovak grumbled as he passed behind them.

"Perhaps we like it better if they can't," Haber said pointedly. Smovak raised his eyebrows and moved on.

Mungabo climbed up onto his bunk above McCain's and clasped his hands behind his head as he lay back to stare at the ceiling. "There's never any ass in them Russian movies," he complained. "Nobody cares about all that political shit, and some of the action was okay . . . but there's never any ass." Luchenko moved past the bunk, heading toward the far end of the billet, with Maiskevik and Nolan close behind. "Never any ass," Mungabo repeated in a louder voice for his benefit.

"Imperialist decadence," Luchenko tossed back. "That's all they have to offer."

"I'll take it, I'll take it," Mungabo murmured, eyeing his pinups.

McCain grinned to himself as he folded his jacket and stowed it in the flat drawer beneath his bunk. Yevgenni Andreyov, who was following, stopped by the end of their bunk. Andreyov was probably around sixty, with patches of white hair on either side of a balding dome, and a white beard, but twinkling gray eyes that could have belonged to somebody thirty years younger. McCain always found him genial, and trusted him more than he did the others at the far end of the billet.

"They brought it upon themselves, you know—the Germans," Andreyov said. "In 1917 they sent Lenin back so that he would take Russia out of the war. But the state that Lenin created was the one that finally destroyed Germany. That's irony for you."

"You seem to know a lot about all that," McCain commented.

"Yes, well, my father was there, you know—with Konev's army in 1945."

Scanlon came in just as McCain turned to head for the washrooms at the far end of the billet. He was carrying a string bag containing grapefruits, which he deposited on his bunk. McCain indicated them with a questioning motion of his head. "A fella who has a friend who works in one of the ag zones," Scanlon said. "I got them during the movie. It's legal. You can get your bonus in kind instead of in points if there's a surplus."

"I haven't seen one of those since I left the States. How much?"

"A point . . ." Scanlon caught the look on McCain's face, "for two."

"Capitalist!" McCain snorted.

"Sure, a man has to live."

McCain picked up the bag containing his toilet gear and began walking through to the far end of the billet. At the middle table of the next section, Smovak and Vorghas were sitting down to a card game with Charlie Chan, the Amurskayan whose name nobody else could pronounce. Chan was slenderly built and studious-looking, with olive skin, slit-eyes, and a pencil-line mustache. He was notorious for his appalling jokes, which the other Siberians seemed to find as hilarious as he did. Behind them the Hungarian, Gonares, was already asleep in his bunk. Gonares was currently on outside work assignment, shifting freight in the cargo bays at the hub. Farther along, a Yakut called Nunghan and an Afghan were experimenting with the latest gambling creation—a pinball game that involved shooting glass marbles up an inclined wooden board to roll down again through an obstacle course of holes and nails. The idea had been Rashazzi's, who had charmed "the Dragoness"—the stern-faced woman-mountain who ran the OI store—into getting a box of marbles from a children's toyshop in Novyi Kazan specially for the purpose.

McCain now hardly noticed the strange smell that had greeted him the day he first entered the billet. It was due, he had since discovered, to a kind of wild garlic that certain Siberians, Yakuts in particular, once ate traditionally during the long winters when no other vegetables were available, and now chewed through habit. The scent reeked on the breath and exuded from the pores. "Yes, I know what you mean—we've got it, too," Peter Sargent had said when McCain tried to describe it. "An extraordinary olfaction—fermenting birdseed in a crappy petshop," which at least conveyed the intensity, if not the precise quality. McCain wondered if they'd bribed somebody in the ag zones to grow a patch of the awful stuff for them specially. He couldn't imagine it being included in the production lists drawn up by the omniscient planners in Moscow.

On the far side, Taugin, the Frenchman, was stretched out with his head propped on one hand, staring mournfully at a woman's picture framed on the locker next to him, as he seemed to do for most of his free time. The rest of it he spent prowling morosely about the compound or along Gorky Street. From time to time he would murmur things like, "Mimi, where are you now?" or "Oh, Mimi, where did we go wrong?"—but the name was different on different days, and the pictures changed.

Luchenko, Maiskevik, and Nolan were together in the rear section. On the other side of the table from them, Borowski, the Pole, was getting up from his bunk. In contrast to his Gallic neighbor, Borowski was pragmatic, cheerful, and always willing to help. But how much did that mean? He was still one of the group at the far end, which McCain looked upon as Luchenko's personal circle. Russia was notorious for nothing being what it seemed. Zamork was a good microcosm of it.

"Profits before people," Nolan fired at McCain as he passed. "That's capitalism. It destroys life. There used to be beavers on Manhattan Island. Did you know that? And what about the passenger pigeon?"

"Ask the Siberian mammoth," McCain said, and went through into the washroom. A moment later he stuck his head out again. "And there's plenty of beaver in Manhattan. Ask Mungabo." He disappeared back inside to relieve himself.

The door opened again a second later, and Borowski came in. They stood side by side, staring at the wall. Abominable noises and odors came from the cubicles behind, where two of the Siberians were entrenched. The damn garlic affected everything. "It's a miracle that Razz's mice survive in here," Borowski commented. A flurry of scampering in the cage behind the door acknowledged the remark. McCain didn't answer. He'd caught the expressions on Luchenko's and Maiskevik's faces when he poked his head back out to retort at Nolan. The back of his neck was prickling.

"What did you think of the movie?" Borowski asked.

"Hmm? . . . Aw, standard stuff."

"You know, in Russia they teach that it was their entry into the Japanese war that brought victory there, too. But that was only a week before it ended, wasn't it? Hadn't America already dropped the first atomic bomb by then?" Borowski saw that McCain wasn't listening. As he zipped himself up he leaned closer and murmured, "Watch yourself out there." Then he left.

The sound of flushing came from one of the cubicles behind. McCain recreated in his mind every detail that he could recall of the situation in the end section just beyond the door when he had passed through. Luchenko had been sitting to the right of the end table, about midway along, with Maiskevik standing behind him and Nolan farther back by his bunk. Taugin was on his bunk to the left, and Borowski would probably have gone that way, too, after leaving the washroom. On the table in front of Luchenko there had been a pack of cigarettes, a book, a tin lid used as an ashtray, and at the near end a couple of magazines. Near the far end there had been a large enamel mug almost full of steaming tea, perhaps left there by Borowski. McCain thought carefully; then he opened the door of one of Rashazzi's cages of mice and scooped a large fistful of feed grain into his left hand.

When McCain came out, Luchenko was still at the table, and Nolan had sat down on his bunk. But Maiskevik had moved to stand in the center aisle at the far end of the table, covering the way through to the rest of the billet. To the left, Taugin hadn't moved, and Borowski was getting something from his locker. The mug of tea was still standing where it had been. McCain moved to the left to pass by the table.

"Earnshaw." Luchenko's voice was unusually clipped. "I may have some information on your colleague." McCain stopped and looked inquiringly. "But first, of course, there is a price."

"You never mentioned anything about that," McCain said.

"I must have forgotten. Nothing is free here. I'm sure that being American, you will understand."

"You expect me to pay you for doing your job?"

"It is the custom here."

"No, thanks."

McCain turned in the direction he had been heading, but Maiskevik moved to block the way. "If you choose not to avail yourself of the service, that's up to you," Luchenko said. "But I have done my part. It must still be paid for."

Maiskevik shoved McCain roughly in the chest with the flat of his hand to stop him, and stood stroking the knuckles of his clenched fist. "Everybody in here pays their taxes," he growled. It was one of the few occasions on which McCain had heard Maiskevik speak. The message was clear enough. On the fringe of his awareness, McCain registered that the rest of the billet had suddenly gone quiet. He heard somebody come out from the washroom behind him and stop.

McCain looked quizzically at Luchenko. "I thought you said we could always discuss these things reasonab—" His left hand shot the grain into Maiskevik's face, and as the Bulgarian blinked reflexively McCain's other hand swept the mug up off the table to follow with the tea. Maiskevik bellowed and staggered back, clawing at his scalded face. McCain kicked hard into his crotch, then seized the lapels of his jacket with both hands to pull the Bulgarian forward onto a murderous head-butt full in the face. Maiskevik fell back against the end of Borowski and Taugin's bunk, his eyes glazed and blood gushing from his ruined nose. McCain kicked his feet away, and he crashed into a sitting position on the floor. Incredibly, he was trying to get up again. McCain grabbed a fistful of hair to jerk Maiskevik's head back and delivered a straight-fingered jab to the exposed throat. Maiskevik gagged and crumpled to sit with his head lolling to one side, with rivulets of blood from his nose running down the front of his clothes.

It had been too fast and violent for anyone else to react. Luchenko was gaping from his chair across the table, Nolan was staring ashen-faced from behind, while a few feet from McCain, Borowski was still frozen in the act of turning from his locker. Forcing himself to be calm externally despite the adrenaline charge pulsing through his body. McCain replaced the mug on the table. "I've just filed for an exemption," he told Luchenko. Then he stepped over Maiskevik's legs to continue on his way. The others who had come forward from the other sections of the billet parted to let him through. He stopped halfway to pour himself a cup of tea at the center table, and carried it back to his bunk.

Slowly the billet came back to life behind him. At the far end, Luchenko was still sitting, stunned, while Nolan, Borowski, and a couple of others hauled Maiskevik to his feet and steered him into the washroom.

Scanlon was leaning forward on the edge of his bunk when McCain sat down opposite him. "Here," he said, holding out his flask. "A little drop o' the hard stuff will do you more good than that."

McCain took a long swig and nodded. "Thanks." He handed back the flask and sipped his tea.

Scanlon regarded him curiously for a while. Then he took a sip from the flask himself and looked across at McCain again. "So, Mr. Earnshaw," he said at last, "what kind of a school of journalism was it, I'm wondering, that they sent you to, now?"

Inside the Government Building at Turgenev, General Protbornov and the three other men with him watched a replay of the incident as it had been recorded through a wide-angle lens built into one of the ceiling lights in billet B-3. The title on the thick, red-bound folder laying in front of Protbornov read, MC CAIN, LEWIS H., U.S. UNIFIED DEFENSE INTELLIGENCE AGENCY. ABSOLUTE TOP SECRET.

Sergei Kirilikhov, from the Party's Central Committee, nodded tight-lipped and pivoted his chair to face away from the screen. "You were right after all, General," he said to Protbornov. "He reacted just as your people predicted he would. My compliments."

Protbornov patted the folder on the table affectionately. "When he was a teenager in California, there was a gang of bullies at the school he attended who liked to terrorize other students, especially Hispanics. Well, one day they made the mistake of picking on a new batch of students who turned out to be the children of Nicaraguan mountain guerilla fighters recently arrived in the country, and almost got themselves killed. The affair made a deep impression on McCain. Later, when he was with NATO, he hospitalized a would-be mugger in Berlin. What we have just seen was fully in character."

Maxim Sepelyan, from the Ministry of Defense, stroked his chin dubiously. "You, ah . . . you don't think that this man could be too headstrong—too impulsive, perhaps?"

Protbornov shook his head. "We have studied his motivational psychology intensely. Despite what you just saw, he is not a person primarily disposed toward violence. He only resorts to force when compelled to in self-defense. His ideological convictions reflect the same principle. When given a choice, he bases his relationships on reason, persuasion, and patience. But he is defiant, and he has a strong sense of loyalty to his beliefs. Those are exactly the qualities we want."

The other man present, General Andrei Tolomachuk, from the KGB's Ninth Directorate, gestured toward the screen from Protbornov's other side. "I presume that what we saw there was genuine. The Bulgarian wasn't acting under instructions?"

"Definitely not," Protbornov said. "That was all quite genuine, I assure you. Part of the objective was to test that McCain's ability and determination are as we have assessed them."

The four exchanged inquiring looks. "Very well, I am satisfied," Kirilikhov pronounced. Tolomachuk agreed. Sepelyan thought for a moment longer, then nodded. "When I get back to Moscow, I will advise that the next phase of the operation proceed as planned," Kirilikhov said.

Protbornov looked pleased. "So the countdown remains on schedule. We're still talking about a November seventh D-day." Kirilikhov nodded.

"Four months from now," Sepelyan mused. "The waiting will make it seem like a long time."

"It's the centenary," General Tolomachuk said. "We've been waiting a hundred years. What are four more months compared to a hundred years?"

"What are they compared to owning the world?" Protbornov asked.

❀ CHAPTER EIGHTEEN ❀

Maiskevik was taken to the infirmary the next morning for treatment following an "accident," and Luchenko was summoned to a talk with Major Bachayvin, the block commandant. An hour later two guards appeared at the billet to collect Maiskevik's things, and by lunchtime the prevailing opinion was that he wouldn't be coming back. No official reason was given. Luchenko reappeared later and had nothing to say on the matter except that two replacements would be coming to B-3 in Maiskevik's place. McCain carried on in the metalworking shop through the afternoon, expecting to be hauled away at any time, but by the end of the shift nothing had happened. He could only conclude that the management, for reasons best known to themselves, were going along with the accident story officially. Maybe Luchenko was on the take to a greater degree than he cared to make known to his bosses, McCain reflected. Or maybe they were all part of it, too. Either way, it could add up to possible opportunities to be exploited.

When McCain arrived back at the billet, Nolan brought him a note from the mail pouch that a messenger delivered every day to Luchenko. It advised that the book McCain had reserved was being held in the library. McCain hadn't reserved any book. He went to the library and was handed a gaudy paperback entitled *A Hero's Sacrifice*. It was one of the standard pulp inspirational pieces churned out for

152

the masses by Party hacks, and carried a cover picture of a standard Soviet workaholic hero, muscles taut beneath bronzed skin, steely-eyed, and complete with hard hat and jackhammer, shown against a background of cranes, bulldozers, and an oil refinery under construction.

McCain took the book to the general compound and shielded himself among a group of prisoners placing bets on a Siberian variation of the shell game before he ruffled through the pages. The slip of paper that dropped into his hand read:

SUBJECT OF QUERY WAS DETAINED IN SOLITARY AT SECURITY HQ TURGENEV UP TO FOUR DAYS AGO FOR CONTINUING INTERROGATION. CONDITION GOOD. NO GROUNDS FOR CONCERN. HAS RECENTLY BEEN MOVED TO ZAMORK, RESTRICTED SECTION, BLOCK D.

The message also included instructions for McCain to follow to reestablish contact, should he need further information on anything. McCain wasn't sure whether he felt reassured or not, although, according to Scanlon, the source had proved consistently reliable in the past. Reputation was everything in any good business, Scanlon had reminded him.

He saw Andreyov approaching as he was about to begin walking back across the compound, and stopped to wait for the older man to join him. "Have you met the two new arrivals yet?" Andreyov asked. He had a thick woolen cardigan beneath his jacket and swung his arms across his body as he spoke, as if it were cold. McCain could picture him in a black overcoat and fur hat in a Moscow street scene.

"No, I've been in the library," McCain said. "So they're here already, eh?"

"And straight out of training, if I ever saw KGB before. You've stirred things up properly, you know. They don't trust you an inch now. A bodyguard for Luchenko, that's what they are. Mungabo has christened them King and Kong."

"It seems strange," McCain commented, mainly to see what Andreyov would say. "I've have thought they'd have shipped *me* out."

"Oh, they couldn't leave Maiskevik there, could they? Not any longer—after what happened. He's lost face. . . . Wouldn't be able to carry the same weight any more, in the billet. Not after what happened."

"And I don't get put away for a while to cool down?"

"No, they couldn't do that, could they? Not if they want to pretend it was an accident."

"That's my point. Why would they pretend that?"

"Who knows why they do things?"

McCain gestured at the compound in general. "So, is it likely to be everybody's gossip for the evening?"

"No, it won't be spread around."

"How come?"

"It's best."

They began walking slowly toward the door into the throughway between A and B Blocks. Andreyov turned his head to peer at McCain, as if weighing something in his mind. Finally he said, "You seem to be a man of strong opinions—strong impressions of things."

McCain thrust his hands into his pockets. "Some things, maybe. I don't know. . . . What did you have in mind?"

"The things you argue with Nolan about. You have strong ideals."

"I never really thought of myself as an idealist."

"Principles, then?"

"A few, maybe."

Andreyov hesitated, then said, "I admire that. Everybody who is anything worthwhile has to admire that. But, you know, it troubles me that you should think so badly of Russia." Before McCain could reply, he went on, "It isn't everything you think. We are proud of our country, as you are of yours. Like you, we worked hard and we suffered to make it what it is. And we have transformed our Motherland from backwardness to one of the world's strongest nations, and extended its influence everywhere—out into space, too. There are many positive things that you should remember, things we have achieved. Creative things. Our history, our arts . . . Russia has produced men of words and ideas that have swept through the civilized world as have few others. Russians have brought glory to music and ballet, and at one time to painting and architecture. . . . And hospitality and friendship! Do you know what the educated Russian values more than anything else? Good friends and stimulating conversation. There is nothing anywhere else in the world to match the loyalty of Russians who are close friends. You have to spend an evening at home with an apartment full of them, when the talking goes on over food and vodka until long into the night. Or I am on my own and the telephone rings at three in the morning, and it's my friend Viktor who I have known for forty years and he tells me, 'Yevgenni, I have problems and I need somebody to talk to. I am coming over.' Or it is Oleg, who says, 'I have been thinking about what you said last week. We must discuss it.' So what do I do? I put the water on to boil for some tea. Where would you find that in New York? Oh, no, there I must get up and go to work because I have to be 'successful' all the time, or make money, money, or please the boss whose ass I want to kick, but then he fires me from my job and I sleep in the street. Is it not so?"

They emerged into Gorky Street and turned to follow it for a short distance to reenter the B Block area through its front entrance.

"No, you misunderstand," McCain said. "I don't have any quarrel with the Russian people. I respect everything the Russian tradition stands for—all the things you said. But the present political system is something alien to all that. That's not the real Russia."

"Yes, we've made our share of mistakes, it's true," Andreyov agreed. "Especially in Stalin's time. And I admit we are still too bureaucratic and paranoid about foreigners. Russians worry a lot what people think of them, you see. They can't stand the thought of being compared unfavorably, or of being seen in a bad light. They're like a wife who is too fussy about her house and won't let anyone in when she thinks it's untidy. And we still tend to feel embarrassed by some things, so we hide ourselves from the world. But it's changing. Someday we will show the world. Not in my lifetime, maybe . . . but it will happen."

"Well, when it does, then I'll feel a lot easier," McCain said.

They walked on in silence for a short while. Then Andreyov said, "That movie last night, my father was there, you know—he was with

Konev's army that linked up with the Americans in Germany. Within months there was talk that now they were going to start fighting the Americans. He told me some of the soldiers wept when they heard it. They couldn't understand why."

"Life can be crazy," McCain agreed.

"You don't understand it either?"

"I gave up trying to. I just believe that you pay what you owe, you collect what you're due, you protect what you have, and you help if you can. Otherwise mind your own business and leave people alone."

"You don't want to destroy the Soviet Union?"

"Not unless it tries to destroy me."

"What about if you thought it was about to? Would you attack it preemptively?"

McCain nodded as he saw the point. "Like Maiskevik, for instance?"

"We are taught that the capitalists will start a desperate, last-ditch war to try and save themselves rather than submit to the inevitable triumph of world socialism," Andreyov said. "Doesn't what you've just said confirm it?"

"Look at Japan, China, and the rest of Asia and tell me again about the triumph of world socialism. I'd say it's the other way round: it's not us that's in the ditch. Maybe we feel the same way about you."

Andreyov shook his head sadly. "No trust, no trust," he sighed. "Why does it always have to be that way? You know, I heard a story once about two men from a ship that had sunk, and they were floating on top of a chest full of food and water in a sea full of sharks. But to make enough room to open the door, one of them would have to jump in the water. Now, they had an oar also, which meant that the other one could beat away the sharks. But if he didn't beat away the sharks and allowed the other one to be gobbled up, then he would be left with all the food. They both knew that they would maybe survive if they cooperated with each other, and that they would both die if they didn't; but if one was left with all the food, then he would certainly survive. So neither of them would jump, because neither trusted the other. And they both starved to death, on top of a chest full of food." Andreyov looked at McCain. "It's the same problem, isn't it. What's the solution?"

McCain thought for a while. "I guess first we have to decide who the sharks are," he said. They stopped inside the B Block mess area. McCain took in the usual evening scene, then his eyes came back to Andreyov. He wondered how a seemingly harmless old man came to be shut up in a place like this. "What did you do to get in here?" he asked.

"Oh, it's a funny story. . . . I don't really have any family left now, you see, so I volunteered for the experimental population that they were bringing up to inhabit the colony. But they didn't like some of the things I said, so they put me in here rather than send me all the way back again. Subversive, they said I was."

"Not many guys your age get to go into space," McCain commented.

"Hah! I might as well not have bothered, for all I can remember," Andreyov replied. "Very peculiar, it was. I don't have any clear recollection at all of that trip. A lot of others I was with said the same thing. All like part of a dream, it was . . ." He paused and rubbed his temples. "In fact, even thinking about it makes me tired. And it's past my time to rest, anyway. Not as young as you people. . . . If you'll excuse me, I think I'll turn in."

"Sure. Thanks for the talk. 'Night."

Andreyov went on into the billet. McCain spotted Scanlon and Koh at one of the tables and went over to sit with them. It could have been his imagination, but despite what Andreyov had said about gossip not spreading, McCain got the distinct feeling that many eyes were following him; too many heads seemed to look away suddenly as he let his gaze wander over the mess area. He looked back at the other two.

"How's Andreyov tonight?" Scanlon asked.

"He always strikes me as a lonely kind of person. That's why he talks a lot, and I listen. He only came up here because he doesn't have any family down there." McCain shrugged and gestured at the figures in the mess area. "Maybe this is his family now. I don't think the idea of going home even crosses his mind."

"Ah well . . ." Scanlon looked curiously at Koh. "Don't you ever think about going home?"

"Not a lot." Koh was packing his long, straight-stemmed pipe with the mixture of tobacco and herbs that he smoked.

"There is really no point. And besides, not everyone back where I come from agrees that what I did was an honorable thing." Koh never pinpointed exactly where he considered himself to be from. "And that's very important, of course. It's conceivable that I'd have a harder time back there than up here."

"Don't you want to contribute something to what a lot of people are saying is Asia's century?" McCain said.

Koh chuckled as he lit his pipe. "Maybe I already have." He sucked several times, and was rewarded with a cloud of aromatic smoke that he puffed into the air.

"What did you do?" McCain asked.

"Maybe I'll tell you one day," Koh answered mysteriously. He went on, "In any case, whatever is destined to evolve will do so in the long run, with or without me. With all their glorification, I don't believe that even the Christs, Napoleons, Hitlers, and Genghis Khans really influence history that much. All they do is slightly accelerate or slightly retard what would have happened anyway."

"So Asia was due to take the twenty-first century anyway?" McCain said.

"Yes, eventually," Koh replied. "You had Malthus, and thought you were running out of resources; we had Confucius. But people are the only resource that matters, because human ingenuity creates all the rest—and we have thirty percent of the world's supply. When you think of it that way, the outcome was inevitable sooner or later."

Scanlon was staring with his head cocked to one side, as if this put a lot of things in a perspective that he hadn't seen before. "Go on, Koh," he said. "That's a thought, now. So it was all inevitable, you're telling us?"

Koh shrugged. "Eventually. But the West itself speeded up the process."

"How come?" McCain asked.

"You made the Third World into colonies and held it back for centuries. But in doing that you were compressing a spring. And when the spring was released after the Second World War, nothing could contain the energy and the urgency to make up for lost time. In half a century Asia went through social changes that had taken the West a thousand years. America lost confidence in itself—the very thing we had admired most. You made the same mistake that the British had a hundred years before."

"Trust the Brits to be at the bottom of it," Scanlon muttered.

Koh went on, "The power and wealth of their ruling class was tied to industries that were becoming obsolete. Instead of adapting and moving with the times, they tried to entrench themselves around technology that was being superseded. It can't work. Neither the lion nor the zebra can stop evolving and hope to survive. One would starve; the other would be eaten." It was true, McCain thought to himself. While the two powers that represented the culmination of the Old World remained deadlocked in their military stalemate, the forerunners of the New were racing ahead with developing the energy-dense, nuclear-based industries that would power the twenty-first century and carry mankind across the Solar System.

"Different dogs have their days," Scanlon said.

"Quite," Koh said. "Likewise, human culture as a whole is all the time evolving, but it doesn't evolve evenly, everywhere at once. It's like an amoeba, where first one part moves, than another. The center of action shifts from place to place, and so civilizations rise and fall: the East and Middle East long ago, Greece, Rome, and the classical civilizations of the Mediterranean, the power struggles of Europe, and the rise of America. But there was no law of nature which said that once the focus shifted to America, it had to remain there forever. What we're seeing is simply the next step in the process. The era of Western civilization that sprang from the European Renaissance a thousand years ago is over. . . . Actually, the term is a misnomer. What happened back at that time was not the *rebirth* of anything. It was the *birth* of a completely new culture. Oh, true, a new civilization might pick up a few stones that suit its needs from the rubble of an old one, but that's not the same thing as rebuilding it. . . ." Koh sat back and smiled through the cloud that was beginning to engulf him.

He held out an upturned hand in a gesture that could have meant anything, and an ecstatic light crept into his eyes. "They must free their souls to soar . . ." He paused, looking at the other two for a moment as if they had suddenly materialized there from nowhere. Then he carried on, his voice rising and falling in cadences of lyrical rapture: ". . . unfettered essence of distilled turpentine."

McCain and Scanlon glanced at each other. They knew they wouldn't get anything more that was coherent out of Koh for the rest of the evening. And then, which was just as well, the lights blinked to signal that it was time to move into the billets. They each took one of Koh's arms and helped him to his feet.

"You never struck me as a student of cultural evolution, Kev," McCain said as they steered Koh toward the B-3 door.

"Well, aren't the Irish students of life itself, and isn't that everything?" Scanlon replied. He looked across at McCain for a moment. "Anyhow, it's the evolution of what's going on in this place that ye should be thinkin' more about, yourself."

"How d'you mean?"

"Whatever it is you have in mind to do, you've got it off to a fine beginning. But, Mr. Earnshaw, journalist, as the bishop said to the parlor maid, 'Where do we go next from here?'"

◈ CHAPTER NINETEEN ◈

From its position two hundred thousand miles away from Earth and some distance above Earth's equatorial plane, *Valentina Tereshkova* had permanent lines for its communications lasers to at least two of the Soviet synchronous satellites, which redistributed message traffic among surface locations and other satellites, depending on the signals' final destinations. The West's military establishment also maintained a system of "Auriga" surveillance satellites, which between them were able to keep a constant watch on both the Soviet satellites and *Tereshkova*. The Aurigas were equipped with telescopes designed for operation in the infrared range, which could pick up the stray reflections from both ends of the Soviet communications beams; thus they were able to eavesdrop on the message-flow to and from *Tereshkova* as it took place. From space, the intercepted stream of Soviet communications code was routed down through a complicated chain of links and relays, eventually becoming grist for the computer batteries of the National Security Agency's code-cracking mill at Fort Meade, Maryland.

For as long as *Tereshkova* had been operational, a portion of its signal traffic had used virtually impregnable top-security coding algorithms—which had done little to alleviate the West's suspicions over what was supposed to be an innocuous social experiment in space-living. By summer of 2017, however, the hungry NSA cryptoanalysts in the section that handled "Teepee," as the intercept traffic to and from *Tereshkova* was code-named, had received a windfall of a different kind.

The standard procedure followed by both sides for sending encrypted messages over communications links was to transmit the code as a stream of five-digit number groups. That way, anyone intercepting the transmission with the intention of decoding its content would receive none of the clues that a structure reflecting the varying word-lengths would have supplied. To complicate the task further, the transmitting computers then obscured where the different messages in a stream began and ended, by filling the gaps between them with random five-digit number groups so that the channel simply transmitted continuously twenty-four hours a day. A message buried in the stream carried a special number sequence that the computers at the receiving end were programmed to watch for.

For some time the pattern-searching routines that the NSA computers subjected incoming material to as a first pass had been detecting irregularities in the filler groups used to pack the gaps in Teepee transmissions from *Tereshkova* to Earth: the random numbers weren't as random as they should have been. Further analysis revealed a concealed coding system. It suggested that the West had unwittingly tapped into illicit traffic between personnel at two of the Soviet Union's own establishments—an intriguing notion. The "Blueprint" code, as this traffic buried inside Earthbound Teepee was designated, turned out to be comparatively unsophisticated, and clearly not a creation of professional Soviet cryptographers; furthermore, its sender was too chatty, providing the Fort Meade veterans with sufficient material to break it fairly quickly. In late June the names "Earnshaw" and "Shelmer" appeared in the plaintext translation of one of these signals, which, from the lists that the NSA kept of who was likely to be interested in what, caused copies to be routed, via Litherland at CIA, Langley, to Bernard Foleda.

Three weeks previously, the CIA had arranged for a message to be beamed into the Soviet communications net in accordance with the protocols that Dyashkin had passed to Dr. Bowers in Japan, indicating interest and a willingness to "talk" further. Dyashkin had acknowledged, and in the ensuing unusual dialogue—phrased very obliquely to keep the Soviet counterpart of NSA off the scent of who was talking to whom—the Americans had requested Dyashkin, implicitly as a test of good faith, to try to find out if the two visitors who had disappeared on *Tereshkova* at the beginning of May were still being held there. A week later, a response from Dyashkin had stated that they were.

What was interesting about the Blueprint intercept that contained the references to Earnshaw and Shelmer was that it occurred a day before Dyashkin's reply. In other words, a message from the mysterious correspondent up in *Tereshkova* was known to have contained the answer a day before Dyashkin sent it to the CIA. Here, then, was evidence that Dyashkin was the hitherto-unknown recipient at the Earth end of the Blueprint line; also, it corroborated that his information was in fact coming from where he said it was coming from.

Bernard Foleda looked at the report that Barbara had brought in and studied the figures on the appended sheet. It was an estimate of the amount of political indoctrination included in the Soviet school curriculum for various grades. "They always go for the children," he murmured as he read.

"Who do?" Barbara asked.

"Fanatics, extremists, every kind of nut with a cause. The way to their utopia is by getting at the minds of the children, so they try to control the schools. Instead of getting educated, the kids end up as political putty. Maybe the Chinese are right: governments should stay out of the whole business."

"Is that what they're saying?"

"It was something that Myra and I talked about a while back." Foleda sat back and tossed the report down on his desk. "Did I ever tell you?—that might have had something to do with how I got into this kind of work."

Barbara sat down on one of the chairs at the meeting table and looked at him curiously. "I don't think so."

Foleda stared at the window. "There was something that happened when I was a teenager—not really so sensational, but it's always stuck in my mind, so I suppose it must have made some kind of impression. Two people came to have dinner with us one night— a Jewish couple that my parents had been friends with for a long time. They talked about the past year that they'd spent traveling around overseas. All their lives they'd been busy with their own affairs, until one day they looked at each other and realized they hadn't seen anything of the world, and if they didn't do something about it soon, they never would."

"Too wrapped up with family and business, you mean?" Barbara said.

"Yes, exactly. Anyhow, I can remember Ben—that was his name—saying to my father, 'You've known us for a long time, Chuck. I've never had any time for politics. But, do you know, after what we saw in other places, I *never* want to set foot outside this country again. I don't want to see our grandchildren growing up the way we saw others made to. And I'll tell you something else: I would give thousands of dollars, no, *tens* of thousands, to any political party— Republicans, Democrats, I don't care; they're all the same to me—just so long as they're committed to defending this country.'"

"That was how you got into intelligence?"

"Oh, I wouldn't exactly say that. But I think it played a part. I'd been looking for a way to express what I felt about the world, and that just about summed it up."

Barbara was used to Foleda's inclination to ramble off like this for no obvious reason. It usually happened when he was preoccupied with something that he hadn't said much about. Some people claimed that they did their hardest thinking while asleep. She had come to see this as his way of distracting his consciousness while a deeper part of his mind tussled with something else. "Do you think everyone in this business needs an ideology like that?" she asked.

Foleda shook his head. "I don't know of any rule that says they have to. Take Lew McCain for instance. Totally pragmatic. He's not interested in keeping the world free for democracy. He just likes challenges with some risk thrown in, and believes in being free to be himself. In fact, the way he operates, an ideology would probably be more of a hindrance. Maybe that's why he's a good field man and I fit in better behind a desk. And yet in another way . . ." Foleda looked away from the window. "How do you feel about this whole Dyashkin business?" he asked Barbara suddenly.

She had worked with him long enough not to have to ask pointless questions. "What bothers you about it?"

Foleda stared down at the papers strewn across his desk. "It's coming together too easily. . . . Look at it. First, two of our people get stuck up on Mermaid. A month later this professor shows up in Japan with a story that he wants to defect, and he just happens to run the primary groundstation that Mermaid talks to. And while all that's going on, the hackers at Meade find a code that turns out to be easier to break than it ought to be, and they discover that somebody up there has their own private line down to him." He tilted his chin questioningly.

"Even if NSA hasn't found it yet, he has to have some way of talking back," Barbara said.

"Right. What does that make you think?"

Barbara shrugged. "Maybe we can get the use of his line to make contact with our two people up there somehow."

"Why would you need to do that?"

"Because the Soviets are coming up with any excuse not to let us talk to them officially . . ." Barbara's eyes narrowed as she began to see what Foleda was driving at.

"Nine out of ten. And what else does it make you think?"

She frowned for a few seconds, then said, "Is that what somebody somewhere wants me to think?"

Foleda nodded. "Ten out of ten." He got up and moved over to the window, where he stood staring out silently for a while. "Anything that involves Mermaid is serious. There are questions we need answers to before we can let this go farther. Who is this line to Dyashkin from? What was it set up for? Why does he want to defect? And most important, is he genuine? We can't go walking blind into something like this."

Barbara waited. She understood the situation, but at the same time could see no immediate pointer to a way of getting the answers that were needed. It would be another exercise in the long, uphill grind that was ninety percent of intelligence work: sifting through uninteresting-looking scraps, looking for patterns and connections, and hoping something useful might emerge. Where, then, would they begin accumulating more background information on somebody like Dyashkin?—personal things, glimpses of his character and loyalties, things that might help fill in the blanks. Barbara looked over the desk for possible clues to the way that Foleda's mind had been working. One of the reference screens was displaying a summary of notes he had extracted from various databank records. At the top was the heading, *Dorkas, Anita Leonidovich. Codename "Cellist."*

Foleda had turned away from the window and was watching her. "The Aeroflot administrator," he commented. "Dyashkin's former wife."

"Yes, I know," Barbara said.

"Except she's not with Aeroflot anymore." Foleda moved to where he could see the screen. "In 2014, three years after she and Dyashkin went separate ways, she remarried, this time to a character by the name of Enriko Dorkas, who's listed as a foreign correspondent with *Novoye Vremya.*"

Barbara pursed her lips silently. *New Times* was a magazine of news and current affairs that had been founded in 1943 for the specific purpose of providing cover for Soviet intelligence officers abroad. "Which presumably means he's KGB," she said. "Where are they posted?"

"He's a colonel," Foleda confirmed. "They're both in London, with the Soviet Residency in Kensington. Officially she's a clerk at the embassy. But it gets more interesting. You see, according to a report that we have on file from SIS, Anita Dorkas—Penkev before she married Enriko—is connected with an underground Soviet intellectual dissident organization known as the Friday Club. As is often the case with senior officers, she and her husband don't live in the embassy quarters, but have an apartment in Bayswater. A double advantage for somebody mixed up in dissident activities: one, opportunities to travel abroad; and two, a lot of freedom to meet with outside groups and sources of foreign aid. The SIS desk that's been dealing with her says she's being extremely cooperative."

"You mean the British have recruited her?"

"So they claim."

Barbara nodded and was about to reply, but then she checked herself and sat back to stare at the screen again thoughtfully. "Unless, of course . . . she's really with the KGB too. The dissident story could be a cover for tracking down the dissidents' overseas connections."

Foleda gave a satisfied nod. "And that's the key question: Did she maneuver her way into marrying an upward-bound KGB man to gain a unique base for her dissident activities? Or is she a loyal Party agent-wife posing as a dissident? Which way round is it?"

"How confident do the British sound about her?" Barbara asked.

Foleda shrugged. "She's provided personnel lists of embassy staff that they requested, organization charts, the names of some contacts over there who are passing information to the Soviets. It was material that we already had from other sources, so we could tell if what she was producing was authentic. But on the other hand, if the Soviets already figured we had it, they wouldn't be losing anything by letting her give it to us again. So it doesn't really prove anything."

"Hmm . . ." Barbara sat back in her chair. "How long ago did you say she married this Enriko?"

"Three years—since 2014," Foleda replied.

"If she's a genuine dissident, she must have set herself up with him that far back. What do our people in Moscow have on her?"

"A lot that corroborates her claim. But then, the Soviets have been known to plant agents with covers long before they're activated. However, there is evidence that she's been mixed up with the Friday Club for at least eight years." Foleda looked at Barbara curiously as he said this, as if inviting her to read the implication.

"Eight years," she repeated. "That would take us back to 2009 . . . while she was still married to Dyashkin."

"Ye-es."

Now Barbara saw the point. "If Anita is genuinely a dissident, and was that long ago, then possibly Dyashkin is too."

"Right." Foleda moved around the desk and sat down in his chair again. "Wouldn't that be a worthwhile thing to find out about him?" And finding out shouldn't prove too difficult, for Anita was not only accessible outside the Eastern bloc, but was already talking to British intelligence.

"Okay, I get it," Barbara said. "So what now? Do you want me to start getting questions together for the London people to work on?"

Foleda shook his head. "No, not them."

"Who, then?"

"When was the last time you had a trip to England?"

Barbara's eyes snapped wide in surprise. "Me? I haven't done anything like that for years."

"Then, let's get rid of some cobwebs. Don't you have a pet ideology to save the world or bring in the millennium?"

"Me? No. Didn't Thoreau say that as soon as something starts ailing people, even constipation, they're off trying to change the world? I'm happy minding my own business."

Foleda's craggy, dark-chinned face split into a grin. "Then, that makes you a natural for the field, like Lew. Maybe we should have left you there in the first place. Let's just say that I'd like to keep this business in the family for the time being."

❀ CHAPTER TWENTY ❀

The woman the others called Nasha brought to mind a vision of an obscenely fat toad. Stiff black hairs bristled from the warts on her multiple chins, her arms creased at the joints like columns of boneless brawn, and her piglike eyes darted constantly this way and that in their fleshy slits, pouring disapproval on everything they surveyed. "They're not even half done yet," she scolded as she waddled up to deposit another wire basket full of dirty crockery and cutlery on top of the one that Paula hadn't had a chance to empty yet. An odor of stale perspiration accompanied her. "There's more to come, and after that the floor needs doing. What's the matter—haven't you ever worked before in your life? I suppose you always had oppressed blacks to take care of you in America, eh? Well, here it's different. Everyone works to eat." She bustled away with a final remark in Russian that Paula didn't catch.

Paula lifted a stack of plates from the basket into the sink full of hot, greasy water and poured in more detergent. The scum coated her arms, and her hair clung to her forehead in the clammy air. Her hands were sore, because the gloves they'd given her had holes in them. "There are no others available." Couldn't we get some? "That is impossible"—the eternal Russian answer to everything. They could build an artificial world in space with materials mined from the Moon, but they couldn't make a dishwasher that worked. Why couldn't the dishwasher be fixed? "That is impossible." Why? "It is impossible."

They had brought her to a place on the edge of the urban zone called Novyi Kazan—the women's section of what was apparently a sizable detention facility located below the surface. After a degrading physical examination and search during the admission process, she had been issued a two-piece tunic of light gray and a few personal effects, and brought to a barred cell that held seven other women in addition to herself. They ate and slept there, and the few amenities they enjoyed were brought there. Life alternated between the cell and the workplace, which in Paula's case meant the same hot, noisy kitchens for ten hours a day, and the drab-paneled corridors that she walked through from one to the other. She longed to be back in solitary. At least on her own she'd had time to think.

"What do you call this? Do you call this clean?" The toad was back again. "You have to press harder to wipe off the grease. Are people expected to eat off this? What's the matter—are you worried your arms might ache?"

"The detergent is almost gone. It needs more detergent."

"There is no more detergent."

"Why can't we get some more?"

"That is impossible."

"Why?"

"It is impossible."

She ate alone at one end of the cell's single table, doing her best to ignore the taunts that the novelty of having an American among them provoked from the rest of the company.

"What is the matter with her this evening, do you think?"

"Her hands are chapped. Can't you see her hands? Obviously she's not used to working."

"Why not? Doesn't anyone work in America?"

"Well, of course somebody has to work. The blacks work, and the oppressed classes work, for their capitalist masters."

"Then, she must be a capitalist."

"A capitalist's princess daughter—much better than the likes of us."

"Sophisticated, you see."

"Very noble and haughty."

"It won't do her much good here, though, will it?" Giggling.

"Hey, is that right, Princess? Is your father a capitalist? Did you grow up in a big mansion with silk sheets and servants to wipe your nose for you?"

"And her behind!" Shrieks of laughter.

"Now you know how much fun it was for your servants."

"In Russia, everyone wipes their own nose."

A small washroom containing two basins and a single, unscreened toilet bowl opened off the rear of the cell. Paula was attempting to clean off the day's grease with lukewarm water and the gritty, seemingly unlatherable soap provided, when Katherine, a thinly built Byelorussian with long black hair and pale skin, came in. Katherine had a comparatively reserved disposition bordering on aloofness, and said little; but her eyes had a studied look as they took in the surroundings, and her words when she did speak were those of a person with a different background from most of the others. She hung her towel on one of the hooks behind the door and set down a plastic bag that she had been carrying. From it she took a piece of soap, a toothbrush, a tin of tooth powder, and a comb, and then turned on the faucet without saying anything. The faucet shuddered violently, hissed with the release of trapped air, and then began emitting a trickle of yellowish water. Water in the colony was supposed to be recycled through a closed ecological system. Sometimes Paula wondered.

The soap Katherine had laid out was whiter and creamier looking than the gray cake that Paula was holding. Paula looked at it, then she shifted her eyes to catch Katherine's in the metal mirror and inclined her head. "Where did you get that?"

"It was issued."

"I got this. Why is it different?"

"Oh . . . sometimes it varies. If the storewoman has preferences . . ."

"Some people are favored, you mean."

"You have to be accepted."

"And I take it I'm not."

"She maybe has something against Americans."

"But not just her."

Katherine shrugged and hung her shirt and pants next to the towel. Paula carried on scrubbing her arms in silence for a while. Then she said, "Can I talk to you, Katherine?"

"I cannot prevent you from talking."

"There's something I don't understand. Look, *why* do Russians believe all that propaganda? I mean, they've got eyes, haven't they? They've got brains—they can think. Surely you people don't believe everything they tell you about us. I mean . . ." Paula made a helpless gesture in the air. "After a hundred years of it, you *must* know . . . Our politicians tell us stupid things about Russians, too, but we know that's just the way they are. We might not like everything the Soviet system stands for, but we don't confuse that with the *people*. We don't have anything against you as individuals."

"You talk about having eyes and brains, and about people, but it is you who serve the system that crushes people."

"But that's not true. The things they tell you aren't true. People are free under our system. It's—"

"Then, that makes it even worse. If you had no choice because you were forced to be slaves, that would be oppression. But if you are free and choose to be slaves . . . And it is us who you say are propagandized?"

Paula shook her head wearily. "You really believe that every American is hostile to all Russians?"

"America is the heart of capitalism. It is inevitable that the capitalists must try to destroy progressive socialism before they themselves are swept away. Our priority has always been to defend ourselves against this. It had to be. Look how many times you have attacked us. . . . And you accuse *us* of hostility!"

Paula stared at her bemusedly. "We attacked? . . . I don't understand. What are you talking about? No Western nation has ever attacked you—except Hitler, and then we were all on the same side. No Western democracy ever attacked Russia."

"You see, they lie to you," Katherine said. "In the very first year of the nation, in the summer of 1918, the capitalists sent their armies into Russia in an attempt to help treacherous counterrevolutionary forces destroy the new Soviet state. Is that not attacking us?"

History had never been one of Paula's consuming passions. She shook her head. "I don't know. . . .I guess I never really looked into that particular period."

Katherine nodded. "There, you see. Yes, American, British, French, Japanese, they all came. You didn't know? And even after Russia had been weakened by four years of war in Europe and then torn apart by the Revolution, still the people's Red Army was invincible. And then you say Hitler was not one of you, because you are the democracies. But it was the so-called democracies that rearmed Germany and allowed Hitler to rise, so they could send him against Russia to fight the war for them that they were too cowardly to fight themselves. They tried to start a war that they would wriggle their way out of like worms, but they underestimated Stalin."

"I'm not so sure about that. I—"

"Pah! What do you know? You know nothing. And then, when the tiger they had tried to ride about-turned, it was Russia that killed it and saved them. And then it was Russia that drove the Japanese invaders out of China and ended the war. Russia has always defended countries that were invaded. After the war, you Americans and your puppets tried to invade Korea. And you tried to invade the Middle East, you tried to invade Cuba, you tried to invade Vietnam."

Paula stared. "You mean that's what they teach?"

Katherine shook her head uncomprehendingly. "And you say we have never been attacked, that we are being paranoid. You think you are victimized, and wonder why. It is we who have *always* been attacked."

Paula sighed. "I don't know, your propaganda, our propaganda . . . Who's to say what's right? But neither one of us is responsible for whatever really goes on. Why should any of it affect us here, personally? In here of all places, I'd have thought we had enough in common to outweigh all that, whatever the real story is."

Katherine looked at her coldly. "The reason I'm in here is that my loyalty is in question," she said. "I used to have a husband. He went to London with a Soviet trade mission, and while he was there he met a reporter from a New York art magazine, and she seduced him. The Americans let him return with her, and now they are living down there somewhere with a family. So, you see, Princess, I do not exactly have strong reason to be fond of Americans, American women in particular, and especially American women journalists. Does that answer your question?"

Paula lay in the dark, clutching the coarse blanket around her and staring up into the black shadow of the bunk above. She was picturing teenage days of sailing among the islands in Puget Sound, the shining towers of downtown Seattle across the water, and the Olympic Mountains, green in the sunlight, rich with recent rain. As she thought back, she wondered what had become of the self-assurance and single-mindedness that she thought she had learned from her mother, Stephanie. With Paula's father being so long away at sea, and having come from a naval family before that, Stephanie had always been in control of herself and her life. She'd socialized a lot and thrown lots of parties. There was always a stream of visitors calling at the house. Hence, for Paula, learning to assert herself with people around had been simply another part of growing up. One thing that had made an impression on her, she remembered, was her mother's adroitness in handling the advances—usually tactful, but sometimes crude—that an attractive woman left on her own for long periods of time was subjected to by the men who came to the house. Ever since then she'd tended to regard men as polarizing into two groups: either they were strong, or they were weak; they were either smart, or stupid; worth getting to know, or not worth wasting time on. She could respect the ones who met her standards . . . but there weren't many of them. When she was about fifteen, by which time they had moved to the East Coast, she remembered one of those intimate mother-daughter conversations, in which Stephanie had confided that, yes, sometimes she had gone along with those propositions when Paula was younger—with discretion, naturally. Intrigued, Paula had wanted to know which ones. Stephanie mentioned a couple of names, and Paula had found that she approved the choices. Instead of feeling indignation as she had half expected, she had found her mother to be a suddenly far more human and exciting person.

"Hello, American Princess," a voice whispered from nearby. "Are you awake?"

Paula turned her head and made out a figure crouched by the bunk in the darkness. "Who is it?"

"It is I, Dagmar." Dagmar was an East German girl, about the same age as Paula, auburn-haired, not unattractive, with a firm, shapely body and freckled face.

"What do you want?"

"To say hello—to be friends. Is not right they all mean to you like this. I think is not Princess's fault if world can't get along, yes? So I come, make good. We can be friends together, yes?"

Paula blinked sleepily—she had been farther gone than she'd realized. "Why not? . . . Maybe."

She sensed the face coming closer in the darkness. There was alcohol on the other woman's breath. "Yes, Dagmar and Princess can be good friends. No sense to fight . . ."

Paula felt the blanket being lifted and the hand sliding softly over her breast. "Fuck off!" She knocked the hand away sharply, pulled the blanket back around her neck, and turned away.

"Stuck-up bitch!" Dagmar's voice hissed.

Paula heard her straighten up and stamp away to the far end of the cell. Peals of female laughter came through the darkness a moment later. "What, Dagmar, no luck? What did we tell you?"

"*Der Seicherin!* That's it. She can rot for all I care now."

"How much did we say you owe me, Dagmar? Or would you rather climb in here instead and call it quits?"

Paula pulled the blanket around her face and put everything out of her mind but sleep.

☸ CHAPTER TWENTY-ONE ☸

"I remember an American couple I met last year, when I was on vacation with a girlfriend over in Connemara on the Irish Atlantic coast. Nice looker, too: used to model flimsy knickers and things—you know, the kind you see on the posters in the tube stations. . . . Anyway this couple—a carpenter of some kind and his wife, they were, from Michigan—had bought a porcelain figurine, you see, that they'd found in some little antique shop in a fishing village they'd driven through. It was rather attractive, I must say—two leprechauns with long pipes and evil grins, hatching mischief over jugs of grog. It could easily have been a hundred years old or more. . . ."

"Jeremy," from the British Special Intelligence Service, paused to smile at the recollection as he sat between the two women in the rear seat of the London taxicab. He was suave, urbane, smooth-shaven, wavy-haired, and nattily dressed in a dark three-piece suit with a buttonhole carnation. His speech and manner evoked something of an image that Barbara thought had gone out of style with tailcoats and dreadnoughts.

He continued, "Well, this figurine had an inscription round the base in Gaelic which had been intriguing them for days, but nobody they'd met had been able to translate it for them. But Gaelic poetry was something I used to dabble in, back at university. Would you have believed I'd decided to try and become a playwright, years ago?

I actually got a couple of things staged, too—the usual provincial kind of thing, you know."

"So what did it say?" Sylvia asked from his other side. She was also from SIS, and had been carefully picked for the job because of her tall, lean build, tapering face, and black, shoulder-length hair. She was wearing a navy two-piece costume with polka-dot scarf and trim, white shoes and matching purse, a floppy white hat, and carrying a lightweight pastel-blue shoulder wrap over her arm.

"That was the funny part," Jeremy said. "You see, it said, ha-ha . . . it said, 'Made in Taiwan.' "

Barbara smiled and looked away at the crowd thronging the sidewalk on Oxford Street, a few hundred yards east from Marble Arch. It was well into July, and the summer sun and blue skies had brought out the colors on the London streets: the shirts and dresses of the tourists and late-morning shoppers, the seasonal offerings in the windows of the fashion houses, and riotous displays of orchids, roses, and lilies on the carts of streetcorner flower vendors. There were couples old and young, some arm in arm, some with children; businessmen strolling to lunch, jackets slung over their shoulders, women in colored slacks and bright summer dresses; two Arabs studying a painting in one of the shop windows; an Indian in a turban, munching an ice-cream cone. Just ordinary people, wanting nothing more than to be left alone.

Barbara liked watching people minding their own business. It summed up her outlook on life, as she'd said to Foleda. She thought it a pity that so many people were incapable of doing likewise. And always the wrong people. For invariably, it seemed, it was those of mediocre talents but inflated ambitions, with no affairs of their own worth minding, who meddled the most in other people's. So the people most likely to end up making decisions about other people's lives were usually the last ones anyone would want doing the job. Although she worked for a government, privately she thought they were not unlike germs: the only thing anyone really needed them for was to protect themselves from other people's.

The cab crossed the end of Baker Street, and Jeremy glanced at his watch. They were exactly on time. The driver slowed down and cruised for a block. A woman was waiting on the corner of Duke Street. She was tall and lean, with a tapering face, black shoulder-length hair, and wearing a navy two-piece costume with polka-dot scarf and trim, white shoes and purse, a floppy hat, and carrying a light-weight pastel-blue shoulder wrap. "That's her, Freddie," Jeremy said, pointing. The woman was looking at the taxi-cabs in the oncoming traffic. She saw the yellow-bound notebook wedged on top of the dashboard inside the windshield and raised her arm. The cab pulled over, and she climbed in, seating herself next to Sylvia, who was on the curb side. Because of the tinted rear windows and the high upright back with just a tiny window in the center that London taxis had, it would not be apparent to anyone watching that it was already occupied. The woman would seem to have simply hailed a cab and climbed in.

"Gawd, it's 'er twin sister!" Freddie chirped.

"Just drive, there's a good fellow," Jeremy said. He closed the driver's partition, and they pulled back out into the traffic.

"This is Anita Dorkas," Jeremy said to Barbara. "Anita, this is the American who wants to talk to you. Don't worry about this other person. She's you, as you've probably gathered already, so there's nothing I can tell you about her. So how are things? Do you still have the afternoon free?"

Anita nodded. "I need to be back at the embassy by five, though." She spoke English competently, though her Russian accent was distinctive. "I'm pleased to meet you," she said to Barbara.

"Me, also."

"Did you arrive in England this morning?" Anita asked.

"Nobody said I'd just come here from anywhere," Barbara pointed out. "Only that I'm American."

"Incurably Russian and suspicious," Jeremy said breezily. "She fishes compulsively."

Sylvia was scrutinizing Anita carefully, from her hat down to her shoes. "Tch, tch. You're not wearing lipstick," she said reproachfully.

Anita raised a hand to her mouth involuntarily. "I forgot. I'm sorry—I hardly ever use it."

"Terrible capitalist muck, anyway," Jeremy remarked.

Sylvia produced a handkerchief and mirror from her purse, moistened the handkerchief with her tongue, and wiped her own lips clean. "How's that?"

Jeremy looked her up and down, then Anita, and nodded. "Splendid. Two peas in a pod."

They made a right into New Bond Street, followed it down to Picadilly, and there turned left to head toward the Circus. Jeremy slid the partition open again. "Here'll do, Freddie." The cab pulled over and stopped. Sylvia squeezed by in front of Anita's knees to open the door and climb out. She paid Freddie the fare and added a tip, then strolled along the sidewalk for a few yards before stopping to admire a diorama of the South Seas in a travel agent's window. A half block back along the street, the thickset man in the felt hat and baggy blue suit, who had gotten out of another cab following a few cars behind, stopped in a doorway and studied his newspaper. After a few seconds Sylvia began moving again, and so did he. By that time the cab carrying Barbara, Anita, and Jeremy was already lost in the traffic and on its way to a hotel near Regent's Park, where a suite had been reserved. Meanwhile Sylvia had a slow, solitary but relaxing afternoon ahead of her, leading her tail, whom she had already spotted, around the circuit that Anita had memorized: window shopping along Picadilly and Regent Street, lunch in Leicester Square, a visit to the National Gallery, and then a walk across St. James's Park and coffee over a magazine in a boulevard cafe near Victoria Station before the rendezvous in Buckingham Palace Road to work the switch back again. And she was getting paid for it. There could be worse ways of making a living, she supposed.

Barbara stuck her head through into the bedroom of the hotel suite. "Don't hang up. Anita wants milk, not cream, for the coffee," she told Jeremy, who was sitting propped on the bed with his back against a stack of pillows and his legs stretched out in front of him. His jacket and shoulder strap with holster containing a .38 were draped over the back of a chair, and he was holding a book lying open on his lap.

He addressed the viphone by the bed, which was switched to voice only and at that moment connected to room service. "Oh, one moment. Could we have some milk as well as cream for the coffee, please?" He glanced at Barbara. "Is that it?" She nodded. "That will be all, thank you."

"Thank you, sir," a dignified voice acknowledged from a grille in the unit. "It will be about fifteen minutes." The voice signed itself off with a click.

"Everything going all right?" Jeremy asked.

"Better than we hoped," Barbara said.

"Good-o. The firm likes to please, you know." Jeremy settled himself back more comfortably and returned his attention to his book.

Barbara turned from the doorway and walked back across the lounge to where Anita was sitting in one of the two easy chairs at the table by the window. The view outside was a rolling green sea of Regent's Park treetops, with the buildings of the zoological gardens visible above like white cliffs in the distance. Anita resumed talking as Barbara sat down.

"It was a difficult decision in many ways, but I came to the conclusion that there are basic human values that have to come before patriotism. Certainly that's true if one defines loyalty to the present Soviet regime as patriotism. But that isn't how we see it. Before 1917, Russia was socially and politically backward compared to Western Europe, I admit, but when you allow for the effect of a czar who was living in a different age and an emotionally unbalanced empress, it was making tremendous strides to catch up. Russia was starting to assert itself as a modern state. The charade of archaic pomp, royal courts, and fairy-tale palaces was played out. Nothing could stop the tides of industry and trade that were sweeping Russia into the twentieth century. The uprising in March was the voice of the real Russia. That was the direction that it should have kept going in. What happened in November was all wrong, an aberration. That is what has to be undone. At the time of the Revolution, Maxim Gorky—and he was no lover of czarism—warned the people not to destroy the palaces and treasures of the old order, because those things represented a cultural heritage that would continue to grow in the new Russia. But instead, it was stunted. What we have seen in the last hundred years is a cancer of barren political dogma and mindless slogans that has suppressed culture. That is what we are committed to ending. Our loyalty is to the Russia that should have been, and which will be one day."

Anita sat on the edge of her chair, polite, but at the same time tense and unsmiling. Her face, though at first sight attractive in proportion and line, revealed an undertone of pallor and tiredness in the daylight by the window which seemed to accentuate the spareness of her frame. Barbara's impression was of someone very serious and very dedicated, for whom one ideal had come to dominate all other considerations in life. Her instinct was to accept Anita as being what she claimed to be—but, of course, something more substantial than that would be needed eventually.

"What I wanted to ask you about was something else," Barbara said. "It goes back a number of years, now. Your former husband, Igor. What can you tell me about him?" She watched Anita's face but was unable to detect an immediate reaction that hinted either of aversion, lingering affection, or any other emotion.

"A lot of things," Anita replied. "What would you like to know?"

"You don't seem surprised or curious about why we should be interested in him."

"Nothing surprises me anymore. I'm sure you have your reasons."

"You were a member of the Friday Club as long as eight years ago," Barbara said, making it a matter-of-fact statement rather than a question.

"Yes."

"And other affiliated groups before that." That was a guess, but worth a stab.

"Yes," Anita answered.

"What kinds of activities were you involved in back then?"

"Is this really necessary? I've been through this over and over with the British. Don't you people talk to each other? I'm sure I don't have to remind you that we have limited time. My understanding was that you considered this meeting to be very important. I would like to make it as useful as possible."

Barbara conceded the point with a nod. "Tell me, then, was your husband also involved in the dissident movement? Did you work together? How close were his views to the ones you expressed a few minutes ago?"

"We were in Sevastopol then. He was working on submarine communications," Anita said distantly. "Then we moved to Moscow. He was made a professor at the university."

"Yes, I have seen his chronological record."

A pigeon alighted on the sill outside the window. It strutted a few steps with its chest pouting and its head extending and retracting like that of a comical clockwork toy, then stopped and cocked an eye to peer in through a pane for a couple of seconds. Then it flew away.

"He was one of us," Anita said. "He lived for the same cause. But he was never as passionate about it as some of them were. Maybe it had something to do with his being a scientist. Or maybe he became a scientist because he was that way to begin with. . . . But he was always more unexcitable and analytical. And very patient. He could have waited a hundred years for the system to change."

"Does that mean he might still be actively involved?" Barbara asked.

"Oh, I don't doubt it," Anita said without hesitation. "He's not the kind to be easily changed."

"Do you know where he is now?"

"The last I heard was that he'd moved to Siberia, some kind of scientific establishment somewhere—but that was several years ago now."

"You haven't kept in touch since you separated?"

"No."

Barbara looked surprised. "I'd have thought your work would have required it."

Anita hesitated, then said, "My marriage to Enriko—my present husband—was a very fortunate occurrence for our group. As you can see, it provides opportunities for extending our contacts and gaining overseas support. It seemed better, in order not to risk jeopardizing such a stroke of good luck, to cut my connections with the past." The explanation didn't stand up. If Dyashkin were ever exposed by the

KGB, his ex-wife would automatically be on the suspect list regardless of whether she stayed in touch with him or not. That Anita's marriage to a KGB officer had been allowed to go through said, as clearly as anything could, that so far Dyashkin had managed to stay clean. Barbara stared back and said nothing.

Anita became agitated and reached for her purse, which she had set down by the window. She rummaged inside and took out a box of pills. Barbara picked up the jug of fruit juice from the tray standing on the table by the recorder taping the conversation, filled one of the glasses, and held it out. Anita took one of the pills and recomposed herself. "There was more to it than that," she said. "Igor always had an eye for women—maybe you already know that. They responded to him, too, even though he never said very much. He had a way of radiating an aura of . . . well, call it mystery, or dominance, if you will. You know the kind of thing."

Barbara smiled and tried to look encouraging. "Sure. Who hasn't met a few like that?"

Anita went on, "Perhaps our getting married was a mistake. Igor was a brilliant man. Sometimes I felt I couldn't provide the amount of intellectual stimulation he needed. He was in the Navy when we met, and for a time things seemed to go all right. But after he got his doctorate and we began meeting more academic kinds of people . . ." Anita drained the rest of the glass of juice. "One of his affairs became serious. Of course, the woman was also a scientist—a nuclear expert of some kind. I met her a few times. A very spirited woman. Her hair was the most noticeable thing. Like fire. Yellowy red, almost orange."

"Can you tell me her name?" Barbara asked.

"Oshkadov. Olga Oshkadov."

"Where was she from?"

"I don't know. But she worked at the science city, Novosibirsk."

"I see. Go on."

Anita shrugged. "There isn't really a lot more to tell. He was adamant that he wanted to separate. Because of our underground activities, however, we both saw that it was in our interests not to quarrel or get emotional about the situation. He agreed to a generous settlement financially to smooth things over. I have no complaints, really."

"Was Olga also a dissident?"

"I don't know. If she was, I was never told. But then, you'll appreciate that we were hardly in the habit of publicizing such matters."

Barbara nodded. "And your present marriage to Enriko. Would you say it was, well . . ."

"How far does affection enter into it?" Anita shook her head and smiled humorlessly. "Oh, there's no need to worry about that. I've had my share of those kinds of delusions. Now only the cause matters to me. Enriko means nothing. This time it's purely a matter of expedience—an opportunity that was too good not to seize."

There was a tap on the door. Jeremy ambled out of the bedroom and opened it to admit a waiter with a cart loaded with plates, silver dishes, and pots. "Oh, jolly good. Just leave it there, would you? Here, buy yourself a drink on us."

"Thank you very much, sir." The waiter left.

"Just one last thing," Barbara said.

Anita looked at her. "Yes?"

"Were you or your husband ever involved with a group known as the Committee for Freedom and Dignity?"

Anita looked puzzled. "No."

"You didn't deal with a person who went by the name of 'Tortoise'?"

"No."

"You're sure?"

Anita shook her head. "I've never heard of either of them. Who are they?"

"You really don't know?"

"No. . . . Can't you tell me who they are?"

Barbara finished the notes she had been making and closed her book. "It doesn't matter," she said. "It's time for lunch."

It was hardly surprising that Anita had never heard of either the Committee or the Tortoise, for neither of them existed. The terms had been invented purely for introduction into the conversation as "tracers." If they turned up in the official Soviet communications traffic intercepted by the Western intelligence in the weeks ahead, it would be a give-away that Anita's loyalties were not as she claimed.

❊ CHAPTER TWENTY-TWO ❊

It hit Paula first when she was on her way to the kitchens, a half hour after the cell's cheerless breakfast of watery oatmeal, black bread with margarine and jam, and tea. A hot flush came over her suddenly. She found herself fighting for breath, and her legs became lead. She tottered against the corridor wall and put a hand out to steady herself.

The female guard who was leading stopped and looked back, while the other three prisoners in the detail waited with no show of concern. "What's the matter with you? Come on."

"You by the wall, move!" the second guard snapped from the rear. She poked Paula sharply in the back with the baton she was carrying.

Paula lurched a couple of paces along the wall, tried to stand, and fell back against it once more. Her chest was pounding, and she could feel perspiration trickling down her body inside her shirt. Nausea welled in her throat. "Can't . . ." she gasped.

"Oh, you don't feel like working today? Is that it? What do you take us for, fools? You don't get away with that kind of thing here. You and you, take her arms. We'll take her to work if she won't walk."

Paula felt two of the other women hold her on either side, and then she was on her way along the corridor again. She had a fleeting impression of somebody going the other way stopping to look curiously, two prisoners in work smocks wheeling a cart into an elevator on one side, and all the time the back of the guard striding ahead . . . wide hips swinging beneath the plain brown military skirt; massive calves encased in thick tan stockings; heavy, flat-heeled shoes. Now they were at the doors leading into the kitchens.

Her first breath inside was like an intake of hot, fetid gas from a furnace, and sent her reeling against one of the aluminum worktables. The Toad was there suddenly, saying something, but all Paula could hear was incoherent snatches of her voice mixed with the guard's.

". . . matter with her? Doesn't she . . ."

"I think it's . . . on the way here . . . malingering?"

"Yes, *you!* I'm talking to you! What do you *babble-babble, cluck-cluck-cluck-cluck-cluck* . . ."

Paula was distantly aware of her knees buckling. Her arm pushed out against something as she slid down the side of the table to the floor. There was a crash and the sounds of breaking glass. The faces of the Toad and the guard were peering down at her with their mouths moving, but both the sight and the sounds were out of focus. After the effort of trying to stand, the relief of sitting was like an escape to nirvana. She let her head fall back against the metal door behind her and closed her eyes, not minding if she stayed there forever. She couldn't get up again, didn't want to get up. Nothing could make her. That was all there was to it.

. . . Then she was being stretched out along the floor. A coat or something was being tucked around her. She drifted. . . .

"Hey, can you hear me?" Someone was slapping her cheek lightly. She was still lying on a hard floor, feeling cold and shivery now. A hand was feeling her pulse . . . then her eyelid was being lifted. A bright light . . . Collar being opened, dermal diffusion capsule taped to the side of her neck. She opened her eyes briefly and saw a woman in a white cap and a medical smock lowering a red blanket. Warmth, blessed warmth . . .

Voices echoed from far away. "Oh no, she's got something all right . . . Couldn't guess at this stage . . . will be notified in due course . . ."

Hands were lifting her. . . .

�֍   ✖   ✖

She was watching Mike showering. Mike had been the oldest of the lovers she'd had. She liked his body the most. He had big shoulders and a barrel chest, and even the thickening around his midriff had excited her as a sign of maturity. He reminded her of Robert Mitchum, one of her favorites from the old-time movies, before they'd been taken over by health-faddist adolescents. She and Mike used to shower together after they made love. The best times had been late in the evening, before going out to dinner, or maybe to a party somewhere in Washington. He grinned and gestured for her to join him. But as she moved he began changing into the Toad. The closer she approached, the more he transformed. She recoiled, and it was Mike again. There was no way to get to him.

The dream dissolved, leaving her tense and agitated. She turned her head to the side and felt it resting on a pillow that felt soft and smelt clean. The remnant of the image in her mind died away, and her tension with it. Her toes were rubbing on the luxury of smooth linen. The sounds of a woman's footsteps on a hard floor, lasting for a few seconds, stopping, then starting again, and a man's voice talking in Russian, filtered through into her awareness.

She opened her eyes and saw a room with beds and lockers, pastel-yellow walls, and some kind of wheeled apparatus consisting of metal flasks, rubber tubes, and a panel with lights and switches standing at the far end. Raising her head, she saw she was in a small medical ward. A blond orderly was collecting dishes from the other beds and taking them to a cart standing in the center aisle, and a woman on the far side was watching something on a flatscreen mounted on a hinged arm extending across the bed. Another woman was reading, others were sleeping. Paula tried to sit up, but she was too weak and her head swam from the attempt. She followed the orderly with her eyes, licked her lips as she summoned up the effort, and finally managed to croak, *"Pozalsta . . ."*

The orderly looked round, put down the plate she was holding, and came over. She had blue eyes and a pretty face. "So, you are awake now," she said in Russian. "How do you feel?"

"Could I get something to drink?"

"Water, yes? I don't know if anything else would be good." She half-filled a glass from a pitcher on the locker by the bed and helped Paula to lift her head. Nothing had ever tasted so good.

"Better? I'll get the nurse to come and look at you. Sleep some more, now."

"Spasiba, spasiba." Paula lay back and closed her eyes. Simply to be talked to like a human being again . . . She put out of her mind any thought about how long it was likely to last.

They told her it was food poisoning. She told them she wasn't surprised. It would soon pass, they said. One more day of rest, and then there would be no reason for her not to return to work. No, she protested, surely not so soon. She didn't feel up to walking, let alone laboring for ten hours. One more day—they were adamant.

Paula found herself dreading the thought of going back. Several of the other women with her in the ward were also Russians, but they exhibited nothing comparable to the hostility she had been subjected to back in the cell. It seemed she'd managed to get herself confined with just about the worst mix of personalities that she could have run up against.

The woman across the aisle was called Tanya and came originally from Volgograd. It used to be Stalingrad before the Party went through one of its periodic interchangings of black and white and deglorified the great dictator's memory. Tanya was a teacher, and had been arrested for promoting among her pupils ideas that conflicted with the official ideological doctrines. "I couldn't care less about their stupid doctrines," she told Paula. "And that's one of the worst crimes for a teacher. I couldn't make the bureaucrats understand that objective reality *is* what it is, and that it doesn't care what any Party tries to say it should be. We can only discover. Children should be taught *how* to think, not *what* to think. That was all I cared about—children's minds."

"And that can be a crime?"

"A potential threat to the regime—the ultimate crime. But surely it's the same everywhere. Isn't religion used in America for the same purpose—to instill obedience and stifle questions?"

Paula shook her head. "No—it's just there if people want it. In fact, you can't mix it with education, by law."

Tanya looked at her curiously. "Really? That's interesting. I didn't know that. I haven't met many Americans. They don't give you permission to travel to other countries very easily over there, do they?"

"You don't need any permission. Anybody can just get on a plane and go where they want."

"I hadn't heard that before. . . . You *are* being serious, I suppose?"

In the next bed was Anastasia, from Khabarovsk on the Pacific side of Siberia, who said her brother had been convicted of passing secrets to the Chinese. "I hope it doesn't affect my son's career," she told Paula. "He's such a bright boy. At school they're teaching him to program computers. Do American boys ever get to see a computer when they're only fifteen?"

Paula was told she would be moving back to her cell after the evening meal. As the afternoon wore on, she grew quieter, and became inwardly nervous to the borderline of being fearful. She tried to read and rest to recover her strength as best she could, but the emotional strain was draining energy out of her faster than it was recharging. She even toyed with the thought of staging an accident—anything to put off the moment of having to return to the kitchens and the cell.

And then, when there was less than an hour to go before the evening meal was brought in, she heard a voice that she recognized remonstrating loudly in the corridor beyond the ward door, which was open. "I don't care if you are a doctor. It isn't doing her any good, I tell you. It isn't of medical knowledge, it's a matter of common sense." Paula looked up sharply. The Russian woman with fiery, shoulder-length hair had stopped just outside. She was wearing a light-green two-piece tunic and talking to a gray-bearded man in a knee-length white coat. Paula caught a glimpse of her firmly defined, high-cheeked features and determined chin as she half-turned and raised a hand to make her point. The man said something in a lower voice that Paula couldn't catch, and then they moved on. "Then, I'll make sure that somebody in higher authority is informed. If you won't sign a simple . . ." The orange-haired woman's voice faded away.

Suddenly Paula was seized by uncontrollable desperation. "Anna!" she called out.

The blond orderly came out of the instrument room at the far end of the ward. "You wanted something?"

"Yes, look, somebody I know just went past, out there in the corridor. She went that way, with a doctor. Please catch her and tell her I have to talk to her, would you? It's very important. She has red hair, and she was wearing a green suit."

Anna nodded and hurried out into the corridor. Paula lay back against her pillow and found that she was trembling. But she couldn't let the chance pass by. Slowly she calmed down. Chance? . . . Chance of what? Now she didn't even know what she was going to say.

Footsteps sounded outside, and a moment later Anna came back in. "I found the lady," she announced, looking at Paula oddly. "She doesn't know an American woman called Paula Shelmer. But she will come and see what you want. She'll be here in a minute or two, she says." Anna disappeared back into the room at the rear.

Paula looked around. Tanya was sleeping, and Anastasia was sitting at the table at the far end of the ward, writing something. Of the other three from the nearby beds, two were away undergoing therapy, and the other was at the table with Anastasia. So it would be possible to speak with some privacy at least. She lay back, trying to force herself to breathe normally and relax.

The orange-haired woman reappeared in the corridor outside, entered, saw Paula without showing a flicker of recognition, and continued looking around. Eventually her eyes wandered back. Paula nodded and mustered a smile. The Russian woman came over to the bed and stood looking down with a puzzled expression on her face. "You are the American?" she said in excellent English. "Do I know you? . . . But yes, your face does seem familiar."

"Turgenev six weeks ago—the Security Headquarters. You were giving two officers a tough time. I was outside. You came out and spoke to me."

Comprehension flowed into the Russian woman's face. It was an amazingly expressive face. "Yes, of course! The nervous girl in the corridor. I was trying to place you somewhere here, not back there. So, we both wound up in Zamork." She waved a hand briefly. "But why are you in here?"

"Food poisoning, they said. A bug or something. . . . I don't know."

"You are an American, so. And your name is Paula. I am called Olga. But the girl said there was something important. What is it?"

Paula looked over her shoulder and then back. "It's not really something I'd want to make public knowledge . . ."

Olga moved closer and sat down on the edge of the bed. She looked at Paula questioningly. "Well?"

"You said not to be intimidated."

"That's right. They will try, but you mustn't let them. Once they find a crack, they have you. Then they keep hammering in wedges. But strength, they respect. It's all they respect. If only America had understood that sixty years ago."

"The place they've put me in is dreadful. And the people there . . . It's not so much intimidation as degradation."

"Yes, that is another of their nasty tricks. I sympathize. Make a fuss until they change it. You Americans are like the British and try to compromise to please everybody. It can't be done. You just end up pleasing nobody. That's not the way to deal with Russians. They all shout, and whoever shouts the loudest and longest gets his way." Olga patted Paula's arm affectionately and started to rise. Paula caught her by the sleeve.

"I heard you telling those officers that you are a scientist."

Olga hesitated, then sat down again. "So, what of it?"

"And that's how you come to speak English so well?" Olga nodded but didn't reply. Paula went on, "What does a scientist do in a place like this? I mean, are there opportunities to use your mind, to think? Are there others you can communicate with?"

"Naturally there are. This is a space habitat. Resources are limited. They don't ship people this far to open doors and count heads."

Paula took a long breath. "I am a scientist, too," she said. She'd decided before Olga came in that she could hardly do any damage by revealing no more than Protbornov and his interrogators had already established.

"Well, that's very good, and I respect you as a fellow professional. But I still don't see what—"

"You have influence. You can persuade people. Look, I scrape grease off dishes in a stinking kitchen and scrub floors, day after day. Can you talk to someone who might get me moved out? I can do more good somewhere else—better for me, and better for the colony."

Olga frowned. "Are you saying you want to work for them?" Paula noticed she said "them" and not "us."

"I'm not talking about changing sides," Paula said. "I just want to work as a person—on something that has no military value. There must be such things here. You just said yourself that resources are valuable here. Why waste any? There are children in the colony—I could teach science, maybe; or there might be something connected with medicine, agriculture . . . anything."

Olga looked dubious. "Well, I really don't know what I can do. . . ." She caught the imploring look in Paula's eyes, but that only seemed to make her more defensive. She got up and began turning. "My own problems are one thing—I can shout at them about things like that. But interfering in policy on something like is different. I am sorry, but I'm sure it will all straighten itself out in good—" she stopped as if a new thought had just struck her, and turned back. "What kind of scientist are you?"

"Communications electronics. Computers . . ."

"Where did you learn that?"

"I'd rather not say."

"Hmm . . ." Olga regarded her with what seemed like a new interest. "You know something about communications-system protocols and operating software? Encryption routines and hardware microcode?"

"Some," Paula replied cautiously.

"What about Russian systems?"

"I've dealt with them."

"I see." Olga brought a hand up to her chin and stared at Paula for what seemed a long time. Then, abruptly, she seemed to make up her mind. "I can't make promises, and I don't do miracles," she said. "So don't hope for too much. But we'll see." With that she turned away again and left the room.

The women who were attending therapy returned a short while later, and Paula did her best to match their chatter through the evening meal. When it was over, the same two guards who had escorted the work detail arrived to collect her. Anastasia and Tanya gave her a bag of candies to take back, which they had put together between them. "To show how Russians and Americans ought to be," Anastasia told her. Tanya smiled and patted Paula's arm. Paula kissed both of them and found that her eyes were watery.

"They would be, if only they were left alone," she said. Then, with a sickening feeling of dread rising in her stomach, she went back to her bed and picked up the bag into which she had already put her things, while the guards waited stone-faced just inside the door.

At that moment hurried footsteps sounded in the corridor outside, and Dr. Rubakov, the senior physician, came in, waving some papers. "Ah, good, she's still here." Rubakov turned to the two guards. "The order has been rescinded. The American woman is to remain here for a further three days' rest and recuperation. Here is the countermanding order and papers, all signed and approved. You may go." He showed the papers to the senior of the two guards. The guard took them, scrutinized the top sheet carefully, turned it over, and nodded finally to her companion with a shrug. They left, closing the door behind them.

The reprieve had been so sudden and so overwhelming that for a moment Paula thought she was going to collapse again. She sat down shakily on the end of her bed. Rubakov looked pleased. "I'm glad they changed their minds," he said. "You need more time to get over it." He moved closer and studied Paula for a few seconds, at the same time stroking his mustache with the knuckle of his forefinger. "So perhaps we can do a deal, eh?" he murmured in a lower voice. "I can get good cosmetics—French brands, no less. Make you feel and look a new person. Interested, maybe?"

Paula closed her eyes and sighed. "What kind of deal?"

Rubakov looked suddenly alarmed and embarrassed. "Oh no! You misunderstand." He shook his head and spread his hands. "I just want lessons to improve my English!"

⚛ CHAPTER TWENTY-THREE ⚛

It was like a reprieve from a death sentence. Paula couldn't be sure that the last-minute change of plan had anything to do with Olga's intervening somewhere, but for the moment she was content to make the best of the opportunity to regain her strength, and leave the question to answer itself in due course. But secretly the hope was there, though she tried not to admit it to herself consciously because of the risk of a greater disappointment later. She became brighter and more cheerful toward everyone around her.

Dr. Rubakov appeared the next day with the ultimate luxury in the form of a box of milk bath salts, with some lotion and even nail polish for her hands, and a lipstick to add some color for her face—tawny pink, just right for her complexion. After a breakfast of poached eggs and ham with a spiced potato-onion hash, buttered toast, and real coffee, she kept her side of the bargain by giving an impromptu one-hour English lesson before he went on duty. He came back for another hour during his midday break, and again in the evening.

"I never realize is so, so . . . *uzasno?*"

"Terrible."

"*Da,* terrible!" Rubakov threw up his hands and shook his head despairingly at the pieces of paper that he and Paula had accumulated between them on the table. "Here words are spelt the same but sound different; those ones have same sounds, all written different. Where is sense? How can anyone know ever what to write? But children, they learn this?"

"I didn't invent it. I'm just telling you how it is," Paula said. "Maybe that's why your guys and our guys have had such a hard time getting along." They both laughed.

"It's all a result of ancient vernaculars, you know," Tanya, who had been listening, said in Russian from her bed behind them.

"What do you mean?" Rubakov asked, turning.

"Ever since long ago, back to the time of the Greeks and Romans, people had the problem of trying to talk to the slaves that were brought back from conquered nations," Tanya explained. "So 'vernaculars' emerged between household members and servants— simplified mixtures of languages which combined all the oddities from the originals. Over the centuries that followed, waves of successive migrants from religious and political persecutions, and so on, came to Britain, all bringing their own languages with them. They landed at different places, and by the time they all met in the middle, all the conventions were firmly established and nobody was going to change. So, you see, English came out of it as *the* vernacular of all the vernaculars of Europe."

"And now America has continued the process by mixing in Yiddish, Negro, Hispanic, Amerind, and heaven knows what else," Paula said. "It's a superset of English."

"Russians have never had the problem," Anastasia commented from the far side. "Nobody is clamoring to get in. They all want to get out."

The next morning, Rubakov told Paula that General Protbornov would be arriving later to talk to her. The announcement jolted her back to reality, and for the next couple of hours she became subdued, viewing her prospects with a mixture of excitement, which she didn't dare let herself dwell upon, and trepidation. Protbornov appeared shortly before lunch, accompanied by Major Uskayev. They collected Paula and went into the duty nurse's office, just inside the ward door. Protbornov took the chair behind the desk and motioned Paula to sit opposite. Uskayev sat by the wall to one side.

Protbornov emitted a heavy sigh that made Paula think of a

lumbering bear. He rested an elbow on the arm of his chair and stroked the sides of his craggy face with thumb and fingers for a few seconds. "I gather you have met Comrade Oshkadov," he said at last.

"Oshkadov? Is that Olga, the scientist from Novosibirsk?"

"A spirited woman, even if misguided in some ways. A kindred spirit of yours, I would imagine. In fact, you told her that you are also a scientist."

Paula shrugged. "It's not as if it were something you didn't already know."

"You value science highly, don't you, Lieutenant Bryce," Protbornov said. The fact that he knew her identity was no reason for her to make it public knowledge. If Earnshaw, wherever he was, found a way to contact her, he would seek her by her cover name. "You show a total dedication to its ideals."

"I value worthwhile knowledge and methods for acquiring it that have been shown to work," Paula agreed. "Things that matter."

"But ideas, laws, how societies should be structured and governed—such things do not matter?"

"Politics, you mean?"

"Politics, religion, ideology—call it what you will."

Paula wrestled with the question. Obviously the proposition couldn't be denied outright. "Of course things like that make a difference to the lives of people—a big difference," she said finally. "But the things that interest me are the ones that were true long before there were any people, and which will remain true if people disappear."

"You just want to get to the stars. It doesn't matter who with, under what flag?"

"I didn't say that. The stars can wait a bit longer. They're good at it."

Protbornov's mouth twitched in what could almost have been a smile to acknowledge the rebuffed gambit. "You say these things. Yet you are with the United States Air Force, engaged in espionage. A strange career to pick, for a woman of such a political disposition, wouldn't you think?"

Paula sighed and brushed a curl of hair away from her brow. "It was personal. I joined the service for the independence . . . to be away from home, and for the education. Understanding science was important to me. This other business . . . it was something I got talked into. It's not what I do."

"What do you do?"

"We've been through all that. I won't answer."

"So you say you were talked into espionage work. You were forced to spy for the American military? Would you be willing to make a statement to that effect?"

"No, I wouldn't."

"You know, for someone asking favors, you could be more cooperative."

"I didn't ask for favors. I offered a trade."

Protbornov glanced at Major Uskayev, at the same time raising his eyebrows and straightening his fingers momentarily from his chin. The gesture seemed to say, well, it had been worth a try. He paused, giving the subject a moment to fade into the background, then came to the main point. "I understand that you indicated to Comrade Oshkadov that you are willing to be more useful to us."

"Within limits."

"Why should you wish to benefit us?"

"I don't. I wish to benefit myself."

"Frankness is something I respect. So, what are the limits?"

"I have no desire to defect. I wouldn't work on anything of military significance, or act against the interests of my country. But outside that, I'd be willing to explore possibilities for mutual accommodation."

"Why should we be interested in coming to any accommodation?" Protbornov asked.

"Because your resources are limited up here," Paula replied. "You can't afford people who are dead weight." Protbornov grunted and shifted his eyes inquiring to Uskayev.

"We are told that you have expertise in the field of communications," the major said, leaning forward.

"Some."

"Would you be prepared to do work involving communications?"

"Such as what?" Paula asked guardedly.

Uskayev pouted his lips. "Oh, development and improvement of facilities for communicating to Earth and other space stations, perhaps."

"No. I said I won't get involved in anything military."

"But *Valentina Tereshkova* is not a military facility. It is purely an experiment in sociology."

"Oh, come on. You know that anything developed here would have potential everywhere else."

"How about high-speed data-compression and -protection techniques?"

"No. Look, why don't we forget about my specializations altogether. They're not for sale. But apart from that, I'm familiar with basic scientific principles that apply to any field—teaching, maybe, or medicine. There has to be room for some kind of deal that we can come away from and both be better off than we would have been without any deal at all. That's all I'm saying."

Uskayev studied his hands, paring one thumbnail against the other. Finally he looked up and shook his head dubiously. "I don't think she can be of very much use to us," he said to Protbornov.

Protbornov, however, didn't seem satisfied. He started to reply, then changed his mind and looked at Paula. "I'd like to speak to Major Uskayev privately for a few minutes. Please wait outside."

Paula sat at the table in the ward aisle, turning the pages of a magazine but not seeing them. Wrong, wrong, wrong, she told herself. She'd blown it. She had been too stubborn. As Protbornov had said, a person in her position could hardly expect to get away without making a few concessions. She could see the two officers arguing and gesticulating through the observation window of the nurse's office. She should have indicated a tentative compliance for the time being—to get herself transferred out of those dreadful kitchens—and worried about the specifics later, when it would have been more trouble for them to move her back. Why did she always try doing things all at once, instead of taking them a step at a time? Olga had told her how the Russians achieved their ends slowly, by working wedges into cracks. Here had been her chance to delicately insert a wedge of her own. Instead she'd swung a sledgehammer.

At last they called her back in. "We have agreed on a compromise offer," Protbornov said. "We will assign you to work with Comrade Oshkadov for a probationary period. She will be able to give you a better idea of the possibilities available. During that time you must consider what you would be prepared to contribute that might justify a more permanent arrangement. The situation will be reviewed in one month. In the meantime, we accept your claim of being a scientist and not a professional spy. Your status will be adjusted accordingly if you accept. Well?"

"I'll take it," Paula said at once. By this time, she had no stomach left for being obstinate.

They gave her a light-green tunic like the one Olga had been wearing in the infirmary, and moved her upstairs to an above-surface part of Zamork that she hadn't known existed. The terrain sloped upward to the containing wall in keeping with the general layout of the central valley, and westward toward Novyi Kazan a high-level reservoir bounded the detention facility and separated it from the urban center.

Within this area, the privileged category of prisoners, which Paula learned she had now joined, lived in four-person huts beneath *Tereshkova*'s ribbon-suns and peculiar, curving sky. Although the surroundings of coarse grass, leathery scrub plants, and some uncertain-looking trees holding their own in the cindery soil formed a setting that would have fitted a refugee camp more than a Florida country club, after the cells and the kitchens below it was idyllic. Some of the huts boasted patches of flowers. There was even a beach fringing the reservoir, with a bathing area enclosed by a wire fence twenty yards or so out—admittedly not in use currently because of oil leaks from somewhere and a problem with algal blooms—but the feeling of wind blowing across open water after seeing nothing but bare cell interiors and drab, riveted walls for more weeks than she had been able to keep track of was exhilarating.

And on her first evening there, when she walked down through the rows of huts to the reservoir, along by the water, and back following the outer hull wall via the hill at the rear, it rained.

❀ CHAPTER TWENTY-FOUR ❀

At the end of July, the Russians privately released to a number of selected Western and Asian governments a recording of what they claimed was a voluntary confession by Magician. In it, Magician appeared at ease, composed, and in good health. In their consensus, the doctors, psychologists, and experienced interrogators who viewed the recording found no evidence of coercion.

Magician claimed that for many years he had been obsessed with concern over the international situation. He abhorred the distrust the Communist world and the West, and the prospect of its leading to a global calamity horrified him. So, when what seemed like a unique opportunity presented itself, he had attempted to make his own single-handed contribution to easing world tensions. The file of information he had compiled to substantiate the claims of advanced weapons systems being concealed on *Valentina Tereshkova* was a fake. He had invented the data and misled Western intelligence deliberately, in order to provoke public accusations and denials. He had believed at the time that this would force the Soviet government into a more open policy and lead eventually to full international inspection. Thus a major source of potential misunderstanding would have been defused. His intentions had been for the best, as he saw it. However, since then he had come to realize that he had acted naively, and in fact had aggravated the situation instead. He hoped that in setting the record straight he would undo some of the damage he had caused. He regretted his actions, asked the West to understand, and expressed thanks to the Soviet counselors and doctors who had helped him see everything more clearly.

"What do you make of it?" Philip Borden, the UDIA's director, asked Foleda after they had viewed the recording with others in a conference room inside the Pentagon.

Foleda shrugged. "How can anyone know what to make of it? You know as well as I do, Phil, that with the things they've got these days, they could have turned the pope into an atheist since Magician was grabbed. I'd be closer to being convinced if they let some of our people talk to him freely, face-to-face. If he's genuine, what would they have to lose?"

Foleda wasn't the only person to feel that way. After consultation, the US ambassador in Moscow, on behalf of a number of interested nations, challenged the Soviet government to make Magician available for unsupervised interviews by experts freely selected by the West. To the surprise of everyone involved, the Soviets readily agreed.

◎ CHAPTER TWENTY-FIVE ◎

". . . in the formation of a class with *radical chains,* a class of civil society which is not a class of civil society, an estate which is the dissolution of all estates, a sphere which has a universal character by its universal suffering and claims no *particular right* because no *particular wrong* but *wrong generally* is perpetrated against it; which can invoke no *historical* but only its *human* title, which does not stand in any one-sided opposition to the consequences but in all-round opposition to the presuppositions of . . ." The tall, bearded Estonian standing on the box in the general compound delivered his reading from the works of Marx in an untiring, strident monotone that sounded like the long-playing version of a Moslem call to prayer from the top of a minaret. The audience before him continued murmuring among themselves with total inattention, reasonably confident that even the most diligent KGB eavesdropper who might still be glued to a directional microphone capable of distinguishing anything intelligible would long since have been put to sleep.

"We could pool some points and try getting approval to start glassblowing as a hobby, for ornaments or something," Rashazzi suggested. "That would get us some basic equipment and materials. For the optical cavity we'd need, oh . . . say, a meter or two of Pyrex tube. Then for—"

"Sealing it would require a gas-oxygen torch," Haber said. "Soda lime glass could be worked with a propane torch, which would be easier to get hold of."

"Okay, soda-lime glass. Then we'd need some optical-quality glass to make Brewster windows, an abrasive powder for sawing and grinding, and components for the end-mirror cells. . . ."

Haber was still shaking his head. "It's formidable. You still need a vacuum pump and manometer . . ."

"We use the glassblowing setup," Rashazzi said.

"And then the electronics."

"I know where I can get neon-sign electrodes from somebody in the town. A plain, double-sided, epoxy-glass PCB could be made into a twenty-kilovolt capacitor. We've already got some rectifiers."

McCain kept quiet. There wasn't much he could have contributed, anyway. He'd asked them if it would be feasible to home-build a suitable laser device for the method that Scanlon had first speculated about to communicate messages out of *Tereshkova*.

"Gas-dynamic would be simpler to construct," Haber said. "Although there would still be the problem of procuring suitable nozzles and fuel supplies."

After more than two months of observing, listening, and getting to know how the system at Zamork worked, McCain had come to the conclusion that there might still be a chance of carrying out the mission he'd come here to accomplish. True, there was scant likelihood of obtaining the Tangerine file now; but that had been only a means to the end of ascertaining *Tereshkova*'s true nature. His unique situation compared to the rest of the interested section of the West's intelligence community put him in an ideal position to do just that. It couldn't be a one-man operation, however, and that raised the eternal Zamork problem of trying to decide who was reliable. He'd already recruited Scanlon and Mungabo, and now he was putting out feelers to Rashazzi and Haber. It was difficult to imagine anyone with their kind of knowledge earning a living as jailhouse stool pigeons.

"Perhaps you're right," Rashazzi said resignedly to Haber at last. "It's complicated. Maybe the answer isn't to try making our own laser at all. Suppose we just get enough pieces to make what looks like a broken Russian one. Then we find some way to switch it with a working one—there must be some in the labs in Landausk, for example. Or what about alignment lasers? There's still construction going on in some areas."

Haber admired the young Israeli's enthusiasm, but remained pessimistic. "It's no good," he told McCain. "There simply aren't enough places to hide all the parts we'd need, never mind to assemble and test the finished device. Such a task could never be concealed from surveillance."

In the background, the Marxian chant continued with no sign of abatement. "What we need is somewhere permanent to do it, free from surveillance," Rashazzi muttered, staring down at the floor.

"Something like a workshop," McCain said.

"Yes, that's it exactly. We need a workshop."

If Andreyov was a plant, it was the best piece of acting McCain had ever come across. But that in itself didn't make him potentially useful—he was getting old, and he had a loose tongue. All the same, McCain tried making a few indirect references to subverting the system to see if he would catch the gist. Andreyov missed the point and responded typically.

"The system wasn't always like that. The czars, oh yes, they were authoritarian all right, but then Russia has always been authoritarian. It wasn't the same kind of thing. The arts flourished then, because artists were allowed to express what they felt. It wasn't all political. There were Tolstoy and Tchaikovsky, Borodin . . . And there were some executions, yes—a few, mainly criminals—but nothing compared to what came later. Political prisoners weren't treated badly under the czars, you know. The jailers got reprimanded if they didn't address them respectfully. Most of them were cultured, you see. Gentlemen. Not like the rubbish that took over later—murderers and thieves, the lot of them, no better than Hitler. Worse than Hitler.

"Do you know what lost Hitler the war? It was the Nazi racial lunacies. When the Germans invaded Russia in 1941, whole nations of people that the Bolsheviks had taken over wanted to help throw the Communists out—Estonians, Latvians, Lithuanians, Ukrainians.

Eager to fight they were. But Hitler thought they were subhumans and wouldn't use them. He wanted Russia to be defeated by Germans. But it wasn't, of course."

"I heard a joke about Russians," Charlie Chan said, who was listening. "Ivan and Boris meet in the square outside a railroad station in Moscow, you see. Ivan says to Boris, 'Where are you going?' and Boris says, 'I'm catching the train to Minsk, to get bread.' 'But you can get bread right here, in Moscow.' Boris says, 'I know, but the line starts in Minsk.'"

Antonos Gonares, the Hungarian who shared a partitioned bay with Smovak and Vorghas, interested McCain because he often went on work details to the hub. The official plans of *Tereshkova* showed the zone behind the docking ports as housing the nuclear reactors that powered the main generating plant and provided process heat for some of the manufacturing operations. Other reports, however, held that the manufacturing was less extensive than claimed, and that most of the space in those compartments held other installations.

"What kind of work do you do in the hub?" McCain asked Gonares casually one day.

"It varies. Sometimes we move freight around in the cargo bays. Sometimes it's cleaning out tanks or scraping down metal for repainting."

"In the cargo bays? You mean behind the docking ports, back near the nuclear area?"

"Yes, sometimes. Why?"

"Oh, you know journalists—always curious. I was just trying to get a clear picture in my mind of the layout. Who knows?—I might end up writing about it someday. I, ah, I'm sure I could persuade my editors to cash a few points for more details . . . if they proved useful."

"Ah, I see. . . . What kind of details?"

"Oh, nothing very demanding. What's inside which compartment. The positions and directions of the bulkheads. What kind of security they operate there. Maybe a sketch or two?"

"How much might we be talking about?"

"What are the risks, and what would make them worthwhile?"

"Well, maybe. . . . Let me think about it."

Oskar Smovak rubbed his bushy, Fidel Castro beard as he stood watching McCain, who was staring out across the B Block mess area. "What do you see?" he asked after a while. For once, his usually cutting voice was low and measured.

McCain turned his head. "How to you mean?"

"You watch people, and you think. You say little. What are you looking for?"

"I'm just a compulsive people-watcher."

"Is that a common habit among journalists?"

"Probably. How can you report what you don't see?"

"Come on, you're no journalist, Lew. I just wanted to say that if I can, I'd like to help. Okay?"

"Help? What with?"

"Whatever you're planning."

"If I find myself planning something, I'll bear it in mind."

Smovak sighed. "Yes, I know, it's difficult knowing who to trust, isn't it. But for what it's worth, I've managed to get some information for you about the American woman that you came here with." McCain looked round at him sharply. Smovak went on, "She was in a close-confinement cell in D Block up to about a week ago, but she got sick and was taken to the infirmary. She hasn't come back since."

"Who told you that?"

"A nameless friend in another billet who screws an East German wench from the cell she was in. It sounded as if the others gave her a hard time."

"I see. . . . Okay, thanks, Oskar. And I'll let you know if I need a hand."

Borowski, the Pole, had warned McCain minutes before the incident with Maiskevik. "How did you know?" McCain asked him one day as they talked in the compound.

"I just had the feeling they were setting somebody up that night. I figured it had to be you."

"So how come I was left alone afterward?" McCain asked.

"You would have exposed Luchenko's sidelines. He probably bribed someone higher up not to pursue the matter."

"Wouldn't that someone have guessed already?"

"Probably. But why go looking under shitty stones when you can be paid not to?"

Which was pretty much what Andreyov had said. But McCain had never been fully satisfied with that explanation. If the authorities already knew about the graft systems that were operating around the place, Luchenko wouldn't have stood to lose much from exposure. So he could have continued with his taxation racket *and* have kept face by having McCain put through the mill. Something didn't add up—but McCain wasn't about to get to the bottom of it just then, and there would be no point in pursuing the matter. "Why'd you do it?" he asked instead. "Did you have something personal against Maiskevik?"

"We all had something personal against Maiskevik. But on top of that, I'm Polish. I've heard you talk; you know our history—how Stalin carved Poland up with Hitler and stabbed us in the back in 1939, and Katyn, and what happened to the Warsaw resistance army. The Russians have always dreaded the thought of a strong Poland. We've never had any reason to feel exactly charitable toward the Russians."

"'Tis very sociable you're becoming all of a sudden, I can't help noticing," Scanlon said over lunch. "Little tête-a-têtes going on all the time wherever I turn my head. I take it you're recruiting."

"As you said, just being sociable."

"Oh, come on now, I thought we were supposed to be partners. Don't I even get to know who it is I'm likely to find meself working with?"

"If there's a need."

"Aha, always the cautious one, eh?"

"You know the rules. It avoids risking embarrassing complications."

"You went to a good school, I see. Purely out of curiosity, what part of Western intelligence were you with?"

"SIS—the Brits. They infiltrated me in here specially to keep an eye on you. You got yourself such a reputation in London."

"Oh, it's like that, is it? Very well, Mr. Earnshaw, journalist, then here's me with a little tip for ye that'll make your life a whole lot easier. Talk to Koh. He'll put you in touch with the escape committee. They're the people with information of the kind ye could be using."

McCain stared incredulously. "Escape committee? You're joking!"

Scanlon gave a satisfied nod of his gaunt, hollow-cheeked face. "Yes indeed, now, that's put a different tune in your fiddle, hasn't it? I hope ye've a conscience in you, Earnshaw, because it's shame ye should be feelin'."

"Who's on this committee?"

"Ah, come on, now. You know the rules. I've given you my tip. It's Koh that you need to be talking to."

❀ CHAPTER TWENTY-SIX ❀

The Soviet embassy in Kensington was an eleven-story gray stone building of solid, uncluttered lines, built in the last ten years, standing in a walled enclosure of well-tended lawns and shrubbery behind a thick screen of trees. Inside the same compound, an adjacent apartment building of similar size housed most of the Soviet diplomatic personnel stationed in London. Despite such comforts as the swimming pool, sauna, gymnasium, and tennis courts that life within the compound offered, Anita Dorkas was more than grateful to live outside, a privilege that a *Novoye Vermya* correspondent enjoyed.

For one thing it meant she and Enriko could usually manage to skip the dreary weekly Party meetings that were obligatory for everyone else, and live their private lives away from the stultifying cloistered existence led by those within—most of whom knew no more about the world outside than they were permitted to see on supervised tours made in groups. But more important, it enabled them to escape the omnipresent web of informants competing to discover anything derogatory. The wives were notorious for courting mutual confidences in order to curry favor with the chiefs by disclosing what they had learned, while two men would spend the night drinking together and then race to file reports on each other the next morning. The privilege existed to allow Enriko, in his capacity as a KGB case officer responsible for recruiting sources among British nationals and foreign residents, to operate more freely, since the embassy itself was under constant surveillance by the British; the irony of it was that the same convenience made it easier for Anita to conduct her own extramural dissident activities, too.

As was her habit on days when she was on duty, she took the tube to Holland Park station and walked from there. Enriko was using the car that day, anyway, to go to Hatfield for a luncheon interview with the chairman of a British industrial association. The Englishman prided himself on his political astuteness and was flattered at the suggestion of being quoted in a restricted-circulation newsletter that Enriko had assured him was read daily by the top Soviet leaders. Enriko would insist on making a small payment, of course, because ". . . our accounting procedures require it." In time, as what had ostensibly begun as a friendship based on common business interests deepened, Enriko would ask for gradually more demanding favors and the payments would get bigger, until one day the victim would wake up to find himself way out of his depth. Then the high-pressure business would begin. There were four basic vulnerabilities that led people into being recruited, Enriko sometimes said, quoting an American acronym that the CIA taught their people. "MICE"— Money, Ideology, Compromise, Ego. In the case of the soon-to-be-recruited British industrialist, clearly it was Ego.

The gate attendant waved her on through, and she entered the marble foyer of the embassy building through the main entrance. An elevator took her up past nine floors of regular embassy rooms and offices to the tenth, where she emerged into the windowless anteroom of the London Residency of the KGB's First Chief Directorate, which handled all operations abroad. As with its counterparts in Washington, Paris, Bonn, Rome, Brasilia, Bangkok, New Delhi, and elsewhere, it existed solely for the purpose of subversion and information gathering. Anita's special key opened the outer steel door. The security officer on duty checked her ID via a remote viewpanel and opened the second door, three feet beyond the first, from inside. She entered, nodding a good morning to him in his guardpost as she passed, and went through into the central corridor of the lower level.

The thing that most people noticed immediately upon entering the Residency for the first time was the sepulchral quiet pervading the place. It was because the outer walls, floors, and ceilings of the building's entire top two floors were all double to ensure soundproofing, with electronic noise beamed through the spaces between to frustrate listening devices. The few windows were formed from a one-way opaque glass that was also soundproof and impervious to all known types of eavesdropping equipment. A whole social order based on treachery, deceit, mistrust, and paranoia, Anita thought to herself. How was it possible to avoid becoming embroiled in it along with everyone else?

She passed the large General Programs room, with twenty-odd work booths at which a number of case officers were already busy drafting reports, translating documents, and formulating operational plans. The important work of the case officers was considered to be not the obtaining of restricted information and documents—although this was valuable enough—but the discovering, cultivating, and eventual recruiting of "agents of influence": politicians, government officials, journalists, academicians, and the like—persons able to influence policy-making and public opinion. For the mission of the KGB was still what it had always been: to preserve and expand the power of the Soviet Communist Party oligarchy throughout the world by essentially clandestine means.

Across the corridor, on the far side of a wood-paneled outer room furnished with antique cabinets, a sofa, leather-backed chairs, and a conference table, was the office of the Resident, Major General Dimitri Turenov. Beyond that were two more offices. The first was shared by two of the line chiefs: the chief of Line X—the KGB field term for Directorate T, which collected foreign scientific and technological data—and the chief of Line N (Directorate S), which was responsible for supporting "illegals"—Soviet-bloc nationals infiltrated into other countries under various identities. The next office belonged to both the chief of Line KR (Directorate K), whose task was countering British counterintelligence, and the internal-security officer, who looked after the embassy's protection, the guarding of important Soviet visitors to the country, and recapturing defectors. Opposite these was the larger office shared by the chief of the American Group, who compiled dossiers on resident American businesspeople, scientists, technicians, servicemen, and others who had come to their attention as potentially useful; the chief of a similar group that watched West Europeans; and the active-measures officer, who handled covert operations and orchestrated disinformation and propaganda campaigns among the British news media.

Halfway along the corridor she came to the stairway and elevator connecting the tenth and eleventh floors. Halfway up the stairs she met Ivan, one of the case officers, and Anatoli on their way down. Anatoli was one of the technicians who monitored local British police and counterintelligence-service radio frequencies. If, for example, a sudden increase in British surveillance communications activity occurred just before an agent from the Residency was due to meet with one of his contacts, the agent would be signaled by radio to abort the appointment.

"Good morning," Anita said to them.

"Did Enriko come in with you?" Ivan asked.

"I'm afraid not. He'll be out until the afternoon. Is it important?"

"Popovechny wanted to talk to him. He asked me to mention it if I saw him, that's all." General Vadim Popovechny was the Residency's second-in-command and also the head of Line PR, specializing in political intelligence. He was dedicated, ambitious, and injected the ideal measure of toughness into the place to complement Turenov's more intellectual and sophisticated management style.

"Any idea what it's about?" Anita asked.

"Sorry, no."

"Where's he gone?" Anatoli inquired.

"Hatfield, I think he said."

"Oh well, see you later, anyhow," Ivan said.

"Yes. Maybe at lunch."

"See you later," Anatoli said.

The eleventh floor contained the electronics-surveillance officer's domain, which included an enormous room packed with radio and microwave receivers, recorders, computers, terminals, and equipment that communicated with satellites via antennas on the roof. Next to that were the Technical Operations and Photography labs, and then the Translation Office, which Anita entered. Grigori and Eva were already there. Anastasia had a dental appointment and wouldn't be in until later, she remembered, and it was Viktor's day off. "Good morning," she said.

"Hello, Anita," Grigori answered. He was in his late twenties, and had come out from Moscow fairly recently to spend a couple of years familiarizing himself with overseas routine before becoming active in the field.

Eva, cheerful and freckle-faced, was both physicist and linguist, and had taught English at the Foreign Intelligence School of Moscow University's Institute for International Relations. She looked around from the screen that she was working at and grinned. "Hi. Say, I like the coat. Is it new?"

Anita took her coat off, held it up for Eva to see, then hung it on the rack inside the door. "I got it a couple of days ago in Queensway. On sale, too."

"I love the color. And that collar has such a stylish look."

"Oh, Viktor worked late and finished the Chalmers article, so you don't have to worry about it," Grigori informed her. "It's all filed and logged."

"Good," Anita said. "I don't like dealing with that heavy technical material, anyway." She sat down at her own terminal, activated it, and entered a call to the classified section of the computer records for the file she had saved yesterday. "It's going to be a hot day."

"I was thinking of going for a swim in the compound at lunchtime," Eva said.

"Sounds like a good idea. Maybe I'll join you." Anita produced her magnetic key and inserted it in her desk to open the drawer containing the original documents that she had been working from. She was about to say something further, then stopped and frowned down at the drawer as the lock failed to disengage. Either it was faulty, or her key had been invalidated—all the electronic locks in the building could be reprogrammed remotely from the Security Office downstairs. An instant later a message on her screen announced: illegal access code. request denied.

Anita stared perplexedly at the screen. Then she realized that

Maria Chorenkov, the section's supervisor, was standing in the doorway of her office adjoining the Translation room. "Comrade Dorkas, would you step this way, please," she said. She was a tall, straight-bodied woman with a sharp face, thin-rimmed spectacles, and graying hair tied in a bun, who always wore thick, utilitarian stockings and drab tweedy clothes. Her voice just at this moment fitted the image. Confused, Anita followed her into the office. Behind her, Eva and Grigori exchanged apprehensive glances.

"You won't be needing access to the records, since you will no longer be working with this section," Chorenkov told her without preliminaries when the door was closed. "You are being transferred downstairs to the Secretariat, effective immediately. Collect your personal belongings, please. And thank you for your help during the time you have been with us."

Anita was flummoxed. "But this is so sudden. I don't understand . . ."

"All I know is that I have direct instructions from General Popovechny."

"He gave no reason?"

"Not to me. And I didn't ask."

"But . . . Could I speak with him, please?"

"That is impossible. He will be out until tomorrow."

Anita collected her personal belongings, mumbled a bewildered farewell to Grigori and Eva, and went back downstairs to report to the Secretariat, which provided the Residency's clerical services. She was given the job of searching through British newspapers, magazines, specialist journals, and the public dataservice for references to certain listed topics. All the information was freely available in the public domain; it gave her the uneasy feeling that her security clearance had been suspended.

But by lunchtime she was telling herself that she had overreacted. The mundane work had to be done, after all, and somebody had to do it. Maria Chorenkov's brusqueness and insensitivity had been typical. Tomorrow there would be a simple explanation. By midafternoon she had just about recovered from the shock, when Colonel Felyakin, the internal-security officer, called her into his office.

"You are scheduled for leave tomorrow, I see," he said.

"Yes," Anita replied.

"I hope you haven't made any important plans, because it will be necessary to change your arrangements," he told her. "A couple of people from Moscow will be here, and one of the things they want to look into involves you and your husband. Apparently there has been an administrative mix-up over the dates and durations of some of the postings, and we'd like to get it straightened out. Can you manage that all right?"

"Why, yes . . . I suppose so."

"Thank you. Shall we say ten o'clock? Oh, and your husband also. I've checked, and he is due in tomorrow, anyway."

"I'll tell him."

"And make sure you have your passports. We'll need to check the dates and visas in them."

"Yes. Ten o'clock tomorrow," Anita repeated mechanically.

"Excellent."

By evening Anita's imagination had turned her fears into certainly. Somehow they were on to her. Enriko called to say he had been detained during the afternoon and would be going straight back to the embassy for an evening appointment with the Line KR chief, Colonel Shepanov. The solitude aggravated Anita's nervousness. She paced restlessly about the apartment, smoking more cigarettes than she was accustomed to and fussing with knickknacks and ornaments that didn't need rearranging. She poured herself a drink and sat staring unseeingly at the television for an hour, searching back in her mind over the events of the past few weeks for a hint of anything that might have gone wrong or something indiscreet that she might have said. She could find nothing, but that didn't really amount to much. The biggest danger in this kind of business was having to depend on other people.

Every time she looked at the clock, another slice of time had been shaved off the interval that remained until ten tomorrow morning. She found herself dreading the thought of reentering the embassy. If a KGB officer's wife had come under suspicion, it would be automatic for his reliability to be questioned too. Who were these people from Moscow who wanted to talk to them? Why the need for passports? She didn't believe the explanation that Felyakin had given.

It was around midnight when Enriko finally appeared, having left the car at the embassy and taken a taxi. He and Shepanov had been drinking together, and although he wasn't sufficiently far gone to be called drunk, it showed. This happened from time to time. Anita saw it as a safety valve against the stresses that made ulcers, high blood pressure, and nervous problems routine occupational hazards of a KGB officer's life—and Enriko always had enough sense not to let it get out of hand. But whereas he usually came home bright-eyed and talkative after an evening of drinking with friends, on this occasion he returned morose and distracted. Obviously there was something heavy weighing on his mind.

"What is it?" Anita asked him.

"Nothing."

"Look, I can see something's wrong. But I can't read minds. How can I help if you won't say what's the matter?" He just looked at her strangely for a while and wouldn't answer.

Finally, after he had poured himself another drink and was sitting opposite her on the couch in the lounge, he said, "Shepanov is heading for trouble, you know. He has problems with his marriage, and that is leading him into a problem with drink. It's a familiar story."

"I've heard gossip around the compound about his wife and one or two names," Anita replied. "Yes, it happens."

"And he's lonely away from Russia and his friends. He likes having someone to talk to. But sometimes he opens up too much and says things that he shouldn't." Enriko seemed to be working up to something. Anita waited. Then he took a gulp from his glass and asked suddenly, "How much do you know about that woman scientist from Novosibirsk that your former husband took up with?"

Instantly Anita stiffened. Normally her reaction would have been to remind him that they had agreed not to talk about such matters, but it was too close to the things that had been preying on her mind all evening. Instead she asked, "What do you mean? What about her?"

"Oh, I'm not interested in your personal affairs or anything like that. But what about her . . . politically?" Enriko took another drink, and for the first time Anita wondered if he really had gone past the limit. "Was her loyalty ever in question?"

Anita stared at him for a few seconds, trying to fit what he was saying in with the other things that had happened that day. "Why?" she asked. Her voice was strangely dry and hollow. "What's happened?"

Enriko looked up to meet her eyes directly. "Shepanov told me tonight that she was arrested three months ago on charges involving illegal dissident activity. That, of course, would put Dyashkin under suspicion straight away." Enriko didn't have to spell out the rest. All of Dyashkin's close associates and relatives would also be subject to investigation, and especially Anita as his ex-wife. That was something that Enriko could have done without as far as his own career prospects were concerned. "Were you ever mixed up in anything like that?" he demanded.

"Of course not. I went through enough screening before we were married. You know yourself how rigorous they are."

"They have made mistakes, nevertheless."

Anita felt herself grow cold and start to shake. She needed to escape for a moment to compose herself. "Let me get you a coffee," she said.

"Anita, look at me. I ask you again—Were you ever involved in anything like that?"

She forced herself to react angrily. "I told you, no! Sober up, you're being ridiculous. Would you like a coffee?"

Enriko slumped back on the couch. "Yes, maybe I should. . . ."

Anita got up and hurried through to the kitchen. Her mind was too agitated to think while she opened a cabinet and took out the coffee and two mugs. Then, as she stood staring at the jar in her hands, the realization came over her that if she went back to the embassy tomorrow morning, the only way she would ever leave it again would be under escort, heading for the airport to board a Moscow-bound plane. Enriko would no doubt weather through eventually. She wouldn't last a day. Very likely she was finished already.

She stood there, gnawing at her lip, dismissing from her mind preposterous thoughts of what she could do. Then she slowly raised the jar of coffee in both hands, hesitated for a moment, and smashed it on the floor. By the time Enriko appeared in the lounge doorway, she was already past him in the hall, slipping on her coat. He looked at her uncertainly. "What was that? Are you all right? Where are you going?"

"The coffee jar—it slipped. I'm just going to get some more at the shop on the corner. Be a dear and clean it up while I'm gone, would you?" And before Enriko could reply, she had let herself out the hall door and was heading for the stairs. The apartment was only one floor up, and instead of using the front entrance, she went on down another level and left the building via a side door from the parking basement.

Anita walked several blocks, then took a cab to Knightsbridge on the south side of Hyde Park. She went into a hotel that she knew there and sat for a while, steadying herself with a drink in the upstairs bar and thinking what to do next. Then, reaching the conclusion that she had no other choice, she went to a phone booth in the lobby and called the special number she had been given by her contact at SIS.

In an operations room of the British Special Intelligence Service located in a labyrinth that had existed beneath Whitehall since the days of World War II, the duty officer who took the call consulted a supervisor, and then sent out a radio signal coded for emergency priority. Two miles away in Chelsea, the signal activated an ordinary-looking communicator in the pocket of a jacket that had been thrown over the back of a chair, underneath a pile of clothes. The unit had been set to reject incoming calls. However, it contained special-purpose circuitry that caused the standard setting to be bypassed.

Jeremy had been waiting months for this. The chateaubriand for two had been splendid, the wine impeccable, and the atmosphere enchanting. Now, with the soft strains of violins and the scent of roses pervading her bedroom, the evening was almost complete.

Daphne kissed him on the mouth and lay back, smiling seductively as she opened her robe to uncover her perfect body. Jeremy allowed his eyes to feast on the sight. "I say," he murmured.

"I've always had a thing about flimsy little knickers like those. Is what's underneath as pretty as the rest?"

"Why don't you find out?" she whispered.

His hand stole down from her cheek, lingered at her breast to excite her nipple, then stroked downward, over her stomach, as the muscles tensed in eager anticipation.

Beep! Beep! Beep! Beep! . . .

"Bloody Christ, not now! . . . Blast! Blast! Damn and blast the buggering sods! They can't—"

"What is it?" Daphne shrieked, sitting up.

"I have to call in."

"You said you were off all night."

"I am. I mean . . . Oh, it's too complicated to explain now."

"Can't you turn the bloody thing off?"

"It's somewhere under all this stuff . . ."

"Be careful with that dress, darling."

"There. Oh, God! . . ."

Daphne pulled her robe back around her and reached for a cigarette. She sighed resignedly. "The phone's there. Better luck next time?"

"Oh, there will be a next time, then?"

"But of course. In fact, I think you did it on purpose, just to heighten the suspense."

"You really are insane. But I'll still take the rain check."

"Rain check?"

"Oh, it's what the Americans say."

"What does it mean?"

Jeremy stopped as he was about to punch in the number. "Do you know," he said, suddenly bemused, "I have absolutely no idea."

Jeremy collected Anita in a cab from a rendezvous at Hyde Park Corner and took her to an address south of the river, in Lambeth. When they arrived, Sylvia was already there with another woman from SIS. Two agents would be there twenty-four hours a day until Anita was moved, and the police would be keeping a watch on the outside discreetly.

"What do you think will happen next?" Anita asked them.

"That's not up to us," Sylvia answered.

"Since the Americans have been showing so much interest in you, it wouldn't surprise me if you ended up being whisked off over there," Jeremy said.

"I do hope I haven't been a nuisance," Anita told them.

Sylvia laughed. "Of course not. It's our job. What a silly thing to say!"

"Never let it be said that we allowed anything to come before King and Country," Jeremy recited staunchly. Sylvia gave him a curious look. He sniffed disdainfully. "I rather think I'll go and put on some tea." With that he marched out of the room and across the hallway outside—stopping to deliver a hefty kick at the umbrella stand on the way.

❁ CHAPTER TWENTY-SEVEN ❁

Getting anything organized in Zamork on the systematic basis that McCain had in mind would require ways of evading the informers and electronic surveillance devices—and if McCain's theory of the whole operation having been set up as an "information mine" was correct, the Russians were unlikely to have settled for half-measures.

Rashazzi and Haber had developed several techniques for locating and disabling concealed microphones, and were experimenting with ways of neutralizing the bracelet monitors. To mask these activities and at the same time provide some amusement for himself, Rashazzi had been training his mice to eat the polyvinyl insulating coatings of Russian electrical wiring, and then releasing the mice into the spaces behind the floors and walls. When Russian technicians arrived to trace the faults that the two scientists' tamperings sometimes caused in the security system, they invariably found short-circuited wiring that looked for the world as if it had been nibbled by busy rodent teeth, usually with mouse droppings nearby. The ruse didn't last long, however, and instructions came down through Luchenko for Rashazzi to get rid of the mice. Then they mysteriously escaped from their cages and presumably disappeared into the hole that just as mysteriously appeared in the wall underneath the tank in one of the B-3 toilet cubicles. Their mobility must have been extraordinary, for within days repair crews were rushing frantically all over Zamork in response to a plague of electrical failures and burned-out lighting circuits. Luchenko was in trouble with the block supervisor, and Rashazzi lost a stack of accumulated privileges, but the reactions went no further than that.

The exercise provided a smoke screen for finding out more about the security system, but it really didn't solve the overall problem. The Russians had long been adepts at deception, and it was never possible to be sure that the surveillance measures uncovered at one level were not decoys intended to divert the prisoners' attention while a more cunningly hidden level continued operating unimpaired. Long after Rashazzi and Haber had become experts at ferreting out wired microphones, for example, they discovered another kind embedded in the walls, which operated without any telltale leads at all: they were connected by strips of conducting paint, which were then concealed by a layer of ordinary paint. Rashazzi made a probe tipped by a pair of fine needles that could detect the strips, but it was tedious work.

It was possible to play various games to try and deduce if a particular location was being monitored, such as deliberately staging a provocative-sounding dialogue there and watching for any Russian response. The trouble was that Russians could play games like that too, by weaving their net with a wide mesh and purposely allowing the small fry through in order to catch the bigger fish later. How many were willing to be fall guys to find out?

McCain concluded there could be no safe way of communicating inside Zamork's regular environment. The outside work details offered better prospects, but he had no control over who was assigned to them—and he himself was confined to working inside Zamork, anyway. But then, he asked himself, was it so essential to get out of Zamork itself, after all? Surveillance devices would be in the places where people went: in the billets, corridors, mess areas, and so on. But in addition to places like those, the structure included spaces behind the walls, machinery compartments between decks, and shafts carrying cables and ducting off in all directions. If there were some way of getting into places like that . . .

McCain put the question to Rashazzi one morning as they were walking along Gorky Street, staying close to a tractor hauling a trailer loaded with trays of rattling pipe fittings.

"Albrecht and I have been looking into that for some time," Rashazzi said. "The problem is that the wall- and floor-panels everywhere carry a system of conductive strips on the back that will cause open circuits and set off alarms if they're moved."

"Couldn't you jumper the connections or something before the panels were lifted, so the circuit wasn't broken?" McCain asked.

"You could, if you knew the circuit layout. But you can't trace the layout until you lift the panels. So it's a vicious circle. A lot of people around Zamork have gotten themselves stretches in solitary through fooling with it. It's a tricky business."

McCain fell silent and stared moodily at the floor as they walked. Without some way of being able to talk and exchange information freely, he wasn't going to get anywhere.

The outer torus of *Valentina Tereshkova* was a little over three miles around, which meant that the total length of the colony's road system was not large. Therefore the Russians hadn't bothered shipping up heavy road-maintenance machinery to stand idle most of the time; they made use of the labor force already available there instead. When centralized planning failed to produce enough bolts to match the number of holes that Scanlon was drilling, bedframe production ceased while the planners brooded over their schedules, and McCain was sent on an outside assignment with the road-resurfacing gang that Koh was with, working near the edge of one of the agricultural zones. He hoped this would give him the chance he'd been waiting for to talk with Koh in less restrictive surroundings.

The road that the gang was working on ran between rows of corn, at the base of a series of terraced plantations of vines, fruit trees, soybeans, and tomatoes. Above, through the transparent roof section by the nearby agricultural station, one of the minor spokes soared upward to merge into the clutter of the hub structure a half mile overhead. A mild breeze was blowing from the west, and the environment provided a welcome change from Zamork for the guards as well as for the prisoners, which meant that nobody was in any hurry to get the job done, so supervision was minimal. Two of the guards were playing cards across the hood of one of the trucks and another was sitting reading in the driver's seat, while the rest sauntered about casually, sometimes exchanging words with the prisoners. McCain was working with Koh a short distance away from the others, using rakes to spread a sticky gray concoction of lunar-rock furnace slag and binding compound processed from industrial leftovers.

"So, what did you do?" McCain asked.

"How do you mean?" Koh replied. McCain had the feeling that Koh knew quite well what he meant.

"You said once that you'd tell me sometime about what you did to wind up in here."

Koh worked on in silence for a while. McCain thought he was ignoring the question, when suddenly Koh chuckled. "Do you remember the incident at the Asian Industrial Fair in Chungking a couple of years ago?"

"Seems to ring a kind of a bell. . . . There was a fire, wasn't there? Something to do with the KGB."

"A Chinese traditionalist movement called White Moon was making a nuisance of itself, campaigning against industrialization and modernization," Koh said. "They staged a demonstration at the Chinese pavilion . . . or at least, that was the way it was supposed to look."

McCain nodded. "Now I remember. Except they weren't White Moon people at all. They were imposters. It was a stunt set up by the Chinese intelligence service to discredit them and justify imposing tighter restrictions. But later, the guy who authorized it admitted he was working for the KGB. So all the time, it was a deception orchestrated by Mosc . . ." McCain's voice trailed away. He stopped what he was doing and looked up suddenly. "Wait a minute. Nakajima-Lin Kohmei-Tso-Liang—it was *you!* You were the KGB's inside man, the head of Chinese intelligence."

"Deputy head," Koh said.

"Whatever. So what went wrong? How'd you wind up in here?"

Koh chuckled again. "Yes, it was my idea—a bit unfair, I suppose, but you've no idea how difficult White Moon was becoming. It was just intended to be a demonstration. The people we hired weren't supposed to burn the whole pavilion down. That was entirely due to an overzealous subordinate. But it was my responsibility, and we do have a strong sense of honor . . ." Koh shook his head from side to side, and his breath came in quick, shaking gasps, as if what was amusing him was too much to bear. "But, you see, the KGB had nothing to do with it, hee-hee-hee. . . . I only made that confession after everything was blown anyway."

"You mean you never worked for the KGB?"

"No. It was probably the first piece of international mischief in which they were genuinely innocent, ha-ha-ha . . . and nobody believed them!"

McCain smiled and turned back to his raking. "And so?"

"So, the KGB kidnapped me to make sure I wouldn't do anything like that again, and here I am."

The dump truck arrived to deposit another load of material and then went to collect a fresh charge from the mixer at the far end of the workings. One of the guards came close to inspect what they were doing, then moved away. They worked on in silence for a while. Finally McCain said, "Scanlon told me I should talk to you."

"Oh yes?"

"Have you ever heard of an escape committee, back at Zamork?"

"One hears all kind of things in Zamork."

"Do you think it's possible at all—escaping from here?"

"They say all things are possible."

It seemed McCain was going to have to work for it. He tried a more oblique approach. "If there were an escape committee, and if it were up to you, who would you trust to recruit into it?" he asked.

"I get the impression that you are already doing an excellent job of working that out for yourself," Koh said.

"Who are the dangerous ones? Who would you leave out?" Koh didn't answer at once, and McCain prompted, "I'd assume not Luchenko and that bunch at the far end, for a start—Nolan and the rest."

Koh frowned. "I'm not so convinced Nolan is one of them," he said at last. "I don't doubt he's a true believer, but that doesn't mean they'd trust him enough to be a plant. Their leaders tend to be contemptuous of true Marxists, you know. Stalin wasn't at all happy when Beria proposed recruiting upward-bound idealists from English universities back in the nineteen-thirties. He didn't think people who believed such twaddle could make reliable spies."

At least Koh was talking more out here than he usually did. McCain sought to keep it going. "What motivates people like Nolan?" he asked.

"Fear of freedom."

"That sounds like a strange thing to say."

"Not if you think about it. In the long term, humanity is evolving toward the emergence of individualism. Merging the Western philosophy of individual freedom and the political and economic principles that go with that into its own culture is probably the greatest single thing that has happened to Asia. It's the force that is shaping the twenty-first century."

"The good old American system."

"Yes. But nobody ever said it had to stay in America. In any case, it originated in Europe."

"Okay."

Koh went on, "But sometimes social changes are too fast for people to adapt to. When that happens, people are left feeling insecure, threatened by forces they don't understand and can't cope with. So they try to escape by turning the clock back. Early social orders like the feudal systems suppressed individuality, but in return they provided security and certainty. You knew who you were, where you belonged, and what was expected of you—as in childhood, where the authority of the family constrains, but at the same time protects."

"Children have to grow up eventually."

"Yes, and so do people. But when the change is too fast and leaves them feeling isolated, people turn to authoritarianism for the certainty and security they have lost. Hence the rise of Reformation religions of Luther and Calvin when European feudalism collapsed. The middle classes flocked to prostrate themselves before an all-powerful God whose strength would protect them."

"That's just about what happened with Nazi Germany, too," McCain said as he worked.

"Precisely. They weren't ready to become a liberal democracy when the Allies tried to impose it on them after 1918. They, too, yearned for the kind of authority they were used to, and for a strong leader who would take responsibility and make the decisions." Koh shrugged. "And they found one." He lifted a hand from his rake to gesture vaguely at the colony around them. "And the same thing is true of this Soviet political monstrosity. Progressive? Pah! Nothing of the kind. It's the last relic of an order that's on its way out."

"You and Scanlon seem to talk about that kind of thing a lot," McCain said.

"Aren't all the Irish supposed to be philosophers of life, 'which means everything'?" Koh replied.

McCain straightened up and drew a handkerchief from his pants pocket to wipe the sheen of perspiration from his forehead. "Getting back to Scanlon," he said. "About four days ago he told me—"

Koh cut him off with a wave of his hand. "You can save yourself the lengthy explanation." He nodded toward the truck a hundred yards back along the road, which carried the tools, lunch bags, and other oddments. "When you pick up your jacket, look in the inside pocket. You will find something there that should answer your questions. Think of it as a gesture of good faith by the escape committee. They feel there might be grounds for you and them to get together. I get the impression that you feel the same way."

"Then it does really exist?"

"Certainly."

"But how? . . ."

Koh smiled and shook his head. "Never mind how I know the things I know. Let's just say, Mr. Earnshaw, that both of us know something about the intelligence business."

CHAPTER TWENTY-EIGHT

When the gas pedal of an automobile is pressed harder, the vehicle goes faster. Within the throttle's operating range, the output of the process changes smoothly with input. The mathematical relationship connecting the two is an example of a "linear" function. When pressure is steadily increased on the trigger of a gun, on the other hand, the operation is markedly nonlinear: nothing much happens until the mechanism is on the point of tripping, after which an infinitesimally small further increase of input brings about an abrupt and spectacular change in system output—the gun fires.

Most mathematical representations of nature take the form of functions that change smoothly. The real-world processes that they model, however, invariably lead to discontinuities when taken far enough, and the models turn out to be merely approximations that are close enough to be useful over limited ranges. Thus, solids eventually melt, liquids boil, a star condenses, or a new species emerges: suddenly a phase change occurs in which the former behavior breaks down, new laws supplant the old, and all the previous limits and projections cease to mean anything. These boundaries are the places where the really interesting things in nature happen. Crossing them is what is called Evolution.

Paula had received her first insight into the astonishing complexities that can arise from nonlinear systems when she was studying complex-number theory at college. A "complex" number consists of two independent parts, like the latitude and longitude components of a map reference. And like the points on a map, the total field of all complex numbers can be represented by the infinity of points on a plane—unlike ordinary, one-part numbers, all of which can be represented by the points on an endless line. Now, infinitely many points exist between any two points on a plane, however close to each other they might be; and an infinity of numbers exists between any two of the numbers in the complex-number plane. Therefore, if an arbitrary path is traced across the plane, the value of the numbers that the path passes over will change smoothly with the distance moved: an infinitesimally small change of position will yield an infinitesimally small change in number value. There are no sudden jumps.

The function that particularly excited Paula is called the "Mandelbrot Set," and has been described as the most complicated object known to mathematics. Yet the method of generating it is amazingly uncomplicated. A point is taken on the complex plane, and the number that it corresponds to is used as the input to a simple equation. The equation is then evaluated to produce a result. Depending on the range that the result falls in, a color is assigned to the corresponding point on a display screen. Repeating the procedure for all the other points generates a color map of how the result obtained changes from place to place for the originally smooth-changing number field. The outcome is not a mixture of formless patches as might be supposed, which would denote lumplike properties varying steadily from region to region. Instead, what emerges is highly organized, infinitely detailed *structure!* Totally unexpected discontinuities and instabilities appear, in which the minutest variations of input send the results fleeing away to infinity; and yet a curious connectedness remains, producing spirals, snowflakes, filaments, and strangely beautiful compound forms, ever-varying in an unending regress of successive levels of detail down to whatever resolution might be explored.

Reflecting on how a simple mathematical relationship could create such astounding richness of form out of nothing more than a smoothly graded number field, Paula had suddenly made the connection to the generation of form and structure in the natural world—for the shapes and whirls and connecting threads revealed in the graphics imagery *were* compellingly evocative of the structures found in nature. And was not the entire physical universe the product of physical "processors" operating analogously upon steadily varying gradients of electric and magnetic fields, chemical concentrations, pressures, temperatures, velocities, and densities, from the molecular fields that guide the differentiation of growing embryos to the ridges and chasms of space-time that mold galaxies? That was when she had experienced her first true excitement at the world of physical sciences, from which had grown the compulsion to comprehend more of its workings that she had known ever since.

She was reminded of those natural hairspring mechanisms now, as she sat staring at a display screen in a computer-graphics lab in the Government Center at Turgenev. One of the things the *Valentina Tereshkova* experiment was revealing already was that there was still much to be learned about maintaining complex closed ecologies. With Olga's help, Paula had ended up working in a section of the Environmental Department, creating computer models of plant and microorganism interaction cycles. The hope was eventually to integrate such models into a comprehensive simulation of the colony's entire biology—although that goal could easily be still many years away. She traveled with an escorted party of others to Turgenev every day through a five-day week, and back to Zamork in the evening. She spent most of her time there in the graphics lab of the central computer facility. The lab was located in a less restricted part of the same general computing complex in which Magician had met his downfall.

On the screen, an intricate, constantly changing network of colored symbols interconnected by flow lines and feedback loops modeled dynamically the collective metabolism of one of the closed aquatic ecosystems being tested in the biolab area at Landausk. Currently the ecology inside *Valentina Tereshkova* was sustained by using industrial engineering processes to produce atmospheric gases, recycle water, and remove wastes. The longer-term intention was to develop a self-regulating biological system to perform these functions—an Earth-type ecology in miniature. But the subtleties and complexities of the interactions involved, even in a small, isolated aquatic system simpler than any farmyard pond, were endless and fascinating. She had thought for a long time at the back of her mind about quitting the Air Force and defense work for a field to which she could devote herself with total absorption. But for some reason she had always put it off for just one more year. . . .

The door of the room opened and Olga came in. She had tied her orange hair high and was carrying some books and a sheaf of papers, which she set down on the desk behind Paula's chair. "Still busy, I see," she said. "I talked to Stefan and got the things you said you wanted to read. Here they are."

Paula turned her chair away from the screen. "Thanks."

"How are things going?"

"Oh . . . more complicated than we expected, but interesting. How much longer before the Zamork bus leaves?"

"About an hour. Why? Do you want to take the later one again? I'm sure it can be arranged."

"Yes."

Olga smiled. "A prisoner applying for overtime. Whoever heard of anything like it?"

"I feel like a person again."

"I was only teasing. I understand." She nodded at the screen. "Are you on the track of what went wrong in test tank three?"

"I think so. The green algae blooms support the fish as food and produce oxygen. Also, they detoxify some of the harmful gases, such as ammonia. The problem with the way it's set up is that the system won't produce a dense algae population, no matter what you do. So it pollutes itself through oxygen starvation."

"Any idea why?"

"The macrophytic plants that they put in as purifiers upstream to oxygenate the shell-bacterial filters also produce an antibiotic that interferes with the reproduction cycle of the algae," Paula said. "But it would be difficult to eliminate them, since they supply feed for the White Chinese Amur fish. So we need some way to break down the antibiotic. Bigheaded carp cause blue-green algae to predominate, whereas Silver Chinese carp, which are phytoplankton eaters, produce a shift toward diatom algae." She sighed. "The whole ecology changes completely with even a slight shift in fish-species composition. In other words, the way they're trying to do it doesn't have enough resilience against change. It's too sensitive. It needs more negative feedback."

Olga looked impressed. "Did you work all this out?"

"No I picked it up from the biologists. I'm just helping out with the software."

Olga moved round the desk and sat down in the chair on the far side. "This kid of thing really interests you, doesn't it," she said.

"Biology?"

"Not that, so much. I know you're a physicist."

Paula leaned her chair back and stretched out a leg to rest her foot on the edge of the console. "Evolution interests me—not in the biological sense especially, but the way order and complexity emerge out of chaos, generally."

"That's what I mean: the underlying processes common to all of science." Olga seemed to be trying to say that science, the common search for truth, was something that united people of all races and nationalities. They adhered to the same standards of ethics and intellectual honesty, and spoke the same language. Deception—especially self-deception—was the only enemy, and it was the enemy of all of them.

Paula looked across the desk and met the Russian woman's questioning look. "Yes, exactly," she said. In other words, they were both on the same side of something that had nothing to do with flags or frontiers. She looked around the room and up at the ceiling, shrugged, and sighed. Olga nodded her head, acknowledging that there was nothing more they could safely say just there and then. But Paula sensed that Olga had accomplished what she'd come in for.

The met again later that evening back at Zamork, on the gray beach fringing the reservoir. The strip-suns overhead were fading in simulated dusk, and other figures were out, making the best of the brief evening that would persist until the perimeter lights were switched on. A cool breeze was coming across the water. Olga turned up the collar of the coat she was wearing over her tunic, and they began walking slowly along the water's edge toward where the beach ended at the hull wall.

"Would it come as any great surprise to you to learn that I might have had my own reasons for agreeing to help you that day back in the infirmary?" Olga asked.

At the time, Paula had been too overwrought with her own circumstances, and later too relieved to know she would be escaping from them, to think about it. But since settling in to her new status, she had wondered. "No, it wouldn't," she answered honestly.

"I have no interest in political ideologies," Olga went on. "They are nothing but medieval religion and superstition, hiding behind different slogans. Their purpose is the same: to control the minds of people through dogmatism and manipulation. Neither system respects truth, freedom, or any form of independent thinking, or tolerates opposing opinions. The inquisitors of Galileo were no more interested in the way the Earth moves than American creationists care about the true origins of life on this planet. The real issue in both cases is that of traditional, unquestioned authority being challenged."

"But with science it's different," Paula completed. "Okay, we see eye to eye on all that. So, where is this leading?"

"Along with others, I came to the conclusion that the ethic and rationality of the scientific approach to understanding reality could help form the basis of a saner world," Olga replied. "But Neanderthal political systems stood in the way—particularly the ones like ours that suppress free expression, which is essential if anything better is to evolve. So I became politically active as a dissident, and upset a lot of people in the process. To cut a long story short, I ended up losing my academic titles, being arrested, and eventually getting shipped up here."

Paula nodded. "So?"

"The dissidents that I worked with are still active back there," Olga said. "Most of them are the kind of people that we have talked about—*our* kind of people: scientists, intellectuals, and thinkers who believe in the possibility of a safer, more civilized world based on reason and honesty." They had neared the point where the wall of the outer hull rose sheer at the water's edge. Behind them, the ground above the beach rose steeply to become the hill forming the valley side, lined with the huts of the special VIP's. They stopped, and Olga turned to face Paula directly. "Many others were arrested over the years. We could never find out what had happened to them. But when I came to Zamork, I found many of them up here, alive and well."

"Go on," Paula said, still not seeing any connection with herself.

Olga's voice dropped instinctively, even though they were alone. "I managed to establish a way of communicating with somebody down there."

"To Earth?"

"Yes. I was able to send information about the people who were up here—there were colleagues down there who could make good use of such information, besides friends and relatives who needed to be told. And more than that. With early notification of the new arrivals up here, our people down in Russia knew who else was at risk—the KGB works in predictable patterns. Many were smuggled out of the country in good time. The KGB was going insane trying to discover where the information was coming from."

"Well, that great, but why are you telling me all this?" Paula said.

"The channel was cut, due to an accident. I need a communications specialist to restore it. Now I'm asking you to help me."

So *that* was what had caught Olga's interest in the infirmary. Now it all fitted together. They turned and began retracing their steps slowly along the beach. Lights were coming on around the perimeter and along the wire barrier twenty yards out in the water. "How did it work?" Paula asked.

"Does that mean you will help?"

"I don't know at this stage if I can. You'll have to tell me more about it."

"I once had a lover who was a university professor," Olga replied. "Let's call him Ivan. Oh, it wasn't so terribly serious—he was formerly a Navy man, and quite active with the ladies from Archangel to

Vladivostok, I suspect. But whatever, we found that we shared certain values, and we remained good friends even after the passionate stage wore off."

"What kind of professor is he?"

"Was—communications engineering. But now he's at a research establishment in Siberia. It also happens to be the groundstation that handles the main communications link from *Valentina Tereshkova.*" Olga turned her head to glance at Paula as they walked. "Now do you see?"

Paula stopped walking, and her eyes narrowed. Olga waited. "The place you've got me into at Turgenev . . . that's no coincidence either, is it?" Paula said slowly. "It's practically next door to the Communications Center."

"You catch on fast," Olga murmured. They resumed walking. Olga continued, "I assume you're familiar with the random-number streams that are used as fillers between messages on secure channels as routine procedure."

Paula saw the implication immediately. "You piggy-backed on the beam, using the gaps."

"Right."

"How?"

"Ivan smuggled a specially programmed electronic chip up to me via a flight-deck officer on one of the transporters. It was designed to replace the random-number generator in the encoding processor of the primary Earthside commlink, inside the Communications Center. The way it worked was, first I'd plug the chip into a BV-Fifteen and preload it with the message text that I wanted to send—I could do that myself anywhere. Then a certain insider whose name doesn't matter would switch the chip inside the Communications Center for me, and the message was transmitted automatically."

"Okay, I get it." Paula nodded. The BV-15 was a standard Soviet general-purpose computer, used as a net terminal or stand-alone system and found all over *Tereshkova.* There were two of them in the graphics lab where Paula worked. "So what went wrong?"

"There was an equipment fault that caused a power surge and blew up the chip," Olga replied simply. "I still have my contact inside the Communications Center. The procedure should still work. But we no longer have the hardware."

"And you want me to program a new chip," Paula concluded.

"Exactly. I have specifications of the BV-Fifteen program for loading the chip, and I can get documentation for the transmission encoders. You already have access to the equipment you need in the graphics lab. There would be no need for you to physically enter the Communications Center itself, or any other secure area."

"What about the messages coming in from Earth?" Paula asked. "How do you handle them?"

"I can take care of that myself," Olga answered.

"If we do it, is there any guarantee Ivan will still be listening after all this time?"

"No. Let's just hope that he is."

They stood looking in silence at the lights and the water for a while. "When do you want an answer?" Paula asked at last.

"I was hoping for one now."

"I have to think about it."

"Tomorrow, then?"

"Okay, tomorrow."

When they met the next day, Paula had been having some ideas of her own about how a private communications link to Earth might prove useful, too—except that the people she had in mind to communicate with had nothing to do with Soviet intellectual dissidents or with spiriting fugitives out of Russia. How she might be able to extend the link from the groundstation in Siberia to the West's military-communications network, she at present hadn't the faintest idea. But in the meantime, the opportunity for setting up the first phase was too good to miss. Her fingertips were already itching impatiently at the prospect.

"All right," she told Olga. "You've got yourself a deal. Let's hope Ivan's still listening—I'll give it a try."

◎ CHAPTER TWENTY-NINE ◎

McCain rinsed off the suds and dried his face briskly with his towel in front of the mirror. Gonares was working at the hub again that week, and had been bringing back descriptions and sketches as McCain had asked. From his initial perusals of them, they seemed to McCain to bear out the officially published construction plans. Maybe Foleda had allowed himself to get carried away for once.

The door opened as if a grizzly bear had swiped at it, and Oskar Smovak came in. He threw down a plastic box containing his soap and shaving gear, and began peeling off his shirt. "Sounds as if we're going to be getting the place spruced up before very much longer, eh, Lew?" he said, leaning forward to examine his beard in the mirror.

"How come?"

"This place is going to be the big attraction."

"Zamork?"

"No, the whole of *Tereshkova*. Haven't you heard?"

"Heard what?"

"Big celebrations for the centenary. All the Russian bigwigs will be coming here—First Secretary Petrokhov, Chairman of the Council of Ministers, Kavansky, the whole Politburo, most of the Central Committee . . . *Tereshkova* will be the showpiece of the Communist world." November 7 was the day the Soviets traditionally celebrated the Revolution. This year would be extra special, since it was the centenary.

"Well, don't forget to write down all your complaints and suggestions," McCain grunted.

When McCain came out of the washroom, he found Luchenko sitting with Nolan at the end table. Andreyov was reading something to Borowski nearby, and Taugin was lying morosely on his bunk. King and Kong, as usual, were hovering not especially inconspicuously in the background. Luchenko caught McCain's eyes and tilted his head to beckon him over. McCain stopped.

"You have been getting good reports from your work detail," Luchenko said. "I'm glad to see it."

"I like to think I earn my keep," McCain answered.

"You seem to be behaving yourself more these days."

"People are leaving me alone more these days."

Luchenko let the remark pass. "Just to show that such things do not go unrecognized, I will be assigning you to more outside duties around the colony," he said. "I trust you will find that agreeable."

McCain raised his eyebrows in genuine surprise. It fitted in with his own aims perfectly. "Sure," he replied. "I like to be out and about."

"Of course. Well, just so you know what to expect." Luchenko stared up with an expression that said he had made a concession and would be expecting some reciprocation. McCain returned a look that said maybe, and moved on. He guessed that Luchenko had had no choice, so was making it look like a favor. In other words, Luchenko had been notified that there was going to be need for a lot of outside work around the colony. It fitted with what Smovak had just said.

Charlie Chan was with Irzan and Nunghan, who were dealing cards over a bunk in one of the middle sections. "I know a funny joke," he said, catching McCain by the sleeve as he passed.

"Oh?"

Charlie Chan shook, barely able to contain himself. "A Russian from Moscow goes into a Yakut's hut on the tundra and sees a glove hanging from the ceiling. He says, 'What's that?' And the Yakut replies, 'A cow's udder.'"

"Go on."

"That's it. A cow's udder!"

Chan collapsed onto his bunk, where he lay shrieking and writhing with mirth. McCain walked on, shaking his head. He still hadn't managed to fathom Charlie Chan's weird humor. Maybe it was a glimpse of how it had all begun, he mused—the first dazzling insight to metaphor, back in the winter gloom of some Neanderthal cave, which had evolved down through the ages from those beginnings through the court jester and the music hall, to Buster Keaton, Laurel and Hardy, the banana peel and the custard pie.

"I know another one just as good," Charlie Chan's voice offered behind him as he reached the front section.

"Tomorrow," McCain called back. "I couldn't stand it."

Mungabo was sitting on the top bunk, sewing a tear in his pants, and Rashazzi and Haber were debating something abstruse at the center table. Scanlon and Koh were sitting on opposite bunks in the bay on the far side, and seemed to be talking about the evolution of cultures again. McCain wandered around the table behind the two scientists and sat down next to Koh. "Smovak tells me we're going to be getting some visitors," McCain said.

Koh nodded. "So it appears. I've also heard a rumor of amnesties being granted—part of the public-relations spectaculars. They plan on making this a big event."

"Does that mean we're all going home?"

"I wouldn't hold my breath. If there's anything to it at all, it probably only applies to the privs."

The talking and the activity among the occupants of the billet's front section were to cover their underlying tension in the time left before lights-out. For tonight was when they would make their first attempt at breaking through into the underfloor space.

"Koh was just saying some fascinating things about history," Scanlon told McCain. "And isn't that something you're always talking about yourself?"

"It was one of my majors, sure," McCain replied.

Koh nodded. "We were discussing the European Renaissance."

"Except that the man's saying it wasn't a Renaissance at all," Scanlon said.

"The term is a misnomer." Koh settled himself more comfortably on the bunk. "It was the *birth* of a new culture, not a rebirth of anything." McCain remembered hearing this before. But on the last occasion, Koh had been smoking his herbal mixture and had become incoherent before he could get any further. Koh went on, "Teachers and professors like to think that their subjects are part of a glorious legacy that spans down through the ages in an unbroken succession from the distant past. It gives them a feeling of noble pedigree. So they present architecture, or art, or mathematics, or whatever as a continuum and divide it into periods that they call Classical, Medieval, Modern, and so on. But the continuity they see is an illusion. Each culture possesses its own unique way of conceptualizing reality—a collective mindset that determines how the world is perceived. And everything which a culture creates—its art, its technology, its political and economic system—is unavoidably part of an expression of its unique worldview. Oh, it's true that a culture might adopt some things it finds useful from others that went before, but that doesn't constitute a lineage. The splendor of Rome was the voice of the Roman worldview; the New York skyline spoke of America. They were products of different minds and perceptions. There was no line of descent from one to the other."

The ceiling lights blinked three times to signal five minutes to lights-out. Haber and Rashazzi got up from the table and came over. McCain moved his legs to make room for Haber to sit down. Rashazzi stepped up to the top bunk and turned to sit with his legs dangling over the side.

Koh continued, "Rome was an expression of Classical Man who never mastered the concept of infinity, but shrank from it at every encounter. Look at his pictures and vase paintings. They show only foregrounds, never any background. You see—they avoid the challenges of distance and limitless extent. His temples were dominated by frontages that denied and suppressed inner space. He shunned the open ocean and seldom sailed out of sight of land. His world was timeless: its past lay hidden in an obscure, unchanging realm of gods, and he made no plans or provision for any future. . . . In other words, everything that Classical Man created expressed the same thing: perception of a world that was finite and bounded. Even his mathematics confined itself to the study of finite, static objects: geometric figures bounded by lines; solids bounded by planes. Time was never recognized as a dynamic variable—that was what confounded Zeno and led to insoluble paradoxes. And Classical Man's number system contained no negatives and no irrationals—not because he was intellectually incapable of dealing with them, but simply because his worldview encompassed nothing that such entities were needed to describe. In a finite, tangible world, numbers merely enumerate finite, tangible objects. And it was perfectly natural that the form of art that dominated his culture should be sculptures: static, finite objects bounded by surfaces."

Rashazzi seemed about to say something, then rubbed his chin thoughtfully and nodded, evidently deciding not to interrupt. The sound of Smovak bellowing about something came from farther along the billet.

"But Classical Man died, and Europe stagnated through the centuries of its Dark Ages before Western Man appeared. That's the way every new culture arises: nothing significant happens for thousands of years, and then, suddenly, a new breed of Man with a new worldview bursts forth in a frenzy of creativity that sweeps the old order away. Western Man appeared out of the wreckage when European feudalism collapsed—not as a reincarnation of Classical Man, who was gone forever, but born in his own right, from his own beginnings.

"Western Man not only comprehended change and infinity, he delighted in them—with a restless, thrusting energy, the like of which the world had never seen. After the stagnation of the Dark Ages, everything that spoke for him was an exultation of the newfound freedoms that they symbolized. The calculus of Newton and Leibnitz was the language of a universe no longer static and bounded, but dynamic and unlimited, to be explored through the scientific passion for discovery and the voyages of the global navigators. His mastery of perspective and soaring Gothic arches rejoiced in the experience of boundless, endless space. And what was his dominant form of art, which reached its zenith of expression along with the high point of his culture in the eighteenth century? Music, of course. For what else is the music of Mozart and Beethoven than flute and strings exploring vast, orchestra-created voids—the flourishes of baroque porticoes and the curves of the infinitesimal calculus, the commitment to reason and the power of intellect—set to sound?"

Koh paused and stared solemnly into the space opposite him. His voice took on an edge of regret. "But, like Classical Man before him—in fact, any organism that is born lives out its span and dies—he was not immortal. And like Classical Man he balked before realities that his nature was unable to assimilate. The problems that have plagued him since are the consequences."

"You mean the problems we're in right now, today?" Rashazzi said.

"Yes. Whereas Classical Man couldn't come to terms with infinities of space and time, what confounded Western Man was the confrontation with physical infinities: the infinity of potential growth and achievement that is implicit in the evolutionary process itself and in the creative power of the intelligent mind. For although free of the tyranny of feudalism, Western Man is essentially Malthusian in his worldview: always bounded by the currently perceived limits and possibilities. He extended his vision to the horizon, but not beyond it. As the continuous functions of his mathematics aptly symbolize, his is a world that changes smoothly, an orderly, civilized world, unable to accommodate to sudden leaps. Was it mere coincidence, then, that the world of Western Man fell apart at the end of the nineteenth century, when it came face-to-face with the discontinuities of relativity, quantum mechanics, evolution, and the implications of industrialized economic growth? He couldn't cope with phase changes. Oh, some individuals played with the concepts academically in the same way that Zeno played with mathematical infinities; but the collective mind-set of Western Man was unable to *feel* what the concepts *meant*. And so, he has foundered into his own, cultureless, Dark Age."

The lights-out warning flashed. "Time to break it up, you lot at the end," Smovak's voice called out. "Let's have some quiet."

"Oskar, you make more noise than all of those guys put together,"

Mungabo shot back from the far side of the table. The group dispersed back to their own bunks.

"'Tis a small part we are of everything, when ye think about it, and that's the truth," Scanlon said from across the aisle as McCain climbed into bed.

"What makes you so interested in all that stuff of Koh's?" McCain asked.

"I'm not sure. It's a new way of looking at things." Scanlon paused. "I suppose a man likes to think that what he is and what he does will add a little to something that matters. Like them stones that Koh talks about . . . Wouldn't anyone rather think that what he did would be built into something worthwhile than be left in the rubble?" McCain turned his head and looked across at him. Scanlon was staring up at the ceiling, deep in thought. Then the lights went out.

A half hour later, McCain was lying in the dark, waiting for his senses to register the pattern of stillness that would tell him that the billet had settled down for the night. It was possible that the surveillance might include infrared sensors capable of tracking body movements in the darkness or other devices that Rashazzi had failed to detect—but there had to be some risks.

"Okay?" he breathed into the darkness when he judged the time to be right.

"Okay," Scanlon's voice whispered back.

"On your way," Mungabo muttered above.

McCain raised his head and whistled quietly through his teeth. A similar signal acknowledged from the far side, which meant Rashazzi agreed. McCain lifted his blanket aside and rolled noiselessly onto the floor. He slid the drawer out from underneath his bunk and placed it on top, then turned and removed Scanlon's drawer also, lifting it up on top of his own. Then he moved out between his and Scanlon's bunks toward the center space of the billet. The black-clad shape of Rashazzi was already wriggling along the floor on the far side of the table to meet him. McCain reached under the table and grasped the ends of the wires that Rashazzi pushed through for him. Then he crawled back between the bunks, passed one wire to Scanlon, and drew the other into the space underneath his own bunk, where the drawer had been.

The "gesture of good faith" that Koh had brought for McCain from the escape committee had turned out to be a set of wiring diagrams showing the layout of heating, lighting, and security circuits, which were standardized and the same for every billet. In particular, they showed the locations of the conducting strips on the backs of the structural panels, and their connection points to the alarm wiring. The information would make it possible to bore holes in just the right places to attach jumper leads for bypassing the breaks, *without* having to disturb any panels beforehand. Then, with luck, they would be able to lift the bypassed floorpanel and explore the recesses beneath without triggering the alarm system. That was the purpose of the night's experiment.

Apparently the escape committee had obtained the diagrams through bribery followed by blackmail from a Russian electrician. Exactly who the committee were, or at least which of them were responsible for this particular venture, Koh hadn't said. Their problem was that they were in a billet on the upper level, and going down from there would simply have brought them through the ceiling of the billets below. Hence they needed the cooperation of people who were already on the lower level.

McCain and Scanlon had spent much of the previous night taking turns to lie in the narrow space between the bunks, laboriously cutting two saucer-size holes through the soft-alloy floorplates in the positions indicated on the diagrams. McCain removed the disk on his side, which had been resealed with a compound of aluminum dust and a nonsetting goo that Rashazzi had concocted, and felt beneath the floorplate for the low-voltage cable running beneath the hole. He scraped an inch of the cable bare and attached the wire that Rashazzi had passed from across the room, securing it with adhesive tape. Meanwhile Scanlon had done the same on his side, hanging his arm around the edge of his bunk. There was nothing more for them to do now until Rashazzi completed the more complicated connections on the far side of the room. When that was done, they would have constructed a bridge circuit across the end of the billet, bypassing the pattern of contact strips beneath the floor. While Rashazzi worked on the wiring, Haber and Koh, working from the bunks on either side, should already have taken the heads off the remaining rivets holding down the panel.

"How are we doing?" Scanlon's voice whispered from the darkness close to McCain's ear.

"It's attached. I'm waiting for Razz." Rashazzi would be measuring resistances and voltages before he risked breaking the circuit.

"Any bets on what's downstairs?"

"Probably bilgewater." Only McCain and Rashazzi would actually be going. There was no need for a circus.

At last, the wire in McCain's fingers jerked three times. He acknowledged. "That's it," he told Scanlon. "They've got the plate up. I guess this is it."

"Good luck, Lew."

McCain crawled back to the center space and stopped to listen, but could detect nothing abnormal. Moving slowly and soundlessly, he crossed the center between the end of the table and the door, and then moved toward the space between the two opposite bunks.

He found the edge of the hole with his fingers. Rashazzi had already gone down. Haber reached out in the darkness and handed him a purloined flashlight and a cloth bag containing tools, some nylon rope, and other items that might come in useful. McCain patted the German's arm, and then lowered himself full-length down into the opening between the bunks. He felt hard protrusions and structural beams around him, all the more constricting and entombing in the total darkness now pressing in from every side. Then he heard the floorplate being replaced above him.

Light appeared ahead, silhouetting Rashazzi's form against a clutter of supporting members, pipework, and cabling. There was little clearance, and McCain's first thought was to wonder if the expedition might have ended already, right there. They began examining the surroundings methodically inch by inch, shifting their flashlights to opposite hands and rolling over to study first one side, then the other. Rashazzi spent some time on his back, examining the conduction strips from the underside. One of the tasks for tonight would be to install a second bypass circuit below the floor, so that in future they'd be able to lift the plate up again without repeating the whole procedure every time. They found no sign of surveillance devices in the below-floor space. Then Rashazzi began worming his way forward. McCain could see nothing of what lay ahead, since Rashazzi's body was between him and the light.

After he had progressed eight feet or so, Rashazzi stopped and began moving the light around to reconnoiter. McCain moved up behind him. It was a tight squeeze. Than, as Rashazzi continued angling his lamp this way and that, a glint of light caught McCain's eye for an instant, reflecting off something *below*. He pointed his own lamp down between two of the metal ribs he was lying on, and brought his face close to peer along the beam. There was a much roomier space down there, with glimpses of machinery. Suddenly McCain realized that he and Rashazzi were not truly in the below-floor space at all. They were lying in a shallow frame carrying pipes and cables immediately beneath the flooring; the true interdeck compartment was still beneath them. He tapped Rashazzi's leg, and light blinded him as Rashazzi aimed his lamp back to look over his shoulder. McCain pointed at the metal work beneath them and jabbed his finger up and down several times. Rashazzi understood and probed the darkness beneath with his beam, but from where they were, there was no way down. Rashazzi continued wriggling forward, stopping after another ten feet or so to let McCain catch up.

By now they were well under the next billet, if not beyond, with a steady background of humming and throbbing coming from the darkness beneath. Rashazzi shone his lamp ahead to check the next stretch. Then he emitted a soft "Ahah!" and resumed crawling. McCain followed and saw that a large pipe that had been walling them in on the right made a sudden turn away, leaving a gap in the side of the frame large enough to squeeze through. Rashazzi was already lowering himself down. Then he provided the light while McCain joined him.

They were in a space barely high enough to stoop in, standing on a metal floor. Around them were runs of ducting, blowers and other machinery, pillars and braces supporting the deck above, and a maze of pipework. Shining their lights upward, they could see the frame they'd been crawling inside. They spent some time checking again for surveillance devices, but could find nothing. "It looks clean," Rashazzi whispered, finally. "You know, I think we might just have done it—a place where we can avoid surveillance, without having to get out of Zamork."

"Maybe," McCain replied. "Let's check out some more of it."

They had already agreed that to get as far from the known parts of Zamork as they could, they would continue exploring downward rather than laterally if they did get below the billet, and accordingly they set to work examining the floor. It consisted of reinforced metal plates secured by spotwelds. Rashazzi had made a hand-operated trepan-like device for cutting sheet metal away around such welds, but it would be tedious and time-consuming. Rather than commit themselves to such a task, they moved along to the next panel, but found the same thing. And with the next; and the next. But the one after that was different: it was secured not by welds, but by snap fasteners.

"Considerate," McCain grunted. "Must be removable for maintenance or something."

Rashazzi shrugged in the torchlight. Without further ado, he loosened the panel and lifted it aside. Below was a shallow space containing a lighting fixture in what was apparently the ceiling of yet another level below. The Israeli felt in one of his pockets for an electrician's screwdriver tipped with a neon indicator and squatted down to probe around the connections. The neon failed to light. "It's not live, anyway," Rashazzi said.

They turned their lamps off while McCain tested the ceiling panel. It lifted freely and showed no trace of light from below. Rashazzi switched his lamp on again, while McCain swung the panel upward on its cables and lodged it to one side. They peered down through the gap and made out more machinery, with portions of metal flooring some distance below; but it was difficult to judge how far. McCain unraveled the rope from his bag and lowered one end down while Rashazzi tied the other end to a pillar. McCain checked that his bag was securely tied at his waist, then swung his legs into the hole and lowered himself down hand over hand until his feet found the floor below. Rashazzi followed.

They were in a narrow walkway that could have been intended for maintenance. It led between pumps, transformers, and large, squat cylinders wreathed in pipes, that seemed to be storage tanks. Or perhaps it could have been used during construction of *Valentina Tereshkova,* for the absence of power in the ceiling light suggested that the place was visited infrequently. "I wonder where this leads," McCain said. "We might have an open gateway here, right out of Zamork, anytime." The floorplates this time, however, were solidly seam-welded, precluding any possibility of penetrating further in the downward direction without enormous effort. They began exploring the surroundings.

Farther on, another walkway went off to one side. They followed it between the last of the storage tanks and girderwork abutting a bulkhead to a series of bays containing power-distribution equipment and banks of enormous batteries—a backup supply system for emergency power. An intermediate deck split the space beyond into two levels. The upper level was cluttered with more piping and structural work. But the lower space, the floor of which was actually sunken a few feet to make it considerably deeper and roomier than it appeared from even a short distance away, was comparatively empty. Conceivably it had been left as expansion space in which to install more equipment at some later date. McCain and Rashazzi glanced at each other in the torchlight, then moved closer and lowered themselves down into the space.

It went back perhaps twenty feet, ending at a solid bulkhead wall, which Rashazzi estimated could well be the near side of Gorky Street, extending down to the lower levels. That fitted with the mental map that McCain had been constructing, too. A wall of cable guides running between roof supports closed in one of the sides, while the other was semi-open to a forest of supports and tiebars that disappeared into the blackness behind the storage tanks.

Rashazzi stroked his chin and looked around. "I don't know where we might be able to get to from here," he said. "It will take some time to check. But you know something, Lew? Think of it—here we are in a pretty secluded place, with another whole level above full of machinery making nice background music to screen out noise. If we could run some power into here from somewhere, this would make the perfect workshop that Albrecht and I were looking for." He nodded and looked around again with evident satisfaction. "Yes, I'd say that tonight's expedition has already been well worth the effort."

◉ CHAPTER THIRTY ◉

The warm, dry summer had done wonders for Myra's health, and by the middle of August her face had regained its color and filled out again. "Yeah, I figure you'll last a few more years yet, at least," Foleda told her approvingly as they sat sipping iced orange juice at a sunshaded table on the veranda at the back of the house.

"Doesn't she look so much better," Ella said from where she was sitting with her legs dangling in the pool, watching Johnny and two other boys of about his age from along the street playing in the water on the far side. "You look like a brand-new woman, Mother."

"I feel like one," Myra replied.

"See," Foleda said. He always managed to look outrageous on his days off, and on this occasion was wearing Bermuda shorts of a deafening tartan, sunglasses, and a straw hat. It reminded Ella of pictures she had seen of Churchill in some of his wartime outfits. "That's what having an attentive husband does for you."

"Are you going to let him get away with that, Mother?" Ella asked Myra.

"Sure, if it works both ways," Myra said. "Because I score higher. I mean, look at the state of him. He hasn't had a day sick for years."

"And people always think that kind of work is so stressful. You're a fraud, Dad—and living off us taxpayers, too."

"Nonsense. I work hard all the time. It's the best deal you people ever got—worth every penny."

"How come no heart attacks, then?"

"The light heart and inner tranquility that come from being honest."

Myra laughed delightedly. "How can you possibly mean it, Bernard? What about the fuss you had last week with the attorney general over that Argentinean minister's hotel suite your people bugged?"

"Hell," Foleda grunted. "I said honest, not legal."

A call-tone came from the screenpad lying by the tray on the table. Myra picked it up and acknowledged. It was Randal, Ella's husband, from inside the house. "Is Bernard there?" he asked. Myra passed the pad over.

"What?" Foleda said.

"There's a news item just coming in about that Russian space colony you're always interested in," Randal told him.

"*Tereshkova*?"

"Yes. I thought maybe you'd like to see it right away. . . . Or I could store it for later."

"No, I'd like to see it now," Foleda said. He started to get up.

"Want me to put it through on the pad out there?"

"No, I'll come inside. Why spoil the party?"

A bright-red beach ball bounced on the surface of the water and bobbed against the poolside, with Johnny splashing after it. "Where are you going, Grandpa?" he called up.

"Just inside for a minute."

"Ask them, they'll know," one of Johnny's friends said, coming across behind him.

"We'll know what?" Ella asked them.

"Which *did* come first, the chicken or the egg?"

"Ask your grandma," Ella answered. Johnny looked at Myra.

"Ask your grandfather," Myra said.

"Didn't they teach you at school that birds evolved from reptiles?" Foleda said as he made to leave.

"Sure."

"Well, there's your answer: dinosaurs were laying eggs before there were any chickens."

Foleda found Randal sprawled along a couch in the window-lounge a half level below the kitchen and dining area, a handpad resting on his knee. "What have we got?" Foleda said, perching himself on an arm of one of the chairs facing the wallscreen across the room.

Randal touched a button and the screen came to life with a view of Moscow's Red Square, showing the Kremlin wall and St. Basil's Cathedral. After a few seconds it switched to columns of parading tanks and missile carriers, and then a line of heavily muffled Soviet leaders saluting from the reviewing stand atop the red-marble mausoleum of Lenin's Tomb. "It came in live a few minutes ago," Randal said.

The commentator's voice-over narrated: "News from Moscow today of a big break with tradition. The customary military parade held every November seventh to celebrate the uprising that brought the Communist Party to power, which has long seemed an inviolable national institution, will not take place in this, the Revolution's centenary year. A spokesman for Tass, the Soviet news agency, announced this morning that this year the occasion will be commemorated out in space. Instead of reviewing the traditional military parade in Red Square—which tends to be a cold business around November in Moscow—the Soviet leaders will be traveling en masse to the experimental space colony *Valentina Tereshkova,* two hundred thousand miles from Earth"—a view had appeared of *Tereshkova* hanging in space, followed by standard shots of a transporter docking at the hub, a view of the Turgenev urban zone, and a harvesting machine at work in one of the agricultural sectors, while the voice continued—"to see not marching soldiers and rockets, but scientists, engineers, farmers, and spaceborne factories. So, what does it mean? Are they sending us one of those famous 'signals' we're always being told about? Some of the experts will be giving us their interpretations later. Frank Peterson talked in Moscow with Mr. Gorlienko, the Soviet foreign minister."

"What do you think?" Randal said to Foleda. "Doesn't that look like a change? Come on, Bernard, give them some credit when it's due. This is exactly the kind of initiative we need more of. We have to reciprocate."

"We'll see." Foleda sounded skeptical.

"Dammit, anyone would think you people wanted a war," Randal said, shaking his head in exasperation.

It was a subject they often argued about. Randal was a psychiatrist. He considered all nuclear weapons immoral and had pronounced the world leadership collectively insane. Foleda, on the other hand, contended that the nuclear-tipped ICBM was the most moral weapon to have been invented since the days when kings led their soldiers into battle. It put the wealthy and powerful of all nations right up in the front line, where the risks were no longer exclusively other people's. "With true democracy," Foleda maintained, "everybody is in the trenches."

On the screen the Soviet foreign minister was telling an interviewer, "Yes, you could describe it as a gesture. We see it as symbolizing the direction of the Soviet Union's commitment to the twenty-first century. Coming in the one hundredth year of our existence as a modern nation, the completion of *Valentina Tereshkova* is a model to the world of what can be accomplished under a communist system. Your economists and experts said it couldn't be done—that our system was too inefficient to achieve any significant nonmilitary goals. They discouraged the emerging nations of the world from trying to emulate us. But we have shown them! Tell us now what we are or are not capable of achieving. That is the direction in which we will continue to grow—stronger and more prosperous. And is it not appropriate that on our centenary, when this policy becomes demonstrable reality, that is where our leaders should be?"

"It's an honest, straightforward, goodwill gesture," Randal said across at Foleda. "Somebody has to start trusting somebody."

Foleda didn't reply, but stared hard at the screen, trying in his mind to reconcile what he had just heard with the most recent trends to be distilled from the various intelligence sources that his people tapped. Deliveries of fuel and supplies to Soviet naval bases had been increasing significantly. The Warsaw Pact nations had announced plans in the weeks ahead for military exercises to be held in Eastern Europe and Siberia that would involve large-scale troop and armor movements. Soviet aircraft had been doing a lot of practice flying lately. Fourteen hospitals near major cities had installed emergency generating equipment in the last three months alone. A KGB general had taken charge of the Soviet civil-defense organization. No single item stood out as grounds for anything conclusive, but taken together they added up to precisely the kind of situation that made intelligence analysts nervous.

But the signs didn't seem to anticipate the same level of activity extending into the longer term. The Soviet military units undergoing mobilization, for example, were not being issued with winter clothing and equipment; the quantities of spare parts being ordered from factories were not consistent with demand requirements extending far into the future. It seemed that whatever they were hatching would happen soon, and was expected to be over with quickly. At a time of acute first-strike apprehensiveness everywhere, such a thought was blood-chilling. And now here was a specific date, less than ten weeks away, slap in the middle of the time frame that seemed to be indicated. Suddenly Foleda felt the sickening certainty that he could already look at a calendar and put his finger on doomsday.

". . . you'd think that some people wanted a war." He realized that Randal had been saying something.

"What are you saying we should do, disarm unilaterally?" he asked, snapping himself back to the present.

"Why not? If we did, they would. Then the problem would have gone away. That's simple enough, surely."

"But suppose you were wrong, and they didn't," Foleda said, his voice still numb. "Would you be willing to run *that* risk? Which would you see as greater?"

Before the exchange could proceed any further, a flashing symbol appeared in the bottom corner of the screen to indicate an incoming call. Randal touched a button on the handpad. "Foledas'. This is Randal."

"Hello, Randal, this is Barbara Haynes, calling Bernard," a woman's voice said from the unit. "Is he around?"

"Hi, Barb. Sure—one moment."

"I'll take it up in the kitchen," Foleda said, relieved at the chance to extricate himself. Randal redirected the call, erased the stored bulletin that they had just watched, and settled back to see what else had come in on the news.

Barbara was calling from a house that the CIA owned on some tree-covered acres in Maryland. "We collected Mrs. Jones and took her to the farm. Everything's fine. Shall I confirm that you'll be coming out tomorrow to talk to her? It meant that Anita Dorkas had arrived from London, been smuggled through the airport despite attempts by Soviet officials to intervene, and was now installed at the safe house."

"Good work," Foleda said. "You bet I'll be there."

The room had a large marble fireplace, a molded plaster ceiling, and high windows with rich, heavy drapes, looking out over lawns and a rose garden. It was furnished traditionally with a slender-legged Georgian sideboard, davenport, side tables, and several settees and wing-backed chairs. A grand piano stood at the far end, inside the arched entranceway from the hall. Anita Dorkas was sitting at one end of the long central table, with Foleda across the corner from her on one side and Barbara on the other. Harry Meech, also from the department, sat at the other end with a portable screenpad, surrounded by files and notes. Gerald Kehrn from the Defense Department was pacing around agitatedly, first studying the pictures on the walls, now picking up a vase, then stooping to examine the china in one of the glass-fronted cabinets.

"And that was enough to make you so certain you'd been discovered?" Foleda said again.

"It wasn't just that. It was a combination of several things," Anita replied. She sounded tired, but not resentful. This kind of thing was necessary and not unexpected. "The behavior of my superior at the embassy that day. The fact that they chose a time when Enriko was away. And when he told me what Shepanov had said—about the woman that my ex-husband had taken up with being arrested—the implications were obvious. Igor—my ex-husband, Professor

Dyashkin—would have come under suspicion immediately. We had both been involved in underground dissident activities, and for all I knew he might have been arrested, too, by then. Either way, it was only a matter of time before they got onto me. I was afraid that if I went in to work the next morning, I would only come out again under arrest, en route for Russia."

"You just walked out," Foleda said. "Not a word to your husband? You didn't say anything? You've never seen him since. Isn't that a little odd?"

"I've already explained: I used him. He was head-to-toe KGB. There was never anything between us as far as I was concerned. I had no qualms in that respect."

"How did he feel about it?"

"As far as I could tell, he saw ours as a normal marriage."

"How would you describe his attitude to your relationship?"

Anita hesitated and searched for words. "He was . . . well, considerate enough in our dealings, I suppose . . . not ungenerous. We had ups and downs occasionally, but on the whole we got along all right. You could have described it as a friendly accommodation, not exactly romantic . . ."

"Was it successful sexually?"

Anita nodded. "Yes, I'd say so."

"But you've just said he was pure KGB," Foleda pointed out. "Earlier, you painted a pretty clear picture for us of your ideological convictions. They're very strong. Wasn't there any basic emotional conflict here? A paradox, maybe?"

"I'm not sure I follow you," Anita said.

"Didn't it bother you to go to bed with a dedicated officer of the KGB?" Barbara asked her.

Anita looked at her squarely, then at Foleda. "No. He was quite good, if you must know. And it is fun. Why not make the best of it?"

"Did he have other women, too?"

"If he did now and then, it wouldn't have surprised me."

"Would the thought have troubled you?"

"No."

"How about yourself?"

"Never among the embassy staff. I couldn't afford to risk compromising my own work."

"But elsewhere? Your illegal contacts in London?"

"There was one, yes."

"You didn't contact him the night you decided to get away—before you called the SIS number?"

"No."

"Why not?"

"It simply wasn't that strong a thing. I needed help, not friendship."

Foleda nodded, satisfied, while Meech scribbled furiously at the far end of the table and tapped buttons on his screenpad. It would have been easy for Anita to have tried harder to justify her action by depicting herself as having had a rougher time from her husband, and putting more blame on him for the problem. What she had said didn't have the ring of a cover story about it.

There was a short pause. Anita refilled her water glass from the pitcher on the table, took a sip, and lit a cigarette.

"Getting back to Professor Dyashkin," Kehrn said over his shoulder from across the room. "You and he were married when, did you say?"

"August third, 2003," Anita replied.

"And divorced? . . ."

"2011. I forget the precise date."

"In Moscow."

"Yes."

"Which was after he'd begun his affair with Olga . . ."

"Olga Oshkadov. Yes."

"But before he moved to Sokhotsk."

"Where?" Anita frowned. "I've never heard of that place."

Kehrn made a pretense of forgetfulness. "Oh, that's right, I'm sorry. You didn't keep in touch, did you?" Meech nodded to himself unconsciously as he recalled earlier answers onto the screen for comparison. Kehrn came back to the table and rummaged through some papers. "Presumably you have heard of *Valentina Tereshkova,* though," he said.

Anita shrugged lightly. "The space colony? Why, of course. In fact, wasn't it in the news yesterday?"

"Does it hold any special significance for you?"

"No, none. Should it?"

"Does it hold any significance for Professor Dyashkin? Do you connect him with it in any way? Did he ever talk about it?"

Anita could only shake her head. "If he was connected with it somehow, I was never aware. He never mentioned it in any special sense—only the casual references that anyone might make concerning things that appear in the news."

"And you said that you didn't know he'd moved to Siberia?"

"No, I didn't say that. I knew he'd moved to Siberia. I didn't know exactly where. Was it to the place you mentioned a moment ago?"

The interview went on in a similar vein until it was time for lunch. Kehrn went through with Anita to the table that the house orderlies had set in the dining room, where two CIA officers who would be questioning Anita further in the afternoon were due to meet them. Foleda announced that he would go for a stroll around the pond at the rear of the house to feed the ducks and get some air before joining the party. Barbara accompanied him.

"What do you make of it?" he asked her.

"I still think she's genuine. In fact, I'm more convinced than I was in London."

"Uh-huh. What else?"

"Well, if Professor Dyashkin is also mixed up with the Friday Club, and his ladyfriend Olga has been arrested, that maybe answers one of the big questions we've been asking: Why does he want to defect? He can feel the heat closing in on him, and wants an option for an out."

"It's obvious, isn't it." There was a note to Foleda's voice that said perhaps it was too obvious. He stopped as a flotilla of ducks arrived from across the pond and waited a few feet out from the bank for pieces of breadrolls he'd picked up from the plates that had come in with the coffee earlier. "Then, how's this for a long shot?" he said. "Let's suppose that Olga was moved up to *Tereshkova* for some reason, and that she's inside the prison camp there. We already know that Dyashkin is at the receiving end of the Blueprint transmissions. See my point?"

Barbara nodded. "It's a good bet that Olga's the person at the other."

"That's the way it looks to me." Foleda broke another roll and tossed the pieces into the water.

"How can we find out for sure?"

"Easily—by asking Dyashkin. He must know who is it he's talking to."

"Would he tell us?"

"Why shouldn't he? He confirmed that Lew McCain and the Bryce girl are up there. And besides, he's sweating and he might want us to get him out, so he's not of a mind to refuse favors." Foleda turned back from the pond. "Now let's string all those facts together. We've never been able to discover how he works his end of the Blueprint line, but we know he's got some way of sending messages up to Mermaid. Now we're pretty certain his contact up there is Olga, and Olga was arrested for anti-Soviet activities. Now let's assume that Olga's inside the same place that Lew McCain and Bryce are in . . . and bearing in mind that we already possess a link between us and Dyashkin . . . See the possibilities?"

Barbara shook her head and blinked at the audacity of what Foleda was suggesting. "Then, maybe we could use his line to get through to our own people up there," she completed.

"A neat idea, eh? Who knows what kind of use we might find for a connection like that?" Foleda threw the last of the bread. "Well, the ducks look happy. Let's go back and get some lunch ourselves."

◉ CHAPTER THIRTY-ONE ◉

The secret belowdecks workshop became known as "the Crypt." By the time McCain, Rashazzi, and Haber got there, Haber was breathing heavily from the exertions of the journey, which was still strenuous, even with the rope ladder that Rashazzi and McCain had attached at the light-fixture panel. The worst part was getting down from the pipe-supporting frame underneath the billet floor. Now that they could examine and neutralize the security circuits from the rear, what they needed was an easier way in. They had identified several out-of-the-way places in the Core where entry might be possible, which would have the added advantage of making the Crypt available during the day. Besides giving them more productive time, this would provide relief from the exhausting loss of sleep that was beginning to affect all of them.

By now the Crypt was powered and lit from a junction box that Rashazzi had tapped into, and had acquired a spacious workbench, boxes, storage racks, and a staggering assortment of tools, test equipment, instruments, electronic components, and jars of chemicals, gadgets, and parts, which the two scientist-thieves had materialized from a score of hiding holes that McCain had never suspected, and the whereabouts of which he still hadn't the foggiest notion. The laser was at one end of the bench. Scanlon had managed to purloin a broken research model from the scrap heap at the university in Landausk, where he'd been working since bedframe production was suspended. It needed some replacement parts, which the two scientists said they could hand-make, and a new electronic control unit. In addition, a number of other contraptions and devices were at various stages of construction.

"Come this way, Lew," Rashazzi said. "This is what we wanted to show you." He beckoned McCain through into the space behind the bench. Haber followed, after collecting a notebook and some other items from the bench. Supported between two boxes was a shallow cylinder cut from one end of a drum about three feet across, containing six inches or so of water. The hole in the center was plugged, and a loop of stiff wire sticking up through the water from the plug formed a handle to pull it out. On the floor between the two boxes and underneath the cylinder was a bowl for the water to drain into. It seemed a very simple arrangement, and McCain could attach no significance to it. He waited curiously.

Haber had placed a meter rule across the dish with its edge above the center of the plug, and was waiting with a pencil and notebook. "Ready when you are," he told Rashazzi.

Rashazzi picked up a dropper and used it to deposit spots of a purple dye at intervals across the liquid. Then he grasped the wire handle and, taking care not to disturb the water, slowly drew the plug out. The water began falling through into the bowl beneath. "The liquid has had over twenty-four hours to settle," Rashazzi said, watching. "That's to allow any swirling introduced during filling it to dissipate completely. Did you know that when water in a bathtub back on Earth forms a vortex, the direction of rotation usually doesn't have anything to do with the way the Earth spins, as most people think? It's an accidental consequence of the motion left over from when it flowed in and how it was sloshed about. To see the true effect of the Earth's rotation, you have to eliminate such residual currents."

"No, I didn't," McCain answered tonelessly, staring at the falling surface of the water and trying hard not to let his feelings show at that particular moment. If they were going to preoccupy themselves with this kind of academic fussing, the whole effort was a waste of time already. What good could come out of it?

As the water level in the dish fell, the drops of dye elongated into threads along the flow lines and traced out the counterclockwise swirl that was beginning to appear, slow on the outside and getting faster nearer the hole. Rashazzi leaned over the dish to read the measuring scale, and used a stopwatch to time the rotation speed at increasing distances from the center. "One, one point three; two, one point nine; three, two point four . . ." he recited to Haber, who scribbled the numbers down. McCain watched the process without interrupting.

When the dish was empty and the experiment over, Rashazzi straightened up and remarked, "Conservation of angular momentum, you know. That's what makes vortexes form."

McCain grunted noncommittally. The principle was the same as with twirling ice skaters, where pulling in the arms causes them to spin faster.

Rashazzi went on, "If an element of the fluid possesses momentum about the center, its rotational rate must increase as the radius it's at decreases. The same thing causes tornadoes and hurricanes. You can see how the water in a tub at Earth's north pole, for example, would be rotating."

"Sure," McCain said.

"And what about at the equator? Would you agree that the water in that case is not rotating?" Rashazzi asked. McCain looked uncertain. "It's not rotating around the hole—in the plane perpendicular to the hole's axis," Rashazzi said.

McCain nodded. "Okay. So?"

Rashazzi looked across at Haber. "The situation on a rotating cylinder, such as a floor inside the ring of *Valentina Tereshkova*, is identical to that at the Earth's equator," the German explained to McCain. "There should be no vortex induced by rotation."

It took a second for the point to register. Then McCain stared bemusedly at the bottom of the empty dish, looked up again, gestured vaguely with his hand. "But? . . ."

"Exactly." Rashazzi nodded. "There's something odd about the mechanics of this place. Since the colony rotates a lot faster than Earth does, the effect is much stronger here. It can overwhelm the residual currents I mentioned earlier. We'd have noticed it long ago if all the sinks and showers here didn't have suction drains—not one good old-fashioned plughole anywhere."

McCain shook his head as if to clear it. This was all completely unexpected. "Have you got any idea what it means?" he asked.

"Not really," Rashazzi admitted. "But the motion of the colony must be more complicated than we've supposed. It wasn't something we wanted to even talk about upstairs. I'm not sure what it might mean."

"That game that Nunghan and his friends play out in the mess area was what first made us curious," Haber said. "If you look very carefully, marbles don't roll straight over long distances. There's a slight curve. That's something else you shouldn't get in a rotating cylinder. We established that it wasn't due to any slope in the floor, but it wasn't possible to measure anything accurately without being conspicuous. That was why we needed a place like this."

"And also the laser," Rashazzi said. "If we can get it up to the surface level somehow, there are some other things we'd like to try with it. For example, if we can—"

At that moment a rasping sound came from a buzzer fastened to one of the supporting pillars. It meant that something had broken one of the infrared beams that Rashazzi had installed to cover approaches to the Crypt. Instantly Haber flipped a switch to put out the light. They moved back against the wall and waited. After a minute or so, lights flickered in the direction of the walkway through the pump and storage-tank area, accompanied by the sounds of people approaching. They came to the side branch that led to the Crypt and followed it. There were three lights, and a muttering of voices. McCain and the others tensed. The approaching figures were moving purposefully, not in the manner of people searching, but of ones who knew where they were going. They reached the edge of the sunken level and shone their beams down into the space below to pick out the three men crouching in the darkness. McCain, Rashazzi, and Haber moved out from the wall resignedly, holding their hands high and empty in front of them.

Then, from out of the darkness beyond the lights that were

blinding them, an English voice said cheerfully, "Sorry, didn't mean to startle you chaps. It's just what you might call a good-neighbor visit." It was Peter Sargent, from upstairs in B-12.

Rashazzi turned on the light again and Haber sat down weakly on a nearby box. McCain glared up as the three newcomers switched off their flashlights and clambered down into the Crypt. "What the fuck are you doing here?" he growled.

One of the two men with Sargent was swarthy-faced, with a short beard and dark eyes that were constantly darting suspiciously this way and that. He looked Indian. McCain knew his face from around the compound but had never talked to him. The other, McCain hadn't seen before. Heavily built, with reddish curls fringing an immense brow, and a face that somehow managed to combine decisive, sharply lined features with a rounded, babyish shape, he was wearing a priv-category green tunic. He moved a pace forward into the light and took in the surroundings with a cool, dispassionate stare that could have signified ownership.

"We thought it was time to introduce ourselves personally," Sargent said. He gestured toward the big man first. "Eban Istamel, who is Turkish. . . . And this is Jangit Chakattar, originally from Delhi." He looked pleasantly at McCain. "We were delighted to hear that the information from the escape committee turned out to be so useful. But we also heard from Koh that you had doubts if the committee exists at all. I can assure you that it does." He gestured toward himself and at his two companions once again. "You see, it was *our* present. We run the escape committee."

McCain looked from one to another for what seemed a long time, in silence, but from the expression on his face his mind was working furiously. Finally he asked Sargent, "Which one is in charge?"

"Eban." Sargent indicated the big Turk. "He is the chairman."

"Very pleased to meet you," McCain said. The Turk extended a perfunctory hand. . . . And McCain hit him squarely on the jaw.

The big Turk sat on a box with his back propped against one of the roof supports, dabbing a folded handkerchief at the swelling on one side of his mouth. McCain, Haber, and Sargent were also sitting in a loose circle, while Rashazzi leaned against the bench and Chakattar stood looking on from behind. "It's all right," Istamel had mumbled to his two astonished companions when McCain punched him. "He had the right. We used them."

For what McCain had realized in the moments following the appearance of Sargent and his two friends was that he and his group in B-3 had been set up. The fact that they had come through without mishap was beside the point. They had been the ones at risk. Supposedly this had been necessary because the committee people occupied an upper-level billet, and penetration belowdecks required access from the lower level. But clearly the new arrivals had not come via the route that McCain's group had been using, through the floor of B-3. That meant they had another way of getting into the belowdecks region. Moreover, Istamel's presence showed that it connected with the privs' level up on the surface, somehow. Very likely they'd had such an alternative all along, but had played safe by getting the B-3 group to try out the method first. McCain had guessed their appearance now represented a bid to take over the operation, and the disdainful manner that the Turk had exhibited did nothing to dispel the suspicion. But McCain's action, in accordance with the rough-and-ready unspoken code by which such things were asserted, had symbolically redressed the imbalance of status which the advantage the escape committee had gained for itself implied. The meeting could now proceed as a discussion between equals.

"You people are really serious?" McCain sounded mildly incredulous. "This escape committee business. You think there's a hope of getting away from a place like this?"

"Probably slim," Sargent admitted. "But studying the possibilities does help keep the mind busy, all the same. It wouldn't do to allow oneself to vegetate, would it?"

"What kinds of possibilities have you identified?" Rashazzi asked curiously.

"Really you can't expect us to divulge details of such things freely," Chakattar protested from where he was standing. "Much effort was involved—all kinds of confidential things. We don't know anything about you three."

"True," Haber sighed. "Nor do we know you."

The eternal Zamork impasse. The position was ridiculous. McCain saw from his expression that the Turk was thinking the same thing. Somebody was going to have to make a first move. "Look," he said, addressing the company in general. "We all know the problem. But we've all put a lot into finding a place like this, specifically to get away from the environment upstairs. You got the information to make it possible; we did the work. Now, if we're not going to pool what we know, what's the point of all this?"

Istamel glanced at his handkerchief and put it back in his pocket. "The problem isn't so much of knowing who's trustworthy, but the risk that if someone were caught, the more he knew, the more would be compromised," he said. "So we are reluctant to give away anything without a good reason. I'm sure the same applies to you, also."

"How are we supposed to help each other achieve our respective goals if we don't share information?" Rashazzi asked.

There was a short silence. "Very well," Chakattar said at last. "You talk about goals. Ours is very simple: to find ways of escaping. What is your goal?" Rashazzi and Haber looked at McCain.

It was McCain who had proposed that somebody had to start trusting somebody, and he accepted that the onus of making the first concession was his. Besides, he could see nothing to lose from appearing to be forthright by revealing to the present company what the Russians would already have concluded for themselves, anyway. "All right, I'll be straight," he said. "I was sent here on a mission by a branch of Western intelligence. That mission involves establishing the nature of equipment believed to exist in locations around *Valentina Tereshkova*. I intend if I can to carry out that mission, and to find a way of communicating the findings back to Earth. In other words, my immediate goal is to conduct a reconnaissance of the entire colony and a detailed examination of certain parts of it. One piece of information that might help a lot would be knowing how you got in here." He looked from the Turk to the Englishman to the Indian and spread his hands. "We have a common need here. You're looking for ways to get out—a detailed knowledge of the place is essential for any specific plan. So, for the time being at least, our goals are identical. When the time comes to revise that, then hopefully we'll all have gotten to know each other better."

Istamel looked at Sargent and Chakattar, in a way that said it was good enough for him. Sargent gave a shrug and nodded. Chakattar, however, was still unhappy. "You want us to give you concrete information," he pointed out. "But all you are offering in return is a promise of good intentions. That doesn't seem like a good trade to me. What do you have that would be of tangible benefit to us right now?"

Rashazzi caught McCain's eye for an instant, and indicated the drum at the rear with a slight questioning motion of his head. He was asking if they should mention the vortex experiment that McCain had just witnessed. McCain returned a barely perceptible shake of his head. They needed to know more about what it meant themselves, first. Instead, he looked back at Istamel. "It's clear that your way in involves access to the surface level."

"Maybe so." Istamel shrugged. The expression on his babyishly round yet shrewd face remained neutral.

"But any serious plans about escaping would require freer movement around *Tereshkova*. You'd need ways of getting out of Zamork entirely. Do you have ways of accomplishing that?"

"There are the outside work details."

"Yes, but they're guarded," McCain said.

"Guards can be bribed."

"Sure," McCain agreed. In fact, some of the things he'd been asking people like Gonares in B-3 to do involved just such arrangements. "But what I'm talking about is freedom of movement anywhere around the colony, without any hassle from guards or limits on time," he said. "Interested?"

Istamel looked very interested. "You can provide this?" he said, sitting forward.

"If we can find a way to get out through the perimeter of Zamork itself," McCain said. "And it sounds as if what you've done could already represent half the job. You see, this is the kind of way I'm saying we can work together."

Sargent held out an arm and pulled back his jacket sleeve to display his wrist bracelet. "But even if you did get out of Zamork, you've still got a problem with these," he said. "You'd trigger an alarm the first time you came within range of an interrogating sensor. And they're all over the place."

"Then, let us show you something we've discovered," McCain said. "Razz?" He got up and walked over to the bench, while Rashazzi went to fetch a flat box from one of the racks before joining him. The others came over and gathered round. McCain took off his jacket and rested his forearm on the bench with the electronic unit of his own bracelet facing upward. As with all of them, it consisted of a square metal frame with rounded corners to which the bracelet attached and, fitted in the frame's recess, a plain black rectangular insert that contained the electronics. Rashazzi took a scalpel and cut along one side of the joint between the edge of the insert and the frame, at the same time swabbing a solvent fluid into the crack. Then he began working along the second edge.

"My unit has been tampered with," McCain said. "The insert is only held by a soluble adhesive that Razz cooked up. You see, whoever designed these devices was careless. The insert in the center contains the ID electronics, but the power cell and the detector for a break in the wristband are housed in the frame. So, the two can be separated without triggering an alarm. What's more, the chip was only secured by cement around the edges, which Albrecht found a way of breaking." As McCain said this, Rashazzi tested the bond by prying an edge of the wafer with the blade, and finding it sufficiently softened, lifted it clear for Haber to remove with a pair of tweezers.

"Well, I'll be damned!" Sargent exclaimed.

McCain held out his arm to show the bracelet with its empty frame. "One way you could use this is to switch ID's," he said. "Suppose you"—he looked at Sargent—"needed to go to Turgenev or somewhere, but I had a work assignment there. We could switch the inserts. Much more flexibility."

Haber pointed at the insert, which he had placed on a glass plate. "But even better, the inserts in the badge ID's that outside civilians wear are identical. If we could get hold of a general-clearance badge somehow, we could substitute its insert for the one in your bracelet, and you'd be able to go anywhere you wanted."

McCain looked at Chakattar. "Is that tangible enough?"

"Would it work, though?" Sargent asked doubtfully. "Wouldn't the ID coding in the security computers be changed as soon as the badge was missed?"

Rashazzi shook his head. "It doesn't work that way. You only get that degree of security here, inside Zamork. Outside, individuals aren't tracked place to place. A general-clearance insert is just like a key that will get you in anywhere. That's all it does. They all transmit the same code."

Istamel and his two colleagues exchanged glances. "And you think you might be able to obtain such a device?" he said.

Haber smiled, and gestured at the workshop around them. "We do appear to have something of a flair for, shall we say, larcenous inventiveness."

"Very good. I am satisfied," Istamel pronounced.

McCain turned from the bench to face him directly. The Turk stared him in the eye and nodded. "You have a deal, Mr. Earnshaw. We have too much in common to waste our energies on rivalry. We work cooperatively, yes? . . ." He bunched a fist and brought it up close to the side of McCain's chin. McCain looked back at him unblinkingly. Istamel thumped the side of his jaw, not hard enough to hurt, but solidly enough to be more than playful. "As partners, eh?" A flicker of a grin crossed his face. McCain grinned back at him. They shook hands.

✸ CHAPTER THIRTY-TWO ✸

Two guards escorted Paula from the interview room in the Surface Level Administration Building to the security post at the door opening out into the general area where the huts were situated. She made her own way back to Hut 19 from there. The climate-control engineers had been experimenting again that day and had created strange conditions around Novyi Kazan, in which evaporation from the reservoir and other nearby bodies of water formed a mist below the roof that reduced the ribbon-suns to indistinct, watery blurs. A month previously they had managed to produce a miniature cyclone that wrapped itself around the town's central tower and sucked all its windows out. Half of them still hadn't been replaced.

She walked past the Recreation Building, where the gymnasium and hobby rooms were located, and turned right onto the path running between Huts 10 and 17. Several of the green-clad figures who were out nodded or called a greeting as she passed. The session with Protbornov and Major Uskayev had followed the course that had long ago become usual. Why couldn't she communicate with her government? she had demanded to know yet again—they must be pressing for information. She could, the Russians replied, if she would only agree to be more cooperative. How did she like her new work? It was fine. She did realize, of course, that they could always send her back to the lower levels? That was up to them. Unnerving as she found the thought inwardly, she was keeping to the tactic that Olga had urged. And although as yet she hadn't won her battle, the contest was beginning to feel more equal.

She shared Hut 19 with three Russian women. Elena came from Minsk and was a sociologist, a field of study traditionally frowned upon by the authorities, since from the time of the state's inception "hard" science and engineering had been viewed as more relevant to its industrialization goals. Elena had been a little too zealous in compiling and supplying to foreign publishers statistics on health and wealth in the people's utopia that the people's leaders had found embarrassing, and found herself consigned to Zamork as the only place sufficiently safe and far away to keep her out of mischief. Svetlana was a deactivated agent of the KGB. After undergoing years of tutoring and training, she had been infiltrated into Austria posing as a German immigrant, and had been granted Austrian naturalization. But then she had gone on to develop a taste for Western living and an open disdain for Marxist orthodoxy that had made her superiors nervous, and Zamork became her destination after recall to Moscow. Lastly, Agniya was a former Moscow art and literature critic. She had persisted in criticizing the censors instead of the artists, and dismissed the officially promoted idols as mediocrities. After Paula's experiences on the lower level, their company and intellectual stimulation was like a release from the grave.

Svetlana, the former KGB agent, was in when Paula got back to the hut, trying a new picture in different positions on the walls. It was a scene in a city of tall buildings. The city was inhabited by a mixture of all the monsters that had ever crashed, roared, terrorized, and demolished their way across the world's movie screens—Godzillas, mutant spiders, giant ants, barrel-chested gorillas, creaking Frankensteins, and shapeless blobs. But these monsters were panicking, fleeing in wide-eyed terror through the streets and pulling their baby monsters after them, while others shrieked from windows. It was also, evidently, a city of monsters-in-miniature . . . for looming above the buildings in the background, silhouetted against the sky as it lumbered closer, was a spacesuited human figure. Paula studied it and managed a smile despite her weariness after the past few hours. "Cute," she pronounced. "Where'd it come from?"

"You met Maurice, the Frenchman who paints," Svetlana replied. "It's one of his."

"I thought he was going back. Wasn't there an exchange deal that the Russians worked out with the French and the West Germans, or something?"

"Yes, that's right. He went a couple of days ago. This picture is a parting gift that he left for me, but I only got it this morning. . . . I was thinking, maybe here, by Elena's baskets. How does it look?"

"Perhaps a little more to the right . . . there, that's good. Want me to hold it?"

Paula watched while Svetlana fixed the corners of the picture with pieces of adhesive tape. Svetlana had dark hair with a reddish tint, brushed into long waves that curled forward beneath her ears, and a trim figure whose curves not even the standard baggy green priv's tunic could hide. People got along well with her, and it seemed natural that the Frenchman should have left her a farewell present. It was strange, Paula thought. She had been arrested while on a professional espionage assignment for the United States government, Svetlana was a former KGB agent, and yet here they were living together and acting naturally like affectionate sisters. It said how people everywhere could be if only those who aspired to power would leave them alone. Or was it the people's own fault for taking any notice in the first place of those who presumed to command them?

Svetlana finished fixing the picture and stepped back. "Yes, I think that looks fine. We'll leave it there." She put the tape back on a shelf. "I've just made some tea. Would you like some?"

"I could use something," Paula said.

"How was it today?"

"The usual. They want me to take a guided tour around the colony and send a vigram home saying there are no nasty things hidden up here." Since the West had never concealed its suspicions about weapons on *Valentina Tereshkova,* Paula wasn't revealing anything that Svetlana didn't already know about.

Svetlana poured strong tea into two cups and topped them up

with hot water. She handed one to Paula, added sugar and a drop of lemon juice to her own, and sat down on one of the hut's two double-height bunks. Paula sat down at the table and sipped her tea, savoring the taste and the feeling of the hot, refreshing liquid moistening her dried mouth. The Russian woman lit a cigarette. "Well, why don't you do it?" she asked Paula. "Surely it can't do any harm. I mean, if what they say is true, it could only be for the best if the West were told about it."

"I don't know," Paula said after considering the question. "I guess I don't like the thought of being used as a political mouthpiece. It's not my kind of business. I'm a scientist."

"Then, what are you doing here?" Svetlana asked.

"That's what I mean—I've gotten mixed up in more than enough of what I should have stayed out of, already." Paula seemed dissatisfied with her own answer and frowned while she drank from her cup again. "Anyway, it shouldn't be up to me. If the Russians want to convince the Americans that this place is legitimate, all they have to do is bring them here and let them walk around. Why should it need to be my problem?"

Svetlana sighed. "You know how it is with stubborn old men who worry about what history books might say about them." She fell silent for a while, contemplating the smoke from her cigarette. "We got to be quite friendly, Maurice and I," she said at last in a distant voice that seemed to change the subject.

Paula smiled. "I can't say I'm surprised. You are quite attractive, after all, and he was, well . . . very French."

"No, I didn't mean that way. I meant just as friends. We used to talk a lot. He was very intellectual as well as artistic."

"Oh, I thought—"

"That's all right. He seemed to know a lot about science—to me he did, anyway, which doesn't say all that much. You'd have liked him. It's a pity he's gone." Svetlana hoisted her legs up onto the bunk and shifted back to prop herself against the end wall. She looked at Paula quizzically. "Were you really a spy?" she asked matter-of-factly.

"Come on. You know better than that."

Svetlana didn't seem to have expected a straight answer. "You know, I think Maurice might well have been. He never said so, but when you've worked as I have, you develop an instinct for these things."

"With the French intelligence people, you mean?"

"Yes. You know it's funny, the different reasons why people get involved in espionage. With me it was virtually automatic. My father was a KGB colonel, and I went into the academy at Bykovo straight from university. It was just a job that the family expected me to go into, and quite an exciting one, too—almost a game, in fact. But some people do it for very deep, premeditated reasons, such as ideological beliefs. Maurice was like that. He was one of those serious minded people, always worried about humanity and where it was heading for a thousand years from now."

Paula thought instinctively about Earnshaw, but couldn't place him in that category. For him it came closer to soldiering—a job that had to be done that obviously everyone couldn't leave to everyone else. His motivation reflected short-term realities more than distant ideals.

Svetlana went on, "Maurice worried that the stubborn old men might get the world into a war. They were all just as paranoid, he thought—yours as well as ours—all equally responsible for the lunacy that things have come to. 'Impotent dinosaurs, stuck in a swamp with nothing but umbrellas,' he used to say. And finding out the truth about the weapons that some people say are hidden up here concerned him a lot."

"What bothered him so much about that?" Paula asked.

"The thought that all the suspicions might be nothing more than the products of fantasies and preconceptions. If that turned out to be so, then how many more crucial judgments are being based on equally wrong perceptions?"

Paula was staring at the far wall. Suddenly she glimpsed the entire situation and her own relationship to it from a new perspective. What she saw didn't make her feel entirely comfortable. "It would be insane," she agreed in a faraway voice.

"Yes. And the really insane part is that we could end up blowing everything for no other reason than wrong information. Maurice's big obsession was to make sure that the right people got the right facts. You see, intelligence work was almost a religion with him. That was why the Russians were always moving him around the colony so much. Probably that was why they let him go."

"How do you mean?" Paula asked.

"They offered him the same kind of deal as they did you: a tour around, if he would agree to relay back what he saw. And he went along with it."

"Did he ever say what he found?"

"Not in so many words—not to me, anyway," Svetlana said. "But think about it. If he discovered anything that shouldn't have been there, would he be on his way home right now? That must say something." Paula cast an eye around at the walls and ceiling and gave Svetlana a cautioning look, querying if they ought to be talking aloud like this about somebody who was quite possibly not out of the Russians' hands yet. Svetlana laughed. "What does it matter if they are listening to us?" she said. "He would only be confirming what they themselves have been telling the world for years." She lifted her head and called out in a louder voice, "Can you hear me, former comrades? Am I right? Are we saying anything you don't agree with?"

Paula fell quiet as she sipped the rest of her tea. Suddenly she saw the role that she had been slipping into as one of mere academic detachment—an irrelevancy. The thought made her feel, in a way . . . irresponsible. It was the first time that the job she'd come to *Tereshkova* to do had felt like something that really mattered.

◉ CHAPTER THIRTY-THREE ◉

The big news in the second week of September was that the Russians had yielded suddenly and unexpectedly to the international pressure that had been building up for several years. In a surprise announcement from Moscow, the Soviet foreign minister stated that *Valentina Tereshkova* would be opened to unrestricted international inspection immediately following the November 7 celebrations. This was also the colony's official completion date. The Russians pointed out that it was not normal to permit outsiders into any site while construction was still in progress. It had always been their intention to declare an open policy, they claimed; but the persistent Western harassment would have been an affront to anyone's dignity. As a further gesture toward reconciliation, and to mark the departure from precedent, they invited the nations of the West to send delegates to join the Soviet leaders for the centenary, to symbolize their common commitment to a harmonious and prosperous future.

The banner headline of *The New York Times* read: DRAMATIC CONCESSIONS IN SURPRISE SOVIET INITIATIVE. Philip Borden, director of the UDIA, tossed a copy of the morning's San Francisco *Chronicle* down on top of it. MOSCOW SAYS "DA"!

"The news grid and networks are full of it. Peacenik lobbyists have been hounding congresspeople around Washington all morning," he told Foleda across his desk. "I've got to present our assessment to the

Security Council at three this afternoon. Half the country's clamoring for a big gesture of reciprocation, and some of the European governments are already indicating a willingness to accept. The secretary of state says he agrees, and we expect the other intelligence agencies to be cautiously in favor. But you're not happy, and you think we should sit tight."

"It was also the Europeans who went rushing off to Munich, don't forget," Foleda reminded him. "I don't like the passive position it puts us in. I don't like a precedent where they call the tune and we jump. I don't like the thought of our making a spectacle of falling over ourselves with gratitude just because they've said they'll act reasonably for once—as if that represented some kind of favor. Hell, when did they ever make a big show of being grateful all the times we acted reasonably?"

Borden stared for a moment. "There's more, though, isn't there?"

Foleda thought for a second, then looked up to return Borden's look directly and nodded. "I think this whole business about November is a cover for something else—something a lot bigger. I still think it could be a strike. We're talking about eight weeks to go, Phil."

Borden sighed. They had been through all this with the Security Council and the defense chiefs, and the consensus had been that the fears were exaggerated. "Hell, I can't go back with that again. Don't you think that just maybe, this time you're being a little too suspicious?"

"We're paid to be suspicious. We're good at it, too. That's why we've worked together for a long time."

Borden drew a long breath and looked dubious. He gestured at the headlines lying on his desk. "It would mean making myself about as popular as smallpox this afternoon. I mean, do we have anything new to go on? Everything the Dorkas woman says checks out. NSA's tracer scans didn't turn up anything, and some of the information she's come up with is too valuable to have been a gift pack. What else can we say about her?" The tracer scans referred to the Committee for Freedom and Dignity and the Tortoise that Barbara had mentioned during her meeting with Anita in London. The National Security

Agency had reported no occurrence of these terms in the Soviet communications traffic that they listened in on. Although it constituted negative evidence, it did support Anita's story.

"No, that's not it. They can run all the checks they like. I'm satisfied that she's okay," Foleda said.

There was other evidence supporting the Soviets' proclaimed position, too. A confidential report recently received from the French Deuxieme Bureau concerned a French agent by the name of Maurice Descarde, who had been released in an exchange deal from internment in *Valentina Tereshkova*. Apparently Descarde had returned to Earth a week previously and was now back in Paris. During interrogation he had stated that on numerous occasions he had worked in parts of the colony where weapons systems and ancillary equipment were supposed to exist, but had never seen any signs of them. Physiological and psychiatric tests indicated that he was in good health, functioning normally, and in complete command of his faculties.

"Okay, Bern, I'll try stalling things for a bit longer and push for using Cabman," Borden said finally after more wrangling. "We've all done our evaluations of Anita Dorkas—us, CIA, the British—and as far as it's ever possible to be sure, we all think she's clean. So we'll assume that Cabman's straight and play your hunch that he's got some way of getting messages up to Oshkadov that NSA hasn't uncovered, and that Oshkadov is inside the same place that Sexton and Pangolin are in." The names were McCain and Paula's code designations. "Let's stop pussyfooting around and tell Cabman now that we know who he's talking to, and that we want a through-channel to our people up there. I'll stall at the meeting on the grounds that we're trying to get independent confirmation."

Foleda sat back and massaged his eyebrows uneasily for a few seconds. He started to reply, but then stopped, sighed, and then nodded his head in a way that said he was as satisfied as he could expect to be. "Okay."

"We can't do a lot more." Borden waited, looking at Foleda curiously. "What is it that's really bothering you about this whole thing?"

Foleda took a moment to choose his words. "Go right back to the beginning and work through everything that's happened since. Now ask yourself, What would the implications be if Magician had been a double agent all along?" he replied.

❀ CHAPTER THIRTY-FOUR ❀

The escape committee's route led out through the ceiling of B-12 billet, which had the advantage of an unusually cooperative foreman, and from there climbed to the surface through an intermediate level of pipework and plumbing. It emerged in the basements of the Services Block, a building at the east end of the surface level that contained the canteen and other amenities that privs enjoyed, and the back of which screened a drop down to the general compound used by the prisoners on the lower levels. From the Services Block it connected across the surface to Hut 8, which Eban Istamel occupied with three others. The hut was situated roughly in the center of the surface residential area, which put it above the Core zone of the lower levels. Istamel and the others had tunneled down through the floor of Hut 8 and penetrated the upper subsurface machinery galleries, and from there gained access to one of the elevator shafts running down through the Core and continuing on down past the lowest billet level. A maintenance cover in the side of the shaft opened through to the machinery deck where the Crypt was located.

The ways of escape that the committee had been looking into all involved gaining access to the hub—as was inevitable, since that was where the Soviet transporter ships, the only means for leaving the colony, docked. The possibilities that Sargent outlined included stowing away in the consignments of materials and equipment shipped up the spoke elevators to the hub, impersonating Russian personnel going there on official duties, getting there concealed illicitly among the work details assigned to the hub, and making the half-mile climb through the systems of ducting, conduits, and structural supports outside the elevator shafts.

The big problem with all of these proposals was the stringent security measures that the Soviets enforced to protect every conceivable way to entry to the spokes. Every car destined for the hub was combed inside and out three times before departure. The ID checks of Soviet personal were impregnable. The structure surrounding the elevator ports was a jungle of alarms and detectors. As the inmates who knew the tricks for vanishing from work details had found out, the security that applied to movement among the various places around *Tereshkova*'s outer ring could be surprisingly lax. But getting into the spokes, as most of the escape committee's guinea pigs had discovered to their cost, was a different matter. But since the spokes represented the only way out of the colony, and at this distance from Earth guards came at a premium, it probably made sense that things should be so.

After thinking the matter over, however, McCain wasn't so sure that the only way to the hub was indeed through the spokes. "Why," he asked Rashazzi and Haber when they were alone in the Crypt one day, "can't we go *outside* them?"

"Sure, why not?" Rashazzi shrugged. The proposition was too absurd to argue about.

"No, think about it," McCain urged. "It would exploit the very weakness that the Soviets have built into their own system. Apart from in Zamork, security around the ring isn't very tight—in fact, in most places it's nonexistent. They only bother seriously guarding the access routes into the spokes. Why? Obviously because there isn't anyplace else to go. It never occurred to them that anybody might ever want to break through to the outside!"

Rashazzi was staring at Haber with an expression that said his initial reaction was already giving way to second thoughts. Haber blinked back at him. Clearly there were problems to be solved, but the idea was starting to make a crazy kind of sense. McCain waited. "Do you think it's feasible, Razz?" Haber asked.

"I'm not sure. . . . Maybe."

"Obviously such a scheme would require protection and life support," Haber said. "The Russians must keep regular EVA suits at maintenance and emergency posts around the ring. . . . What do you think?"

"Mmm . . ." Rashazzi looked dubious. "They'd be difficult places to get into. And I can't think of anywhere they're likely to be here, in Zamork."

"Do you need them?" McCain asked. "What about improvising something? Is that such a crazy idea?"

"Homemade spacesuits?" Haber evidently thought it was.

This time Rashazzi wasn't so sure. "No . . . perhaps we don't need regular suits," he said slowly. "You know, Lew might be onto something. There are places we can get into that contain firefighting and rescue equipment that includes various kinds of breathing gear. That would take care of the hardest part." He paused, thinking rapidly. "The other part would be maintaining a pressured environment for the body. Actually that's not as much of a problem as most people think—not for what we need, anyway. In fact, you can stand up to about ten seconds in a hard vacuum without any protection at all."

"Very well, now tell us how we climb a kilometer up to the hub in ten seconds," Haber said.

"Obviously we'd need longer," Rashazzi agreed.

"But maybe only enough to get past the high-security zone at the base of the spoke," McCain pointed out. "An hour or even less, say. Then you get back inside again."

Rashazzi nodded. "Breathing pure oxygen would require a pressure of about two psi," he said to Haber. "That's not such a big difference over the outside. It should be possible to seal a mask over the face and eyes so that it doesn't blow off. It might leak a bit. But as long as the supply's enough to hold out, so what?"

"Would your eyes and ears be okay?" McCain said. "How about the rest of your body?"

"Not too big a problem," Rashazzi answered. "People in space vehicles and simulators work in low pressures all the time. The biggest thing to watch is gases in the body expanding or coming out of solution in fluids to form bubbles. So, you don't eat the wrong food before you go out, and you breathe pure oxygen for an hour to denitrogenate the blood. There isn't any gas in the eye structure to expand, and because of the way ears are made, they get uncomfortable from ambient overpressure, not underpressure."

Haber's attitude seemed to warm as he listened. He began nodding. "It would be necessary to prevent fluids from migrating, and evaporation from the skin. Some kind of elastic wrapping garment to maintain a pressure around the body would probably be sufficient, but not so tight as to restrict breathing and movement. A material that expanded up to a point and then went rigid would be ideal."

"Stretchy stuff with some kind of slack fiber woven into it, maybe," Rashazzi agreed. "What can we get hold of that's like that?"

"Getting an outside view of the place would answer a lot of questions," Haber mused thoughtfully.

McCain thrust his hands in his pockets and paced a few yards to the bench. He stared down at the laser for a moment, then turned back to face them. "Okay, supposing it works and we get to the hub. The next thing we need to know more about is Sargent's ideas for getting into one of the transporters . . ." He realized suddenly that Haber's remark had had nothing to do with escape bids, but had gone off on a different tangent that meant something to the two scientists but not to him. "What's wrong?" McCain asked. "Have I missed something?"

"We were going to mention it anyway," Haber said to Rashazzi.

"You're talking in riddles," McCain said to both of them. "Mention what?"

"We've found something else that's odd," Rashazzi said. "Come and look at this." They led McCain to the rear of the work area. Suspended from a support quite high up in the girders overhead was a line with a metal ball at the end. A pointer attached to the ball extended downward, almost scraping a large sheet of card marked with a circular scale graduated in degrees, which was lying flat on the floor. Rashazzi reached out and set the line swinging.

"From the length and period of a pendulum, a simple formula

gives the local acceleration due to gravity," he said. "That in turn determines the force with which an object presses down on the floor—in other words, what you weigh." He looked up at McCain. "Do you remember feeling a little heavy when you first came here? But after a couple of days it had gone away? Most of us did. You thought it was due to fatigue, maybe? Well, it wasn't so. The rotationally induced 'gravity' in *Valentina Tereshkova* is approximately ten percent greater than Earth-normal."

"Seems strange," McCain commented.

"It's very strange," Rashazzi agreed. "If anything, you'd expect a space colony to be designed for a level somewhat *lower* than Earth's—to reduce the stresses upon the structure, and hence permit lighter and cheaper construction. But why would any designer go the other way?"

"I don't know. Do you?"

"No. But that's not all." Rashazzi motioned toward the pendulum as it passed over the centerpoint of the circle, slowed to a halt a couple of inches outside the scale, and began its swing back again. "This is what's called a Foucault pendulum. That means it's free to swing in any direction."

"Unlike the kind in a grandfather clock, which is constrained to move in a plane parallel to the back wall of the cabinet," Haber interjected.

McCain nodded. Rashazzi went on, "Like a gyroscope, a pendulum tries to conserve momentum by continuing to swing in the same direction in space. Imagine one set up at the north pole on Earth. Pick an arbitrary direction—that of the constellation Aries, for example. Pull the pendulum back in that direction, and release it. Now imagine it continuing to swing in the same plane, away from Aries and then back toward it again for a whole day. The Earth will have turned a full three hundred sixty degrees beneath it. Or, if you were standing on the ground next to the pendulum, you would have observed the Earth as staying still and the plane of the pendulum's swing rotating through a circle—in fact, as Aries moves in its circle around the pole"—Rashazzi pointed at the card on the floor—"you could measure its rotation rate on a scale."

McCain remembered seeing this in science museums when he was younger. "Okay," he agreed. "Now what?"

"Now let's repeat the procedure at the equator," Rashazzi said. "Aries no longer moves in a circle around the center of the sky overhead, but rises and sets. We start the pendulum moving just as Aries peeps over the eastern horizon, and it continues to swing east-west. But six hours later, Aries will be overhead. Now, is the pendulum still moving toward and away from Aries as it was before? Hardly. It would have to be yo-yoing up and down, which would be a miracle. No, instead it's still moving east-west with respect to Earth. In other words, an observer there would see no rotation of the plane it swings in. Between the pole and the equator both effects combine, and the plane will rotate not through a full circle, but through a certain angle and back again, which depends on latitude."

McCain had been on *Tereshkova* long enough to know of the rim's equivalence to Earth's equator. "So a pendulum here should keep going in the same direction," he concluded.

Rashazzi nodded. "Quite. But it doesn't. The plane of the swing rotates. We've measured and timed. Its oscillation period is eighty-eight seconds."

"As the colony spins," McCain said.

"Except that with the official dimensions as given by the Russians, and allowing for ten percent above Earth-normal weight, it ought to be about a minute," Haber said.

Rashazzi looked at McCain quizzically for a second, as if challenging him for an explanation. "One answer that would give a slower rotation rate would be if the diameter of *Tereshkova* were considerably larger than it's supposed to be." He showed his palms briefly. "But that's impossible, of course. Ever since the Russians started building it, *Valentina Tereshkova* has been studied by enough groundbased and spacebased telescopes and other instruments for us to be under no doubt that it is the size they say it is."

McCain could only look at them in bafflement. "So what do you make of it?" he asked them. "Anything?"

Haber shook his head.

"There's something very strange about the geometry of this whole place," Rashazzi said. "Never mind Eban's escape projects. Even without them, we need to get out and conduct more tests all over *Tereshkova*. One look at it from the outside would tell us a lot. That's one attraction of the idea you had. But right now, I can't tell you what this business means."

"Should we tell the escape committee about this?" Haber asked.

McCain shook his head. "Not until we know what's behind it. Right now they don't have any inkling of this. So it's not something that could reach the wrong ears if any of them were careless. Let's keep things that way for the time being."

❀ CHAPTER THIRTY-FIVE ❀

The amenities for privileged-category inmates at Zamork included a library that was larger and more diverse than the one available in the subsurface Core. In particular it possessed a more comprehensive reference section. Now, reference books tend to weigh a lot, and payloads hauled up out of Earth's gravity well at considerable expense could be better devoted to other things. So the bulk of the reference material in the Zamork library resided in electronic form, and was updated by periodic transmissions from Earth. In fact, it was a subset of the main public library maintained in Turgenev.

Since Communists are supposed to exhibit a passionate zeal for setting constantly new records of production, this material included vast tables of industrial-output statistics, construction figures, agricultural yields, and five-year forecasts of everything from zip fasteners on Aeroflot flight attendants' uniforms to millions of barrels of oil from the drilling platforms in the Caspian Sea. In reality, few people were even remotely interested, and none of those who were believed the official numbers anyway. Hence, for all of the technological ingenuity and organizational skills that beaming these tables from Earth to *Valentina Tereshkova* and having them instantly accessible on library screens represented, they were hardly ever read by anyone, let alone checked. Hence, anyone who wanted to, and who had access to the necessary facilities down on Earth, could encode messages into those data with little risk of being discovered. Of course, the intended recipient would have to know what numbers to watch and how to interpret them. This was the method that "Ivan" had used to communicate from Earth into *Tereshkova*—the other half of the Blueprint dialogue, which had persistently eluded the NSA.

After the accident that lost Olga the special chip which Ivan had provided, the transmissions from *Tereshkova* had ceased. Coded messages from the Earth end had continued to appear, embedded in the statistical updates beamed into the library, but Olga had had no way of responding until she acquired the electronic chip that she had asked Paula to program for her. Three days after Paula gave her back the finished chip, Olga was waiting in the hut when Paula returned from her day at the Environmental Department. They chatted about local matters with Svetlana and Elena for a while, and then Olga suggested a walk on the hill above the reservoir.

"I was in the library today," Olga said when they were alone. "A reply from Ivan has come in. He received our message. The link is working again!"

Paula was pleased. "So, there were no hitches. You're in business again. I'm glad I was able to help."

"I'm sure Ivan is feeling relieved now," Olga said. "He must have been getting quite worried."

They walked on for a while. Paula became thoughtful as some of the things that she had been brooding over during the past few days came back to her. "What kind of a person is he—Ivan?" she asked at last. "How well did you know him?"

A surprised look flashed across Olga's face, but she shrugged and replied, "Well, I told you we were lovers once. He's . . . well, quite sophisticated in many ways, I suppose you'd say, cultured—"

"No, I meant politically. You said he belonged to that dissident organization that you were part of back on Earth. Does that mean he's opposed to the Soviet system? Is he . . . well, how loyal does that make him?"

Olga frowned. "That depends. Obviously he's less than completely happy with the present regime and what it represents. But he's a strong nationalist. He loves everything Russian."

"What about the international situation—all the tensions?" Paula asked.

"It's something that concerns him deeply," Olga answered. She slowed her pace and studied Paula's face searchingly. "Very deeply, in fact. His main reason for being active in the dissident movement is to promote greater understanding worldwide. Why do you ask?"

Paula struggled for the right way to put the question. "How far would he go to achieve that, do you think?"

"I'm sorry. You'll have to explain what you mean."

"Well, take this channel that we've got now, down to Siberia. He's in a communications station, with access to all kinds of equipment. From the way he's able to read our signals and inject his own into the upbound beam, I'd assume his position there must be a fairly senior one."

Olga nodded slowly, still looking puzzled. "Yes."

"Do you think he might be willing to extend the link farther if we had a good reason to ask him—beyond the borders of the Soviet Union, for example?"

Olga stopped and turned to face Paula fully. "What strange questions you're asking all of a sudden. Extend the link farther to *where* beyond the borders of the Soviet Union?"

Paula hesitated, then drew in a long breath. "Do you think he might relay a message from us here, into the Western military-communications system?" Before Olga could reply, she plunged on to explain. "You knew Maurice, the Frenchman who was exchanged. Svetlana told me he'd seen for himself that at least some of the weapons that are supposed to be up here don't exist. He'll have told his people as much of course, but it'll only be one man's word. Would he be believed? It's information that could be crucial to policy decisions at a time like this. Through Ivan we could be in a position to corroborate it. Or even to find out more . . . I don't know . . ." But then, suddenly, a feeling of futility at even thinking about it overwhelmed her. She shook her head with a sigh and resumed walking. "Oh, forget it, Olga. It was a stupid idea. Why should a senior scientist want to risk his neck transmitting messages to the West? It just seemed—"

"Now wait a minute. I'm not sure it is such a stupid idea." Olga was staring at her keenly. "Ivan is already risking his neck—I told you, he is very concerned about the present tensions. And look at it this way: if all we were asking him to do was relay confirmation to the West from a source it might trust—one of its own agents—of what the Soviets have been saying publicly anyway, they could hardly accuse him of betraying secrets or being disloyal, could they? I wouldn't write it off so quickly as a lost cause. It might be worth a try."

Paula frowned uncertainly. Olga continued to shoot questioning looks at her as they walked, but she kept quiet. Finally Paula asked, "Have you managed to get any news on Lew Earnshaw yet? If I could talk to him about it somehow, it would help a lot."

"I'm still trying. As soon as I hear anything, of course I'll let you know."

"I see."

"I could include a feeler to Ivan in my next message," Olga offered.

"Don't rush me. I need to think about it some more," Paula said.

"As you wish."

But inwardly Paula had already as good as conceded that in the end the decision was probably going to have to be hers. She didn't even know if Earnshaw was anywhere within two hundred thousand miles.

Less than a hundred feet below the hill in an entirely different environment, McCain, Scanlon, Istamel, and Sargent were sitting, like a conspiratorial circle in some smugglers' cave of old, in a pool of yellow light surrounded by darkness around a makeshift table of aluminum drums and wall paneling. McCain unwrapped the package that Rashazzi had left for them, revealing two pieces of charred, twisted plastic about the size of a credit card but thicker, which had obviously been severely burned. Istamel picked one of them up and examined it.

For the frame, Rashazzi had welded together plastic pieces cut from a razor-blade dispenser of an acceptably close shade of blue, which he had found in the general store. He had fashioned the securing clip from the clip of a ballpoint pen, using as a guide for its shape and dimensions the imprints of a genuine clip that Peter Sargent had somehow obtained in a bar of soap; and for the plastic-encapsulated electronics insert in the center, he cut a square out of a slice sawn from the base of a black chess king. Then he had incinerated his handiwork in a bowl of shredded rags soaked in alcohol. To a casual inspection, the result looked impressively like a standard Russian general-clearance badge that had been in a fire.

Istamel gave a satisfied grunt and placed the fragile object down again carefully. "It's good," he pronounced. He picked up the other and looked at it briefly. "I see no problem. These are fine."

"Well, I'm pleased to hear it," Scanlon said, sitting forward. "And now maybe ye can tell us what it is ye have in mind that we'll be needing them for."

The Turk drew his hands back to the edge of the table and ran his eyes quickly around the group. "I know of a situation that would suit our purpose," he told them. "I am a doctor by profession—of physiology. In particular I specialize in the regulatory mechanisms of the circulatory system. I have privileged status here in Zamork because I agreed to work cooperatively in the Space Environment Laboratory at the hub. They develop different kinds of spacesuits, do research into conditions and effects of working outside—things like that." He shrugged and thrust out his lower lip as if acknowledging that some kind of explanation was called for. "It enables me to pursue my own work and keep my knowledge up to date. So if helping their interests to a degree also serves my interests, why not? We're all traders at heart, yes?"

McCain nodded curtly. "Sure, we hear what you're saying. And?"

"The technical people there are Russian civilians—doctors and technicians from around the colony. Most of them carry general-clearance badges—which will give access to anywhere within the colony's regular environment outside a few restricted zones, such as parts of Landausk and the Government Center, which require various grades of special-clearance badges." McCain and Scanlon glanced at each other and looked more interested. Istamel went on, "I've noticed that when they change into their lab coats and working clothes, they tend to leave the badges on their regular coats, which they hang in a closet by the lab entrance. Now here's the interesting part. Heavy-current cabling to an air compressor and some welding equipment passes through the bottom of that closet. Also, the space below the hanging rail is always piled with bags and boxes that contain who-knows-what. Now you see my point: if a fault developed that caused those cables to heat up and ignite something that happened to be in one of those boxes . . ."

"You mean you'd put a package in there of your own to make sure that a couple of the coats at least were destroyed," Scanlon said, nodding.

"Exactly," Sargent threw in.

"But could you guarantee that the cable would set fire to the package?" McCain queried.

"We don't have to," Istamel replied. "We make the package a self-igniting incendiary device—something that Razz and Haber can put together. We fake some kind of fault in the electrical system and cover the cables in the closet with something that will burn, simply to make it look like an accidental fire. So the way it works is, first we switch these"—he indicated the burned dummies lying on the table—"for two of the badges, and at the same time plant the materials to start the fire. Then, just when it's due to go up, we put a short-circuit somewhere in the electrical system. Afterward, the Russians recover the two dummies, write them off officially as destroyed, and supply replacements to whoever they were issued to. Meanwhile, we have the real ones in working order."

McCain thought for a while but couldn't fault it. "Can you manage it all on your own?" he asked.

"Given the materials, then everything in the closet, yes," Istamel replied. "But the electrics, I'm not so strong on."

"Now, that would be my department if there was a way of getting me there," Scanlon said. "The IRA gives a good apprenticeship in things like that."

"But there isn't," McCain said.

"I'm not so sure," Istamel murmured thoughtfully. "We do have regular-category prisoners on work assignments around the hub. They deliver materials to the lab sometimes, cart away the trash, and so on. If we could get you on something like that . . ."

"But Luchenko isn't in the habit of handing out favors on request, and my bracelet isn't programmed for the hub," Scanlon said.

They debated various possibilities at some length, but got nowhere. Then Sargent returned to their first thought by asking, "What about this scheme that Razz came up with for swapping the inserts between two bracelets? Maybe we could find somebody assigned to the hub who'd appreciate an extra holiday in exchange for letting us borrow his insert for a day. Maybe we could get Kev to the hub that way—with the insert that's programmed for the hub mounted in his bracelet."

"Wouldn't the guards notice his face was different?" Istamel asked.

"Possible, but unlikely," Sargent said. "They're not exactly the most diligent or the brightest in the place. So, fair enough—it's a risk."

McCain looked inquiringly at Scanlon. "What do you think, Kev?"

"Ah, and why not? I've done riskier things in me time. Sure, I'll go with it."

"We seem to have settled it, then," McCain said. "So let's get it moving as quickly as possible. The sooner we have the badges, the sooner we can be mobile. There's a lot I want to find out about this place." He turned again toward Istamel. "Changing the subject back, you said you're a doctor of physiology?"

"Yes," Istamel replied.

"And you're helping develop designs for spacesuits?"

"In the Space Environment Laboratory. That's right."

"That's interesting," McCain said. "Let us tell you about something else we're working on that maybe you can help us with. . . ."

◎ CHAPTER THIRTY-SIX ◎

Russians, Paula decided, simply weren't happy unless they were suffering. From what she had read of their poets, dramatists, novelists, and historians, their compulsion expressed itself in the sense of tragedy and glorification of sacrifice that permeated their national spirit. Another manifestation, she thought, could be the innate genius they displayed for creating agricultural disasters. Peasant revolts had been a standard part of the czarist background scenery. Stalin's forced collectivization of the farms had produced starvations on a scale that even now could only be guessed at; Lysenko had risen to become head kook in charge of biology with state backing; successive disastrous postwar harvests had been offset only by exports from the evil West; and now, three quarters of the farming experiments in the sector known as Ukraine—between Turgenev and Landausk—were turning out to be dismal failures.

The reason, as the Soviets had now admitted publicly, was clear to Paula from the dynamics of the simulation she was running to test a program modification before finishing for the day. The notion that lunar dust could be force-fed into becoming living, tillable soil by introducing a few selected bacteria strains and saturating it with bulk nutrients might have been attractive to quota-obsessed bureaucrats, but the problem was that it didn't work. The process wasn't amenable to brute force. The Western and Asian space programs had opted for an approach based on self-evolved biosystems, where all the ecological subtleties were allowed to develop in their own time, even though nobody could say for sure why all of them were needed. It was a far slower method, and helped explain why the non-Soviet programs had not gone for large-scale colony construction yet. But it was showing positive results. Now, goaded by we-told-you-so jeers from the rest of the world's biological community, the Soviets had commenced a crash program to ship thousands of tons of terrestrial soil up to *Valentina Tereshkova* for enriching certain areas, then dressing those areas with huge quantities of transplanted crops and plants to provide an acceptable setting for the Soviet leaders to make speeches about progress in when they came up for the November 7 celebrations.

Dr. Brusikov, the Russian section-head whom Paula worked under, came in from the corridor. In his dealings with her he always confined himself to business, never alluding to personal or political matters. "I wanted to catch you before you went," he said. "How does it look?"

"It's running and seems to be okay. I've added the defaults."

"Excellent." Brusikov rubbed his palms together and moved over to the screen. "Well, I'll carry on playing with it for a while this evening. Same time tomorrow, is it? You're not off, are you?"

"No." At that instant a double beep sounded from the unit on Paula's wrist. It meant that the computers monitoring the security and access system had noted the time, and she was now free to move beyond her working vicinity.

"There's your signal," Brusikov said. "Very well, we'll see you tomorrow. Good night."

"Good night." Paula went out into the corridor and turned in the direction of the elevator. Two more figures, one of them dressed in the familiar green priv tunic of Zamork, emerged from another door and headed the same way.

The Zamork inmate's name was Josip. He was a statistician from Yugoslavia, who was also working on ecological models. "I see they're going ahead with this idea of sending tons of dirt up to us," he said. "Have you ever heard of anything so crazy? All to avoid embarrassing their illustrious leaders. It's Potemkin villages all over again."

The civilian was called Gennadi. He was a Russian, younger than Josip, with fine, handsomely lined features, blond hair, and blue eyes that shone with devotion to the Party and the system. In an earlier period, allowing for the turnabout of ideology—which wouldn't have made a lot of difference, since all fanatical ideologies are interchangeable, anyway—he would have qualified as the Nazis' Nordic ideal. He detested everything Western, and anything American in particular. Whenever possible Paula avoided him.

"Well, aren't you going to tell us how incompetent we are?" he asked her as they stopped to wait at the elevator. Paula sighed and said nothing while she continued staring at the doors.

"Oh, lay off, Gennadi," Josip said. "We've all had a hard day. Your great Russian bosses blew it. There's no getting away from the fact, so why not shut up?"

Gennadi took no notice. "You see, it's not really the soil we need. It's the bacteria and things that come with it. But then, *we* are only fallible mortals. We don't have supernatural beings to help us." His tone was sarcastic. Ridiculing religion was one of Gennadi's favorite lines.

"What's that got to do with it?" Josip asked.

"Didn't you know? Why do you think their God told Noah to build the ark? You didn't imagine it was to save all those animals, did you, Josip? Oh, my word, no! The animals were simply the vehicles to carry God's most precious creations, you see: the flea, the hookworm, the body louse, the intestinal parasite, the polio virus, and the dysentery bacterium. Aren't malaria, cholera, yellow fever, and bubonic plague the punishments that this infinitely wise, compassionate, and forgiving Father preserved to inflict upon His children? The victims that He hounds the most gleefully are always the poor, the hungry, the defenseless. What kind of a fiend would we brand any human father who treated his children like that?"

They stepped into the elevator, but Gennadi continued, "Does it make any sense to you, Josip? I say, if the suffering people of this world have anywhere to turn for help, it's their fellow man: engineers, scientists, builders, doctors, farmers. But when a disease is finally eradicated after causing untold misery for thousands of years, what do they do? They thank their God! I ask you! What did He have to do with it? Why did He make it happen in the first place?" Gennadi looked at Paula. "What I can't understand is that you're a scientist. How can you respect a government that does nothing to stop such fairy tales? Is it right that you force children to pray to this absurd God every morning in school?"

"That went away a long time ago," Paula said as the door opened and they got out. "How merciful has the god been that you force children to pray to in *your* schools?" But the answer didn't satisfy her.

They came out into the ground-level concourse of the building, where the inmates due to return to Zamork were assembling from various parts of the surrounding complex. Paula moved to the far end of the group, and to her relief Gennadi didn't stay around but left via the main entrance. She stood without speaking to anyone until the bus drew up outside the main doors to take them back. Minutes later the bus had negotiated the geometric maze out of central Turgenev and merged onto the roadway running above the monorail track in the direction of Novyi Kazan.

The galling part of it all was that the things Gennadi said mirrored her own views on religion almost perfectly. There had been many times when she had pointed out the same nonsenses to the fundamentalist fanatics she'd come across back in the States. That was why she was always so disarmed by Gennadi's arguments: she had never before been in the position of hearing virtually her own words turned back upon her, and of being able to find no way to respond.

And even more disturbing, what did it signify that he should be ascribing the same attributes to her, now, that she had always seen in people like him? She thought of Olga, and how their common appreciation of science bonded them into a global community that stood apart from superficial divisions of people into nations and creeds—meaningless divisions based not on comprehension of reality and truth, but on prejudice, myth, wishful thinking, and unreason. On both sides of the world, reason was subordinated to systems that were equally irrational, and yet were just as certain of themselves. Such systems couldn't be entrusted with the future. Now, she thought, she understood how Maurice had felt.

✻   ✻   ✻

When Paula arrived back at Zamork, she went for her evening meal—yellow-pea soup and bread, a potato, stewed pulp of cabbage leaves, and a slice of gelatinous processed meat that the cook insisted was ham—in the communal canteen of the Services Block. It was a busy time with the day workshift trickling in, but she spotted Elena, one of her companions from Hut 19, alone at one of the tables, and joined her.

Elena had somehow managed to retain her chubby build despite the unspectacular diet. She had straight brown hair, which she wore short with a fringe, ruddy cheeks, a second chin, and ample hips. Paula always pictured her as a farmer's wife, but in fact she was a sociologist, and for that reason was out of favor with the authorities who decided what the mainstream lines of learning and thinking should be. Thus, with typical topsy-turvy Communist logic, only in the society that claimed to comprehend the social struggle as a science was its study by scientific processes actively discouraged—or banned outright if the findings didn't support what doctrine said had to be true. Elena's counterparts in the West usually made prime-time TV.

"I never used to consider social science a 'science' at all," Paula confessed after they had talked for a while. "I'm not sure if I do now."

"Oh?" Elena continued eating and didn't seem perturbed.

"A science means being able to predict confidently what causes will produce what effects. It works with things like physics, but the processes that physics describes are really simple—particles and forces and how they interact. Yet it took centuries to get where it is, and we got it wrong at every opportunity. But you know, Elena, even the ecological webs that I've been working with for two months are simple compared to a nation's social system, never mind the whole world's. Nobody knows what changes will produce what results, whatever else they say to get funding. It's all still at the voodoo stage: eventually it'll rain if you dance long enough."

Elena smiled. Paula admitted inwardly that she sometimes took advantage of Elena's disposition in order to dump her own emotional charge when she was agitated about something. "I suppose you're right," Elena said. "Certainly sociology never managed to become very strong as an experimental science. You can't very well go around putting people in cages to study them. . . . But then, of course, that was mainly all you Americans' fault if anybody's." Elena's eyes were twinkling.

Paula realized that she wasn't about to be let off the hook so easily. "What do you mean?" she asked.

"If your really believe all the things you say about freedom and the rights of people to govern themselves, why didn't you allow the United States to become a huge, natural sociological laboratory?" Elena replied. "You could have let every part of the country try out whatever kind of system appealed to it—liberal or authoritarian, secular, religious, whatever—and found out from experience what worked and what didn't. Then you'd have seen which of the experts' predictions succeeded, and been able to evaluate the worth of the experts doing the predicting. Instead, you introduced those big federal programs that cost fortunes and which I'm not convinced did much good—straight from untested speculation to national law, without any experimental stage in between. And the irony is, it's exactly what you've always accused us of."

"Touché," Paula acknowledged. "I asked for that."

"But it's going to happen, nevertheless," Elena went on.

"You think so?"

"It's starting already—look at China. They've got cities that are rigidly Marxist just twenty miles from others that are totally laissez-faire. One area is run by a traditionalist religious sect that rejects technology, another has no laws at all relating to personal morality, and in another everyone carries a gun. Everyone migrates to where they think it'll suit them best, and if they find they were wrong they try somewhere else."

"It sounds like chaos."

"It is in many ways, while they're finding out how to make it work without fragmenting in all directions. But it's true evolution in action. That's why they'll lead the migration out into space when it comes. What they're doing is a foretaste of how it will be, but on a vaster scale. We haven't seen diversity yet. It will be an explosion, not a migration."

"If it happens," Paula had said before she realized it.

Elena looked at her curiously. "Naturally it will happen. Why shouldn't it?"

"Oh . . ." Paula sat back on the bench and looked around. "The way the world is. . . . Are the leaders on both sides smart enough to handle it? Take all the fuss there's been about this place, for example. You'd think it would be a simple enough matter to settle once and for all if it's a battle platform, wouldn't you? But apparently it's not so simple. Now they're saying—"

"Of course it isn't a battle platform," Elena said. Her tone of voice left no room for doubt. "I'm sorry, but that really is a figment of your Western imagination—paranoia at its worst."

"How can you be so sure?"

"Common sense tells you." Elena inclined her head to indicate a bespectacled man with a ginger beard, who was talking animatedly to a group at the next table. "Do you know who that is? Professor Valdik Palyatskin, one of the Soviet Union's authorities on low-temperature fusion. The woman across from him is a specialist in genetic diseases. The skinny man over there, in the center on the far side, is one of the engineers who built the largest aluminum refinery in Siberia. I know it's insane that such people should be in here because of their political views, but what matters for now is that they constitute a valuable potential resource to the state—in fact, if you want my opinion, I think that's the whole reason why this place was set up as it is. This is the last place anyone would concentrate them in, if it were a battle platform. It would be a prime target. They'd be much safer down underneath Siberia somewhere."

Elena pushed her plate away and looked up; but Paula's face had taken on a distant look, and she didn't answer. Of course. It was so obvious. But Western intelligence didn't know the caliber of the people who were interned up here—not to mention many of the civilian population, who had come by choice. The Russians didn't publish directories of names for anyone who might be curious. Here was something else that the intelligence advisers to the West's decision-makers needed to know about.

For a moment Paula thought of simply going to General

Protbornov and telling him that she wanted to communicate with the West, and why. Surely it would be in everyone's interests. And as Olga had said when they talked about using Ivan, it would only be corroborating what the Soviets themselves had been saying publicly. But as she thought more about it, her enthusiasm waned. Coming through on an official Soviet communications channel, what would the chances be that her story would be believed? True, as was standard practice with all agents, she had memorized a coding method to indicate whether a communication was being sent freely or under coercion. But agents could be genuinely turned; the best people could be fooled and misled. And besides, the thought of cooperating with the Russians and then having to face Earnshaw later was enough to put the idea out of her head without further consideration.

But there was still Ivan.

"Are you going?" Elena asked, surprised, as Paula started to rise.

"Excuse me. Yes, I have to leave."

"Why? What's the matter?"

"I have to find Olga urgently."

⊚ CHAPTER THIRTY-SEVEN ⊚

Water pumped up by subterranean backstage machinery emerged near the top of the hill abutting the outer-hull wall to feed a stream that flowed back down to enter the reservoir at the beach. Behind the beach, the stream curved around a flat, open stretch of grass and sand that the privs used as a recreation area. Paula found Olga there, with a group of spectators who were watching some gymnasts vaulting. It seemed that Olga had been searching for her, too. Two Russian guards were looking on idly from a distance.

"Very well, I've decided," Paula said without preliminaries. "I want to try making contact with the West through Ivan." Olga opened her mouth to speak, but before she could say anything Paula went on, "I've just been talking with Elena. There are more things that they ought to know about this place—more than Maurice will tell them. When do you plan to send your next message?"

"That's what I was looking for you to tell you about," Olga said. "We already have it!"

"Already have what? I don't understand. . . . What are you talking about?"

"We have a channel to your people in the West, via Ivan."

"That's impossible. How could we?"

Olga moved her face closer to Paula's ear. "If I told you that a communication has come in over it from Tycoon, directed to

Pedestal/Fox, would that mean anything to you?" She leaned closer and slipped a piece of paper into Paula's jacket pocket. "That is a copy of it."

For a few moments Paula could only stand and stare, dumbstruck. In front of them, one of the performers took a tumble, provoking derisive comments from the group watching.

"We should get some of the dirt they're sending up from Earth. Maybe it would grow better grass for you to fall on."

"Let's hope it's good, black soil from the Ukraine," another said. "I'd rather have better food."

"The whole business is so stupid," someone grumbled.

"Well, that was how a Party bureaucrat somewhere obeyed orders when he was told to send Russia into space," the first replied. The others laughed.

"Tycoon" identified Bernard Foleda in his capacity as head of the mission that had brought Paula and Earnshaw to *Valentina Tereshkova*. "Pedestal" was the code name for that mission, while "Fox" was part of the validation-coding system that labeled the message as authentic and would permit her, by her form of reply, to do likewise. "But how? . . ." she stammered.

Olga took her elbow and steered her away from the crowd, in the direction of rising terrain toward the hill. "I've learned more from Ivan since we restored the link. As was to be expected, he's been under observation by the KGB since my arrest. But with somebody of his status, they have avoided confronting him directly until they have solid evidence. Well, apparently he felt the way the wind is blowing and is looking for insurance—he's talking to the West about defecting."

"Talking? . . ." Paula checked herself and nodded. "Yes, of course. In his position it wouldn't be difficult, would it?"

"Exactly. And he'd have told your people about his position at the groundstation. My guess is that they put pressure on him to see if he could make contact, just as you wanted to."

Paula frowned. "But how could they have known about his private line to you?"

"I'm not certain that they did," Olga said. "Maybe that was just a gamble."

They sat down on a couple of rocks in a cluster that had doubtless originated from some part of the Moon. Forty years ago the material would have been priceless. Now it was used for unremarkable landscaping props—or, more likely, had simply been dumped by a construction team.

"I assume you'll want to reply," Olga said.

As things stood, Olga used any BV-15 computer to load her messages to Ivan into one of the chips that Paula had programmed—after what had happened to Ivan's original, they weren't relying on having just one—and then her undisclosed accomplice substituted the chip for a standard one contained in the encoding equipment inside the Communications Center. Although this method did not require the chip to be switched every time there was a message to go out, they had judged it safer than leaving the chip in place permanently and attempting to access it from a remote terminal, which would have left a nonstandard piece of hardware waiting to be discovered. To send a message of her own, Paula could handle the first part of the operation herself, but not the second.

"I can use the spare chip," she told Olga. "But I'll need your accomplice to switch it for me."

Olga nodded. "There should be no difficulty." Obviously it would make no difference to Olga's accomplice whose message was in the chip.

The signal that she finally composed during her next session in the graphics lab was headed TYCOON/HYPER FROM PANGOLIN/TROT, 09/22/17. It read: MESSAGE RECEIVED. PEDESTAL NEGATIVE FOLLOWING DISCOVERY/ARREST DURING ACCESS TANGERINE. CURRENTLY DETAINED MERMAID/ZAMORK. CONDITION GOOD BUT DENIED COMM'N RIGHTS. NO NEWS SEXTON BUT BELIEVED ELSEWHERE HERE. MUST CONSIDER TANGERINE LOST. HOWEVER, BELIEVE OTHER INTELLIGENCE MIGHT ASSIST EVALUATION, E.G. KEY INMATE NAME LIST. CAN SUPPLY. CONFIRM INTEREST. ENDS ENDS.

"Sexton" and "Pangolin" were Earnshaw's and her code designations respectively. Paula strung three copies end-to-end as a single data block for redundancy and tagged the message for transmission.

The validation system was based on a list of unique key words that each agent memorized, which were known to nobody else. Foleda's department kept a master file of all the lists. Each word in a list was a compound of two parts, chosen such that the first part could be combined naturally in English with many second parts to give a valid completion. For example, the word "ice" could combine with "cube," "bucket," "berg," "breaker," and many more equally valid completions. Only one, however, was correct for a particular list. Thus, whether a message originated from the agent or from the department, a correct completion from the same list confirmed both that the message was authentic, and that it was not being sent under coercion.

In the specific case of the reply sent by Paula, the "Trot" after her code name completed the compound word that Foleda had cued with "Fox." She in turn had selected the first part, "Hyper," of another compound and included it in her response. The completion "Golic" in the next message she received would confirm that it was indeed from Foleda, and not a forgery manufactured by someone with access to the communications medium.

The medical orderlies took Albrecht Haber away again halfway through the afternoon of McCain's day off. It was his second relapse in a week. An hour after the midday meal, he had gone to lie down, complaining of nausea and stomach pains, and not long after that he had become feverish.

"Barbarians, that's what they are, keeping an old man like him in a place like this," Oskar Smovak declared to the others sitting at one of the tables out in the B-Block mess area. "What harm can he be to anybody? He ought to be sent home."

"Did anybody notice what he was eating at lunch?" Luchenko asked, standing a few feet away accompanied by Kong.

"What does it matter?" Smovak replied. "With the muck they serve, it's a wonder we're not all in the infirmary." Luchenko grunted and walked back into the billet, followed by his wooden-faced shadow.

"It's your move," Leo Vorghas said.

"Oh, was it?" Smovak returned his attention to the chessboard between them.

"Charlie Chan's got a new joke about the food."

"Thanks, but I'd rather not hear it."

At the end, near Smovak, Koh turned a page of the book he was reading. McCain was sitting a couple of feet away, leaning forward with his arms folded on the edge of the table while he watched four of the Siberians rolling marbles across a pattern of chalked lines and symbols on an open area of the floor. It was a new game they had worked out with Rashazzi. As usual there was a lot of arguing and cursing, with tokens and slips of paper changing hands constantly to keep track of the scores and bets. Buried in the design were special marks that Rashazzi had made to measure accurately the trajectories of the rolling balls across the surface. But on this particular occasion he wasn't present. He had worked a series of bracelet-swapping deals and was now able to remain virtually full-time in the Crypt without interruption.

"So you really never had heard of Sam Caton, eh?"

McCain realized Smovak had moved a piece and was talking to him. He turned his head back. "Nope. Never had."

"I thought everyone in America must have heard of him. I was testing you, you see."

"I know."

"You can't be too cautious." Smovak looked at Koh. "Did you ever visit America?"

"Of course he has," Vorghas threw in without looking up from the board. "Where hasn't he visited?"

"You were in California at one time, I think you mentioned once, Mr. Earnshaw," Koh said, lifting his face toward McCain. "I know some parts of it. Where exactly did you live?"

"I was born in Iowa. But I grew up some of the time in and around Bakersfield. Went to college in L.A."

"Ah yes, Bakersfield. I have a cousin not far from there—in Fresno, as a matter of fact. He's an attorney, and he also restores antique clocks and musical machines."

"We should have guessed." Smovak shook his head disbelievingly.

"He's even got a cousin in Moscow, did you know that? Has the franchise to run a Japanese restaurant there. I ask you—a Japanese restaurant in Moscow! There isn't anywhere on the planet that the Koh tribe hasn't reached."

Koh marked his place with a piece of card and set down the book. "It's just as well, too," he said. "It was mainly immigration from the East that saved the United States. Fifty years ago, everyone was being frightened by scare-stories about runaway population explosion. But even at the time, the facts were exactly opposite. It's perfectly natural and healthy that when nations industrialize and their living standards improve, their populations should grow geometrically for a while— it happened in Europe in the eighteenth century, America in the nineteenth, and is still happening to a degree in Asia. However, they level out again as lifestyles change. . . . But the wise man looks at the dry distant mountains and prepares for a drought, even while the river is in flood. The point everyone missed was that populations *decrease* geometrically too. And even while the panic was at its highest, the West's birthrate had not only declined, but fallen below the replacement level. They were facing a catastrophic population collapse. That was what almost ruined West Germany. So I'm afraid, gentlemen, that you'll have to resign yourselves to being a small minority in the world ahead. Fortunately, with the kind of civilization that I see emerging, I don't think it will matter very much."

Mungabo and Scanlon had come in from Gorky Street and sat down to catch the tail end of what Koh had been saying. Scanlon pulled a box of playing cards from his pocket and began laying out a solitaire array. "And what do you see emerging, Koh?" he inquired. "Will this be the fella to replace Western Man?"

"Maybe," Koh said.

"Got a name for him yet?" Mungabo asked.

"Next will come the Nonlinear Man—Interplanetary Man—who will emerge among the offplanet worlds that will soon take shape," Koh replied. "He will take Classical beauty, Western science, Chinese pragmatism, Japanese dedication, and maybe Russian realism, along with other stones from other rubble, but he will build them into a new edifice which will be his own. His children will accept as self-evident the concept of evolution as a succession of discontinuities, and take for granted the impossibilities of today becoming commonplace tomorrow. They will go out to populate a universe which by its very size and extent, stretching away beyond the range of the most powerful instruments, symbolizes a reality that imposes no limits on how far their civilization can grow, how much it may achieve, or what they may become." Koh looked around the table. "There are no finite resources, only finite thinking." He opened his book again, looked down, and resumed reading.

Scanlon continued moving and turning the cards. Smovak picked up a knight and thumped it back down on the board. "Check." Vorghas put his chin between his hands to study the new position.

McCain leaned forward and moved a red five onto a black six. "Busy day at the hub?" he asked Scanlon casually.

Scanlon scooped up the cards again and dealt two gin-rummy hands. McCain picked up his hand and inspected it. "As a matter of fact, I heard they had a little bit of excitement there today," Scanlon said. "A fire, no less—in the Space Environment Lab, it was. An electrical fault, by all accounts."

"That's too bad," McCain murmured. "Anyone hurt?"

"Ah, no, it was nothing serious. . . . But I'm told some things in a closet up there were burned pretty badly."

McCain sent a questioning look over the top of the fan he was holding, and Scanlon returned a faint nod. They played for a while. When they finished, Scanlon put the cards back in the box, slipped it into his jacket pocket, and rose to leave. Then, as if struck by an afterthought, he turned back, took the box from his pocket again, and handed it to McCain. "If you're going back inside the billet, do me a favor and give these back to Chan, would you? I've to meet a man in the compound in a couple of minutes."

"Sure," McCain said, dropping the box into his own pocket. But it wasn't the same box, and there weren't any playing cards inside. Instead, it held a package containing two functioning general-clearance civilian badges.

A day later, Haber had undergone an amazing recovery and was returned to the billet. With him he brought the remaining components which, together with the ones he had purloined from the pharmaceuticals lab during his previous two visits from the infirmary, enabled him and Rashazzi to construct an accurate balance scale in the Crypt workshop. They used it to measure the weights of objects at various heights in the elevator shaft that connected the Crypt deck, via the surface and Hut 8, back down to B-12 billet and gave the escape committee's "elevator route" its name.

"Things should weigh less at higher levels as you get nearer to the spin axis," Rashazzi explained to McCain after the results had been compared. "And in fact they do. But the decrease is far less than it ought to be. At this level in the rim, a weight should change by two point one percent if it's moved twenty meters nearer the axis. But the amount we measured was less than half that."

Haber took off his spectacles and began polishing the lenses with a handkerchief. "The baffling thing is that once again the results are consistent with the idea of the colony's being larger than is officially stated." McCain had been thinking about that since the scientists described the results of their tests with the pendulum. He wondered if weapons could be concealed in the extra volume that seemed to be indicated. But Haber demolished the notion when he continued, "But to give these figures, the diameter of the ring would have to be something like four and a half kilometers, which is well over twice the quoted figure. I really don't know what to make of it. A discrepancy that large would have been public knowledge years ago."

Nobody could offer any satisfactory answers. But the matter was put aside for the time being when Peter Sargent and Eban Istamel brought more news from the escape committee. In the course of exploring farther down below the elevator-route shaft, they had gained entry to a tube that appeared to be part of a robot freight-transit system that possibly ran all the way around the ring. If so, then it offered not only a way out of the limits of Zamork, but a ticket to anywhere else in the colony.

So at last it looked as if McCain and his group were about to become fully mobile. Now, perhaps, they'd begin shedding light on some of the perplexing questions that had been accumulating.

❄ CHAPTER THIRTY-EIGHT ❄

Deep in the Pentagon's labyrinth of corridors and offices, Bernard Foleda and Gerald Kehrn came out of an elevator and turned in the direction of Foleda's office. Foleda pounded along irascibly, setting the pace. Kehrn was looking worried.

"Dirt!" Foleda snorted. "Who ever heard of shipping thousands of tons of dirt up into orbit? Not even their cloud-cuckoo-land economics could justify it. What do they take us for? It smells to high heaven, Gerry."

A lot of other people thought so, too. That was why the United States, representing a number of concerned Western nations, had demanded the USSF vessels be permitted to monitor the operations, going on in low-Earth orbit, of transferring cargo from Soviet surface shuttles into longer-range transporter ships. To everyone's surprise, the Soviets had agreed.

"Well, don't forget that their ideas on what's efficient don't exactly tally with ours," Kehrn said. "To them, efficiency is directing all the resources you've got onto whatever objective the Party says is top priority. That was how Mermaid got to be built in the first place. It isn't simply the sum total of a lot of individually profitable businesses. They wouldn't be able to see how running a pet-food factory profitably can be efficient when pet food isn't important. So maybe to them it makes sense."

"Yes, and what caused Mermaid to be their top priority?" Foleda growled. "They're up to something."

Barbara got up from a chair opposite Rose in Foleda's outer office as they appeared. Rose began leafing through a wad of papers and message slips. "It's been all hell let loose . . . Borden has called three times in the last half hour. The President's chief of staff called. The CIA director. . . . Whaley over in Defense . . ."

"Hold the trench just a little longer, Rose," Foleda said without slackening his pace. "We've got something really urgent."

"Okay, but I'm telling you, the ammunition's running low here." As she spoke, a call-tone sounded from the screen-panel beside her desk. The others went on through.

Barbara closed the door of the inner office. "What have we got?" Foleda asked her. She had beeped him via his pocket handpad a few minutes earlier and told him only that she had news from Mermaid concerning Pedestal.

Barbara opened the folder she was carrying and handed him a sheet of printout. He sat down at his desk, and Kehrn moved around to read it with him over his shoulder. "In from NSA eight minutes ago," Barbara said. "They show the time of receipt as ten-thirty-nine hours today. The validation completion is correct for Pangolin."

"My God, we did it!" Foleda breathed as his eyes read rapidly down the paper. "It's from Bryce. Our signal got through. She *is* still up there. . . . No news of Lew, though, eh?"

Kehrn nodded. "She's the communications whiz. It figures."

"Your hunch must have been right," Barbara said to Foleda. "It must be Oshkadov that Dyashkin has been talking to."

"He did what we wanted," Kehrn said. "The guy's busting his ass over there to please. It's starting to look as if he's clean." He looked down questioningly, but Foleda was leaning back in his chair and staring at the far wall without seeming to have heard.

Kehrn was about to say something more when Foleda's desk screen began emitting its priority tone. Barbara answered it. "Yes, Rose?"

"Fix bayonets. I'm out of bullets. Borden's on his way."

Moments later the door burst open and Philip Borden strode in, looking strained. "What the hell, Bern? I've been calling you. I was told you were out."

"Sorry, Phil, I was. We only got back this second." Foleda showed him the transcript of the message from *Tereshkova*. "Take a look at this. It just came in. We've got a line to Bryce. Sounds as if Lew might be there someplace, too."

Borden took the sheet and scanned down it. "Holy cow, I don't believe this . . . a private channel to our own people inside a Soviet space station. Honestly, Bern, when you first sprung this on me I thought you'd flipped. . . . What's this bit about key inmate names?"

"I don't know. Like I said, I only saw it for the first time myself a few seconds ago."

The diversion had calmed Borden down a little from the agitated state he'd been in when he entered. He set the folder down on Foleda's desk and sighed wearily. "Well, let's hope that now you've got it, it can do some good. They sure made us look a bunch of assholes this time."

"Who did?"

"Moscow, of course. What else do you think the flap's all about out there? Don't tell me you haven't heard yet."

"I just this second got back," Foleda said again. "I've been giving a talk to that conference of Stan's all morning."

Borden waved a hand vaguely overhead. "We've sent three USSF interceptors in to monitor those Soviet transfer operations in orbit. They used X-ray detectors, magnetometer detectors, visual observation, and Christ knows what. The reports are in. They're all the same."

"What did they find?" Kehrn asked.

Borden threw up his hands. "What do you think they found? Dirt. Just lots of dirt. Nothing else. The President's mad as hell about it, we're a laughingstock, and some of the Asian states are wondering if maybe we have been crazy all along. This isn't my best day, Bern."

For once Foleda looked dumbstruck. It was he who had predicted that the Russians would never permit the payloads of the Soviet shuttles to be inspected. There was no risk that they might be decoys: the transporter ships loaded from them could be tracked clearly all the way to *Tereshkova*. Nothing could be substituted with any chance of escaping detection.

"Does that mean we've got a decision for November?" Barbara asked.

Borden nodded. "We're accepting. It hasn't been announced publicly yet, but I got it from the White House an hour or so ago. We'll be sending the Vice President and Secretary of State. The President's view is that we don't have any choice now if we want to avoid being written off by half the world as paranoids. He didn't want to force this inspection issue, and he feels that we pushed him into it. This is his way of telling us, 'screw you.'"

Foleda stared gloomily at his desk. This was what he had been fearing. In the tide of euphoria and hopes for a sudden easing of tensions that had swept the world, most of the leading European and Asian nations had already announced that they would be sending representatives. The party would travel from Earth orbit to *Valentina Tereshkova* in a neutral ship carrying a mixed United Nations crew. The President, he knew, had expressed displeasure at what he saw as the US's failure to seize an important initiative, and he held excessive caution and unwarranted suspicion on the part of the UDIA as largely to blame. "So the rest of it didn't make any difference, eh?" Foleda concluded.

Borden shook his head. "Not after this. They think we're seeing shapes in tea leaves. And to be frank, I'm half inclined to think they might be right."

"We walked right into it," Foleda said. "I was a chump. Of course there's nothing but dirt in those shuttles. Whatever they needed up there went up months ago. This dirt thing was a deliberate provocation for us to call them, and we did. Now our credibility's shot."

"You still think it's a blind for something, then," Borden said.

"No, I don't think. I'm sure of it. They wanted to make sure we'd be embarrassed enough to make amends by sending our people there, along with everyone else's."

"What for?"

Foleda looked up. "Hostages. What else? And they don't even

have to hijack them—we're sending them voluntarily. Mermaid is a battle platform. Those VIPs are its protection. They guarantee we won't fire at it preemptively, and they constitute insurance against *us* having possible weapons up *our* sleeve. Hesitation and disagreement in our camp at a crucial moment could prove decisive."

Borden nodded. He had heard this before. "But aren't you overlooking one thing, Bern?" Kehrn said. "All the *Soviet* VIPs will be there too—and I mean practically *all* of them. Their tops, too: bigger than the ones everybody else will be sending. That has to count for something."

"And suppose they don't," Foleda countered. "Suppose it's all phony, and they don't send any of them up there—just empty ships for us to watch through telescopes. Do you think our people would insist on checking them out after this latest fiasco? No way. See— they've covered that base too."

Kehrn looked uneasy. "Well . . . they'd have to be there." He frowned, as if, having stated it, he wasn't sure why. "I mean, they couldn't not be there when all the rest arrive, could they? And the place will be declared open after that . . ."

Foleda looked hard at him for a few seconds, then leaned back in his chair and shook his head. "No. They don't have to do any of that. By that time, none of it will matter. Whatever it is they're planning will have happened by November seventh. A month. That's all we've got to find out."

He sounded more certain than ever before. This time the others remained quiet and didn't argue.

❁ CHAPTER THIRTY-NINE ❁

Agniya left Hut 19 early in October. She had accepted an offer of a teaching position in Turgenev on condition of good behavior, and was released for a three-month probationary period to take up normal accommodations in the town.

"That's how they get you," Svetlana said to Paula as they stood watching with some other friends as Agniya sent back a final wave before disappearing into the Administration Building. The second of the two guards who had helped her carry her belongings from the hut closed the door behind. "They gave her a work assignment at the elementary school. She's always loved children. Now she'll cooperate and do what they want—and not only that, but be grateful for it, too. With you it will be computers."

"I doubt if it'll come to that," Paula said.

"We'll see."

"That's what this whole place is for," Elena said as they began retracing their steps down toward the huts. "At one time they used to punish dissenters, but it was so wasteful. Then they tried brainwashing, but it destroyed the creativity that they wanted to use. Now they rehabilitate people without losing them."

Agniya's replacement arrived that evening. A guard showed her to the hut and deposited her bags inside the door, while a second waited outside. She stepped in and looked around, nodding a greeting to Svetlana and Elena. Then she shifted her eyes to Paula, who had risen to her feet and was staring wide-eyed. They gazed at each other in amazement for several seconds, and then hugged warmly. It was Tanya, the schoolteacher whom Paula had last seen in the infirmary, before her transfer to the surface level.

"So it was true, they did move you up here!" Tanya exclaimed. "Anastasia and I often wondered about you. You remember Anastasia?"

"Of course. How is she?"

"Up and about again. And you! You're looking so well compared to how you were. Things must really be a lot different up here."

"Yes, you'll find it quite a change. Oh, but I'm being rude—these are the other two ladies who live here." Paula introduced Svetlana and Elena. They showed Tanya the bunk that Agniya had vacated. Svetlana offered her a cigarette. She declined and began unpacking her things. Paula helped her put them away while Elena made tea.

"Is it true you have a beach up here?" Tanya asked.

"Yes—kind of," Paula said. "And more. I'll show you around before dark. But how did you get here?"

Tanya sighed. "The usual kind of deal, I suppose. There are a lot of new arrivals at *Tereshkova* these days—moving into quarters that have recently been completed at Turgenev and Landausk. They include many families with children. Apparently the place is short of teachers. I was offered a transfer up here in return for helping out at one of the schools . . . And here I am."

"You're a teacher, then?" Svetlana said.

"Yes."

"Isn't that interesting. Agniya—the woman you're replacing here—she went to teach at Turgenev, too. She was released, in fact."

"Subsurface Zamork is filling up, too," Tanya said. "New faces appearing every day."

"I wonder what's going on," Svetlana mused.

"They want the place full and bustling with people for November seventh," Tanya said. "And this year it's going to be sun-bronzed youth and gymnastics displays. Troops and tanks are out." Potemkin villages, Paula thought. Yet at the same time the news made her stop and think. It was hardly the kind of population that anyone would want on a battle platform.

They finished getting Tanya settled in, and talked while finishing their tea, after which Paula and Tanya got up to leave for a tour of the surface level. But just as they came out of the hut, Olga appeared.

"Olga, I'd like you to meet Tanya, a friend of mine from when I was Sub. She's just moved in as Agniya's replacement. Isn't that wonderful? Tanya, this is Olga. If you really want to find out how to get anything done up here, she's the woman to know."

"A pleasure," Tanya said, extending a hand.

Olga shook it lightly and smiled, but she seemed distracted. "Paula, look, there's someone I want you to talk to. He has some news you'll be interested in."

"Now? I was just about to show Tanya around."

"It is urgent." Olga's voice was serious.

"Of course you must go," Tanya told Paula. "I'm sure everything will still be here in the morning. And to tell you the truth, I am rather tired. I'm sorry we had to meet in such a rush, Olga. We'll see each other again soon, I'm sure. Good night." And with that, Tanya turned and went back into the hut.

Olga took Paula to Hut 8, which was close to Hut 19, in the next row downhill toward the Administration Building. She tapped on the door, which was opened almost immediately by a big, heavyset man with a fleshy, smooth-skinned, olive complexion, wide eyes, and reddish curls framing a high brow. His face was familiar, but Paula had never had reason to talk to him. He had evidently been expecting them, and stepped outside. The three of them began walking slowly in the direction of the reservoir.

"Paula, this is Eban," Olga said. "You've probably seen him around. I think Eban can help you with regard to the other American you've been asking about."

"Lewis Earnshaw? You know where he is?"

"Hmm, I've possibly heard tell of him," Eban said noncommittally. "Describe him to me."

"Oh, about six feet in height, I'd guess. One-eighty-pounds, probably—solid, lean kind of build. Black, wavy hair. It used to be short, parted on the left. Brown eyes, alert, taking things in all the time. Clean-shaved face."

"Why is he here?"

"He came here with me on May first, as a journalist for Pacific News Services of California. We were arrested on charges of espionage."

"Why did he really come here?"

"I've given you my answer."

Eban sniffed and looked at Olga questioningly. "She's reliable," Olga said. "I've worked with her for a long time now. Have you ever regretted trusting my judgment?"

"I don't like the part about showing her the Crypt and the way into it," Eban said, speaking as if Paula wasn't there. "It's not necessary for her to know of it at this stage. Why can't we bring him up here instead?"

"There are reasons, as you know," Olga replied.

"Hmm." Eban reflected for a moment longer, then nodded. "Very well. But I will need to make arrangements. Come by the hut at the same time tomorrow. Knock if a pot with yellow primroses has been put in the window by the door. Otherwise don't bother—it will mean the hut is being watched."

The next day, Olga visited the library and brought Paula the transcript of a reply from "Tycoon/Golic," addressed to "Pangolin/Hot." "Tycoon" was Foleda's code name, while "Golic" completed the compound "Hypergolic," the first half of which Paula had supplied in her transmission. It acknowledged receipt of Paula's message, asked a few specific questions, and expressed interest in the list of inmates' names that Paula had referred to. She decided to put off responding until she'd allowed some time for the promised contact with Earnshaw—which with luck might be imminent.

That evening, the flowers had been placed in the window by the door of Hut 8 when Olga and Paula approached. Paula hadn't asked how Eban knew whether or not the place was under observation. It was the kind of thing that could happen at any time for no particular reason in Zamork. Olga was carrying a book. They went up to the door and knocked, and Eban let them in. Inside was another man, late thirties or thereabouts, with flat, sandy-colored hair and a ragged mustache. He was wearing the gray uniform of regular-category inmates from the subsurface levels. Paula's first thought was to wonder how he had gotten into the hut, almost in the center of the surface level compound, without being seen. Before Paula could say anything, Eban touched his lips with a finger and shook his head as a signal for her to remain quiet.

"I've brought your book back, Eban," Olga said. "Most of it was good, but I didn't agree with the last part. Do you really go along with that?"

"Yes, but I'm not in a mood to argue about it now. Oh, did you want to hear that tape I was telling you about?"

"The American one?"

"They call it piano blues. I wonder why we never invented anything like it." Eban started a player on a shelf in one corner, and twangy music turned to high volume filled the room. Silently the mustached man handed Paula a flashlight, and then he and Eban went through to the small bathroom and shower closet at the rear of the hut, motioning for Paula to follow. Olga came after them.

The mustached man knelt down by the shower and felt with his fingertips under the edge of the lip enclosing the cubicle floor. The click of a catch sounded, and the whole square of tiling surrounding the drain hinged upward. A section of pipe below the drain had been replaced by a loop of flexible tubing to allow the trapdoor to swing free. Below was a vertical shaft, shored with strips of metal and plastic panels. It was lit by a small bulb fixed in one of the corners a short distance down. The mustached man swung his legs into the shaft and climbed down out of sight. Eban nodded for Paula to follow. She crouched down and sat on the edge of the opening. Below, the head and shoulders of the mustached man were silhouetted dimly against the light. She turned and braced her arms on the edge, and a hand from below guided her foot toward a rung fastened to the shaft wall. Paula felt with her other foot, found the next rung, and began climbing carefully down. Above her head, the trapdoor swung back over the top of the shaft and clicked shut.

They had climbed down through no more than ten feet of the surrounding soil, or whatever else lay beneath the huts, when Paula felt herself stepping out of the shaft into thin air. The hand caught her foot again and moved it onto a solid surface. She ducked out of what turned out to be an opening in a roof, and found herself standing on a steel housing of some kind, partly visible in the feeble light from a second bulb at the bottom of the shaft they had emerged from. Machinery hummed in the space she could sense around her, and there was a current of warm air smelling of oil. Then even the light from the shaft vanished, plunging the place into complete darkness. A moment later a flashlight beam appeared, illuminating the hole in the roof above them. "Give me some light there with yours," the mustached man hissed. Paula did so while he attached a panel over the opening. Then he turned back toward her.

Paula shone her lamp at his face. "We can't go on meeting like this," she said.

He grinned apologetically. "A dreadful way to introduce myself, I know." He was obviously English. "Hello. My same is Sargent— Peter Sargent. I'm taking you to Lewis Earnshaw."

"Paula Shelmer. How long has this tunnel been here?"

"Well, now, that would be telling, wouldn't it?"

They climbed down to the floor, and Sargent led the way through a fragmented world of machines, pipes, ducting, structural supports and cable runs glimpsed briefly in the dancing flashlight beams and made all the more unreal by the suddenness of the contrast with the world they had just left. A bridge of braced girders spanning a drop into black nothingness pointed to a wall reinforced with metal ribbing, which appeared to extend beyond the containing decks above and below. Heights had never been one of Paula's strong pints, and she made the crossing with trembling legs and a dry mouth. At the far end, Sargent straddled the topmost girder and removed a section that had been cut out of the wall in front, then drew Paula close by him to look through.

She felt as if her heart had dropped down to somewhere in her stomach. The shaft she found herself staring down plunged away to lose itself in blackness beyond the range of the light from Sargent's flashlight. It was like looking down a bottomless mine.

"Down there?" Paula croaked.

"It's one of the main Core elevators," Sargent replied cheerfully. "The problem is that we're up at the top, and the place we want to get to is down near the bottom. The part that the car runs over is in between, which means we have to get underneath it."

"Wonderful."

"Nothing to worry about. First we have to get across to the other side, which we do by dropping down into that horizontal strip and following it around. There's a space across there, behind the rails the car runs on, that we can use to get down. I'll go first. If you're not happy about the traverse, I can bring a line back to clip on you that'll catch you if you slip."

"No, I'll make it. Let's get it over with. But what happens if the car comes up while we're only halfway over?"

"It's all right. It doesn't come up this high. But it causes quite a strong draft of air. Be ready for it."

Sargent led off, and Paula tracked him with her light. He moved surely and unhurriedly, finding his holds and shifting position with effortless catlike grace. He reached the far side in no time and lodged himself in the recess behind the vertical rails. Moments later, the beam from his lamp came on to light up the first stretch immediately below Paula. She was already wishing she'd accepted the offer of a safety line, but a streak of pride prevented her from calling out after him now. She lowered herself from the hole to the level of the horizontal strut and edged sideways onto it, feeling ahead with a hand, finding a hold, and pulling herself another step toward the first corner.

"Great stuff!" Sargent's voice called from across the shaft. "There's a plate just above your head that you can hold onto there. The next bit's a little tricky because there's nothing for your hands. Take it slowly and press your palms flat against the wall for balance." Paula looked sideways and down over her shoulder. A metal bracing strip about three inches wide ran along the wall, a short distance out from it, with nothing within reach above but smooth, featureless metal. She swallowed hard and gulped a breath. Flattening her chest and the side of her face against the wall, she moved out from the corner, her arm stretched to the side, fingertips inching their way along the surface, feeling for the first edge or crack. Her breath came in short, uneven gasps. Sargent had made it look like a stroll. Probably one of those people who relaxed by walking up walls in Yosemite, she thought savagely.

It had to happen. Just as she reached the midpoint, the cables on the far side kicked into motion with a jolt that almost caused her to fall off there and then, and suddenly the whole shaft seemed to be filled with motor noise. Paula closed her eyes and pressed herself against the wall, feeling it throb with vibrations. Air surged around her, and her fingers clawed instinctively at the cold metal. The vibrations intensified, and the terror that is triggered only by the self-preservation instinct compelled her to open her eyes and look down. The roof of the car was rushing upward at her, into the part of the shaft illuminated by the flashlight. It wasn't going to stop. She could see herself being smeared like . . .

Everything had gone quiet. She looked down and saw the top of the car just a few feet below, stationary. Then her hand gave way suddenly as the palm slipped on its own perspiration. A hand gripped her elbow and steadied her as she tottered. Sargent had moved back out of the recess and was bridging the gap that remained between her and the final corner, one hand steadying her and the other anchored on a firm hold. He drew firmly before she could panic, and seconds later she was perched next to him on a section of supporting frame, safely inside the recess.

"All right?" he asked.

Paula nodded, although she was breathing shakily. "I haven't had so much fun since my draft physical."

To get them down, Sargent produced a line that had been hidden behind a girder and uncoiled it, letting the free end drop into the darkness below. He showed her how to run it around her back and thigh to regulate her speed by friction, and then he went first again. A short while afterward, Paula felt two sharp tugs on the line to signal that the way was clear for her to follow. After her experience at the top of the main shaft, the descent seemed uneventful.

They left the elevator shaft through a maintenance hatch which Sargent replaced behind them, and came out onto a narrow steel-floored walkway leading between rows of large tanks and piping. After a short distance Sargent held a hand up for Paula to stop. "We've installed our own intruder alarms," he explained. "There's an infrared beam right here. Step over it carefully. It saves them having heart attacks in the Crypt every time someone goes down there."

"What is this Crypt? Eban mentioned it to Olga yesterday."

"You'll see."

They turned off to the side and passed by a series of bays containing transformers and power-distribution equipment. Beyond, light showed from a space underneath an intermediate-level deck. It was so obscured by the forest of support works and engineering that Paula didn't realize its extent until they were almost on top of it. As they stepped down inside, she saw that the space had been improvised into a workshop-laboratory, with a couple of large benches, tool racks, a table covered with drawings, and all manner of components, assemblies, and devices in various stages of construction. Three figures were waiting, presumably alerted to their approach by the flashlights. The youngest was swarthy-skinned, with black hair and alert, lively eyes. The man next to him was lean in build, with sparse hair, hollowed cheeks, and protruding eyes, giving Paula an instant impression of a human weasel. The third stepped forward and stood looking her up and down for a few seconds, a grin playing at the corners of his mouth. Then he grasped her by the shoulders with both hands and stared at her face. "Hi," Earnshaw said.

"Hi." She returned his gaze for a moment, then reached up and squeezed his forearms affectionately. "So, you are here. The Russians wouldn't tell me."

"They're like that." Earnshaw looked down at her green tunic. "What's this—a priv? You're doing okay. And I was worried that you were getting a hard time."

"I was at first, but it changed. It's a long story. I have news, too. A lot's been happening." Paula waved an arm at the surroundings. "But it looks as if you haven't been exactly idle either. What's this all about?"

"Another long story. One part of it is we're fixing a laser. But we need help with the electronics."

"So that's why you finally brought me down here?"

"Of course. What else did you think?"

"Lew, you never change. You're hateful."

"A much better relationship for business," Earnshaw said. He motioned with his head to the other two men waiting behind. "This is Paula, my partner that I told you about. Paula, meet Razz and Kev, two more of the crew."

❀ CHAPTER FORTY ❀

McCain's brow knotted in open disbelief. "Tycoon?" he repeated. "You're in touch with Tycoon? How could you be?" They were sitting on a couple of boxes off to one side at the edge of the lighted work area and speaking in lowered voices out of earshot of the others, who were carrying on with their work. This was company business.

"It's a complicated story," Paula replied. She had anticipated problems in convincing him. "Basically it works like this. I've gotten to know a Russian woman up on the priv level called Olga. She's a scientist, too—in the nuclear field—but also a human-rights dissident. That's why she's here." McCain nodded and listened intently. Paula went on, "The point is that a colleague of hers—one of her dissident colleagues, that is—who's also one of her long-standing personal friends, happens to hold a high position in the communications groundstation in Siberia that handles the main link up to here. To cut a long story short, they found a way of sending messages to each other by concealing them in the regular traffic in a way that's transparent to the standard handling system."

"That much I can buy," McCain agreed. "But how did you get in on it?"

"They lost an electronic chip that was vital to the process, and needed somebody who could program a new one. Olga and I had gotten to know each other by then. It was in my field. She took a chance."

McCain looked derisive. "*She* took a chance? How much do you know about this Oshkadov woman?"

"Look, she's a scientist. We understand a lot of things in common. I'd still be down in that pit if it wasn't for her. She got me out."

"She needed someone to program the chip."

"Sure. So it's a selfish world. But it was still her neck."

"Okay, okay." McCain raised a hand. "So you're in the picture regarding this private line they've got. Now, how did you persuade this guy down in Siberia . . . What's his name?"

"Ivan."

"How did you persuade Ivan to send a message off to our side for you? Give me one good reason why a Soviet official in a high position—I don't care if he's a dissident or not—should agree to risk getting himself shot by sending—"

"I didn't get him to send anything," Paula said. "I thought of it, but Tycoon beat me to it. He sent a message through Ivan to me first."

McCain sat back on the box and stared at Paula incredulously. He closed his eyes momentarily, shook his head, and rubbed his brow with a knuckle. "You mean Tycoon just happens to be in touch with this Ivan, and Ivan, for no particular reason, tells him all about his secret line up to *Tereshkova*. Come on, what have they been putting in your coffee? . . . Code names get broken pretty easily—you know that. And yet somebody in a place like this shows you a message that says it's from Tycoon, and you swallow the whole—"

"It carried a correct validation-code initializer," Paula said. "I included one from my list in my response, and since then a reply has come back with the right completion. What more do you want? If we're not going to trust the code system, what's the point of setting it up in the first place?"

McCain looked nonplussed. "That's impossible," he declared. "Or else they've got your completion list. How much to do you remember from when you were interrogated?"

"You don't have to look for something like that to explain it," Paula insisted. "Ivan has approached our side with an offer to defect. Think about it. He and Olga were both mixed up in illegal goings-on together. She was discovered somehow, the KGB grabbed her, and she wound up here. Obviously Ivan could be next. He can see that as much as anybody, so the idea of him suddenly getting a divine revelation to make himself scarce would make sense. Now put yourself in Tycoon's place. To make the deal sound attractive, Ivan would have told who he is and how valuable he'd be if he came over. He's hardly in a position to refuse favors right? So if you were Tycoon, what's the first thing you might think of trying? What would there be to lose if it was Ivan's neck on the line? Wouldn't you give it a shot? Well, that's what Tycoon did."

McCain exhaled a long breath and rubbed his chin. He couldn't fault her reasoning, but he still didn't like the situation. There were coincidences involved, and he was always suspicious of coincidences. In the end he seemed to dismiss the subject for the time being, and got up from the box. "Razz will have to tell you what he wants with the laser," he said, turning toward where the others were working. "But apart from that, come and see some of the other things we've got going down here."

Rashazzi and Sargent had made a dummy head from plaster and used it as a template for various patterns of rubber headpieces, which they made by cutting and regluing sections of used inner tubes. The tubes were used on the general-purpose groundcars found all over *Tereshkova*; Sargent and Mungabo had obtained them from a recycling plant they'd discovered in the course of exploring beneath Landausk. Over the open face-section they had attached a mask assembled from stolen pieces of firefighters' breathing apparatus and experimented with ways of sealing it to contain four pounds per square inch overpressure, filling it from an improvised air pump. They had settled on a method that seemed to work acceptably, and now Sargent was donning the equipment to try it out as the first live subject.

"What about the rest of the body?" Paula asked after McCain had explained the idea of going outside using homemade spacesuits. "You'll need some kind of restraint to maintain pressure."

Rashazzi pointed at an oil drum standing by the rear wall, partly covered by a sheet of tin but emitting fumes of a not-entirely-pleasant odor. "We've found that elastic surgical bandages plasticized in the concoction that's brewing in there give the properties we need. Wrapping the body mummy-fashion would probably work, but we're going to try welding sheets of the stuff into parts of stretch-suits. Getting dressed would be a lot quicker."

Paula looked dubiously at the pump that Rashazzi was connecting to the mask over Sargent's face. "You'll need something a lot more powerful than that for a full-size vacuum chamber." A large chamber would be necessary to test the complete suits. Nobody in their right mind would try out something like that for the first time by leaping out into space and trusting to luck.

"We can rig up a natural one," Rashazzi said. Already Paula was developing the impression from listening to him that with his enthusiasm and energy, anything might be possible. "We find an outer compartment against the hull wall, drill a hole through to the outside, and fit a valve in it. Then we shut off the room and decompress it gradually by means of the valve to provide a test chamber. When we're happy the suits work, we make a hatch through with the chamber evacuated, and it becomes our airlock for getting in and out."

"How far away from the outer surface is the cosmic-ray shield?" Paula asked. An important point. The shield was a detached structure outside the hull, and since it didn't rotate with the colony, it would be moving with a relative speed of something like a hundred fifty miles per hour. That was something that McCain realized he'd forgotten in his discussions with the scientists.

"It is only a matter of feet," Rashazzi agreed. "But it's something we can only know for sure by cutting the hatch and looking out." So somebody would have to work his way across the outside skin of the structure without being thrown off, in darkness, with the inner surface of the shield flashing by probably within inches of him all the time. Paula shuddered at the thought of it. She'd done her share of heroics, she decided.

At the table near the bench, Scanlon was updating the maps which the group was producing from information gathered in their reconnaissance expeditions carried out via the freight-transit system that the escape committee had discovered. "And 'tis fortunate lads we are, indeed," Scanlon said, looking up at her. "The traffic down there is busy these days so we've no problem getting rides to anywhere we want."

"Why's that?" Paula asked him. McCain had drifted away and was staring out into the darkness again, obviously deep in thought.

"All the good earth from Mother Russia that's coming down the spokes from the hub and having to be distributed around," Scanlon said.

"So it is true, then—they are really sending soil all the way here?"

"As true as we're here, talking." Scanlon gestured casually at a bin standing beside the plasticizing drum. "There's a pile of it in there, if you're interested. We're sick of coming back covered in the stuff."

"What did you bring it back here for?" Paula asked, walking over to the bin.

"Ah, that was Razz. It was there and it was unguarded—too much for the poor man to resist."

She stood looking down at the dark soil, then on impulse stooped and let some trickle through her fingers. It felt dry, probably partly dehydrated for shipment, but could doubtless be reconstituted on-site. "Do you need it, or can I take some?" she asked absently.

"And what would anyone be needing the likes of that for?"

"I have some friends up on the surface who might like some—real Russian soil to grow flowers in, maybe."

"Did you want it for anything in particular?" Scanlon called to Razz.

"Not really. We can get plenty more, anyway," Rashazzi answered.

Scanlon shrugged. "Help yourself. You'll find some empty cans on the shelf behind the rack there."

Paula found a can with a lid and scooped some of the soil into it. McCain came over to her as she screwed on the lid. He seemed to have arrived at some decision in his mind and drew her aside again. "There's one way I can check out this channel of yours," he said. "Can you send off a response from me to Tycoon's last message, with an initializer that *I'll* select from *my* list? If we get an answer with the right completion, I'll accept it as genuine."

It was what Paula had been expecting him to say, but as usual Earnshaw had had to check through all the alternatives and possible objections first. She nodded. "Write out what you want to send, and I'll take it back up with me."

"Exactly what do you do with it then?"

"The chip is programmed, but the transmission text has to be loaded into it. I do that on an offline system—there are several that I can get access to up there."

"Inside Zamork?"

"I'm working in a place at Turgenev in the day. Olga fixed it. That was how I got out of the kitchens."

"What kind of work?"

"Eco-modeling."

"Go on."

"Then Olga takes the chip back and passes it to an associate she's got, who substitutes it for a chip in the outgoing coding processors."

"How do you get the replies back?"

"They're encoded in statistical updates beamed up into the library. Olga transcribes them and brings me the copy."

"So Russians have access to the plaintext going both ways."

"How else could it be? Two separate systems are involved: here down to Siberia, and from there into our commnet. There has to be a conversion from one to the other."

McCain nodded reluctantly. "Okay. Let's sit down again. I won't be a second." He went over to the table where Scanlon was working, and returned with a notepad and a pencil. They sat down on the boxes again, and he handed her the pencil and pad. "What was Tycoon's last initializer?" he asked.

"Hot," she told him.

"My completion is 'Gospel,'" McCain said. Only he had known that. Paula's completion code for the same word would have been "Rod."

"Initializer?" Paula asked.

McCain thought for a second. "Trans." Paula might have chosen the same word too, for it was also on her list. *In her case only,* a valid reply from Foleda would carry the completion "Locate"; for a valid reply to McCain, however, she had no idea what the completion should be.

Paula wrote: SEXTON/GOSPEL TO TYCOON/TRANS. She waited. McCain whistled tunelessly through his teeth for a few seconds and then dictated a straightforward, innocuous statement to the effect that he was being detained on *Tereshkova,* and that he was in good shape and being treated fairly, apart from denial of communications rights.

Paula looked up questioningly. "That's it?"

"That's it."

"You're not going to say anything else?"

"What else do you want me to say?"

"Well, you could answer some of the questions that Tycoon asked in his message. We could give the names of some of the VIPs upstairs that he sounded interested in. Or mention that the place is taking in new batches of civilians with lots of children. Or that tons of soil from Earth are arriving here. Wouldn't that be considered useful intelligence material?"

McCain shook his head. "Not until I've a better idea who I'm talking to."

Paula sighed with exasperation. In her own mind she had no doubt that the link was genuine. "You're talking to Tycoon," she said. "Believe me, I *know.*"

"Let's wait and see, shall we?"

"God, why are all you intelligence people so suspicious of everything?"

"We're not. But the ones who aren't don't last too long. So your impressions end up being formed only by the rest. Scientists call it statistical bias. We call it survival. But isn't that what eco-modeling is supposed to be all about?"

On her next day at Turgenev, Paula composed the message as Earnshaw had directed. She had thought of sending a separate communication along with it under her own code to supply the additional information she had suggested, but on further reflection decided against it. It would be tantamount to a direct violation of orders, for one thing—Earnshaw was still the senior member of the mission—and for another, it would only be a matter of days at the most before Tycoon replied. Then, with Earnshaw finally reassured, all would proceed much more smoothly.

Sure enough, a couple of days later Olga brought Paula a transcript of a message from Tycoon to "Sexton/Vaal." This time Paula was spared another ordeal in the elevator shaft, for Earnshaw came up to meet her in the machinery gallery at the bottom of the shaft beneath Eban Istamel's hut. Earnshaw confirmed that "Vaal" was the correct completion for "Trans" from his own personal list. Therefore there could no longer be any doubt that the channel did connect all the way through to Foleda in Washington. To Paula's chagrin, however, he still declined to supply the information she had suggested. But he did give her a reply in which he hinted that he was in a position to enjoy virtually unlimited freedom of movement around the colony's outer ring.

The tone of the response that came back from Foleda gave the impression that he was in trouble and having credibility problems back home. Uncharacteristically throwing caution to the winds, he specified the precise locations around *Tereshkova* where weapons installations were suspected to exist, described their nature, and requested Sexton to check the sites and report as quickly as possible. The message ended, REPEAT, OBJECTIVE SUBORDINATES OTHER CONSIDERATIONS. POSSIBILITY OF COMPROMISE ACCEPTABLE. EXPEDITE BY ALL AVAILABLE MEANS.

Which meant, "Risk your ass if you have to. We need this."

❂ CHAPTER FORTY-ONE ❂

The two principal factors that made *Valentina Tereshkova* potentially so formidable were its distance from Earth and its sheer size. Whether driven by high-power pulsed reactors located in the hub or rim, or in the form of ejectable bomb-type devices, its weaponry would be based on transforming nuclear energy into beams of concentrated firepower traveling at the speed of light and impacting on their targets at a rate equivalent to tens or even hundreds of tons of high explosive per second. Since nuclear processes produce energy at an intensity millions of times greater than anything attainable from conventional sources, which involve only the outer electron shells of atoms, the resulting hardware would be extremely compact, and thus easily hidden in lots of unlikely places.

This had caused a lot of headaches among the Western analysts whose job was to come up with credible ways to attack the platform, should the need ever arise—the military had contingency plans filed away for just about every eventuality conceivable. True enough, a single nuclear warhead would have sufficed to destroy it totally, but missiles of any kind were ruled out. With the target at almost-lunar distance—ten times that to geosynchronous orbit—surprise would be out of the question: in the long climb from near-Earth space an attacking wave of missiles would have no hope of surviving. Yes, the West did have beam weapons of its own deployed in near-Earth orbits. But this was where *Tereshkova*'s size made the telling difference. For the West's weapons were comparatively small, special-purpose types designed to attack pinpointable targets such as missiles and satellites at shorter ranges. Hence they couldn't hope to knock out the hidden weapons on something like *Tereshkova* in a surprise attack. Counterfire from *Tereshkova*, on the other hand, would be instantly devastating to clearly defined targets sitting in space. The answer, of course, would have been to build something comparable in size at the proper time, but it was a little late to catch that boat now, and the political arguing was still going on.

Also significant was *Tereshkova*'s capacity to accommodate a variety of weapons. The essence of directed-beam strategy was to be able to deliver a wide range of wave-lengths from the electromagnetic and particle energy spectra, generated by a series of devices differently "tuned" to exploit the weaknesses of a given target type. Typically, hardening or protecting a target against one of the spectrum would render it more vulnerable in another part. For example, crudely focused, intense bursts of microwave energy would act by becoming trapped and concentrated, waveguide-fashion, in the structural cavities of the target, causing intense internal currents to circulate as if the target had been struck by lightning. Effective shielding against such a microwave attack could be achieved by cladding the target with an insulated metal skin. But this would make it more susceptible to pulsed diffuse X-rays, which when deposited upon an insulated metal layer induce strong electro-magnetic emissions inside the shield, fatal to electronic equipment. Heavy ions carried kinetic energy deep into solids faster than it could dissipate, causing materials to explode. Muons made lightning with two hundred times the mass of electron beams. Neutrons induced premature fission in warheads, degrading them to uselessness.

Symphony for full orchestra.

One of the suspected weapons that Foleda had communicated details of to McCain was a tunable, high-power, free-electron laser. That meant that the laser beam drew its energy from accelerated electrons that could be made to vibrate at any of a range of frequencies by a variable magnetic field. This contrasts with methods employing an excited solid, liquid, or gas medium, where the frequency is fixed and depends on the medium used. The system in question, it was claimed, operated across the optical spectrum from infrared to ultraviolet, and was aimed by the optical-mirror system located around the hub. According to the information received, it existed beneath the confused pile of buildings, tanks, conveyer ramps, and elevator machinery known as Agricultural Station 3, at the base of the minor spoke between Turgenev and Novyi Kazan.

McCain was far from certain what a tunable, high-power, free-electron laser installation ought to look like. In fact, he hadn't a clue. But as long as he was able to describe accurately what lay in there, the experts could worry about interpreting what it meant. Moreover, he had reasoned, if it existed it would be securely contained and guarded. So even if it proved impossible to actually get inside, the existence of obstacles too formidable to penetrate would say enough about the kind of place it was. And if the obstacles turned out to be no more than would allow them to simply test and withdraw? . . . Well, as Foleda had so thoughtfully reminded him, that was part of the job.

He felt the car slowing down in the darkness. Then it clattered over a series of switches before stopping for a few seconds, lurched a short distance forward, and then stopped again. From a point beside him, Scanlon's flashlight beam came on to reveal another stationary car filling the tunnel ahead, and a narrow maintenance walkway on one side, behind a handrail. It meant they were joining the line of waiting cars that often formed at the approach to the loading point below Agricultural Station 3. They had come out of the regular transit tube, and the roof here was somewhat higher.

"This will do us as good as anywhere," Scanlon's voice said from the darkness.

"Sure. Let's go."

McCain raised himself out of the hollow in the car's load of kidney beans that he had been lying in, and shone his own light while Scanlon hauled himself over the side and onto the walkway. Then McCain joined him. Even when they were heading for a destination farther on around the ring, they had learned from experience to get off the transit system here, work around the loading area on foot, and catch another car on the far side. On an earlier expedition that McCain had made with Mungabo, the load of corn they were riding had been switched up a ramp and emptied into a silo by physically inverting the car, almost suffocating both of them. McCain was beginning to feel like an unnatural denizen of some strange subterranean world of pipes, girders, ducting, and metal, whose proper inhabitants were not creatures of flesh and blood at all, but the ubiquitous, tireless machines.

An opening off the walkway brought them into an upward-sloping passage that bent through an angle to join a large compartment containing motors and winches, with cables disappearing up into the space overhead. The flashlights picked out more passages going off in other directions and walls meeting in strange combinations of angles. As with the oddly-flung-together jumbles of constructions surrounding the spoke-bases on the surface, there didn't seem to be a straight edge or surface anywhere that ran direct from one side of the torus to the other—like a bulkhead in a ship. Even Rashazzi, for all his sightings and measurements, had confessed to getting confused in the process of passing through the spoke zones, and frequently found himself coming out of them in a direction he hadn't expected. The others who had reconnoitered long-distance around *Tereshkova* had all reported similar difficulties.

They stopped here to exchange the coveralls that they had taken to wearing when riding the tubes for standard light-blue smocks and white caps, as worn by the agricultural technicians, which Koh had stolen on a work assignment. The coveralls hadn't been really necessary this time, as it turned out, but on other occasions they had dropped into cars full of the earth still coming down the spokes from transporters unloading at the hub and come out looking like mud-wrestlers. The smocks carried their two general-clearance badges, enabling them to move around. Having only two badges exacerbated the problem of limited time, and Istamel was working on a scheme for acquiring more.

McCain unfolded a sheaf of papers containing extracts from

Foleda's instructions and sketches from previous reconnaissances. "Section of bulkhead to the east. Inspection ladder leading to catwalk below cable bank," he read.

Scanlon aimed his light upward and swung it from side to side. "Well, there's what some people might call a bulkhead, and that's a ladder. It's close to east, I'd say, but how can a man be sure?"

"That has to be the way. Are you all set?"

"To be sure, hasn't it been me that's been waiting for the last five minutes? So let's be off."

McCain's group had established that one of the colony's waste-reduction and water-recycling plants was situated in that direction, as indeed was shown in the public information released by the Soviets. Beyond it, the official plans showed a long space, radial to the main axis—thus pointing, interestingly, at the mirror system surrounding the hub—which was described vaguely as "Materials Storage." That, according to the information that Foleda had assembled, was where the laser emplacement was supposed to be located.

The area they entered higher up was illuminated by pilot lights, and on an earlier visit Sargent and another from the escape committee had observed technicians working there. The choice was either to move carefully and try to stay under cover, or simply walk through brazenly and trust in their appearance to avoid drawing attention. Since it seemed probable that the vicinity of a high-security installation would be under observation, acting furtively was as likely as not to do more harm than good. Therefore they had decided on the impertinent approach.

The surroundings they passed through were reminiscent of parts of an oil refinery or chemical plant, with large domed vessels wreathed in piping and supports, pumps, compressors, and tubes zigzagging their way through heat exchangers. They passed two figures working on equipment inside a hatch they had opened on a railed platform overlooking the through-walkway. One of them raised a hand casually as McCain and Scanlon passed below. Scanlon waved back.

On Earth, the atmosphere, soil, and oceans provide huge

reservoirs in which the breakdown of dead matter and wastes, the return of gases into the air, and the removal of moisture by rainfall can all proceed at a relatively leisurely pace—even slow, inefficient processes operating on a planetary scale add up at the end of a day to a lot of materials processed. But *Valentina Tereshkova* had nothing of comparable capacity. Instead, the colony relied on mechanical condensers to dehumidify the atmosphere, and the extracted water resupplied drinking, irrigation, and industrial needs. Most of the moisture came from plant and animal respiration, which was why the dehumidifiers were located by the agricultural zones. Bulk condensation of water releases large amounts of energy, and the condensation process operated in conjunction with heat exchangers which carried the excess away to be radiated into space. Wastes were broken down through a wet-oxidation process, carbon dioxide returning to the atmosphere and solid nutrients being filtered out and shipped away for incorporation into animal feed and fertilizers. The Soviets had expressed pride in the accomplishment of their designers in devising a complete recycling process that eliminated the need to transport anything away from the habitat, thereby avoiding its expensive replacement from Earth. But that had been before more recent events, of course. McCain had no idea what they were telling everyone now.

On the far side of the recycling plant they came to a sturdy-looking wall, extending up beyond the level they were in, which looked as if it was part of the main supporting structure. It emerged on one side from behind a confusion of platforms and pipes, crossed squarely across in front of them for a distance, and then angled back on a different tack through a girderwork maze. McCain and Scanlon stopped and exchanged quick glances. The line was just about where, according to the official plans, the side of the "Materials Storage" compartment ought to be.

But McCain grew puzzled as he surveyed the scene. There was nothing resembling a guardpost, no observation ports anywhere that he could detect—no warning signs, even. They moved over to a cluster of valves on some pipes coming up from below and pretended to be inspecting them. While McCain studied the wall in detail,

Scanlon made notes of their route and the things they had observed, to add to their maps when they returned.

It seemed to be, for all that McCain could make of it, just a wall. Its only feature was a single, small, insignificant-looking door with the numeral "15" stenciled on it. Camouflage, McCain decided. The real installation was on the other side. He looked at Scanlon and motioned with his head to indicate approaching the door.

"It was your boss that told you to go sticking your fool neck out, not mine," Scanlon said.

"Come on, you Irish asshole."

They crossed the floor and came to the door. It looked ordinary enough, with no sign of anything suspicious close-up. Scanlon moved a pace forward and tried it. It opened. The sound of voices came from beyond, and instinctively McCain and Scanlon flattened themselves out of sight on either side. But then they realized that the voices were raised and coming from a distance. After a few seconds McCain eased himself forward and peered around the edge of the doorway. Scanlon did the same on the other side. They stared, then looked at each other perplexedly. McCain stepped out and went through. Scanlon followed. They looked around and found themselves standing in . . . a Materials Storage warehouse.

It was certainly spacious, and reminded McCain of a walk-around contractors'-supplies yard back in the States. They had come in through a side door. Arrayed along wide aisles were stacks of all the standard structural modules used to build the apartments, public buildings, factories, and office units found all over *Tereshkova*: wallboards, floor strips, roof frames, ceiling panels; windows, doors, stairs, partitions. There were plumbing sections, electrical sections, kitchen-equipment sections, decorating sections . . . "Holy Mother of God, wouldn't Razz be in his element here!" Scanlon breathed.

A forklift truck passed, carrying a pile of metal sheeting. The voice they had heard belonged to a man with a clipboard, who was standing about ten yards away and reading a list of items to two others: "We'll need ten of those, ten of those, and twenty two-point-seven flanges . . . Now, not that kind . . . Right, those." None of them took any notice of the two newcomers.

McCain and Scanlon walked slowly on through. There were ceramic bricks, blocks, tiles, and slabs; metal strips, rods, bars, and sheets; piles of sand, grit, chips, and gravel; wire in coils; paint in drums. None of it suggested a high-power, tunable, free-electron laser.

"Are you two looking for something?" a voice asked.

They turned and found a broad, bearded man in a brown workcoat standing at an intersection of two of the aisles.

"Er, just looking around," Scanlon said.

"Which unit are you with?"

McCain remembered what Paula had told him about new arrivals, and gambled on a bluff. "We're not, yet. We've only just shipped up from Earth. Trying to get our bearings. It's very confusing."

"I see. Well, glad to have you here. Look around if you want." The man turned to carry on in the direction he had been heading.

"One moment," McCain called.

"Yes?"

McCain gestured toward the far side of the warehouse, opposite where they had entered. "What lies that way, behind there?" According to the official plans, it should have been a crop-drying plant.

"A crop-drying plant," the man said.

"Thank you."

When the man had gone on his way, they continued on to the far side of the warehouse, which was formed by two walls meeting asymmetrically at an angle a third or so of the way along. They went through another open door, crossed an alley behind it, and came to a steel structure supporting a complex of large hoppers and interconnecting conveyors. "What place is this?" McCain asked one of the two women they found monitoring panels in a control room nearby.

"Number-Three Crop-Drying Plant," she told him.

"What's above?"

"Hydroponic recirculators and a crushing mill."

"And below?"

The woman laughed. "Oh, that's a long drop. There's nothing

until you get to Earth, Moon, or somewhere else, depending on which way we're turned at the moment. Are you lost?"

"Er, yes, I suppose we are. New arrivals. . . . Thank you."

"And I think it's about time we were trying to find our way back," Scanlon said. "There's nothing more to interest us down here."

"No . . ." McCain sounded bemused. "No, Kev, I guess you're right."

❁ CHAPTER FORTY-TWO ❁

When the reports were in, every one of the specific reconnaissance objectives listed by Foleda had yielded similar results. Gonares had seen nothing at the hub resembling the launching guns for ejectable, fission-pumped, X-ray laser modules that McCain had described. Rashazzi and Sargent had penetrated into where the aluminum-smelting plant was supposed to be below Landausk and found no sign of a nuclear-driven microwave projector there; instead, they had found aluminum-smelting furnaces. And McCain himself had verified that there were no particle accelerator tubes running deep down in the ring at Novyi Kazan, and others had confirmed it at two other places. Yes, it was inevitable that in a volume as large as that of *Valentina Tereshkova,* there were still a lot of places they hadn't seen. A complete search would take months. But the fact remained that without exception, *all* of the findings prophesied by Western intelligence had turned out dead wrong.

"So what does that tell you about all the other suspicions and delusions you people have been suffering from for years? Oh, I don't mean just on our side—the same mentalities exist on both sides. The whole problem with the world has always been the kinds of people who end up running it. It never mattered so much in the past, because they could always go off to fight in out-of-the-way places and keep it between themselves and anyone stupid enough to follow them. But that started to change when we"—Paula was referring to the general category of scientists—"gave them knowledge that allowed them to fly, and they used it to bomb cities. Now things have gone way past that and it affects everybody. You want to play at being scientific, and test the hypothesis. Okay, it's tested. Now we have to tell the people who matter what the results are. There isn't any choice, morally, or whatever other way you want to think of it." She pushed her hair from her brow and turned to face Earnshaw, who was standing impassively on the other side of the Crypt, his arms folded across his chest. For the moment they were alone. Paula was tired, and her voice had been rising with emotion and exasperation.

Earnshaw breathed in heavily and shook his head. "I still don't like it. I say no."

Paula stared disbelievingly. "Why, for Christ's sake? You can't give me one single reason . . ."

"So I'm pulling rank. That means I don't need a reason."

"Beliefs without evidence . . . No, not even that. In the face of evidence."

"Call it uncertainty and caution."

"How can there by any uncertainty? Look, you can't argue with facts. Why do so many people act as if refusing to accept facts that don't conform to their preconceptions can change reality? Reality doesn't care about anyone's preconceptions. The only way to learn anything is by allowing facts to shape beliefs. Aren't you doing just the opposite by letting preexisting beliefs decide what you're prepared to accept as fact? That's called prejudice and superstition."

"I call it gut-feel."

"It's the same difference."

Earnshaw sighed and turned away for a moment. His voice grated, as if he was managing to control his patience only with an effort. "What happened to probability in this all-very-scientific analysis of yours? There are too many facts that look suspiciously to me like unlikely coincidences . . ."

"Suspiciously, suspiciously. See, there you go again. Is there anything you're not suspicious about?"

"And I don't like the thought of having to communicate everything openly through Russians."

"You're obsessed with Russians. Because this place doesn't match your preconceptions about Russian prisons, you're convinced it has to be a cover for something. You never stop to think it might be *you* that's wrong—that your whole set of ideas about their prisons and everything else might be behind the times. Maybe they *are* changing, and people like you just haven't woken up to it yet."

"It's a nice thought," Earnshaw agreed. "But it could turn out to be wrong. What makes you as confident as you sound?"

"Gut-feel." Paula smiled icily and turned away.

"Well, maybe now you're not being so smart. Gut-feel might not be a strong point in your department. What do you know about Olga, apart from that after they'd given you a hard time and kept you on your own for a while, she showed up friendly and understanding just when you needed someone to talk to. Did you ever wonder about that?"

"That's not the way it was. *I* approached *her*—in the infirmary. I'd only seen her for a few seconds before that, by chance."

"By chance. And she just happened to walk through the infirmary."

"Oh, Jesus Christ, don't you ever quit? . . ."

"Look," Earnshaw said, finally sounding sharp. "I've never disputed that you're good at what you do. Don't start trying to tell me how to do what *I* do. That's my job. Okay?"

Paula glared back at him. "Okay. But isn't the main part of that job to communicate back what you find out? We've got information. There are lots of civilians arriving here, lots of children, lots of dirt, and no weapons. Doesn't it occur to you that sending that information back might be a duty?"

Earnshaw held her gaze long and steadily. When he spoke, his voice had returned to normal. "And hasn't it occurred to *you* that *that* might be exactly what somebody somewhere wants us to do?" he asked.

McCain should have been out with a labor detail assigned to soil spreading and planting, but he had used Rashazzi's bracelet-insert-swapping trick to buy enough free time from a couple of Siberians and a Japanese in A Block, a Russian and an Arab in E Block, and a Finn in F Block to be virtually free of work commitments. He had also made it worth Luchenko's while not to notice. For the rest of the day, he prowled around Gorky Street and the general compound alone, reflecting on all the impressions and oddities that he had registered since his coming to Zamork, and seeing if he could fit them into a different pattern from the one that had taken root in his head.

For one of the things that Paula had said was true: the way the place was run was unlike any Russian prison system that he had ever heard of, and was out of character with the mentalities of totalitarian bureaucrats. It was too free and easy, too unrestrained: prisoners from different nations and backgrounds, convicted for different reasons, mixed and moved around inside Zamork with minimal supervision; there was too much lenience toward things like alcohol, Rashazzi's wire-stripping mice, stealing, and absconding. Then there was the Exchange system, which made bribery and corruption rampant—yet surely it could have been curbed had there existed a will to do so—and the distinctly un-Russian practice of operating by incentives rather than by fear and intimidation. Paula thought it was all just part of the Russians' catching up with the times at last. McCain wasn't so sure.

Naturally, others had noticed this, too. Some of the inmates argued that it simply reflected the pointlessness of having Earth-style security in a space colony; others saw it as consistent with a purpose of rehabilitation and reeducation, not punishment; while McCain for his part had come to the conclusion that the Russians had cultivated these impressions deliberately to camouflage the real purpose of Zamork, which he had described as an "information mine." It was all designed to *encourage* people to mix freely, and therefore talk. And there were many people around who would have much to talk about that the Russians would be very interested to hear. Oh, true, the Russians did go through the motions of interrogations, searches, punishments for infractions, and the like, but with time it had all come to strike McCain more and more as not quite genuine—a charade to dull critical examination by satisfying expectations.

Very clever, McCain had conceded. Everything operated at a

double level. There were the apparent reasons for things being as they were, which most people worked out for themselves and were happy with, as they were meant to. And then there was the real reason, which only a few, such as he, had fathomed. And taking advantage of that insight, he had turned the Russians' own tactic back on them by exploiting the very freedoms that they had built into the system—for their own purposes—to set up and run his own miniature espionage operation. Even cleverer.

Now he was beginning to suspect there had been not two, but three levels to the deception all along. And far from being cleverer, he had been duped all the way down the line.

For the same facts that had led him to the information-mine explanation were also consistent with the supposition that he had been meant to believe just that, and that the actions he'd imagined himself to be carrying out freely had in reality all been part of the same plan. In other words, what he'd been doing was exactly what the Soviets had wanted him to do. And now it all made sense why prisoners inside Zamork should have found all the resources they needed to organize themselves as they had, why the security system had turned out to be ridden with loopholes, and why Paula had just happened to gain access to a supposedly secret communications channel back to Western intelligence at the same time: The weapons did exist. The information that Foleda had supplied regarding their locations, however, was false—planted over a period of several years though phony defectors and leaks. The whole thing had been staged to feed misinformation to the West from a source they would believe: their own, trusted agents on the inside. The real weapons were in the places that McCain and his people had never been able to get into.

McCain stopped suddenly, staring at the compound wall in front of him, as the full implication of that line of thought became clear. If Magician had been a double agent and part of that same stratagem, then the Tangerine file had never existed. The whole story had been fabricated to lure the US into doing exactly what it had done: send somebody after it. That explained his and Paula's capture. They hadn't goofed somehow. The Soviets had set the whole thing up from the beginning, specifically so that the agents the US sent would be captured. That was how they had obtained the "inside people" whom Western intelligence would trust. It wasn't an information mine at all; it was a misinformation factory.

He sought out Rashazzi. "Razz, have you ever gotten the feeling that everything we've been doing has been steered?"

One thing McCain had noticed over the months was that Rashazzi was never surprised by anything. "I'm listening," was all Rashazzi said.

McCain went on to summarize his latest thoughts. The young Israeli listened intently, nodding and agreeing occasionally, but without interrupting. "Just for two people?" he queried dubiously when McCain had finished. "They would set up a deception as elaborate as that, just for two people?"

McCain shook his head. "I never said that. My guess is that they've been grabbing all kinds of different candidates and shipping them up to Zamork on one pretext or another for a long time—people like Peter Sargent, for example, who I'm sure is from British intelligence. You might have been on the list, even. The Russians have been auditioning for months before they made a final choice of which ones to use."

"And these weapons we've been looking for. You think they really are here, but in the places we haven't been to."

"The places we haven't been *steered* to," McCain said. "Our side was fed faked information to make us look in the wrong places."

"So where ought we to start looking?"

"In the places we've been steered away *from.*"

"For example?"

"Underneath Zamork, for a start."

Rashazzi frowned, trying to follow what McCain meant. "Explain," he invited finally.

"Think back nine weeks to when you and I found the original route, underneath B-three. One level down, in the first machinery space, the floorpanels were spot-welded—which we could have cut around with the tool you'd made. But just in case we didn't have anything like that, there was also an easy way down through the lighting panel, and we took it. Our original intention was to keep on going down. But the floor of the pump bay below was solid and seam-welded. Yes? That was why we started exploring outward at that point. Doesn't that say to you that perhaps we were deliberately headed off in that direction? And what do you think we might find if we went back now and carried on going straight down?"

"But . . . Are you saying we were *meant* to find that route down from under B-three? Wouldn't that mean that the Russians knew all along that we'd set up the Crypt?"

"Or something like it, somewhere down there." McCain nodded. "Sure. That's what I think. It was essential to their plan. Without some of the stuff that we thought we were making secretly, we wouldn't have been able to get out and about. And that would explain why they put scientists like you and Albrecht in with us, too. The effort had to be real to make the setup look genuine." Rashazzi cupped a hand over his mouth as he strove to assimilate the torrent of new suggestions. He shook his head wonderingly. McCain stared at him expectantly. "Well, what do you think it would take to cut down through the floor of the pump bay? Could we do it?"

"Would we be allowed to?" Rashazzi asked. "From what you've just said, mightn't that whole area—the Crypt, all of it—have been under surveillance all along? I know we've checked it enough times and never found anything, but still . . ."

"I've got a hunch that it really might be clean," McCain said. "If there were bugs and we discovered them, the whole game would be up. So maybe the Russians wouldn't risk it."

"You mean they'd rely on stooges to know what's going on down there?"

"Exactly."

Rashazzi's eyes flickered over McCain's face. "Any guesses who?"

"Any of the escape committee, maybe. I've never trusted that Indian, Chakattar. Then there's our bunch . . . Who knows?"

"Albrecht is okay," Rashazzi said.

"I guessed that." McCain nodded. "Okay, so how about that floor? Let's assume that whatever's down there, nobody will be expecting anyone to be coming through that way."

Rashazzi thought for a while before replying. "With a slow drill and plenty of lubrication, we could bore a pilot hole through quietly, with a good chance of not attracting attention. Then we could push a fiber-optic pipe down for a look around. We've got a good range of tools now. The only real limit on how long a man-size hole would take is the amount of noise we could afford to risk. That would depend on what we find down there."

"Then, let's start right away," McCain said.

Rashazzi nodded. "I assume this like the geometric anomalies— we keep it to ourselves?"

"Absolutely." McCain nodded emphatically. "And one more thing. Obviously we can't trust any method of communication out of here that's controlled by the Russians. That means we'll want the laser. How's it going? Has Paula finished what you wanted on the power supply?"

"Yes, just about."

"So you and Albrecht can do the rest?"

"I think so."

"Good. I want to have it operating ASAP."

◉ CHAPTER FORTY-THREE ◉

It was late morning. In Hut 8 on the surface level, Eban Istamel had connected the output from a cassette player to the wire that had been uncovered from the bug hidden in the ceiling vent, in order to confound any unwelcome listeners. Two of the hut's other occupants were on work assignments at Turgenev and one of the agricultural stations, and the third was away in the Services Block library. Paula sat staring wearily across the table at the electronic chip that Olga was showing in the palm of her hand.

Olga's voice was appealing but firm. "There isn't a lot of time, Paula. The bus will be leaving soon, and I'm due to be back at work in Turgenev for the rest of the day. From the way you described it, the situation sounds serious. Nobody could blame you for deciding to act on your own initiative. So I did take it upon myself to preload the message that I asked you to draft this morning. It's in this chip now, ready to be sent." She gestured toward the sheet of paper lying by Paula's elbow. The message Olga had written was directed to Tycoon/ from Pangolin/ in the standard format that Paula used, but had blank spaces after the slashes.

The text listed the hub X-ray-module emplacement, the Agricultural Station 3 laser, the Landausk microwave projector, and the other installations that Tycoon had specified in his request to Sexton. Along with each item was a summary of what had been found there and a terse concluding assessment: FINDINGS

NEGATIVE—SOURCE INVALIDATED. FINDINGS NEGATIVE—
SOURCE INVALIDATED . . . FINDINGS NEGATIVE—SOURCE
INVALIDATED. "All I need from you now," Olga said, "is your
completion code for Moon and a new initializer." "Moon" had been
the initializer in Foleda's last incoming communication.

Paula got up and crossed the room to stare out through the
window. The Polish historian from the hut in the next row higher up
the slope was out fussing with his tomato plants again. Paula crossed
her arms in front of her and rubbed her shoulders as if she were cold.
They had been through all this earlier, before Olga went to Turgenev.
Although Paula was surer than ever of the stand she had taken with
Earnshaw, her anger had abated. Now she just felt tired of it all.

"If the information is true, what harm can it do to set the West's
suspicions at rest?" Istamel asked from where he had been leaning by
the side of the washroom door, listening. "They're always telling
everybody about how incurably suspicious *Russians* are, after all. And
don't get me wrong—I've got no reason to feel especially friendly
toward Russians. But I've always said American propaganda
exaggerates everything just as much. They're all as bad as each other.
It's the line of work that does it. Which side they're on doesn't make
any difference."

Olga had told Istamel simply that they had a way of
communicating secretly with one of the American intelligence
services. She hadn't said how. Paula would have been happier if Olga
hadn't said anything at all, but Olga evidently regarded the whole
business as sufficiently serious to warrant his involvement and advice.
Paula wasn't sure what position or influence the Turk had that should
cause Olga to value his opinion in this way—but people didn't ask
unnecessary questions in Zamork. And besides, Olga must have had
good reason to consider him reliable, for they were talking about her
own channel to Ivan, too.

"Look, I'm not sure you quite understand," Paula said. "What
my opinions might be as an individual, and my capacity in the
mission that I came here on, are not the same thing. Intelligence
work isn't what I do. I'm a scientist. I was only in a technical-
support role."

"But you came on an intelligence mission, all the same," Olga said. "Doesn't that make it just as much your duty to report back what you can?"

Paula drew a deep breath. "I still don't like the thought of deciding something like this on my own. Why can't we get Lew Earnshaw up here? Maybe if you two tried talking to him, it might make him see sense. Couldn't we at least give it a try first?"

"The Crypt is cut off," Istamel reminded her. "We can't get him up here."

"Is that maintenance crew still working down the shaft?"

"It's worse than it was this morning. They've got half the wall opened up and cables everywhere. It could go on for days."

"And do you have days?" Olga asked. "Remember how urgent Tycoon's last message sounded. We don't know what might be going on down there. A crucial situation may have developed, and its outcome could depend on what we know. Nobody's going to hold anything against you for doing what you thought might help prevent a war."

"Yes, it might prevent a war," Eban repeated, nodding gravely as if the realization had only just struck him. "A war that would affect everybody in the world, wherever they are, whatever side they are on, and even if they're not interested in either side. Perhaps this is a situation where it is not possible to permit the luxury of thinking like an American. You must try to think just as a member of humanity— of a community that knows no frontiers, whose only interest lies in truth."

"Like a *scientist!*" Olga said.

A long silence followed. Paula continued staring out the window. The scene outside hadn't changed, and wouldn't change. Neither would her predicament. The decision had to be faced. There was no escaping it. She turned. Olga and Istamel were waiting silently, she at the table, he still leaning by the far door. Paula looked at them for a moment longer, but capitulation was already written in her eyes. She came back to the table, sat down heavily, looked across to Olga, and nodded. "The completion for 'Moon' is 'Rise,'" she said.

Olga drew the sheet of paper over and wrote the word in the first of the blank spaces. She looked up. "And a new initiation word from your list?"

There was a silence. Olga and Eban remained motionless while moments passed that seemed to drag like hours. A woman's voice called out to somebody on the pathway between the huts outside.

"'Pin,'" Paula answered.

They had cut a section out of the floorplating, guided by the small test holes that Rashazzi had drilled to keep them inside the square of underfloor ribbing. Below was an interdeck space one to two feet deep. McCain sat by the edge and watched, while Rashazzi used a holder fashioned from stiff wire to push the fiber-optic cable down into the hole they had drilled through the lower surface at one of the corners. Rashazzi peered into the viewing piece attached to the other end of the cable, and after a few seconds began rotating the top of the holder for an all-round view of whatever was below.

"See anything?" McCain asked.

"Nothing. It's all dark." Rashazzi passed the viewer to McCain. McCain hunched forward and lifted it to his eyes. The entire field of view was pitch black. He spent longer than Rashazzi had, panning slowly through a full circle, but there wasn't a glimmer of anything. McCain withdrew the holder and held it up over his head while he looked into the viewer again. A fuzzy but discernible image of the shapes and shadows produced in the pump bay around them by the lamp that Rashazzi had hung overhead marched across his field of vision. The fiber optic was working okay.

"We could drill a second pilot hole and put a light down," Rashazzi suggested.

"We could fart around like this for weeks, too," McCain said.

"You want to carry on?"

"It looks dead enough down there to me, Razz. Hell, we've gotten this far. Sure, let's go the rest."

Rashazzi probed with a gauge to assess the thickness of the panel, and selected a sawblade with the pitch he estimated would work the most quietly. He fitted it into the handle and began cutting two-handed with slow, deliberate motions, using the hole to gain a start.

They had experimented with a power saw in the Crypt, but rejected it as too noisy. After a few minutes, Rashazzi rested his hands and McCain took over.

"I've been thinking about something," Rashazzi said after a while as he watched.

"So what's new? You're always thinking about something."

"About the laser."

"What about it?"

Rashazzi reached up and moved the lamp to illuminate better the area that McCain had cut to. "You don't trust this communications channel that they've got upstairs . . . because it goes through Russian intermediaries."

"Damn right."

"Just because they're Russians? The fact that they are dissidents doesn't carry any weight?"

"I don't *know* that. I've only been told it—secondhand, thirdhand, who-knows-how-many-times-hand. Who can believe anything they're told in this place?"

"You think the KGB might be reading it?"

"Let's just say it wouldn't be on the list of things I'd be most surprised to learn about the world."

Rashazzi rubbed the tip of his nose with a knuckle, as if pondering how to put what was on his mind. Finally he said, "But you wouldn't be any better off with the laser, even if you did get it talking straight into the US military network. You'd have to use the existing channel to advise them what frequency they should watch for, the code you plan to use, and so on. If the KGB get that information too, they'll be able to intercept anything that comes or goes over the laser, just as easily. You won't have gained anything."

McCain sat back and returned the saw to Rashazzi. "True," he agreed.

"But you must have figured that out already."

"Yes, I had."

Rashazzi looked up and frowned. "So, what use is it?"

"Camouflage," McCain said. "If we've got informers around, I wouldn't want word to get back that we've stopped working on the laser. It would be too much of a giveaway that we're suspicious. Also, my partner from upstairs is in on it, and I don't like the sound of the people around her up there. It reeks of a setup. I don't want her carrying back an impression that anything's changed down here. We carry on with the laser as planned." Rashazzi nodded in a way that said it made sense, and resumed cutting.

When the panel was fully cut, they lifted it clear and lodged it to one side. The beams from their flashlights failed to reveal anything significant in the darkness below. The space seemed to be quite large and open. McCain lowered a weighted line, which bottomed at ten feet or so. He swung his legs down and let himself down hand over hand, and Rashazzi followed.

This was not another machinery compartment. They were in a long, bare room, entirely without furnishings or contents of any kind. And yet, strangely, there seemed to be something familiar about it as they probed upward and around with the beams from their lamps. They were near one end of the room, and in the middle of the end wall was a doorway. Rashazzi directed his lamp along the length of the room and picked out the shape of another door at the far end. And then McCain realized why it looked familiar: it was a standard Zamork-style billet, without partitions or any of the fittings, but the same shape and size. Rashazzi had noticed it too. He moved toward the door and hesitated, but there was no bracelet-interrogation signal from above. He tried the lights, but they were dead. The door opened when he pushed it. He went through, and McCain joined him outside.

They were looking down into a larger space now, from a railed walkway. There was a similar door behind them to the left of the one they had come out of, and another to the right. There was a whole row of them they saw, no longer with surprise, as they proceeded along the walkway.

"We're not going to find any weapons down here, Razz," McCain said.

"I know."

"You know what this is?"

"Yes. What's it doing down here?"

"I don't know. Are they planning to turn the whole place into a prison?"

For they were in a standard Zamork billet block. They had come down through the ceiling of one of the upper-level billets, and knew where the stairs down to the lower level would be even before they saw them. They went down, moved out into the central mess area, and sure enough, there were the two levels of billets facing them from the other side. All empty and silent. They walked to the end of the mess area, but instead of the bars and gate as existed in all of the blocks above, they found a solid wall with ordinary-looking double doors. McCain tried one of them, found it unlocked, and eased it open an inch, then instantly caught Rashazzi's shoulder as a signal to keep back and stay quiet. There was light outside, and the sounds of voices and movement. They moved closer to the crack to peer through.

Outside was a broad thoroughfare which in every way resembled Gorky Street. The layout was the same, the directions were the same, and there was another set of large double doors farther on and across the corner, just where the next block would be. They seemed to have emerged inside a whole, new, unsuspected level of Zamork that existed deeper down beneath the regular complex, except it wasn't fitted out in the fashion of a detention facility. It seemed more like a normal residential complex. The large double doors that they could see were open, and inside them—in the mess area of the block they opened into—a work crew was unloading furniture from a truck. Whatever the place was, it was evidently being prepared for occupation. Suddenly McCain remembered all the bedframes that he and Scanlon had made when they were in the metalworking shops in the Core.

"What do you make of it?" Rashazzi whispered.

McCain watched through the crack and shook his head. "I don't know what to think. But it looks as if they're expecting more guests. That means this block we're in could be next. We'll have to patch up that hole we made in the ceiling back there."

"No problem. It'll fix so that nothing will show unless you're looking for it," Rashazzi said.

"But while we're here, I want to measure the layout," McCain muttered. "We need to make another hole to get down into here, but in another place—somewhere concealed—that won't be right in the middle of someone's ceiling."

"One of the service ducts, maybe . . . or through the utilities bay?"

"Yes." McCain eased the door shut again and turned to face Rashazzi.

"That should be easy enough," Rashazzi agreed. "But what for? Why do you want to be able to get in and out of here?"

"Because," McCain said, "it looks as if it's being fitted out for civilians. In other words, this place must connect out to the rest of the colony."

"Of course. That truck got down here somehow."

McCain nodded. "Exactly. And if we were *meant* to get out and about to collect wrong information on all those weapons installations, then the Russians know all about our freight-line route out of Zamork, too." He gestured over his shoulder with a thumb at the doors behind them. "Well, maybe here's a way out for us that they won't know about."

☷ CHAPTER FORTY-FOUR ☷

It was not customary for the deputy director of the UDIA to attend the meetings of the National Security Council, normally held in Washington's Old Executive Building. Nor for that matter the UDIA director, since intelligence matters were usually covered by the director of the CIA, who presented the findings and recommendations of all departments. But Borden had been called in to this session because of the importance that the link into *Valentina Tereshkova* was assuming, and he had brought Foleda with him to permit Foleda to voice his disagreement for himself. Foleda felt privately that Borden's dissociating himself from Foleda's view in this way was uncalled for and fell short of the degree of reciprocation that Foleda's support on previous occasions warranted—but that was the way of politics. For his part, he had decided the situation justified stating his opinions bluntly, without making concessions to anyone's sensibilities.

President Warren Austin gestured at the report lying on the table in front of him, with its appended sheaf of Pedestal-Sunflower transcripts. "Sunflower" was the new code designation for the complete link from Foleda, through Cabman, to the Pedestal-mission operatives up in the Soviet space colony. "And that covers all the weapons installations that we've compiled from various sources— Magician and the rest?" he said.

"The main ones that we specified," Borden confirmed. "Every one that our people penetrated has turned out to be negative. In each case, what was found conformed to published Soviet information."

"Hmm, so when this gets to be made public, we'll all look like bozos again," the President murmured. Borden shifted uncomfortably in his chair. Apparently UDIA wasn't among the President's favorite outfits again today.

At the far end of the table, General Thomas Snell of the Army, chairman of the Joint Chiefs of Staff, looked up from contemplating his fingers. "One question," he said. "All we know for sure is that this information is coming into our network from Cabman in Siberia. How certain are we that he is in fact getting it from where he says he's getting it from? Could the Soviets be managing the operation?"

"We know from the validation codes that it is coming from our agents," Borden said.

Snell nodded. "I know that, but agents have been turned before."

"True," Frank Collins, the CIA director, agreed. "But on top of that, NSA has intercepted Teepee-Blueprint transmissions that correlate with every Sunflower message. So we have confirmation that it's coming down from Mermaid." In fact, they no longer really needed Cabman's transmissions from Siberia, since NSA could read the signals coming down to him from Mermaid before he relayed them on to the West. But to reveal that to Cabman would have been giving away too much.

The President looked at Foleda. Other eyes followed forbearingly, with okay-Foleda-let's-hear-it-for-the-record expressions. Borden stared down at the table.

Foleda returned the President's stare directly. "I don't trust the Sunflower transcripts. Our agent on Pedestal has the code designation 'Sexton.' Sexton is an experienced operative whom I've known personally for years, whose judgment I trust, and whose reliability I wouldn't question. But the messages we've seen from Sexton have all been neutral, with no content of any substance. The reports pertaining to weapons are from Pangolin *only*—a technical-support person, not of the department. I move that all incoming

Sunflower material not validated by Sexton be discounted." That was out of order. In the chair next to Foleda, Borden winced.

Robert Uhl, the defense secretary tossed out a hand. "We have to make allowances . . . They're in a *prison* up there. I don't know exactly what the conditions are, but does it seem reasonable to *expect* that Sexton is even able to be present all the time? They might have all kinds of problems getting together to collaborate. Pangolin could well be doing the best job that's possible."

Collins shrugged. "I could buy that." Beside him the secretary of state, Joseph Myers, nodded agreement.

"Motion denied," the President ruled. He reached for a file in front of him.

"I haven't finished," Foleda said.

"Shut up, Bern," Borden hissed. "This is an NSC meeting. There are recognized procedures . . ."

"I'm saving you from having to say it," Foleda muttered back. "That's why I'm here, isn't it?"

"Go ahead, Mr. Foleda," the President invited.

"We're continuing to get reports from all sources of ominous developments throughout the Soviet-bloc nations. The number of warships at sea is unprecedented. Military-communications traffic in all bands has been abnormally heavy for days." Foleda gestured toward a folder on the table. "A new item in yesterday of food-canning plants switching to three-shift working a month ago. It can all be construed as indicative of hostile intentions. In such a climate we can't afford to dismiss anything that casts doubts on the reliability of Sunflower material. I repeat my previous motion. I would also recommend that we consider raising the readiness level of our armed forces until Mermaid has been opened to international inspection and cleared."

The secretary of state heaved himself restlessly forward in his chair and shuffled about among some papers. "Look, we know it's your people's job to worry, but I think this is going too far. We've wanted a breakthrough for years to relax the tension. I'll put my money on this being it. I say we have to try for it." Interestingly, he directed his words at Borden, not Foleda.

General Snell rubbed his chin hesitantly. "Although, I don't know
. . . Maybe there could be something to it . . ."

"We've been through all this," the defense secretary said. He
nodded toward Foleda to concede the point. "Yes, I agree with Mr.
Foleda; under normal circumstances all the things he's reminded us
of would constitute grounds for concern—serious concern. But there
is one fact that outweighs those considerations: virtually the entire
Soviet leadership—its top leadership, including the First Secretary of
the Party, chairman of the Council of Ministers, chiefs of the KGB
and the military—are either there already, or will be within the next
couple of days. We've asked ourselves, Is that where anyone in their
right mind would concentrate the brain of the entire national
organism at a time of intended conflict? On a battle station out in
space that would be bound to be a first target? Of course not. It just
wouldn't make sense. A more plausible explanation for all the Soviet
military activity we're seeing is that since they won't be having their
big parade this year, they're organizing exercises instead."

It was the first week of November, and Soviet television was
already broadcasting live coverage into the world news grid of the
first groups of Soviet leaders arriving inside *Valentina Tereshkova*.
More transporters were en route, and others, including the UN vessel
with the Western VIPs, would be departing from Earth orbit in the
next day or so. As the defense secretary had pointed out, they would
all be very vulnerable if there were hostilities.

The factors that made *Valentina Tereshkova* a virtually unassailable
weapons platform didn't make it automatically a safe haven for people.
The reason was that to disable its weapons effectively, the West's
orbiting lasers and other beam projectors would have to knock them
all out simultaneously with a first shot. With the devastating and
instantaneous return-fire that *Tereshkova*—if the rumors were true—
could bring to bear, there would never be a chance for a second shot.
But such a first-shot knockout would be impossible for the simple
reason that the West's weaponry was designed to attack pinpoint
targets in space; without knowing exactly where to aim, it would have
no chance of surviving long enough to find a few compact, hardened
spots on a structure measuring miles around.

But for people loose in the general volume of the main torus, the situation was different. A salvo from all the West's orbiting beam weapons fired in unison could blow away enough of the relatively thin skin to decompress the whole ring in seconds. Even if the Soviet weapons operators were protected inside their hardened emplacements, the chances for survival of anyone out in the general colony areas would be slim. That was why the consensus had gone the way it had, leaving Foleda out on his own. If there was anything to what he said, nobody for a moment could see the Soviets acting the way they had.

The large screen at one end of the room was showing a still picture of the Soviet chairman of the Council of Ministers standing on a rostrum, a garland of flowers hanging down over the front of his suit, addressing a crowd in the main square of Turgenev, inside *Tereshkova,* minutes after his party had descended from the docking facilities at the hub. It was from a clip of the latest Soviet news bulletin, which the people at the meeting had watched earlier and not bothered to turn off. Behind the crowd were glimpses of *Tereshkova*'s bewildering, Oz-like architecture, and above, the strange curving sky with its elongated suns.

Foleda leaned back and extended a hand briefly to indicate the screen. "Just suppose," he suggested, "that what we saw there a little while ago isn't happening at all. Wouldn't that make a difference?"

The President shook his head and pinched the bridge of his nose. "What do you mean, not happening, Mr. Foleda? I'm not sure I follow."

"Of course it's happening," the secretary of state muttered impatiently. "I'm starting to wonder if this is happening."

"We know the transmission is coming in from the Soviet news service, that's all," Foleda said. "But how do we know that the events it's showing are happening *now*—up there inside Mermaid, right at this moment?"

"NASA's picking up the TV transmissions from Mermaid independently of the Soviet news broadcasts down here," Collins said. "There's no question that's where it's coming from, if that's what you mean."

"Look at the screen," the secretary of state said, gesturing. "You can see where it is."

"That only demonstrates that a signal is being transmitted down from Mermaid," Foleda persisted. "No, that wasn't my question. What I said was, how do we *know* that the events that it depicts are actually taking place right now?" He looked around the table. Nobody seemed to be quite with him. He drew a breath. "How do we know that it isn't all something they did months ago—that what they're transmitting isn't a recording, just like what we're looking at on the screen here?"

"We can see the ships arriving up there . . ." the secretary of state started to answer automatically, but then his voice trailed away as he realized that it didn't mean very much. Everyone else saw it too, and Foleda didn't bother pointing out the obvious.

"That has to be ridiculous," the defense secretary declared, sitting back abruptly.

Collins looked at Foleda, frowned, then looked away again. Borden had half-turned and was sitting with his face propped on a hand, staring as if Foleda had just grown another head. The President was shooting looks all around the table to get someone to respond. Everyone seemed to be thinking that someone ought to say why the idea was crazy, but no one wanted to say it first.

"Well?" Foleda challenged. "Okay, I agree I'm suspicious, but that's what you pay me to be. Our job is to make worst-case assumptions. I've made one. Show me I'm wrong."

The secretary of state spread his hands. "There have to be some things you can't always prove. Some things you just have to take on trust and hope you're right. It's possible that anyone in this room could be a KGB spy. We don't *know* it isn't true. We just have to carry on and hope it isn't. If everyone waited for everything to be proved, they'd never do anything. Who was the general who said that if you wait until all the information's in, you'll be bound to be too late?"

"I'm not so sure, Joe." General Snell was leaning back, rubbing his chin thoughtfully. "Maybe there is a way we can find out if those Russians are really where they say they are."

"How?" the President asked them from the end of the table.

"We've got agents up there, right now. And we've got a means of communicating with them. We don't have to rely on what the Soviet news service says. Can't we ask our own people if they can see with their own eyes the same things we're seeing on screens down here? If they say they can, that would be good enough for me."

The heads turned back toward Foleda. Foleda blinked. He had discredited Sunflower so much in his own mind, he realized, that the possibility of using the link for this purpose hadn't occurred to him. An unskilled agent's failing to find weapons that might be there was one thing—negative evidence was always questionable. But confirmation of something taking place right in front of one's eyes constituted positive evidence. That was a different matter.

"What do you say, Mr. Foleda?" the President asked. "You have expressed the greatest skepticism toward Sunflower. If we took up General Snell's suggestion and got confirmation from our own agents there, would that satisfy you?"

Foleda's brow creased into a frown. The truth was that he didn't trust the Soviets an inch, and didn't like the West in general—and the US in particular—were dancing eagerly to the Soviet tune to demonstrate their inoffensiveness. But those were prejudices pure and simple, and there was no way to defend them now. He looked up and nodded.

"Yes, Mr. President, I guess that would change the picture a whole lot," he agreed unhappily.

◎ CHAPTER FORTY-FIVE ◎

In the background, the large screen in the graphics lab at Turgenev still displayed the exchange cycle of gases between soil bacteria and the atmosphere. But Paula and Olga were more interested in the smaller deskscreen pivoted to face them on the console below, which was showing on a local channel the crowd gathering in the square outside the building. The second transporter bringing Soviet government and Party officials had arrived at the hub twenty minutes previously, and they were expected to emerge from the spoke at any time. There was considerable excitement among the privileged-category inmates back at Zamork, too. Rumors had been circulating of large-scale amnesties to be announced during the November 7 celebrations, and the compound was alive with speculations about whose names might have been chosen.

"But why?" Olga asked again. She shook her head and moved over to a worktop at the side of the room and stared down again at the transcript of the latest request to come in from Tycoon. "They can see on the public television channels that there are important people arriving here. Why should they want corroboration from you? And why does it matter so much, anyway?"

"It's strange . . ." Paula answered in a faraway voice, leaning back and staring at the large screen but not seeing it. They had established some time ago now that since it was part of the Environmental

Department, which was classed as a normal civilian work area, the graphics lab was not wired for surveillance. Therefore they could speak freely there.

Olga turned and came back to stand behind Paula's chair. "Why should the Americans doubt it? Do they think that what they're watching down there might be recordings or something? Maybe they still believe this is a war platform." She tapped her lips with her fingertip for a moment. "Could they be afraid that the Russians might be planning to hijack the Western VIPs who are on their way here? You know them better than I do. Are they capable of dreaming up something like that?" Paula didn't answer. Olga waited, then looked at her. "What are you thinking?"

Paula swiveled the chair slowly, her elbow resting on the armrest, and looked up over her loosely closed fist. "I think it's worse than that," she said.

Olga frowned. "Worse?"

"A lot."

"What do you mean?"

Paula pushed herself up from the chair, paused to choose her words, and then turned to stand with her back to the console, resting herself against the edge. "We don't know what's been going on down on Earth between your side and mine over the past few months. But we do know they're run by some people who can be pretty irrational."

Olga nodded. "Yes, I would agree with that. So?"

"Well, if you were the Americans," Paula said, "what would the fact that practically the entire Soviet leadership had gone up to *Valentina Tereshkova* for the November seventh celebrations say to you?"

"Why . . . that they were taking time off to go away and enjoy themselves for once, I suppose. And since a potential target would be the last place they'd pick, I'd be pretty happy that they weren't planning to—" Olga broke off and turned her head toward Paula quizzically as she saw what Paula was implying.

"Yes," Paula said. "And what would it say if they hadn't gone there at all, but wanted you to think the things you've just said?"

Olga stared incredulously. "No!"

"I think so." Paula nodded somberly. She met Olga's eyes fully. "I think the Americans believe you're about to launch." Olga sat down weakly and shook her head. "And worse," Paula said. "What if the West decides to preempt?"

"Oh, God . . ." Olga licked her lips and turned her head first one way and then the other. She seemed to be having trouble coming to terms with the enormity of it. Paula watched silently. At last Olga gestured at the transcript, then indicated the BV-15 terminal standing in a corner. "We must do something . . ." Her voice choked. She waved a hand again. "The channel. We must send them an answer."

"Yes, I know." Paula straightened up from the console, gathered the transcript, and sat down at the terminal. Her movements were purposeful and resolute, as if she had been giving Olga time to catch up with the conclusion she had already recognized in her own mind as inevitable. Paula took a screwdriver from a drawer and removed the BV-15's cover. Then she reached in her pocket, took out a small plastic box containing one of the preprogrammed chips, and plugged the chip into the socket that it was coded to work in. Then she replaced the cover, sat down, and activated the screen. Olga moved her chair closer to watch.

Then a frown crossed Paula's face. She sat back uncertainly and turned her head to glance at the small screen showing the scene outside the building. The crowd was denser now, and officials were buzzing excitedly around the doors that opened from the concourse outside the spoke elevators. Paula looked back at the terminal again with a suddenly numb expression. "I can't do this," she said.

"What's the matter?" Olga asked. She sounded alarmed.

"This message. I can't send it. I *can't* tell them those leaders are arriving here."

"But why not?"

"Because I don't *know* that they are." Paula turned her head and looked at Olga oddly. "Am I being paranoid too, now? But don't you see? All I have to go by is a TV picture, just like the people down there in America. I can't tell if it's real any more than they can."

Olga was shaking her head. "But . . . but that's ridiculous. You're *here*. They're not." She waved frantically at the deskscreen. "That's all happening right outside the building we're in." They couldn't simply walk out and look, of course, because their Zamork bracelets would trigger alarms if they tried leaving their authorized working vicinity, which would achieve nothing but get them spells in solitary.

Paula was adamant. "If I sound silly, I'm sorry, but I think it's important. You're always reminding me that we're scientists. Well, this would be confirming reported data that we haven't observed for ourselves. Scientists can't do that."

Olga was looking dazed. "But . . . we're talking about possibly averting *war!*" she insisted. Her voice was pleading, her face strained. "Global war. How many times we've talked about this, what it would mean . . . You can't stop because of something like this." She got up from her chair and stood with her hands pressed flat together against her face. Her eyes darted this way and that, as if seeking answers on the walls. "I can show you. . . . Yes, look, wait there. I'll go and get Gennadi."

Paula turned her head and watched, puzzled, as Olga hurried across the room and opened the door. She went out into the corridor and her footsteps retreated. Then Paula heard her say, "Oh, Dr. Brusikov, are you leaving?"

Brusikov's voice answered, sounding surprised. "I was going out to watch the arrival of the foreign minister and his party, and then have lunch. Why?"

"Oh, good. Then, you are going out into the square?"

"Yes." The voices were right outside the door now.

"Could I ask a favor?" Olga ushered Brusikov into the room. He nodded perfunctorily to acknowledge Paula's presence. Olga glanced quickly around the lab and took a bright-blue cylindrical cardboard container, three feet or so long, from a stack lying on a shelf—the kind commonly used for carrying things like rolled technical drawings. "I promised these to somebody urgently, but missed him. He's outside in the square now, but I can't go out there. I wonder if you'd be so kind . . ."

"Oh, I see." Brusikov nodded. "Very well. But how will I know him?"

Olga turned to the screen showing the scene outside and pointed to a man in a yellow jacket and green hat, standing on the edge of the crowd, near the main door of the Government Building. "That's him. He's very distinctive. His name is Zavdat."

Paula had stood up from her chair behind them. As Brusikov turned to leave, she said suddenly, "No, that's the wrong one."

He stopped and looked back questioningly. Paula held Olga's eyes steadily while she drew a red cylinder off the shelf. "I put them in *this* one."

Olga didn't falter. "Oh yes, that's right . . . I must have got them mixed up." She took the red cylinder and exchanged it for the blue one that Brusikov was holding. He nodded and left, closing the door.

A strained silence descended while the two women watched the screen, Paula looked remorseful now, Olga tight-lipped and flushed. After a minute or so the figure of Dr. Brusikov came out of the Government Building entrance, carrying the red cylinder. He stopped and looked about for a few seconds, then approached the man in the yellow coat and green hat. Brusikov said something and offered the cylinder. The man in the yellow coat shook his head, shrugged, and waved a hand. Brusikov remonstrated and pointed back at the Government Building. The man shook his head again. Finally Brusikov, looking disgruntled and not a little mystified, moved away to find a different spot in the crowd.

Paula turned away but avoided facing Olga directly. "I'm sorry," she whispered.

Olga shook her head. She was her usual calm self once again. "No, you were quite right," she said. "Neither of us knew for sure. It is I who should apologize."

"For a moment I didn't trust you."

"At times like these, it's a wonder anyone trusts anybody."

On the screen the doors on the raised level above the square opened and a group of smiling figures came out to be greeted by cheers and applause. Paula sat down at the terminal again and pushed the curl from her forehead. "Then, let's get on with the job," she said.

Dressed in a selection from the civilian attire accumulated in the

Crypt, Rashazzi took the laser outside to repeat over longer ranges some tests that he and Haber had conducted inside the structure which had yielded odd results. He emerged at the surface in a ventilator outlet above some apartments on the far side of the reservoir, and spent more than an hour surreptitiously aiming pulses at parts of the buildings of central Novyi Kazan and timing the returns on an electronic interferometer that Paula had built. He explained the results to McCain later, after returning to the Crypt. Haber was with them.

"Since we are on the inside of a cylinder, the verticals of buildings converge toward the center, like the spokes of a wheel. And since we know the size of *Valentina Tereshkova,* it's easy to calculate how much the convergence ought to be: verticals spaced two hundred meters apart at the base ought to converge by about three meters through a fifteen-meter difference in height."

McCain nodded. That much was straightforward enough. "Okay."

"But they don't," Rashazzi said. "It works out at closer to one point three meters. So what's happened to the difference?"

McCain could only shake his head. "It fits with this idea that keeps coming up, of the whole place being bigger than it's supposed to, doesn't it," he said.

"Yes," Haber agreed. "And not only that. To give the amount of convergence that Razz had measured, the colony would have to be just the diameter that was indicated by the experiments we did with the balance scale: almost four and a half kilometers instead of less than two kilometers."

McCain made a face. "I hate coincidences."

"Oh, I don't think this could properly be called a coincidence," Haber said.

"Probably not. But we still don't have any explanations, huh?"

Rashazzi looked at McCain with a strange, unsmiling expression for a second. Then he picked up a sheet of paper that he and Haber had been poring over when McCain arrived. "Yes," he replied in a curious voice. "As a matter of fact, Lew, this time I believe we do have an explanation. . . ."

※ ※ ※

Brusikov came in again on his way back from lunch to return the cylinder and ask what the hell Olga had been playing at. Paula apologized and explained that Olga had been fooled by the yellow coat and green hat—hardly the most common of outfits to be seen around *Tereshkova*, she pointed out with as much charm as she could muster—and had not paid enough attention to the face. It wasn't the right man. Brusikov went away grumbling about being made to feel a fool, but accepted it.

Paula remained, staring at the work she had been doing on the larger screen, but no longer interested in it. How was anybody supposed to care about the flatulence of microbes when the world might be about to cremate itself?

She thought about the message she had composed for Foleda, and how inadequate it seemed compared to the scale of what was at stake. Her conviction grew that the nature of *Valentina Tereshkova* had become a major factor in the equations being juggled in Washington and in Moscow. Here she was, not only present at that fulcrum of events, but singled out through a strange series of twists of fate for a unique perspective that should surely be crucial to any decisions embarked on at such a moment. She remembered reading somewhere that Napoleon scoffed at the notion of luck. "Lucky" people, he maintained, were the ones who put themselves in the right place and at the right time for the right things to happen.

In other words, they rose to the occasion. Here was an occasion that surely beckoned.

She was still feeling despondent when Olga returned. The Russian woman slipped in without knocking, and closed the door behind her.

"Did the message go off all right?" Paula asked.

Olga nodded and stood leaning against the door with her eyes closed for a moment, as if allowing tension to drain away. "Top priority, so Ivan will send it straight on." She went over to the empty chair in front of the console and sat down, noticing as she did so the red cylinder, which Paula had put back on the shelf. "Has Brusikov been back?"

"Yes. He wasn't very amused."

"What did you tell him?"

"That it was the wrong man. You were misled by the hat and the coat—an unlikely similarity in appearance."

Olga nodded, and sat staring at the console for what seemed a long time. Paula watched her but had nothing to say. Eventually Olga turned her chair to face across the room. They looked at each other. At last Olga said, "It doesn't seem enough, somehow."

Paula nodded in a way that said Olga didn't have to elaborate. "I've been thinking the same thing. And on reflection I'm not even sure they'll believe that much."

"Why shouldn't they?"

"Who am I? Just the support half of the team." Olga gave the impression that she had expected the reply but had allowed Paula to make it all the same, just to be sure they both understood the same things. Paula got the feeling that Olga's thoughts had been running parallel to her own. Olga hesitated visibly. "Yes?" Paula prompted.

Olga looked up. "There is another way."

"What way?"

"Ask the Russians to connect you to America via one of their regular channels—it could be a private military link, not public TV. Show yourself here, in *Valentina Tereshkova,* alongside the Soviet leaders. Let your own people talk with you over the link, ask questions, and observe you responding and interacting. That way they will know that the Soviet leaders are here, and that they are here now." Paula was so surprised by the proposal that for a moment she could only shake her head and stare incredulously. "Say you wish to talk with General Protbornov urgently, and tell him everything," Olga urged. "He has access to the people who can arrange it."

"But . . . everything? We'd have to reveal the channel. You'd lose your communications to Ivan. Ivan would be exposed."

"I know. I've already thought of all that. What do things like that matter now? If there's a war it will all be lost anyway."

Paula swallowed hard. "That's . . . that's some decision you're asking."

"Is it? What is the alternative?"

A good point, Paula conceded. For when she thought about it, the only alternative to trying was to live the rest of her life, irrespective of the outcome, with the knowledge that she hadn't tried. Put that way, it didn't really leave much of a choice.

◉ CHAPTER FORTY-SIX ◉

Major General Protbornov stared back across the desk in his office at the Internal Security Headquarters in Turgenev. For several seconds his rugged, heavy-jowled face was completely blank, as if it had just been solidly punched. Then he blinked and raised a hand to rub the corner of his eye. "Communications?" The heavy, rumbling voice assembled the word slowly, a syllable at a time, as if they were steps he was having to mount to overcome his disbelief. "Communications into American intelligence, from inside Zamork? How could this be possible?" Beneath their puffy lids, his eyes had taken on a bleak expression that already seemed to be looking into the face of demotion, arrest, and possibly even a firing squad.

Uskayev—the same blond, gray-eyed major whom Paula had last seen with Protbornov in the infirmary—drew a notepad closer across the top of his desk, which stood by the window to one side of the office. "Describe the mechanism of this communications method," he said. "What form does it take?"

Olga sighed in the chair beside Paula. "We possess an electronic chip that is programmed to insert encoded text into the random-number-group fillers in the regular message stream to Earth," she replied, speaking in a tired voice. "The chip is substituted for the standard one in the outgoing encryption processor located in the Communications Center."

"How do you gain access to the Communications Center?"

"I don't. I have an associate."

"The name?"

Olga hesitated. Uskayev looked up sharply. Clearly if she'd come here asking for favors, she couldn't expect to hold anything back. "Andrei Ogovoy, an engineer at the Communications Center," she said. Uskayev wrote rapidly on his pad.

"Go on," Protbornov said.

Olga described her channel down to the groundstation at Sokhotsk and the technique of disguising encoded replies as statistical data. She said that the channel had been extended to connect into the US military and intelligence communications system, but insisted, correctly, that she didn't know how the link from Sokhotsk to the US operated.

"You say this person at Sokhotsk was communicating with you privately before there was any contact with the Americans," Protbornov said when she had finished.

"Yes."

"So this person must have set up the link to the Americans, and managed the transfer of messages after it was established. Who was this person who commanded such extraordinary opportunities?"

"The name?" Uskayev said, pen poised.

Paula stared woodenly ahead and heard Olga take in a long breath beside her. "Professor Igor Dyashkin," Olga said. "Director of the operational facility at Sokhotsk." Despite herself, Paula raised her eyebrows. Protbornov and Uskayev exchanged ominous glances.

Protbornov stared down at his hands in a way that said the sky might as well fall now, for all the surprises life had left to offer. He looked up. "So, you have your channel to the professor. And how did you progress from there to initiating contact with the Americans?"

"We didn't," Olga said. "They initiated contact with us." Protbornov stared at her incredulously.

That had been expected. Paula explained, "I'm not a journalist with Pacific News Services. My companion and I came here on a mission for US military intelligence. It was our people. A message came over the channel from them, to us." She looked at Uskayev and nodded resignedly before he could say it. "Bryce, Paula M., second lieutenant, United States Air Force, serial number AO 20188813, temporarily attached to the Unified Defense Intelligence Agency."

"And your colleague?" Protbornov clearly wasn't going to quit while he was on a roll.

"I only know him as Lewis Earnshaw. He's with the UDIA. That's all I know."

Protbornov nodded, having disposed of those preliminaries, and clasped his hands. "So, you say the UDIA contacted you here, using the link through Professor Dyashkin. But how could they possibly have known about it?"

"I don't know," Paula replied.

"You can't expect us to believe that," Protbornov scoffed.

"She's telling the truth," Olga said. "We are both scientists. We don't know what kinds of intrigues go on among you people. But that's all immaterial now, compared to the reason why we've decided to come here and reveal everything." She paused to let the point sink in. Protbornov waited. Olga went on, "To us, the messages we have been receiving indicate that the West believes the Soviet Union is about to launch a first strike. We think there's a strong possibility that the West will decide to attack preemptively. Preventing such a catastrophe must take priority over other considerations—that is why we have been frank. We think there is a way it can be prevented, but we will need your help."

Protbornov was looking astounded. "A first strike . . . by us? Preemptive attack? But this is ludicrous. Our whole leadership is up here, practically on vacation. Tomorrow we will be declaring *Valentina Tereshkova* open to international visitors. The ship bringing the first representatives from all nations, including the United States, is on its way here at this very moment. There will be celebrations, games, amnesties . . . Why would anyone be worrying about a strike at *this* of all times? Have they all gone mad down there?"

Olga was nodding. "I know, I know. It sounds insane. The irony is that those very things are what has caused the concern. It's all a misunderstanding, and it mustn't be allowed to lead to a calamity.

But since the problem is one that stems from misinformation, it can be rectified by correct information. That is what we need you to help us do."

Uskayev had put his pen down and was listening with a dazed look on his face. Protbornov moistened his lips and nodded curtly without change of expression. "Explain what it is you wish us to do," he said.

Olga told him about the reconnaissance expeditions by Zamork prisoners to investigate alleged weapons installations around the colony. The muscles in Protbornov's throat convulsed in spasms as one revelation followed another, but he heard her through without interrupting. "But from the tone of their responses, the Americans didn't seem satisfied by the negative findings," Olga concluded. "We think they suspect that false information concerning the locations was planted to mislead them." She described the Americans' latest request for confirmation that Soviet leaders were in fact at *Tereshkova*, and interpreted it as indicating Western suspicions that the Soviet broadcasts might be prerecordings made months ago. If the West so concluded, then the only motivation they'd be able to deduce would be that the Soviets were about to launch a strike. Olga ended, "The only way to eliminate that risk is to convince them of their mistake. Paula has agreed to talk to her own people over a live connection into the US communications network is one can be set up. If she's seen here, alongside the arriving leaders and conducting a responsive dialogue with Washington, all doubts would be dispelled. Can you do it?"

Protbornov's bushy eyebrows knotted. "What you're asking, and in so little time . . . It would require the highest authority. And with all of them so preoccupied at this time . . ."

"This is a state emergency," Olga said. "I know the procedures exist. We have volunteered everything. Will you try?"

The general sat immobile for almost a minute, staring at the desk, his expression unchanging. Finally he spread his hands wide along the edge of the desk and stood up. "Wait here," he instructed, and left the room.

Major Uskayev busied himself with completing his notes and

then entering them into a terminal by his desk. Paula and Olga waited without speaking. There was a tap on the door, and a woman in uniform entered to deposit some papers in a basket by the door. She took more papers from another basket and left. Paula thought of all the effort, ingenuity, perseverance, and courage that had gone into setting up Olga's channel to Ivan—now revealed as Dyashkin—the link to Foleda, the secret workshop below Zamork, and Earnshaw's private espionage operation. Now that she had a moment to reflect, she was horrified at how much would be lost because of what she and Olga were saying here today. But if they were right, all that and infinitely more would otherwise have been lost anyway. She tried not to dwell on what it meant if they were wrong. . . . No, that wasn't possible. They *had* to be right. She convinced herself with the certainty that comes only with the knowledge that being wrong would be to lose everything.

Protbornov returned twenty minutes later with a captain and four armed guards. The entire party, including Uskayev, took an elevator down inside Security Headquarters and followed a series of passages that took them underneath the Government Building. Here they ascended again and came to a corridor, where the escort conducted them to one of the doors and took up positions outside. Inside was a conference room, where two men were waiting. One was in his early forties, short, with thick black hair and bushy brows. Protbornov introduced him as Comrade Kirilikhov from the Party's Central Committee. The other was older, with thinning hair and a sallow, tired complexion; his name was Sepelyan, and he was from the Soviet Ministry of Defense. An orderly brought in tea. Protbornov said that Turgenev was keeping a channel open to Moscow, where the appropriate people to take the matter higher were being sought.

Step by step and in greater detail, the two women went through the whole story again. Kirilikhov expressed amusement at the suggestion of Western doubts about Soviet leaders really coming to *Tereshkova,* since he himself had arrived from Earth a mere twelve hours previously. Protbornov listened glumly while Olga described once more how prisoners inside Zamork had talked with American military intelligence in Washington, and Paula told how they had been burrowing around the whole colony like rabbits. She listed the locations that they had checked, and summarized the findings she had communicated to Washington. "It was hardly something that could be called espionage," Olga pointed out. "She simply confirmed what the Soviet government itself had been saying publicly for years."

"Yes, that point has not been missed," Kirilikhov said, nodding. He shifted his gaze to Paula. "But you say you have reason to believe that the credibility of your reports was not rated highly in Washington?"

"From the tone of the responses, yes," Paula said. "Probably because of my position."

"As a support specialist, not a trained agent," Olga explained.

"Ah." Kirilikhov nodded.

Sepelyan studied his fingers while he weighed up the things that had been said. "So why should they believe you any the more if we put you on a line to Earth? You could have been turned—brainwashed. They still think we do things like that, don't they? Or maybe we have somebody standing off-camera, pointing a gun at your head. After what you've told us, would it be enough to convince them?"

There was a short silence. Protbornov shrugged. "What else can we do?"

"It's something, at least," Kirilikhov said.

Sepelyan sat forward to the table. "I was thinking about this other agent that came with you, this . . ."

"Lewis Earnshaw," Uskayev supplied.

"This Mr. Earnshaw. He is the professional, you say, yes? Experienced. Believable. If we could get *him* to appear on the line also and confirm the story, might that do the trick? Those who know him, his own boss, maybe . . . Would they believe their own man?"

"I've interrogated him many times," Protbornov said. "Yes, professional. Impossible to intimidate or persuade. You get nothing from him, nothing. If he were *my* man, I would believe him. Unquestionably, I would believe him."

"He couldn't have been brainwashed?" Kirilikhov inquired.

Protbornov shook his head emphatically. "Him? Never."

"Why couldn't he have a gun pointing at him too, then?"

"He'd tell you to pull the trigger and be damned. He wouldn't compromise."

The Russians began warming to the idea, but then noticed that Paula had sat back and was shaking her head. "What is wrong?" Protbornov asked her.

Paula sighed hopelessly. "I just can't see him agreeing to it. . . . You have to understand what he's like: stubborn, antagonistic, indoctrinated with fixed views. He won't even consider the possibility that there might be alternatives to the way he thinks." She raised her opened hands. "He abhors everything about the Soviet system. The general said it—he wouldn't compromise. As a matter of principle, he'd never be seen going on television, public or private, and voluntarily cooperating with Russians. That's the way he is. It won't work. Forget it."

Protbornov pulled a face. "On reflection, I have to admit that she's probably right," he said. "That does sound like him."

"It was just an idea," Sepelyan said.

"A pity," Kirilikhov murmured.

Silence fell. Then Olga, who had been sitting and thinking to herself in silence, said, "I don't know . . . perhaps there is a way in which we could get him to do it." She glanced at Paula. "Or maybe you could."

"How?" Paula asked.

"The laser that they've got," Olga said. "Wasn't that the idea of it in the first place? And you said it's working now. Well, maybe he won't go on a live TV transmission with Russians—but he might say the same thing privately, over his own personal link. Might he be persuaded to do that?"

Protbornov was looking bewildered. "Laser? What laser? What are you two women talking about now?"

They told him about Earnshaw's laser and its intended use for communicating with Earth. Protbornov sat looking stunned. The two men from Moscow glanced at him from time to time like officials from the head office of a bank with a branch manager whose staff had been giving away notes on the street. If Earnshaw believed he was acting independently, possibly he could be induced to send a personal confirmation from *Tereshkova* of what his own eyes were seeing there, Olga said. All Protbornov would need to do was make sure the guards stayed out of the way.

Paula thought it was worth a try, but she pointed out a problem that still remained. Communications only work when the person on the receiving end is listening. For a signal from the laser to get through, somebody down on Earth would have to be expecting it, and know what frequency and code to look for. Furthermore, in view of the minuscule amount of energy that would actually reach Earth, they would need to be using more than just any equipment for the looking.

Olga was aware of that. "But I understand that you helped them build the electronics," she said to Paula. "Could you provide the operating frequency and whatever else somebody would need to know to set a receiver up?"

"Sure—actually there isn't that much," Paula said. "What have you got in mind?"

"We use the existing channel through Sokhotsk to give that information to the Americans," Olga replied. "We're here now, in Turgenev. We can send it off right away. You can tell Earnshaw it was your idea—that you did it in anticipation, hoping he would agree. We will have to hope that the Americans can arrange a suitable method for reception in time. It might take, what . . . a day, maybe?"

"A lot less is they use emergency procedures," Paula replied. "But that only applies to relaying a signal through the communications net. I don't know how they'd pick it up in the first place."

"We can only leave that side to them," Olga said. "Once they're set up, then all Earnshaw would need to do is get himself to a place where he can witness what's happening here, and point the laser at the roof. That shouldn't be too difficult if the guards stay away from him—but nobody tells him that, of course."

"Will he know if he's getting through?" Sepelyan asked. "Does this device receive also?"

"Yes," Paula said. "A reply signal comes back along the same path in the opposite direction."

"Along with the sunshine? Wouldn't the signal get lost in it?"

"It shouldn't. We picked the operating frequency to coincide with one of the dark absorption lines in the solar spectrum. And at the Earth end, they'll be able to use a powerful transmitter, don't forget."

Sepelyan nodded in a way which said that was all right with him, whatever it meant. Everyone looked at everyone else. Evidently there was nothing more to be said.

"Then, we seem to be agreed to give this suggestion a try," Protbornov announced. "We have little time. Therefore I propose that Lieutenant Bryce be taken back to Zamork at once to contact Mr. Earnshaw and explain the situation. Comrade Oshkadov goes downstairs to the Communications Center to send the message to the Americans via the Sokhotsk channel, advising the laser frequency and other details. Lieutenant Bryce can write them down before she leaves."

"Very well," Olga agreed.

Protbornov looked inquiringly at Kirilikhov and Sepelyan. They returned nods that said they were satisfied. "I'd better go and check on what's happening in Moscow," Kirilikhov said. He gave Protbornov a withering look as he rose from his chair. "After the present situation is resolved, we can discuss Zamork and the effectiveness of its security measures. Out of curiosity, have you ever been down a salt mine in Siberia, General?"

❄ CHAPTER FORTY-SEVEN ❄

Inquisitive visitors waiting to board the spoke elevators after their arrival at *Valentina Tereshkova* had always been told that behind the bulkhead facing the boarding area at the hub were storage tanks for water and liquid chemicals, as the official plans showed. In fact there were no storage tanks there. The small amount of agriculture and industrial processing that had been staged purely for show had never required much in the way of chemicals. And neither were there any manufacturing facilities worth speaking of next to the hub nuclear reactors behind the docking ports. The dummy bulkhead with its pipes, and the rest of the facade, had been dismantled now. What the reactors actually powered were capacitor banks feeding a battery of electromagnetic coil guns capable of imparting an acceleration of hundreds of g's into their drum-shaped projectiles to hurl them miles clear of the platform in seconds. Each projectile consisted of a fission bomb contained in an ellipsoidal cavity shaped to feed a configuration of lasing material that would transform a large proportion of the detonation energy into fifty independently aimable beams of high-density X-rays.

Field Marshal Vladislav Kyrenko, Commander in chief of "Anvil"—the designation of the entire space bombardment system that the superficialities of *Valentina Tereshkova* had disguised—steadied himself against a handrail while the general in charge of

Battle Station 2 at the hub finished his report. One of the things the planners of space warfare hadn't taken into account was the difficulty of maintaining dignity under conditions of negligible weight.

"All mechanical and hydraulic systems tested and functional. Registration computers have been tracking assigned targets for twelve hours and check positively. All projectile onboard computers have been updating continuously without errors. Power-plant and launch systems are fully operational."

"Sounds good," Kyrenko said. "So what odds should I bet on our zapping every American lasersat with the first salvo?"

The general smiled faintly. "Oh, pretty good, I'd say."

"And the morale of the crew?"

"Just waiting to go for it."

Kyrenko nodded. "Good. Carry on." He watched as the general went back into the armored fire-control center from which the hub batteries would be directed. Inside, through the opening next to the massive door that would be closed before the action commenced, he could see technicians and operators busy at their rows of consoles. And that was merely the inner defense. The space between the inner and outer skins held a layer of pulverized moonrock several feet thick at the strongpoints.

That completed the hub part of the inspection. Kyrenko turned to Lt. General Churenev, his principal aide, who was standing with the party of officers waiting behind. "Everything looks fine here. Let's move on down."

They bobbed and pulled themselves across the deck and entered the elevator waiting at the top of one of the shafts from the Turgenev spoke. The doors closed, and moments later they were descending toward the ring. The outer tube of the spoke was armored, too; but since it was more exposed than the hardened battle stations at the hub and various locations around the rim, it would not be used while combat conditions prevailed. Once hostilities commenced, the garrison at the hub would be sealed in there for the duration.

At Turgenev they came out of the elevator into the main concourse of the skeleton that had once been the Government Building and crossed the dusty, derelict space to come out onto the raised terrace bordering the main square, where two staff cars were waiting. All was darkness, broken only by pools of light from the floodlamps set up at ground level by the military. The lines of reflecting slats in the roof had been closed to prevent their directing hostile laserfire into the interior. Kyrenko halted with his party, and stood for a while staring out at the black, empty shapes of the deserted ghost city. On the far side, the bones of what had been Internal Security Headquarters stood silhouetted against one of the lamps, picked clean by an army-engineer squad collecting materials for a piece of last-minute improvised construction. A row of groundcars stood silent and abandoned in the shadows beneath.

"It's hard to imagine it the way it was," Churenev commented. "With light, color, people, children . . ."

Kyrenko nodded distantly. "The day has come at last, Oleg. For a hundred years we have been treated like lepers. The capitalists sent Lenin back from Switzerland because they thought his Revolution would destroy Russia. When that failed, they set up Hitler and the Nazis, and sent them against us, but we destroyed them. Then they encircled us with guns and bases and missile sites, as if we were a disease that had to be contained. They spread lies, waiting . . . thinking they could wear us down by siege. But they forgot the Mongols, Napoleon, Hitler—how many times Russia has come back to bury those who thought they had destroyed her. And so it will be again. They say we are on the verge of collapse. But soon they will learn." He turned his head. "Am I not right?"

Churenev sighed. "If that is how it must be . . ."

The party descended the steps to the square, climbed into the cars, and left Turgenev. For a little over a quarter mile they drove through a desolation of bare metal terraces and piles of rotting vegetation that had been one of the agricultural sectors. In fact, only the crops along the valley center, lining the route along which visitors had been taken, had ever been real. The wheat, sorghum, vegetables, and rice terraces higher up the sides, which foreign observers had admired so enthusiastically from afar—apart from one show-piece section that they climbed laboriously to inspect more closely for themselves—had been planted with plastic imitations.

They came to Agricultural Station 3 and parked outside the waste-recycling plant that consisted mainly of dummy tanks, pipes, and reactor vessels. Its processing capacity was only a fraction of the publicized value—for the simple reason that there had never been that much waste to process. The field marshal and his aides walked through an opening in the side of an armored enclosure and entered the space that the public plans described as "Materials Storage." The commander of Battle Station 4, free-electron-laser emplacement, was waiting with his senior officers.

The party moved through the bays of windings and super-conducting magnets, the linac tunnel, and the control room. Accelerator potentials and field frequencies had been tuned to take out the West's communications and instrumentation satellites, checks were positive, and there were no problems to report. Emergency generators, local backup life-support systems, and escape chute down to the armored ring-transit tunnel were all operational. The men were in good shape.

"Very good, General," Kyrenko approved. "First-rate. So, we will meet in Washington, eh?"

"Yes, sir—to help burn down the Pentagon." Everyone laughed.

Kyrenko turned to Churenev and the others. "Very well, gentlemen. That completes the tour. My compliments to all of you. Let us return to HQ."

They reembarked in their vehicles and drove the remaining distance to Novyi Kazan, climbing the ramp by the emptied reservoir to the main entrance. On the way in, Kyrenko stopped in the upper-level communications room to send a signal to Moscow. It read: ANVIL AT BATTLE READINESS, CONDITION ORANGE 1. ALL UNITS OPERATIONAL. COUNTDOWN STATUS TO PLAN IS CONFIRMED.

Then he continued on down into the hardened zone containing the command center from which he and his staff would direct and coordinate all the battle stations. It was a place that had never been included in the official tours. On the publicly released plans, however, it was described as a detention and rehabilitation facility. Its name was Zamork.

✹ CHAPTER FORTY-EIGHT ✹

The speeches were over, but the main square in Turgenev was still alive with people when Paula came out from the main concourse of the Government Building, accompanied by Major Uskayev, the captain, and two guards. The sight of a woman in a plain green tunic under armed escort contrasted with the colorful, holidaylike atmosphere that had taken over, and heads turned to watch them curiously as they crossed the terrace outside the main doors and descended the steps to the square, where a security-police van was waiting.

As the van entered an underpass, changed direction, and emerged again to negotiate the tortuous route out of the town, Paula saw that the bridges and pedestrian ways were bustling with people. Many of them were acting like tourists, rubbernecking at the sights and posing for pictures—no doubt recent arrivals out viewing their new home, she thought. On the edge of town they passed a large, open area of grass, where teams of children in white and red outfits were putting final touches to their gymnastics routines for the celebrations. For a moment the brightly lit tunnel of the colony's valley curved upward before them, with the green and yellow arms of the agricultural terraces spreading upward on either side, and then the van entered another tunnel to descend from town-center level to the valley floor.

The agricultural sector looked presentable again after the heroic efforts that had gone into saving its face—not to mention those of the Soviet leaders—and terraces of grain, fruit, and vegetables, and pastures with reasonably contented-looking cows lined the route beneath the inverted blue-yellow skybowl all the way past Agricultural Station 3 to Novyi Kazan. Here, they exited from the throughway by the reservoir, where a couple of boats were out sailing, and ascended the ramp to the gate in front of the surface buildings of Zamork. They passed through the checkpoint into the outer yard, where they disembarked from the van and entered the Administration Building.

A few minutes later, Paula came out on her own through the rear guardpost into the surface-level compound. In talking the situation over, she had agreed with Olga and Protbornov that the best chance of succeeding with Earnshaw lay in sustaining an appearance of everything's being normal, which meant he couldn't be allowed to know that the Russians were involved. Obviously the days of the elaborate clandestine operation that had run from B-3 were now over. But before they intervened to close it down, the authorities would permit it to serve this one final purpose.

Istamel was reading on his bunk in Hut 8 when Paula arrived. Seeing from her face that something urgent was afoot, he got up and went over to the cassette player. For some time now the occupants of Hut 8 and the regular visitors to it had been recording assorted conversation, usually arranged to be as boring as possible, between different individuals for occasions like these. Istamel selected one that featured just the two of them talking interminably about medieval Turkish poetry, dropped it into the player, and connected the output into the microphone circuit. That way the conversation would correlate with who had been seen entering the hut, if it happened to be under observation.

Paula had decided during the drive from Turgenev that there wasn't time to go through the whole thing again to let Istamel know what had happened. Besides, the whole ploy was to tell Earnshaw only that Olga had sent a message alerting the West to receive the laser signal, and to make him believe everything beyond that was normal. Istamel would play his part better if that was as much as he knew, too—and he could find out when she told Earnshaw. "I have to go down to the Crypt immediately," she said. "Do you know if Lew is there?"

"He should be. I was there earlier and left him with Razz and Albrecht. They seemed busy. Where's Olga? I thought you'd both be back together."

"A lot has happened. Look, it's too much to explain now. Come back down and hear it with the others."

Istamel nodded and asked no more. They went through to the shower and opened the hatch in the cubicle floor. Istamel went down first, and Paula followed, closing the hatch over them. They came out of the roof where the ladder ended, threaded their way through the machinery compartment, and crossed the girder bridge to the outside of the elevator shaft. Paula had been over this route many times now, and the traverse across the shaft to the recess on the far side no long troubled her. On the next two crossings after her first introduction by Peter Sargent, she had balanced with the help of a handrope that was stowed nearby to be temporarily strung across if needed, but now she could manage without. Istamel still used the rope, which inwardly gave her a certain satisfaction. They completed the descent, left the shaft through the maintenance hatch at the lower level, and made their way between the lines of tanks toward the Crypt, taking care not to trigger Rashazzi's alarm system on the way. As they came within sight of the Crypt's lights, they caught the sound of raised voices arguing excitedly. That in itself was unusual. Paula pursed her mouth determinedly and steeled herself for the coming confrontation.

Earnshaw was with Rashazzi and Haber, as Istamel had said. In addition, Koh had appeared. They were standing around the large table, which was strewn with pieces of paper, and they continued gesticulating and making sketches even while Paula and Istamel were climbing down into the workspace, as if unaware of their approach. Then Earnshaw turned his head to acknowledge their presence, and the others fell silent.

It wasn't a time for observing niceties. Paula drew up facing the group and moved her arm in a brief gesture that took in the whole of the workshop and its contents. "All of this can wait for a while," she told them. "I've just come from Turgenev. Olga is there, sending off a message. It's an important message. A lot of things have been happening that you don't know about down here." Haber motioned to one of the sheets of paper that he and the others had been talking over and started to say something, but Paula cut him off with a wave of her hand. "We received a message from Tycoon this morning which said, in effect, that the West believes the Soviets are about to launch a first strike. I mean, they're not fooling. This is *it!*"

Istamel was staring at her incredulously. "But you never mentioned anything about this . . ."

"There wasn't time up there. I'm mentioning it now."

"But what did it say? Why should they think the Russians would attack now, with all their leaders here? It doesn't—"

"That's the whole point," Paula said. "They don't believe the Russian leaders are here. They're suspicious that the TV broadcasts going out might be recordings—in other words, a deception concocted to cover a strike. Anyhow, Olga and I have already sent a signal back confirming that the leaders are up here. That was as much as we could do right away. But we don't think it's enough. What we want you to—"

"Shut up." Earnshaw's voice wasn't loud, but it carried such an unexpected whiplike snap that Paula did shut up. He acknowledged with a nod. "Now, run that by me again." Paula was too taken aback to reply. He said it for her. "Our side has reasons for thinking the Soviets might be about to strike if their leaders aren't really up in *Tereshkova*—is that right? But you know it's all a mistake, because the leaders really are here. And that's what you've told Tycoon."

Paula nodded and returned a puzzled look. When he didn't respond immediately, she collected herself together again and got back into stride. "We did what we could, but the signal only had my validation code. I'm not sure that would carry enough weight in Washington. To really convince them . . ." Her voice trailed away as she saw that Earnshaw and the two scientists were not listening, but exchanging ominous looks among themselves. Koh had backed inconspicuously into the shadows, but Paula's confusion just at that moment was such that she didn't notice.

"It fits," Earnshaw murmured. "They've put them all down a big hole, somewhere out of the way. Jesus, they *are* about to launch a strike. They're on their countdown right now!"

"The whole thing is a super-battlestation," Rashazzi whispered. "They're probably only waiting for that UN ship to arrive."

"About sixteen hours from now," Haber said numbly.

It was dawning on Paula that she'd been running off the tracks since somewhere way back up the line. She sent an uncomprehending look from one to another. "I . . . don't understand what you're talking about. What's going on?"

Earnshaw exhaled a long sigh and turned away, as if needing a moment longer to integrate the new information into his thinking. Rashazzi turned absently away toward the bench, lost in a world of his own and thinking furiously. Haber still looked thunderstruck. Paula looked around for Koh and noticed for the first time that he had disappeared. Earnshaw saw the question forming on her face and stepped forward, cutting her off before she could speak. "Maybe there are a few things that *you* ought to know before you do any more talking," he said. Just for an instant, Paula sensed the tenseness in his voice, an urgency to divert her attention.

Without warning Earnshaw whirled round and his fist streaked out in the same movement, bunched karate-style to deliver a devastating blow to the V below Istamel's ribs. The Turk emitted a strained gurgling sound and dropped to his knees as his legs buckled. In the same instant Koh materialized from the darkness behind and slid his right arm around Istamel's neck to seize the jacket collar high on the opposite side below the ear, while his left arm came round from the other side to grasp the right lapel. Koh drove his knee into the Turk's back, gaining leverage to tighten his arms scissor-fashion in a way that slid aside the muscle covering the carotid artery and exposed it to the full pressure of the bony edge of Koh's forearm— cutting off the brain's blood supply brings unconsciousness much faster than strangulation. Rashazzi turned from the bench with a heavy metal bar in his hand, ready to help out if needed. Istamel tried to struggle, but the blow from Earnshaw had paralyzed his breathing. His efforts became feeble, then his eyes rolled upward and he went limp. Koh sustained the pressure for a few seconds longer and shook his head regretfully. "Something like this seems to happen whenever you two meet," he commented to Earnshaw as he released the body and let it crumple to the floor.

Earnshaw squatted down and opened Istamel's jacket. He undid the shirt and uncovered a Soviet communicator pad secured on a waistband. A quick but thorough search added a .45 automatic in an underarm sling, some extra clips of ammunition, and a general-clearance badge. Haber produced some cord, and Earnshaw helped him truss up the Turk out of the way in a sitting position with his back to one of the supporting pillars. Rashazzi tied a gag around his mouth.

Paula could only shake her head in helpless bewilderment as she watched. Earnshaw straightened up and turned back toward her. "You pick nice friends," he commented.

"What is this?" Paula mumbled. "Will somebody tell me what's going on? How did you know he was a plant?"

Rashazzi, Haber, and Koh moved back around the table. "He said he went to the hub on one of our missions," Earnshaw said.

Paula still hadn't fully accommodated to what had just happened. "So?"

"There isn't any hub," Rashazzi said.

Paula shifted her gaze uncertainly from one to another of them, finally letting it come to rest on Earnshaw. His face had an odd, challenging expression. "Suppose we told you that this place we're in is not *Valentina Tereshkova*," he said. "In fact, it isn't even in space at all."

The statement was so preposterous that for a moment it didn't register and Paula answered mechanically. "That's crazy. Of course it's in space. Go to one of the ag sectors and look up through a window. Everyone knows they came here from Earth, don't they? I know that you and I did."

"Do you?" Rashazzi's quietly reasonable tone broke her stupor and made her look away from Earnshaw. Only now did her face show its first sign of any willingness to try to understand. Rashazzi went on, "You may know that you were taken out to *Tereshkova* on a transporter from Earth over six months ago, but that's not quite the same thing. A lot has happened since then."

"Just out of curiosity . . ." Earnshaw said. Paula's head jerked back to face him. "Were you taken sick soon after we were arrested?" Her expression supplied the answer. He nodded. "So was I. And when you came round, did a doctor tell you you'd been out for a couple of days? These guys had similar experiences, too. Now, isn't that strange? What do you think might have happened during that couple of days?"

"That's . . . absurd," Paula said. This time, however, her voice had lost its earlier conviction. Instead it was asking how what they were saying could be possible.

Rashazzi stepped over to the table and picked up a pencil. Paula moved forward, while the others closed around. Taking a blank sheet of paper, Rashazzi sketched a shallow, truncated, inverted cone—a circular strip, banked all the way round, like a racetrack.

"Suppose this were a large platform, miles in circumference, with miniature cities, agricultural sectors, and landscaping on it, all contained in a big, donut-shaped tunnel deep underground somewhere," he said. "Now support the entire platform on a system of superconducting magnetic fields and rotate it at such speed that the force vectors of gravity and centrifugal force combine into a single resultant perpendicular to the floor. If you want some specific numbers, from the tests we've conducted I'd estimate a banking angle of twenty-five degrees and a rotation period of ninety seconds, which implies a radius of a little under a kilometer, or about six tenths of a mile."

Paula shook her head in the way of somebody trying to wake up. "It can't be . . . I mean, adding the vectors like that . . . Everything would weigh more."

"By about ten percent, with the figures I've just quoted," Rashazzi agreed. "Which is about the most you could expect people to adjust to reasonably quickly, and why you couldn't go to a larger banking angle. And in fact, the gravitational acceleration as measured in Zamork is ten percent greater than Earth-normal. A strange way to design a space colony, wouldn't you think?"

"And incidentally, the scales they weigh you on in the infirmary are calibrated to read ten percent light," Haber interjected. "That is very interesting, yes?"

"Do you remember feeling weak and heavy in the limbs when you woke up?" Earnshaw asked her. "We did, too. It wore off after a few days."

Paula was looking at Rashazzi's sketch with a changed expression, as if she wanted to be convinced. But now the scientist in her asserted itself, searching for the flaws. "Why rotate it at all?" she asked. "If it's on Earth and in a gravity field to begin with, why bother?"

"Because of the curvature that can be built into the structure," Rashazzi answered. "A static platform would have to be flat, like a washer. It could never support the illusion of being the inside of a big hamsterwheel, as it would have to do to look real. But banking it introduces a vertical component of curvature and gives you a floor that does indeed bend upward as it recedes."

Paula stared down at Rashazzi's sketch dubiously. She thought for a while, then took the pencil and on another sheet drew a pair of curves coming inward from the sides as if from behind an observer, and then retreating and converging to one side. It was a representation of Rashazzi's racetrack as seen by somebody standing on it. She added a series of radial lines sloping down at intervals from its higher, outer edge to the inner, and then some crude human figures at varying distances.

She inspected the result critically, tipping her head first to one side, then to the other. The others remained silent. Finally she said, "No, I still can't buy this. However much you try and disguise it, it's still going to look like a banked racetrack. The people will start to lean over as they get farther away. It won't look anything like this." Beside it she drew another perspective view, this time with the two curves converging upward and away directly in front of the observer, and with the cross-lines appearing as horizontal rungs. It was a hamster's view of the inside of its wheel. Again she added some human figures.

"See, they're nothing like each other. The people should stay vertical, and foreshorten." Paula gestured back at her first sketch. "If you blocked off all the long sight lines, then maybe you could get away with it. But this place isn't built like that. I've just driven from Turgenev, and everyone here's been outside. You can see all the way from Novyi Kazan to the edge of Ag Station Three. It's the same everywhere. Long lines of sight aren't obstructed around the colony, yet you don't see a banked racetrack. So how could it be the way you're saying?"

Rashazzi took back the pencil. "That was something that puzzled us for a long time, and why we at first rejected the racetrack explanation," he said. "This is how you do it." He drew an imitation of Paula's first sketch and superimposed on it a pair of lines cutting across the curve of the track and forming a section of straight strip, as would the edges of a piece of ribbon laid flat along the sloping rim of a dinner plate. Then he added a series of verticals along the lines, connected them with horizontals to complete the illusion, and added a couple of figures as Paula had done.

Rashazzi covered the parts outside the walls with his hands to leave just the view looking along between them. The result came uncannily close to the second sketch that Paula had made. "You build walls," he said. "The colony we are inside is a replica of the real *Tereshkova*—the one you were taken to in May. But it is a replica with a difference. Instead of being circular, it consists of a series of straight segments with sides that don't veer off laterally, just like the real one, and by the geometry I've described, with floors and roofs that curve and yet possess perpendicular gravity everywhere, just like the real one. There are six long segments, running between the bases of the spokes. In addition there are what amount to another six short segments that form the complexes around the spoke-bases themselves—three towns and the three agricultural stations." Rashazzi rummaged through some of the papers that he and the others had been discussing when Paula and Istamel arrived, and produced a plan view to show what he meant.

"That means you'd have to turn through a thirty-degree angle between segments," Paula commented. "Then—" She broke off as the further implication struck her.

"The architect who designed the towns wasn't a nut," Earnshaw supplied, as if reading her mind. "They're that way on purpose, to make you lose your sense of direction."

"Or at least, sufficiently mislead you into not realizing that you're coming out thirty degrees off from the direction you went in," Rashazzi said.

And that explained why the towns and the agricultural stations forming the intersection zones were all built high: to obscure the views to the far side. From relatively close distances the rising structures formed a screen, while from farther back the dip of the roof interceded before it was possible to see over the top of any of the zones and into the next long, straight section.

"The odd bits of sky that you think you see behind the intersection zones from some places are no doubt optical images projected onto screens built in among the higher levels of the architecture," Haber said. "from even a short distance away, the difference would be impossible to distinguish. The overhead views of the hub and the stars at some places are also graphics simulations."

"And so there isn't any hub, and that's why he couldn't have gone there," Earnshaw said, gesturing at Istamel's inert form. "And why security is so tight around the spokes." Paula looked back at the papers on the table, accepting what was on them now, but still needing time to absorb it fully. "And suggestion did the rest," Earnshaw said. "There is some residual distortion, but the unevenness of the valley-sides hides it—you won't see it if you're not looking for it. The gravity does vary a bit from the centers of the long sections to the ends, and the banking angle increases slightly toward the outside. . . . But what dominates everything else is that you *know* you came here physically through space, and that knowledge shapes your perceptions—it was your own first reaction. And being surrounded by people who reinforce the belief . . ." He shrugged. "What reason would there be to question it?"

"Why did *you* question it?" Paula asked.

"Me? I didn't. Ask these guys. They were being scientists while you were saving the world."

Paula had asked for that, and let the remark go. There were so many questions bubbling in her head now that she didn't know where to begin. "*All* the people out there? Surely they couldn't all have been through the same treatment. Not on that scale."

"The Russians officers and so on are no doubt just playing parts," Earnshaw said. "And probably a lot of the prisoners are, too. But some are genuine, like us—probably to give us an authentic layer of immediate contacts to interact with."

"I meant the inhabitants of the colony generally," Paula said.

"I don't know. They could have been told they were taking part in a simulation experiment, and have a taboo about mentioning it—to preserve the realism. On the other hand, I've talked to some people who don't seem to have any clear recollection of how they got here. They think they do, until you question them about details. Then you find it's all vague and muddy."

"Drugs," Haber said. "It would be possible to transport many people on a simulated two-day flight under the influence of sense-disorienting substances that would dull memory and increase suggestibility."

"A weightless flight?" Paula queried.

"Later, they wouldn't remember," Haber said. "They could recall it as having been weightless if that was suggested to them."

Paula closed her eyes and nodded that she was finally persuaded. "Why?" She asked in a voice that sounded suddenly tired. "What would be worth so much effort . . . the cost of it all?"

"The world," Earnshaw said simply. "They saw years ago which way the game was going for them, and this was their last-ditch gamble. They built a weapons platform in space, thinly disguised as a colony—enough to fool visitors on the guided tours. At the same time they built this replica, with all the trappings of the complete colony. Then they hatched a scheme to get people inside the replica whose credibility the West would trust, and allowed them to set up supposedly secret communications channels to report back through. They staged this stunt with the November celebrations and the leaders to put everyone off guard. Sure there were people on the dummy we went to months ago, but they'll have been taken off since."

Now a lot of things were becoming clearer. "The dirt," Paula said slowly. "That's what that business was all about. Those ships didn't come here . . . go there to take dirt *up*. They went there to bring the people *down*."

Earnshaw nodded. "Sure. And where have the Russians *really* been putting their leaders in the meantime—with all their families, generals, Party hacks, and lots of people who'd be too useful to risk losing if there was a lot of rebuilding to do afterward? Down here, wherever here is—in a self-contained world with its own industry, agriculture, life-support, and a population ready-installed to keep it running for years, if need be, if the predictions turn out wrong and bad conditions on the surface last for a long time. What we're in is a giant-size bomb shelter."

Paula went very quiet as the full extent of how completely she had been taken in and how willingly she had fallen for it all became sickeningly clear to her. It must have shown on her face, she realized when she looked up and found Earnshaw watching her. "Oh, don't worry too much," he said. "You weren't the only one. They were thorough. They even stripped the fittings from the cells they put us in after we were arrested up in the real *Tereshkova*, and transferred them down here with us to the cells in the replica. I remember a vent in the ceiling of mine that had the same scratch in it. And don't think you were the only one they managed to hang a stooge on, either." He indicated Istamel with a turn of his head. "He wasn't the only one who was supposed to have been to the hub. I had my own Olga, too, and I fell for it."

Paula looked at him uncertainly. "Scanlon," Rashazzi said. It was the first time that Paula had ever heard a note of hopelessness in the Israeli's voice. "He's known everything, right from the start. They've been playing us like fishes all the time."

Paula stared back, horrified. She looked across at the bench and the things around it that had been constructed with so much effort: the laser, to signal across a void that wasn't out there; the survival suits—four of them—to get to a hub that didn't exist; the detectors, circuit-test meters, RF monitors, IR sensors, badges, bracelet solvents, and all the other paraphernalia devised to evade a surveillance system that had never been intended to contain them. She shook her head in mute protest, struggling to take in the full magnitude of the disaster.

And then a new voice spoke softly from the shadows in an Irish brogue. "Is that a fact, now?" They turned as Scanlon moved out into the light. Earnshaw started forward, then froze as he saw the automatic in Scanlon's hand. The others remained motionless on either side of him. Scanlon stopped far enough back from them not to be rushed. "No, to give credit where credit's due, Lew never told me that you were on your way to working out where we really are." He looked around the circle of grim faces. "My compliments, gentlemen. As the barmaid told the parson, 'It gets more interesting as you uncover more of it.' Wouldn't you agree?"

❧ CHAPTER FORTY-NINE ❧

"Now what?" Scanlon asked them. "It was an interesting conversation and I'm impressed by your ingenuity, but what did you imagine you were going to do next? There wasn't so much of a mention of any suggestion, unless I'm mistaken."

McCain didn't bother replying, but continued staring back woodenly. It was true. There was no way out, and the Russians controlled all the communications—as they had done all along. Scanlon doubtless had a communicator like Istamel's and would have summoned for help before revealing himself. Now he was simply waiting for it to arrive. Although Paula hadn't had a chance to say so, McCain guessed that the errand she'd come here on after sending the message to Foleda had been to try getting him to endorse it personally. Scanlon had waited long enough to see if she would succeed. Now the whole sorry charade was over. There was nothing left to do but await the appearance of the show's stagehands and producers from the wings.

A whole pattern now became clear, which McCain could have kicked himself for not having spotted earlier. Of course the Russians would have ensured that there was always somebody at his elbow to steer and prompt him, making sure he played his part according to the design. Scanlon had ingratiated himself with McCain from the beginning, by arranging—so he'd said—for McCain to get news of

Paula via the library from the phantom Russian officer, who probably didn't exist. It was Scanlon who had urged him to take on Maiskevik, which McCain could see now had been intended to equip him in the eyes of the billet with the image his role would require. Scanlon had steered McCain's group to Istamel's escape committee, and the committee had steered them to the freight system, which had doubtless been monitored all along by the Russians. McCain burned inwardly with anger at his own failing as much as at Scanlon's duplicity. He stared at the gun in Scanlon's hand, judging the distance and weighing up the chances—if everything was lost anyway—of taking the Irishman with him.

And then Scanlon did something very strange. He checked that the gun's safety catch was on, reversed it, and tossed it to McCain. McCain caught it reflexively but was too astonished to do anything more than blink. "I didn't want to risk you fellas being too impetuous," Scanlon said with a shrug. "Not after watching what happened to the sleeping beauty over there." Everybody was still too dazed to move or say anything. Scanlon regarded them all quizzically for a few seconds more, like a professor waiting for a class of slow students to catch on. "Well?" he asked them. "Doesn't a man have a right to change his mind?"

For once, Rashazzi could do no more than stammer. "Change? . . . Change how? Are you saying you're with us?"

"To be sure, what else do you think I'm saying?"

"But why?" Haber was shaking his head, equally bemused.

"I found the way I thought about things and people changing as time went by," Scanlon said. "Being among the likes of yourselves had a lot to do with it. But there isn't the time now to be going off into grand speeches. The fact of the matter is that you're stuck with me. And you'd be best advised to trust me whether you like it or not, because I'm the one chance you've got of getting out of here. And that's the only way you'll ever tell anyone what you know."

Haber looked baffled. "Get out of here? Tell what we know? How could anything like that be possible now? The Russians know everything."

"Ah well, that's not quite so," Scanlon said. "Aren't I just after saying that the way I see things has been changing for a while now? There are some things they don't know about. For one thing, they don't know you've worked out that the place we're in isn't in space— for haven't I only this minute found out that you know that much meself? And they don't know that you've burrowed your way into the civilian levels underneath Zamork that have just been opened up. You were supposed to find the freight system and go joyriding around, but you weren't supposed to go that deep."

"Who are the other informers?" McCain asked, finding his voice at last. "They wouldn't rely on just one."

"You've already got him," Scanlon said, nodding toward Istamel. "But he never got to know that you'd found the deep levels. You did a good job of covering up. You were supposed to include more plants in your team than you did. Maybe you've a nose for sniffing them out."

"Chakattar?" McCain said.

Scanlon nodded. "All the escape-committee crowd, except Sargent. He's straight."

"I was never happy about them," McCain said. The way they'd gotten hold of the wiring diagrams had seemed too easy in retrospect. "What about in our billet? Gonares was supposed to have been at the hub, too, so we know about him. What about Mungabo? He's been down in the deeper levels."

While McCain was speaking, Rashazzi went over to check on Istamel, whose breathing was more regular again now. Rashazzi poured an ethery-smelling liquid onto a gauze pad and applied it to the Turk's nose. "This will keep him out of it for a while," he said. "He might be a bit sick when he comes round."

"Mungabo's okay," Scanlon said. "I was the only plant in the front section. Nolan, Andreyov, Borowski, Irzan, and Charlie Chan are clean. The rest are fakes."

McCain looked genuinely surprised. "Smovak? Vorghas?"

"Both with Czech political intelligence. Luchenko is a KGB colonel. The other Asiatics are with GRU."

"So Creeping Jesus isn't in on it, eh—a true disciple?"

"Do me a favor. Who in their right mind would depend on the

likes of him? He was put there to be a source of provocation to draw you out, and it worked like a charm."

"What about Maiskevik?" McCain asked. That was something he'd often wondered about. "Was that for real, or did he take a dive?"

"Oh, you clobbered him all right," Scanlon said, grinning. "It was real enough—part of the test, you might say. They wanted a man with fight in him, to be sure he'd hit back at the system when he got the chance. And they made sure the only chance he got would be by setting up a spy operation. They had about a dozen or more people they might have used, scattered around in Zamork. But not all of them managed to set up a communications link back to wherever it was they came from, and others didn't measure up in other ways." Scanlon looked at Paula. "That was why the Russians waited until the Earth-end connection into Washington—the end they couldn't control—was working before they involved you. If that had failed, they'd have concentrated on one of their other candidates."

"Where is this place?" Rashazzi said. "Where are we all?"

"Underneath some hills near a place called Sokhotsk, in Siberia—where the groundstation is located that handles communications to the real *Tereshkova*," Scanlon replied. "There's been a genuine exchange of message traffic with the real *Tereshkova* for your people to follow, to keep up appearances. The Russian code name for this place is 'Potemkin.' How's that for being appropriate? Or maybe there's someone in the Kremlin with a sense of humor, after all. Now, if—"

"Why?" McCain demanded. He had recovered from the shock, and his mind was starting to work again. "Why are you doing this? It's not exactly a job they'd have picked anybody for. You must have been pretty hot. What happened?"

Scanlon scratched the side of his sparse head of hair and sighed. "Yes, it's true that at one time I was mixed up with the IRA. But when I got to thinking about it I found meself asking, Are these really the kind of people I'd like to see running Ireland if the Brits left and they did win? They were not. And they're not the kind of people you stay around for very long if you've crossed them, either. I decided I'd be safer heading East. But I found myself asking the same question about the Russians and the world as I'd asked about the Provos and Ireland: Are these really the kind of people I'd like to see in charge of it? And the answer came out the same." Scanlon tossed out an arm to dismiss the subject. "But are we to be getting on with what needs to be done, or stand here prattling like old women all day? Olga and the general are waiting in Turgenev for Paula to get back and make her TV debut, and I've decided to take my chances with the rest o' ye and have a shot at getting us out."

"What's this about TV?" McCain asked, giving Paula a mystified look.

She avoided his gaze, feeling sheepish now. "Olga and Protbornov asked me to appear on a connection to Washington to back up the signal that we sent. I agreed. They wanted me to try and persuade you to do the same thing—because you'd have better credentials."

"Some goddam hope! And you actually—"

"No, that's what I told them . . . really. Then Olga had this idea that maybe you'd confirm the message if you thought you were doing it independently—using the laser. I came here to try and sell you on that." Paula exhaled a sharp breath and showed her empty hands. The gesture said that that was the way it was, that she couldn't change it now, that he could think whatever he liked.

McCain stared at her for a second, then nodded. It was all under the bridge now. "That would have been their trump. Well, at least we didn't . . ." He looked at her again, frowning. "Olga suggested that?"

"Yes."

"But she knows this place isn't in space. The laser couldn't communicate out. Why would she come up with a damn fool idea like that?"

Paula bit her lip awkwardly. "I've been wondering the same thing," she said. "It had to be part of what they'd set up all along, too. They could intercept the laser signal at the roof, relay it up to *Tereshkova*, and repeat it on another laser set up inside. They could handle replies from Earth in the same way. That was how they planned to involve *you*. And I walked straight into it."

McCain shook his head. "Surely not. That has to be too—"

"She's right," Scanlon said. "That's exactly how it was. Don't you remember back in June, it was *me* who put you onto the idea for the laser. And it was me who found the broken one that's now fixed and lying on the bench there—but it wasn't *too* broken. And it's me who's supposed to go with you to Turgenev now, to make sure it's aimed at the right place on the roof—where the detector to relay the signal up to the groundstation has been fixed."

McCain stared as if he was having a hard time believing it. "That far back? It was all planned that far back? We were *supposed* to build the laser for this all along? . . . Jesus Christ!"

"And we thought we were being so cunning," Rashazzi muttered despondently.

Paula sat down on one of the stools. "My God, and it came so close . . ." She looked at McCain. "Would you have? If I'd told you the story and you went to Turgenev to see the VIPs for yourself, would you have confirmed it to Washington with the laser?"

McCain turned his face toward her, thought about the question, and then nodded with a strange, glassy-eyed expression. "Yes," he told her. "To be frank, I think I might."

"And perhaps we won't disappoint them yet," Scanlon said. Everyone turned to look back at him curiously. He nodded, satisfied that he had all their attention again. "Right, are we through with the talking now?" he asked. There was silence. "Good. Now, they say the best way to catch a thief is with a thief. It might be, I'm thinking, that the best way to outwit deceivers is with deception. And there's something all the more poetic when it's by turning their own deception around on them, which has a natural appeal to an Irishman. The first thing we have to do is collect Sargent and Mungabo. And let's get Charlie Chan and Borowski down here, too, since they're okay and we'll need all the help we can get. After that, this is what I'm proposing . . ."

◉ CHAPTER FIFTY ◉

The Infra-Red Orbiting Observatory (IROO) was a permanently manned astronomical space observation platform operated jointly by the Jet Propulsion Laboratory in California, NASA, and the East Asiatic Scientific Research Council. Designed for studying the universe at high resolution in the longer-than-optical wavelengths that the Earth's atmosphere blocks almost completely, it boasted a main telescope built around a 200-centimeter-diameter primary mirror, which was cooled with liquid helium to avoid polluting its sensitive detectors with heat radiated from the structure. Since becoming fully operational five years previously, the observatory had penetrated the screening dust clouds that attend both the births and deaths of stars, bringing a new understanding of stellar evolution; it had mapped the inner regions of the Milky Way and pinpointed the supermassive black hole centered there; and it helped reveal the dynamics of energetic distant galaxies. Its instruments were sensitive enough to detect a speck of dust thirty miles away by its heat radiation alone; also, it was in an almost-polar orbit oriented such that for the next several days it would be able to train those instruments on *Valentina Tereshkova* continuously.

"We're keeping a line open to Tokyo," Kay Olson, a special assistant at the State Department, said from one of the screens in Foleda's outer office. "The Japanese prime minister is talking to

Professor Kobasuka at this moment. Meanwhile the IROO crew have been alerted via JPL to stand by for a special operational directive. The President has asked to be kept informed, and we'll advise you of further developments at they happen." Kobasuka was chairman of the committee that selected the program of objectives for IROO to study from proposals submitted by scientists all over the world.

"Fine," Foleda acknowledged. He turned his head toward Barbara, who was waiting for a response from a man looking offscreen on another display. "How's it going?"

"Defsec C-three-I has ordered an emergency-band connection into MILCOM from the NASA tracking net. They're testing it now. JPL has confirmed that the IROO high-power signal-laser can be tuned to the frequency specified in Pangolin's message."

"Anything on Sunflower from Sexton?"

"No."

Foleda grunted. "Stay with it and let us know straightaway when anything new comes up."

"Will do."

Foleda walked back to the interview room next door to his office, where Philip Borden and Anita Dorkas were sitting at the table with a heavily built, bearded man. Foleda waited inside the door without interrupting. "You're certain," Borden was saying to Anita. "You arrived that morning and were transferred to low-security work without explanation, and Colonel Felyakin talked to you the same day. What did he say, exactly? It's important."

"He told me to reschedule the day's leave I had listed for the next day, because some people were due to arrive from Moscow to straighten out an administrative mixup. He said it involved the durations of some of the postings in England, and asked me to be there at ten o'clock with Enriko, and to make sure we had our passports."

Borden nodded. "And Enriko came home drunk that same night?"

"I don't know that I'd say drunk. He had been drinking."

"With the Line KR chief, Colonel Shepanov."

"Yes."

"And what did Enriko say?"

Anita sipped from a glass of water on the table. "He was very quiet and preoccupied—not the way he usually was when he and Shepanov got together . . ."

"Go on."

"He mentioned that Shepanov had been having personal problems and sometimes talked too much. Then, quite suddenly, he asked about the scientist from Novosibirsk that my ex-husband went off with seven years ago. Shepanov had let slip that she'd been arrested for dissident activities."

"Did he say when she was arrested?" the bearded man interjected. He had a strong East European accent.

"About three months previously—that would have been April— May, I'd guess."

The bearded man nodded. "And you assumed that your ex-husband had been under investigation, too, and that as a matter of standard KGB procedure all his close relatives and associates would be suspect, including you."

Anita nodded. "Yes, exactly."

"And what was your reaction?" Borden asked her.

"I was terrified, naturally, because of the work I'd been doing for the British. From the other things that had happened that day it seemed likely that I'd been found out already, that Enriko was under suspicion, too, and that the people from Moscow were coming to take us both back."

"So you ran away, and sought asylum with the British."

"Yes."

"Leaving your husband?" the bearded man queried, raising his eyebrows.

"There was no love in our relationship. He was pure KGB. His postings abroad were useful to my own work."

"That never struck you as just too convenient?" Foleda asked, still near the door, and speaking for the first time.

Anita looked uncomfortable. "Not at the time . . . although since you mentioned it, I've been wondering."

Borden looked inquiringly across the table. He had been through this many times, but wanted the bearded man to hear it firsthand for himself. Voldemar Zatin, former chief of the KGB's training academy at Bykovo, forty miles north of Moscow, whose defection to the West five years previously had been a minor sensation, leaned back in his chair and thought for a few moments over the things that had been said. Then he looked at Borden and gave his opinion.

"The business at the London Residency—that is not how they would do it. You would never be permitted to leave the building in a situation like that. The first thing you know is when the KGB men from Moscow come in, and then you stay there in the embassy until you leave for the airport. Complete surprise. No opportunity to suspect or do anything. The passports? Bah!" Zatin waved a hand in front of his face. "They send someone to your apartment for them, if that is where they are."

"All a setup, then, you think?" Borden said.

"I'm certain of it. It was all so that she would bring a story to the West that would make them believe that Dyashkin was genuine and had a legitimate reason to defect. He was part of it from the start. His dissident activities—all part of his cover."

Anita stared in astonishment. "But that was over seven years ago."

Zatin pulled a face and tilted his head indifferently. "Seven years, ten years—what of it? Some operations they plan twenty years ahead. Thirty years, even. The husband was another part of it—from the beginning. They allowed the marriage to happen, exactly so she would get into compromising situations on foreign postings, from which she could defect easily. She was allowed to believe she was using him; in reality, they were using her. I have seen similar schemes."

Stunned, Anita stared down at the table. Borden looked over at Foleda and exhaled a long breath. "You were right all down the line, Bern. . . . Look, it's kinda late in the day to say so, I know, but—" Foleda waved his hand in a way that said it was okay, save it till later. Borden nodded. "So what's the situation out front?" he inquired, nodding toward the door.

"Technically it looks good," Foleda said. "State is talking to the Japanese now, and we've got an emergency military hookup through

NASA. The President's being kept posted, and the defense secretary and Chiefs of Staff are standing by."

Borden got up from his chair. "Then, let's get on down and see what comes in," he said. And to Anita and Zatin, "You've helped a lot. Thanks. We'd like you to stay around for a while."

As they passed by Foleda's outer office, Foleda stopped to poke his head in. "Have Security send someone to take care of the visitors while they're in the building," he said to Barbara. "We're going on down to Communications. Anything new here?"

"The Japanese want to know if we're willing to underwrite the cost of lost research time on IROO if they reassign it to Mermaid," she told him.

"Shit," Foleda said over his shoulder as he turned to follow Borden again. "Tell 'em I'll write a personal check."

⦿ CHAPTER FIFTY-ONE ⦿

Paula's feelings as she drove back to Turgenev in the security police van with Major Uskayev and their escort were very different from the zeal that had carried her in the opposite direction just a few hours earlier. Although it was a source of wonder to think that the valley packed with buildings and trees beyond the roadway, the Russian television crews filming decorations being set up for tomorrow's celebrations, and the panoramic view of the hub and starfield overhead in the agricultural sector were all parts of an illusion manufactured underground in Siberia, she remained quiet and subdued.

Thinking back over everything that had happened in the six months since it had all begun, she could see now how systematically and ruthlessly she had been deceived. And what had made the deception possible was her own intellectual conceit and a conviction of infallibility that it had never crossed her mind to question. The irony was that it was she, the scientist, who had taken her assumptions for granted; Earnshaw, the cavalier, had questioned every assumption. That, of course, was the way the Russians had set it up. That, precisely, had been their whole intention.

The Tangerine file had never existed. The story had been planted on Western intelligence as the irresistible lure that it had turned out to be, guaranteeing they would send somebody to try and retrieve it.

Depicting it as a computer file—but one held inside a low-security maintenance computer, and hence not impossible to extract—ensured they would send somebody expert in Soviet computer techniques, and hence qualified to be duped into setting up the communications channel later.

What stung most of all was the realization that the long period of isolation and interrogation after her arrest had constituted an elaborate process of observation and testing by the Russians to find the right combination of vanity, stubbornness, exaggerated self-confidence, and political naivete that they needed for their purpose. And out of all the candidates who had been brought to *Tereshkova* in various ways during the past year or so, hers was the dubious distinction of having passed every test with honors. "The whole problem with the world is that fools and fanatics are always so certain of themselves, but wiser people are full of doubts," she remembered quoting pompously to Earnshaw on their voyage up. "How come he didn't add, 'I think'?" Earnshaw had asked. It had taken her this long to understand what he'd meant.

A lot of things were painfully clear with hindsight. The women who had been such obvious plants in her cell during the initial interrogation period had been meant to be obvious—to entice her into a mood of self-congratulation for having spotted them, and contempt toward those whom she had mistaken for fools. Thus they had established in her a conviction based on false security that *she* couldn't be fooled; or, if she was more honest with herself, they had simply built upon the belief they found existing there already. She remembered a stage magician she met at a party once, who had talked about how easily some scientists were fooled by claims of paranormal phenomena. "Basically it plays upon conceit," the conjurer had said. "They don't like to think they can be taken in by 'mere entertainers.' Therefore their subconscious thinking runs something like: If *I* can't spot the trick, then there can't be a trick. The only choice they've got left then is to accept what they think they've seen as genuine."

The spell in the kitchens, the environment she'd been put in, the degradations she'd been subjected to—all calculated to create a readiness born of desperation to throw herself at the first promise of escape back to anything resembling her kind of world, with her kind of people. And so they'd drugged her food to make her sick, and that had gotten her into the infirmary, ready for Olga's appearance, staged after their "coincidental" encounter in the corridor outside Protbornov's office. That, of course, had been to make sure that Paula would approach Olga first, thus avoiding any of the suspicions that might have been caused by Olga's coming to her. The position in the Environmental Department, the link to "Ivan" that had needed a technical expert to restore it, and the manipulation to make her believe that extending the link to the West had been her own idea— all parts of the plan. And then, playing on the personality traits that she recalled snatches of having revealed during the drugged, hazy period of her early interrogation, there had been Svetlana, Elena, Gennadi, and others—all acting out roles calculated to echo and amplify her own prejudices and perceptions, and reinforce her private self-image.

The hardest part of all to swallow was Olga's treachery. Paula had not only trusted her, but had admired and accepted her as sharing a common ethic based on truth, honor, and integrity that put them above the irrationalities of a lesser world. Truth, honor, integrity! Olga had baited her line with those very sentiments. As Scanlon had said, the thought of turning their own deceptions back on them by continuing to play their own game had a very sweet, poetic appeal to it.

They arrived at the Government Center in Turgenev and went straight up to a room full of maps, screens, and communications equipment, where Olga and Protbornov were waiting. Some other officials and officers were doing a good job of pretending to be anxious. Olga played her part with nauseating perfection. "Thank heavens you're all right, Paula. You were gone a long time. I was beginning to worry. Did you speak to Earnshaw? What did he say? Will he do it?"

Paula looked Olga straight in the eye and nodded. "Yes, he's convinced. He'll do it. He and Scanlon are going to try getting up onto the roof of the air-processing plant next to the Security Headquarters building, where they can observe the main square and operate the laser." Despite himself, Protbornov was unable to suppress a triumphant gleam in his eyes at Paula's confirmation that Scanlon would be accompanying Earnshaw. This was the last of the possible problems that the Russians had anticipated. It was important that Scanlon go too. He knew where on the roof to point the laser.

"Which route will they be taking?" Protbornov asked.

"Up from the freight line through the terminal below Turgenev center," Paula replied. "From there they'll come into the square through the shops on the north side disguised as civilians, with the laser and spectrometer dismantled, rolled up inside bundles that look like parade banners. With the square crowded, they figure on slipping in to the garage below the air-processing plant, finding a way up to the roof, and tapping into a power line somewhere to run the equipment."

"When will they be coming?"

"Three hours from now—when the crowd starts getting big for the First Secretary's arrival." The final shipload of Soviet VIPs, including the First Secretary of the Communist Party, Chairman of the Supreme Soviet, and the whole of the top cadre of government, would arrive in time for its passengers to rest and freshen up before welcoming the UN ship bringing the rest of the world's delegates twelve hours later.

Protbornov looked over at Major Uskayev. "Did you get that? Get on to Security control and make sure they have the details. Under no circumstances are any of the police to interfere. Make sure Earnshaw and Scanlon have an unobstructed route up to the roof, and clear any watchmen, or anyone else who might interfere, off the premises."

"Right away, sir," Uskayev said, and left the room.

"And for you, we have something special," Protbornov told Paula. He slipped an arm around her shoulder in an almost fatherly fashion and steered her over to two men in suits who were waiting nearby. "Here are the engineers who will brief you. You came here as a television journalist, yes? Well, now we are going to make you into a real one. Very appropriate, don't you think? Would an American find it funny?" His eyes twinkled, and the craggy, heavy-jowled face actually contorted itself into a laugh. "But not public television, of course—as we promised. Just a private transmission to your own people. Our embassy in Washington is making the arrangements now." He presented her to the two men. "This is the American lady who might save the world." They smiled dutifully and said it was a pleasure to meet her. Olga, who was on Paula's other side, actually had the nerve to turn and kiss her on the cheek. At least the ecstatic shine in Olga's eyes was genuine.

"No, the pleasure's mine," Paula told them. And that statement was quite genuine, too.

Meanwhile, in a compartment in the deeper levels below Zamork, McCain, Scanlon, Koh, and Rashazzi, assisted by Mungabo, Charlie Chan, and Borowski, had finished their preparations and were almost ready to begin cutting through the outer hull wall. . . .

❂ CHAPTER FIFTY-TWO ❂

The tank was made of heavy-gauge steel sheet, solidly riveted. Before they drained it, it had contained fresh water and been one of a row of several such tanks in a compartment on the service deck beneath the recently opened civilian level below Zamork. Then they had cut off the top five-foot section with an acetylene torch from the engineers' stores they had broken into, lifted it off, and turned it on its side to form an open box, with the inspection hatch that had been on top now in the side opposite the open one. Getting down into the service deck had proved easier than expected—the place was virtually deserted, no doubt because of the holiday and the celebrations commencing up on the surface.

Rashazzi had guessed, and Scanlon had confirmed, that even though the structure they were in was not in space, nevertheless it was rotating in a vacuum—in fact, inside an evacuated toroidal tunnel. Besides reducing power requirements, the vacuum would eliminate wind noise from the outside—a strange thing for people to hear who were supposed to think they were in space—and it would insulate the structure from the surroundings, avoiding the risk of unusual heat patterns on the surface that might arouse the curiosity of Western surveillance satellites. Hence a breakout party would still need the survival suits, and it would need an airlock. However, they hadn't been able to find a chamber small enough and strong enough, adjacent to the outer wall, to use as one. The compartment holding the water tanks and associated pumping machinery came closest, but its volume was still much too large to evacuate in a reasonable time— other than explosively. And even if they did evacuate it, Rashazzi was doubtful that the walls could withstand the load that would have resulted from the normal pressure in the rooms surrounding it.

Therefore they had improvised their own airlock. The section of tank now stood with its open side butted up against the outer wall and secured by crude welds to the reinforcing ribs. Rolls of rubber padding and thick plastic sheet, stiffened by metal plates and heavy with "Razz-goo," were wedged all around the joint, which had then been heavily dusted with powdered chalk. The packing would be sucked in tighter when the box was evacuated, and the seal didn't have to be a perfect seal anyway—moderate leakage from the huge volume outside the tank would be of no consequence.

Mungabo, with Charlie Chan and Borowski, now recovered from their initial amazement at what had been going on not so far beneath their feet, had finished cutting away a section of the inner wall— Scanlon had confirmed that the outer wall was also a pressure vessel and would be able to take the load. The tank would be evacuated by the simple expedient of drilling holes through the final skin to the vacuum outside, and then cutting away the entire section as soon as the pressure had fallen low enough. A thick steel plate over the inspection hatch on the other side of the tank would be adequate to close it off, since the pressure of the air outside would keep the plate in place.

Suited up already, McCain, Scanlon, Rashazzi, and Koh had spent the last hour sitting against a step in the floor, resting and breathing oxygen, to denitrogenate their body tissues, from a large cylinder connected to the four hoses. McCain found the garment heavy and constricting, like a stiff scuba wetsuit, and it seemed to stick to itself and everything else where the sealing compound that Rashazzi had concocted oozed from the joints. In front of them, Mungabo climbed out of the hatch in the side of the box and began passing items of equipment that Borowski checked off against a list to Charlie Chan, who was still inside. There were two battery-operated inspection lamps and a regular flashlight apiece, for there was no reason to expect the outside to be lit—Scanlon didn't think it was; four heavy-duty electric hand-drills, and a reel carrying hundreds of feet of cable connecting back through a packed hole in the side of the tank to an electrical junction box; two satchels full of large aluminum eyebolts, S hooks, snaplinks, and miscellaneous lines and slings accumulated during the two months since they'd had the idea of crossing over the outside to get to the spokes; a hundred-foot rope ladder formed by making loops at intervals along a nylon line and tying them to a second line; spare oxygen bottles; two bags containing clothes to change into when they got out; and a bag of assorted tools.

Borowski checked the final items and Mungabo passed them inside. Then Chan climbed out. The four figures on the floor stood up awkwardly, and working in pairs—McCain and Scanlon, Rashazzi and Koh—checked each other's face seals one more time. The other three helped them fix webbing harnesses over the suits to carry the equipment, and switched their oxygen hoses to the smaller bottles they would be taking with them. At last all was ready. The four who were going and the three who would be staying behind exchanged final handshakes.

"You'll do just great, guys," Mungabo said, talking loudly to be heard through their head coverings. "Don't forget to send us a card, huh?" McCain nodded and made a female shape in the air with his hands. Mungabo laughed and slapped him on the shoulder.

Borowski checked each one's oxygen valve and connections as they stepped up to the hatch, where Charlie Chan helped them through. "Good luck. I'm only sorry that you didn't bring us in on this sooner. We would have liked to help more." Rashazzi made a palms-up gesture. Borowski nodded. "It was never possible to be sure who you could trust, eh? Well, a pity all the same."

Charlie Chan was looking somber. "Let's hope that you can manage to do something out there, if you make it. This time I don't have a joke."

The four squeezed into the box, wedging themselves into the corners to avoid sticking together when they bumped. Rashazzi nodded, and the others outside lifted the coverplate into position over the hatch. The box was lit by an inspection lamp the others had used while cutting through the wall's inner skin. McCain concentrated on his breathing. It felt smooth and trouble-free, and he had no sensations of light-headedness or reduced vision. He recited a list of arithmetic multiplications in his head, and judged his faculties to be unimpaired. When Rashazzi looked at him questioningly, he returned a nod with a thumb-up sign. Scanlon and Koh did likewise. Scanlon pulled the gas cylinders connected to the cutting torch toward him to make room, and Rashazzi drilled a close pattern of holes through the exposed wall of outer skin facing them.

Rashazzi watched a pressure gauge as plumes of white dust began appearing around the wall joint at places where air was being drawn in from the outside. Koh at one end, and Scanlon at the other, signaled to the three outside where the worst leaks were by tapping on the sides, and after some minutes the currents had diminished. Even so, it was not long before the total flow into the tank balanced the flow out, and the pressure stabilized. Rashazzi drilled more holes to increase the outflow, and the pressure dropped farther. Everyone checked their respirators and seals again, and waited for more leaks to be plugged. Because of the lack of time, the whole business was going to be riskier than it would have been with the kind of airlock they had envisaged originally: the lock they had been forced to improvise would only work one way. Had an emergency developed up to this point, they could have aborted the operation by covering the drilled holes with rubber pads and steel plates, which had been brought into the tank for the purpose, and repressurized the box by opening the large oxygen cylinder. But once they cut away the final wall and opened the box completely to the vacuum, the air pressing on the hatch coverplate would exert a force of over three tons. After that, there could be no going back.

A strange stillness came over McCain as the pressure continued falling and the world of all the sounds that he had been registering unconsciously receded. He felt completely isolated now, cut off from the light, air, and the life of Zamork, and already a part of whatever existed on the outside. Rashazzi turned out the light for a second, and a crushing, total darkness added its weight to the silence. As they had guessed, no light showed through the holes from the far side. Rashazzi turned the light on again and continued drilling. Nobody indicated experiencing any ill effects, and when the pressure had fallen to a level where the flow to the outside was diminishing, McCain began using another drill to speed things up. At the joint, the remaining leaks showed as fast, fine jets now, accompanied by faint vaporlike fans where the cooling of rapidly expanding air turned its moisture content into ice. Then Rashazzi pointed to the gauge, made an O with his thumb and forefinger to indicate zero pressure. The others acknowledged that they were okay. Rashazzi nodded, lit the torch, and began cutting away a small rectangle of metal.

When the section broke free, Koh lifted it clear and Scanlon directed one of the inspection lamps outward to reveal a vast, dark void, and on the far side of it an immense gray wall, broken at intervals by vertical supports, rushing past at what Rashazzi and Haber had calculated would be a hundred fifty miles per hour. Rashazzi commenced cutting an enlargement of the hole for them to climb through. Because of the confined space he was only able to cut half the rectangle they needed, and then he passed the torch to McCain to finish it on his side. McCain did so, but the section refused to budge. He looked out through the small hole and found that the piece he had been trying to move was attached to a diagonal rib running across a corner on the outside. He made a new cut following the line of the rib, and the section came free, leaving behind a triangular corner piece. But the hole was large enough for their purpose.

Scanlon leaned out and pointed the lamp sideways, down, and up. McCain peered out with him and found himself staring out of the sheer face of a monstrous precipice of metal. The wall was reinforced by a square grid of heavy stiffening members spaced ten feet or so apart horizontally and vertically, with thinner tension bars running diagonally and crossing at riveted gussets in the centers— one of these diagonals partly crossed the section that McCain had tried to cut first, which was why he had been unable to move it. Rashazzi had estimated that above them this wall would extend at least two hundred fifty feet vertically before it began curving over to form the roof.

Looking down, they were about forty feet above the platform supporting the colony, which, McCain recalled from Rashazzi's sketches, was in the form of a tilted circular track, like the rim of a dinner plate. The wall they were looking out of, however, was straight, cutting across an arc of the platform's circumference like the outer edge of a strip of ribbon laid along the dinner-plate rim—in fact it was one of the long sections connecting the spoke-base zones. Hence the floor at the base of the wall was an exposed part of a circle, with the enclosing tunnel forming the far side and roof. To the left, the floor narrowed toward tunnel-side; immediately below them it was about a hundred feet wide; and to the right it continued to broaden beyond the range of their lamps as the tunnel-side receded. According to Rashazzi's drawings, the exposed arc of floor would reach a maximum width of about two hundred feet at its midpoint.

McCain had to force himself to remember that since the supporting platform was banked at twenty-five degrees and they had emerged at its upper edge, the wall they were looking out of was in reality tilted back from vertical by that amount, with respect to the Earth's surface. But the combination of gravity and centrifugal force generated a "local vertical" within the spinning reference frame of the colony, and that was what the senses responded to—as indeed they had been doing for six months on what was, after all, simply the other side of the same wall.

Scanlon was to lead the first pitch of the climb. He attached one of the lines to a snaplink on his harness, and McCain ran the line around his shoulder and back, bracing himself to be ready should Scanlon fall. Scanlon clipped a satchel to his harness at one hip, one of the drills to the other, then turned around on the edge of the drop and leaned back the length of his arms to inspect the area overhead. Then he selected one of the S hooks, attached a sling to it, and stretched to reach sideways along the outside. One foot remained visible, and the fingers of his other hand curled around the edge of the opening. The foot vanished, then the fingers, and he was gone. Koh stood by, ready to pay out the cable of the drill, and Rashazzi moved into the now-vacated opening to shine a light upward for Scanlon.

The line moved intermittently through McCain's hands and

around his body. He could read Scanlon's progress from its motion: stationary while he worked at preparing holds, then moving up onto them, then stopping again to survey the next part. When about twenty-five feet had run out, there was another halt. Then the line went taut, and after a short pause, jerked three times. Scanlon was signaling that he had anchored himself to the structure and wanted to bring McCain up—they had decided to move in short pitches if they found the outside in darkness, to stay within range of each other's lamps. McCain gathered a coil of extra line and the second satchel, and Rashazzi squeezed out of the way to let him move forward. McCain tugged twice on the safety line, and Scanlon drew in the slack from above. Then McCain turned around, grasped the sides of the opening, and backed himself out.

Scanlon's lamp was sending down enough light from above to show the first sling, which he had hung as a stirrup from one of the gussets where the diagonal ribs crossed. McCain leaned sideways as Scanlon had done, leaving one foot in the opening and a hand gripping the edge, and stretched out his other leg to find the stirrup with his foot. He grasped the gusset and pulled himself across, transferring his weight slowly until he could crouch in the stirrup. A moment later Rashazzi reappeared in the opening behind him with another light. Scanlon had drilled a hole into the skin above the crossover and hung the next sling from an eyebolt. A snaplink was also attached to the eyebolt, with the safety line and drill cable running up through it. Scanlon would have placed "runners" like this at intervals as a safeguard. Thus, had he fallen, he would only have dropped through twice his height above his last runner before McCain checked the fall from below. Without threading the line through the runners, he would have dropped through twice his height above McCain before the line tightened.

McCain slipped the lines out of the snaplink—if *he* fell, Scanlon would catch him from above, now—and grasped the higher sling to straighten himself up, which brought his face level with the first of the horizontal ribs. There was a bolt inserted immediately below this rib, attached to a short loop of rope threaded through another snaplink. The end of a longer sling hung down from above the rib.

Scanlon must have stood in the sling that McCain was clutching and clipped the loop above it to his waist to hold him while he leaned out around the overhanging rib to attach the sling above. McCain pulled himself up as high as he could using the loop, then stepped out into the long sling, found another one above as he had expected, and moved up to stand on the rib itself, where he could reach the next diagonal crossover. From there the sequence of movements repeated itself. After the next panel, the light from above showed him he was getting close to Scanlon, and one more panel later they were side by side.

Scanlon was standing on a horizontal rib with his harness fastened to two separate bolts. He passed the drill across and McCain took over the lead, now threading the line as Scanlon had done on the previous pitch, since his protection was now from below and no longer from above. The psychological effect was to make him feel less secure, and as soon as he was more than a few feet above Scanlon, he found himself perspiring and breathing heavily. Physically he was beginning to feel the strain, too. The routine became a torment of forcing aching muscles to stretch and pull, fighting to gain every inch of movement against the drag of the suit. Fatigue dulled his mind and sapped his concentration. He placed the next bolt and attached a sling, but even as he began hauling himself up on it, he remembered too late that he hadn't tested it before trusting his weight. The thought had barely formed in his mind when the wall and the surrounding void merged into a blur. There was a sensation of falling, then a jolt as if he were being cut in half, and almost simultaneously he felt a painful blow to his shoulder and a crack on the head that set lights exploding before his eyes . . . and the next he knew, he was hanging limply in his harness against the wall, his ears ringing.

He stirred, and looked about him in a daze. His lamp was hanging a couple of feet below him on the loop of line attached to his harness, still lit. He pulled it in and shone it upward. From him the line went up about five feet to the runner that had caught him, and from there back down past him again to where Scanlon was. So he'd fallen about ten feet. He hung for a few more seconds to regain his breath, then pulled himself back into the nearest sling and climbed laboriously back to the place where he had fallen from. He replaced the bolt that had come out, testing it thoroughly this time, and carried on. And then, when he stretched up to start on the next hole, the drill seized up with a burned-out motor.

They had expected it. The drills were designed to be air-cooled, and hence overheated rapidly in the vacuum. That was why they had brought several spares and why McCain had brought an extra line. He tied the drill and lowered it to Scanlon, who in turn lowered it on down to Rashazzi at the opening. One drill gone in less than fifty feet, McCain reflected as he waited for a tug on the line to tell him that a replacement was ready for him to pull up. They had over two hundred feet to go, and only three more drills. The odds weren't reassuring.

The next drill did even worse. McCain continued to the end of his pitch after the replacement came up, and anchored himself as Scanlon had done; then Scanlon came on up and took the drill to leapfrog as McCain had before and lead the next pitch. He was halfway up it when the second drill burned out. They had planned on getting both of them a full hundred feet above the opening before Rashazzi and Koh moved up to join them—that was how long the rope ladder was. The seriousness of the situation was enough to change that, however, and a series of violent tugs on the line from below told them that Rashazzi wanted them to hold everything right there and to come up himself, now.

A cardinal rule of roped climbing is that only one person moves at a time. Unable to progress farther, Scanlon secured himself where he was above McCain and lowered the auxiliary line again, this time to pull up the coiled rope ladder. Scanlon secured the top of it at the high point where he was, McCain guided the rest down as it unrolled, and Koh climbed right on past him to join Scanlon, carrying one of the remaining two drills, plus some of the extra gas cylinders and bags. Finally Rashazzi came up, similarly loaded. He stopped when he reached McCain, and, standing on the rope ladder, beckoned urgently for McCain to follow what he was doing. Rashazzi pointed at the vent inlets on the drill he had with him, then held the nozzle from one of the gas cylinders close and with his other hand made the motion of opening the valve. McCain understood. Rashazzi was telling him to use the cooling effect of high-pressure gas expanding into a vacuum. Rashazzi jabbed a finger at the wall, then held it up. Cool the drill after every hole. McCain nodded that he understood. Rashazzi resumed climbing, and vanished around the next horizontal rib above.

McCain stayed in that position for some time. When he finally got a signal to follow, he moved quickly on the ladder, past Scanlon, who was still just a short distance above, and on to where Rashazzi and Koh had pushed while Scanlon and McCain rested, a hundred feet or so from the top. And they were still using the third drill. From there Scanlon led off again, and McCain followed through. Only fifty feet to go.

Topmost on the rope once again, McCain anchored himself and took up position with the line around him in preparation to bring Scanlon up. He noticed with a feeling of vague detachment that he seemed to be running in slow motion, like an action replay: leadenly deliberating every movement, and then having to exercise inordinate concentration to execute it. He hung, staring out into the void, and the realization slowly came to him that everything was going to be fine. Not jut fine, but—wonderful! The certainty washed over him in a wave, sweeping away his discomfort and bringing, instead, relief. Suddenly all their worries seemed comical through being so trivial. He began giggling behind his facepiece at the thought. The world was going to be just fine. War? There wasn't going to be a war. . . . He realized that somebody below was trying to pull him off. They were jerking on the line and trying to pull him off. That wasn't very friendly. . . . Why would anybody want to be unfriendly on a day like this? He let the slack of the line fall away from him. Scanlon didn't need the protection, anyway—nobody was going to fall. He hung in his harness, laughing into the dark around him, then singing. "Home, home at Lagrange . . ." The world was beautiful, and everybody in it wonderful. . . . After that he remembered nothing until a light shone straight into his facepiece from immediately outside, blinding him. Scanlon must have arrived. McCain grinned back into the light and waved.

Scanlon caught McCain's body as it slumped down in the harness, and clipped on an extra sling to hold the inert form fast to the wall. Then he dropped the auxiliary line for the others to send up the ladder, signaling frantically for them to move fast.

◎ CHAPTER FIFTY-THREE ◎

They took Paula down to a room looking out over the main square of Turgenev, where a standard two-way videophone was connected through to Washington via Moscow and the regular international telecommunications system. Olga, Protbornov, and a group of others crowded in to witness the proceedings. A technician in contact with the Russian embassy in Washington on an adjacent panel announced that they were through, and moments later Bernard Foleda, poker-faced, was looking at her from the screen.

" 'Micro,'" he said.

" 'Phone,'" she responded.

There was a short delay. The transmission time to *Tereshkova* was a little over a second each way, the engineers had reminded Paula. Also, Soviet censors would be monitoring the broadcast to delete any undesirable material before it went out, which would introduce an additional short delay—Americans did the same thing on most of their "live" TV shows. Also, of course, it masked the additional turn-around time of the transmission's being sent up from Earth before it was relayed back again.

Foleda nodded. "Glad to see you're looking okay. It's been quite a while. People here were getting worried. There's a lot been going on back here to try and get you out."

"I guessed."

Again there was a delay before the image of Foleda responded.

"Do you have any news of Sexton?" He was playing his part straight, not knowing what the score was.

"He's here, and they know I know he's here. I assume you received the previous message that I sent, validation initializer 'Pin.'" That had been the message confirming the presence of the Soviet leaders.

A flicker of genuine surprise crossed Foleda's face. "They've found out about that?"

"I revealed it," Paula told him.

Foleda drew in a long breath, containing his emotions with obvious effort. "Go on," he said curtly.

"You wanted confirmation that the Soviet leaders are really here. The tone of your request implied that if the facts were otherwise, you had reason to believe that the Soviets were intending attack. You suspected that the broadcasts you're receiving might be recordings. Obviously a mistaken impression couldn't be risked. I *know* their leaders are up here, because I'm up here and I've seen them. I sent the 'Pin' message to say so. But I wasn't sure that it would carry enough weight in itself. The accomplices I have here, who helped me operate the channel that we've been communicating over, convinced me that the situation was serious enough to go to the Russians and get them to let me talk direct to you, to do whatever I have to do to make sure there's no misunderstanding." Following cues from one of the Russians across the room, Paula walked across to the window. A technician followed her with a camera. "This is the central square of Turgenev, in *Valentina Tereshkova*," Paula said. "I'm in a building looking down over it. The people you can see down there are waiting for the arrival of the Soviet First Secretary and his party. If you're getting Russian news coverage of this, compare what they're showing you with what I'm seeing. What I'm offering to do is go down into the square and describe the scene from there as the first Secretary actually arrives. I have approval from the Russian authorities here to talk with some of his party on-camera, if you request it. They're all extremely concerned here."

"If they're so concerned, why don't they let Sexton come on with you?" Foleda asked.

"I tried to get him to do just that, but he refused. He wouldn't cooperate with Russians in any way."

Back across the room, Foleda's face stared out of the videophone screen for a long time, unmoving and unblinking. Paula hadn't said anything about a message giving the laser frequency, and neither had he. That, of course, was still supposed to be a secret. Suddenly, Foleda seemed to arrive at a decision. "Wait," he said. "There are other people that I have to bring in on this." With that he stood up abruptly and disappeared from the picture.

Mutters of approval came from the audience that had been watching from around the room. In the midst of the hubbub, Major Uskayev came in and drew Protbornov over to the window. He pointed down at the far side of the square outside, where two figures were working their way along the edge of the crowd. One was wearing a knee-length tan coat with a black hat; the other had workman's coveralls and a floppy brown peaked cap. Both were carrying long, rolled bundles. They looked casual, but were moving closer to the doors of the garage underneath the air-processing plant. Protbornov pointed them out to Paula. "Those are Earnshaw and Scanlon?" he asked.

She nodded. "Yes, that's them."

"Is their way clear?" Protbornov asked Uskayev.

"Yes, sir. All police have been moved back from that side of the square. The building is cleared but under observation."

"Excellent." Protbornov raised a pair of binoculars and gazed down through them. "My word, what theatricals!" he commented. "One has put on a beard. The other has a beard and spectacles."

"They believe in being thorough," Olga said, next to him.

Paula watched the two figures saunter to the back of the crowd, stand looking around them for a few seconds, and then vanish quickly inside one of the garage doors. For an instant no one was looking at her, and she smiled to herself. "Yes, very thorough," she agreed.

Then, Foleda reappeared and stated that the transmission from *Tereshkova* was being put onto a conference circuit to involve other US officials also. He requested live coverage from the square outside as Paula had offered. Accordingly, she went on down and out of the building with a party that included a number of Russian officers, engineers, and the camera and sound operators. Protbornov, Olga, and the remainder of his group went back upstairs to follow the exchange from the control room that Paula had been taken to on her return from Zamork. A number of screens had been hooked into the conference circuit by the time they arrived. On them, the Russians had so far identified Foleda's chief, Philip Borden, the director of the CIA and his deputy, two senior military assistants to the defense secretary, a White House presidential aide, and several faces from the offices of the Joint Chiefs of Staff. Protbornov was radiating triumph, and Olga looked coolly pleased with herself.

Then a thunderous applause went up from the crowd on the screen showing Paula in the square outside, as the doors at the rear of the terrace in the background opened. The dignitaries who were already gathered parted to make way for the familiar stock figure of First Secretary Vladimir Petrokhov, flanked by his most senior ministers and key Party members. "Describe what's happening now," Foleda said from one of the screens.

"Petrokhov and his group are coming out onto the terrace in front of me now," Paula replied on the other screen.

At that instant one of the engineers at the consoles on the other side of the room looked up sharply. "Laser contact! We're picking up a laser transmission from the roof. Positive acknowledgment from Sokhotsk. It's relaying out to *Tereshkova* now."

"Text?" Protbornov snapped.

"Just a call for acknowledgment, sir, coded 'Tycoon/High from Sexton.'"

Absolute silence descended on the room. Even while the operator was speaking, the signal had been repeated on a portable laser set up by the military inside Anvil two hundred thousand miles away, and transmitted back out in the direction of Earth. Now everything depended on whether the Americans had managed to organize some means of receiving it. Tension mounted as the dialogue between Paula and Foleda continued on the screens. Then, on the screen showing Foleda, a woman approached him from behind, caught his shoulder, and whispered something urgently in his ear. He promptly excused himself and left. In the Russian command room, the suspense became agonizing. Shortly afterward, Borden was summoned away, too. More minutes of agony dragged by. And then the engineer who had spoken previously shouted out in jubilation, "Acknowledgment! A response is coming in from the Americans, via Anvil!"

"Source identification?" another general, who was with Protbornov, queried.

Another of the engineers consulted readouts and tapped keys. "First report indicates they're using the IROO observatory, sir."

"As we expected," the general said, sounding satisfied.

"Text?" Protbornov called.

"Text from Tycoon reads, 'Sexton/Two from Tycoon/Ball. Signal received. Reading clear. Standing by. Over.'"

"By the czars, we've done it!" Protbornov breathed.

"Response intercepted from Sexton," the first engineer sang out again. "Text reads, 'Consider it imperative that arrival Soviet VIP cadre Mermaid be confirmed. Voluntary cooperation via Soviet TV judged inappropriate. Am occupying position affording direct visual observation Turgenev center. Personal positive identifications confirmed, list of names follows: Petrokhov, Kavansky, Sanyiroky, Vlasov—'"

Whoops and shouts of jubilation broke out all around the command room. Protbornov emitted a loud belly laugh and slapped Olga heartily on the back, causing her to gasp, while the other senior officers crowded round to pump his hand and offer congratulations. Across the room, on the far side of it all, Major Uskayev smiled as he watched on one of the screens the view being picked up through a telescopic lens by one of the KGB teams posted among the roofs surrounding the air-processing-plant building. It showed the hatless head of whoever was wearing the sandy-colored beard—with the heavy-rimmed spectacles and hair tinted to match the beard, it could have been McCain or Scanlon—peering down from behind a cowling at the edge of the roof, then turning to say something, presumably to the one who was operating the laser. Then the head withdrew from view.

"How are we doing here?" Protbornov asked, having moved across the room.

"They're like puppets dancing on our strings," Uskayev said. "And they tried so hard. . . . It's almost possible to feel sorry for them."

Behind the cover of the parapet of the air-processing-plant roof, Peter Sargent unstuck his beard for a second to scratch underneath his chin. A few feet back, sitting comfortably in the recess between a ventilator housing and a stanchion supporting some pipes, Albrecht Haber finished tapping a sequence into the keyboard connected to the laser.

"Bloody stuff makes you itch," Sargent said. "Where did Razz get it—off a horse or something?"

"Who knows?" Haber answered. "That's the last of the names. What do you have now?"

Sargent consulted the list of information that he'd compiled in a notebook. "Ah yes, this should take a while. Ready? Message begins: 'Previously advised data confirmed as follows . . .'" Sargent started working through the list of weapons emplacements that Paula had described before, going into greater detail about how they had been penetrated and reiterating that the weapons didn't exist.

"Let's hope that Protbornov's people leave us alone for a while," Haber said as he worked.

"Oh, I think they will," Sargent replied breezily. He stretched back and looked up at the sky. "As long as we find things to say, we're doing a great job of distracting the opposition for them. That means they'll be perfectly happy to let us stay up here all day if we choose— certainly until their zero hour, anyway. . . . Care to pass the coffee and one of those sandwiches, old chap?"

☸ CHAPTER FIFTY-FOUR ☸

Many airplane pilots have crashed to their deaths singing and laughing in their last moments before losing consciousness. What makes hypoxia, or oxygen starvation, so dangerous is its insidious onset and the delirious sense of euphoria that comes just before total collapse, which makes the victim the least qualified to judge the seriousness of the situation.

McCain felt anything but euphoric when he came round. His head felt as if it had been split with a butcher's cleaver, everything spun nauseatingly, his throat was raw, and his lips stung. He was lying back and being supported, but he couldn't see anything and was aware only of the pressure against his face. He tried to move his arms to push it off, but had no strength. Pressure around his middle forced him to exhale, then release. He breathed in again.

Where was this? Had he been in an accident? . . . The fragments of his mind slowly came back together and started functioning again. He was lying on his back, which meant they were off the wall. The others must have gotten him to the top. He couldn't remember anything of what had happened. Then sudden light blinded him. He tried to turn his head away, but the pressure around his face remained. Someone was shining a lamp in through his facepiece, but the facepiece was being forced down. The urge to struggle welled up, but he didn't have the strength. After a few seconds it subsided, and he lay with his eyes closed.

He understood now. They had turned his oxygen pressure up and were holding his facepiece down against the seal to stop it from being blown off. Everything was starting to feel quite warm and pleasant. He settled back to doze. Somebody struck him a couple of sharp blows on the side of the head. Now someone was pinching his upper arm through his sleeve—with pliers or something. Jesus—it *hurt!* He shook it off angrily . . . but the effort had started him moving again. He felt himself being hauled into a sitting position, and opened his eyes to see just a confusion of shapes, lights, and forms. Dizziness swept over him again, and he fought not to vomit inside his mask. The feeling gradually passed.

Now they were tapping him insistently on the shoulder. He opened his eyes again and saw they were on what looked like the same wall of metal panels contained behind reinforcing girders, except that the pattern was now sloping instead of vertical. It curved over and fell away steeply to the right, but seemed to level out above them to the left, like the ridge of a hill. Ahead, the whole ridge curved up and away. Somebody swung a lamp to illuminate a figure standing in front of him, and McCain caught a glimpse of a roof flying by not far above their heads. The figure—McCain wasn't sure who it was— gestured urgently for him to stand up, and at the same time the two who were supporting him pulled at his arms. They carried him the first few yards with his legs trailing and feet bumping over the metal ribs. Then his legs began working again, feebly at first but improving quickly as blood brought oxygen to his starved muscles.

They continued edging upward to the left as they followed the ridge, and continued crossing its flat top when it leveled out. In the center they came to a ready-made metal walkway, and continued along it without having to step over ribs and gussets every few feet. The tunnel roof curved upward ahead of them as it receded, paralleling the top of the structure they were on—although they had no more uphill work to do, since the geometry ahead became "level" as fast as they moved onto it. Nevertheless, McCain was exhausted and had to be helped all the way. But the two who were supporting him urged him on relentlessly and permitted no rest.

They reached the end of the long section they had been following, which meant they were over Novyi Kazan. Here, unlike the situation inside the colony, the sudden leftward change in direction to the next section was unmasked, although the stretch ahead seemed to continue curving upward. The walkway brought them to the side of a rounded, turretlike structure that was just about in the position of the spoke elevator at the center of Novyi Kazan. They followed around it to the left, and the surface they were on began sloping downward noticeably again, but in the opposite direction from before; this meant that they had crossed over the center of the roof and were approaching the inner edge of the racetrack. A bridge from the turret projected out horizontally, with the colony's inner wall falling away below on the near side. The others sat McCain down at the base of the turret's side and shone their lamps outward.

The chasm facing them was difficult to judge because of the unfamiliar scale of everything and the feebleness of their lamps in the great void of darkness. The outward curve of the ridge-side below them prevented their seeing to the bottom. On the far side, the chasm ended at a sheer wall that moved with the tunnel roof. The wall carried a horizontal groove which the bridge from their side disappeared into. According to Scanlon, the far end of the bridge was supported by a wheeled cradle running on rails. The rails formed a circular track inside the racetrack's nonrotating core—the solid hole in the middle of the empty donut.

Unlike the real *Valentina Tereshkova*, Potemkin—the replica beneath Siberia—didn't possess a hub. The main reason was the impossibility of engineering a cavern over a mile in diameter with an unsupported roof—as would have been necessary, since spokes connecting a hub to the rim would have swept through that whole volume; another reason was that a hub couldn't have contributed to the deception: it would have had to exhibit reduced gravity, which couldn't be reproduced on Earth. The elevators that departed from the spoke-bases at Turgenev and elsewhere stopped inside turrets protruding above the roof like the one McCain was sitting outside, and then engaged a horizontal drive to travel inward through the bridges—of which there were six in all, one for each spoke. Thus, to return to terra firma, the escapees would have to get across the bridge.

However, that promised to be simpler now, with the guards on the inside and them on the outside; furthermore, they could see a railed catwalk running the full length of the outside of the bridge, which they could reach from a steel ladder not far from where they were standing. . . . But making this part of the task easier had been the whole point of breaking through to the outside in the first place, after all—before anyone had known that there wasn't a hub out there to get to.

The others came back to McCain and changed his oxygen bottle and their own for the spares they had brought. Then they climbed the ladder to the catwalk, Scanlon going first, with Rashazzi and Koh still assisting McCain behind. McCain had recovered his senses sufficiently by now to know he'd gone down with hypoxia. Probably the fall that he'd taken earlier had loosened his facepiece or breathing tube. The trouble, he recalled vaguely, was that the physical and mental disablement following acute hypoxia could persist for hours. And he couldn't really remember, he realized, why it was so important for them to get out at all.

As they moved out onto the bridge, they could look down into the chasm and see they were high above an exposed arc of the racetrack platform once again, but an inner arc this time, not an outside one as they had looked down over from the wall. Far below, they could make out jumbles of pipework, cabling, and gigantic windings in the space enclosed by the platform, while ahead of them the curve of the wall they were approaching grew more apparent as they got closer. Behind, they could trace out with their lightbeams the full height of the wall enclosing the dummy colony, from its base far below on the supporting racetrack, up through tier after tier of diagonally-crossed square lattice, until it curved to become the flat roof that they had so recently been walking along. Except, it wasn't flat anymore. Looking back along the bridge, they could see its lines to be curved concavely upward; and the farther along it they moved, the more the angle of the far end that they had come from increased. By the time they were almost across the chasm and nearing its inner wall, the distant end of the bridge, and with it the ridgetop that it projected from, had taken on a distinct tilt toward them. What was happening was that since they were moving inward along a radius, the centrifugal force they were experiencing was getting less. This in turn required a progressively smaller banking angle to compensate, and the architecture curved accordingly. Nevertheless, when they entered the groove which they had seen from the far side—now revealed as a deep gallery twenty feet high at least, cut into the cylinder forming the tunnel's inner wall—the floor below and the roof above were still racing by at well over a hundred miles per hour.

Inside this gallery, the bridge ended in a large boxlike construction cluttered with cables, motor housings, and catwalks, supported by a set of wheeled bogies. Scanlon had described this assembly as a "terminal." The bogies ran on four rails, which the escapees could see flashing by below as they reached the end of the bridge and clambered across the outside of the terminal to reach its inward-facing side. Here, a mating port, set above a system of guides and lifting gear, faced another pair of rails that ran alongside the ones the terminal rolled upon, thus tracing a smaller circle inside. The port mated with airtight vehicles called gondolas, which accelerated along the inner track until their speed matched the terminal's—that was how transfers of people and materials in and out of Potemkin were effected. In itself, this arrangement would have permitted the use of one gondola only—obviously, since having more than one speeding up and slowing down on the same track would have been unworkable—and with six terminals to service, would have been inadequate. The problem had been solved by having a gondola, after it had matched speed with a terminal, physically lifted from the track and up onto the guides to mate with the port, which immediately freed the track for other traffic. Similarly, after a gondola had slowed down from Potemkin's speed, it exited from the ring formed by the through-track to come to a halt in a side loop.

With the current level of traffic between the "hub" and rim, the escape party hadn't anticipated difficulty in finding a ride to hitch. Sure enough, the port of the terminal they had arrived at had a gondola already docked. They worked their way over the port and across onto the gondola's roof. After a wait that seemed interminable but in fact had probably been less than ten minutes, the gondola detached from the port. A pair of hydraulic rams pushed it down the guides and set it on the inner track. The rams disengaged, and the entire, uncannily silent rolling assembly of terminal box, port, lifting gear, and bogies moved away into the darkness as the gondola began shedding speed.

Shortly afterward, another, identical terminal appeared from the other direction as the spoke that had been following behind them—the one that connected to Agricultural Station 3, if McCain had been visualizing things correctly in his muddled condition—caught up and then overtook them. The strange thing now was that the whole terminal was tilting down at them. The body of the gondola pivoted about its long axis, McCain realized—like some carnival rides. As the gondola slowed down, its body was returning to Earth's horizontal from the banking angle it had assumed while at the terminal's speed. When the next spoke passed them, moving much faster this time, its tilt was noticeably greater, and the next raced by tipped at what must have been almost the full angle corresponding to terminal-radius speed.

The roof and inner wall of the gallery moved by very slowly in the flashlight beams now. Then the gondola exited into a side tunnel and came to rest at a port similar to the one it had docked with at the terminal, but on the opposite side. While whatever transfer it had come to make was in progress inside, the four men lowered themselves down from its roof. The first thing McCain noticed on regaining his feet, despite his condition, was how light he felt. He looked down and stamped one foot, then the other. It was elating to stand on real, solid ground once again—even Siberian. The others seemed to be having a similar reaction. But there was little time for celebrating just now. The next job was to get out of the vacuum.

This part had been taken care of for them by safety-conscious Soviet design engineers, and involved procedures that Scanlon had been familiarized with during his training after being posted to Potemkin. Maintenance workers sometimes needed to come out and work in the transfer bay where the gondolas docked. Since the bay contained a hard vacuum, that meant putting on suits and going out through airlocks. To prevent anyone's getting trapped out there, the airlocks could be opened from the outside; Scanlon, moreover, knew where they were located and how to open them. The only problem was that opening an airlock would trigger an indicator in the maintenance control room.

Scanlon had selected an airlock situated at a remote end of the transfer bay—unlikely, therefore, to have many people in its vicinity inside. A line of small orange lights in the bay led the party to it, and a larger external light above, showing green, marked its location. Lower down, beside the outer door of the lock, was an illuminated panel with several buttons. Scanlon pressed one of the buttons and the door opened, bathing them in sudden light that dazzled them after the hours of working in blackness. They crowded through, shielding their faces with their hands, and Scanlon used an inner panel to close and pressurize the lock.

Sound!

McCain wanted to shout out with sheer joy and relief as the world of sound re-formed itself around them. There was humming and vibration that seemed like a hurricane, hissing from the air system, rustling and movement from the bodies around him . . . and yelling and laughing! Rashazzi had warned them against the risks of aching ears and sinuses from repressurizing too quickly, but nobody cared. Scanlon pulled away his facepiece, drew in a chestful of air, and whooped. Rashazzi and Koh helped each other, then both of them removed McCain's. The rush of cool, fresh air after hours of claustrophobic confinement made all the more isolating by the silence was overwhelming. He stood and gulped, and sucked it into his lungs.

"Does it taste good?" Rashazzi asked them, grinning.

"It beats even Dublin Guinness," Scanlon sighed, pausing for just a moment.

"Definitely one of life's more . . . memorable moments," Koh said, savoring.

McCain didn't care at the moment whether the Russians appeared or not.

But Scanlon cared. He had already opened the control box of the airlock doors and was detaching a wire that would make it appear that the control-room indicator had been triggered by a fault. Then he opened the inner door. On the far side was an anteroom with rows of steel closets and some seats, and behind that a corridor, many doors, and a steel-railed stairwell visible at the far end beside an elevator.

Scanlon led the way along the corridor to the stairs, hustling the others along after him. They went down a level to an intersection of two more corridors, with a well opening down onto a maze of piping on one side, and then through one of the doors into a cluttered machinery compartment reminiscent of the ones they had known below Zamork. It was warm and smelled oily, and the noise inside sounded to McCain like Niagara. But it was deserted, and it promised rest. . . .

McCain eased himself painfully down against a wall. Rashazzi had already flopped out on an open expanse of floor and was lying with his eyes closed and his mouth wide open gulping in air, but also with a smile of weary triumph on his face. Koh collapsed next to him with a barely audible, grateful moan. Scanlon closed the door quietly, turned on a light, and looked at McCain. "Will you be staying with us in the land of the living for a little longer, then?" he inquired. McCain nodded but didn't reply. "Ah, sure, that's a good thing to be knowing. As the strip dancer said to the reverend's wife . . ."

But McCain had slumped back and was out of it before he heard the rest.

⊚ CHAPTER FIFTY-FIVE ⊚

Americans sometimes described things as being almost crazy enough to work. And Lt. General Vladimir Fedorov's initial reaction to the proposal for replicating a two-kilometer-diameter space colony underground and using it as the basis of such a deception had certainly been that it was crazy. In fact, that was the one time when he'd found himself wondering if the leaders of his country had gone collectively insane, and had seriously contemplated defecting to the West. Now, as he stood with his adjutant, Colonel Menikin, and several aides, watching the activity in the mess area of B Block, after two years as the governor of Zamork, he had to admit that it all seemed to have been sufficiently crazy to have worked.

The atmosphere was abuzz with excited murmurings as guards shepherded the prisoners out of the billets and down from the upper level to be formed into ranks for general assembly on the mess-area floor. Work assignments had been canceled, and more prisoners were coming in from the compound, Gorky Street, and the Core. There were rumors of mass amnesties about to be announced, that the Moscow government had fallen, and that war had broken out back on Earth. One squad of guards was particularly busy in billet B-3, which had been cleared out. Outside its door the block commandant, Major Bachayvin, and several officers were talking with the block supervisor, Supeyev, and the billet foreman, Luchenko.

Zamork had served its purpose. The things that mattered now were happening outside its boundaries, and whichever way the outcome of it all went, the charade inside was over. It was time to reestablish proper discipline and security, and to commence sorting out from the individuals who had been brought here as inmates those who showed the most promise and willingness to be useful in the new era of the regime. Fedorov wondered what kind of place the new era would have for him.

A communicator beeped on the belt of one of the aides standing near him. The aide answered it, listened for a moment, and passed the unit to Colonel Minikin. "From Colonel Gadzhovsky, sir."

"Very good," Menikin acknowledged. Gadzhovsky was in command of the guard detail that had been sent to open up the supposedly secret workshop that the prisoners had set up in the machinery deck below. Menikin talked to Gadzhovsky, then reported to Fedorov. "Three prisoners were apprehended down there, all members of McCain's billet: the Zigandan Mungabo, the Pole Borowski, and the Buryat. They're being brought up now."

Fedorov nodded. "Good. You'd better go and inform Major Bachayvin." He watched as Menikin walked over and said something to the group outside the door of billet B-3. Then his brow furrowed. Bachayvin, Supeyev, and Luchenko were gesticulating vigorously as they answered, and seemed agitated. A few moments later, a foreman from one of the upper-level billets came hurrying across the floor, went over to join them, and started saying something to Supeyev. Fedorov cast a general eye around the rest of the mess area, and when he looked back again, Menikin, Bachayvin, and Supeyev were coming toward him. The expressions on their faces gave him his first inkling that something was wrong.

"There are still three prisoners from B-three unaccounted for," Menikin said. He looked inquiringly at Supeyev.

"The two scientists, Rashazzi and Haber, and the Asiatic, Nakajima-Lin," Supeyev said. "Also the Englishman, Sargent, is not present with the contingent from B-twelve."

Fedorov frowned uncertainly. "They can't be out in the colony somewhere. We've been covering their access to the freight line at all times. They must be loose somewhere down in that machinery deck." He turned to Menikin. "Have Gadzhovsky seal all exits down there, and send Major Kavolev down with his men to help with a search. The whole place is to be combed—every inch of it."

"Yes, sir." Menikin took his own communicator, contacted Gadzhovsky again, and began speaking.

"I never did like this policy of relying on informers to tell us what was going on down there," Fedorov growled to Bachayvin. "The whole place should have been wired so tight that a bug couldn't have moved without our knowing."

"But if the prisoners had discovered it, sir? . . ."

"Bah! It could have been done invisibly. Everyone must take risks sometimes."

Menikin looked up from the communicator to interrupt. He looked concerned. "There's more from Major Gadzhovsky."

"Well?"

"We know now why Istamel failed to report in on time. He's just been found unconscious in the elevator shaft. They're taking him to the infirmary now. There as a piece of broken rope near him. The three prisoners who were detained down there say that he fell, and that they were on their way up to report it."

"Any sign yet of the four others who are missing?"

"Negative, sir."

Fedorov didn't like it. He turned away and stared morosely out at the lines of prisoners and guard details now coming to order. If he waited a few more minutes and the four were found, nothing more would come of it. But if he delayed and they weren't found, the consequences for him would be worse. Such was the justice of life that withholders of bad news could lose their heads just as easily as the bearers. Americans called it "Catch-22" for some reason he'd never understood.

He turned back toward Colonel Minikin. "Call General Protbornov's office in Turgenev," he ordered.

✸ CHAPTER FIFTY-SIX ✸

The human body is a continuous liquid system. Blood must flow to and from every part of it to bring oxygen to its cells and remove the waste products of metabolism from them, and the intercellular volume supporting this flow is connected throughout. Hence, if pressure differences exist between parts of the body, blood, like any other fluid, will migrate from high-pressure regions to lower-pressure ones, and the delicate skin capillaries will rupture if the pressure across them exceeds their strength.

When, after resting for some time in the machinery compartment, the four escapees cut and peeled away the survival skins they had used to make the crossing through the vacuum, they found their bodies covered with long, painfully swollen, black and purple weals. The worst were around their waists and major limb joints. Inevitably, the stretching and exertion of climbing the first wall had opened cracks in their suiting despite the improvised seals, into which the flesh had literally been sucked in elongated blood blisters that only the inner clothing had contained. The middle of Rashazzi's back looked as if it had been beaten with a rubber hose, Scanlon's left wrist was swollen into a balloon that practically immobilized the hand, and Koh had the same trouble with an elbow and a knee. Between them, a pretty sorry team, all in all, McCain thought. In addition to a collection of blemishes pretty much the same as the others', he had two hideous black eyes.

"I feel like I've been breathing powdered glass," he said as they sat cleaning the worst of the goo from themselves and putting on the clothes they had brought to change into. "What happened back there?"

"Your face seal had been knocked crooked on one side and had started leaking," Rashazzi told him. "I had to lift part of it away briefly to fix it."

"You mean my whole face was open?"

"Yes . . ."

"Holy shit!"

"For about five seconds, maybe. The reason you feel all dried up is that gas and moisture poured out of your lungs and mucous tissues into the vacuum. It's possible that the evaporative cooling caused ice to form on your tongue."

"It feels like I've been eating ashes."

"Be thankful it's us and not you who have to look at that face of yours," Scanlon said. "You look like me uncle Mick, the morning after a night out enjoying himself."

"Be thankful there aren't any gas pockets behind the eyes," Rashazzi said matter-of-factly. "Otherwise they'd have blown out like champagne corks."

Scanlon had stayed by the door to peep out from time to time, but had seen no signs of excitement or searching. They concluded, therefore, that if the opening of the airlock had triggered an indicator, either it hadn't been noticed, or it hadn't been deemed serious enough to investigate yet, or it had been put down to a wiring fault as they'd intended. Whichever, it seemed they were in no immediate danger. But they had far from unlimited time.

McCain winced as he stretched an arm up into the sleeve of the baggy gray sweater that he'd unrolled. "So what are the possibilities now?" he said to the company in general. "Where do we go from here?" He pulled the sweater down over himself and pushed his head through. "Which one said that—the bishop to the barmaid?"

"Do we all feel up to surprising a guardpost full of KGB and overpowering them, stealing their uniforms, and bluffing our way through in disguise?" Scanlon asked. The looks from the others answered the question and said they weren't in a mood for Irish humor just then.

"How far above us is Sokhotsk?" McCain asked.

"We're under a range of hills to the northwest," Scanlon answered. "Elevator systems from here go up five hundred feet to Potemkin's transportation and control center. From there, Sokhotsk is about three miles away, connected by a road and rail tunnel. The tunnel comes out in a staging area below the main Sokhotsk administrative complex."

"Which is presumably in a high-security area," Rashazzi said.

"The whole place is a high-security area," Scanlon replied.

"Against outside penetration, anyhow?" Rashazzi suggested. "But in a way, we're already on the inside."

"It doesn't make any difference," Scanlon said. For once he sounded pessimistic. "The security is as strict every way. Let's face it, getting into Sokhotsk isn't going to be a piece of cake by anybody's definition."

There was a glum silence. Then McCain said, "What about the rest? You said something about mining and some kind of industrial center."

"Scientists, VIPs, and the like—small numbers of people—they come and go through Sokhotsk," Scanlon said. "But building and operating Potemkin meant moving materials and people on a scale that would never be seen going in and out of a research establishment. So some industry was sited nearby as a cover. There's a bauxite-mining operation on the other side of the hills from Sokhotsk, and an aluminum-smelting plant and rolling mill at a new town called Nizhni Zaliski, about five miles away from it—places where trains and trucks don't attract attention."

That sounded closer to what McCain had in mind. "So Potemkin, the place we're at, connects to the mining operation, and to Sokhotsk," he concluded.

"That's right," Scanlon said. "But the mining side doesn't connect direct to Sokhotsk. The only way into Sokhotsk is from where we are, and getting in will be the devil of a job that I'm already after telling you."

"Hmm . . ." McCain sat back, rubbing his chin.

"What about other ways in?" Rashazzi asked Scanlon. "Pipes, ducts, drains . . . How tight is the protection on things like that?"

"As tight as the arse on a fish, and that's watertight," Scanlon said.

McCain finished dressing. He tried stooping to pull on the canvas shoes that he'd brought, but the soreness around his waist prevented him from bending. Rashazzi put them on and laced them for him. "Well, that's just great, Kev," McCain couldn't stop himself from saying. "Why couldn't you have thought of all that before we bothered coming this far?"

"There wasn't a hell of a lot of time for speculating, for one thing, if you remember," Scanlon said. "And for another, I assumed your interests would lie in getting away from the Russians—it never occurred to me that anyone would want to get closer to them. And for another, if you want me to be honest, I never thought we'd make it this far."

Koh had been sitting quietly and staring into space while he listened. When silence fell again, he remarked, "You know, the deviousness of the Western mind will never cease to mystify me. Why do you always look for the most difficult way of doing everything? Does it have something to do with inscrutable Puritans and their unfathomable work ethic?"

"What are you talking about?" McCain asked.

"Why do you imagine that you must get into Sokhotsk?"

McCain looked nonplussed for a moment, then shrugged as if dismissing the obvious. "There might be a war about to start out there. We know something that nobody else on our side knows, which might be vital. We have to try to communicate that information back if there's any possibility at all for doing so, no matter how slim the chances."

Koh looked back unblinkingly in a way which said that whatever was obvious to McCain wasn't obvious at all to him. "Well?"

McCain shrugged again, started to speak, then looked at Rashazzi. "It is a communications establishment," Rashazzi said. "We're in the middle of Siberia, and we need to communicate with the West." He spread his hands briefly, in the manner of a person not wishing to offend someone who was being obtuse. "We'll need access to the kind of equipment that's inside Sokhotsk."

Koh looked unimpressed. "And what will you do with it?" he asked. "Could any of you operate sophisticated Russian equipment that you haven't been trained to use, even if you knew the right access codes? I certainly couldn't. So what else do you think we'll do—sneak in somehow, just happen to find somebody who knows how everything works, hold a gun to his head, and make him do as we say?"

"Maybe," McCain mumbled, taken aback slightly by the realization that he hadn't thought it through. "Who knows?"

Koh snorted. "Very derring-do. And the type of people you'll find in there will probably tell you to go ahead and shoot. So what good would it do?"

Koh was right, but McCain couldn't let himself concede defeat now. "We won't know until we get in there." He sat back wearily against the wall. "Like I said, however slim the chances . . ."

"Zero is a pretty slim number," Koh agreed. "Taking on those chances would be the same as throwing your vital information away."

"What else can we do?" Rashazzi asked. "We can't just sit here without trying anything."

"Why do you insist that you have to use sophisticated equipment in a top-security Soviet research establishment at all?" Koh asked. "What's wrong with simply picking up a phone?" The others all started to speak, then stopped again at the same instant. They looked at each other, each waiting for one of the other two to tell Koh why it was crazy. "Scientists!" Koh sighed, shook his head, and continued looking distant while he waited for them to get there in their own time.

"What phone?" Scanlon asked at last.

"You're all asking how to get *in*to Sokhotsk," Koh said. "I'm saying let's think about going the other way. You said this place connects out through the bauxite-mining complex to Nizhni Zaliski, an industrial town. Well, a town ought to have phones in it. And very possibly the freight going out that way isn't checked as thoroughly as anything going into a place like Sokhotsk. If anything's worth a try, surely this is."

The others exchanged looks again, but with more interest this time. "You know, it might just be crazy enough to work," McCain murmured, half to himself.

Scanlon had steepled his hands in front of his nose and was staring wide-eyed over them, thinking furiously all of a sudden. He stood up, walked a few paces stiffly toward the far wall, then turned to face the others again. "The containers," he said. "All those containers full of soil that have been coming down the spokes . . . they're the kind that deep-space transporters use—designed for automatic handling. That means they probably came in by rail through Nizhni Zaliski to the transportation center upstairs, and were offloaded into the elevators, transferred via the gondolas, and sent down the spokes without any unloading."

"So?" McCain asked.

"They'll be going back the same way, empty," Scanlon said. "They're probably still going back now, because there were a lot of them. And if I'm right in what I'm thinking, I know where they'll be collected together to go onto the trains. If we could get into one of those, we might find ourselves with a clear run out to Nizhni Zaliski. . . . Koh's right. We were all talking about going the wrong way."

McCain was frowning, however, as he considered the implications. "What's up, Lew?" Rashazzi asked. "Is there something wrong with it?"

"Not as far as it goes," McCain said. "But what then? Okay, so we find a phone. Exactly who are we intending to call with it? An international call to Washington—from here, at a time like this? No way. What else is there? The US embassy? Sure, they're in radio contact with Washington all the time, but what about a line to their number in Moscow? Don't tell me the KGB won't be monitoring it twenty-four hours a day. We'd never get through, and we'd be picked up in minutes."

Scanlon nodded resignedly. "Lew's right."

"We call my cousin in Moscow," Koh said simply. "The KGB aren't interested in his number."

McCain blinked. "Who?"

"My cousin—the one who has the restaurant franchise in

Moscow. I told you about him once. He's only a fifteen-minute walk from the American embassy. I'll call him, and he can go there and tell them whatever you want him to say."

For several seconds there was one of those sudden silences that descends when everybody realizes that there's nothing left to say. McCain stared at Koh disbelievingly, and shook his head—but still couldn't fault it. They got up and gathered together the rest of the things that were worth taking. Then Scanlon turned off the light, opened the door a fraction, and brought an eye close to the crack. "It looks clear," he hissed. "Lew and I'll go first. The other two of you follow when we've made it to the top of those stairs."

"Then, let's go," McCain said.

"Just a minute," Rashazzi's voice whispered from the shadows behind.

McCain turned his head. "What?"

"I don't have any money for the phone. Does anyone else?"

"Holy Mother of God," Scanlon breathed disbelievingly.

"Scientists!" Koh muttered at the rear.

"Razz, let's worry about that after we get out of this goddam place," McCain groaned tiredly.

❈ CHAPTER FIFTY-SEVEN ❈

President Warren Austin of the United States stood in the center of the Pentagon War Room floor, looking grimly up at the situation displays. General Snell, other senior officers of the Joint Chiefs of Staff, and advisers watched from one side as Borden summarized the latest analysis. "What it boils down to is that our agents there are telling us it's not a weapons platform and that the top Soviet leaders are arriving, and at the same time not to believe what they're telling us—Pangolin and the sender designating himself Sexton have both returned incorrect validation codes."

Defense Secretary Robert Uhl, who had only recently arrived, shook his head and hesitated. Nothing was making any sense. He gestured at one of the screens monitoring the Soviet TV connection from Paula, who at that moment was talking to others in another part of the Pentagon. "How can they be telling us not to believe what they're saying? They're telling us they're up there where the Russian leaders are, and we can see it with our own eyes."

"We think it could be for the Russians' benefit rather than ours," Foleda said from beside Borden. "Somehow they're controlling all the communications, in and out. Sexton—if it is Sexton—seems to be letting them hear what they want to hear."

"But how could it not mean what it says when we can see that what it's saying is right?" Uhl asked again.

"Could that TV transmission with the woman in it be recorded?" an aide asked.

Somebody else shook his head. "No. We're interacting with her live."

"So what does it mean?" Uhl asked.

Borden could only shake his head. "We don't know. There are all kinds of theories . . ."

"Theories!" Uhl snorted and turned away, rubbing his hands together nervously.

The President stared up at the displays again. "If Mermaid is a weapons platform as we've been fearing, its mission will be to take out our spacebased systems from long range in an opening strike," he said slowly. "That would deprive us of two things: our Starshield defense against a strategic attack down on the surface, and our ability to knock out their shield. Agreed?"

"That's the way we see it," General Snell confirmed. In other words, the Soviets would be able to launch virtually unopposed from behind a now-immune defensive screen that would reduce any retaliatory strike from the West down to ineffective proportions.

"Would we accept the odds under those conditions, or would we back down without a fight?" Austin asked. "Could that have been their aim all along?"

"It would make a lot of sense," Uhl agreed. Who wouldn't have liked an intact global economy to dictate terms to, rather than a mess that would take fifty years to rebuild?

Austin paced a yard or two with his hands clasped behind him. "So what are our options?" he asked the room in general.

"Well, as long as those Soviet leaders are walking around out in the towns up there, they're vulnerable," Snell said. True, US weapons firing from Earth orbit could blow away the roof and wipe out everybody unprotected, even if they couldn't damage hardened weapons emplacements. But this was really ruling out an option rather than offering one. It would be unacceptable morally to resort to anything that drastic purely as a precautionary measure—and the consequences if the fears subsequently turned out to be unfounded would be unthinkable. As a retaliation, yes. But the problem there was that if the fears were well grounded and *Tereshkova* was permitted to fire its weaponry first, the US would have nothing left to retaliate with.

Uhl chewed unhappily on his lip for a moment. "I wish I had something else to offer, but I don't. I have to agree with the intelligence people." He glanced quickly in Borden and Foleda's direction. "We eliminate part of Mermaid's advantage by a preemptive strike against the Soviet shield, and hope we can take out a large part of it before Mermaid replies. That would leave them exposed—partially, anyhow—to our missiles. Then, after Mermaid takes out our shield—which we can't stop it from doing, anyway— we'd be left set for a slugging match, eighties-style."

"In that case, they might end up being the ones who back down," somebody suggested.

Snell shook his head. "They'd still have the edge. Besides, they're desperate; we're not. Time isn't on their side."

Uhl accepted the statement with a heavy nod. "What about the UN ship?" he asked, looking at the President. "There's still time to try and get it diverted."

Austin thought for a while. "I'm not sure we should try," he said at length. "If we're likely to end up depending on surprise, it might be the wrong thing to do. The Soviets would be alerted through their UN people." Snell nodded his agreement without saying anything. "I'm afraid they'll have to take their chances with everyone else," Austin said. He turned to take in the whole of the waiting assembly. "We go to General Readiness Orange, and Red Standby One for the spacebased orbital systems. Send it out right away. And find out how we're doing with that conference hookup to the Europeans."

◉ CHAPTER FIFTY-EIGHT ◉

"Yes, hello? This is the Tunguska Cement Works. . . . Comrade Gorzchenko? One moment." Mariana Porechny plugged a line into a socket on the switchboard in front of her and keyed in an extension number. "So I told her not to be stupid," she continued saying to Eugenia, her only companion in the exchange. "If you can't keep your boy from climbing over fences, I said, it's not my fault if he goes and cuts his leg. I mean, the nerve of the woman—complaining about us leaving *our* tools out in our *own* yard. You'd think it was your job to mind everybody else from their own stupidity, wouldn't you. And it's not as if it was the first time, either. And her husband's always blocking our gate in that wreck they drive around in. And then there was the time when—No, he isn't answering. . . . The works manager? Wait, I'll try it. . . ."

"I tried to call my son in Moscow yesterday," Eugenia said distantly. "He said it's like a graveyard there. They're having rallies outside the city this year because there's no parade. The funny thing is, he said they were on alert for civil-defense drill. Did you ever hear of anything like that before? It gets worse. What a thing to go and do on a holiday. I sometimes think they haven't got anything worthwhile to do at all—any of them."

"Nasty kids they've got—especially him, that one. That day there was paint all over our window and down the wall, they tried to say it was the two little Bryokov boys from round the corner—and they're

455

no angels, mind—but I knew straightaway it was them. I even saw the tin—it was the one her creepy-crawly husband had the day before, when he painted their door. A real mess he made of it, too. You've never seen such an ugly color. Kind of purple, like the stuff that tart across the street plasters all round her eyes when she goes out, wobbling along on those heels with her skirt up the top of her legs—you can tell she's up to no good. And do you know what time she comes prancing back, brassy as you please? And then her mother told me one day—Hello? The general manager? . . . Well, that's not my fault, is it? . . . Yes, wait a minute. I'll try it. . . . No patience, some people. They're the kind who make the world what it is—never a good word to say for anyone. I can't understand them at all."

"He sounded as if he'd caught a cold," Eugenia said absently.

Neither of them noticed the door inching inward until it opened all the way suddenly. A tall, heftily built man in a gray sweater, followed instantly by another one, scrawnier, with bulging eyes, came though so swiftly that the two women found hands clamped over their mouths before they'd had a chance to react or make a sound. Another man, younger than the other two, and swarthy-skinned, with wavy black hair—definitely a killer, from the intense look in his eyes—moved in between them and the switchboard, while a fourth closed the door softly and bolted it.

Mariana quivered with terror. The four intruders looked mean and desperate, with blotchy, unshaven faces, disheveled hair, and scruffy, grease-stained clothes—escaped convicts if she'd ever seen one. The face of the man staring down at her was grotesque: wild eyes staring from a mask of bloated purple. Psychotic murderers were often physically deformed or mutilated, and they killed compulsively to get revenge on the society they felt rejected by—she'd read it in a magazine somewhere. Eugenia had slumped over in her chair and seemed to be in a swoon. The man at the door turned, revealing cruel, slant-eyed, Oriental features. That meant for a certainty they'd be raped. Mariana's chest pounded, and every reflex drove her to struggle and scream in mindless panic. But the two killers were holding her so tightly that she couldn't move, and the hand over her mouth stifled her shouting.

"We don't want to hurt you," the big man said slowly. His voice had a foreign accent. "There's no need to be afraid. All we need is your cooperation. Nod your head if you understand me." They held her until her strength was exhausted. "There is no danger. Do you understand?" At last the meaning sank in. She nodded her head twice. "I'm going to let go so that you can breathe. Please do not make any noise."

The hand on her mouth loosened, and she gasped in air gratefully. The hand drew away. "Who are you?" she asked fearfully. "What do you want?"

The Oriental wrote something on her notepad and pushed it across the console. "Merely your help, if you would be so kind, madam," he said. "Please call that number in Moscow for us. It is extremely urgent."

"That's all?"

"Please. It is urgent."

Mariana nodded. She indicated a handset on the console, and the Oriental picked it up. Then she looked at the notebook and keyed in the number with trembling fingers. It rang for four or five seconds. Then a voice answered, "Willow Garden restaurant."

"I—I have a call for you," Mariana said in a shaking voice. The Oriental began chattering excitedly in a strange tongue. It sounded to Mariana like an obscure dialect of Chinese.

General Snell listened while the two Defense Department scientists explained the figures being displayed on one of the War Room consoles. Snell nodded, and turned back to the President and his group. "The next thirty minutes will be the crucial period. Three of our biggest space lasers will come out from eclipse behind Earth during that time. If Mermaid is going to take out our system with a surprise strike, it will be in that time frame." Austin nodded somberly.

"We have to go for the Soviet shield, now," Uhl implored. "Okay, so it's an act of war. But if that colony really is clean, they should have been open about it from the beginning. If it isn't clean, we've got a good reason. The world will understand that."

"If it leads to an all-out exchange, the world will remember that it was us who struck first. Will it understand that?" Austin asked.

"They haven't left us with a choice," Uhl said. "It wouldn't be striking first. It would simply be getting us back toward more of a balance. We hold right there. The next step would be up to them."

"God, I don't know . . ." Austin stared up at the situation displays again.

On one side of the room, an aide approached Foleda, who was standing with Borden. "You have an urgent call from your office," he said in a low voice.

"Where do I take it?" Foleda asked.

"Follow me." The aide led Foleda into a side room, packed with consoles and operators, off the central floor near the main door. Barbara's face was waiting on one of the screens.

"What is it?" Foleda asked.

"A call's come in for you from the Moscow embassy. It—"

"At a time like this?" For an instant Foleda had trouble keeping his voice down. "What do they want, for chrissakes?"

"Apparently somebody who runs a Japanese restaurant there walked in off the street and said he got a phone call from Siberia . . ." Barbara's voice faltered at the look on Foleda's face.

"Are you serious? We've got a war about to—"

"The call was to 'Tycoon/Shot/Line/Rise/Glove' from Sexton."

Foleda blinked, frowned, and shook his head bemusedly. "Those codes check?"

"All of them. 'Glove' is Sexton's exceptional-status verifier."

"From Siberia? How the hell can he be calling from Siberia?"

"You'd better hear the text. . . ."

Footsteps pounded in the corridor outside Lt. General Fedorov's office in the administrative sector of Zamork. Moments later, a major strode in, followed by several guards who between them were hustling the three prisoners Mungabo, Borowski, and the unpronounceable Asiatic. "Block Supervisor Supeyev and Foreman Luchenko are here also," the major reported.

Fedorov gave a curt nod. "Have them wait outside." He licked his lips nervously and surveyed the three prisoners as they were lined up before his desk. They stared back at him impassively. "This is urgent, and I have no time for politeness," he said. "You understand? The Turk, Istamel, who was taken to the infirmary." There was no response. "You know who I'm talking about?" he demanded in a louder voice.

The major punched Mungabo in the stomach. "Yes, sir," Mungabo wheezed.

"Then say so when I ask you," Fedorov shouted at him. "The doctor says he has no broken bones, no bruises, and shows no signs of having fallen. He does show symptoms of being drugged. What do you know about this?"

"Nothing . . . sir," Mungabo replied. The major drew back his fist. Mungabo braced himself.

Then a tone sounded from the terminal next to Colonel Menikin, who was looking on. Fedorov held up a hand and turned to watch while Menikin took the call. It was from Major Gadzhovsky, who was commanding the search of the lower levels. Alarm was showing on his face. "Yes?" Menikin snapped at the screen.

"Still no sign of the four missing prisoners," Gadzhovsky reported. "But we have found an additional hole cut through into the public levels below Zamork. Major Kavolev and his section have already left and are on their way down there now. Also, we can find no trace of the escape suits that the prisoners are known to have been manufacturing." Istamel had been keeping the Russians updated on the progress of the suits. Since the proposed date for the prisoners' ridiculous intended attempt at breaking out had been given by Istamel as weeks after November 7, the authorities had seen no harm in allowing them to carry on distracting themselves with the idea.

Menikin swallowed hard and flashed an apprehensive glance at Fedorov. "They can't have done anything with them," he protested. "They haven't even begun work on an airlock." Just then, another call came in on an adjacent screen. "It's Kavolev," Menikin said.

"Major Kavolev reporting from Level Four-H in the public sector. We've discovered an engineers' store that's been broken into. I'm having the engineering supervisor brought here to give us a list of what has been taken. From a screenview of the interior that we sent him, he says there's an acetylene torch missing and a number of gas cylinders."

There was a long silence when Kavolev had finished. "We just collect things," Mungabo offered, and shrugged.

The color was draining from Fedorov's face. "Get me a line to Turgenev," he said in a suddenly weak voice.

The senior Russian leaders had withdrawn, and the speeches being given now were from secondary officials. The crowd had thinned somewhat. On the roof of the air-processing plant above the square, Albrecht Haber sat forward suddenly and gave the laser terminal a couple of raps. Then he picked it up and shook it. "Something wrong?" Peter Sargent asked from his vantage point by the edge.

"The screen just went blank. I don't think we're getting anything."

"Oh-oh. Do you think it spells trouble?"

"I'm not sure." Haber tried tapping in some test codes, and fiddled with a control. "It's dead. I suspect they've cut us off."

Sargent looked out over Haber's head, and his eyes took on a sober expression. "Yes, you're right. I rather think the show's over, old boy."

Haber looked up, and Sargent nodded to indicate the direction behind him. Several figures in KGB uniforms were scrambling frantically across the rooftop toward them. "So it would appear," Haber agreed, nodding. "I would say that we put on an acceptable performance, wouldn't you?"

"Absolutely. I see no bouquets, though. But we should go out in style nevertheless, don't you think?"

Haber nodded solemnly. "Yes indeed," he agreed. "In a manner that befits gentlemen of the acting profession."

So saying, the German and the Englishman stood up in full view to face the windows of the Government Building opposite. They took off their beards and hats, and extending their arms wide, bowed as if acknowledging applause. They were still taking encores when the first KGB arrived and dragged them away out of sight.

❈ ❈ ❈

Confusion had taken over the command center in the Government Building. One of the console operators was yelling something, Uskayev was trying to make sense out of what the KGB squad commander was saying via a handpad from the rooftop opposite, and Fedorov was babbling something else from Zamork. What was clear was that the faces of the two men being held up on the roof were not those of Scanlon and McCain. Major Uskayev used another screen to call up shots of the prisoners who had been reported missing. "The German, Haber, is one," he announced. "The other is Sargent."

Protbornov was wearing the expression of a skydiver who had just realized he'd forgotten something important before he jumped. On another screen to the side, Fedorov at Zamork waited for orders but was now forgotten. "What . . . What does this mean?" Protbornov choked. "Where is the American? If those two have returned wrong codes . . ."

Olga was gaping, horrified, as she took in what it meant. The color drained from her cheeks, and her face became a strained, pallid mask of wax. She turned her head slowly and found Paula watching her with a quiet, satisfied expression. "You betrayed me!" Olga whispered.

Paula almost burst out laughing. "*Me?* You wanted me to try to stop a war. Well, that's what I've been doing—what *you* wanted, in *your* way. So screw you, too, lady."

Total shock had seized the room. Seconds ticked by with nobody speaking or moving. Protbornov stared fixedly ahead of him, heedless of his surroundings as the full enormity of the catastrophe unfolded. In the background, the faces on the screens continued making noises but were no longer saying anything.

Then the shrill tone of a priority call broke the silence. Major Uskayev answered it woodenly. It was from the duty controller in the Strategic Headquarters located beneath the Government Building, which was where the Soviet leaders had withdrawn to direct the forthcoming operations. He looked dazed. "Please advise General Protbornov that American battle lasers have just fired without warning on our spacebased missile defenses," the controller said. "The whole shield has been crippled."

Down below, inside Strategic Headquarters, the First Secretary of the Communist Party and his immediate circle were staring dumbfounded at a message appearing on one of the main display screens. It had started coming in over a priority link from Moscow just as the Soviet supreme commander was about to send the order for Anvil to commence return-fire.

The message, signed by President Warren Austin of the United States and endorsed by all the Western European and East Asian premiers, was addressed to the First Secretary personally. But instead of being addressed to him at the *Valentina Tereshkova* space colony, it was addressed to him at "Potemkin, Ground Zero," and specified correctly the latitude and longitude coordinates of the replica beneath Siberia.

The West, the message said, had retargeted three thousand of its strategic warheads on those coordinates. The final move of the endgame was up to him.

◉ EPILOGUE ◉

"Good evening, Mr. McCain."

"Hi, Jerry. That light seems to be fine."

"Yes, the maintenance man said it should be okay now. Your cab's waiting out front." Jerry took in the dark suit, crisp white shirt, and tie with jeweled clip beneath the overcoat as McCain crossed the rooftop lobby to the main doors. "Going to a party tonight?"

"No, just a quiet dinner with an old friend."

"Have a nice evening."

"I'll try."

McCain went out and found the cab waiting on the pad in front of the doors. "Is it the Milburn Towers, sir?" the cabbie checked as McCain climbed in.

"That's right. We've plenty of time." The engine note rose, and McCain settled back in the comfortable leather upholstery of the rear seat. Moments later, the brightly lit roof of the apartment building with its garden and pool was falling away below. Lights were coming on in the twilight, and as the cab's nose swung around, the glow of the Washington, D.C., area moved into the frame of the windshield against the darker sky on the horizon to the east.

So, the war that would end wars had done precisely that—by never happening. With an entire strategic arsenal ready to rain down on the very point where they had concentrated everyone they had judged as worth the most to preserve—including themselves—what else could the Soviet leaders have done but capitulate? The hills overhead would have made little difference to the size of the hole that would have been made in Siberia.

Thus in a position to dictate terms, the West had obtained a reconnection to its agents and allies inside Potemkin, and used them to ensure that the Soviets stayed put while an international inspection force was dispatched to *Valentina Tereshkova*. What they found there, with the world looking on, was enough to topple the Soviet empire, and a modern democratic state eventually emerged from the ensuing internal chaos. Some observers described the process as "1917 played backward."

It was November 7 again, and on that date McCain usually found his mind going back to the events that had culminated on that day in 2017. It was customary when thinking over things like that to say that it didn't seem like ten years, he reflected as he looked up through the cab roof at the stars that were starting to come out—some of them were the artificial worlds being built out there, which at certain times were visible to the eye; he'd seen all he wanted to of artificial worlds and was content to make the best of the real one. But the truth was, it did seem like ten years. A lot of things had happened in that time.

With the big standoff between the giants at last resolved, the world had been left with little more than local squabbles and police actions to occupy its military minds while it completed its process of growing up. Defense institutions had shrunk accordingly, and the release of creativity and resources from all nations into more productive enterprises had made visible already the beginnings of a social and economic upheaval that promised to dwarf the Agricultural, Industrial, and Information Revolutions put together. The human race would soon explode outward across the Solar System. Real colonies were taking shape in the Earth-Moon vicinity now—in fact, the interior of *Valentina Tereshkova* had been rebuilt, and it was now one of them. There was a permanent base on Mars, which was mushrooming as new arrivals poured in. Gigantic manned ships for voyaging to the outer planets were under construction in lunar orbit, and robot starprobes were at the design stage. And the underground space colony that had been called Potemkin was still there and working underneath Siberia, as a familiarization and training simulator for would-be colonists. Earth's population was plateauing out; that of the Solar System, the experts said, was about to take off. The late twentieth century of McCain's boyhood, with its endless pessimisms about imminent doom and declining everything, seemed a long way away.

The cab joined one of the traffic corridors into the city, and minutes later was over the rainbow-lit heights and glass canyons of the metropolis. It singled out the blue-frosted pinnacle of the Milburn Towers, circled into its descent, and let McCain off outside the doors leading in from the roof-level parking area, where other vehicles were discharging their loads of evening diners, hotel guests, and revelers. McCain walked through the lobby to the Orchid Lounge adjoining the restaurant, checked his coat, and gave his name to the host, who showed him through to the booth where he was expected.

The figure that rose to greet him was wearing a dark gray suit, maroon tie, and matching handkerchief protruding from the breast pocket. The face had filled out a little since McCain had last seen it, although the eyes still had a noticeable bulge. It showed the lines of ten additional years, but at the same time had mellowed out and lost the tenseness it had once radiated. It was a face that seemed more at peace with itself and the world now.

"Hello, Mr. Earnshaw, journalist," Scanlon said. "It's been a long time. Your face has undergone some improvement, I see."

McCain grinned. "You're not looking so bad yourself."

They shook hands warmly, and Scanlon dropped the act. "Lew, I'm glad to see you so well. This is a fine place you picked."

"One of the best in town. Have you been here before?"

"I can't say that I have. Washington isn't a place I've ever had an opportunity to get to know."

"The restaurant's beautiful—looks right down over the center of the city. You'll like it."

The cocktail waiter appeared at the booth. He was Oriental in appearance. McCain ordered a Napoleon cocktail, and Scanlon took a refill of Bushmill's Irish with a touch of water. It was getting on near ten years since they'd last seen each other at the end of the winding-down after it all, when Scanlon had disappeared to pursue his own life. Then, a month or so ago, he had called out of the blue to say he would be in Washington in early November. November 7 had seemed a good day to choose for getting together.

"So, this is one of your regular haunts, eh?" Scanlon said, raising his glass.

"Oh, I wouldn't say regular. Once in a while, maybe. . . ."

"And a fine place for charming the ladies out of their wherewithals, too, I wouldn't wonder. 'Tis a grand view out there on that side. Do you live near here?"

"No, not in the city. I've got a place at Warrenton, in Virginia—west from here."

"How far would that be?"

"Oh, about thirty miles."

Scanlon sat back and looked McCain up and down. "And speaking of ladies, do you ever see the blond partner in crime that you had back then? A bit skinny if I remember, but not bad-looking for that. She had a temper on her, too, that'd put many a man to shame."

McCain shook his head. "Not these days. We were just doing a job, that's all. She got together with Razz in the end. I guess they had some things in common. . . . At least he could hold his own with her. They both went off on one of the lunar projects."

"Is that a fact, now?"

"Something to do with beaming power out to spaceships."

"Since you're still in the area, I suppose you keep in touch with your pals from your old firm," Scanlon said.

"I still see Bernard Foleda and his family from time to time," McCain replied. "You remember him from all the debriefings—the guy I worked for."

"I liked him. He said what he had to, without any frills or fancy airs and graces. How's he doing?"

"He retired after they started closing chunks of the Pentagon down and the excitement went out of life. Myra—that's his wife—told me once that he couldn't get used to not having the KGB tailing him to work every morning. It was as if he'd lost old friends. So he quit. He does things with his grandchildren and drinks with old cronies from the Pentagon Mafia." McCain made a brief openhanded gesture. "I do see Koh every now and again. He's into big-time politics in Asia again, and travels backward and forward to Washington. He's always on a tight schedule, but he makes time if he can."

The drinks arrived. McCain looked across, hesitated for a moment, then raised his glass in a toast. "Well . . . to old times, I guess."

"And old friends." They drank, and stayed silent for a few seconds. "And what about yourself?" Scanlon asked at last. "Is the world managing to keep you well enough supplied with mischief?"

McCain set his glass down and shrugged. "Oh, they gave me an allowance that'll see me okay permanently, so money's no problem. I fly a plane and keep pretty active. There's a woman called Donna that I stay friendly with—I am a one-at-a-time kind of guy, whether you believe it or not. She's a lawyer and doesn't need full-time entanglements either, so it suits both of us. Politics and history still interest me—I read a lot." He sipped his drink again. "And I'm collecting information on the history of espionage technology. I'm thinking maybe I'll try writing a book about it one day." He smiled wryly. "The only problem is, I'm not sure if there are many people left who'd have any use for it these days. Maybe commercial espionage is the only field left that pays."

"Try writing one on mountaineering, then. Ye've some experience of that, too."

McCain grinned. "Anyhow, what about you? When you called, you said something about teaching? You? Surely not."

Scanlon looked upward and rubbed his neck in a guilty kind of way with his fingertips. "Ah, well now, it's teaching of a kind, all right—'security adviser,' I suppose you might call it. Some of these new nations that are appearing in Asia and all over . . . the people who are mixed up in the jockeyings to run them tend to worry about their safety and such, you understand. They'll pay well for good instructors to teach their bodyguards the business, if you follow my meaning."

McCain nodded in a resigned kind of way. "I might have guessed: know-how for sale, eh? Homicide, mayhem, explosives, booby-traps . . ."

"A man has to make a living," Scanlon said, using a phrase from the past. "And besides, hasn't anyone a right to sleep easy in their own beds?"

McCain fell silent and studied his glass for a while. When he finally looked up, his face was more serious. "Kev, there's one thing I always wanted to ask you about. What did make you switch sides back in Zamork?"

Scanlon shrugged. "Ah well, now, the KGB were never happy about having to use a foreigner for a job like that. But then, they could hardly have used a Russian with a fella like you, could they? So they took the risk and lost. I think maybe the let themselves believe too much of their own propaganda on Irish-English-American relationships. . . . And then, who ever understood how the Irish tick, anyhow?"

McCain drank, thought, and shook his head. "That was what you said at the debriefings and interrogations, but it never rang true—not to me. What was the real reason?"

Scanlon looked across, not answering at once, but his expression showed no surprise. Finally he said, simply, "It was Koh that did it."

"Koh?" McCain looked genuinely astonished.

Scanlon turned his head away to gaze out through the glass wall that formed the far side of the lounge. "It was them things he used to say about civilizations: Greeks, Romans, Europe, America . . . even the Brits. How they all were born suddenly like living things, grew and flourished and expressed what they were in everything they did . . . and then they died. A few stones from the rubble are picked up by the next one and built into something better, but the race as a whole moves on and that's what matters." He gestured up at the darkening sky outside. "And that's what's going on out there, right now. Wouldn't anyone like to think that what he did helped make a brick or two of what went into it? And when I got to thinking about it that way, how could I carry on working for the crowd I was with? Everything about that system represented where the rest of the world that mattered had come from, not where it was going to."

McCain leaned back and looked at him wonderingly. "So it was all those hours you used to spend talking to him. Koh did it, eh? He sweet-talked an Irishman around. I wonder if he knew what he was doing."

"Ah, to be sure he knew. . . . And it was watching the likes of yourself, and Razz, and the rest, and thinking what it all stood for," Scanlon said. "I'd seen a regime that could only survive through fear—that destroyed people's minds. And then I saw the power of the human mind, and people who would survive through overcoming fear. And I made my choice."

McCain drained his glass, then nodded. "Poetic, and philosophical," he complimented.

"And isn't that what you'd expect from the Irish?"

McCain looked across the booth. "I never had any quarrel with the people, you know, Kev," he said. "It was only the system. Look how well they're doing now. . . . Oh, and guess who I got a letter from a little while ago—Andreyov. Remember him?"

"The old fella, with the white hair."

"Yes, him. He's back in the Ukraine."

"Did you know that his father was there—in Germany in 1945, with Konev's army?" Scanlon asked. They both laughed.

"He mentioned the first Russian Disney World that's opened up outside Moscow," McCain said. "He says Protbornov's running it. I couldn't make out if he was being serious or not."

At that moment the host came back to the table and announced, "More of your party have arrived, gentlemen." McCain looked up, puzzled, just in time to catch Scanlon giving the host a wink.

Then a woman's voice said from behind him, "I thought you'd have picked a Japanese restaurant, Lew."

McCain turned disbelievingly. She still had the obstinate curl of hair on her forehead that said so much about her personality, but her figure was more full now. He half-rose to his feet, speechless.

Rashazzi was behind her, grinning from ear to ear. "It's our first Earthside leave for eighteen months," he explained. "We couldn't let it go by without looking you up. And the timing was perfect." McCain shook Rashazzi's hand, then gave Paula a warm hug.

"It was her idea," Scanlon said. "She tracked me down and called me from the Moon six weeks ago."

"So we're a little late," Rashazzi said. "You know how it is—women . . ."

"Er, your table is ready," the host informed them. "But if you'd like a cocktail first, we can get you another one later. Mr. Nakajima-Lin called a few minutes ago to say he'd been detained slightly, and for you to go ahead. He'll join the party shortly."

"No, let's wait for him," Rashazzi said. "I'm not starving yet."

"We're in Washington for a week," Paula told McCain. "Why hurry?" Paula and Rashazzi sat down.

McCain was looking astounded. "Koh? Koh's coming here too?"

"One of his little jaunts that you mentioned," Scanlon aid. "Just between the four of us, I think the tribe is planning on colonizing the United States."

"So, what's it like being scientists on the Moon?" McCain asked.

"Indescribable," Rashazzi said. "Exhilarating. The sense of vastness, the sheer rawness of nature up there . . . You can't imagine it."

"You're sure that's where you really are?" McCain said over the top of his glass. "It couldn't be down underneath Brooklyn or somewhere?" Rashazzi laughed.

"And being a scientist . . ." Paula said. She gave McCain a long look that was suddenly serious, just for the moment. "You had a lot to do with that, you know, Lew. I learned a lot about people, yes . . . But I learned what *real* science means, too."

"How d'you mean?" he asked.

"You know what I mean. Science is realism—eliminating wishful thinking. If you can't do that, you can't begin. You'll never know what truth is. You can make your own Potemkin in your head. And sometimes it can be just as difficult to break out of. But when you do, and you look back at the prison you were living a whole make-believe life in and mistaking it for reality, it's the same feeling of release and endless room to grow."

"Just like Koh's ideas about evolution," Scanlon commented.

"They're the same thing," Rashazzi said.

The Oriental cocktail waiter came back to the booth, and McCain stared up at him while he took Paula's and Rashazzi's order. His features seemed to be a mixture of Japanese and Chinese, with neither predominating—McCain had learned to distinguish them during his earlier years in the East. Then he frowned uneasily as a new thought struck him. "Your name wouldn't be Nakajima-Lin by any chance, would it?" he asked the waiter.

"No, sir. It's Jones."

McCain sat back with a sigh of relief. "That's good to know, anyway."

"Why do you want to know?" the waiter inquired curiously.

McCain looked out at the stars beyond the far wall. "Oh, that's a long, long story. Let's just say that it would have been a coincidence. I've never been very comfortable with coincidences."

The other smiled. Scanlon and McCain ordered refills.

Meanwhile, high in the sky outside, a particular pinpoint of light was just becoming visible, close to the Moon.

VOYAGE FROM YESTERYEAR

Dedication

❀ ❀ ❀

To ALEXANDER JAMES—
who was conceived at about the same time as the book.
Nature delivered faster.

◈ PROLOGUE ◈

". . . Ladies and gentlemen, our guest of honor tonight—Henry B. Congreve." The toastmaster completed his introduction and stepped aside to allow the stocky, white-haired figure in black tie and dinner jacket to move to the podium. Enthusiastic applause arose from the three hundred guests gathered in the Hilton complex on the western outskirts of Washington, D.C. The lights around the room dimmed, fading the audience into white shirtfronts, glittering throats and fingers, and masklike faces. A pair of spotlights picked out the speaker as he waited for the applause to subside. In the shadows next to him, the toastmaster returned to his chair.

After sixty-eight years of tussling with life, Congreve's bulldog frame still stood upright, his shoulders jutting squarely below his close-cropped head. The lines of his roughly chiseled face were still firm and solid, and his eyes twinkled good-humoredly as he surveyed the room. It seemed strange to many of those present that a man so vital, one with so much still within him, should be about to deliver his retirement address.

Few of the younger astronauts, scientists, engineers, and North American Space Development Organization executives could remember NASDO without Congreve as its president. For all of them, things would never be quite the same again.

"Thank you, Matt." Congreve's voice rumbled in a gravelly

baritone from the speakers all around. He glanced from side to side to take in the whole of his audience. "I, ah—I almost didn't make it here at all." He paused, and the last whispers of conversation died away. "A sign in the hall outside says that the fossil display is in twelve-oh-three upstairs." The American Archeological Society was holding its annual convention in the Hilton complex that week. Congreve shrugged. "I figured that had to be where I was supposed to go. Luckily I bumped into Matt on the way, and he got me back on the right track." A ripple of laughter wavered in the darkness, punctuated by a few shouts of protest from some of the tables. He waited for silence, then continued in a less flippant voice. "The first thing I have to do is thank everybody here, and all the NASDO people who couldn't be with us tonight, for inviting me. Also, of course, I have to express my sincere appreciation for this, and even more my appreciation for the sentiments that it signifies. Thank you—all of you." As he spoke, he gestured toward the eighteen-inch-long, silver and bronze replica of the as yet unnamed, untried SP3 starprobe that stood on its teak base before Congreve's place at the main table.

His voice became more serious as he continued. "I don't want to go off into a lot of personal anecdotes and reminiscences. That kind of thing is customary on an occasion such as this, but it would be trivial, and I wouldn't want my last speech as president of NASDO to be marked by trivia. The times do not permit such luxury. Instead, I want to talk about matters that are of global significance and which affect every individual alive on this planet, and indeed the generations yet to be born—assuming there will be future generations." He paused. "I want to talk about survival—the survival of the human species."

Although the room was already quiet, the silence seemed to intensify with these words. Here and there in the audience, faces turned to glance curiously at one another. Clearly, this was not to be just another retirement speech. Congreve went on. "We have already come once to the brink of a third world war and hung precariously over the edge. Today, in 2015, twenty-three years have passed since U.S. and Soviet forces clashed in Baluchistan with tactical nuclear weapons, and although the rapid spread of a fusion-based economy at last promises to solve the energy problems that brought about that confrontation, the jealousies, mistrusts, and suspicions which brought us to the point of war then and which have persistently plagued our race throughout its history are as much in evidence as ever.

"Today the sustenance that our industries crave is not oil, but minerals. Fifty years from now our understanding of controlled-fusion processes will probably have eliminated that source of shortages too, but in the meantime shorter-sighted political considerations are recreating the climate of tension and rivalry that hinged around the oil issue at the close of the last century. Obviously, South Africa's importance in this context is shaping the current pattern of power maneuvering, and the probable flashpoint for another East-West collision will again be the Iran-Pakistan border region, which our strategists expect the Soviets to contest to gain access to the Indian Ocean in preparation for the support of a war of so-called black African liberation against the South."

Congreve paused, swept his eyes from one side of the room to the other, and raised his hands in resignation. "It seems that as individuals we can only stand by as helpless observers and watch the events that are sweeping us onward collectively. The situation is complicated further by the emergence and rapid economic and military growth of the Chinese-Japanese Co-Prosperity Sphere, which threatens to confront Moscow with an unassailable power bloc should it come to align with ourselves and the Europeans. More than a few Kremlin analysts must see their least risky gamble as a final resolution with the West now, before such an alliance has time to consolidate. In other words, it would not be untrue to say that the future of the human race has never been at greater risk than it is at this moment."

Congreve pushed himself back from the podium with his arms and straightened. When he resumed speaking, his tone had lightened slightly. "In the area that concerns all of us here in our day-to-day lives, the accelerating pace of the space program has brought a lot of excitement in the last two decades. Some inspiring achievements have helped offset the less encouraging news from other quarters: We have established permanent bases on the Moon and Mars; colonies are being built in space; a manned mission has reached the moons of Jupiter; and robots are out exploring the farthest reaches of the Solar System and beyond. But"—he extended his arms in an animated sigh—"these operations have been national, not international. Despite the hopes and the words of years gone by, militarization has followed everywhere close on the heels of exploration, and we are led to the inescapable conclusion that a war, if it comes, would soon spread beyond the confines of the surface and jeopardize our species everywhere. We must face up to the fact that the danger now threatening us in the years ahead is nothing less than that."

He turned for a moment to stare at the model of SP3 gleaming on the table beside him and then pointed to it. "Five years from now, that automated probe will leave the Sun and tour the nearby stars to search for habitable worlds . . . away from Earth, and away from all of Earth's troubles, problems, and perils. Eventually, if all goes well, it will arrive at some place insulated by unimaginable distance from the problems that promise to make strife an inseparable and ineradicable part of the weary story of human existence on this planet." Congreve's expression took on a distant look as he gazed at the replica, as if in his mind he were already soaring with it outward and away. "It will be a new place," he said in a faraway voice. "A new, fresh, vibrant world, unscarred by Man's struggle to elevate himself from the beasts, a place that presents what might be the only opportunity for our race to preserve an extension of itself where it would survive, and if necessary begin again, but this time with the lessons of the past to guide it."

An undercurrent of murmuring rippled quickly around the hall. Congreve nodded, indicating his anticipation of the objections he knew would come. He raised a hand for attention and gradually the noise abated.

"No, I am not saying that SP3 could be modified from a robot craft to carry a human crew. The design could not feasibly be modified at this late stage. Too many things would have to be thought out again from the beginning, and such a task would require decades. And yet, nothing comparable to SP3 is anywhere near as advanced a stage of design at the present time, let alone near being constructed.

The opportunity is unique and cannot, surely, be allowed to pass by. But at the same time we cannot afford the delay that would be needed to take advantage of that opportunity. Is there a solution to this dilemma?" He looked around as if inviting responses. None came.

"We have been studying this problem for some time now, and we believe there is a solution. It would not be feasible to send a contingent of adult humans, either as a functioning community or in some suspended state, with the ship; it is in too advanced a stage of construction to change its primary design parameters. But then, why send *adult* humans at all?" He spread his arms appealingly. "After all, the objective is simply to establish an extension of our race where it would be safe from any calamity that might befall us here, and such a location would be found only at the end of the voyage. The people would not be required either during the voyage or in the survey phase, since machines are perfectly capable of handling everything connected with those operations. People become relevant only when those phases have been successfully completed. Therefore we can avoid all the difficulties inherent in the idea of sending people along by dispensing with the conventional notions of interstellar travel and adopting a totally new approach: by having the ship *create* the people after it gets there!"

Congreve paused again, but this time not so much as a whisper disturbed the silence.

Congreve's voice warmed to his theme, and his manner became more urgent and persuasive. "Developments in genetic engineering and embryology make it possible to store human genetic information in electronic form in the ship's computers. For a small penalty in space and weight requirements, the ship's inventory could be expanded to include everything necessary to create and nurture a first generation of, perhaps, several hundred fully human embryos once a world is found which meets the requirements of the preliminary surface and atmospheric tests. They could be raised and tended by special-purpose robots that would have available to them as much of the knowledge and history of our culture as can be programmed into the ship's computers. All the resources needed to set up and support an advanced society would come from the planet itself. Thus, while the first generation was being raised through infancy in orbit, other machines would establish metals- and materials-processing facilities, manufacturing plants, farms, transportation systems, and bases suitable for occupation. Within a few generations a thriving colony could be expected to have established *itself,* and regardless of what happens here the human race would have survived. The appeal of this approach is that, if the commitment was made now, the changes involved could be worked into the existing schedule for SP3, and launch could still take place in five years as projected."

By this time life was flowing slowly back into his listeners. Although many of them were still too astonished by his proposal to react visibly, heads were nodding, and the murmurs running around the room seemed positive. Congreve nodded and smiled faintly as if savoring the thought of having kept the best part until last.

"The second thing I have to announce tonight is that such a commitment has now been made. As I mentioned a moment ago, this subject has been under study for a considerable period of time. I can now inform you that, three days ago, the President of the United States and the Chairman of the Eastern Co-Prosperity Sphere signed an agreement for the project which I have briefly outlined to be pursued on a joint basis, effective immediately. The activities of the various national and private research institutions and other organizations that will be involved in the venture will be coordinated with those of the North American Space Development Organization and with those of our Chinese and Japanese partners under a project designation of Starhaven."

Congreve's face split into a broad smile. "My third announcement is that tonight does not mark my retirement from professional life after all. I have accepted an invitation from the President to take charge of the Starhaven project on behalf of the United States as the senior member nation, and I am relinquishing my position with NASDO purely in order to give undivided attention to my new responsibilities. For those who might believe that I've given them some hard times in the past, I have to say with insincere apologies that I'm going to be around for some time longer yet, and that before this project is through the times are going to get a lot harder."

Several people at the back stood up and started clapping. The applause spread and turned into a standing ovation. Congreve grinned unabashedly to acknowledge the enthusiasm, stood for a while as the applause continued, and then grasped the sides of the podium again.

"We had our first formal meeting with the Chinese yesterday, and we've already made our first official decision." He glanced at the replica of the star-robot probe again. "SP3 now has a name. It has been named after a goddess of Chinese mythology whom we have adopted as a fitting patroness: Kuan-yin—the goddess who brings children. Let us hope that she watches over her children well in the years to come."

PART ONE

THE VOYAGE OF THE MAYFLOWER II

◎ CHAPTER ONE ◎

About two hundred feet below the ridgeline, the Third Platoon of D Company had set up its Tactical Battle Station in a depression surrounded by interconnecting patches of sagebrush and scrub. A corner in a low rock wall sheltered it on two sides, a large boulder closed in the third, and a parapet of smaller, flat rocks protected it from the front; a thermal shield stretched across the top hid the body heat of its occupants from the ever-vigilant sensors of hostile surveillance satellites.

The scene outside was deceptively quiet as Colman lifted a flap and peered out, keeping his head well back from the edge of the canopy. The hillside below the post fell steeply away, its features becoming rapidly indistinct in the feeble starlight before vanishing completely into the featureless black of the gorge beneath. There was no moon, and the sky was clear as crystal. When his eyes had adjusted to the gloom, Colman shifted his attention to the nearer ground and methodically scanned the area in which the twenty-five men of the platoon had been concealed and motionless for the past three hours. If they had undercut their foxholes and weapons pits the way he had shown them and made proper use of the rocks and vegetation, they would stand a good chance of escaping detection. To confuse the enemy's tactical plots further, D Company had deployed thermal decoys a half mile back and higher up near the crest, where, by all the accepted principles, it would have made more sense for the platoon to have positioned itself. Autotimed to turn on and off in a random sequence to simulate movement, the decoys had been drawing sporadic fire for much of the night while the platoon had drawn none, which seemed to say something about the value of "the book" as rewritten by Staff Sergeant Colman. "There are two ways to do anything," he told the recruits. "The Army way and the wrong way. There isn't any other way. So when I tell you to do something the Army way, what does it mean?"

"It means do it your way, Sergeant."

"Very good."

A tiny pinpoint of orange glowed bright for a second, about fifty feet away, where Stanislau and Carson were covering the trail from the gorge with the sub-megajoule laser. Colman scowled to himself. He turned his head a fraction to whisper to Driscoll. "The LCP's showing a cigarette. Tell them to get rid of it."

Driscoll tapped into the fingerpanel of the compack, and from a spike pushed into the ground, ultrasonic vibrations spread outward through the soil, carrying the call sign of the Laser Cannon Post. "LCP reading," a muted voice acknowledged from the compack.

Driscoll spoke into the microphone boom projecting from his helmet. "Red Three, routine check." This would leave an innocuous record in the automatic signal logging system. In the darkness Driscoll pressed a key to deactivate the recording channel momentarily. "You're showing a light, shitheads., Douse it or cover it." His finger released the key. "Report status, LCP."

"Ready and standing by," the voice replied neutrally. "Nothing to report." Outside, the pinpoint of light vanished abruptly.

"Remain at ready. Out."

Colman grunted to himself, made one final sweep of the surroundings, then dropped the flap back into place and turned to face inside. Behind Driscoll, Maddock was examining the bottom of the gorge through the image intensifier, while in the shadows next to him the expression of concentration on Corporal Swyley's face was etched sharply by the subdued glow of the forward terrain display screen propped in front of him.

The image that so held his attention was transmitted from an eighteen-inch-long, infantry reconnaissance drone that they had managed to slip in a thousand feet above the floor of the gorge and almost over the enemy's forward positions and was supplemented by additional data collected from satellite and other ELINT network sources. The display showed the target command bunker at the bottom of the gorge, known enemy weapons emplacements as computed from backplots of radar-tracked shell trajectories, and the locations of observation and fire-command posts from source analysis triangulations of stray reflections from control lasers. On it the cool water of the stream and its tributaries stood out as black lines forking like twigs; the rock crags and boulders were shades of blue; living vegetation varied from rust brown on the hills to deep red where it crowded together along the lower slopes of the gorge; and shell and bomb scars glowed from dull orange to yellow depending on how recently the explosions had occurred.

But what Corporal Swyley was concentrating on so intently were the minute specks of brighter reds that might or might not have been imperfectly obscured defensive positions, and the barely discernible hairline fragments that could have been the thermal footprints of recent vehicle movements.

How Swyley did what only he did so well was something nobody was quite sure of, least of all Swyley himself. Whatever the reason, Swyley's ability to pick out significant details from a hopeless mess of background garbage and to distinguish consistently between valid information and decoys was justly famed—and uncanny. But since Swyley himself didn't understand how he did it, he was unable to explain it to the systems programmers, who had hoped to duplicate his feats with their image-analysis programs. That had been when the "-ists" and the "-ologists" began their endless batteries of fruitless tests. Eventually Swyley made up plausible-sounding explanations for the benefit of the specialists, but these were exposed when the programs written to their specifications failed to work. Then Swyley began claiming that his mysterious gift had suddenly deserted him completely.

Major Thorpe, Electronics Intelligence Officer at Brigade H.Q., had read somewhere that spinach and fish were sure remedies for failing eyesight, so he placed Corporal Swyley on an intensive diet. But Swyley hated spinach and fish even more than he hated being tested, and within a week he was afflicted by acute color-blindness, which he demonstrated by refusing to see anything at all in even the simplest of training displays.

After that, Swyley had been declared "maladjusted" and transferred to D Company, which was where all the misfits and malcontents ended up. Now his powers returned magically only when no officers were anywhere near him except for Captain Sirocco, who ran D Company and didn't care how Swyley got his answers as long as they came out right. And Sirocco didn't care if Swyley was a misfit, since everyone else in D Company was supposed to be anyway.

It probably meant that there was no easy way of getting out of D Company again let alone out of the regular service, Colman reflected as he watched in the darkness and waited for Swyley to deliver his verdict. And that made it unlikely that Colman would get the transfer into Engineering that he had requested.

It seemed self-evident to him that nobody in his right mind would want to get killed, or to be sent to places he'd never heard of by people he'd never met in order to kill other people he didn't know. Therefore nobody in his right mind would be in the Army. But since the Army was full of people whom it had judged to be acceptably sane and normal, it seemed to follow that the Army's ideas of what was normal had to be very strange. Now, to transfer into something like Engineering seemed on the face of it to be a perfectly natural, reasonable, constructive, and desirable thing to want to do. And that seemed enough to guarantee that the Army would find the request unreasonable and him unsuitable.

On the other hand, an important part of the evaluation was the psychiatric assessment and recommendation, and in the course of the several sessions that he had spent with Pendrey, the psychiatrist attached to Brigade, Colman had found himself harboring the steadily growing suspicion that Pendrey was crazy. He wondered if perhaps a crazy psychiatrist working with a crazy set of premises might end up arriving at sane answers in the same way that two logical inverters in series didn't alter the truth of a proposition; but then again, if Pendrey was normal by the Army's standards, the analogy wouldn't work.

Sirocco had endorsed the request, it was true, but Colman wasn't sure it would count for very much since Sirocco ran D Company, and anything he said was probably inverted somewhere along the chain as a matter of course. Perhaps he should have persuaded Sirocco not to endorse the request. On the other hand, if anything recommended by Sirocco was inverted to start with, and if Pendrey was crazy but normal by the Army's standards, and if the premises that Pendrey was working with were also crazy, then the decision might come out in Colman's favor after all. Or would it? His attempt to think the tortuous logic of the situation once again was interrupted by Swyley at last leaning back and turning his face away from the screen.

"They've got practically all their strength out on the flanks both ways along the gorge," Swyley announced. "There are some units moving down the opposite slope, but they won't be in position for about another thirty minutes." The glow from the screen highlighted the mystified look that flashed across his face. He shrugged. "Right now they're wide open, right down below us."

"They don't have anything here?" Colman checked, touching the screen with a finger to indicate the place where the bottom of the trail emerged from a small wood on the edge of a grassy flat and just a few hundred feet from the enemy bunker. The display showed a faint pattern of smudges on either side of the trail in just the positions where defensive formations would be expected.

Swyley shook his head. "Those are decoys. Like I said, they've moved practically all the guys out to the flanks"—he jabbed at the screen with a finger—"here, here, and here."

"Getting round behind B Company, and up over spur Four-nine-three," Colman suggested as he studied the image.

"Could be," Swyley agreed noncommittally.

"Looks dead as hell down there to me," Maddock threw in without taking his eyes from the viewpiece of the intensifier.

"What do the seismics and sniffers say about Swyley's decoys?" Colman asked, turning his head toward Driscoll.

Driscoll translated the question into a computer command and peered at the data summary on one of the com-pack screens. "Insignificant seismic above threshold at eight hundred yards. Downwind ratio less than five points up at four hundred. Negative corroboration from acoustics—background swamping." The computers were unable to identify vibrational patterns correlating with human activity in the data coming in from the sensing devices quietly scattered around the gorge by low-flying, remote-piloted "bees" on and off throughout the night; the chemical sensors located to the leeward of the suspected decoys were detecting little of the odor molecules characteristic of human bodies; the microphones had yielded nothing in the way of coherent sound patterns, but this was doubtless because of the white-noise background being generated in the vicinity of the stream. Although the evidence was only partial and negative at that, it supported Swyley's assertion that the main road down to the objective was, incredibly, virtually undefended for the time being.

Colman frowned to himself as his mind raced over the data's significance. No sane attacking force would contemplate taking an objective like that by a direct frontal assault in the center—the lowermost stretch of the trail was too well covered by overlooking slopes, and there would be no way back if the attack bogged down. That was what the enemy commander would have thought anyone would have thought. So what would be the point of tying up lots of men to defend a point that would never be attacked? According to the book, the correct way to attack the bunker would be along the stream from above or by crossing the stream below and coming down from the spur on the far side. So the other side was concentrating at points above both of the obvious assault routes and setting themselves up to ambush whichever attack should materialize. But in the meantime they were wide open in the middle.

"Alert all section leaders on the grid," Colman said to Driscoll. "And open a channel to Blue One."

Sirocco came through on the compack a few moments later, and Colman summarized the situation. The audacity of the idea appealed to Sirocco immediately. "We'd have to handle it ourselves. There isn't enough time to involve Brigade, but we could pin down those guys on the other side while you went in, and roll a barrage in front of you to clear obstacles." He was referring to the Company-controlled robot batteries set up to the rear, below the crestline of the ridge. "It would mean going in without any counterbattery suppression when you break though. What do you think?"

"If we went fast, we could make it without." Colman answered.

"Without CB suppression there wouldn't be time to move any of the other platoons round to back you up. You'd be on your own," Sirocco said.

"We can use the robot batteries to lay down a close-cover screen from the flanks. If you give us an optical and IR blanket at twelve hundred feet, we can make it."

Sirocco hesitated for a split second. "Okay," he finally said. "Let's do it."

Ten minutes later, Sirocco had worked out a hastily contrived fire-plan with his executive officer and relayed details to First, Second, and Fourth platoons, and Colman had briefed Third Platoon via his section leaders. Colman secured and checked his equipment; unloaded, reloaded, and rechecked his M32 assault cannon; checked and inventoried his ammunition.

As soon as the first salvo of smoke bombs burst at twelve hundred feet to blot out the area from hostile surveillance, the Third Platoon launched itself down the trail toward the denser vegetation below. Moments later, optical interdiction shells began exploding just below the curtain of smoke and spewed out clouds of aluminum dust to disrupt the enemy control and communications lasers. Ahead of the attacking troops, a concentrated point-barrage of shells and high-intensity pulsed beams fired from the flanking platoons rolled forward along the trail to clear the way of mines and other antipersonnel ordnance. Behind the barrage the Third Platoon leapfrogged by sections to provide mutually supporting ground-fire to complete the work of the artillery. There was no opposition. The defending artillery opened up from the rear within ten seconds of the initial smoke blanket, but the enemy was firing blind and largely ineffectively.

In thirteen minutes the firefight was all over. Colman stood on the gravel bank of the stream and watched as a bewildered major was led from the enemy bunker, followed by his numb staff, who joined the gaggle of disarmed defenders being herded together under the watchful eyes of smirking Third Platoon guards. The primary objective had been to take prisoners and obtain intelligence, and the crop had yielded two captains in addition to the major, a first and a second lieutenant, a chief warrant officer, a sergeant major, two sergeants, and over a dozen enlisted men. Moreover, the call-sign lists and maps had been seized intact, along with invaluable communications and weapons-control equipment. Not a bad haul at all, Colman reflected with satisfaction.

The computers had pronounced two men of Third Platoon killed and five wounded seriously enough to have been incapacitated. Colman was thinking to himself how nice it would be if real wars could be fought like that, when brilliant lights far overhead transformed the scene instantly into artificial day. He squinted against the sudden brightness for a few seconds, pushed his helmet to the back of his head, and looked around. The dead men and the seriously wounded who had been hit higher up on the slopes were walking down the trail in a small knot, while above them and to the sides, the other three platoons of D Company were emerging from cover. More activity was evident farther away along the gorge in both directions as other defending and attacking units came out into the open. Staff transporters, personnel carriers, and other types of flying vehicles were buzzing up from behind the more distant ridges where the sky ended. Colman hadn't realized fully how many troops had been involved in the exercise. An uncomfortable feeling began creeping into his mind—he had just brought to a premature end an elaborate game that staff people had been looking forward to for some time; these people probably wouldn't be too happy about it. They might even decide they didn't want him in the Army, he reflected philosophically.

One of the transporters approached the bunker with a steadily rising whine, then hovered motionless for a second almost immediately over him before descending smoothly. Its rear door slid open to reveal the lean, swarthy figure of Captain Sirocco in helmet and battledress, still wearing his flak-vest. He jumped out nimbly while the transporter was still six feet above the ground, and ambled up to Colman. Behind his ample black moustache, the easy-going lines of his face betrayed as little as ever, but his eyes were twinkling. "Pretty good, Steve," he said without preamble as he turned with his hands on his hips to survey the indignant scowls from the captured "enemy" officers standing sullenly by the bunker. "I don't think we'll get any Brownie points for it though. We broke just about every rule in the book." Colman grunted. He hadn't expected much else. Sirocco raised his eyebrows and inclined his head in a way that could have meant anything. "Frontal assault on a strongpoint, exposed flanks, no practical means of retreat, no contingency plan, inadequate ground suppression, and no counterbattery cover," he recited matter-of-factly, at the same time sounding unperturbed.

"What about leaving your chin wide open?" Colman asked. "Isn't there anything in the rules about that?"

"Depends who you are. For D Company all things are relative."

"Ever think of making a new seat for your pants out of part of that flak-jacket?" Colman asked after a pause. "You're probably gonna need it."

"Ah, who gives a shit?" Sirocco looked up. "Anyhow, won't be much longer before we find out."

Colman' followed his gaze. An armored VIP carrier bearing a general's insignia on its nose was angling toward them. Colman shifted his M32 to the other shoulder and straightened up to watch. "Smarten it up," he called to the rest of Third Platoon, who were smoking, talking, and lounging in groups by the stream and around the bunker. The cigarettes were ground out under the heavy soles of combat boots, the chattering died away, and the groups shuffled themselves into tidier ranks.

"On what did you base your analysis of the situational display, Sergeant?" Sirocco asked, speaking in a clipped, high-pitched voice mimicking the formal tones of Colonel Wesserman, who was General Portney's aide. He injected a note of suspicion and accusation into the voice. "Was Corporal Swyley instrumental in the formulation of your tactical evaluation?" The question was bound to arise; the image analysis routines run at Brigade would have yielded nothing to justify the attack.

"No, sir," Colman replied stiffly, keeping his eyes fixed straight ahead. "Corporal Swyley was manning the com-pack. He would not have been assigned to ELINT analysis. He's color-blind."

"Then how do you explain your extraordinary conclusions?"

"I suppose we just guessed lucky, sir." Sirocco sighed. "I suppose I'll have to put it in writing that I authorized the assault on my own initiative and without any substantiating data." He cocked his head at Colman. "Happen to know anyone around here who makes a good pair of pants?"

Ahead of them the door of the VIP carrier opened to expose the rotund form of Colonel Wesserman. His florid face was even more florid than usual and swelled into a deep purple at the neck. He seemed to be choking with suppressed fury.

"I guess he doesn't have a nose for the sweet smell of success," Colman murmured as they watched.

Sirocco twirled one side of his moustache pensively for a second or two. "Success is like a fart," he said. "Only your own smells nice."

❁ **CHAPTER TWO** ❁

A sudden change in the colors and format of one of the displays being presented around him in the monitor room of the Drive Control Subcenter caught Bernard Fallows's eye and dismissed other thoughts from his mind. The display was one of several associated with Number 5 Group of the Primary Fuel Delivery System and related to one of the batteries of enormous hydrogen-feed boost pumps located in the tail section of the vessel, five miles from where Fallows was sitting.

"What's happening on Five-E, Horace?" he asked the empty room around him.

"Low-level trend projection," the subcenter executive computer replied through a small grille set to one side of Fallow's console. "Booster five-sub-three's looking as if it's going to start running hot again. Correlation integral sixty-seven, check function positive, expansion index eight-zero."

"Reading at index six?"

"Insignificant."

Fallows took in the rest of the information from the screen. The changes that the computers had detected were tiny—the merest beginnings of a trend which, if it continued at the present rate, wouldn't approach anything serious for a month or more. With only another three months to go before the ship reached Chiron there was no cause for alarm since the rest of the pump-group had enough design margin to make up the difference even without the backup. But even so, there was little doubt that Merrick would insist on the primary's being stripped down to have its bearings reground, alignment rechecked, and rotor rebalanced again. They had been through that routine twice already in the three months that the main drive had been firing. That meant another week of working in near-zero g and klutzing around in heavy-duty protective suits on the wrong side of the stern radiation shield. "Bloody pump," Fallows muttered sourly.

"Since a pump is not an organic system, I presume the expression is an expletive," Horace observed chattily.

"Aw, shuddup." The computer returned obediently to its meditations.

Fallows sat back in his chair and cast a routine eye around the monitor room. Everything seemed to be running smoothly at the crew stations beyond the glass partition behind his console, and the other displays confirmed that all else was as it should be. The reserve tank to Number 2 vernier motor had been recharged after a slight course-correction earlier and was checking out at "Ready" again. All the fuel, coolant, primary and standby power, hydraulic, pneumatic, gas, oil, life-support, and instrumentation subsystems servicing the Drive Section were performing well within limits. Way back near the tail, the banks of gigantic fusion reactors were gobbling up the 35 million tons of hydrogen that had been magnetically ramscooped out of space throughout the twenty-year voyage and converting over two tons of its mass into energy every second to produce the awesome, 1.5-mile-diameter blast of radiation and reaction products that would have to burn for six months to slow the 140-million-ton mass of the *Mayflower II* down from its free-cruise velocity.

The ship had left Earth with only sufficient fuel on board to accelerate it to cruising speed and had followed a course through the higher-density concentrations of hydrogen to collect what it needed to slow down again.

Fallows glanced at the clock in the center of the console. Less than an hour before Walters was due to take over the watch. Then he would have two days to himself before coming back on duty. He closed his eyes for a moment and savored the thought.

Only three months to go! His children had often asked him why a young man in his prime would turn his back on everything familiar and exchange twenty years of his life for a one-way journey to Alpha Centauri. They had good reason, since their futures had been decided more than a little by his decision. Most of the *Mayflower II*'s thirty thousand occupants were used to being asked that question. Fallows usually replied that he had grown disillusioned by the spectacle of the world steadily rearming itself toward the same level of insanity that had preceded the devastation of much of North America and Europe and the end of the Soviet empire in the brief holocaust of 2021, and that he had left it all behind to seek a new start somewhere else. It was one of the standard answers, given as much for self-reassurance as anything else. But in his private moments Fallows knew that he really didn't believe it. He tried to pretend that he didn't remember the real reason.

He had been born almost at the end of the Lean Years following the war, so he didn't remember about that period, but his father had told him about the times when fifty million people lived amid shantytown squalor around the blackened and twisted skeletons of their cities and huddled in lines in the snow for their ration of soup and bread at government field-kitchens; about his mother laboring fifteen hours a day cutting boards for prefabricated houses to put two skimpy meals of beef broth and rice from the Chinese food ships on the table each day and to buy one pair of utility-brand pressed-paper shoes per person every six months; about his older brother killed in the fighting with the hordes that had come plundering from the Caribbean and from the south.

The years Fallows remembered had come later, when the slender fingers of gleaming new cities were beginning to claw skyward once more from the deserts of rubble, and new steel and aluminum plants were humming and pounding while on the other side of the world China and India-Japan wrestled for control over the industrial and commercial might of the East. Those had been stirring years, vibrant years, inspiring years. Fallows remembered the floodlit parades in

Washington on the Fourth of July—the color and the splendor of the massed bands, the columns of marching soldiers with uniforms glittering and flags flying, the anthems and hymns rising on the voices of tens of thousands packed into Capitol Square, where the famous building had once stood. He remembered strutting into a high-school ball in his just acquired uniform of the American New Order Youth Corps and pretending haughtily not to notice the admiring looks following him wherever he went. How he had bragged to his envious friends after the first weekend of wargaming with the Army in the New Mexico desert . . . the exhilaration when America reestablished a permanently manned base on the Moon.

Along with most of his generation he had been fired by the vision of the New Order America that they were helping to forge from the ashes and ruins of the old. Even stronger than what had gone before, morally and spiritually purer, and confident in the knowledge of its God-ordained mission, it would rise again as an impregnable sanctuary to preserve the legacy of Western culture from the corrosive flood of heathen decadence and affluent brashness sweeping across the far side of the globe. So the credo had run. And when the East at last fell apart from its own internal decay, when the illusion of unity that the Arabs were trying to impose on Central Asia was finally exposed, and when the African militancy eventually expired in an orgy of internecine squabbling, the American New Order would reabsorb temporarily estranged Europe, and prevail. That had been the quest.

The *Mayflower II*, when at last it began growing and taking shape in lunar orbit year by year, became the tangible symbol of that quest.

Although he had been only eight years old in 2040, he could remember clearly the excitement caused by the news that a signal had come in from a spacecraft called the *Kuan-yin*, which had been launched in 2020, just before the war broke out. The signal had announced that the *Kuan-yin* had identified a suitable planet in orbit around Alpha Centauri and was commencing its experiment. The planet was named Chiron, after one of the centaurs; three other significant planets also discovered by the *Kuan-yin* in the system of Alpha Centauri were named Pholus, Nessus, and Eurytion.

Ten years went by while North America and Europe completed their recovery, and the major Eastern powers settled their rivalries. At the end of that period New America extended from Alaska to Panama, Greater Europe had incorporated Russia, Estonia, Latvia, and the Ukraine as separate nations, and China had come to dominate an Eastern Asiatic Federation stretching from Pakistan to the Bering Strait. All three of the major powers had commenced programs to reexpand into space at more or less the same time, and since each claimed a legitimate interest in the colony on Chiron and mistrusted the other two, each embarked on the construction of a starship with the aim of getting there first to protect its own against interference from the others.

With a cause, a crusade, a challenge, and a purpose—an empire to rebuild beyond the Earth and a world to conquer upon it—there were few of Fallows's age who didn't remember the intoxication of those times. And with the *Mayflower II* growing in the lunar sky as a symbol of it all, the dream of flying with the ship and of being a part of the crusade to secure Chiron against the Infidel became for many the ultimate ambition. The lessons of discipline and self-sacrifice that had been learned during the Lean Years served to bring the *Mayflower II* to completion two years ahead of its nearest rival, and so it came about that Bernard Fallows at the age of twenty-eight had manfully shaken his father's hand and kissed his tearful mother farewell before being blasted upward from a shuttle base in Arizona to join the lunar transporter that would bear him on the first stage of his crusade to carry the American New Order to the stars.

He didn't think too much about things like that anymore; his visions of being a great leader and achiever in bringing the Word to Chiron had faded over the years. And instead . . . what? Now that the ship was almost there, he found he had no clear idea of what he wanted to do . . . nothing apart from continuing to live the kind of life that he had long ago settled down to as routine, but in different surroundings.

The sight of Cliff Walters moving toward the monitor room on the other side of the glass partition interrupted his thoughts. A moment later the door to one side opened with a low whine and

Walters walked in. Fallows swung his chair round to face him and looked up in surprise. "Hi. You're early. Still forty minutes to go."

Walters slipped off his jacket and hung it in the closet by the door after taking a book from the inside pocket. Fallows frowned but made no comment.

"Logging on early," Walters replied. "Merrick wants to talk to you for a minute before you go off duty. He told me to tell you to stop by the BCD. You can take off now and see him on the company's time." He moved over to the console and nodded at the array of screens. "How are we doing? Lots of wild and exciting things happening?"

"Five-sub-three primary's starting to play up again, you'll be happy to hear. Low-level profile, but it's positive. We had a one-fifteen second burn on vernier two at seventeen hundred hours, which went okay. The main burn is behaving itself fine and correcting for trim as programmed. . . ." He shrugged. "That's about it."

Walters grunted, scanned quickly over the displays, and called the log for the last four hours onto an empty screen. "Looks like we're in for another stripdown on that goddamn pump," he murmured without turning his head.

"Looks like it," Fallows agreed with a sigh.

"Not worth screwing around with," Walters declared. "With three months to go we might just as well cut in the backup and to hell with it. Fix the thing after we get there, when the main drive's not running. Why lose pounds sweating in trog-suits?"

"Tell it to Merrick," Fallows said, making an effort not to show the disapproval that he felt. Talking that way betrayed a sloppy attitude toward engineering. Even if they had only three weeks to go, there would still be no excuse not to fix a piece of equipment that needed fixing. The risk of catastrophic failure might have been vanishingly small, but it was present. Good practice lay with reducing possibilities like that to zero. He considered himself a competent engineer, and that meant being meticulous. Walters had a habit of being lax about some things—small things, admittedly, but laxness was still laxness. To be ranked equally irked Fallows. "Log change of watch duty, Horace," he said to the grille on the console. "Officer Fallows standing down. Officer Walters taking over."

"Acknowledged," Horace replied.

Fallows stood up and stepped aside, and Walters eased himself into the subcenter supervisor's chair. "You're off on a forty-eight, that right?" Walters asked.

"Uh-huh."

"Any plans?"

"Not really. Jay's playing on one of the teams in the Bowl tomorrow. I'll probably go and watch that. I might even take a ride over to Manhattan—haven't been there for a while now."

"Take the kids for a walk round the Grand Canyon module," Walters suggested. "It's being resculpted again—lots of trees and rocks, with plenty of water. Should be pretty."

Fallows appeared surprised. "I thought it was closed off for another two days. Isn't the Army having an exercise in there or something?"

"They wound it up early. Anyhow, Bud told me it'll be open again tomorrow. Check it out and give it a try."

"I might just do that," Fallows said, nodding slowly. "Yeah . . . I could use being out and about for a few hours. Thanks for the tip."

"Anytime. Take care."

Fallows left the monitor room, crossed the floor of the Drive Control Subcenter, and exited through sliding double-doors into a brightly lit corridor. An elevator took him up two levels to another corridor, and minutes later he was being shown into an office that opened onto one side of the Engineering Command Deck. Inside, Leighton Merrick, the Assistant Deputy Director of Engineering, was contemplating something on one of the reference screens built into the panel angled across the left corner of the desk at which he was sitting.

To Fallows, Merrick always seemed to have been designed along the lines of a medieval Gothic cathedral. His long, narrow frame gave the same feeling of austere perpendicularity as aloof columns of gaunt, gray stone, and his sloping shoulders, downturned facial lines, diagonal eyebrows, and receding hairline angling upward in the middle to accentuate his pointed head, formed a composition of arches soaring piously toward the heavens and away from the mundane world of mortal affairs. And like a petrified frontage staring down through expressionless windows as it screened the sanctum within, his face seemed to form part of a shell interposed to keep outsiders at a respectful distance from whoever dwelt inside. Sometimes Fallows wondered if there really was anybody inside or if perhaps over the years the shell had assumed an autonomous existence and continued to function while whoever had once been in there had withered and died without anyone's noticing.

Despite having worked under him for several years, Fallows had never been able to master the art of feeling at ease in Merrick's presence. Displays of undue familiarity were hardly to be expected between echelon-six and echelon-four personnel, naturally, but even allowing for that, Fallows always found himself in acute discomfort within seconds of entering a room with Merrick in it, especially when nobody else was present. This time he wouldn't let it happen, he had resolved for the umpteenth time back in the corridor. This time he would be rational about how irrational the whole thing was and refuse to be intimidated by his own imagination. Merrick had not singled him out as any special object of his disdain. He behaved that way with everybody. It didn't mean anything.

Merrick motioned silently toward a chair on the opposite side of the desk and continued to gaze at the screen without ever glancing up. Fallows sat. After some ten seconds he began feeling uncomfortable. What had he done wrong in the last few days? Had there been something he'd forgotten? . . . or failed to report, maybe? . . . or left with loose ends dangling? He racked his brains but couldn't think of anything. Finally, unnerved, Fallow managed to stammer, "Er . . . you wanted to see me, sir."

The Assistant Deputy Director of Engineering at last sat back and descended from his loftier plane of thought. "Ah, yes, Fallows." He gestured toward the screen he had been studying. "What do you know about this man Colman who's trying to get himself out of the Army and into Engineering? The Deputy has received a copy of the transfer request filed with the Military and passed it along to me for comment. It seems that this Colman has given your name as a reference. What do you know about him?" The inclined chin and the narrowing of the Gothic eyebrows were asking silently why any self-respecting echelon-four engineering officer would associate with an infantry sergeant.

It took Fallows a moment or two to realize what had happened. Then he groaned inwardly as the circumstances came back to him.

"I, er . . . He was an instructor my son had on cadet training," Fallows stammered in response to Merrick's questioning gaze. "I met him at the end-of-course parade . . . talked to him a bit. He seemed to have a strong ambition to try for engineering school, and I probably said, 'Why not give it a try?,' or something like that. I guess maybe he remembered my name."

"Mmmm. So you don't really know anything about his experience or aptitude. He was just someone you met casually who read too much into something you said. Right?"

Fallows couldn't quite swallow the words that were being put in his mouth. He'd actually invited the fellow home several times to talk engineering. Colman had some fascinating ideas. He frowned and shook his head before he could stop himself. "Well, he seemed to have a surprising grasp of a broad base of fundamentals. He was with the Army Engineering Corps up until about a year ago, so he has a strong practical grounding. And he's studied extensively since we left Earth. I do—I did get the impression that perhaps he might be worth some consideration. But of course that's just an opinion."

"Worth considering for what? You're not saying he'd make an engineering officer, surely."

"Of course not! But one of the Tech grades maybe . . . Two or Three perhaps. Or maybe the graduate entry stream."

"Hmph." Merrick waved a hand at the screen. "Doesn't have the academics. He'd need to do at least a year with kids half his age. We're not a social rehabilitation unit, you know."

"He has successfully self-taught Eng Dip One through Five," Fallows pointed out. Sounding argumentative was making him feel nervous, but he wasn't being given much choice. "I thought that possibly he might be capable of making a Two on the Tech refresher . . ."

Merrick glared across the desk suspiciously. Evidently he wasn't getting the answers he wanted. "His Army record isn't exactly the best one could wish for, you know. Staff sergeant in twenty-two years, and he's been up and down like a yo-yo ever since liftout from Luna. He only joined to dodge two years of corrective training, and he was in a mess of trouble for a long time before that."

"Well, I—I can't pretend to know anything about that side of things, sir."

"You do now." Merrick arched his fingers in front of his face. "Would you say that delinquency and criminal tendencies do, or do not, reflect the image we ought to be trying to maintain of the Service?"

Faced with a question slanted like that, Fallows could only reply, "Well. . . no, I suppose not."

"Aha!" Merrick seemed more satisfied. "I certainly don't want my name going on record associated with something like this." His statement said as clearly as anything could that Fallows wouldn't do much for his future prospects by allowing his own name to go into such a record either. Merrick screwed his face up as if he were experiencing a sour taste. "Low-echelon rabble trying to rise above themselves. We've got to keep them in their places, you know, Fallows. That was what went wrong with the Old Order. It let them climb too high, and they took over. And what happened? They dragged it down—civilization. Do you want to see that happen again?"

"No, of course not," Fallows said, not very happily.

"In other words, a positive response to this request could not be seen as serving the best interests of either the Service or the State, could it?" Merrick concluded.

Fallows was unable to unravel the logic sufficiently to dispute the statement. Instead, he shook his head. "It doesn't sound like it, I suppose."

Merrick nodded gravely. "An officer who abets an act contrary to the best interests of the Service is being disloyal, and a citizen who acts against the interests of the State could be considered subversive, wouldn't you agree?"

"Well, that's true, but—"

"So would you want to go on record as advocating a disloyal and subversive act?" Merrick challenged.

"Definitely not. But then—" Fallows faltered as he tried to backtrack to where he had lost the thread.

"Thank you," Merrick said, pouncing on the opportunity to conclude. "I agree with and endorse your assessment. Very good, Fallows. Enjoy your leave." Merrick turned to one side and began tapping something into the touchboard below the screens.

Fallows stood awkwardly and began moving toward the door. When he was halfway there he stopped, hesitated, then turned round again. "Sir, there's just one thing I'd like—"

"That's all, Fallows," Merrick murmured without looking up. "You are dismissed."

Fallows was still brooding fifteen minutes later in the transit capsule as it sped him homeward around the *Mayflower II*'s six-mile-diameter Ring. Merrick was right, he had decided. He had been a fool. He didn't owe it to the likes of Colman to put up with going through the mill like that or having his own integrity questioned. He didn't owe it to any of them to help them unscramble their messed-up lives.

Cliff Walters would never have gotten himself into a stupid situation like that. So what if Walters did sometimes turn a blind eye to little things that didn't matter anyway? Walters was a lot smarter when it came to the things that did matter. So much for Fallows, the smartass kid shuttling up from Arizona to save the universe, who still hadn't learned how to keep his nose clean. Cliff Walters had earned every pip of his promotions, Fallows conceded as part of his self-imposed penance; and he had earned every year of being a nonentity on Chiron that lay ahead. Someday, maybe, he'd learn to listen to Jean.

❀ CHAPTER THREE ❀

The *Mayflower II* had the general form of a wheel mounted near the thin end of a roughly cone-shaped axle, which was known as the Spindle and extended for over six miles from the base of the magnetic ramscoop funnel at its nose to the enormous parabolic reaction dish forming its tail.

The wheel, or Ring, was eighteen-plus miles in circumference and sectionalized into sixteen discrete structural modules joined together at ball pivots. Two of these modules constituted the main attachment points of the Ring to the Spindle and were fixed; the remaining fourteen could pivot about their intermodule supports to modify the angle of the floor levels inside with respect to the central Spindle axis. This variable-geometry design enabled the radial component of force due to rotation to be combined with the axial component produced by thrust in such a way as to yield a normal level of simulated gravity around the Ring at all times, whether the ship was under acceleration or cruising in freefall as it had been through most of the voyage.

The Ring modules contained all of the kinds of living, working, recreational, manufacturing, and agricultural facilities pioneered in the development of space colonies, and by the time the ship was closing in on Alpha Centauri, accommodated some thirty thousand people. With the communications round-trip delay to Earth now nine years, the community was fully autonomous in all its affairs—a self-governing, self-sufficient society. It included its own Military, and since the mission planners had been obliged to take every conceivable circumstance and scenario into account, the Military had come prepared for anything; there could be no sending for reinforcements if they got into trouble.

The part of the *Mayflower II* dedicated to weaponry was the mile-long Battle Module, attached to the nose of the Spindle but capable of detaching to operate independently as a warship if the need arose, and equipped with enough firepower to have annihilated easily either side of World War II. It could launch long-range homing missiles capable of sniffing out a target at fifty thousand miles; deploy orbiters for surface bombardment with independently targeted bombs or beam weapons; send high-flying probes and submarine sensors, ground-attack aircraft, and terrain-hugging cruise missiles down into planetary atmospheres; and land its own ground forces. Among other things, it carried a lot of nuclear explosives.

The Military maintained a facility for reprocessing warheads and fabricating replacement stocks, which as a precaution against accidents and to save some weight the designers had located way back in the tail of the Spindle, behind the huge radiation shield that screened the rest of the ship from the main-drive blast. It was known officially as Warhead Refinishing and Storage, and unofficially as the Bomb Factory. Nobody worked there. Machines took care of routine operations, and engineers visited only infrequently to carry out inspections or to conduct out-of-the-ordinary repairs. Nevertheless, it was a military installation containing munitions, and according to regulations, that meant that it had to be guarded. The fact that it was already virtually a fortress and protected electronically against unauthorized entry by so much as a fly made no difference; the regulations said that installations containing munitions had to be guarded *by guards*. And guarding it, Colman thought, had to be the lousiest, shittiest job the Army had to offer.

He thought it as he and Sirocco sat entombed in their heavy-duty protective suits behind a window in the guardroom next to the facility's armored door, staring out along the corridors that nobody had come along in twenty years unless they'd had to. Behind them

PFC Driscoll was wedged into a chair, watching a movie on one of the com-panel screens with the audio switched through to his suit radio. Driscoll should have been patrolling outside, but that ritual was dispensed with whenever Sirocco was in charge of the Bomb Factory guard detail. A year or so previously, somebody in D Company had taken advantage of the fact that everyone looked the same in heavy-duty suits by feeding a video recording of some dutiful, long-forgotten sentry into the closed-circuit TV system that senior officers were in the habit of spying through from time to time, and nobody from the unit had done any patrolling since. The cameras were used instead to afford early warning of unannounced spot checks.

"You never know. The chances might be better after we reach Chiron," Sirocco said. Colman's transfer application had been turned down by Engineering. "With the population exploding like crazy, there might be all kinds of prospects. That's what you get."

"What's what I get?"

"For being a good soldier and a lousy citizen."

"Not liking killing people makes a good soldier?"

"Sure." Sirocco tossed up a gauntleted hand as if the answer were obvious. "Guys who don't like it but have to do it get mad. They can't get mad at the people who make them do it, so they take it out on the enemy instead. That's what makes them good. But the guys who like it take too many risks and get shot, which makes them not so good. It's logical."

"Army logic," Colman murmured.

"I never said it had to make sense." Sirocco brought his elbows up level with his shoulders, stretched for a few seconds, and sighed. After a short silence he cocked a curious eye in Colman's direction. "So . . . what's the latest with that cutie from Brigade?"

"Forget it."

"Not interested?"

"Dumb."

"Too bad. How come?"

"Astrology and cosmic forces. She wanted to know what sign I was born under. I told her maternity ward." Colman made a sour face. "Hell, why should I have to humor people all the time?"

Sirocco wrinkled his lip, showing a glimpse of his moustache. "You can't fool me, Steve. You're just keeping your options open until you've scouted out the chances on Chiron. Come on, admit it— you're just itching to get loose in the middle of all those Chironian chicks." The first, machine-generated Chironians were the ten thousand individuals created through the ten years following the *Kuan-yin*'s arrival, the oldest of whom would be in their late forties. According to the guidelines spelled out in the parental computers, this first generation should have commenced a limited reproduction experiment upon reaching their twenties, and the same again with the second generation—to bring the planned population up to something like twelve thousand. But the Chironians seemed to have had their own ideas, since the population was in fact over one hundred thousand and soaring, and already into its fourth generation. The possible implications were intriguing.

"I'm not that hung up about it," Colman insisted, not for the first time. "Maybe it is like some of the guys think, and maybe it's not. Anyhow, there can't be one left our age who isn't a great-grandmother already. Look at the statistics."

"Who said anything about them? Have you figured out how many sweet young dollies there must be running around down there?" Sirocco chuckled lasciviously over the intercom. "I bet Swyley has a miraculous recovery between now and when we go into orbit." Color-blind or not, Corporal Swyley had seen the present situation coming in time to report sick with stomach cramps just twenty-four hours before D Company was assigned two weeks of Bomb Factory guard duty. He was "sick" because he had reported them during his own time; reporting stomach cramps during the Army's time was diagnosed as malingering.

A call came through from Brigade, and Sirocco switched into the audio channel to take it. Colman sat back and looked around. The indicators and alarms on the console in front of him had nothing to report. Nobody was creeping about under the floor, worming their way between the structure's inner and outer skins, tampering with any doors or hatches, cutting a hole through from the booster compartments, crawling down from the accelerator level above, or climbing furtively across the outside. Nobody, it seemed, wanted any thermonuclear warheads today. He rose and moved round behind the chair. "Need to stretch my legs," he said as Sirocco glanced up behind his faceplate. "It's time to do a round anyhow." Sirocco nodded and carried on talking inside his helmet. Colman shouldered his M32 and left the guardroom.

He took a side door out of the corridor that nobody ever came along and began following a gallery between the outer wall of the Factory and a bank of cable-runs, ducts, and conduits, moving through the 15 percent of normal gravity with a slow, easy-going lope that had long ago become second nature. Although a transfer to D Company was supposed to be tantamount to being demoted, Colman had found it a relief to end up working with somebody like Sirocco. Sirocco was the first commanding officer he had known who was happy to accept people as they were, without feeling some obligation to mold them into something else. He wasn't meddling and interfering all the time. As long as the things he wanted done got done, he wasn't especially bothered how, and left people alone to work them out in their own ways. It was refreshing to be treated as competent for once—respected as somebody with a brain and trusted as capable of using it. Most of the other men in the unit felt the same way. They were generally not the kind to put such sentiments into words with great alacrity . . . but it showed.

Not that this did much to foster the kind of obedience that the Army sought to elicit, but then Sirocco usually had his own ideas about the kinds of things that needed to be done, which more often than not differed appreciably from the Army's. Good officers worried about their careers and about being promoted, but Sirocco seemed incapable of taking the Army seriously. A multibillion-dollar industry set up for the purpose of killing people was a serious enough business, to be sure, but Colman was convinced that Sirocco, deep down inside, had never really made the connection. It was a game that he enjoyed playing. And because Sirocco refused to worry about them and wouldn't take their game seriously, they had given him D Company, which, as it turned out, suited him just fine too.

Colman had reached the place where a raised catwalk joined the gallery from a door leading through a bulkhead into one of the booster-pump compartments, where tritium bred in the stern bypass reactors was concentrated to enrich the ramdrive fusion plasma before it was hurled away into space. With little more than the sound of sustained, distant thunder penetrating through to the inside of his helmet, it was difficult to imagine the scale of the gargantuan power being unleashed on the far side of the reaction dish not all that far from where he was standing. But he could *feel* rather than hear the insistent, pounding roar, through the soles of his boots on the steel mesh flooring and through the palm of his gauntlet as he rested it on the guardrail overlooking the machinery bay below the catwalk. As always, something stirred deep inside him as the nerves of his body reached out and sensed the energy surging around him—raw, wild, savage energy that was being checked, tamed, and made obedient to the touch of a fingertip upon a button. He gazed along the lines of superconducting busbars with core maintained within mere tens of degrees from absolute zero just feet from hundred-million-degree plasmas, at the accelerator casing above his head, where pieces of atoms flashed at almost the speed of light along paths controlled to within millionths of an inch, at the bundles of data cables marching away to carry details of everything that happened from microsecond to microsecond to the ever-alert control computers, and had to remind himself that it had all been constructed by men. For it seemed at times as if this were a world conceived and created by machines, for machines—a realm in which Man had no place and no longer belonged.

But Colman felt that he did belong here—among the machines. He understood them and talked their language, and they talked his. They were talking to him now in the vibrations coming through his suit. The language of the machines was plain and direct. It had no inverted logic or double meanings. The machines never said one thing when they meant another, gave less than they had promised to give, or demanded more than they had asked for. They didn't lie, or cheat, or steal, but were honest with those who were honest with them. Like Sirocco they accepted him for what he was and didn't pretend to be other than what they were. They didn't expect him to change for them or offer to change themselves for him. Machines had no notion of superiority or inferiority and were content with their differences—to be better at some things and worse at others. They could understand that and accept it. Why, Colman wondered, couldn't people?

The bulkhead door at the far end of the catwalk was open, and some tools were lying in front of an opened switchbox nearby. Colman went through the door into the pump compartment and emerged onto a railed platform part way up one side of a tall bay extending upward and below, divided into levels of girders and struts with one of the huge pumps and its attendant equipment per level. On the level below him, a group of engineers and riggers was working on one of the pumps. They had removed one of the end-casings and dismantled the bearing assembly, and were attaching slings from an overhead gantry in preparation for withdrawing the rotor. Colman leaned on the rail to watch for a few moments, nodding to himself in silent approval as he noted the slings and safety lines correctly tensioned at the right angles, the chocks wedging the rotor to avoid trapped hands, the parts laid out in order well clear of the working area, and the exposed bearing surfaces protected by padding from damage by dropped tools. He liked watching professionals.

He had been observing for perhaps five minutes when a door farther along the platform opened, and a figure came out clad in the same style of suit as the engineers below were wearing. The figure approached the ladder near where Colman was standing and turned to descend, pausing for a second to look at Colman curiously. The nametag on the breast pocket read B. FALLOWS. Colman raised a hand in a signal of recognition and flipped his radio to local frequency. "Hey, Bernard, it's me—Steve Colman. I don't know if you're heard yet, but that transfer didn't go through. Thanks for trying anyway."

The features behind the other's visor remained unsmiling. "*Mister* Fallows to you, Sergeant." The voice was icy. "I'm sorry, but I have work to do. I presume you have as well. Might I suggest that we both get on with it." With that he clasped the handrails of the ladder, stepped backward off the platform to slide gently down to the level below, and turned away to rejoin the others.

Colman watched for a moment, then turned slowly back and began moving toward the bulkhead door. He didn't feel resentful, nor particularly surprised. He'd seen it all too many times before. Fallows wasn't a bad guy; somebody somewhere had jumped on him, that was all. "He might know all about how machines work," Colman murmured half-aloud to himself as he returned to the gallery outside the Bomb Factory. "But he doesn't understand how they think."

❀ CHAPTER FOUR ❀

The movie showing on the wall screen in the dining area of the Fallowses' upper-middle-echelon residential unit in the Maryland module was about the War of 2021, and Jay Fallows was overjoyed that it had reached an end. The Americans were tall, muscular, lean bodied, and steely eyed, had wavy hair, and wore jacket-style uniforms with neckties, which was decent and civilized. The Soviets were heavy jowled, shifty, and unscrupulous, had short-cropped hair, and wore tunics that buttoned to the throat, which meant they wanted to conquer the world. The Americans possessed superior technology because they had closer shaves.

"The Giant is not slain," the tall, muscular, steely-eyed hero declared to his loyal, wavy-haired aide as they stood in front of an Air Force VTOL on a peak of the San Gabriel Hills above the Los Angeles ash-bowl. "It must sleep a while to mend its wounds now its task is done. But it will rise again, hardened and tempered from the furnace. This will not have been for naught." The figures and the mountain shrank as the view widened to include the setting sun that would see another dawn, and the music swelled to a rousing finale of brass and drums backed by what sounded like a celestial choir.

Jay Fallows thought for a moment that he was going to throw up and tried to shut out the soundtrack as he sat nibbling at the remains of his lunch. An astronomy book lay propped open on the table in front of him. Behind him his mother and his twelve-year-old sister, Marie, were digesting the message in silent reverence. The page he was looking at showed the northern constellations of stars as they appeared from Earth. They looked much as they did from the *Mayflower II*, except in the book Cassiopeia was missing a star—the Sun. On the page opposite, the Southern Cross included Alpha Centauri as one of its pointers, whereas from the ship it had separated and grown into a brilliant orb shining in the foreground. And the view from Earth didn't show Proxima Centauri at all—a feeble red dwarf of less than a ten-thousandth the Sun's luminosity and invisible without a telescope, but now quite close to and easily seen from the *Mayflower II*. Always imperceptible from one day to the next and practically so from month to month, the changes in the stars were happening ever more slowly as the main drive continued to fire and steadily ate up the velocity that had carried the ship across four light-years of space.

Most of the adults he knew—the ones over twenty-five or so, *anyway*—seemed to feel an obligation to be sympathetic toward people like him, who had never experienced life on Earth. From what he had seen he wasn't sure that he'd missed all that much. Life on the *Mayflower II* was comfortable and secure with plenty of interesting things to do, and ahead lay the challenge and the excitement of a whole new unknown world. Certainly that was something no one back on Earth could look forward to.

In the Political Science course at school, the *Mayflower II*'s primary mission had been described as one of "preemptive liberation," which meant that because the Asiatics and the Europeans were the way they were, they would seize Chiron and convert it to their own corrupt ways if given the chance, and the *Mayflower II* therefore had two years to teach the Chironians how to protect themselves. There were other, more abstract reasons why it was so important for the Chironians to be educated and enlightened, which Jay didn't fully understand, but which he accepted as being among the many mysteries that would doubtless reveal themselves in their own good time as part of the complicated business of growing up.

Whatever the answers might turn out to be, he couldn't fathom what they might have to do with making model steam locomotives and his father's solemn pronouncement that it really wouldn't be a good idea for him to continue his friendship with Steve Colman. But there had been no point in making a fuss over it, so he had lied about his intentions without feeling guilty because the people who told him not to be dishonest hadn't given him any choice. Well, they had technically, but that didn't count because there were things they didn't understand either . . . or had forgotten, maybe. But Steve would understand.

"I'm glad I wasn't alive *then*," Marie said from behind him. "I can't imagine whole cities burning. It must have been *horrible.*"

"It was," Jean agreed. "It's a lesson that we all have to remember. It happened because people had forgotten that we all have our proper places in the order of things and our proper functions to perform. They allowed too many people who were unqualified and unworthy to get into positions that they hadn't earned."

"Pay our debt, collect our due
Each one proud for what we do"

Marie recited.

"Very good," her mother said.

Little snot, Jay thought to himself and turned the page. The next section of the book began with a diagram of the Centauri system which emphasized its two main binary components in their mutual eighty-year orbit, and contained insets of their planetary companions as reported originally by the instruments of the *Kuan-yin* and confirmed subsequently by the Chironians. Beneath the main diagram were pictures of the spectra of the Sunlike Alpha G2v primary with numerous metallic lines; the cooler, K1-type-orange Beta Centauri secondary with the blue end of its continuum weakened and absorption bands of molecular radicals beginning to appear; and M5e, orange-red Proxima Centauri with heavy absorption in the violet and prominent CO, CH, and TiO bands.

"There won't be a war on Chiron, will there?" Marie asked.

"Of course not, dear. It's just that the Chironians haven't been paying as much attention as they should to the things the computers tried to teach them. They've always had machines to give them everything they want, and they think life is all one long playtime. But it's not really their fault because they're not really people like us." The conviction was widespread even though the *Mayflower II*'s presiding bishop was carrying a special ordinance from Earth decreeing that Chironians had souls. Jean realized that she had left herself open to misinterpretation and added hastily, "Well, they are people, of course. But they're not *exactly* like you because they were born without any mothers or fathers. You mustn't hate them or anything. Just remember that you're a little better than they are because you've been luckier, and you know about things they've never had a chance to learn. Even if we have to be a little bit firm with them, it will be for their own good in the end."

"You mean when the Chinese and the Europeans get here?"

"Quite. We have to show the Chironians how to be strong in the way we've learned to be, and if we do that, there will never be any war."

Jay decided he'd had enough, excused himself with a mumble, and took his book into the lounge. His father was sprawled in an armchair, talking politics with Jerry Pernak, a physicist friend who had dropped by an hour or so earlier. Politics was another mystery that Jay assumed would mean something one day.

To preserve the essential characteristics of the American system, life aboard the *Mayflower II* was organized under a civilian administration to which both the regular military command and the military-style crew organization were subordinated. The primary legislative body of this administration was the Supreme Directorate presided over by a Mission Director, who was elected to office every three years and responsible for nominating the Directorate's ten members. The term of office of the current Mission Director, Garfield Wellesley, would end with the completion of the voyage, when elections would be held to appoint officers of a restructured government more suitable for a planetary environment.

"Howard Kalens, no doubt about it," Bernard Fallows was saying. "If we've only got two years to knock the place into shape, he's just the kind of man we need. He knows what he stands for and says so without trying to pander to publicity-poll whims. And he's got the breeding for the position. You can't make a planetary governor out of any rabble, you know."

Pernak didn't seem overeager to accept the implied invitation to agree. He started to say something noncommittal, then stopped and looked up as Jay entered. "Hi, Jay. How was the movie?"

"Aw, I wasn't watching it." Jay waved vaguely with the book and returned it to its shelf. "Usual stuff."

"What are the girls still talking about in there?" Bernard asked.

"I'm not sure. I guess I couldn't have been listening that much."

"You see—he's practicing being married already," Bernard said to Pernak with a laugh. Pernak grinned momentarily. Bernard looked at his son. "Well, it's early yet Figured out what you're doing this afternoon?"

"I thought maybe I'd go over to Jersey and put in a few hours on the loco."

"Fine." Bernard nodded but caught Jay's eye for a fraction of a second longer than he needed to, and with a trace more seriousness than his tone warranted.

"How's it coming along?" Pernak asked.

"Pretty good. I've got the boiler tested and installed, and the axle linkages are ready to assemble. Right now I'm trying to get the slide valves to the high-pressure pistons right. They're tricky."

"Got far with them?" Pernak asked.

"I had to scrap one set." Jay sighed. "I guess it's back to square one on another. That's what I reckon I'll start today."

"So when are you going to show it to me?"

Jay shrugged. "Any time you like."

"You going to Jersey right now?"

"I was going to. I don't have to make it right now."

Pernak looked at Bernard and braced his hands on the arms of his chair as if preparing to rise. "Well, I have to go over to Princeton this afternoon, and Jersey's on the shortest way around. Jay and I could share a cab."

Bernard stood up. "Sure . . . don't let me keep you if you have things to do. Thanks for letting me have the cutter back." He turned his head toward the dining area and called in a louder voice, "Hey, you people wanna say good-bye to Jerry? He's leaving." Pernak and Jay waited by the door for Jean and Marie to appear.

"On your way?" Jean asked Pernak.

"Things won't do themselves. I'm stopping off at Jersey with Jay to see how his loco's coming along."

"Oh, that locomotive!" Jean looked at Jay. "Are you working on it again?"

"For a few hours maybe."

"Well, try not to make it half the night this time, won't you." And to Pernak: "Take care, Jerry. Thanks for dropping by. Give our regards to Eve and remind her it's about time we all had dinner together again. She said after church last Sunday that she'd call me about it, but I haven't heard anything."

"I'll remind her," Pernak promised. "Ready, Jay? Let's go."

Pernak had short, jet-black hair, a broad, solid frame, and rubbery features that always fascinated Jay with their seemingly endless variety of expressions. He had lectured on physics topics several times at Jay's school and had proved popular as much for his entertainment value as for his grasp of the subject matter, which he always managed to make exciting with tantalizing glimpses inside black holes, mind-bending accounts of the first few minutes of the universe, and fantastic speculation about living in twisted spacetimes with unusual geometries. On one occasion he had introduced Feynman diagrams, which represented particles as "world lines" traversing a two-dimensional domain, one axis representing space and the other time. Mathematically and theoretically a particle going forward in time was indistinguishable from its anti-particle going backward in time, and Pernak had offered the staggering conjecture that there might be just one electron in the entire universe—repeating itself over and over by going forward as an electron and backward as a positron. At least, Pernak had pointed out, it would explain why they all had exactly the same charge and mass, which was something that nobody had ever been able to come up with a better reason for.

Pernak had a surprisingly long stride for his height, and Jay had to hurry to keep up as they walked a couple of blocks through densely packed but ingeniously secluded interlocking terraces of Maryland residential units. It wasn't long before Pernak was talking about phase-changes in the laws of physics and their manifestation through the process of evolution. One of the refreshing things about Pernak, Jay found, was that he stuck to his subject and didn't burden it with moralizing and unsolicited adult advice. He had never been able to make up his mind whether Pernak was secretly a skeptic about things like that or just believed in minding his own business, but he had never found a way of leading up to the question.

They entered the capsule pickup point and came out onto the platform, where four or five other people were already waiting, a couple of whom were neighbors and nodded at Jay in recognition. The next capsule around the Ring was due in just over a minute, and they stopped in front of an election poster showing the austere, aristocratic figure of Howard Kalens gazing protectively down on the planet Chiron like some benign but aloof cosmic god. The caption read simply: PEACE AND UNITY.

"Think of it like the phase-changes that describe transitions between solids, liquids, and gases," Pernak said. "The gas laws are only valid over a certain limited range. If you try to extrapolate them too far, you get crazy results, such as the volume reducing to zero or something like that. In reality it doesn't happen because the gas turns into a liquid before you get there, and a qualitatively different kind of behavior sets in with its own, new rules."

"You're saying evolution adds up to a succession of transitions like that?"

"Yes, Jay. Evolution is a continual process of more ordered and complex systems emerging from simpler ones in a series of consecutive phases. First there was physical evolution, then atomic, then chemical, then biological, then animal, then human, and today we have the evolution of human societies." Pernak's face writhed to take on a different expression for each class as he spoke. "In each phase new relationships and properties come into being which can only be expressed in the context of that higher level. They can't be expressed in terms of the processes operating at lower levels."

Jay thought about it for a few seconds and nodded slowly. "I think I get it. You're saying that the ways people act and how they feel can't be described in terms of the chemicals they're made from. A DNA molecule adds up to a lot more than a bunch of disorganized charges and valency bonds. The way you organize it makes its own laws."

"Exactly, Jay. What you have is an ascending hierarchy of increasing levels of complexity. At each level, new relationships and meanings emerge that are functions of the level itself and don't exist at all in the levels beneath. For instance, there are twenty-six letters in the alphabet. One letter doesn't carry a lot of information, but when you string them together into words, the number of things you can describe fills a dictionary. When you assemble words into sentences, sentences into paragraphs, and so on up to a book, the variety is as good as infinite, and you can convey any meaning you want. Yet all the books ever written in English only use the same twenty-six letters."

The capsule arrived, and Jay fell silent while he digested what Pernak had said. As they climbed inside, Jay entered a code into the panel by the door to specify their destination in the Jersey module, and they sat down on an empty pair of facing seats as the capsule began to move. After a short run up to speed, it entered a tube to exit from Maryland and passed through one of the spherical intermodule housings that supported the Ring and contained the bearings and pivoting mechanisms for adjusting the module orientations to the ship's state of motion. For a brief period they were looking out through a transparent outer shell at the immensity of the Spindle, seemingly supported by a web of structural booms and tie-bars three miles above their heads, with the vastness of space extending away on either side, and then they entered the Kansas module where the scene outside changed to animal grazing enclosures, level upon level of agricultural units, fish farms, and hydroponic tanks.

"Okay, so you track it all back to the Big Bang," Jay said at last. "Then where do you go?"

"Classically, you can't go anywhere. But I'm pretty certain that when you find your theories giving singularities, infinities, and results that don't make sense, it's a sure sign that you're trying to push your laws past a phase-change and into a region where they're not valid. I think that's what we're up against."

"So where do you go?" Jay asked again.

"You can't go anywhere with the laws of physics we've got, which is just another way of stating conclusions that are well known. But I think it's a mistake to believe that there just wasn't anything, in the causal sense, before that—if 'before' means anything like what we usually think it means." Pernak sat forward and moistened his lips. "I'll give you a loose analogy. Imagine a flame. Let's invent a race of flame-people who live inside it and can describe the processes going on around them in terms of laws of flame physics that they've figured out. Okay?" Jay frowned but nodded. "Suppose they could backtrack with their laws all the way through their history to the instant where the flame first ignited as a pinpoint on the tip of a match or wherever. To them that would be the origin of their universe, wouldn't it."

"Oh, okay," Jay said. "*Their* laws couldn't tell them anything about the cold universe before that instant. Flame physics only came into existence when the flame did."

"A phase-change, evolving its own new laws," Pernak confirmed, nodding.

"And you're saying the Big Bang was something like that?"

"I'm saying it's very likely. What triggers a phase-change is a concentration of energy—energy *density*—like at the tip of a match. Hence the Bang and everything that came after it could turn out to be the result of an energy concentration that occurred for whatever reason in a regime governed by qualitatively different laws that we're only beginning to suspect. And that's what my line of research is concerned with."

Another flash of stars and they were in Idaho, one of the two fixed modules that carried the main support arms to the Spindle. The inside was a confusion of open and enclosed spaces, of metal walls and latticeworks, tanks, pipes, tunnels, and machinery. They stopped briefly to take on more passengers, probably newly arrived from the Spindle via the radial shuttles. Then the capsule moved away again. "It could open up possibilities that'll blow your mind," Pernak resumed. "Suppose, for instance, that we could get to understand those laws and create our own concentrations on a miniature scale to inject energy from . . . let's call it a hyperrealm, into our own universe—in other words make 'small bangs'—mini white holes. Think what an energy source that would be. It'd made fusion look like a firecracker." Pernak waved his hands about. "And how about this, Jay. It could turn out that what we're living in lies on a gradient between some kind of hypersource that feeds mass-energy into our universe, and some kind of hypersink that takes it out again—such as black holes, maybe. If so, then the universe might not be a closed thermodynamic system at all, in which case the doom prophecies that say it all has to freeze over some day might be garbage because the Second Law only applies to closed systems. In other words we might find we're flame people living in a match factory."

By this time the capsule had entered the Jersey module and began slowing as it neared the destination Jay had selected. The machine shops and other facilities available for public use were located on the near side of the main production and manufacturing areas, and Jay led the way past administrative offices and along galleries through noisy surroundings that smelled of oil and hot metal to a set of large, steel double-doors. A smaller side door brought them to a check-in counter topped by a glass partition behind which the attendant and a watchman were playing cribbage across a scratched and battered metal desk. The attendant stood and shuffled over when Jay and Pernak appeared, and Jay presented a school pass which entitled him to free use of the facilities. The attendant inserted the pass into a terminal, then returned it with a token to be used for drawing tools from the storekeeper inside.

"There's something for you here," the attendant noted as Jay was turning away. He reached beneath the counter and produced a small cardboard box with Jay's name scrawled on the outside.

Puzzled, Jay broke the sealing tape and opened the box to reveal a layer of foam padding and a piece of folded notepaper. Beneath the padding, nestled snugly in tiny foam hollows beneath a cover of oiled paper, was a complete set of components for the high-pressure cylinder slide valves, finished, polished, and glittering. The note read:

Jay,

I thought you might need a hand with these so I did them last night. If my hunch is right, things have probably gotten a bit difficult for you. There's no sense in upsetting people who don't mean any harm. Take it from me, he's not such a bad guy.

STEVE

Jay blinked and looked up to find Pernak watching him curiously. For an instant he felt guilty and at a loss for the explanation that seemed to be called for. "Bernard told me about it," Pernak said before Jay could offer anything. "I guess he's under a lot of pressure right now, so don't read too much into it." He stared at the box in Jay's hand. "I don't see anything—not a darn thing. Come on, Jay. Let's take a look at that loco of yours."

✸ CHAPTER FIVE ✸

Chiron was almost nine thousand miles in diameter, but its nickel-iron core was somewhat smaller than Earth's, which gave it a comparable gravitational force at the surface. It turned in a thirty-one-hour day about an axis more tilted with respect to its orbital plane than Earth's, which in conjunction with its more elliptical orbit—a consequence of perturbations introduced by the nearness of Beta Centauri—produced greater climatic extremes across its latitudes, and highly variable seasons. Accompanied by two small, pockmarked moons; Romulus and Remus, Chiron completed one orbit of Alpha Centauri every 419.66 days. Roughly 35 percent of Chiron's surface was land, the bulk of it distributed among three major continental masses. The largest of these was Terranova, a vast, east-west sprawling conglomeration of every conceivable type of geographic region, dominating the southern hemisphere and extending from beyond the pole to cross the equator at its most northerly extremity. Selene, with its jagged coastlines and numerous islands, was connected to the western part of Terranova via an isthmus that narrowed to a neck below the equator; Artemia lay farther to the east, separated by oceans.

Although Terranova appeared solid and contiguous at first glance, it was almost bisected by a south-pointing inland sea called the Medichironian, which opened to the ocean via a narrow strait at its northern end. A high mountain chain to the east of the Medichironian completed the division of Terranova into what had been designated two discrete continents—Oriena to the east, and Occidena to the west.

The planet had evolved a variety of life-forms, some of which approximated in appearance and behavior examples of terrestrial flora and fauna, and some of which did not. Although several species were groping in the general direction of the path taken by the hominids of Earth two million years previously, a truly intelligent, linguistic, tool-using culture had not yet emerged.

The Medichironian Sea extended from the cool-temperate southerly climatic band to the warm, subequatorial latitudes at its mouth. Its eastern shore lay along narrow coastal plains, open in some parts and thickly forested in others, that rapidly rose into the foothills of the Great Barrier Chain, beyond which stretched the vast plains and deserts of central Oriena. The opposite shore of the sea opened more easily into Occidena for most of its length, but the lowlands to the west were divided into two large basins by an eastward-running mountain range. An extension of this range projected into the sea as a rocky spine of fold valleys fringed by picturesque green plains, sandy bays, and rugged headlands, and was known as the Mandel Peninsula, after a well-known statesman of the 2010s. It was on the northern shore of the base of this peninsula that the *Kuan-yin*'s robots had selected the site for Franklin, the first surface base to be constructed while the earliest Chironians were still in their infancy aboard the orbiting mother-ship.

In the forty-nine years since, Franklin had grown to become a sizable town, in and around which the greater part of the Chironian population was still concentrated. Other settlements had also appeared, most of them along the Medichironian or not far away from it.

Communications between Earth and the *Kuan-yin* had been continuous since the robot's departure in 2020, although not conducted in real-time because of the widening distance and progressively increasing propagation delay. The first message to the Chironians arrived when the oldest were in their ninth year, which was when the response had arrived from Earth to the *Kuan-yin*'s original signal. Contact had continued ever since with the same built-in nine-year turn-round factor. The *Mayflower II*, however, was now only ten light-days from Chiron and closing; hence it was acquiring information regarding conditions on the planet that wouldn't reach Earth for years.

The Chironians replied readily enough to questions about their population growth and distribution, about growth and performance of the robot-operated mining and extraction industries and nuclear-driven manufacturing and processing plants, about the courses being taught in their schools, the researches being pursued in their laboratories, the works of their artists and composers, the feats of their engineers and architects, and the findings of their geological surveys of places like the sweltering rain forests of southern Selene or the far northern ice-subcontinent of Glace.

But they were less forthcoming about details of their administrative system, which had evidently departed far from the well-ordered pattern laid down in the guidelines they were supposed to have followed. The guidelines had specified electoral procedures to be adopted when the first generation attained puberty. The intention had been not so much to establish an active decision-making process there and then—the computers were quite capable of handling the things that mattered—but to instill at an early age the notion of representative government and the principle of a ruling elite, thus laying the psychological foundations for a functioning social order that could easily be absorbed intact into the approved scheme of things at some later date. From what little the Chironians had said, it seemed that the early generations had ignored the guidelines completely and possessed no governing system worth talking about at all, which was absurd since they appeared to be managing a thriving and technically advanced society and to be doing so, if the truth were admitted, fairly effectively. In other words, they had to be covering a lot of things up.

Although they came across as polite but frank in their laser transmissions, they projected a coolness that was enough to arouse suspicions. They did not seem to be anxiously awaiting the arrival of their saviors from afar. And so far they had not acknowledged the

Mission's claim to sovereignty over the colony on behalf of the
United States of the New Order.

"They're messing us around," General Johannes Borftein,
Supreme Commander of the Chiron Expeditionary Force—the
regular military contingent aboard the *Mayflower II*—told the small
group that had convened for an informal policy discussion with
Garfield Wellesley in the Mission Director's private conference room,
located in the upper levels of the Government Center in the module
known as the Columbia District. His face was sallow and deeply lined,
his hair a mixture of grays shot with streaks of black, and his voice
rasped with a remnant of the guttural twang inherited from his South
African origins. "We've got two years to get this show organized, and
they're playing games. We don't have the time. We haven't seen any
evidence of a defense program down there. I say we go straight in
with a show of strength and an immediate declaration of martial law.
It's the best way."

Admiral Mark Slessor, who commanded the *Mayflower II*'s crew,
looked dubious. "I'm not so sure it's that simple." He rubbed his
powerful, blue-shadowed chin. "We could be walking into anything.
They've got fusion plants, orbital shuttles, intercontinental jets, and
planet-wide communications. How do we know they haven't been
working on defense? They've got the know-how and the means. I can
see John's point, but his approach is too risky."

"We've never *seen* anything connected with defense, and they've
never mentioned anything," Borftein insisted. "Let's stick to reality
and the facts we know. Why complicate the issue with speculation?"

"What do you say, Howard?" Garfield Wellesley inquired, looking
at Howard Kalens, who was sitting next to Matthew Sterm, the grim-
faced and so far silent Deputy Mission Director.

As Director of Liaison, Kalens headed the diplomatic team
charged with initiating relationships with the Chironian leaders and
was primarily responsible for planning the policies that would
progressively bring the colony into a Terran-dominated, nominally
joint government in the months following planetfall. Hence the
question probably concerned him more than anybody else. Kalens

took a moment to compose his long, meticulously groomed and attired frame, with its elegant crown of flowing, silvery hair, and then replied. "I agree with John that a rigid rule needs to be asserted early on . . . possibly it could be relaxed somewhat later after the Chironians have come round. However, Mark has a point too. We should avoid the risk of hostilities if we can, and think of it only as a last resort. We're going to need those resources working *for* us, not against. And they're still very thin. We can't permit them to be frittered away or destroyed. Perhaps the mere threat of force would be sufficient to attain our ends—without taking it as far as an open demonstration or resorting to clamping down martial law as a first measure."

Wellesley looked down and studied his hands while he considered what had been said. In his sixties, he had shouldered twenty years of extraterrestrial senior responsibilities and two consecutive terms as Mission Director, Although a metallic glitter still remained in the pale eyes looking out below his thinning, sandy hair, and the lines of his hawkish features were still sharp and clear, a hint of inner weariness showed through in the hollows beginning to appear in his cheeks and neck, and in the barely detectable sag of his shoulders beneath his jacket. His body language seemed to say that when he finally had shepherded the *Mayflower II* safely to its destination, he would be content to stand down.

"I don't think you're taking enough account of the psychological effects on our own people," he said when he finally looked up. "Morale is high now that we're nearly there, and I don't want to spoil it. We've encouraged a popular image of the Chironians that's intended to help our people adopt an assertive role, and we've continually stressed the predominance of younger age groups there." He shook his head. "Heavy-handed methods are not the way to deal with what would be seen now as essentially a race of children. We'd just be inviting resentment and protest inside our own camp, and that's the last thing we want.

"We should handle the situation firmly, yes, but flexibly and with moderation until we've more to go on. Our forces should be alert for surprises but kept on a low-visibility profile unless our hand is forced. That's my formula, gentlemen—firm, low-key, but flexible."

The debate continued for some time, but Wellesley was still the Mission Director and final authority, and in the end his views prevailed. "I'll go along with you, but I have to say I'm not happy about it," Borftein said. "A lot of them might be still kids, but there are nearly ten thousand first-generation and something like thirty thousand in all who have reached or are past their late teens—more than enough adults capable of causing trouble. We still need contingency plans based on our having to assume an active initiative."

"Is that a proposal?" Wellesley asked. "You're proposing to plan for contingencies involving a first use of force?"

"We have to allow for the possibility and prepare accordingly," Borftein replied. "Yes, it is."

"I agree," Howard Kalens murmured. Wellesley looked at Slessor, who, while still showing signs of apprehension, appeared curiously to feel relieved at the same time. Wellesley nodded heavily. "Very well. Proceed on that basis, John. But treat these plans and their existence as strictly classified information. Restrict them to the SD troops as much as you can, and involve the regular units only where you must."

"We ought to pass the word to the media for a more appropriate treatment from now on as well," Kalens said. "Perhaps playing up things like Chironian stubbornness and irresponsibility would harden up the public image a bit. . . just in case. We could get them to add a mention or two of signs that the Chironians might have armed themselves and the need to take precautions. It could always be dismissed later as overzealous reporting. Should I whisper in Lewis's ear about it?"

Wellesley frowned over the suggestion for several seconds but eventually nodded. "I suppose you should, yes." Sterm watched, listened, and said nothing.

⚙ CHAPTER SIX ⚙

Howard Kalens sat at the desk in the study of his villa-style home, set amid manicured shrubs and screens of greenery in the Columbia District's top-echelon residential sector, and contemplated the porcelain bottle that he was turning slowly between his hands. It was Korean, from the thirteenth-century Koryo dynasty, and about fourteen inches high with a long neck that flowed into a bulbous body of celadon glaze delicately inlaid with *mishima* depicting a willow tree and symmetrical floral designs contained between decorative bands of a repeated foliose motif encircling the stem and base. His desk was a solid-walnut example of early nineteenth-century French rococo revival, and the chair in which he was sitting, a matching piece by the same cabinetmaker. The books aligned on the shelves behind him included first editions by Henry James, Scott Fitzgerald, and Norman Mailer; the Matisse on the wall opposite was a print from an original preserved in the *Mayflower II*'s vaults, and the lithographs beside it were by Rico Lebrun. And as Kalens's eyes feasted on the fine balance of detail and contrasts of hues, and his fingers traced the textures of the bottle's surface, he savored the feeling of a tiny fraction of a time and place that were long ago and far away coming back to life to be uniquely his for that brief, fleeting moment.

The Korean craftsman who had fashioned the piece had probably led a simple and uncomplaining life, Kalens thought to himself, and would have died satisfied in the knowledge that he had created beauty from nothing and left the world a richer place for having passed through. Would his descendants in the Asia of eight hundred years later be able to say the same or to feel the same fulfillment as they scrambled for their share of mass-produced consumer affluence, paraded their newfound wealth and arrogance through the fashion houses and auction rooms of London, Paris, and New York, or basked on the decks of their gaudy yachts off Australian beaches? Kalens very much doubted it. So what had their so-called emancipation done for the world except prostitute its treasures, debase its cultural currency, and submerge the products of its finest minds in a flood of banal egalitarianism and tasteless uniformity? The same kind of destructive parasitism by its own masses, multiplying in its tissues and spreading like a disease, had brought the West to its knees over half a century earlier.

In its natural condition a society was like an iceberg, eight-ninths submerged in crude ignorance and serving no useful purpose other than to elevate and support the worthy minority whose distillation and embodiment of all that was excellent of the race conferred privilege as a right and authority as a duty. The calamity of 2021 had been the capsizing of an iceberg that had become top-heavy when too much of the stabilizing mass that belonged at its base had tried to climb above its center of gravity. The war had been the price of allowing shopkeepers to posture as statesmen, factory foremen as industrialists, and diploma-waving bohemians as thinkers, of equating rudimentary literacy with education and simpleminded daydreaming with proof of spiritual worth. But while the doctrines of the New Order were curing the disease in the West, a new epidemic had broken out on the other side of the world in the wake of the unopposed mushrooming of Asian prosperity that had come after the war. Mankind as a whole, it seemed, would never learn.

"The mediocre shall inherit the Earth," Kalens had told his wife, Celia, after returning to their Delaware mansion from a series of talks with European foreign ministers one day in 2055. "Or else, eventually, there will be another war." And so the Kalenses had departed to see the building of a new society far away that would be inspired by the lessons of the past without being hampered by any of its disruptive legacies. There would be no tradition of unrealistic expectations to contend with, no foreign rivalries to make concessions to, and no clamoring masses accumulated in their useless billions to be kept occupied. Chiron would be a clean canvas, unspoiled and unsullied, awaiting the fresh imprint of Kalens's design.

Three obstacles now remained between Kalens and the vision that he had nurtured through the years of presiding over the kind of neo-feudal order that would epitomize his ideal social model. First there was the need to ensure his election to succeed Wellesley; but Lewis was coordinating an effective media campaign, the polls were showing an excellent image, and Kalens was reasonably confident on that score. Second was the question of the Chironians. Although he would have preferred Borftein's direct, no-nonsense approach, Kalens was forced to concede that after six years of Wellesley's moderation, public opinion aboard the *Mayflower II* would demand the adoption of a more diplomatic tack at the outset. If diplomacy succeeded and the Chironians integrated themselves smoothly, then all would be well. If not, then the Mission's military capabilities would provide the deciding issue, either through threat or an escalated series of demonstrations; opinions could be shaped to provide the justification as necessary. Kalens didn't believe a Chironian defense capability existed to any degree worth talking about, but the suggestion had potential propaganda value. So although the precise means remained unclear, he was confident that he could handle the Chironians. Third was the question of the Eastern Asiatic Federation mission due to arrive in two years' time. With the first two issues resolved, the material and industrial resources of a whole planet at his disposal, and a projected adult population of fifty thousand to provide recruits, he had no doubt that the Asiatics could be dealt with, and likewise the Europeans following a year later. And then he would be free to sever Chiron's ties to Earth completely. He hadn't confided that part of the dream to anyone, not even Celia.

But first things had to come first. It was time to begin mobilizing the potential allies he had been quietly sounding out and cultivating for the three years since the last elections. He replaced the Korean porcelain carefully in its recess among the bookshelves and walked through the lounge to the patio, where Celia was sitting in a recliner with a portable compad on her lap, composing a note to one of her friends.

The young, sophisticated wife that Howard Kalens had taken with him to Luna to join the *Mayflower II* was now in her early forties, but her face had acquired character and maturity along with the womanly look that had evolved from girlish prettiness, and her body had filled out to a voluptuousness that had lost none of its femininity. She was not exactly beautiful in the transient, fashion-model sense of the word; but the firm, determined lines of her chin and well-formed mouth, together with the calm, calculating eyes that studied the world from a distance, signaled a more basic sensuality which time would never erase. Her shoulder-length auburn hair was tied back in a ponytail, and she was wearing tan slacks with an orange silk blouse covering firm, full breasts.

She looked up as Howard came out of the house. Her expression did not change. Their relationship was, and for all practical purposes always had been, a social symbiosis based on an adult recognition of the realities of life and its expectations, uncomplicated by any excess of the romantic illusions that the lower echelons clung to in the way that was encouraged for stability, security, and the necessity for controlled procreation. Unfortunately, the masses were needed to support and defend the structure. Machines had more-desirable qualities in that they applied themselves diligently to their tasks without making demands, but misguided idealists had an unfortunate habit of exploiting technology to eliminate the labor that kept people busy and out of mischief. Too, the idealists would teach them how to think. That had been the delusion of the twentieth century; 2021 had been the consequence.

"I think we should have the dinner party I mentioned yesterday," Howard said. "Can you put together an invitation list and send it out? The end of next week might be suitable—say Friday or Saturday."

"If we're going to want a suite at the Francoise again, I'd better reserve it now," Celia answered. "Any idea how many people we're talking about?"

"Oh, not a lot, I want it to be cozy and private. Here should be fine. Probably about a dozen. There's Lewis, of course, and Gerrard. And it's about time we started bringing Borftein closer into the family."

"That man!"

"Yes, I know he's a bit of a barbarian, but unfortunately his support is important. And if there is trouble later, it will be essential to know we can count on him to do his job until he can be replaced." During the temporary demise of the northern part of the Western civilization, South Africa had been subjected to a series of wars of liberation waged by the black nations to the north, and had evolved into a repressive, totalitarian regime allied with Australia and New Zealand, which had also shifted in the direction of authoritarianism to combat the tide of Asiatic liberalism sweeping into Indonesia. Their methods had merit, but produced Borfteins as a by-product.

"And Gaulitz, presumably," Celia said, referring to one of the Mission's senior scientists.

"Oh, yes, Gaulitz definitely. I've plans for Herr Gaulitz."

"A government job?"

"A witch doctor." Kalens smiled at the frown on Celia's face. "One of the reasons America declined was that it allowed science to become too popular and too familiar, and therefore an object of contempt. Science is too potent to be entrusted to the masses. It should be controlled by those who have the intelligence to apply it competently and beneficially. Gaulitz would be a suitable figure to groom as a . . . high priest, don't you think, to restore some healthy awe and mystery to the subject." He nodded knowingly. "The Ancient Egyptians had the right idea." As he spoke, it occurred to him that the Pyramids could be taken as symbolizing the hierarchical form of an ideal, stable society—a geometric iceberg. The analogy was an interesting one. It would make a good point to bring up at the dinner party. Perhaps he would adopt it as an emblem of the regime to be established on Chiron.

"Have you made your mind up about Sterm?" Celia asked.

Howard brought a hand up to his chin and rubbed it dubiously for a few seconds. "Mmm . . . Sterm. I can't make him out. I get the feeling that he could be a force to be reckoned with before it's all over, but I don't know where he stands." He thought for a moment longer and at last shook his head. "There are some confidential matters that I'll want to bring up. Sterm could turn out to be an adversary. It wouldn't be wise to show too much of our hand this early on. You'd better leave him out of it. Later on it might change . . . but let's keep him at a distance for the time being."

◉ CHAPTER SEVEN ◉

Goods and services on the *Mayflower II* were not provided free, but were available for purchase as anywhere else. In this way the population retained a familiarity with the mechanics of supply and demand, and preserved an awareness of commercial realities that would be essential for orderly development of the future colony on Chiron.

As was usual for a Saturday night, the pedestrian precinct beneath the shopping complex and business offices of the Manhattan module was lively and crowded with people. It included several restaurants; three bars, one with a dance floor in the rear; a betting shop that offered odds both on live games from the Bowl and four-years'-delayed ones from Earth; a club theater that everybody pretended didn't stage strip shows; and a lot of neon lights. The Bowery bar, a popular haunt of off-duty regular troops, was squeezed into one corner of the precinct next to a coffee shop, behind a studded door of imitation oak and a high window of small, tinted glass panes that turned the inside lights red.

The scene inside the Bowery was busy and smoky, with a lot of uniforms and women visible among the crowd lining the long bar on the left side of the large room inside the door, and a four-piece combo playing around the corner in the smaller room at the back. Colman and some of D Company were sitting at one of the tables standing in a double row along the wall opposite the bar. Sirocco had joined them despite the regulation against officers' fraternizing with enlisted men, and Corporal Swyley was up and about again after the dietitian at the Brigade sick bay had enforced a standing order to put Swyley on spinach and fish whenever he was admitted. Bret Hanlon, the sergeant in charge of Second Platoon and a long-standing buddy of Colman, was sitting on the other side of Sirocco with Stanislau, Third Platoon's laser gunner, and a couple of civilian girls; a signals specialist called Anita, attached to Brigade H.Q. was snuggling close to Colman with her arm draped loosely through his.

Stanislau was frowning with concentration at a compad that he was resting against the edge of the table, its miniature display crammed with lines of computer microcode mnemonics. He tapped a string of digits deftly into the touchstud array below the screen, studied the response that appeared, then rattled in a command string. A number appeared low down in a corner. Stanislau looked up triumphantly at Sirocco. "3.141592653," he announced. "It's *pi* to ten places." Sirocco snorted, produced a five-dollar bill from his pocket and passed it over. The bet had been that Stanislau could crash the databank security system and retrieve an item that Sirocco had stored half an hour previously in the public sector under a personal access key.

"How about that?" Hanlon shouted delightedly. "The guy did it!"

"Don't forget—a round of beers too," Colman reminded Sirocco. The girls whooped their approval.

"Where did you learn that, Stan?" Paula, one of the civilian girls, asked. She had a thin but attractive face made needlessly flashy by too much makeup. Her clothes were tight and provocative.

Stanislau slipped the compad into his pocket. "You don't wanna know about that," he said. "It's not very respectable."

"Come on, Stan. Give," Terry, Paula's companion, insisted. Colman gave Stanislau a challenging look that left him no way out.

Stanislau took a long draught from his glass and made a what-the-hell? gesture. "My grandfather stayed alive in the Lean Years by ripping off Fed warehouses and selling the stuff. He could bomb any security routine ever dreamed up. My dad got a job with the

Emergency Welfare Office, and between them they wrote two sisters and a brother that I never had into the system and collected the benefits. So life wasn't too bad." He shrugged, almost apologetically. "I guess it got to be kind of a tradition . . . sort of handed down in the family."

"A real pro burglar!" Terry exclaimed.

"You son-of-a-gun." Hanlon said admiringly.

"Son-of-a-something, anyway," Anita added. They all laughed.

Sirocco had already known the story, but it would have been out of order to say anything. Stanislau's transfer to D Company had followed an investigation of the mysterious disappearance from Brigade stores of tools and electrical spares that had subsequently appeared on sale in the Home Entertainment department of one of the shopping marts.

Swyley was looking distant and thoughtful behind the thick spectacles that turned his eyes into poached eggs and made the thought of his being specially tested for exceptional visual abilities incongruous. He was wondering how useful Stanislau's nefarious skills might be for inserting a few plus-points into his own record in the Military's administrative computer, but couldn't really say anything about the idea in Sirocco's presence. There was such a thing as being too presumptuous. He would talk to Stanislau privately, he decided.

"Where's Tony Driscoll tonight?" Paula asked, straightening up in her chair to scan the bar. "I don't see him around anywhere."

"Don't bother looking," Colman said. "He's got the late duty."

"Don't you ever give these guys a break?" Terry asked Sirocco.

"Somebody has to run the Army. It's just his turn. He's as qualified to do it as anyone else."

"Well what do you know—I'm on the loose tonight," Paula said, giving Hanlon a cozy look.

Bret Hanlon held up a hand protectively. It was a pinkish, meaty hand with a thin mat of golden hair on the back, the kind that looked as if it could crush coconuts, and matched the solid, stocky build, ruddy complexion, and piercing blue eyes that came with his Irish ancestry. "Don't look at me," he said. "I'm contracted now, all nice and respectable. *That's* the fella you should be making eyes at." He nodded toward Colman and grinned mischievously.

"Do him good too," Sirocco declared. "Then they might make him an engineer. But you'll have a hard time. He's holding out till he's found out what the talent's like on Chiron."

"I didn't know you had a thing about little girls, Steve," Anita teased. "You don't look the type." Hanlon roared and slapped his thigh.

"I've got two sisters you can't get in trouble with," Stanislau offered.

"You got it wrong,"' Colman told them. "It's not the little ones at all." He widened his eyes in a parody of lewd anticipation and grinned. "Think of all those *grandmothers.*" Terry and Paula laughed.

Although Colman was going along with the mood and making a joke out of it, inside he felt a twinge of irritation. He wasn't sure why. Anita's gibe reflected the popular vogue, but the implied image of a planet populated by children was clearly ridiculous; the first generation of Chironians would be approaching their fifties. He didn't like foolish words going into people's heads and coming out again without any thought about their meaning having transpired in between. Anita was an attractive girl, and not stupid. She didn't have to do things like that. Then it occurred to him that perhaps he was being too solemn. Hadn't he just done the same thing?

"Some grandmothers!" Terry exclaimed. "Did anybody see the news today? Some scientist or other thinks the Chironians could be building bombs. There was an interview with Kalens too. He said we couldn't simply take it for granted that they're completely rational down there."

"You're not suggesting there'll be a fight, are you?" Paula said.

"I didn't say that. But they're funny people . . . cagey. They're not exactly giving straight answers about everything."

"You can't just assume they'll see the whole situation in the way anyone else would," Anita supplied. "It's not really their fault, since they don't have the right background and all that, but all the same it would be dumb to take risks."

"It makes sense, I guess," Paula agreed absently.

"Do you figure they might start trouble, chief?" Stanislau asked, turning his head toward Sirocco.

Sirocco shrugged noncommittally. "Can't say. I wouldn't worry too much about it. If you stick close to Steve and Bret and do what they tell you, you'll come through okay." Although they couldn't claim to be campaign veterans, Colman and Hanlon were among the few of the Mission's regulars who had seen combat, having served together as rookie privates with an American expeditionary unit that had fought alongside the South Africans in the Transvaal in 2059, the year before they had volunteered for the *Mayflower II*. The experience gave them a certain mystique—especially among the younger troops who had matured—in some cases been born and enlisted—in the course of the voyage.

"I think it will be all right if Kalens gets elected," Terry told them. "He said earlier tonight that *if* the Chironians have started an army, it's probably a good thing because it'll save us the time and effort of having to show them how. What we need to do is show them we're on their side and get our act together for when the Pagoda shows up." The EAF starship was designed differently from the *Mayflower II*. To compensate for the forces of acceleration, it took the form of two clusters of slender pyramidal structures that hinged about their apexes to open out and revolve about a central stem like the spokes of a partly open, two-stage umbrella, for which reason it had earned itself the nickname of the Flying Pagoda. Terry sipped her drink and looked around the table. "The guy's got it figured realistically. You see, there's no need for a fight. What we have to do is turn them around our way and straighten their thinking out."

"But that doesn't mean we have to take chances," Anita pointed out.

"Oh, sure . . . I'm just saying there doesn't have to be anything to get scared about."

Colman was becoming irritated again. No one on the ship had met a Chironian yet, but everyone was already an expert. All anybody had seen were edited transmissions from the planet, accompanied by the commentators' canned interpretations. Why couldn't people realize when they were being told what to think? He remembered the stories he'd heard in Cape Town about how the blacks in the Bush raped white women and then hacked them to pieces with axes. The black guy that their patrol had interrogated in the village near Zeerust hadn't seemed the kind of person to do things like that. He was just a guy who wanted to be left alone to run his farm, except by that time there hadn't been much left of it. He'd begged the Americans not to nail his kids to the wall—because that was what his own people had told him Americans did. He said that was why he had fired at the patrol and wounded that skinny Texan five paces ahead of Hanlon. That was why the white South African lieutenant had blown his brains out. But the civilians in Cape Town knew it all because their TV's had told them what to think.

Corporal Swyley wasn't saying anything, which was significant because Swyley was usually a pretty good judge of what was what. His silence meant that he didn't agree with what was being said. When Swyley agreed with something, he said he didn't agree. When he really didn't agree, he said nothing. He never said he agreed with anything. When he had decided that he felt fine after the dietitian discovered the standing order for spinach and fish, the Medical Officer hadn't been able to accuse him of faking anything because Swyley had never agreed with anybody that he was sick; all he'd said was that he had stomach cramps. The M.O. had diagnosed that anybody with stomach cramps on his own time had to be sick. Swyley hadn't. In fact, Swyley had disagreed, which should have been obvious because he hadn't said anything.

"Well, I think there's something to be scared about," Paula said. "Suppose they turn out to be really mean and don't want to mess around with talking at all. Suppose they send a missile up at us without any warning or anything . . . I mean, we'd be stuck out in space like a sitting duck, wouldn't we. Then where would we be?"

Sirocco gave a short laugh. "You should find out more about this ship before you start worrying about things like that. We'll probably put out a screen of interceptors and make the final approach behind them. They'll stop anything before it gets within ten thousand miles. You have to give the company some credit."

Hanlon made a throwing-away motion in the air. "Ah, this is all getting to be too serious for a Saturday night. Why are we talking like this at all? Are we letting silly rumors get to us?" He looked at Sirocco. "Our glasses are nearly empty, Your Honor. A round was part of the bet."

Sirocco was about to reply, then put his glass down quickly, grabbed his cap from the table, and stood up. "Time I wasn't here," he muttered. "I'll be up in Rockefeller's if anyone wants to join me there." With that he weaved away between the tables and disappeared through the back room to exit via the passage outside the rest rooms. "What in hell's come over him?" Hanlon asked, nonplussed. "Aren't they paying captains well these days?"

"SDs," Swyley murmured, without moving his mouth. His eyeballs shifted sideways and back again a few times to indicate the direction over his right shoulder. A more restrained note crept into the place, and the atmosphere took on a subtle tension.

Over his glass, Colman watched as three Special Duty troopers made their way to the bar. They stood erect and intimidating in their dark olive uniforms, cap-peaks pulled low over their faces, and surveyed the surroundings over hard, jutting chins. Nobody met their stares for long before looking away. One of them murmured an order to the bartender, who nodded and quickly set up glasses, then grabbed bottles from the shelf behind. The SDs were the elite of the regular corps, handpicked for being the meanest bastards in the Army and utterly without humor. They reminded Colman of the commando units he had seen in the Transvaal. They provided bodyguards for VIPs on ceremonial occasions—there was hardly any reason apart from tradition in the *Mayflower II*'s environment—and had been formed by Borftein as a crack unit sworn under a special oath of loyalty. Their commanding officer was a general named Stormbel. B Company made jokes about their clockwork precision on parades and the invisible strings that Stormbel used to jerk them around, but not while any of them were within earshot. They called the SDs the Stromboli Division.

"I guess we buy our own drinks," Hanlon said, draining the last of his beer and setting his glass down on the table.

"Looks like it," Stanislau agreed.

"I got the last one," Colman reminded them. Somehow the enthusiasm had gone out of the party.

"Ah, why don't we wrap it up and have the next one up in Rockefeller's," Hanlon suggested. "That was where Sirocco said he was going."

"Great idea," Colman said and stood up. Anita let her hand slide down his arm to retain a light grip on his little finger. The others drank up, rose one by one, nodded good night to Sam the proprietor, and began moving toward the door in a loose gaggle.

Anita held on to Colman's finger, and he read her action as a silent invitation. He had slept with her a few times, many months ago now, and enjoyed it. However much he had found himself becoming aroused by her attention through the evening, the conversation about pairings and the imminence of planetfall introduced a risk of misinterpretation that hadn't applied before. Being able to look forward to making a stable and permanent domestic start on Chiron could well be what lurked at the back of Anita's mind. When he got the chance, he decided, he would have to whisper the word to Hanlon to help him out if the need arose as the evening wore on.

The precinct outside was full of people wasting the evening while trying to figure out what to do with it, when Colman and Anita emerged from the Bowery and turned to follow the others, who were already some distance ahead. Anita stopped to fish for something in her pocketbook, and Colman slowed to a halt to wait. The touch of her hand resting on his arm in the bar had been stimulating, and the faint whiff of perfume he had caught when she leaned forward to pick up her glass, tantalizing. What the hell? he thought. She's not a kid. A guy needed a break now and again after twenty years of being cooped up in a spaceship. He turned back to find her holding a phial of capsules. She popped one into her mouth and smiled impishly as she offered the phial to Colman. "It's Saturday, why not live it up a little?" He scowled and shook his head. Anita pouted. "They're good. Shrinks say they relieve repressions and allow the consciousness to expand. We should get to know ourselves."

"I've talked to shrinks. They're all crazy. How do they know whether I know me or not? Do you know how your head works inside?" Anita shook it in a way that said she didn't care all that much either. Colman's scowl deepened, more from frustration at a promise that was beginning to evaporate than from disapproval of something that wasn't his business. "Then how do you expect a pill to figure it out?"

"You should try to find yourself, Steve. It's healthy."

"I never lost myself."

"Zangreni needs stimulants to catalyze her psychic currents. That's how she makes predictions."

"For Christ's sake, that's TV fiction. She doesn't exist. It's not real life. There isn't anything like that in real life."

"Who cares? It's more fun. Why be a drag?" Colman looked away in exasperation. She could have been a unique, thinking person. Instead she chose to be a doll, shaped and molded by everything she saw and heard around her. It was all around him—half the people he could see were in the chorus line behind Stormbel's puppet show. They could be told what to think because they didn't want to think. Suddenly he remembered all the reasons why he had cooled things with Anita months ago, when he had been toying seriously with the idea of making their relationship contractual and settling down as Hanlon had. He had tried to tune into her wavelength and found nothing but static. But what had infuriated him more was that her attitude had been unnecessary—she had a head but wouldn't use it.

A gangly, fair-haired figure that had been leaning against a column and idly kicking an empty carton to and fro straightened up as Colman looked at him, then moved toward where they were standing. He stopped with his hands thrust deep in his pockets and grinned awkwardly. Colman stared at the boy in surprise. It was Jay Fallows. "What the hell are you doing here?"

"Oh, I figured you'd be around here somewhere."

"Is this the guy who makes trains?" Anita asked.

"Yeah. This is Jay. He's okay . . . and smart."

"Smart . . . brains." A faraway look was coming into Anita's eyes. "Brains and trains. I like it. It's lyrical. Don't you think it's lyrical?" She smiled at Jay and winked saucily. "Hi, Jay." The pill was mixing with the drinks and getting to her already. Jay grinned but looked uncomfortable.

"Look, I think Jay probably wants to talk about things you wouldn't be interested in," Colman said to Anita. "Why don't you go on after the others. I'll catch up later."

"You don't want me around?"

Colman sighed. "It's not anything like that. It's just—"

Anita waved a hand in front of her face. "It's okay. You don't want me around . . . you don't want me around. It's okay." Her voice was starting to rise and fall singsong fashion. "Who says I need anybody to have a good time, anyhow? I'm fine, see. It's okay. . . . You and Jay can go talk about brains and trains." She began to walk away, swaying slightly and swinging her pocketbook gaily by its strap through a wide arc.

"Look, I-I didn't mean to bust into anything," Jay stammered. "I mean, if you and her are . . ."

Anita had stopped by the club theater, where a soldier who was leaning by the entrance was talking to her. She slipped an arm through his and laughed something in reply. "About as much as that." Colman said, nodding his head. "Forget it. Maybe you did me a favor." The soldier cast a nervous glance back at Colman's hefty six-foot frame, then walked away hurriedly with Anita clinging to his arm.

Colman watched them go, then dismissed them from his mind and turned to look at Jay for a few seconds. "Can't figure life out, huh?" he said gruffly. It saved a lot of pointless questions.

Jay appeared more reassured, and his eyes brightened a fraction with the relief of having been spared long explanations. "It's all screwed up," he replied simply.

"Would you feel better if I said I haven't figured it out yet either?"

Jay shook his head. "It'd just mean we've got the same problem. It wouldn't solve anything."

"I didn't think it would, so I won't say it."

"So does that mean you've got it figured?" Jay asked.

"Would it make any difference to your problem if I had?"

"No. It'd be your solution, not mine."

"Then that's the answer."

Jay nodded, straightened his arms into his pockets with his shoulders bunched high near his ears, held the posture for a few seconds, and then relaxed abruptly with a sigh. "Can I ask you something?" he said, looking up.

"Do I have to answer it?"

"Not if you don't want to, I guess."

"Go ahead."

"Why is it the way it is? How does what you and I do in Jersey have anything to do with my dad's job? It doesn't make any sense."

"Did you ask him about it?"

"Uh-huh."

"And?"

Jay squinted into the distance and scratched his head. "Pretty much what I expected. Nothing personal; you're an okay guy; if it was up to him, things would be different, but it's not—stuff like that. But he was only saying that so as not to sound mean—I could tell. It goes deeper than that. It's not a case of it being up to him or not. He really believes in it. How do people get like that?"

Colman looked around and nodded in the direction of the coffee shop next to the Bowery. "Let's not stand around here all night," he said. "Come on inside. Could you use a coffee?"

"Sure . . . thanks." They began walking toward the door. "And thanks for the valves," Jay said. "They fit perfectly."

"How's it coming along?"

"Pretty good. The axle assembly's finished. You'll have to come and take a look."

"I sure will."

Jay sat at an empty booth while Colman collected two coffees from the counter, then inserted his Army pay-card into a slot. In a lot of ways Jay reminded Colman of himself when he was a lot younger. Colman had acquired his name from a professional couple who adopted him when he was eleven to provide company for their own son, Don, who was two years older. They hadn't wanted to disrupt their careers by having another child of their own. Colman's stepfather was a thermodynamics engineer involved with heat exchangers in magnetohydrodynamic systems, which accounted for Colman's early interest in technology. Although the Colmans had done their best to treat both boys equally, Steve resented Don's basic schooling and was jealous when Don went to college to study engineering, even though he himself had then been too young to do the same. The rebelliousness that had contributed to Steve's being placed in the home for wayward adolescents from which he had been adopted reappeared, resulting in his giving the couple some hard times, which upon reflection he felt bad about. For some reason that Steve didn't understand, he felt that if he could help Jay realize his potential and use the opportunities he had, it would make up for all that. Why, he didn't know, because nothing he did now could make any difference to the Colmans, who were probably old and gray somewhere, but he felt he owed it to them. People's minds worked like that. Minds could be very strange.

He set the coffees down and slid into the seat opposite Jay. "Ever been thirsty?" he asked as he stirred sugar into his cup.

Jay looked surprised. "Why . . . sure. I guess so. Hasn't everybody?"

"Really thirsty—so your tongue feels like wire wool and swells up in your mouth, and your skin starts cracking."

"Well. . . no. Why?"

"I have. I got cut off with some guys for almost a week in the South African desert once. All you think about is water. You can't describe the craving. You'd cut off your arm for a cup." He paused, and Jay waited with a puzzled expression on his face. "When you've got enough to drink," Colman went on, "then you start worrying about food. That takes longer to build up, but it gets as bad. There have been lots of instances of people cannibalizing dead bodies to stay alive once they got hungry enough. They've killed each other over potato peels."

"So-o-o-o?"

"When you've got enough to eat and drink, then you worry about keeping warm. And when you're warm enough, you start thinking about staying safe." Colman opened his hands briefly. "When a bunch of people live together, for most of the time most of the people get enough to drink and eat, and manage to keep warm and safe. What do you think they start worrying about then?"

Jay frowned and looked mildly uncomfortable. "Sex?" he hazarded.

Colman grinned. "You're right, but you're supposed to pretend you don't know about that. I was thinking of something else— recognition. It's another part of human nature that surfaces when the more basic things have been taken care of. And when it does, it gets to be just as powerful as the rest. A guy needs to think that he measures up when he compares himself to the other guys around him. He needs to be recognized for what's good about him and to stand out. Like you said, it's probably sex, because he thinks the girls are taking notice, but whatever the reason, it's real."

Jay was beginning to see the connection. "Measures up with respect to what?" he asked. "What's the standard?"

"It doesn't matter," Colman told him. "It's different in different places. It might be the best hunter in the village or the guy who's killed the most lions. It might be the way you paint your face. Through most of history it's been money. What you buy with it isn't important. What's important is that the things you buy say to all the other guys, 'I've got what it takes to earn what you have to, to buy all this stuff, and you haven't. Therefore I'm better than you.' That's what it's all about."

"Why's it so important to be better than somebody?"

"I told you, it's an instinct. You can't fight it. It's like being thirsty."

"Am I supposed to feel that way?"

"You do. Don't you like it when your team wins in the Bowl? Why do you work hard at school? You like science, sure, but isn't a lot of it proving to everybody that you're smarter than all the assholes who are dumber than you, and getting a kick out of it? Be honest. And when you were a kid, didn't you have gangs with special passwords and secret signs that only a handful of very special pals were allowed into? I bet you did."

Jay nodded and smiled. "You're right. We did."

"We all did. And it doesn't change when you get older. It gets worse. Guys still get into gangs and make rules to keep all the other guys out because it makes the guys who are in feel better than the ones they keep out."

"But the rules are so dumb," Jay protested. "They don't make sense. Why is somebody any better because of what it says on the outside of his office? It's what he does inside that matters."

"They don't have to make sense. All they have to do is say you're different. Now do you get it? Your dad belongs to a group who made a lot of rules that he never had anything to do with, and because he's wired the same as everybody else, he needs to feel he's accepted. To be accepted, he has to be seen to go by the rules. If he didn't he'd become a threat to the group, and they'd reject him. And nobody can take that. Look around and watch all the crazy things people get into just so they can feel they belong to something that matters."

"Even you?"

"Sure. What could be crazier than the Army?"

"You're not crazy," Jay said. "So what made you join?"

"It was a group, just like I've been saying—something to belong to. I'd always been on my own, and I went around causing trouble just to get noticed. People are like that. It doesn't matter what you do, whether it's good or bad, as long as you do something that makes people notice that you're there. Nothing's worse than not making any difference to anything." Colman shrugged. "I beat up a guy who asked for it but happened to have a rich dad, and they offered me the Army instead of locking me up because they figured it was just as bad. I jumped at it."

Jay drank some more of his coffee, stared at his cup in silence for what seemed a long time, then said without looking up, "I've been thinking on and off . . . you know, I think I'd like to get into the Army. What would be the best way of going about it?"

Colman stared hard at him for a few seconds. "What do you think you'd get out of it?" he asked.

"Oh, I dunno—some of the things you said, maybe."

"Get away from being caged in at home, be your real self, break out of the straitjacket, and all the rest, huh?"

"Maybe."

Colman nodded to himself and wiped his mouth with a napkin from the dispenser on the table while he tried to form the right answer. He was stuck in the Army but wanted to become a professional engineer; Jay could walk into being an engineer but thought he wanted to be in the Army. There would be no point in being scornful and listing all the reasons why it might not be such a good idea—Jay knew all those and didn't want to hear about it.

Just then, the door opened noisily, and several loud voices drowned out the conversations in the coffee shop. Colman recognized three faces from B Company, Padawski—a tall, wiry sergeant with harsh, thin lips and hard, black eyes set in a long, swarthy face—and two corporals whose names didn't come immediately to mind. They had been drinking, and Padawski could be mean at the best of times. Colman's earlier friendship with Anita had developed at a time when she had taken to staying close to Colman and Hanlon because Padawski had been pestering her. Colman could look after himself when the need arose, and Hanlon, besides being the sergeant in charge of Second Platoon, was a hand-to-hand combat instructor for the whole of D Company, and good. The combination had proved an effective deterrent, and Padawski had nursed a personal grudge ever since.

"Who are they?" Jay asked as he sensed Colman's tensing up.

"Bad news," Colman hissed through his teeth. "Just keep talking. Don't look round."

"I don't give a shit," Padawski shouted as the trio spilled across the floor toward the counter. "I don't give a goddamn shit, I tell ya. If that asshole wants to—" His voice broke off suddenly. "Say, who've we got over here? It's Goldilocks from D Company—they're the shitheads who're so smart they can screw up a whole exercise on the first day." Colman felt the floor vibrate as heavy footfalls approached the booth. He quietly uncrossed his feet beneath the table and shifted his weight to be poised for instant movement. His fingers curled more snugly around the half-full cup of hot coffee. He looked up to find Padawski leering down from about three feet away.

"This is private," he murmured in a voice that was low but menacing. "Beat it."

"Hey, guys, Goldilocks has got a new girlfriend! Take a look. Is there something you wanna tell us, Colman? I've always had my doubts about you." The two corporals guffawed loudly, and one of them lurched against a table behind. The man sitting at it excused himself and left hurriedly. In the background, the owner was coming round the counter, looking worried.

Jay had turned pale and was sitting motionless. Colman's eyes blazed up at Padawski. Padawski's leer broadened. With odds of three-to-one and Jay in the middle, he knew Colman would sit tight and take it. Padawski peered more closely at Jay and blew a stream of beery breath across the table.

"Hey, kid, how do you like—"

"Cut it," Colman grated. "You leave him out of it. If it's me you want, I'll take the three of you, but some other place. He's got nothing to do with this."

The owner bustled forward, twisting a cloth nervously in his hands. "Look, I don't want any trouble. I just wanna sell food to the people, okay? They don't want no trouble either. Now why don't—"

"Oh, so it's trouble them fellas is looking for, is it?" a voice with just a hint of an Irish brogue asked softly from the doorway. Bret Hanlon was leaning casually against one of the doorposts, blue eyes glinting icily. His huge shoulders seeming almost to reach the other side of the door. He looked completely relaxed and at ease, but Colman registered his weight carried well forward on the balls of his feet and his fingers flexing inconspicuously down by his hip. The two corporals glanced at each other apprehensively. Hanlon's appearance altered the odds a bit. Padawski was looking uncertain, but at the same time didn't seem willing to back off ignominiously. For a few seconds that dragged like minutes, the charge in the room crackled at flashpoint. Nobody moved.

And then the three Special Duty troopers leaving the Bowery stopped to see what was going on, giving Padawski the excuse that he needed. "Let's get out of here," he said. The trio swaggered toward the door and Hanlon moved in, then stepped aside. Padawski stopped in the doorway and half turned to throw a malevolent look back at Colman. "Some other time. Next time you won't be so lucky."

They left. Outside, the three SD troopers turned away and moved slowly off.

Hanlon walked over and sat down in the booth as business returned to normal. "They knew you were here, Steve. I heard them talking in the back of Rockefeller's. So I thought I'd come back down and hang around."

"I've always said you've got a good sense of timing, Bret."

"So, is this fine young fella the Jay you were telling me about?" Hanlon asked.

"That's Jay. Jay, this is Bret—Bret Hanlon. He runs one of the other platoons and teaches unarmed combat. Don't mess with him."

"Was that why those guys took off?" Jay asked, by now having regained most of his color.

"It probably had something to do with it," Colman said, grinning. "That's the kind of trash you have to deal with. Still interested?"

"I guess I'll have to think about it," Jay conceded.

Hanlon ordered three hamburger dinners, and the two sergeants spent a half hour talking with Jay about Army life, football, and how Stanislau could crash the protected sector of the public databank. Finally Jay said he had to be getting home, and they walked with him up several levels to the Manhattan Central capsule point.

"Shall we be getting back to the party then?" Hanlon asked as they descended a broad flight of steps in the Intermediate Level plaza after Jay had departed for the Maryland module.

Colman slowed and rubbed his chin. He wasn't in the mood. "You go on, Bret," he said. "I think I'm just gonna wander around. I guess I'd rather be on my own for a while."

Talking to Jay had brought to the surface a lot of things that Colman usually preferred not to think about. Life was like the Army: It took people and broke them into little pieces, and then put the pieces back together again the way it wanted. Except it did it with their minds. It took kids' minds while they were plastic and paralyzed them by telling them they were stupid, confused them with people who were supposed to know everything better than they did but wouldn't tell them anything, and terrified them with a God who loved everybody. Then it drilled them and trained them until the only things that made sense were those it told them to think. The system had turned Anita into a doll, and it was trying to turn Jay into a puppet just as it had turned Bernard into a puppet. It turned people into recording machines that words went into and came out of again and made them think they knew everything about a planetful of people they'd never seen, just as it blew black guys' brains out because they wanted to run their farms and didn't want their kids nailed to walls, and then told the civilians in Cape Town it was okay. And what had it done to Colman? He didn't know because he didn't know how else it might have been.

"Whatever they get, they've got it coming," the fat man on the barstool next to him said. "Kids running around wild, breeding like rabbits—It's disgusting. And making bombs! Savages is what they are—no better than the Chinese. Kalens has got the right idea. He'll teach 'em some decency and respect." Colman drank up and left.

Jesus, he thought, he was sick of the system. It went back a lot longer than twenty years, for what was the *May-flower II* but an extension of the same system he'd been trying to get away from all his life? Jay was beginning to feel the trap closing around him already. And none of it was going to change—ever. Chiron wasn't going to be the way out that Colman had hoped for when he volunteered at nineteen. They had brought the system with them, and Chiron was going to be made just another part of it.

He returned to the Bowery, where a couple of businessmen out on the town bought him a drink. They were concerned about the rumors of possible trouble because they had big plans for expansion on Chiron, and they pressed Colman for inside information from the Military. Colman said he didn't have any. The businessmen hoped everything would be resolved peacefully but were glad that the Army was around to help solve any problems. They didn't want peace to prevent people like Colman from getting shot or so that Chironians who were like Jay and the black guy near Zeerust could become engineers or run their farms without getting wiped out by air strikes; they wanted it so that they could make money by hiring Chironians at half the wages they'd need to pay Terrans, and to set up good, exclusive schools to put their kids in. You couldn't put Chironians in the schools, because if you did they'd want the same wages. And in any case they'd never be able to afford it. The Chironians weren't really people, after all.

"What does a Chironian computer print when you attempt illegal access?" one of them asked Colman when they had got into their joke repertoires.

"What?"

"HELP! RAPE! Ha-ha, hah-hah!"

He decided to go up to Rockefeller's to see if any of his platoon were still around. On the way his pace slowed abruptly. Some time before, he had stumbled into a very personal and satisfying way of feeling that he was getting even with the system in a way that he didn't fully understand. Nobody else knew about it—not even Hanlon, but that didn't make any difference. He hadn't seen her for a while now, and he was in just the right mood.

To avoid using a compad in not-too-private surroundings, he went to a public booth in the lobby at Rockefeller's to call the number programmed to accept calls only if she was alone. While Colman waited for a response, his mind flashed back six months. He had been standing stiffly at attention in dress uniform alongside a display of a remote-fire artillery control post that was part of the Army's contribution to the Fourth of July celebrations, when she wandered away from a group of VIPs sipping cocktails and stood beside him to gaze admiringly at the screens carrying simulated battlefield displays. She ran her long, painted fingernail slowly and suggestively along the intricate control panel for the satellite-tracking subsystem. "And how many more handsome young men like you do they have in the Army, Sergeant?" she murmured at the displays before her.

"Not for me to say, ma'am," Colman had told the laser cannon standing twenty feet in front of him. "I'm not an expert on handsome men."

"An expert on ladies in need of stimulating entertainment, perhaps?"

"That depends, ma'am. They can lead to a heap of trouble."

"Very wise, Sergeant. But then, some of them can be very discreet.

Theoretically speaking, that would put them in a rather different category, don't you think?"

"Theoretically, I guess, yes, it would," Colman had agreed.

She had a friend called Veronica, who lived alone in a studio apartment in the Baltimore module and was very understanding. Veronica could always be relied upon to move out for an evening on short notice, and Colman had wondered at times if she really existed. Acquiring exclusive access to a studio wouldn't have been all that difficult for a VIP's wife, even with the accommodation limitations of the *Mayflower II*. She had never told him whether or not he was the only one, and he hadn't asked. It was that kind of a relationship.

The screen before him suddenly came to life to show her face. A flicker of surprise danced in her eyes for the merest fraction of a second, and then gave way to a smoldering twinkle of anticipation mixed with a dash of amusement, "Well, hello, Sergeant," she said huskily. "I was beginning to wonder if I had a deserter. Now, I wonder what could be on your mind at this time of night."

"It depends. What's the situation, company-wise?"

"Oh, very boring for a Saturday night."

"He's not—"

"Wining, dining, and conspiring—no doubt until the early hours."

Colman hesitated for a split second to let the question ask itself. "So . . . ?"

"Well now, I'm sure Veronica could be persuaded if I were to call her and talk to her nicely."

"Say, half an hour?"

"Half an hour." She smiled a promise and winked. Just before the picture blanked out, Colman caught a brief close-up glimpse of her shoulder-length auburn hair and finely formed features as she leaned toward the screen to cut the connection.

Colman's top-echelon, part-time mistress was Celia Kalens.

❂ CHAPTER EIGHT ❂

"On this, the eve of the last Christmas that we shall be celebrating together before our journey ends, I have chosen as the subject of my seasonal message to you the passage which begins, 'Suffer little children to come unto me.'" The voice of the Mission's presiding bishop floated serenely down from the loudspeakers around the Texas Bowl to the congregation of ten thousand listening solemnly from the terraces. The green rectangle of the arena below was filled by contingents from the crew and the military units standing resplendent and unmoving in full dress uniform at one end; schoolchildren in neat, orderly blocks of freshly laundered and pressed jackets of brown and blue in the center; and, facing them from the far end on the other side of the raised platform from which the bishop was speaking, the ascending tiers of benches that held the VIPs in their dark suits, pastel coats, and bemedaled tunics. The voice continued. "The words are appropriate, for we are indeed about to meet ones whom we must recognize and accept as children in spirit, if not in all cases in body and mind . . ."

Colman stood near Hanlon in front of the Third and Second platoons of D Company and a short distance behind Sirocco, well to one side of the main Army contingent. Only a few of the Company were absent for one reason or another, conspicuous among them Corporal Swyley, who was in Brigade sick bay and looking forward to a turkey dinner; the standing order for a spinach-and-fish diet had mysteriously erased itself from the administration computer's records. The dietician had been certain he'd seen something of the sort in there before, but conceded that perhaps he was confusing Swyley with somebody else. Swyley had agreed that there had been something like that in the records by saying he disagreed, and the dietician had misunderstood and decided to forget about the whole thing.

". . . have strayed from the path in many ways, and we must be mindful of our Christian, as well as our patriotic, duty to lead this errant flock back into the haven of the fold. Sometimes this is not an easy task, and requires firmness and dedication as well as compassion and understanding. . . ."

Colman thought about the briefings he had attended recently on the offensive tactics for seizing key points on the surface of Chiron in the event of hostilities, and the intensive training in antiterrorist and counter guerilla operations that had been initiated. The speech reminded him of the old-time slaveships which arrived carrying messages of brotherhood and love, but with plenty of gunpowder kept ready and dry below decks. Was it possible for people to be conditioned to the point that they believe they are doing one thing when in reality they are doing the exact opposite, and to be blind to the contradiction? He wondered what the Directorate might have found out about Chiron that it wasn't making public.

"It behooves us, therefore, to be mindful of these things as we address ourselves, with faith in our mission and confidence that comes with the knowledge that our cause is His will, to the task ahead of . . ."

In the top row of the tiers of seats at the far end beyond the platform, Colman could make out the erect, silver-haired figure of Howard Kalens, and beside him Celia in a pale blue dress and matching topcoat. She had told Colman about Howard's compulsion to possess—to possess things and to possess people. He felt threatened by anything or anyone that he couldn't command. Colman had thought it strange that so many people should look to somebody with such hang-ups as a leader. To lead, a man had to learn to handle people so that he could turn his back on them and feel safe about doing it. Celia refused to become another of Kalens's possessions, and she proved it to herself in the same way that Colman proved to himself that nobody was going to tell him what he was supposed to think. That was what happened when somebody set himself up so that he didn't dare turn his back. Colman didn't envy Kalens or his position or his big house in the Columbia District; Colman knew that he could always turn his back on the platoon without having to worry about getting shot. They should issue all the VIPs up in the benches M32s, Colman thought. Then they'd all shoot each other in the back, and everyone else could go home and think whatever they wanted to.

So how did people like Howard Kalens feel about Chiron? Colman wondered. Did they think they could possess a whole planet? Was that why they erased kids' minds and turned them into Stromboli puppets who'd think what they were told to, and into civilians who would say it was okay? But why did the people let them do it? Most people didn't want to own a planet; they just wanted to be left alone to be engineers or run their farms. Because they played along with the rules that said they were better if they thought the way the rules said they should, and no good if they didn't.

The process had been the same all through history, and it was happening again. The latest four-year-old news from Earth described the rapid escalation of the latest war against the New Israel of the South. Only this time the EAF was getting involved. The Western strategists had interpreted it as an EAF policy to provoke an all-out war all across Africa so they could move in afterward and close up on Europe from the south. Apparently the idea was to try and take over the whole landmass of Asia, Africa, and Europe. Why did they want to take over the whole of Asia, Africa, and Europe? Colman didn't know. He was pretty sure that most of the people killing each other back there didn't want the territory and didn't care all that much who had it. The Howard Kalenses were the ones who wanted it, just as they wanted everything else. Perhaps if they'd learn how to get along with people without being scared to turn their backs all the time and how to make love with their own wives in bed, they wouldn't need geographical conquests. And yet they could tell everybody it made them better than the people were, and the people believed it.

He remembered Jay's mentioning a physicist from the labs in the Princeton module who said that human societies were the latest phase in the same process of evolution that had begun billions of years ago when the universe started to condense out of radiation. Evolution was a business of survival. Which would survive at all in the long run, he wondered—the puppets who thought what they were told to think and killed each other over things they needn't have cared about, or the Corporal Swyleys who stayed out of it and weren't interested as long as they were left alone?

Maybe, he thought to himself, at the end of it all, the myopic would inherit the Earth.

◎ CHAPTER NINE ◎

On the day officially designated December 28, 2080, in the chronological system that would apply until the ship switched over to the Chironian calendar, the *Mayflower II* entered the planetary system of Alpha Centauri at a speed of 2837 miles per second, reducing, with its main drive still firing at maximum power. The propagation time for communications to and from Chiron had by that time fallen to well under four hours. A signal from the planet confirmed that accommodations for the ship's occupants had been prepared in the outskirts of Franklin as had been requested.

December 31, 2080

Distance to Chiron 1.9 billion miles; speed down to 1100 miles per second. Progressive phase-down of the main-drive burn was commenced, and slow pivoting of the variable-attitude Ring modules initiated to correct for the effect of diminishing linear force from the reducing deceleration. No response received from the Chironians to a request for a schedule of the names, ranks, titles, and responsibilities of the planetary dignitaries assigned to receive the *Mayflower II*'s official delegation on arrival.

January 5, 2081

Speed 300 miles per second; distance to destination, 493 million miles. Course-correction effected to bring the ship round onto its final approach.

January 8, 2081

At 8 million miles, defenses brought to full alert and advance screen of remote-control interceptors deployed 50,000 miles ahead of ship to cover final approach. Response from Chiron neutral.

January 9, 2081

Communications round-trip delay to Chiron, twenty-two seconds. Formal arrangements for reception procedures still not concluded. Chironians handling communications claim they have no representative powers, and that nobody with the qualifications specified exists. *Mayflower II*'s defenses brought to combat readiness.

January 10, 2081

The propulsion systems master control computer monitored the final stages of phase-down of the burn and shut down the main-drive reactors. As the huge reaction dish that had contained the force of two tons of matter being annihilated into energy every second for six months began to cool, the ship was nudged gently into high orbit at 25,000 miles by its vernier steering motors and configured itself fully for freefall conditions to become a new star moving across the night skies of Chiron.

❁ PART TWO ❁

THE
CHIRONIANS

⚙ CHAPTER TEN ⚙

As the *Mayflower II* wheeled slowly in space high above Chiron, the outer door of Shuttle Bay 6 on the Vandenberg module separated into four sectors which swung apart like the petals of an enormous metal flower to expose the nose of the surface lander nestling within. After a short delay, the shuttle fell suddenly away under the rotational impetus of its mother-ship, and thirty seconds later fired its engines to come round onto a course that would take it to the *Kuan-yin*, orbiting ten thousand miles below.

"Our orders are to . . . precede the Ambassador's party through the docking lock to form an honorary guard in the forward antechamber of the *Kuan-yin*, where the formalities will take place,'" Sirocco read aloud to the D Company personnel assigned as escorts at the briefing held early that morning. "'Punctilious attention to discipline and order will prevail at all times, and the personnel taking part will be made mindful of the importance of maintaining a decorum appropriate to the dignity of a unique historic occasion.' That means no ventriloquized comments to relieve the boredom, Swyley, and the best parade-ground turnout you ever managed, all of you. 'Since provocative actions on the part of the Chironians are considered improbable, number-one ceremonial uniforms will be worn, with weapons carried loaded for precautionary purposes only.

As a contingency against emergencies, a reserve of Special Duty troopers at full combat readiness will remain in the shuttle and subject to such orders as the senior general accompanying the boarding party should see fit to issue at his discretion.'"

"Ever get the feeling you were being set up?" Carson of Third Platoon asked sourly. "If anyone gets it first, guess who."

"Didn't you know you were expendable?" Stanislau asked matter-of-factly.

"Ah, but think of the honor of it," Hanlon told them. "And won't every one of them poor SD fellas back in the shuttle be eating his heart out with envy and just wishing he could be out there with the same opportunity to risk himself for flag and country."

"I'll trade," Stanislau offered at once.

Sirocco looked back at the orders and resumed, " 'The advance guard will fan out to form two files, of ten men each, aligned at an angle of forty-five degrees on either side of the access lock and take up station behind their respective section leaders. Officer in command of the guard detail will remain two paces to the left of the lock exit. Upon completion of the opening formalities, the guard will be relieved by a detail from B Company who will position themselves at the exit ramp, and will proceed through the *Kuan-yin* to post sentry details at the locations specified in Schedule A, attached. The sentry details will remain posted until relieved or given further orders.' Are there any questions so far?"

The Ambassador referred to was to be Amery Farnhill, Howard Kalens's deputy in Liaison. Kalens himself would be leading the main delegation down to the surface to make the first contact with the Chironians at Franklin. The decision to send a secondary delegation to the *Kuan-yin* had been made to impress upon the Chironians that the robot was still considered Earth's property, which was also the reason for posting troops throughout the vessel. As a point of protocol, Wellesley and Sterm would not become involved until the appropriate contacts on Chiron had been established and the agenda for further discussion suitably prepared.

The *Kuan-yin* had changed appreciably from the form shown in the pictures he had seen of the craft that had departed from Earth in

2020, Colman noted with interest as he sat erect to preserve the creases of his uniform beneath the restraining belt holding him to his seat and watched the image growing on the wall screen at the forward end of the cabin. The original design had taken the form of a dumbbell, with fuel storage and the thermonuclear pulse engines concentrated at one end, and the computers and sensitive reconnaissance instruments carried at the far end of a long, connecting, structural boom to keep them safely away from drive-section radiation. The modifications added after 2015 for creating and accommodating the first Chironians had entailed extensions to the instrumentation module and the incorporation of auxiliary motors which would spin the dumbbell about its center after arrival in order to simulate gravity for the new occupants while the first surface base was being prepared.

In the years since, the instrumentation module had sprouted a collection of ancillary structures which had doubled its size, the original fuel tanks near the tail had vanished to be replaced, apparently, by a bundle of huge metal bottles mounted around the central portion of the connecting boom, and a new assembly of gigantic windings surrounding a tubular housing now formed the tail, culminating in a parabolic reaction dish reminiscent of the *Mayflower II*'s main drive, though much smaller because of the *Kuan-yin*'s reduced scale. The *Mayflower II*'s designers had included docking adapters for the shuttles to mate with the *Kuan-yin*'s ports, and the Chironians had retained the original pattern in their modifications, so the shuttle would be able to connect without problems.

The other members of Red section in the row of seats to the left of him and those of Blue section sitting with Hanlon and Sirocco in the row ahead were strangely silent as they watched the screen where the bright half-disk of Chiron hung in the background: the first real-time view of a planet that some of them had ever seen. Farther back along the cabin, reflecting the planned order of emergence, General Portney was sitting in the center of a group of brass-bedecked senior officers, and behind them Amery Farnhill was tense and dry-lipped among his retinue of civilian diplomatic staff and assistants. In the rear, the SD troops were grim and silent in steel helmets and combat

uniforms festooned with grenades, propping their machine rifles and
assault cannon between their knees.

Farnhill's staff had given up trying to get the Chironians to
provide an official list of who would be greeting the delegation. In
the end they had simply advised the *Kuan-yin* when the shuttle would
arrive and resigned themselves to playing things by ear after that. The
Chironians had agreed readily enough, which was why the orders
issued that morning had called for a reduced alertness level. Kalens's
delegation had met with an equal lack of success in dealing with
Franklin, and had elected finally to go to the surface on the same basis
as the delegation to the *Kuan-yin*, but with more elaborate
preparations and ceremonies.

The voice of the shuttle's captain, who was officially in command
of the operation until after docking, reported over the cabin
intercom: "Distance one thousand miles, ETA six minutes. Coming
into matching orbit and commencing closing maneuver. Prepare for
retardation. *Kuan-yin* has confirmed they will open Port Three."

The image on the screen drifted to one side as the shuttle swung
round to brake with its main engines, and then switched to a new
view as one of the stern cameras was cut in. Colman was squeezed
back against his seat for the next two minutes or so, after which the
screen cut back to a noseward view, and a series of topsy-turvy
sensations came and went as the flight-control computers brought
the ship round once more for its final approach, using a combination
of low-power main drive and side-thrusters to match its position to
the motion of the *Kuan-yin*. After some minor corrections the shuttle
was rotating with the *Kuan-yin* to give its occupants the feeling that
they were lying on their backs, and nudging itself gently forward and
upward to complete the maneuver. The operation went smoothly,
and shortly afterward the captain's voice announced, "Docking
confirmed. The boarding party is free to proceed."

"Proceed, General," Farnhill said from the back.

"Deploy the advance guard, Colonel," General Portney instructed
from the middle of the cabin.

"Guard, forward," Colonel Wesserman ordered from a row in
front of Portney.

"Guard detail, file left and right by sections," Sirocco said at the front. "Section leaders forward." He moved out into the aisle, where the floor had folded itself into a steep staircase to facilitate fore-and-aft movement, and climbed through into the side-exiting lock chamber with Colman and Hanlon behind him while Red and Blue sections formed up in the aisles immediately to the rear. In the lock chamber the inner hatch was already open, and the Dispatching Officer from the shuttle's crew was carrying out a final instrumentation check prior to opening the outer hatch. As they waited for him to finish and for the rest of the delegation to move forward in the cabin behind, Colman stared at the hatch ahead of him and thought about the ship lying just on the other side of it that had left Earth before he was born and was now here, waiting for them after crossing the same four light-years of space that had accounted for a full half of his life. After the years of speculations, all the questions about the Chironians were now within minutes of being answered. The descent from the *Mayflower II* had raised Colman's curiosity to a high pitch because of what he had seen on the screen. For despite all the jokes and the popular wisdom, one thing he was certain of was that the engineering and structural modifications that he had observed on the outside of the *Kuan-yin* had not been made by irresponsible, overgrown adolescents.

"Clear to exit," the Dispatching Officer informed Sirocco.

"Lock clear for exit," Sirocco called to the cabin below.

"Carry on, Guard Commander," Colonel Wesserman replied from the depths.

"Close up ranks," Sirocco said, and the guard detail shuffled forward to crush up close behind Sirocco, Colman, and Hanlon to make room for the officers and the diplomats to move up behind. Sirocco looked at the Dispatching Officer and nodded. "Open outer hatch." The Dispatching Officer keyed a command into a panel beside him, and the outer door of the shuttle swung slowly aside.

Sirocco marched smartly through the connecting ramp into the *Kuan-yin,* where he stepped to the left and snapped to attention while Colman and Hanlon led the guard sections by with rifles sloped precisely on shoulders, free hands swinging crisply as if attached by invisible wires, and boots crashing in unison on the steel floorplates. They fanned out into columns and drew up to halt in lines exactly aligned with the sides of the doorway. Behind them the officers emerged four abreast and divided into two groups to follow Colonel Wesserman to the left and General Portney to the right.

"Present . . . *arms!*" Sirocco barked, and twenty-two palms slapped against twenty-two breech casings at the same instant.

Through the gap between the officers, the diplomats moved forward and came to a halt in reverse order of precedence, black suits immaculate and white shirtfronts spotless, and finally the noble form of Amery Farnhill conveyed itself regally forward to take up its position at their head.

"His Esteemed Excellency, Amery Farnhill," the assistant one pace to the rear and two paces to the right announced in clear, ringing tones that resonated around the antechamber of the *Kuan-yin*'s docking port. "Deputy Director of Liaison of the Supreme Directorate of the official Congress of the *Mayflower II* and appointed emissary to the *Kuan-yin* on behalf of the Director of Congress . . ." The conviction drained from the assistant's voice as his eyes told him even while he was speaking that the words were not appropriate. Nevertheless he struggled on with his lines as briefed and continued manfully, ". . . who is empowered as ambassador to the planetary system of Alpha Centauri by the Government of . . ." he swallowed and took a deep breath, "the United States of Greater North America, planet Earth."

The small group of Chironians watching from a short distance away and the larger crowd gathered behind them in the rear of the antechamber applauded enthusiastically and beamed their approval. They weren't supposed to do that. It didn't preserve the right atmosphere.

"They're okay," Corporal Swyley's disembodied voice whispered from no definable direction. "We're making ourselves look like jerks."

"Shuddup," Colman hissed.

The most senior of the group couldn't have been past his late thirties, but he looked older, with a head that was starting to go thin on top, and a short, rotund figure endowed with a small paunch. He was wearing an open-necked shirt of intricately embroidered blues and grays, and plain navy blue slacks held up with a belt. His features looked vaguely Asiatic. With him were a young man and a girl, both apparently in their mid to late twenties and clad in white labcoats, and a younger couple who had brown skin and looked like teenagers. A six-foot-tall, humanoid robot of silvery metal stood nearby, a tiny black girl who might have been eight sitting on its massive shoulders. Her legs dangled around its neck and her arms clasped the top of its head.

"Hi," the paunchy man greeted amiably. "I'm Clem. These are Carla and Hermann, and Francine and Boris. The big guy here is Cromwell, and the little lady up top is Amy. Well, I guess . . . welcome aboard."

Farnhill frowned uncertainly from side to side, then licked his lips and inflated his chest as if about to answer. He deflated suddenly and shook his head. The words to handle the situation just wouldn't come. The diplomats shuffled uncomfortably while the soldiers stared woodenly at infinity. A few awkward seconds dragged by. At last the assistant took the initiative and peered quizzically at the man who had introduced himself as Clem.

"Who are you?" he demanded. The formality had evaporated from his voice. "Are you in authority here? If so, what are your rank and title?"

Clem frowned and brought a hand up to his chin. "Depends what you mean by authority," he said. "I organize the regular engineering crew of the ship and supervise the maintenance. I suppose you could say that's authority of a kind. Then again, I don't have a lot to do with some of the special research programs and modifications but Hermann does."

"True," Hermann, the young man in the white labcoat, agreed. "But on top of that, parts of this place are used as a school to give the kids early off-planet experience. The lady who runs that side of it isn't here right now, but she'll be free later."

"She got tied up over lunch trying to answer questions about supernovas and quasars," Francine explained.

"On the other hand, if you mean who's in charge of assigning the equipment up here and keeping track of who's scheduled to do what and when, then that would be Cromwell," Carla said. "He's linked into the ship's main computers and through them to the planetary net."

"Cromwell knows everything," Amy declared from her perch. "Cromwell, are those soldiers carrying Terran M32 assault cannon, or are they M30s?"

"M32s," the robot said. "They've the enhanced fire-selectors."

"I hope they're not going to start shooting each other up here. It would be pretty scary in orbit. They could decompress the whole ship."

"I think they know that," Cromwell said. "They've spent a lot longer in space than the few trips you've made."

"I suppose so."

The assistant's patience snapped at last. "This is ridiculous! I want to know who is in overall authority here. You must have a Director of Operations or some equivalent. Please be kind enough to—"

Farnhill stopped him with a curt wave of his hand. "This spectacle has gone far enough," he said. He looked at Clem. "Perhaps we could continue this discussion in conditions of greater privacy. Is there somewhere suitable near here?"

"Sure." Clem gestured vaguely behind him. "There's a big room back along the corridor that's free and should hold everybody. We could all get some coffee there too. I guess you could use some—you've had a long trip, huh?"

He grinned at the joke as he turned to lead the way. Farnhill didn't seem to appreciate the humor.

"Ahem . . ." General Portney cleared his throat. "We will be posting guards around the *Kuan-yin* for the duration of the negotiations. I trust there will be no objections." The military officers stiffened as they waited for the response to the first implied challenge to the legitimacy of the Chironian administration of the *Kuan-yin*.

Clem waved an arm casually without looking back. "Go ahead," he said. "Can't see as you really need any, though. You're pretty safe up here. We don't get many burglars." Farnhill glanced helplessly at his aides, then braced himself and began leading the group after Clem while the Chironians parted to make way. The military deputation broke formation to take up the rear with Wesserman tossing back a curt "Carry on, Guard Commander" in the direction of Sirocco.

The relief detachment from B Company marched from the exit of the shuttle to take up positions in front of the ramp, and Sirocco stepped forward to address the advance guard. "Ship detail, *aiten-shun!* Two ranks in marching order, fall . . . *in!*" The two lines that had been angled away from the lock re-formed into files behind the section leaders. "Sentry details will detach and fall out at stations. By the left . . . *march!*" The two lines clumped their way behind Sirocco across the antechamber, wheeled left while each man on the inside marked time for four paces, and clicked away along the corridor beyond and into the *Kuan-yin*.

Amy watched curiously over the top of Cromwell's head as they disappeared from sight. "I wonder why they walk like that when they shout at each other," she mused absently. "Do you know why, Cromwell?"

"Have you thought about it?" Cromwell asked.

"Not really."

"You should think about things as well as just ask questions. Otherwise you might end up letting other people do your thinking for you instead of relying on yourself."

"Ooh . . . I wouldn't want to do that," Amy said.

"All right then," Cromwell challenged. "Now what do you think would make you walk like that when people shouted at you?"

"I don't know." Amy screwed her face up and rubbed the bridge of her nose with a finger. "I suppose I'd have to be crazy."

"Well, *there's* something to think about," Cromwell suggested.

◉ CHAPTER ELEVEN ◉

Clump, Clump, Clump, *clump, clump, clump, clump, clump.*

"Detail . . . *halt!*"

Clump-Clump!

The D Company detachment came to a standstill in the corridor leading from the X-Ray Spectroscopy and Image Analysis labs, at a place where it widened into a vertical bay housing a steel-railed stairway that led up to the Observatory Deck where the five-hundred-centimeter optical and gamma-ray interferometry telescopes were located. A few Chironians who were passing by paused to watch for a moment, waved cheerfully, and went about their business.

"Sentry detail, detach to . . . *post!*" Sirocco shouted. PFC Driscoll stepped one pace backward from the end of the by-this-time-diminished file, turned ninety degrees to the right, and stepped back again to come to attention with his back to the wall by the entrance to a smaller side-corridor. "Parade . . . *rest!*" Driscoll moved his left foot into an astride stance and brought his gun down from the shoulder to rest with its butt on the floor, one inch from his boot. "Remainder of detail, by the left . . . *march!*"

Clump, clump, clump, clump . . .

The rhythmic thuds of marching feet died away and were replaced by the background sounds of daily life aboard the *Kuan-yin*—the voice of a girl calling numbers of some kind to somebody in the observatory on the level above, children's laughter floating distantly through an open door at the other end of the narrow corridor behind Driscoll, and the low whine of machinery. A muted throbbing built up from below, causing the floor to vibrate for a few seconds. Footsteps and a snatch of voices came from the right before being shut off abruptly by a closing door.

Driscoll was feeling more relieved. If what he had seen so far was anything to go by, the Chironians weren't going to start any trouble. He'd had to bite his tongue in order to keep a straight face back in the antechamber by the ramp, and it was a miracle that nobody important had heard Stanislau sniggering next to him. The Chironians were okay, he had decided. Everything would be okay . . . provided that ass-faces like Farnhill didn't go and screw things up.

What had impressed him the most was the way the kids seemed to be involved in everything that was going on just as much as the grown-ups. They didn't come across like kids at all, but more like small people who were busy finding out how things were done. In a room two posts back, he had glimpsed a couple of kids who couldn't have been more than twelve probing carefully and with deep frowns of concentration inside the electronics of a piece of equipment that must have cost millions. The older Chironian with them just watched over their shoulders and offered occasional suggestions. It made sense, Driscoll thought. Treat them as if they're responsible, and they act responsibly; give them bits of cheap plastic to throw around, and they act like it's cheap plastic. Or maybe the Chironians just had good insurance on their equipment.

He wondered how he might have made out if he'd had a start like that. And what would a guy like Colman be doing, who knew more about the *Mayflower II*'s machines than half the echelon-four snot-noses put together? If that was the way the computers had brought the first kids up, Driscoll reflected, he could think of a few humans who could have used some lessons.

His debut into life had been very different. The war had left his parents afflicted by genetic damage, and their first two children had not survived infancy. Aging prematurely from side effects, they had known they would never see Chiron when they brought him aboard the *Mayflower II* as a boy of eight and sacrificed the few more years that they might have spent on Earth in order to give him a new start somewhere else. Paradoxically, their health had qualified them favorably in their application to join the Mission since the planning had called for the inclusion of older people and higher-risk actuarial categories among the population to make room for the births that would be occurring later. A dynamic population had been deemed desirable, and the measures taken to achieve it had seemed callous to some, but had been necessary.

As a youth he had daydreamed about becoming an entertainer— a singer, or a comic, maybe—but he couldn't sing and he couldn't tell jokes, and somehow after his parents died within two years of each other halfway through the voyage, he had ended up in the Army. So now, though he still couldn't sing a note or tell a joke right, he knew just how to use an M32 to demolish a small building from two thousand yards, could operate a battlefield compack blindfolded, and was an expert at deactivating optically triggered anti-intruder personnel mines.

About all he was good with outside things like that was cards. He couldn't remember exactly when his fascination with them had started, but it had been soon after Swyley, then a fellow private, had taught him to shuffle four aces to the top of a deck and feed them into a deal from the palm. Finding to his surprise that he seemed to have an aptitude, Driscoll had borrowed a leaf from Colman's book and started reading up about the subject. For many long off-duty hours he had practiced top-pass palms and one-handed side-cuts until he could materialize three full fans from an empty hand and lift a named number of cards off a deck eight times out of ten. Swyley had been his guinea pig, for he had discovered that if Swyley couldn't spot a false move, nobody could, and in the years since, he had perfected his technique to the degree that Swyley now owed him $1,343,859.20, including interest.

But his reputation had put him in a no-win situation at the Friday night poker school because when he won, everybody said he was sharping, and when he didn't, everybody said he was lousy. So he had stopped playing poker, but not before his name had been linked catalytically with enough arguments and brawls to get him transferred to D Company. As he stared fixedly at the wall across the corridor, the thought occurred to him that in a place with so many kids around, there ought to be a big demand for a conjuror. The more he thought about it, the more appealing the idea became. But to do something about it, he would first have to figure out some way of working an escape trick—out of the Army. Swyley should have some useful suggestions about that, he thought.

Clump, clump, clump, clump. His train of thought was derailed by the sound of steady tramping approaching from his left—not the direction in which the detail had departed, which shouldn't have been returning by this route anyway, but the opposite one. Besides, it didn't sound like multiple pairs of regulation Army feet; it sounded like one pair, but heavier and more metallic. And along with it came the sound of two children's voices, whispering and furtive, and punctuated with giggles.

Driscoll turned his eyes a fraction to the side. They widened in disbelief as one of the *Kuan-yin*'s steel colossi marched into view, holding a length of aluminum alloy tubing over its left shoulder and being followed by a brown, Indian-looking girl of about seven and a fair-haired boy of around the same age.

"Detail . . . *stop!*" the girl called out. The robot halted. "Detail . . . Oh, I don't know what I'm supposed to say. Stand with your feet apart and put your gun down." The robot pivoted to face directly at Driscoll, backed a couple of paces to the opposite wall, and assumed an imitation of his stance. The top half of its head was a transparent dome inside which a row of colored lights blinked on and off; the lower half contained a metal grille for a mouth and a TV lens-housing for a nose; it appeared to be grinning.

"Stay . . . *there!*" the girl instructed. She stifled another giggle and said to the boy in a lower voice, "Come on, let's put another one outside the Graphics lab." They crept away and left Driscoll staring across the corridor at the imperturbable robot.

A couple of minutes went by. Nobody moved. The robot's lights continued to wink at him cheerfully. Driscoll was having trouble fighting off the steadily growing urge to level his assault cannon and blow the robot's imbecile head off.

"Why don't you piss off," he growled at last.

"Why don't you?"

For a moment Driscoll thought the machine had read his mind. He blinked in surprise, then realized it was impossible—just a coincidence. "How can I?" he said. "I've got my orders."

"So have I."

"That's different."

"How?"

"You don't have to do this."

"Do you?"

"Of course I do."

"Why?"

Driscoll sighed irritably. This was no time for long debates. "You don't understand," he said.

"Don't I?" the robot replied.

Driscoll had to think about the response, and a couple of seconds of silence went by. "It's not the same," he said. "You're just humoring kids."

"What are you doing?"

Driscoll didn't have a ready answer to that. Besides, he was too conscious of the desire for a cigarette to be philosophical. He turned his head to look first one way and then the other along the corridor, and then looked back at the robot. "Can you tell if any of our people are near here?"

"Yes, I can, and no, there aren't. Why—getting fed up?"

"Would it worry anyone if I smoked?"

"It wouldn't worry me if you burst into flames." The robot chuckled raspily.

"How do you know there's no one around?"

"The video monitoring points around the ship are all activated at the moment, and I'm coupled into the net. I can see what's going on everywhere. Go ahead. It's okay. The round cover on the wall next to you is an inlet to a trash incinerator. You can use it as an ashtray."

Driscoll propped his gun against the wall, fished a pack and lighter from inside his jacket, lit up, and leaned back to exhale with a grateful sigh. The irritability that he had been feeling wafted away with the smoke. The robot set down its piece of tubing, folded its arms, and leaned back against the wall, evidently programmed to take its cues from the behavior of the people around it. Driscoll looked at it with a new curiosity. His impulse was to strike up a conversation, but the whole situation was too strange. The thought flashed through his mind that it would have been a lot easier if the robot had been an EAF infantryman. Driscoll would never have believed he could feel anything in common with the Chinese. He didn't know whether he was talking to the robot, or through it to computers somewhere else in the *Kuan-yin* or even down on Chiron, maybe; whether they had minds or simply embodied some clever programming, or what. He had talked to Colman about machine intelligence once. Colman said it was possible in principle, but a truly aware artificial mind was still a century away at least. Surely the Chironians couldn't have advanced that much. "What kind of a machine are you?" he asked. "I mean, can you think like a person? Do you know who you are?"

"Suppose I said I could. Would that tell you anything?"

Driscoll took another drag of his cigarette. "I guess not. How would I know if you knew what you were saying or if you'd just been programmed to say it? There's no way of telling the difference."

"Then is there any difference?"

Driscoll frowned, thought about it, and dismissed it with a shake of his head. "This is kinda funny," he said to change the subject.

"What is?"

"Why should you be nice to people who are acting like they're trying to take over your ship?"

"Do you want to take over the ship?"

"Me? Hell no. What would I do with it?"

"Then there's your answer."

"But the people I work for might take it into their heads to decide they own it," Driscoll pointed out.

"That's up to them. If it pleases them to say so, why should we mind?"

582   James P. Hogan

"The people here wouldn't mind if our people started telling them what to do?"

"Why should they?"

Driscoll couldn't buy that. "You mean they'd be just as happy doing what our people told them to?" he said.

"I never said they'd *do* anything," the robot replied. "I just said that people telling them wouldn't bother them."

Just then, two Chironian girls strolled around the corner from the narrow corridor. They looked fresh and pretty in loose blouses worn over snug-fitting slacks, and had lightweight stretch-boots of some silvery, lustrous material. One of them had brown, wavy hair with a reddish tint to it, and looked as if she were in her midthirties; the other was a blonde of perhaps twenty-two. For a split second, Driscoll felt an instinctive twinge of apprehension at the thought of looking ridiculous, but the girls showed no surprise. Instead they paused and looked at him not unpleasantly, but with a hint of reserve as if they wanted to smile but weren't quite sure if they should.

"Hi," the redhead called, a shade cautiously.

Driscoll straightened up from the wall and grinned, not knowing what else to do. "Well. . . hi," he returned.

At once their faces split into broad smiles, and they walked over. The redhead shook his hand warmly. "I see you've already met Wellington. I'm Shirley. This is my daughter, Ci."

"*She's* your daughter?" Driscoll blinked. "Say, I guess that's . . . very nice."

Ci repeated the performance. "Who are you?" she asked him.

"Me? Oh . . . name's Driscoll—Tony Driscoll." He licked his lips while he searched for a follow-up. "I guess me and Wellington are guarding the corridor."

"Who from?" Ci asked.

"A good question," Wellington commented.

"You're the first Terran we've talked to," Shirley said. She nodded her head to indicate the direction they had come from. "We've got a class of kids back there who are bubbling over with curiosity. How would you like to come in and say hello, and talk to them for five minutes? They'd love it."

"What?" Driscoll stared at them aghast. "I've never talked to classes of people. I wouldn't know how to start."

"A good time to start practicing then," Ci suggested.

He swallowed hard and shook his head. "I have to stay here. This conversation is enough to get me shot as it is. Ci shrugged but seemed content not to make any more of it. "Are you two, er . . . teachers here or something like that?" Driscoll asked.

"Sometimes," Shirley answered. "Ci teaches English mainly, but mostly down on the surface. That is, when she's not working with electronics or installing plant wiring underground somewhere. I'm not all that technical. I grow olives and vines out on the Peninsula, and design interiors. That's what brought me up here—Clem wants the crew quarters and mess deck refitted and decorated. But yes, I teach tailoring sometimes, but not a lot."

"I meant as a regular job," Driscoll said. "What do you do basically?"

"All of them." Shirley sounded mildly surprised. "What do you mean by 'basically'?"

"They do the same thing all the time, from when they quit school to when they retire," Ci reminded her mother.

"Oh yes, of course." Shirley nodded. "That sounds pretty awful. Still, it's their business."

"What do you do best?" Ci asked him. "I mean . . . apart from holding people's walls up for them. That can't be much of a life."

Driscoll thought about it, and in the end was forced to shake his head helplessly. "Not a lot that you'd be interested in, I guess," he confessed.

"Everybody's got something," Shirley insisted. "What do you like doing?"

"You really wanna know?" An intense note had come suddenly into Driscoll's voice.

"Hey, back off, soldier," Ci said suspiciously. "We're still strangers. Later, who knows? Give it time."

"I didn't mean that," Driscoll protested, feeling embarrassed. "If you must know, I like working cards."

"You mean tricks?" Shirley seemed interested.

"I can do tricks, sure."

"Are you good?"

"The best. I can make 'em stand up and talk."

"You'd better mean it," Shirley warned. "There's nothing worse than trying to spend money you don't have. It's like stealing from people."

Driscoll didn't follow what she meant, so he ignored it. "I mean it," he told her.

Shirley turned to look at Ci. "Say, wouldn't he be great to have at our next party? I love things like that." She looked at Driscoll again. "When are you coming down to Chiron?"

"I don't know yet. We haven't heard anything."

"Well, give us a call when you do, and we'll fix something up. I live in Franklin, so there shouldn't be too much of a problem. That's where we usually get together."

"Sounds good," Driscoll said. "I can't make any promises right now though. Everything depends on how things go. If things work out okay, how would I find the place?"

"Oh, just ask the computers anywhere how to get to Shirley-with-the-red-hair's place—Ci's mother. They'll take care of you."

"So maybe we'll see you down there sometime," Ci said.

"Well . . . yeah. Who knows? He was about to say something more when Wellington interrupted.

"Two of your officers are heading this way. I thought you ought to know,"

"Who?" Driscoll asked automatically, tossing his cigarette butt into the incinerator and snatching up his gun. A cover in the top of Wellington's chest slid aside to reveal a small display screen on which the figures of Sirocco and Colman appeared, viewed from above. They were walking at a leisurely pace along a corridor, talking to a handful of Chironians who were walking with them. Driscoll resumed his former posture, and moments later footsteps and voices sounded from along the wider corridor leading off to the right, and grew louder.

"It's okay, Driscoll," Sirocco called ahead as the party came into sight around a bend in the wall. "Forget the pantomime. We're back in the Bomb Factory." Driscoll relaxed his pose and sent a puzzled look along the corridor.

"I might have guessed," Colman said, nodding to himself and taking in the two girls as he drew to a halt.

"Very cozy," Sirocco agreed.

"Er . . . Shirley and Ci," Driscoll said. "And that's General Wellington."

"Been having a nice chat, have you?" Sirocco asked.

"Well, yes, actually, I suppose, sir. How did you know?"

Sirocco waved at the corridor behind him. "Because it's happening everywhere else, that's how. Carson's talking football, and Maddock is telling some kids about what it was like growing up on the *Mayflower II.*" He sighed but didn't sound too ruffled about it. "If you can't beat 'em, then join 'em, eh, Driscoll. . . for an hour or so, anyway. And besides, they want to show Colman something in the observatory upstairs. I don't understand what the hell they're talking about."

"Steve's an engineer," one of the Chironians, a bearded youth in a red check shirt, explained, indicating Colman and speaking to Ci. "We told him about the resonance oscillations in the G7 mounting gyro, and he said he might be able to suggest a way of damping them with feedback from the alignment laser. We're taking him up to have a look at it."

"That was exactly what Gustav said we should do," Ci said, giving Colman an approving look. "He was looking at it yesterday."

"I know. Maybe we can get Gustav and Steve working on it together."

"Hey, don't get too excited about this," Colman cautioned. "I only said I'd be interested in seeing it. The Army might have different ideas about me getting involved. Don't bet your life savings on it."

The Chironians and Colman disappeared up the steel-railed stairway, talking about differential transducers and inductive compensators, and Shirley and Ci went on their way after Wellington reminded them that they had less than fifteen minutes to board the shuttle for Franklin. Driscoll and Sirocco remained with Wellington in the corridor.

"If you don't mind my saying so, isn't this a bit risky, sir?" Driscoll said apprehensively. "I mean . . . with all this going on? Suppose Colonel Wesserman or somebody shows up."

"No chance with these Chironian robots around. They've got the place staked out." He wrinkled his nose, and his moustache twitched as he sniffed the air. "Take a break while you've got the chance, Private Driscoll," he advised. "And I'll have one of those cigarettes that you've been smoking."

Driscoll grinned and began feeling more confident. "You see, Wellington," he said. "They're not *all* as bad as you think."

"Amazing," the robot replied in a neutral voice.

A party was thrown in the Bowery that night to celebrate the *Mayflower II*'s safe arrival and the end of the voyage. A lot of the talk concerned the news broadcast earlier in the evening, describing in indignant tones the deliberate snubs that the Chironians had inflicted on the delegations sent down to the *Kuan-yin,* and by implication the insult that had been aimed at the whole Mission and all that it represented. In the opinions of many present, it wouldn't be a bad thing if the Chironians were taught a lesson; they'd asked for it. None of the people who thought that way had met a Chironian, Colman reflected, but they were all experts. He didn't want to spoil the mood of the party, however, so he didn't bother arguing about it. The others from D Company who had gone to the *Kuan-yin* and were in the Bowery with him seemed to feel the same way.

❀ CHAPTER TWELVE ❀

Howard Kalens was not amused.

"A scandalous exhibition!" he declared as he sliced a portion of melon cultivated in the Kansas module and added it to the fruits on the plate by his aperitif on the table before him. "Nobodies and cretins, all of them. Not one of them had any representative powers worth speaking of. Yet it's clear that a governing organization of some kind must exist, though God knows what kind of people it's made up of, judging from the state the town's in . . . a total shambles. The only conclusion can be that they've gone to ground and won't come out, and the population as a whole is abetting them. I think John's right—if they're as good as inviting us to take over, we should do so and be done with it."

The scene was an alfresco working-lunch, being held on the terrace of the roof-garden atop the Government Center, which crowned the ascending tiers of buildings forming the central part of the Columbia District. High above, the shutters outside the module's transparent roof had been opened to admit the almost forgotten phenomenon of natural sunlight, streaming in from Alpha Centauri, as it held a position low in the sky below the nose of the Spindle while the *Mayflower II* rotated with its axis kept steady toward it.

Garfield Wellesley finished spreading liver paté on a finger of toast and looked up. "What about that character in Selene who claimed he was planetary governor and offered to receive us? What happened to him?"

Kalens looked disdainfully down his nose. "My staff contacted him through the Chironian communications system. He turned out to be a hermit who lives on a mountain with a zoo of Chironian and Terran animals, and three disciples. They're all quite insane."

"I see . . ." Wellesley frowned and nibbled off a piece of the toast.

"Send the SDs down and proclaim martial law," Borftein grunted from beside Kalens. "They've had their chance. If they've run away and left it for us, let's take it. Why mess around?"

Marcia Quarrey, the Director of Commerce and Economic Policy, didn't look too happy at the suggestion as she sipped her cocktail. "Obviously that would be possible," she said, setting down her glass. "But would it serve any useful purpose? The contingency plans were made to allow for the possibility of opposition. Well, there hasn't been any opposition. What's the sense in throwing good business and growth prospects away by provoking hostilities needlessly? We can acquire Franklin simply by walking in. We don't have to make a demonstration out of it."

"Exactly what I was thinking," Wellesley commented, nodding. "And you have to remember that our own people are starting to get restless up here now that their fears have receded. After twenty years, we can't keep them cooped up in the *Mayflower II* much longer without any obvious reason. They've got accommodations prepared by the space-base at Franklin. I'm inclined to say we should start moving the first batches down. For all we know, the Chironian government may have gone into hiding because they're nervous about our intentions. It might be a good way of enticing them to come out again."

"I agree," Marcia Quarrey said. She looked at Borftein. "If that's the case, then sending in the SDs would only confirm their fears. It would be the worst thing we could do."

Kalens chewed on a slice of orange but made a face as if the fruit was bad. "But we've been publicly insulted," he objected. "What are you saying—that we should simply forget it? That would be unthinkable. What kind of a precedent would we be setting?"

"You can't be soft with people like this," Borftein said bluntly.

"Give them a yard, and they'll hate you because they want a mile. Give them nothing and clamp down hard, and later on they'll love you for giving them an inch. I've seen it all before."

Quarrey sighed and shook her head. "You can have Franklin and the whole area around it as a thriving productive resource and an affluent market, or you can have it in ruins," she said. "Given the choice, which would you prefer? Well, it's not as if we didn't have the choice, is it? We have."

"A nice sentiment, I agree," Kalens said. "But they still should be taught some manners."

Wellesley raised a hand a fraction. "Be careful you don't allow this to get too personal, Howard," he cautioned. "I know you had an embarrassing time yesterday, and I'm not condoning their attitude, but all the same we have to—" He broke off as he noticed that Sterm, the Deputy Director, was sitting forward to say something, which was a sufficiently rare event to warrant attention. "Yes, Matt?" The others looked toward Sterm curiously.

Sterm brought his fingers together in front of his face—a noble face whose proud, Roman-emperor features crowned by laurels of curly hair combed flat and forward concealed an underlying harshness of line from all but the most discerning—and stared at the center of the table with large, liquid-brown, unfathomable eyes. "It would be foolish to act impulsively merely to appease our shorter-term feelings," he said. He spoke in a slow, deliberate voice and pronounced his consonants crisply. "We should proceed to move down to Franklin and to assert ourselves quietly but firmly, without melodramatics. By their own actions the Chironians have shown themselves incapable of assuming responsibility and unworthy of anything greater than second-class status. Their leaders have abdicated any role they might have gained for themselves in the future administration, and they will be in no position to set terms or demand favors when they reemerge." He paused, and then turned his eyes to Howard Kalens. "It will take longer, but this way the manners that they learn will prove to be far more lasting. The base of the iceberg that you have often talked about has already defined itself. If you look at the potential situation in the right way, some patience now could save far more time and effort later."

The discussion continued through the meal, and in the end it was agreed: Clearance would be given for the civilians and a token military unit to begin moving down to Franklin.

"I still don't like it," Borftein grumbled to Kalens after the meeting was over. "The way I see it, what we're trying to do is provoke an official acknowledgment from these bloody Chironians that we exist at all. If I had my way, I'd soon show them whether we exist or not."

"I'm not sure that I agree as much as I thought," Kalens told him. "Sterm may have a point. We should try it his way to begin with at least. We don't have to stick with the plan indefinitely."

"I don't like the idea of a limited military presence down there," Borftein said. "We're trusting the Chironians too much. I still say they could have strength that they're not showing yet. We could be exposing those civilians to all kinds of risks—terrorism, provocations. What if they get hit by surprise? I've seen it all before."

"Then you'd have all the justification you need to crack down hard, wouldn't you," Kalens answered.

Borftein thought about the remark for a few seconds. "Do you think that could be what Sterm's hoping for?" His tone betrayed that the thought hadn't registered fully until then.

"I'm not sure," Kalens replied distantly. "Trying to elucidate Sterm's motives is akin to peeling an onion. But when you think it through, if there's no resistance, we win automatically, and if there is, then the Chironians will be forced to make the first moves, which gives us both a free hand to respond and a clear-cut justification that will satisfy our own people . . . which is doubly important with the elections coming up. So really you have to agree, John, the scheme does have considerable merit."

❂ CHAPTER THIRTEEN ❂

Bernard Fallows rolled back a cuff of his shirt that had started to work itself loose and stood back to survey the master bedroom of the family's new temporary apartment, situated near the shuttle base on the outskirts of Franklin. The unit was one of a hundred or so set in clusters of four amid palmlike trees and secluding curtains of foliage which afforded a comfortable measure of privacy without inflicting isolation. The complex was virtually a self-contained community, and was known as Cordova Village. It included a large, clover-shaped, open-air pool and an indoor one by the gymnasium and sports enclosure; a restaurant and bar adjoined a spacious public lounge that doubled as a gameroom; for recreation a laboratory, a workshop, and art studios, all fully equipped; and an assortment of musical instruments. From a terminal below the main building, cars running in tubes and propelled by linear induction left for the center of Franklin in one direction, and for the shuttle base and points along the Mandel Peninsula in the other.

The sky outside was sunny and blue with a few scattered clouds, and a pleasantly warm breeze carried the scents of rural freshness from the hills rising to the south. Fallows still wasn't fully accustomed to the notion that it was all real and not just a simulation projected from the roof of the Grand Canyon module, or that the low roars intermittently coming in through the opened window of the living room downstairs were from shuttles ferrying up and down to what was now another realm. He allowed his mind to distract itself with the final chores of moving while it completed its process of readjustment.

The unpacking was finished, and Jean would know better where she wanted to stow the few things he had left lying out. The move had gone very quickly and smoothly, mainly because the Chironians had even furnished the place—right down to the towels and the bed linen, which had meant that the Fallowses could leave most of their own things in storage at the base until something more permanent was worked out.

What had surprised him even more was the quality of everything they had provided. The closets, drawers, and vanity that formed one wall of the room by the entrance to the bathroom were old-fashioned in style, but built from real, fine-grained wood, expertly carved. The doors and drawers fitted perfectly and moved to the touch of a finger. The fabrics and drapes were soft and intricately woven rather than having been patterned by laser impregnation; the carpets were of an organic self-cleaning, self-regenerating fiber that felt like twentieth-century Wilton or Axminster; the bathroom fittings were molded from a metallic glazed crystal that glowed with a faint internal fluorescence; the heating and environmental systems were noiseless. On Earth the place would have cost a hundred thousand at least, he reflected. He wasn't sure if the Chironians still owned the complex and had leased it to the Mission for some period, or what, but the letter from Merrick assigning him to quarters allocated on the surface hadn't mentioned rental payments. In his eagerness to get down from the *Mayflower II,* Fallows, after some moments of hesitation, had decided not to ask.

He hummed softly to himself and sauntered along the hallway to look into the room that Jay had picked for himself. Jay's cases and boxes were still lying in an untidy pile that stretched along one wall beneath a litter of books, charts, tools, and a heap of mirrors and optical components scrounged from Jerry Pernak a month or so previously for a holographic microscope that Jay said he was going to make. The carcass of a stripped-down industrial process-control computer was lying on the floor by the bed, along with more boxes, an Army battle helmet and ammunition belt—both souvenirs of Jay's mandatory cadet training on the *Mayflower II*—and assorted junk from a medium-duty fluid clutch assembly, the intended purpose of which was a complete mystery. Jay himself had disappeared early on to go off exploring. Bernard shrugged to himself. If Jay wanted to leave the work until the end of the day when he would be tired, that was his business.

"Bernie, this is too much!" Jean's voice came up from the lounge area below. "I'm never going to get used to this." Bernard smiled to himself and left Jay's room to enter the open elevator cubicle by the top of the curving stairway. Seconds later he walked out again and into the lounge. Jean was standing in the center of the floor between the dining room and the area of sunken floor before the king-size wall screen that formed a comfortable enclave surrounded by a sofa, two large armchairs, and a revolving case of shelves half recessed into the wall; a coffee table of dark-tinted glass formed its centerpiece. She gestured helplessly. "What are we ever going to do with all this space? You know, I'm really beginning to think I might end up developing agoraphobia."

Bernard grinned. "It takes some getting used to, doesn't it. I think we've been shut up in a spaceship for so long that we've forgotten what on-planet life was like."

"Was it ever like this? I certainly don't remember."

"Perhaps not quite, but that was twenty years ago, remember. Times change, I guess."

Marie, who had been exploring the house, emerged from the elevator. "The basement is huge!" she told them. "There are all kinds of rooms down there, and I don't know what they're for. I could have my own room to draw things in. And did you know there's another door down there that leads out to a tunnel? I think it might go through to where the cab stops because it's got a thing like a conveyor running along next to it. Perhaps we needn't have carried all those things over and in through the front door at all."

"I said you were in too much of a hurry," Jean said to Bernard. "Just think, all that work for nothing. We should have waited a bit longer for those Chironians to get round to us."

Bernard shrugged. "What the hell? It's done now. We needed the exercise."

Marie walked across the room and gazed at the large screen. "Does this work?" she asked.

"I don't know. We haven't tried it yet," Bernard answered. He raised his voice a fraction. "Anybody home? What do we have to do to get a computer in this place?" No response.

"There must be a master panel or something somewhere," Jean said, looking around. "How about that?" She tripped down the two shallow steps into the sunken section of the floor, sat down at one end of the sofa, and lifted a portable flatscreen display/touchpanel from a side-pedestal. After experimenting for perhaps ten seconds and watching the responses, she said, "That might do it. Try again."

"Is there a computer in the house?" Bernard called out.

"At your service," a voice replied from the direction of the screen. "I answer to *Jeeves,* unless you want to make it something different." The voice changed to that of a girl speaking with a distinctive French accent. *"Un petite française, possiblement?"* Then it switched to a guttural male—*"Karl, ze Bavarian butler, maybe?"*—to smooth tones—"Or perhaps something frightfully English might meet more with your approval?"—and finally back to its original American. "All planetary communications and database facilities at your disposal—public, domestic, educational, professional, and personal; information storage, computation, entertainment, instruction, tuition, reference, travel arrangements, accommodations, services, goods, and resources, secretarial assistance, and consultancy. You name it, I can handle it or put you in touch with the right people."

Bernard raised his eyebrows. "Well, hello, Jeeves. How about all that? I guess you'd better stay who you are for the time being. How about giving us a rundown on this place for a start? For instance, how do you . . ."

Jean looked away as she heard the front door open. A few seconds later Jay arrived. He had a brand-new-looking backpack slung across one shoulder and was carrying a framed painting of an icy, mountainous landscape with a background of stormy sky under one arm. His expression was vaguely perplexed.

"Jay!" Jean exclaimed. "Did you find anywhere nice? What are those things?"

"Oh." Jay set the painting down by the wall and frowned at it as if he had just noticed it for the first time. "I thought that might look nice in my room." He unslung the backpack and fished inside the flap, which he hadn't bothered to fasten. "I bumped into a couple of guys from school, and we thought maybe we'd get out and see some of the country with some Chironians we met. There's a lot more of it around here than inside the GC module. So I got these." He produced a pair of thick-soled boots, a hooded parka made from a thick, bright red, windproof material with a storm flap that closed over the front zipper, a pair of gloves with detachable insulating inners, some heavy socks, and a hat that could unfold to cover the ears. "We were thinking of going to the mountains across the sea," he explained. "You can get there in a flyer from Franklin in about twenty minutes."

Jean took the boots and turned them over in her hands. Then she picked up the parka, unfolded it, and studied it in silence for a couple of seconds. "But . . . these are *good,* Jay," she said. A concerned expression spread over her face. "Where . . . how did you get them? I mean . . . what's all this going to cost?"

Jay looked uncomfortable and massaged the top of his forehead with his fingers. "I know you're not going to believe this, Ma," he said. "But they're not going to cost anything. Nothing seems to cost anything. I don't understand it either, but—"

"Oh, Jay, don't be silly. Come on now—tell me where all this came from."

"Really—you just walk in and help yourself. That's how they do things here . . . for everything."

"What's the problem?" Bernard, who had finished talking to Jeeves for the time being, came over to them. Marie followed close behind.

Jean looked at him with a worried face. "Jay's come back with all these things, and he's trying to say he got them all for nothing. He's claiming that anyone can just help themselves. I've never heard such nonsense."

Bernard gave Jay a stern look. "You don't expect us to believe that, surely. Now, tell us where this stuff came from. I want the truth. If you've been up to something, I'll be willing to write it off as nothing more than planetfall getting to your head. Now—are you sure there isn't something you want to tell us?"

"Everything I've said is true," Jay insisted. "There's this big kinda market in town. It's got just about everything, and you just walk in and take what you want. We got talking to some Chironians, and they showed us what you do. I don't understand it either, but that's how things work here."

"Oh, Jay," Jean groaned. "They were probably taking you for a ride to get a laugh out of it. At your age, you should know better."

"They weren't," Jay protested. "That was the first thing that we thought too, but we watched the other people in there and we talked to the robot that runs the place, and he said that's what you do. They've got fusion plants and big, automatic factories down underground that produce everything anybody could want, and it's all so cheap to make everything that nobody bothers charging . . . or something like that. I can't figure it out."

"Is this the truth?" Bernard asked uncertainly with a strong note of suspicion in his voice.

"Of course it is." Jay sighed wearily. "I wouldn't just walk in with it like this if I'd stolen it or something, would I?"

"I bet he did," Marie declared.

"Thanks a lot," Jay said.

"I want to see this place. Is there any reason why you couldn't take me back there right now?"

Jay sighed again. "I guess not. Let's go. It's one stop along the maglev line."

"Can we go too?" Marie asked, evidently having forgotten her previous convictions. "I want to gets *lots* of things."

"Oh, let your father go with Jay, dear," Jean said. "You can help me finish up here. We can go and see it tomorrow."

"Don't you want to come along?" Bernard asked Jean. "It would get you out and give you a break."

Jean shook her head and indicated Marie surreptitiously with her eyes. "It would be best if you went on your own. We've got plenty to do here." Marie made a face but stayed quiet.

Bernard nodded. "Okay. We'll see you later then. Maybe you'd better leave that stuff here for now, Jay. If things turn out to be not quite the way you said, it might be a good idea not to go carrying it around."

Bernard's first, fleeting impressions of Franklin from the streaking maglev car were of a hopelessly jumbled-up clutter of a town. Unlike the neat and orderly models of urban planning that had replaced the heaps of American rubble during the recovery after the Lean Years—with business, entertainment, industrial, and residential sectors segregated by green belts and tidy landsculpting—everything in Franklin seemed to be intermingled with no discernible rhyme or reason. Buildings, towers, houses, and unidentifiable constructions of all shapes, sizes, and colors were packed together, overlapping and fusing in some places while giving way to clumps of greenery and trees in others. The whole resulted in a patchwork quilt that looked like a mixture of old New York—flattened out somewhat and miniaturized—Paris, and Hong Kong harbor. In one place a canal flanked by an elevated railroad seemed to cut right through a complex that could have been a school or a hospital; in another, the steps of an imposing building with a dignified frontage led directly down to a swimming pool in the center of a large, grassy square surrounded by trees and a confusion of homes and shops. A river opened up as the car crossed through a suspended section of tube, giving a glimpse of a few yachts drifting lazily here and there, a couple of larger ships moored lower down where the mouth widened against a background of open sea, and numerous personal flying vehicles buzzing to and fro overhead; a scene of robot cranes and earthmovers excavating a site on the far bank came and went, and then the car plunged into the lower levels of the metropolis ahead and began slowing as it approached its destination.

"It's a bit different from taking a cab round the Ring," Jay remarked as the car eased to a halt.

"You can say that again," Bernard agreed.

"Is this what the cities back on Earth were like?"

"Well . . . some of them, a long time ago, maybe. But not modern ones."

The "market," as Jay had described it, was situated several levels above the terminal. To get to it they used a series of escalators. A lot of people were milling about, dressed in all manner of styles and colors and reflecting the various races of Earth in more or less even proportions, which was to be expected since the genetic codes carried by the *Kuan-yin* had comprised a balanced mix of types. Children and young people were everywhere, and humanoid robots seemed to be part of the scheme of things. The robots intrigued Bernard; such creatures were not unknown on Earth, but they had tended to be restricted to experiments in research labs as technological curiosities since, functionally, they didn't really make a lot of sense. Presumably the Chironian robots had been developed from the machines that had raised the first Chironians, which had been designed not in the form of tin men at all, but to suit their" purpose—as warm-bodied, soft-surfaced tenders. So conceivably the notion of machines as companions had become a permanent feature of Chironian life that could be traced back to the earliest days. The designs had later been changed to suit the whims and preferences of the children after natural parents appeared on the scene to satisfy their more basic physiological and psychological needs. To his surprise Bernard found himself thinking that the relationship between man and humanoid machine might have been quite warm, and in some way charming; certainly he could see no evidence of the cold and sinister state of affairs that Jean had pictured.

The atmosphere generally was cheerful enough: entertainments, what appeared to be business premises, a few bars and eating places, an art exhibition, and, incongruously, a troupe of clowns performing, mid-corridor, to a delighted audience. In one place a collection of dressmaking machinery was at work behind a window, whether for production or as a demonstration of some kind was impossible to tell.

Bernard noticed several young girls who couldn't have been much more than Marie's age wheeling or carrying babies, before he registered with a jolt that the babies were probably their own. Mixed with the shock of the realization came a twinge of relief that he had left Jean and Marie at home. Explaining this was going to require some delicate handling. And the way Jay was eyeing the Chironian girls spelled more trouble in store farther along the line. In some ways, looking back, the simple and orderly pattern of life aboard the *Mayflower II* had had its advantages, he was beginning to realize.

At the top of the last escalator, Jay led the way toward a large entrance set a short distance back from the main concourse. Above it was a sign that read:

MANDEL BAY
MERCHANDISE, FRANKLIN CENTER OUTLET

❊ ❊ ❊

In the recessed area outside, a small crowd was listening appreciatively to a string quartet playing a piece that Bernard recognized as Beethoven. Suddenly, for a moment, Earth seemed less far away. Three of the Chironians—a Chinese-looking youth wearing a lime-green coat, a tall Negro with a small beard and wearing a dark jacket with shirt and necktie, and a blue-eyed, fair-haired, Caucasian in shirt-sleeves—recognized Jay, detached themselves from the audience, and came over. Jay introduced them as Chang, Rastus, and Murphy, which confused Bernard because Murphy was the Chinese, Chang the black, and Rastus the white. Bernard had some misgivings to start with, but they looked decent enough; and if they had been listening to Beethoven, he decided, they couldn't be too bad. He glanced over his shoulder instinctively before remembering that the *May-flower II* was twenty thousand miles away, realized that he could afford to loosen up a little, and said, "I, er . . . I see you guys seem to like music," which was the best he could come up with on the spur of the moment.

"That's one of my sisters playing the cello," Murphy informed him. (Was it? Oh, yes—the Chinese was Murphy.) Bernard looked over at the quartet. The cello player was olive-skinned with Mediterranean features.

"Oh . . . she's very good," Bernard said.

Murphy looked pleased. "Don't you think it has a fine tone? It's one of Chang's. He makes them."

"Very," Bernard agreed. He didn't really have a clue.

"These are the guys I was telling you about," Jay said. "The ones who are with the group that's going to the mountains."

"You'd be welcome to come too if you want," Rastus said.

Bernard managed a weak smile. "That's a nice thought, but I've got a job to do. We're still going to be busy for a while. Thanks anyway." He thought for a few seconds. "I hope you're not planning anything too tough out there. I mean, Jay hasn't exactly had a lot of practice at that kind of thing. He's never even seen a planet before." Jay winced under his breath and looked away.

Chang laughed. "It's okay. We won't be going very high, and it'll be more walking than anything else. There won't be anything more risky than maybe a few daskrends showing up."

"You can use a gun, can't you, Jay?" Murphy asked.

"Well, yes, but. . ." Jay looked taken aback.

"We should have mentioned it," Murphy said. "Bring one along. A forty-five or something like that would be best, if you've got one."

"Wait a minute, wait a minute," Bernard interrupted, raising a hand in alarm. "Just what the hell is this? What's a das?—"

"Daskrend," Murphy supplied. "Oh, they're a kind of wolf but bigger, and they've got poison fangs. But they're pretty dumb and no big deal to handle. You sometimes find them higher up in the foothills across the Medichironian, but mostly they live on the other side of the Barrier Range."

"We're going to have to talk about this, Jay." Bernard's voice was very serious.

"I was teasing, really," Murphy said. "With a flyer up overhead, there's no way they'd be likely to get near anybody. But it's customary to go armed when you're not in places like Franklin . . . just in case."

"Maybe we shouldn't rush things too much," Bernard suggested. He looked at Jay. "You may want to give yourself time to acclimatize before you get into something like this." His tone said that he was being tactful in his phrasing; Jay wasn't going. For the moment, at least, Jay didn't feel inclined to argue too much.

"It's up to you. Just let us know," Murphy said and dismissed the subject with a slight shrug. "So, have you come back for something else?"

"No. My father just wants to see the store."

"Want to come with us?" Bernard invited.

"Sure," Murphy accepted, and they all began walking. On the way, Jay explained the problem to his three friends.

Inside, a large hall of counters and shelves displayed all manner of products from electronic devices and scientific instruments at one end to rainwear and sports equipment at the other. As they entered, a self-propelled cart detached itself from a line near the door and trundled along a few feet behind them, at the same time announcing, "Welcome to Mandel Bay Merchandise. Did you ever think of laying out your own garden and tending it *manually*? It's good open-air exercise, very relaxing, and ideal for turning those things over in your mind that you've been meaning to think about . . . as well as the soil, ho-ho! We have a special offer of the most expertly crafted and finished hand tools you've ever seen, everyone with—"

"Go away," Chang told it. "We're just looking today." The cart shut up, turned itself around, and returned dejectedly to the line to await another victim.

Bernard stopped, frowned, and looked around. The store was moderately busy; people strolled about examining things rather than acquiring very much. An exception was a couple on the far side whom he recognized as Terrans from the *Mayflower II*, conspicuous for the three carts trailing them in convoy and loaded with everything imaginable. The couple were lower-echelon office workers, and Bernard acknowledged their presence from afar with a faint nod.

"I suppose all this seems a bit strange to you folks," Rastus noted. "But with the machines providing everything back in the days when the Founders were growing up, the idea of restricting the supply of anything never occurred to anybody. There wasn't any reason to. We've carried on that way ever since. You'll get used to it."

"But . . . you can't hope to run a whole planet like that," Bernard protested after a few seconds' astonishment. "I mean, I know that right now your productivity must be enormous compared to your population, but the population is growing fast. You've got to start thinking about some kind of . . . system to regulate things. Your resources are only finite."

Rastus looked puzzled. "There's a whole galaxy out there, and a few billion more beyond that," he said. "It'll take a long time for it to get crowded. Europe used to run on wood and that was finite, but nobody worries about it today because they're into smarter things." He shrugged. "It's the same with everything else. The human mind is an infinite resource, and that's all you need."

Bernard shook his head and gestured in the direction of the couple from the *Mayflower II,* who were glancing furtively around them while a handling machine by the exit unloaded their carts onto a conveyor that looked as if it fed down to the level below. "But look what's happening," he said. "How long can you keep up with that kind of thing? What happens when everyone starts acting like that?"

"Why should they?" Chang asked. He looked across at the couple curiously. "I was wondering what they want with all that stuff. Anyone would think it's about to run out."

"For the status," Jay said. Chang looked at him blankly. "It's okay," Rastus said. "As long as they pay for it."

"That's my whole point," Bernard told them. "They're *not* paying for it—not a cent's worth of any of it."

"They will," Rastus replied.

"How?"

Rastus looked mildly surprised. "They'll find a way," he said.

Just then Jerry Pernak came around a corner accompanied by his fiancée, Eve Verritty, and two more Chironians. A cart was following them with a few odds and ends inside. He gaped at Bernard and Jay in surprise, then grinned. "Hey! So Jay dragged you out to see the sights, eh? Hello, Jay. Started making friends already?" Introductions were exchanged with smiles and handshakes. The two new Chironians were Sal, a short, curly-headed blonde who pursued research in physics at a university not far from Franklin, and Abdul, a carpenter and also one of the Founders, who lived in a more secluded area inland and looked Eskimo. Abdul's grandson, he informed them proudly, had hand-carved the original designs from which the programs for producing the interior wood fittings used at

Cordova Village had been encoded. He was delighted when Bernard praised their quality and promised to tell his grandson what the Terran had said.

"And how about this?" Pernak said. "Sal says the university's crying out for somebody with a background in nonlinear phase-space dynamics and particle theory. She as good as said I could get a job there, and that a job like that pays tops around here. What do you think of that for a break?"

Bernard gave a pained smile. "It sounds good," he agreed. "But the Directorate might have a few things to say."

"I know, but I figured I'd go take a look at the place anyhow out of curiosity. That can't do any harm. Later on, well. . . maybe anything could happen."

"How are they going to pay you?" Jay asked.

"We haven't talked about that yet," Pernak told him.

"That's a personal question, Jay," Bernard cautioned. "Anyhow, it's early yet."

"Jay told us you're an engineering officer on the *Mayflower II*," Chang said, sounding interested. "A specialist in fusion processes."

"That's right." Bernard was surprised and felt a little flattered. "I help look after the main drive systems."

"We could probably arrange a visit for you too," Chang offered. "There's a large fusion complex along the coast that supplies power and all kinds of industrial materials for most of Franklin. Another one's due to be built soon, and they'll be needing people too. I could arrange for you to go and see it, if you think you'd be interested."

It was interesting, certainly. "Well . . . maybe," Bernard replied guardedly. "Who do you know there?"

"I've got a friend whose mother works most of her time there. Her name's Kath."

"And that would be enough to fix something?"

"Sure," Chang said confidently. "I'll give you a call when I've talked to Adam. He's the friend. Would Jay like to go too."

Bernard hadn't really thought of that. He saw Jay nodding vigorously, and tossed up his hands. "Why not? If you're sure it's okay, then thanks . . . thanks a lot."

"No problem," Chang told him.

Eve looked at the cart, which was waiting patiently, and then back at Pernak. "We're through, really," she said. "Shall we carry on and see the town?"

"Let's do that," Pernak agreed. "I'll take the things."

"They can go on the maglev on their own," Murphy informed them. "The handler at the village terminal will route them through. You pick them up by the elevator in your basement. What's your number there?"

"Ninetey-seven," Pernak replied. He looked at Eve and shook his head.

"That's all," Murphy said, addressing the cart. "Ninety-seven, Cordova Village. On your way."

"One second," a voice said from behind them. They looked round to find a Chironian robot winking its lights at them. It was a short, rounded type, which made it look tubby. "You haven't taken any of our special-offer hand gardening tools. Do you want to grow fat and old before your time? Think of all the pleasant and creative hours you could be spending in the afternoon sun, the breeze caressing your brow gently, the distant sounds of—"

"Aw, cut it out, Hoover," Rastus told the robot. "These people have only just arrived. They've got more than enough to do." He looked at the Terrans. "This is Hoover. He runs the place. Don't pay too much attention or you'll end up buried in junk up to your eyes."

"*Junk?!*" Hoover's lights blazed crimson in unison. "What do you mean, *junk?* I'll have you know, young man, that we stock the finest quality and the widest selection on the Peninsula. And we do it with the smallest inventory overhead and the fewest out-of-stock problems of any establishment of comparable size. Junk indeed! Have you troubled to inspect our—"

"Okay, okay, Hoover." Rastus held up an apologetic hand. "You know I didn't mean it. You do a great job here. And the displays today are very artistic."

"Thank you, and my compliments to you, sir." Hoover acknowledged in a suddenly more agreeable voice. "I hope you all enjoyed your visit and that we'll see you here again soon." The cart rolled away to deliver its load to the handling machine. Hoover escorted the group back to the entrance. "Now, next week we're expecting a consignment of absolutely first-class—"

"Lay off, Hoover," Chang said wearily. "We'll check it out through the net. Okay, maybe we'll see you next week."

In the corridor, the quartet had shifted to Mozart. "Have the robots been kept on as a kind of . . . tradition?" Bernard asked.

"The kids like having them around," Sal confirmed. "And to be honest, I suppose we do too. We've all grown up with them."

"I can remember the one that first taught me to talk," Abdul said. "It's still operating today, up there on the *Kuan-yin*. But the ones you see today have changed a lot."

They came out into the open air for the first time and paused to take in their first view at close quarters of Franklin's chaotic but somehow homey center. "And what about all this?" Eve asked. "Does it go back to the first days too?"

"Yes," Sal replied. "Forty years ago this was just a few domes and a shuttle port. The main base that you came in through was only built about ten years ago. Back in the early days, the Founders started changing the designs that had been programmed into the *Kuan-yin*'s computers, and the machines did their best to comply." She sighed. "And this is what it ended up like. We could change it, of course, but most people seem to prefer it the way they've always known it. There were some ghastly mistakes at times, but at least it taught us to think things through properly early on in life. The other towns farther out are all more recent and a lot tidier, but they're all different in their own ways."

"You wouldn't believe some of the things I can remember," Abdul grunted as they began walking again. "Darned machines . . . always did just what we told 'em. For a time we thought they were pretty stupid, but it turned out it was us."

"How old were you then?" Eve asked curiously.

"Oh, I don't know . . . four, five, maybe. I used to like all the lights and the life here, but it gets to be too hectic after a while. Now I prefer the hills. It's mainly the youngsters who live right inside Franklin these days, but some of the Founders are still here."

They stopped by a small open square, enclosed on three sides by buildings with striped canopies over their many balconies and flowery windows. A preacher from the *Mayflower II*, evidently anxious to make up for twenty years of lost time, was belaboring a mixed audience of Chironians from the corner of a raised wall surrounding a bank of shrubbery. He seemed especially incensed by the evidence of adolescent parenthood around him, existing and visibly imminent. The Chironians appeared curious but skeptical. Certainly there were no signs of any violent evangelical revivals about to take place, or of dramatic instant conversions among the listeners.

"It seems irrational to me to argue one way or another about things there's no evidence for," a boy of about fourteen remarked. "You can make up anything you want if there's no way of testing whether it's true or not, so what's the point?"

"We must have *faith!*" the preacher roared, his eyes wide with fervor.

"Why?" a girl in a pink jacket asked.

"Because the Book tells us we must."

"How do you know it's right?"

"There are some things which we must *accept!*" the preacher thundered.

"That's my point," the boy told him. "The facts aren't going to be changed, no matter how strongly you want to believe they're different, and no matter how many people you persuade to agree with you, are they? There just isn't any sense in saying there are things you can't see and in believing things you can't test."

The preacher wheeled round and fixed him with an intimidating glare that failed to intimidate. "Do you believe in atoms?"

"Sure. Who doesn't?"

"Aha!" The preacher made an appealing gesture to the audience. "Is there any difference, my friends? Can we *see* atoms? Is this not arrogant insolence?" He looked back at the boy and jabbed an accusing finger at him. "Do you claim to have seen atoms? Tell us that you have, and I will say that you *lie!*" Another appealing flourish. "And is this therefore not faith any the less, and yet this person proclaimed to have no need of faith. Does he not, therefore, contradict himself before us?"

"Your comparison is quite invalid," a girl who was with the boy pointed out. "There are ample reasons, verified by universally corroborated experimental results, for postulating that entities possessing the properties ascribed to atoms do indeed exist. Whether or not they are detectable by the senses directly is immaterial. Where are your comparable data?"

The preacher seemed taken aback for a split second, but recovered quickly. "The world around us," he bellowed, throwing his arms wide. "Is it not there? Do I not see it? Who created it? Tell us. Is that not evidence enough?"

"No," the boy answered after a moment's reflection. "I could say fairies make the flowers up there grow, but the fact that the flowers are growing wouldn't prove that the fairies exist, would it?"

"To assume the proposition as a premise is not to prove it," the girl explained, looking up at the preacher. "Your argument, I'm afraid, is completely circular."

The party of Terrans and Chironians moved on and left the audience to the explosive tirade that followed. "Those were hardly more than children," Eve Verritty murmured.

"You seem surprised," Rastus said to Bernard.

"Those kids," Bernard replied, gesturing behind them. "There are some pretty sharp minds among them. Is everyone here like that?"

"Of course not," Rastus said. "But everyone values what they have. I said the mind was an infinite resource, but only if you don't squander it. Don't you think that makes an interesting paradox?"

❦ CHAPTER FOURTEEN ❦

Still no overture came from the Chironian leaders. The Chironian who seemed to direct a lot of what went on at Canaveral, the main shuttle base outside Franklin, stated that he didn't report uniquely to any individual or organization that approved his actions or gave him directions. So who told him how the place was to be run? It depended. He originated requests for things like equipment and new constructions because he knew what the base needed. How did he know? Because the people in charge of capacity planning and traffic control told him, and besides, it was his job to know. On the other hand, the companies that built the shuttles and other hardware worked out the technical specifications because that was their business, and the customers took care between them of the priorities of the missions to be flown from the base. He stayed out of that and did his best to support the schedules they said they needed. So ultimately, who was in charge? Who told whom to do what, and who did it? It depended. Nothing made any sense.

Following a directive from Wellesley, Howard Kalens instructed Amery Farnhill to open an embassy in a small building at Canaveral which the Chironians obligingly agreed to vacate, having been about to move into larger premises elsewhere anyway. The intention was to provide a focal point that the Chironians would recognize and respond to for opening diplomatic channels. Unfortunately, the natives paid no attention to it, and after two days of sitting at his desk with nothing to do, Amery Farnhill pleaded with Kalens for approval to send out snatch squads from his contingent of SD guards to bring in likely candidates to talk to him. Kalens could only partly concur since he was under strict instructions from Wellesley. "If you can persuade them, then do it," he replied over the communications link from the *Mayflower II* "A calculated degree of intimidation is acceptable, but on no account are they to use force. I don't like it either, Amery, but I'm afraid we'll have to live with the plan for the time being."

"Hey, you. Stop." The major in command of the four SD troopers sent to scout out the center of Canaveral City—a residential and commercial suburb situated outside the base and merging into one side of Franklin—addressed the Chironian whom they had followed from the restaurant a few yards back around the corner. He was well-dressed, in his midthirties, and carrying an attaché case. The Chironian ignored them and kept walking. Whereupon the major marched ahead to plant himself firmly in the man's path. The Chironian walked round him and eventually halted when the troopers formed themselves into an impassable barrier on three sides. "You're coming to talk to the ambassador," the major informed him.

"No, I'm not. I'm going to talk about air-conditioning for the new passenger lounge in the base."

"Say 'sir' when you talk to me."

"If you wish. Sir when you talk to me." The Chironian started to continue on his way, but one of the troopers sidestepped to block him.

"What's your name, boy?" The major thrust his face close and narrowed his eyes menacingly.

"None of your goddamn business."

"Do you want us to have to drag you there?"

"Do you want to get out of here alive?"

The major's jaw quivered; his face colored. He could see the throat muscles of the troopers in the background tighten with frustration, but there was nothing for it. He had his orders. "On your way," he growled. "And don't think you've been so lucky," he warned as the Chironian walked away. "We've got your face taped. There'll be a next time."

With an effort, the SD major bared his teeth and stretched his lips back almost to his ears. "Excuse me, sir, but do you have a few minutes you could spare?"

"What for?" The Chironian in the purple sweater and green shorts asked.

"Our ambassador would like to talk to you. It's not far—just inside the base."

"What about?"

"Just a friendly chat . . . about your government, how it's organized, who's in it . . . a few things like that. It won't take long at all."

The Chironian rubbed his chin dubiously. "I'm not at all sure that I could be much help. Government of what in particular?"

"The planet. . . Chiron. Who runs it?"

"Runs the planet? Gee . . . I don't know anything about that."

"Who tells you what to do?"

"It depends."

"On what?"

"On what I'm doing." The Chironian looked apologetic. "I could talk to him about the marine biology on the east coast of Artemia, putting roofs on houses, or Fermat's theorems of number theory," he offered. "Do you think he might be interested in anything like that?"

The major sighed wearily. "It doesn't matter. Forget it. Do you know anyone else around here we should try asking?"

"Not really. I guess you guys have got a tough job on your hands. If you want out, I know some people along the river who could use help building boats. Have any of you ever done anything like that?"

The major stared at him as if refusing to believe his ears. "Get outa here," he choked in a weak voice. He shook his head incredulously, "Just . . . get the hell outa here, willya. . ."

"It's impossible!" Amery Farnhill protested to a full meeting of the Directorate in the *Mayflower II*'s Government Center. "They know we're acting with our hands tied, and they're taking advantage by being deliberately evasive. The only way we'll get anywhere is if you allow us to get tougher."

Wellesley shook his head firmly. "Not if you're talking about roughing up people in the streets. It would undo everything we've achieved."

"What have we achieved?" Borftein asked contemptuously.

"We have to do something," Marcia Quarrey insisted. "Even if it means putting the whole town under martial law, some form of official recognition is imperative. This has gone on far too long as it is."

Howard Kalens simmered as he listened. Quarrey had changed her tune when the commercial lobby, whose interests she represented, panicked at the prospect of having to compete in the insane Chironian economic system. The signals coming down the line had told her that she'd better get something done about it and soon, if she wanted to see herself reinstated after the elections, which in turn meant that Kalens had better be seen to back her case if he expected her support in his bid for the Directorship.

"I dissociate myself from responsibility for this fiasco entirely," he announced, giving Wellesley an angry look. "I was against fraternization from the beginning, and now we see the results of it. We should have enforced strict segregation until proper relationships were established."

"It wouldn't have worked," Wellesley countered. "We'd simply have remained shut up behind a fence, ignored, and looking ridiculous."

"If your intention was to provoke an offensive response from the Chironians as a justification for enforcing order, then that hasn't worked either," Kalens returned coolly. "Now we must live with the damage and consider our alternatives."

"What are you suggesting?" Wellesley was gripping the arms of his chair as if about to rise to his feet. "Withdraw that accusation at once!"

"Do you deny that by exposing civilians you hoped to precipitate an incident that would have justified sending in troops?"

Wellesley turned pale, and the veins stood out on his temples. "I deny that! I also deny that you urged segregation. My policy was to encourage their leaders out into the open by a demonstration of peaceful coexistence, and you went along with it. Withdraw your statement."

Kalens looked at him calmly for a few seconds, then nodded. "Very well. I withdraw the statement and apologize."

"Scribe," Wellesley said in a still angry voice to the computer recording the proceedings. "Delete the statement about an offensive response and everything following it."

"Deleted," the machine confirmed. "Last line of entry reads: '. . . shut up behind a fence, ignored, and looking ridiculous.'"

The suggestion had served its purpose. Sterm was watching Kalens curiously, and Marcia Quarrey was looking across the table with new respect. Farnhill shuffled his feet uncomfortably.

"So where do we go from here?" Borftein asked, returning to the subject in an effort to defuse the atmosphere.

Sterm studied his fingers for a moment and then looked up. "Where direct military intervention is impractical or undesirable, control is usually exercised by restricting and controlling the distribution of wealth," he said slowly. "Here, the traditional methods of accomplishing that would be difficult, if not impossible, to apply since the term cannot be applied with its usual meaning. This society must have its pressure points, nevertheless. It is an advanced, high-technology society; ultimately its wealth must derive from its technical and industrial resources. That is where we should look for its vulnerable spots."

A short silence fell while the meeting digested the observation. Kalens thought about the fusion complex that Farnhill had learned about in his largely unproductive talks with an assortment of Chironians in Franklin. Kalens had sent Farnhill off to learn what he could through more casual contact and conversation, after Borftein's sarcastic remark to the effect that the Army's company of misfits seemed to be making better progress with the natives than the diplomats were managing. "Yes . . . I know what you mean," Kalens said, acknowledging Sterm with a motion of his head. "As a matter of fact, we have already begun inquiries along those lines." He turned toward Farnhill. "Amery, tell us again about that place along the coast."

"Port Norday?"

"Yes—some kind of industrial complex, wasn't it?"

"It's a centralized, fusion-based facility that provides generating capacity for practically this whole area, and a great deal of materials via a variety of interdependent processes," Farnhill informed the meeting. "Primary metals and chemicals are among its major products, as well as electricity."

"Who operates it?" Marcia Quarrey asked.

Farnhill looked uneasy and seemed a trifle awkward. "Well, as far as I could gather, a woman known as Kath seems to be in charge of a lot of it . . . as much as anybody's in charge of anything in this place. I haven't actually met her though."

"That could be a good place to start," Kalens suggested to Wellesley.

Wellesley seemed thoughtful. "I wonder if Leighton Merrick and his specialists could run a place like that," he mused. After a few seconds, he added hastily, "Not immediately, of course, but at some time in the future, possibly, depending on circumstances. As insurance, it would certainly pay us to know something more about it."

"I don't know," Farnhill said. "You'd have to ask Merrick about that."

"He ought to be given a chance to go and look at it," Borftein agreed with a nod. "What would be the best way to arrange something like that?"

Kalens shrugged without looking up from the table. "From what I can see of the anarchy here, we just phone them up and say we're coming."

"Perhaps we could propose a goodwill exchange visit," Sterm suggested. "In return, we might offer to show some of their technical people selected parts of the *Mayflower II*. A legitimate cover would be desirable."

"It's a thought," Wellesley agreed distantly. He cast his eyes round the table. "Does anybody have a better idea?" Nobody did. "So let's get Merrick here and talk to him," Wellesley said. He sat back and placed his hands on the edge of the table. "This would be a good time to break for lunch. Scribe, adjourn the session here. We will reconvene in ninety minutes. Contact Leighton Merrick in Engineering, and have him join us then. Also ask him to bring with him two of his more capable officers. Advise me at once if there are any difficulties. That's all."

"Acknowledged," the computer replied.

⚛ CHAPTER FIFTEEN ⚛

Mrs. Crayford, the plump, extravagantly dressed wife of Vice-Admiral Crayford, Slessor's second-in-command of the *Mayflower II*'s crew, closed the box containing her new set of Chironian silver cutlery and added it to the pile of boxes on the table by her chair. Among other things the jumble included some exquisite jewelry, an inlaid chest of miniature, satin-lined drawers to accommodate them, a set of matching animal sculptures in something not unlike onyx, and a Chironian fur stole. "Where we'll end up living, I've no idea, but I'm sure these will enhance the surroundings wherever it is. Don't you think the silver is delightful? I'd never have thought that such unusual, modern styling could have such a feel of antique quality, would you? I must return to that place the next time I go down to Franklin. Some of the tableware there went with it perfectly."

"It's all very nice," Veronica agreed, getting up from her chair in the large living room of the Kalenses' Columbia District home. "I'm sure you'll find somewhere wonderful." Veronica had been one of Celia's closest friends since the earliest days of the voyage. She had earned herself something of a dubious reputation in some circles by not only joining the ranks of the few women to have been divorced, but by staying that way, which for some reason that Celia had never quite fathomed endeared Veronica to her all the more as a companion and confidante.

"They're priceless," Celia commented dryly from her chair. They had been, literally, but the irony was lost on Mrs. Crayford. Veronica caught Celia's eye with a warning look.

"They must be, mustn't they," Mrs. Crayford agreed blissfully. She shook her head. "In some ways it seems almost criminal to take them, but. . ." she sighed, "I'm sure they'd just be wasted otherwise. After all, those people are obviously savages and quite incapable of appreciating the true value of anything." Celia's throat tightened, but she managed to remain quiet. Mrs. Crayford fussed with her pile of boxes. "Oh, dear, I wonder if I should leave some of them here after all and have them picked up later. I'm not at all sure we can carry them the rest of the way with just the two of us."

"That would be quite all right," Celia said.

"We'll manage," Veronica promised. "They're more awkward than heavy. You worry too much."

Mrs. Crayford glanced at the clock display on the room's companel. "Well, then, I really must be getting along. I did so enjoy the trip and the company. We must do it again soon." She heaved herself to her feet and looked around. "Now, where did I leave my coat?"

"I hung it in the hallway," Veronica said, getting up. She walked ahead and out the door while Mrs. Crayford waddled a few feet behind. "Don't bother bringing anything out, Celia," Veronica's voice called back. "I'll come back in for the things."

Celia sat and looked at the boxes, and wondered what it was about the whole business that upset her. It wasn't so much the spectacle of Mrs. Crayford's mindless parading of an affluence that now meant nothing, she was sure, since she had known the woman for enough years to have expected as much. Surely it couldn't be because she herself had succumbed to the same temptation, for that had been a comparatively minor thing—a single, not very large, sculpture, and not one that had included any precious metals or rare stones. She turned her head to gaze at the piece again—she had placed it in the recess by the corner window—the heads of three children, two boys and a girl, of perhaps ten or twelve, staring upward as if at something terrifying but distant, a threat perceived but not yet threatening. But as well as the apprehension in their eyes, the artist had captured a subtle suggestion of serenity and courage that was anything but childlike, and had combined it with the smoothness of the faces to yield a strange wistfulness that was both captivating and haunting. The piece was fifteen years old, the dealer in Franklin had told them, and had been made by one of the Founders. Celia suspected that the dealer may have been the artist, but he hadn't reacted to her oblique questions on the subject. Were the expressions on those faces affecting her for some reason? Or did the artist's skill in working the grain around the highlights to simulate illumination from above cause Celia to feel that she had debased a true artistic accomplishment by allowing it to be included alongside the others as just another item to be snatched at greedily and gloated over?

Veronica came back into the room and began picking up Mrs. Crayford's boxes. "It's all right. You stay there, Celia. I can manage." She saw the expression on Celia's face and smiled. Her voice dropped to a whisper. "I know—awful, isn't it. It's just a phase. She'll get over it."

"I hope so," Celia murmured.

Veronica paused as she was about to turn toward the door. "I'm beginning to miss being thrown out in the middle of the night. How's your handsome sergeant these days? You haven't finished with him, have you?"

Celia gave her a reproachful look. "Oh, come on . . . you know that was just a diversion. I haven't seen him for a while now, but then, everyone has been so busy. Finished? Not really . . . who knows?" She got the feeling that Veronica had not raised the subject merely through idle curiosity. She was right.

"I've got one too," Veronica whispered, bringing her face close to Celia's ear.

"What?"

"A new lover. What do you think?"

"Anyone I know?"

Veronica had to bite her lip to suppress the beginnings of a giggle. "A Chironian."

Celia's eyes opened wide. "You're kidding!"

"I'm not. He's an architect . . . and gorgeous! I met him in Franklin yesterday and stayed last night. It's so easy—they act as if it's perfectly natural . . . And they're *so* uninhibited!" Celia just gaped at her. Veronica winked and nodded. "Really. I'll tell you about it later. I'd better go."

"You bitch!" Celia protested. "I want to hear about it *now*."

Veronica laughed. "You'll have to eat your heart out wondering. Take care. I'll call you tonight."

When the others had gone, Celia sank back in her chair and started brooding again. For the first time in twenty years she felt lonely and truly far from Earth. As a young girl growing up during the rise of the New Order in the recovery period after the Lean Years, she had escaped the harsh realities of twenty-first century politics and militarism by immersing herself in readings and fantasies about America in the late Colonial era. Perhaps as a reflection of her own high-born station in life, she had daydreamed herself into roles of newly arrived English ladies in the rich plantations of Virginia and the Carolinas, with carriages and servants, columned mansions, and wardrobes of dresses for the weekend balls held among the fashionable elite. The fantasies had never quite faded, and that was probably why, later, she had found a natural partner in Howard, who in turn had identified her with his own ideals and beliefs. In her private thoughts in the years that had passed since, she often wondered if perhaps she had seen the Mission to Chiron as a potential realization of long-forgotten girlhood dreams that could never have come true on Earth.

Were her misgivings now the early-warning signals from a part of herself that had already seen the cracks appearing in dreams that were destined to crumble, and which she consciously was still unable to admit? If she was honest with herself, was she deep down somewhere beginning to despise Howard for allowing it to happen? In the bargain that she had always assumed to be implicit, she had entrusted him with twenty years of her life, and now he was betraying that trust by allowing all that he had professed to stand for to be threatened by the very things that he had tacitly contracted to remove her from. Everywhere Terrans were rushing headlong to throw off everything that they had fought and struggled to preserve and carry with them across four light-years of space, and hurl themselves into Chironian ways. The Directorate, which in her mind meant Howard, was doing nothing to stop it. She had once read a quotation by a British visitor, Janet Schaw, to the Thirteen Colonies in 1763, who had remarked with some disapproval on the "most disgusting equality" that she had observed prevailing on all sides. It suited the present situation well.

She swallowed as she traced through her thoughts and checked herself. She was rationalizing or hiding something from herself, she knew. Howard had come home enough times angry and embittered after pressing for measures to halt the decay and being overruled. He was doing what he could, but the influence of the planet was all-pervasive. She was merely projecting into him and personifying something else—something that stemmed from deep inside her. Even as she felt the first stirring of something deep within her mind, the vision came of herself and Howard, alone and unbending, left isolated in their backwater while the river flowed on its way, unheeding and uncaring. After twenty years, nothing lay ahead but emptiness and oblivion. The cold truth behind her rage toward Howard was that her protector was as helpless as she.

Now she knew why Earth seemed so far away. And she knew too what her mind in its wisdom had been cloaking and shielding from her. It was fear.

Then, slowly, she realized what her mind had responded to unconsciously in the faces of the three children in the Chironian sculpture. The artist had been not merely an expert, but a master. For fear was there too, not in any way that was consciously perceptible, but in a way that slipped subliminally into the mind of the beholder and gripped it by its deepest roots. That was why she had felt disturbed all the way back from Franklin. But there was still something else. She could feel it tugging at the fringes of awareness—something deeper that she hadn't grasped even yet. She turned her eyes to the sculpture again.

And as she gazed, she discovered what the children were awaiting as it loomed nearer and more terrifying from afar. The realization tightened her stomach. Even from fifteen years ago . . . it was she—for she had come with the *Mayflower II*. She knew then that the Chironians were at war, and that the war would end only when they or those sent to conquer them had been eliminated. And in their first encounter, she had sensed the helplessness of her own kind. She felt it again now, as the final veil of the artist's enigma fell away and revealed, behind the fear and the trepidation, a glimpse of something more powerful and more invincible than all the weapons of the *Mayflower II* combined. She was staring at her own extinction.

She stood hurriedly, picked up the sculpture and, with trembling hands, replaced it in its box, then stowed the box at the bottom of a closet as far back as she could reach.

◉ CHAPTER SIXTEEN ◉

Port Norday was twenty-five miles or so north of Franklin, beyond the far headland of Mandel Bay, on a rocky stretch of coastline indented by a river estuary that widened about a large island and several smaller ones. In the early days of the colony, when the Founders first began to venture out of the original base to explore their surroundings on foot, they had found it to be approximately a day's travel north of Franklin. Hence its name.

It had grown in stages from constructions that began toward the end of the colony's first decade, by which time the Founders, having profited from reflections on some of their experiences at Franklin, had been more inclined to follow the blunt admonition offered by the machines, which had amounted to, "It's going to be an industrial complex. If you mess around with it, it won't work." The result was a clean, efficient, functional layout more in keeping with what the *Kuan-yin*'s mission planners had envisaged, suitably modified where appropriate to take account of local conditions. Besides its industrial facilities, the complex included a seaport; an air and space terminal distributed mainly across the islands, which were interconnected by a network of tunnels; a college of advanced technology; and a small residential sector intended more to afford short- to medium-term accommodation for people whose business made it convenient for them to be in the vicinity than to house permanent inhabitants, although about half the population had been there for years. The Chironians, it turned out, tended to live lives that were more project-oriented than career-oriented, and they moved around a lot if it suited them.

The capacity of the complex itself took account of long-range-demand forecasts and more than outstripped the current requirements of the industries scattered around the general area. Its primary power source was a one-thousand-gigawatt, magnetically confined fusion system which combined various features of the tokamak, mirror, and "bumpy torus" configurations pioneered toward the end of the previous century, producing electricity very efficiently by blasting high-velocity, high-temperature, ionized plasma through a series of immense magnetohydrodynamic coils. In addition, the fast neutrons produced in copious amounts from this process were harnessed to breed more tritium fuel from lithium, to breed fissionable isotopes of uranium and plutonium from fertile elements obtained elsewhere in the same complex, and to "burn up" via nuclear transmutation the small amounts of radioactive wastes left over from the economy's fission component, the fuel cycle of which was fully closed and included complete reprocessing and recycling of reactor products.

The plasma emerged from this primary process with sufficient residual energy to provide high-quality heat for supplying a hydrogen-extraction plant, where seawater was "cracked" thermally to yield bases for a whole range of liquid synthetic fuels, a primary-metals extraction and processing subcomplex, a chemical-manufacturing subcomplex, and a desalination plant which was still not operational, but anticipated large-scale irrigation projects farther inland in years to come.

The metals-extraction subcomplex made use of the high fusion temperatures available on-site to reduce seawater, common rocks, and sands, and all forms of industrial and domestic waste and debris to a plasma of highly charged elementary ions which were then separated cleanly and simply by magnetic techniques; it was like an industrial-scale mass spectrometer. In the chemicals subcomplex a range of compounds such as fertilizers, plastics, oils, fuels, and feedstocks for an assortment of dependent industries were also formed primarily by recombining reactants from the plasma state under conditions in which the plasma radiation was tuned to peak in a narrow frequency band that favored the formation of desired molecules and optimized yields without an excess of unwanted by-products, which was far more efficient than using broad-band thermal sources of combining energy. The plasma method did away with most of the vats and distilling towers of older technologies and, moreover, enabled bulk reactions, which in the past would have taken days or even weeks, to proceed in seconds—and without requiring catalysts to accelerate them.

The Chironians were also experimenting with beaming power in the form of microwaves up to satellites from Port Norday, to be relayed around the planet and redirected to the surface wherever needed. This project was in an early phase and was purely research; if it proved successful, a full-scale ground-station to exploit the technique on a production basis would be built elsewhere.

Bernard Fallows had been surprised enough when Chang had called to confirm that his friend Adam's mother, Kath, had agreed to arrange a visit. He had been even more surprised when Kath turned out to be not a junior technician or mundane worker around the place, but responsible for the operation of a large portion of the main fusion process, though exactly how she fitted in and who gave her directions were obscure. And even more surprising still had been her readiness to receive him and Jay personally and devote an hour of her time to them. The comparable prospect of Leighton Merrick showing Chang and friends round the main-drive section of the *Mayflower II* was unthinkable. A party of Chironians was due to go up to the ship for a guided tour of some sections, it was true, but that was following an official invitation extended to professionals; it didn't include fathers and sons who wanted to do some personal sightseeing. Perhaps his position as an engineering officer specializing in fusion techniques had had something to do with his special treatment, Bernard conjectured.

There didn't seem to be any concept of rank or status here. Bernard had seen orders being given and accepted without question, sure enough, but the roles appeared to be purely functional and capable of being interchanged freely depending on who was considered best qualified to take command of the particular subject at issue. This seemed to be decided by an unspoken consensus which the Chironians appeared somehow to have evolved without the bickerings, jealousies, and conflicts that Bernard would have thought inevitable. As far as he could make out there was no absolute, top-down hierarchical structure at all. It was a microcosm of the whole planet, he was beginning to suspect. Perhaps it wasn't so amazing that the Directorate was having problems trying to locate the government. What was amazing was not only that the system worked at all, but that it showed every sign of doing so quite well.

"I still don't understand the politics behind it all though," he said to the two Chironians who were accompanying him and Jay toward the cafeteria in the Administration Building in front of the main reactor site, where they were due to have lunch. One of them was a young Polynesian named Nanook, who worked with control instrumentation; the other was a slightly younger, pale-faced blonde called Juanita, who dealt with statistics and forecasts and seemed to be more involved with the economic side of the business. Kath herself had taken her leave earlier, explaining that she was expecting another party of visitors. Bernard spread his hands in an imploring gesture. "I mean . . . who owns the place? Who decides the policies for running it?"

The two Chironians frowned at each other. "Owns it?" Juanita repeated. Her voice suggested that the notion was a new one. "I'm not all that sure what you mean. The people who work here, I guess."

"But who decides who works here? Who appoints them to their jobs?"

"They do. How could it be up to anyone else?"

"But that ridiculous! What's to stop anyone walking in off the street from giving orders?"

"Nothing," Juanita said. "But why would they? Who'd take any notice of them?"

"So how does anyone know who to listen to?" Jay asked, every bit as mystified as his father.

"They soon find out," Juanita said it as if it explained everything.

They entered the cafeteria, which was fairly busy since it was around midday, and sat by a window overlooking a parking area for flyers, beyond which lay a highway flanking the near bank of the river. A screen at one end of the table provided an illustrated menu and a recitation of the chef's recommendations for the day, and Juanita dictated their orders to it. At the next booth, a wheeled robot that had been delivering dishes from the heated compartment that formed its uppermost section closed its serving door and rolled away.

Bernard wasn't getting through, he could see. "Take Kath as an example," he said, turning toward Nanook. "A lot of people around here seem to accept her as . . . boss, for want of a better word . . . for a lot of things, anyhow."

Nanook nodded. "Right. I do most of the time."

"Because she knows what she's talking about, right?" Bernard said.

"Sure. Why else?"

"So suppose someone else showed up who thought he knew just as much. What if half the people around here thought so too, and the others didn't? Who decides? How would you resolve something like that?"

Nanook rubbed his chin and looked dubious. "That situation sounds very farfetched," he said after a few seconds. "I can't see how anyone else could walk in with the same experience. But if it did happen, and it was true . . . then I suppose Kath would have to agree with him. She'd be indebted by that amount. And that would decide it for everyone else."

Bernard stared at him in open disbelief. "You're not saying she'd simply back down? That's crazy!"

"We all have to pay our debts," Nanook said unhelpfully.

"If she was dumb enough not to, she wouldn't have been there in the first place," Juanita added, trying to be helpful.

That didn't explain anything. Jay couldn't see it either. "Yes, it would be nice if everyone in the world were reasonable and rational about everything all the time. But they can't be, can they? Chironians have the same mix of genes as everyone else. There can't be anything radically different."

"I never said there was," Nanook answered.

"So what about the nuts?" Jay asked. "What do you do about people who insist on being as unreasonable and obnoxious as they can, just for the hell of it?"

"We get them," Nanook agreed. "But not a lot. People usually get to learn very early on what's acceptable and what isn't. They've all got eyes, ears, and brains."

"But Jay's still got a point," Bernard said, glancing at his son and nodding "What about the people who won't use them?"

"We don't get a lot of those," Nanook told them again. "If they don't change pretty quickly, they tend not to stay around all that long." Juanita looked from Bernard to Jay as if satisfied that everything was now clear. It wasn't.

"Why? What happens with them?" Bernard asked.

Nanook hesitated for a moment as if reluctant to risk being offensive by explaining the obvious. He shrugged. "Well . . . usually somebody ends up shooting them," he replied. "So it never gets to be a real problem."

For a few seconds Bernard and Jay were too stunned to say anything. "But . . . that's crazy," Bernard protested at last. "You can't just let everybody go round shooting anyone they don't like."

"What else can you do?" Juanita asked.

"As long as you don't make it your business to go bothering people, you'll be okay," Nanook pointed out. "So it never affects most people. And when it happens . . . it happens."

After a few seconds of silence Jay conceded, "Okay, I can see how it might be a good way of getting rid of the odd freak here and there. But what do you do when a whole bunch of them get together?"

"How can they when there are hardly any around to start with?" Juanita asked him. "We told you—if they're like that, they don't last very long."

"And in any case, whatever would a bunch like that want to get together for?" Nanook asked.

Jay shrugged. "All the things crazy people usually follow crazy leaders for, I guess."

"Like what?" Nanook asked.

Jay shrugged again. "Protection, maybe."

"What from?"

A good point, Jay admitted to himself. "Security?" he tried. "To get rich . . . Whatever."

"They've already got security," Nanook declared. "And if they're not rich enough already, how is some crazy supposed to help?"

Bernard threw up his hands in exasperation. "Well, hell, let's say because they're just plain crazy. They don't need any reason. Never mind why, but let's say it's happened. What do you do?"

Nanook sighed heavily. "We have had one or two things like that from time to time," he confessed. "But it never lasts. In the end a bigger bunch gets itself together and gets rid of them. It comes to the same thing—they end up getting shot anyhow."

Jay looked worried, and Bernard appalled. "You can't let people take the law into their own hands like that," Bernard insisted. "Unchecked violence—mob rule—God alone knows what else. It's plain uncivilized—barbaric. You're going to have to change the system sooner or later."

"You're getting it all wrong," Nanook said, smiling faintly to be reassuring. "It's not so bad. Things like that don't happen all the time—in fact, hardly ever. Just sometimes . . ."

Juanita saw the expressions on Bernard's and Jay's faces. "Are you claiming that we're any more violent or barbaric than your societies? We've never had a war. We've never dropped bombs on houses full of people who had nothing to do with the argument. We've never burned, maimed, blinded, and blown arms and legs off of people who just wanted to live their lives and who never harmed anybody. We've never shot anyone who didn't ask for it. Can you say the same? Okay, so the system's not perfect. Is yours?"

"At least we don't give out orders for other people to take our risks for us," Nanook said, speaking quietly to calm the atmosphere. Juanita was starting to get emotional. "The people who take the risks are the ones who believe it's worth it. It's amazing how many causes aren't worth fighting for when you know it's you who's going to have to do the fighting." He shook his head slowly. "No, we don't get too much of that kind of thing."

"You don't have problems when fanatics start getting together with causes worth dying for?" Jay asked.

Nanook shifted his eyes and shook his head again. "Fanatics are gullible fools. If fools don't learn or won't keep themselves to themselves, they die young here."

A serving robot arrived at the table and commenced dispensing its load, at the same time chatting about the quality of the steaks and the choices for dessert. Bernard turned to stare out of the window and think. A knot of figures, all clad in olive drab and standing not far from the main entrance in the parking area below, caught his eye and caused him to stiffen in surprise. They were wearing uniforms—U.S. Army uniforms. Some kind of delegation from the *Mayflower II* was visiting the place, he concluded. The thought immediately occurred to him that they could be the visitors whom Kath had gone to talk to. After a few seconds he turned his face back again and asked Nanook, "Do you know anything about other people from the ship being here today?"

Nanook looked mildly surprised. "Sure. I thought you'd know about it. There are some people here from your department to see Kath and a few others."

"My department?"

"Engineering. That's the one you're with, isn't it?"

Bernard frowned suddenly. "Yes, it is. And I didn't know about it." His concern intensified as the implications sank in. "Who are they?"

"Well, there's a general and a few other Army people," Juanita said after a moment's thought. "And from Engineering there's a . . . Merrick—Leighton Merrick, that's right." She looked at Nanook. "And one called Walters, wasn't there . . . and some other guy . . ."

"Hoskins," Nanook supplied.

"Yes, Frank Hoskins," Juanita said. "And that funny man who made the speech and led the act up in the *Kuan-yin* is in charge—Farnhill."

Bernard's concern changed to a deep, uneasy suspicion as he listened. Walters and Hoskins were his equals in rank and duties; this could only mean that he had been left out of something deliberately. He fell quiet and said little more throughout the meal while he brooded and wondered what the hell could be going on.

"I bet she does," Stanislau maintained. "They all do. Carson made it last night with a chick at Canaveral."

"Who says?" Driscoll demanded.

"He did. She's got a place in the city—just across from the base."

"Carson doesn't know what to do with it," Driscoll scoffed derisively. "He still thinks it's for playing with."

"I'm just telling you what the guy said."

"Oh, in that case it just has to be true, doesn't it. Now tell me that Swyley's color-blind."

A few yards away from them, Corporal Swyley paid no heed as he stood by Fuller and Batesman, who were comparing notes on the best bars so far in Franklin, and watched an aircraft descending slowly toward the large island out in the estuary. He couldn't see any reason why travel shouldn't come free on Chiron, just like everything else, and wondered what kinds of connections could be made from Port Norday to the more remote reaches of the planet. Interesting. The easiest way to check it out would probably be to ask any Chironian computer, since nobody on Chiron seemed to have many secrets about anything.

Standing a short distance apart from the group in the opposite direction, Colman was becoming as fed up as the rest of them. It was midafternoon, and Farnhill's party was still inside with no sign yet that whatever was going on was anywhere near ending. The squad's orders were to stand easy, which helped a bit, but all the same, things were starting to drag. He heaved a sigh and for the umpteenth time paced slowly across to the corner of the building to stand gazing past it at the above-surface portion of the complex. Behind him, Driscoll and Stanislau stopped talking about Carson's sex life abruptly as two Chironians stopped by on their way to the main entrance.

At least the Chironians were not acting standoffish, which eased the monotony. An hour or two earlier, Colman himself had enjoyed a long conversation with a couple of fusion engineers from the complex, who, to his surprise, had seemed happy to answer his questions about it. They had even offered him a quick tour. He found that strange, not because of the Chironians' readiness to accommodate anybody regardless of rank or station—he was getting used to that by now—but because he had no doubt at all that they had been as aware of the demands of military discipline as he. Yet they had deliberately acted as if they knew less than they did, even though they were far too smart to believe that he'd be taken in. The Chironians did it all the time. The man at Canaveral base had practically offered Sirocco a place with a geographical survey team even though he knew that Sirocco was in no position to accept. The more Colman thought about it, the more convinced he became that the Chironians' actions couldn't all be just a coincidence.

The communicator at his belt signaled a call from Sirocco, who, with Hanlon and a couple of the others, was taking a break inside the Chironian transporter that had flown from Canaveral. "How's it going?" Sirocco inquired when Colman answered. "Are the troops mutinying yet?"

"Grumbling, but not too bad. Any news from inside?"

"Nothing yet. It's about time you took a breather. I'll be out in a few minutes to take a spell with Carson and Young. Tell Swyley and Driscoll to stand down with you. They've been out there the longest."

"Will do. See you in a few minutes."

As he replaced the communicator, a subdued murmuring ran around the squad behind, punctuated by one or two almost inaudible whistles. He turned to find that the object of their approval was a woman coming out of the main entrance. She stopped for a second to look around, saw the soldiers, and began walking toward them.

She was in her late thirties—evidently one of the Founders—and carried herself with a stately elegance that was proud and upright without crossing the boundary into haughtiness. Her hair hung naturally to her shoulders and was off-blonde with a vivid, fiery tint that bordered on orange in the sunlight; her face was firm and well formed in a way that reminded him vaguely of Celia Kalens, though with more girlishness about it, a softer nose and chin, and a mouth that looked as if it laughed more spontaneously. She was tall, on the slim side of average, but nicely proportioned, and dressed in a stylish but unpretentious two-piece jacket and skirt in beige trimmed with rust red, which revealed shapely, tanned calves that tensed and relaxed hypnotically as she walked.

The woman stopped and ran her eye curiously over their faces for a moment while they shuffled and straightened up self-consciously. "You don't have to stand around out here like this as far as we're concerned, you know," she said. "You can come on inside if you want. How about a coffee, and maybe something to eat?" The faces turned instinctively toward Colman as he rejoined them.

He started to grin automatically. "That's a nice thought, ma'am, but we're under orders and have to stay here. We appreciate it though." And then he frowned. It was happening again. She knew damn well they had to stay there.

Her eyes rested momentarily on his chevrons. "Are you Sergeant Colman—the one who's interested in engineering?"

Colman stared hard at her in surprise. "Yes, I am. How—"

"I've heard about you." It could only have been from the Chironians he had talked with earlier. Why would they mention his name to her? Who was she? She came nearer and smiled. "My name is Kath. I have some connection with the technical aspects of what goes on here. From what I've heard, I'd imagine you'd find this an interesting place. Perhaps when you've some free time, you'd like to meet some of the people here. If you like, I could mention it to them."

Colman was nonplussed. He shook his head as if to clear it. "What—What exactly do you do around here?"

Kath's smile became impish, as if she were amused by his confusion. "Oh, you'd be surprised."

Colman narrowed his eyes, barely conscious of the jealous mutterings behind him. "Well . . . sure," he said cautiously. "If it wouldn't be any trouble to anyone. You must have talked to the two guys who were here earlier."

Kath nodded. "Wally and Sam. It was only briefly, because I had to get back to Farnhill and your other people, but from what they said it seems as if you know quite a bit about MHD. Where did you study?"

"Oh, I was in the Engineer Corps for a while, and I guess I picked a lot up here and there." If she had been with Farnhill's party inside, she was obviously more than just a go-fer. Why in hell did she come out to the parking lot to be nice to the troops?

"How many other engineers do you have here?" she inquired lightly, looking around the rest of the squad. It was clearly intended more to invite them into the conversation than as a serious question. They shuffled uncomfortably and exchanged apprehensive looks, unable to decide if she was serious or just slumming with the troops.

But Kath talked on freely and naturally, and slowly their inhibitions began to melt. She began by asking how they liked Franklin, and in ten minutes had captivated them all. Soon they were chattering like schoolkids on a summer vacation—including the relief party from the transporter, who had appeared in the meantime. The detail due for a break seemed to have forgotten about it. Something very strange was going on, Colman told himself again.

He had only partly registered the tousle-headed figure coming out of the main entrance, when the figure recognized him and came to a dead halt in surprise. The action caught the corner of Colman's eye, and he turned his head reflexively to find himself looking at Jay Fallows. Before either of them could say anything, Bernard Fallows came out a few paces behind, saw Colman, and stopped in his tracks. It was too late for him to go back in, and impossible to walk on by. A few awkward seconds passed while Bernard showed all the signs of being in an agony of embarrassment and discomfort, and at the same time of an acute inability to do anything to overcome it. Colman didn't feel he had any prerogative to make a first move. Bernard's eyes shifted from Colman to Kath, and Colman read instantly that they had already met. Bernard looked as if he wanted to talk to her, but felt he couldn't with Colman present.

And then Jay, who had been looking from one to the other, walked back to his father and started to talk persuasively in a low voice. Bernard hesitated, looked across at Colman again, and then took a deep breath and came haltingly across with Jay beside him. "It's been a long time," he mumbled. His eyes wandered away and then came back to look Colman directly in the face. "Look, Steve, about that time up on the ship in the pump bay. I, er . . . I—"

"Forget it," Colman interrupted. "It happens to everyone. Let's leave it with all the other stuff that's best left up there."

Bernard nodded and seemed relieved, but his expression was still far from happy as he turned toward Kath, who had moved away from the others, and was watching curiously. Bernard seemed to want to say something that he didn't know how to begin.

Jay was evidently developing a feel for Chironian directness. "We're kind of curious about the people inside," he said. "Especially my dad. It's funny that he wasn't told anything about it."

Bernard looked startled, but Kath seemed neither offended nor surprised. "I thought you might be," she said, nodding half to herself. "Nanook told me about that." She looked at Bernard. "We don't have a lot of time for secrets," she told him. "Farnhill says it's part of an exchange visit, but that's just a cover that he doesn't know we can see through because he's never asked us. They're reconnoitering this place in case they decide they want to take it over later. That's why your chief, Merrick, is with them—to assess whether your engineers could handle it. He's picked Walters and Hoskins to put in here if the Directorate goes ahead with the idea."

Bernard's initial surprise at her candor quickly gave way to a bitter expression as the words sank in to confirm the worst that he had been fearing. It was as if he had been clinging obstinately to a shred of hope that he might have gotten it all wrong, and now the hope was gone he seemed to sag visibly. Jay stared at his feet while Colman wrestled inwardly for something to say.

Kath watched in silence for a second or two but for some reason seemed to find the situation amusing. Bernard stared with a mixture of uncertainty and resentment. "I think I know what's going through your mind," she told him. "But don't worry about it. We don't take orders from Farnhill or Merrick here. Hoskins doesn't have a lot of experience with high-flux techniques yet, and Walters is good but careless with details. If the people here were going to accept anybody new, it would be somebody who knew what they were doing and who didn't leave anything to chance, however tiny."

"Just . . . what are you getting at?" Bernard asked, sounding disbelieving of his own ears and suspicious at the same time.

Kath switched on her impish smile again. "That's all I'm prepared to say," she replied. "For now, anyway. I just thought you'd like to hear it." She turned to Jay to change the subject. "Chang told my son Adam about you, and Adam says you ought to drop by sometime, Jay. He lives in Franklin, so it wouldn't be far. Why don't you do that?"

"Sounds great. I will. How do I get directions—from the net?"

"You've got it." Kath smiled.

Jay glanced at Colman, then looked at Bernard. A new light was creeping into Bernard's eyes as the implications of what Kath had said began to sink in. Jay hesitated, then decided that his father was in the right mood. "You know, this is a bit of a risky place, Dad," he said in an ominous voice. "People getting shot all over the place and stuff like that. I could run into all kinds of trouble on my own. I'm sure you'd feel a lot happier if I had some professional protection."

Bernard looked at him suspiciously. "Just what are you up to now?"

Jay grinned, just a trifle sheepishly. "Er . . . would you get mad if I asked Steve to come along too?"

"I'm sure Adam would be more than happy," Kath interjected. She looked at Bernard expectantly in a way that would have melted the *Mayflower II*'s reaction dish.

Bernard looked from Kath, to Colman, to Jay, and then back to Colman. He was beaten, and he knew it. But after Kath's cryptic statement, he wasn't inclined to argue too much. "Hell, it's not so bad. He doesn't need anyone to stop him from getting shot," he replied. Beside him, Jay's face dropped. Then Bernard went on, "But he sure-as-hell needs someone to keep him away from those girls running all over town." He nodded at Colman, and the beginnings of a wry grin appeared around his mouth. "Keep a good eye on him, Steve. He's crafty." He turned his head and stared resignedly at his son. "And you," he grunted. "Get home on time, and don't say anything about this to your mother."

◎ CHAPTER SEVENTEEN ◎

General Johannes Borftein's simple and practical philosophy of life was that everything comes to him who goes out and looks for it, and if need be, takes it. Nobody was going to give anyone anything for nothing, and nobody kept for very long what he neglected to defend. The name of the game was Survival. He hadn't made up the rules; they had been written into Nature long before he existed.

Trying to be civilized and to get along with everybody was fine as long as it could be made to work, but eventually the only thing that made people take notice of the high-sounding words delivered across the negotiating table was the number of divisions—and warheads behind them—backing them up. And if, when all else failed, the only way left for a nation to look after its interests was to defend them by force, then the best chance for survival lay with promoting the cause totally and using every expedient that came at hand; half measures were fatal.

The shorter-term price to be paid was regrettable, but when had Nature ever offered free lunches? And in the longer term, what did it mean anyway? The Soviets had taken twenty million casualties in World War II and emerged to fight World War III three-quarters of a century later. And in that conflict the U.S. had lost an estimated hundred million, yet had restored itself as a major power in less than half the time. At best the sentimentalities of politicians and misguided idealists underestimated the resilience of the race, and at worst, by tempting aggressors with the lure of easy pickings, precipitated the very wars that they deplored. Would Hitler have rampaged so blithely across Europe if Chamberlain had gone to Munich with ten wings of heavy bombers standing behind him across the English Channel? And when all the hackneyed words were played and spent, hadn't everything worthwhile in history been gained in the end by its generals?

Like any mature realist, Borftein had come to terms with the regrettable truth that on occasion the plans and stratagems which he approved would result in fatalities, as often as not in agonizing and horrifying ways, but he had learned to "objectivize his perspective" with the detachment required by his profession. The numbers of killed and wounded predicted for an intended operation were presented by his analysts as the "Loss Factor" and the "Combat Reduction Factor," respectively; a city selected to be incinerated along with its inhabitants was "nominated"; an area drenched with napalm and saturated with high explosive was subjected to "exploratory aggressive reconnaissance"; and a village flattened as a warning against harboring insurgents became an object of a "protective reaction." Such were the rules.

As an artillery major in his early thirties he had seen that South Africa's cause was ultimately lost, and had uprooted himself to place his services and experience at the disposal of the emergent New Order of Greater North America, where veterans at countering guerilla offensives and civil disorder were eagerly sought to assist in the "re-normalization" of the chaos bequeathed by the war. Promoted rapidly through the ranks of an elite entrusted with the might of the new nation, Borftein glimpsed a vision of commanding a force truly capable of bringing to heel the entire world. But the vision had been short-lived. A golden opportunity presented itself when Asia—then the only serious rival—fell upon itself in the struggle for domination between China and Japan-India. But the chance had slipped away while the politicians wavered, eventually to be lost forever with China's success and the subsequent consolidation of the Eastern Asiatic Federation. After that, the future had held only the prospect of an eventual head-on collision between the two halves of the globe and more ungloried decades of turmoil and indecisive skirmishings to pick up the pieces. Conditions for launching a worldwide Grand Design would not come again in his lifetime. And so he had left to seek a more rewarding destiny with the *Mayflower II*. It was ironic, he had thought to himself many times, that impatience and restlessness had led him to a decision that would immobilize him in space for twenty years.

His impatience was asserting itself again now, as Borftein sat in the chambers of Judge William Fulmire, the *Mayflower II*'s Supreme Justice, listening to Howard Kalens and Marcia Quarrey argue over the finer points of the Mission's constitution, while on the surface the troops were fraternizing openly with what could become the enemy, and two years away in space the EAF starship daily drew nearer. The news from Earth told of a three-cornered conflict sweeping through eastern Africa, black nations clashing against Arabs in the north and whites in the south, Australian forces landing in Malagasay, and the Europeans maneuvering desperately to quell the flames while the EAF fanned them gleefully. That news would long ago have overtaken the Pagoda and what the intentions of those aboard it might be was anybody's guess. It wasn't a time to be fussing over ambiguous syntax and legal niceties.

Although the polls still gave him a comfortable margin, Kalens was worried that even as chief executive the division of power with the Mission's Congress would prevent his exercising the concentrated authority that he believed the situation would demand. Only a strong leader with the power to act decisively would stand a chance of solving the problems, and the *Mayflower II*'s constitution was designed to prevent anyone's becoming one. Its spirit was an anachronism inherited from antiquity when a newly founded Federation had sought to guard itself against a renewed colonialism, and the governing system embodied that spirit quite effectively. That was the problem.

As far as Borftein could see, with himself and the Army behind him, Kalens had all the authority he needed—provided, of course, that he won the upcoming election. But after talking to Sterm about it, Kalens had accepted that an attempt to impose authority over Chiron overtly would risk alienating the Mission's population. A more subtle approach was called for. "Ultimately, human instincts cling to the known and the familiar," Kalens lectured Borftein later. "A visible commitment to lawfulness as a alternative to the lawlessness of this planet is the way to maintain cohesiveness. We can't afford to jeopardize that." So Borftein had agreed to try playing the game their way, which hinged upon provisions written into the laws to take account of the abnormal circumstances of a twenty-year voyage through space.

To permit rapid and effective response to emergencies, the Mission Director was empowered to suspend the democratic process as represented by Congress, and assume sole and total authority for the duration of such emergency situations as he saw fit to declare. Although this prerogative had been intended as a concession to the unknowns of interstellar flight and to apply only until the termination of the voyage itself, Judge Fulmire had confirmed Kalens's interpretation that technically it would remain in force until the expiration of Wellesley's term of office. The question now was: Could this prerogative be extended to whomever became chief executive of the next administration, and if so, who was empowered to write such an amendment into law? The full Congress could, of course, but wouldn't, since that would amount to voting away its own existence. Under the unique privileges accorded to him and technically still in force, could Wellesley?

Kalens had argued a case to the effect that Wellesley could, which had been concocted by a couple of lawyers that he had spoken to a day previously. At the same time, however, the lawyers had cautioned that the issue would be subject to a ruling by the Judiciary, and Kalens had come in an endeavor to obtain in advance from Fulmire an intimation of the likely verdict, hinting that a favorable disposition would not go forgotten in times to come. The endeavor had backfired spectacularly.

"I will not be a party to such shenanigans!" the Judge exclaimed. "This is all highly irregular, as you well know. A ruling must be subject to all due process, and only to all due process. There the matter must remain. What you are asking is inexcusable."

"Our own people have a right to expect the protection of a properly constituted legal system, and this planet fails even to possess one," Kalens argued. "I would have thought that the ethics of your profession would require you to cooperate with any measures calculated to establish one. The purpose of this provision is precisely that."

"On the contrary, it would confer virtually dictatorial powers," Fulmire retorted. "There can be no validity in a legality established by illegal means."

"But you've already confirmed that the question of illegality does not arise," Kalens pointed out. "The emergency clauses apply until the elections have been held."

"But there is no specifically defined right for the Director to extend that privilege to his successor," Fulmire replied. "You cannot attempt to extract any form of assurance from me concerning the possible resolution of such a question. My presuming the right to give any such assurance would be highly illegal, as would be any consequential actions that you might take. I repeat, I have no more to say."

"Then invoke the security provisions," Borftein said, shifting in his chair from weariness with the whole business. "It's a security matter, isn't it? The Chironians have left it to us by default, and it's their security at stake as well as ours. The Pagoda's only two years away. Somebody's got to take the helm in all this."

Fulmire gestured over the books and documents spread across his desk. "The security provisions provide for Congress to vote exceptional powers to the Directorate in the event of demonstrable security demands, and for the Directorate to delegate extraordinary duties to the chief executive once *they* are voted that power. They do not provide for the chief executive to assume such duties for himself, and therefore neither can he do so for his successor."

A short silence fell, and the deadlock persisted. Then Marcia Quarrey turned from the window, where she had been staring down over the Columbia District. "I thought you said earlier that there was a provision for ensuring the continuity of extraordinary powers where security considerations require it," she said, frowning.

"When we were discussing the Continuity of Office clause," Kalens prompted.

Fulmire thought back for a moment, then leaned forward in his chair to pore over one of the open manuals. "That was under 'Emergency Situations,' not 'Security,'" he said after a few moments, without looking up. "Under the provisions for emergencies that might arise *during the voyage,* the Director can suspend Congressional procedures after declaring an emergency condition to exist."

"Yes, we know that," Quarrey agreed. "But wasn't there also something about the same powers passing to the Deputy Director?"

Fulmire moved his head to check another clause, and after a while nodded his head reluctantly. "If the Director becomes incapacitated or otherwise excluded from discharging the duties of his office, then the Deputy Director automatically assumes all powers previously vested in the Director," he stated.

Kalens raised his head sharply. "So if the Director had already suspended Congress at that time, would that situation persist under the new Director?" He thought for a moment, then added, "I would assume it must, surely. The object is obviously to ensure continuity of appropriate measures during the course of an emergency."

Fulmire looked uneasy but in the end was forced to nod his agreement. "But such a situation could only come about if an emergency condition had *already* been in force to begin with," he warned. "It could not be applied in any way to the present circumstances."

"You don't think that a ship full of Asiatics coming at us armed to the teeth qualifies as an emergency?" Borftein asked sarcastically.

"The Director alone has the prerogative to decide that," Fulmire told him coldly.

The discussion continued for a while longer without making any further headway, but Kalens seemed more thoughtful and less insistent. Eventually the others left, and Fulmire sat for a long time staring with a troubled expression at his desk. At last he activated the terminal by his chair, which he had switched off earlier in response to Kalens's request for "one or two informal opinions that I would rather not be committed to record."

"Which service?" the terminal inquired.

"Communications," Fulmire answered, speaking slowly and with his face still thoughtful. "Find Paul Lechat for me and put him through if he's free, would you. And route this via a secured channel."

⚛ CHAPTER EIGHTEEN ⚛

"The thing I still can't understand is what motivates these people," Colman remarked to Hanlon as they walked with Jay to Adam's house. "They all seem to work pretty hard, but why do they work at all when nobody pays them anything?"

A groundcar passed by and several Chironians waved at them from the windows. "It can't be quite like that," Jay said. "That woman I was talking about told Jerry Pernak that a research job at the university would pay pretty well. That must have meant something."

"Well, it sure doesn't pay any money." Colman turned his head toward Hanlon. "What do you say, Bret?"

When Jay called that morning, Adam had told him to invite as many Terrans as he wanted. Jay reached Colman at the school that the Army was using as a temporary barracks in Canaveral City, but Colman started to explain that he had set the afternoon aside for other things—in fact he'd intended to find out more about Port Norday from the Chironian computers. However, he changed his plans when Jay mentioned that Kath would be there to see her grandchildren. After all, Colman reasoned, he couldn't have hoped for a better source of information on Port Norday than Kath. As Hanlon was off duty, Colman had invited him along too.

"I hope you're not expecting an answer," Hanlon said. "It makes about as much sense to me as Greek. . . ." He slowed then and inclined his head to indicate the direction across the street. "Now, there's the fella you should be asking," he suggested.

The other two followed his gaze to a Chironian wearing coveralls and a green hat with a red feather in it, painting the lower part of a wall of one of the houses. Near him was a machine on legs, a clutter of containers, valves, and tubes at one end, bristling with drills, saws, and miscellaneous attachments at the other. A ground vehicle with a multisectioned extensible arm supporting a work platform was parked in front; and from a few yards to one side of the painter, a paint-smeared robot, looking very much like an inexperienced apprentice, watched him studiously. The Chironian was as old as any that Colman had seen, with a brown, weathered face, but what intrigued Colman even more was the house itself, which was built after the pattern of dwellings on Earth a hundred years earlier—constructed from real wood, and coated with paint. It was not the first such anachronism that he had seen in Franklin, where designs three centuries old coexisted quite happily alongside maglev cars and genetically modified plants, but he hadn't had an opportunity to stop and study one before.

The painter glanced across and noticed them watching. "Nice day," he commented and continued with his work. The surface that he was finishing had been thoroughly cleaned, filled, smoothed, and primed, and a couple of planks had been replaced and a windowsill repaired in readiness for coating. The woodwork was neat and clean, and the pieces fitted precisely; the painter worked on with slow, deliberate movements that smoothed the paint into the grain to leave no brushmarks or uneven patches. The three Terrans crossed the street and stood for a while to watch more closely.

"Nice job you're doing," Hanlon remarked at last.

"Glad you think so." The painter carried on.

"It's a pretty house," Hanlon said after another short silence.

"Yep."

"Yours?"

"Nope."

"Someone you know?" Colman asked.

"Kind of." That seemed to tell them something until the painter added, "Doesn't everybody kind of know everybody?"

Colman and Hanlon frowned at each other. Obviously they weren't going to get anywhere without being more direct. Hanlon wiped his palms on his hips. "We, ah . . . we don't mean to be nosy or anything, but out of curiosity, why are you painting it?" he asked.

"Because it needs painting."

"So why bother?" Jay asked. "What's it to you if somebody else's house needs painting or not?"

"I'm a painter," the painter said over his shoulder. "I like to see a paint job properly done. Why else would anyone do it?" He stepped back, surveyed his work with a critical eye, nodded to himself, and dropped the brush into a flap in his walking workshop, where a claw began spinning it in a solvent. "Anyhow, the people who live here fix plumbing, manage a bar in town, and one of them teaches the tuba, My plumbing sometimes needs fixing, I like a drink in town once in a while, and one day one of my kids might want to play the tuba. They fix faucets, I paint houses. What's so strange?"

Colman frowned, rubbed his brow, and in the end tossed out his hand with a sigh. "No . . . we're not making the right point somehow. Let's put it this way—how can you *measure* who owes who what?" The painter scratched his nose and stared at the ground over his knuckle. Clearly the notion was new to him.

"How do you know when you've done enough work?" Jay asked him, trying to make it simpler.

The painter shrugged. "You just know. How do you know when you've had enough to eat?"

"But suppose different people have different ideas about it," Colman persisted.

The painter shrugged again. "That's okay. Different people value things differently. You can't tell somebody else when they've had enough to eat."

Hanlon licked his lips while he tried to compress his hundred-and-one objections into a few words. "Ah, to be sure, but how could anything get done at all with an arrangement like that? Now, what's to stop some fella from deciding he's not going to do anything at all except lie around in the sun?"

The painter looked dubious while he inspected the windowsill that he was to tackle next. "That doesn't make much sense," he murmured after a while. "Why would somebody stay poor if he didn't have to? That'd be a strange kind of way to carry on."

"He wouldn't get away with it, surely," Jay said incredulously. "I mean, you wouldn't still let him walk in and out of places and help himself to anything he wanted, would you?"

"Why not?" the painter asked. "You'd have to feel kinda sorry for someone like that. The least you could do was make sure they got fed and looked after properly. We do get a few like that, and that's what happens to them. It's a shame, but what can anybody do?"

"You don't understand," Jay said. "On Earth, a lot of people would see that as their big ambition in life."

The painter eyed him for a moment and nodded his head slowly. "Mmm . . . I kinda figured it had to be something like that," he told them.

Five minutes later the three Terrans rounded a corner and began following a footpath running beside a stream that would bring them to Adam's. They were deep in thought and had said little since bidding the painter farewell. After a short distance Jay slowed his pace and came to a halt, staring up at a group of tall Chironian trees standing on the far side of the stream alongside a number of familiar elms and maples that were evidently imported—genetically modified by the *Kuan-yin*'s robots to grow in alien soil. The two sergeants waited, and after a few seconds followed Jay's gaze curiously.

The trunks of the Chironian trees were covered by rough overlapping plates that resembled reptilian scales more than bark, and the branches, clustered together high near the tops in a way reminiscent of Californian sequoias, curved outward and upward to support domed canopies of foliage like the caps of gigantic mushrooms. The foliage was green at the bottoms of the domes but became progressively more yellow toward the tops, around which several furry, cat-sized, flying creatures were wheeling in slow, lazy circles and keeping up a constant chattering among themselves. "You wouldn't think so, but that yellow stuff up there isn't part of those trees at all," Jay said, gesturing. "Jeeves told me about it. It's a completely different species—a kind of fern. Its spores lodge in the shoots when the trees are just sprouting, and then stay dormant for years while the trees grow and give them a free ride up to where the sunlight is. It invades the leaf-buds and feeds through the tree's vascular system."

"Mmm . . ." Colman murmured. Botany wasn't his line.

Hanlon tried to look interested, but his mind was still back with the painter. After a few seconds he looked at Colman. "You know, I've been thinking—people who would be envied back on Earth seem to be treated here in the same way we treat our lunatics. Do you think we're all crazy to the Chironians?"

"It's a thought," Colman replied vaguely. The same idea had crossed his mind while the painter was talking. It was a sobering one.

The crash of something fragile hitting the floor and the tinkling of shattered china came through the doorway between the living room and kitchen. Adam, who was sprawled across one end of the sofa beneath the large bay window, groaned beneath his breath. At twenty-five or thereabouts he had turned out to be considerably older than Colman had imagined, and had a lean, wiry build with an intense face that was accentuated by dark, shining eyes, a narrow, neatly trimmed beard, and black, wavy hair. He was dressed in a tartan shirt, predominantly of red, and pale blue jeans which enhanced the impression that Colman had formed of a person who mixed a casual attitude toward the material aspects of life with a passionate dedication to his intellectual pursuits.

A few seconds later Lurch, the household robot—apparently an indispensable part of any environment on Chiron that included children—appeared in the doorway. "It slipped," it announced. "Sorry about that, boss. I've wired off an order for a replacement."

Adam waved an arm resignedly. "Okay, okay. Never mind the sackcloth-and-ashes act. How about cleaning it up?"

"Oh, yes. I should have thought of that." Lurch about-faced and lurched back to the kitchen. The sound of a door opening and the brief clatter of something being fumbled from a closet floated back into the room.

"Does it do that a lot?" Colman asked from his chair, which had been cleared of a pile of books and some stuffed birds to make room for him when they had arrived an hour or so earlier.

"It's a klutz," Adam said wearily. "It's got a glitch in its visual circuits somewhere . . . something like that. I don't know."

"Can't you get it fixed?" Colman asked.

Adam threw up his hands again. "The kids won't let me! They say it wouldn't be the same any other way. What can you do?"

"We couldn't let him do that, could we?" Kath said to Bobby, age ten, and Susie, age eight, who were sitting with her across the room, where they had been struggling to master the intricacies of chess, "Lurch is half the fun of coming here."

"You don't have to live with it, Mother," Adam told her.

Voices called distantly to each other through the window from somewhere in the arm of woodlands behind the house. Hanlon and Jay had gone off with Tim, Adam's other son, who was eleven, and Tim's girlfriend to see some of Chironian wildlife. Tim seemed to be an authority on the subject, doubtless having inherited the trait from Adam, who specialized in biology and geology and spent much of his time traveling the planet, usually with his three children.

Or, at least, the three that lived with him. Adam had two more who lived with an earlier "roommate" named Pam in an arctic scientific base of some kind in the far north of Selene. Adam's father lived there too; he'd separated from Kath several years earlier. Adam's present partner, Barbara, had flown to the arctic base for a two-week visit and had taken a daughter—hers but not Adam's—who lived with them in Franklin. Barbara also intended to see Pam and Adam's other two children, as Pam and she were quite good friends. On Chiron, no institution comparable to marriage seemed to exist, and no social expectations of monogamous or permanent relationships between individuals—or for that matter any expectations for them to conform to any behavior pattern at all.

Adam had not seemed especially surprised when Hanlon

expressed reservations about the wisdom of such an attitude, and had replied to the effect that on Chiron personal affairs were considered personal business. Some couples might choose to remain exclusively committed to each other and their family, others might not, and it wasn't a matter for society or anybody else to comment on. As far as he was concerned, Adam had said, the notion of anybody's presuming to decree moral standards for others and endeavoring to impose them by legislation was "obscene."

Adam also had an older sister—to the surprise of the Terrans—who designed navigation equipment for spacecraft at an establishment located inland from the Peninsula, a twin brother who was an architect and rumored to be getting friendly with a lively redhead from the *Mayflower II* whom Colman couldn't place, a younger sister who lived with two other teenagers somewhere in Franklin, and a still younger half-brother, not a son of Kath's, who was with their father in Selene. It was all very confusing.

"But doesn't this kind of thing upset the kids when it happens?" Hanlon had asked uneasily.

"Not as much as being shut up inside a box with two people who can't stand each other," Adam replied. "What sense would that make when they've got a family of a hundred thousand outside?"

"We're dying to meet your sister, Jay," Tim's girlfriend had said, an arm slipped through Tim's on one side and Adam's on the other.

"Her mother's dying too," Jay had replied dryly.

Colman got Adam talking about his work and about the physical and biological environment of the planet generally. Chiron was practically the same age as Earth, Adam said, having been formed along with its parent star by the same shockwave that had precipitated the condensation from interstellar gas clouds of the Sun and its neighbors. It was an intriguing thought, Adam suggested, that the bodies of the people being born now on Chiron and on Earth all included heavy elements that had been formed in the same first-generation star—the one that had triggered the shock wave when it exploded as a supernova. "We might have been born light-years apart," he told Colman. "But the stuff we're made of came from the same place."

Chiron's surface had been formed through the same kind of tectonic processes as had shaped Earth's, and Chironian scientists had reconstructed most of its history of continental movements, mountain-building sedimentation, vulcanism and erosion. Like Earth, it possessed a magnetic field which reversed itself periodically and which had written a coherent story onto the moving seafloors as they spread outward and cooled from uplifts along oceanic ridges; the complicated tidal cycle induced by Chiron's twin satellites had been unraveled to yield the story of previous epochs of periodic inundation by the oceans; and analysis of the planet's seismic patterns had mapped its network of active transform faults and subduction zones, along which most of its volcanoes and earthquake belts were locked.

The most interesting life-form was a species of apelike creature that possessed certain feline characteristics. They inhabited a region in the north of Occidena and were known as "monkeats," a name that the infant Founders had coined when they saw the first views sent back by the *Kuan-yin* reconnaissance probes many years ago. They were omnivores that had evolved from pure carnivores, possessed a highly developed social order, and were beginning to experiment with the manufacture of simple hand tools. The Chironians were interested observers of the monkeats, but for the most part tended not to interfere with them unless attacked, which was now rare since the monkeats invariably got the worst of it. Other notable dangerous life forms include the daskrends, which Jay had already told Colman about, various poisonous reptiles and large insects that were concentrated mainly around southern Selene and the isthmus connecting it to Terranova, though some kinds did spread as far as the Medichironian, a flying mammal found in Artemia which possessed deadly talons and a fanged beak and would swoop down upon anything in sight, and a variety of catlike, doglike, and bearlike predators that roamed across parts of all four continents to a greater or lesser degree.

Colman remembered what Jay had said about the Chironian custom of going armed outside the settlements, and guessed that it traced back to the days when the Founders had first ventured out of the bases. Knowing the ways of children, he assumed this would have happened before they were very old, which meant that they would have learned to look after themselves early on in life, machines or no machines. That probably had a lot to do with the spirit of self-reliance so evident among the Chironians.

"How else could it be?" Adam said when Colman asked him about it. "Sure they had to learn how to use a gun. You know what kids are like. The machines couldn't be everywhere all the time. Ask my mother about it, not me."

Kath smiled on the other side of the room. "I was from the first batch to be created. There were a hundred of us. Leon—he's Adam's father—was another. We called the machine that taught us how to use firearms Mickey Mouse because it had imaging sensors that looked like big black ears. I shot a daskrend when I was six or maybe less. It came at Leon from under a rock which was why the satellites hadn't spotted it He's still got a limp today from that." She emitted a soft chuckle. "Poor Leon. He reminds me of Lurch."

Colman's eyes widened for a moment as he listened. "I'd never really thought about it," he admitted. "But I guess, yes . . . it'd have to have been like that. Your kids today don't seem to have changed all that much either."

"How do you mean?" Kath asked.

Colman shrugged and nodded his head unconsciously in the direction of Bobby and Susie "They've got heads on their shoulders, they've got confidence in their own thinking, and they trust their own judgments. That's good."

"Well, I'm pleased to hear that at least one Terran thinks so," Bobby said. "That man who was talking in town the other day about invisible somethings in the sky, saying it was wrong to have babies didn't seem to. He said we'd suffer forever after we were dead. How can he know? He's never been dead. It was ridiculous."

"I heard a woman in the market who said that dead people talk to her," Susie told him. "That's even more ridiculous."

"They're not all like that, are they?" Bobby asked, looking hopefully at Colman.

"Not all, I guess," Colman replied with a grin. He turned to Adam and then Kath. "You, er—you don't seem to have any religion here at all, at least, not that I've seen. Is that right?" Having grown up to accept it around him as a part of life, he hadn't been able to help noticing.

Adam seemed to think about it for a long time. "No . . ." he said slowly at last. "We're on our own on a grain of dust somewhere in a gas of galaxies. Inventing guardian angels for company won't change it. Whether we make it or not is up to us. If we mess it up, the universe out there won't miss us." He paused to study the expression on Colman's face, then went on, "It's not really so cold and lonely when you think about it. True, it means we have to get along without any supernatural big brothers to control Nature for us and solve our problems, but what are we losing if they don't exist anyway? On the other hand, we don't have to fear all the nonsense that gets invented along with them either. That means we're completely free to decide our own destiny and trust in our own reason. To me that's not such a bad feeling."

Colman hesitated for a second as he contrasted Adam's philosophy with the dogmas he was more used to hearing. "I, ah—I know a few people who would say that was pretty arrogant," he ventured.

"Arrogant?" Adam smiled to himself. "They're the ones who are so sure they 'know,' not me. I'm just making the best interpretation I can of the facts I've got." He thought for a moment longer. "Anyhow, arrogance and pride are not the same thing. I'm proud to be a human being, sure."

"They'd tell you modesty was a better virtue too," Colman said.

"It is," Adam agreed readily. "But modesty and self-effacement aren't the same thing either."

Colman looked unconsciously toward Kath for her opinion.

"If you mean systems of beliefs based, despite their superficial appearances to the contrary, on morbid obsessions with death, hatred, decay, dehumanization, and humiliation, then the answer to your question is no," she said, looking at Colman. She glanced at her grandchildren. "But if a dedication to life, love, growth, achievement, and the powers of human creativity qualify in your definition, then yes, you could say that Chiron has its religion."

✖ ✖ ✖

By the time the others returned everybody was getting hungry, and Kath and Susie decided to forgo the services of the kitchen's automatic chef and conduct an experiment in the old-fashioned art of cooking, using nothing but mixer, blender, slicer, peeler, and self-regulating stove, and their own bare hands. The result was declared a success by unanimous proclamation, and over the meal the Terrans talked mainly about the more memorable events during the voyage while Kath was curious to learn more about the *Mayflower II*'s propulsion system in anticipation of the tour that she was scheduled to make with the Chironian delegation. Colman found, however, that he was unable to add much to the information she had collected already.

Then came the question of what to do with the rest of the evening. "Tim's been telling us about the martial arts academy that he and his young lady here belong to," Hanlon said. "It sounds like quite a place. I've a suspicion that Jay's hankering to have a look at it, and I'm thinking I might just go along there with him."

"Me?" Jay exclaimed. "I'll come long, sure, but I thought it was you who couldn't resist it."

"Bret's an unarmed-combat instructor with the Army," Tim explained.

Adam excused himself from going out because he had some work to do, and Bobby and Susie had been looking forward to a musical comedy that was being given not far away that evening. Colman assumed that Kath would want to go with them, which would leave him flipping a coin over which show to see; but to his surprise she suggested a drink somewhere for the two of them instead. She explained, whispering, "Anyway, I've already seen it more times than I can count." So who was he to turn it down? Colman asked himself. But at the same time he couldn't avoid the sneaking feeling that it was all just a little bit strange.

Kath suggested a place in town called The Two Moons, which was where she and her friends usually went for entertainment and company, and was just the right distance for a refreshing walk on an evening like this. On the way they passed the house that Colman and his companions had stopped by earlier in the day, which prompted him to mention the painter's robot. "It looked as if it was learning the trade," Colman said.

"Very probably it was," Kath replied. "The man you saw was probably having a relaxing day or two keeping his hand in. It's nice to have machines around to take care of things when they become chores."

"People don't worry about being replaced by a chip?"

"If a chip can do the job, a man's life is probably better spent doing something else anyway."

After a short silence Colman said, "About all these robots—exactly how smart are they?"

"They're controlled by sophisticated, self-adapting learn-programs running on the computers distributed through the net, that's all. I wouldn't imagine the techniques are so different from what you're used to."

"So they're not anywhere near intelligent. . . self-aware, anything like that?"

Kath gave a short laugh. "Of course not . . . but they're deceptive, aren't they. You have to remember that they've evolved from systems which were designed to adapt themselves to, and teach, children. You project a lot of yourself into what you think they're saying."

"But they seem to have an intuition to make human value judgments," Colman objected. "They know too much about how people think."

Kath laughed again. "Do they? They don't really, you know. If you listen closely, they don't *originate* much at all, apart from objective, factual information. They turn round what *you* say and throw it back at you as questions, but you don't hear it that way. You think they're telling you something that they're not."

"Catalysts," Colman said after a few seconds of reflection. "You know, you're right, now that I think about it. All they do is make you exercise the brains you never knew you had."

"You've got it," Kath said lightly. "Isn't that what teaching children is all about?"

※   ※   ※

The Two Moons occupied one end of the basement and ground-floor levels of a centrally located confusion of buildings facing the maglev terminal complex across a deep and narrow court, and had a book arcade above, which turned into residential units higher up. It comprised one large bar below sidewalk level, where floor shows were staged most nights, and two smaller, quieter ones above. Kath suggested one of the smaller bars and Colman agreed, permitting himself for the first time the thought that a pleasantly romantic interlude might develop, though why he should be so lucky was something he was far from comprehending. If it happened, he wasn't going to argue about it.

Of course, Swyley, Stanislau, Driscoll, and Carson had to be there. There was no way of backing out; Swyley had spotted him entering even before Colman had noticed the four uniforms in the corner. "Small world, chief," Driscoll remarked with a delighted leer on his face.

"It is, isn't it," Colman agreed dismally.

Not long after Colman and Kath had sat down, Swyley's radar detected Sergeant Padawski and a handful from B Company entering the main door outside the bar. They were talking loudly and seemed to be a little the worse for drink. Colman noticed Anita and another girl from Brigade with them, clinging to the soldiers and acting brashly. He shook his head despairingly, but it wasn't really his business. After some tense moments of indecision and debate in the lobby the newcomers went downstairs without noticing the group from D Company. Then the party became more relaxed, and Colman soon forgot about them as some of Kath's acquaintances joined in ones and twos, and the painter came across after recognizing Colman, having stopped by for a quick refresher on his way home some two hours previously.

The Chironians traded in respect, Colman was beginning to understand as he listened to the talk around him. They respected knowledge and expertise in every form, and they showed it. Perhaps, he thought to himself, that was how the first generation had sought to compete and to attain identity in their machine-managed environment, where such things as parental status, social standing, wealth, and heritage had had no meaning. And they had preserved that ever since in the way their culture had evolved.

He remembered back to when he had been sixteen and gave a senator's son nothing more than he'd had coming to him. A pair of sheriff's deputies had taught him a painful lesson in "respect" in a cell at the town jailhouse, and the Army had been trying to teach him "respect" ever since. But that had been Earth-style respect. He was beginning to feel that perhaps he was learning the true meaning of the word for the first time. True respect could only be earned; it couldn't be extorted. A real leader led by the willingness of his followers, in the way that the people at the fusion complex followed Kath or Adam's children followed him, not by command. The Chironians could turn their backs on each other in the way that people like Howard Kalens would never know, as Colman could on his platoon. These were his kind of people. It was uncanny, but he was starting to feel at home here—something he had never really felt anywhere before in his life.

Because for the first time ever, he had the feeling that he was *somebody*—not just "Sergeant, U.S. Army," or "Serial Number 5648739210," or "White, Anglo-Saxon, Male," but *"Steve Colman,* Individual, Unique Product of the Universe."

It was a nice feeling.

⚙ CHAPTER NINETEEN ⚙

Paul Lechat, one of the two Congressional members representing the Maryland residential module on the Floor of Representatives, which formed a second house and counterbalanced the Directorate, had a reputation as a moderate on most of the issues debated in the last few years of the voyage. Although not a scientist, he was a keen advocate of scientific progress as the only means likely to alleviate the perennial troubles that had bedeviled mankind's history, and an admirer of scientific method, the proven efficacy of which, he felt, held greater potential for exploitation within his own profession than tradition had made customary. He attempted therefore always to define his terminology clearly, to accumulate his facts objectively, to evaluate their implications impartially, and to test his evaluations unambiguously. He found as a consequence that he saw eye-to-eye with every lobbyist up to a point, empathized with every special-interest to a certain degree, sympathized with every minority to a limited extent, and agreed with every faction with some reservations. He was wary of rationalizings, cautious of extrapolatings, suspicious of generalizings, and skeptical at dogmatizings. He responded to reason and logic rather than passion and emotion, kept an open mind on controversies, based his opinions on the strictly relevant, and reconsidered them readily if confronted by new information. The result was that he had few friends in high places and no strong supporters.

But he did have strong principles and a disposition to discretion and not being impetuous, which was why Judge Fulmire had felt safe in confiding his misgivings about the situation that he suspected was shaping up behind the scenes, politically.

Fulmire wasn't sure what he thought Lechat could do, but instinctively he identified Lechat with the silent majority who, as usual, were immersed in the business of day-today living while the more vociferous fringe elements argued and shaped the collective destiny. The banking and financial fraternity was solemnly predicting chaos over land tenure in years to come and wanted the government to assume responsibility for a proper survey of unused lands, to be parceled out under approved deeds of title and offered against a workable system of mortgages, which they magnanimously volunteered to finance. The manufacturing and materials-industry lobbies agreed with the bankers that a monetary system would have to be imposed to check the "reckless profligacy of inefficiency and waste" and to promote "fair and honest" competition; they disagreed with bankers over the mortgage issue, however, claiming that development land on Chiron had already been deemed up for grabs "by virtue of natural precedent"; they disagreed with each other about prices and tariffs, the manufacturers pushing for deregulation of cheap (i.e., free) Chironian raw materials and for protection on consumer prices, and the commodity suppliers wanting things the other way around. The educational and medical professions were anxious to discharge their obligations to teach the Chironians when they were well and treat them when they were not, but were more anxious for a mechanism to raise the taxes for funding them, while the legal profession pressed for a properly constituted judicial system as a first move, ostensibly to facilitate collecting the taxes. The other groups went along with the taxes as long as each secured better breaks than the others, except the religious leaders, who didn't care since they would be exempt anyway. But *they* clashed with the teachers over a move to place ministers in the schools in order to "strangle at its roots the evil and decay which is loose upon this planet," with the doctors over whether the causes were cultural or spiritual, with the lawyers over the issue of making the Chironian practice of serial, and at times parallel, polygamy and polyandry illegal, and with everybody over the question of "emergency" subsidies for erecting churches. And so it went.

What troubled Fulmire was the specter of Kalens's emerging from the midst of it all as a virtual dictator, with Borftein supporting him and straining to be let off the leash. Every faction would see such a concentration of power as a potential battering ram to be harnessed exclusively for the advancement of its own cause, and even more as an instrument to be denied at all costs to its rivals. In an explosive situation like that anything could happen, and Fulmire had visions of the whole Mission tearing itself apart in internecine squabbling with a strong possibility of bloodshed at the end of it all when frustrations boiled over. The only force that he could see with any potential for exerting a stabilizing influence was the more moderate consensus as represented by the *Mayflower II*'s population as a whole; and Lechat, possibly, could provide a means of mobilizing it before things got out of hand.

Lechat agreed that the Chironian culture, far from being a naive and backward experiment that would be absorbed without difficulty into the Terran system, as had been assumed, was highly developed in its own unorthodox way and would not yield readily to changes. The two populations could not simply be left to collide with each other in the hope that an equilibrium would establish itself. Something, somewhere, would blow up before that happened.

The Chironians had both complied with the *Mayflower II*'s advance request for surface accommodation and anticipated their own future needs at the same time by developing Canaveral City and its environs in the direction of Franklin to a greater degree than their own situation then required. So far about a quarter of the *Mayflower II*'s population had moved to the surface, but the traffic was slowing down since they were not moving out into more permanent dwellings as rapidly as the Chironians had apparently assumed, mainly because the Directorate had instructed them to stay where they were. Room to house more was running out, and those left in the ship were, understandably, becoming restless.

Lechat told Fulmire that he no longer thought it advisable to attempt setting up a Terran community alongside the totally unfamiliar experience of Franklin—at least, not immediately. The Terrans would need time to readjust, and in the meantime they would cling to their own familiar ways and customs. The proximity of Franklin would only cause tensions. Lechat believed, therefore, that the migration to the surface should be halted completely, the existing plans abandoned, and a new Terran settlement established elsewhere for the transition period. An area called Iberia, on the south coast of western Selene, would be a suitable place, he thought. Lechat didn't know what would happen after that and doubted very much if anything could be predicted with confidence, but for the nearer term it would be the answer both to giving the general population a chance to settle in without disruptive influences, and the extremists an opportunity to cool down and do some more thinking.

Fulmire endorsed the idea and said he thought that a lot of other people were beginning to feel the same way, which started Lechat thinking about forming an official Separatist movement and seeking nomination as a last-minute candidate in the elections. Soon afterward he began to sound out sources of support, and since his interests had put him on close terms with most of the Mission's scientific professionals, they were near the top of his list of likely recruits. Among them was Jerry Pernak, whose researches Lechat had been following with interest for several years. Accordingly, Lechat invited Pernak and Eve Verritty to dinner with him one evening in the Franchise, a restaurant in the Columbia District frequented mainly by political and media people, and explained his situation.

"I don't think it could work," Pernak said, shaking his head after Lechat had finished. "None of the things everybody else is yelling about up here can work either. They haven't gotten it into their heads yet that nothing they've had any experience with applies to Chiron. This is a whole new phenomenon with its own new rules."

"How do you mean, Jerry?" Lechat asked across the table. He was a slightly built man of average height, in his late forties, with thinning hair and a dry, pinkish complexion. He tended to red at the nose and the cheeks in a way that many would have considered indicative of a fiery temperament, but this was totally belied by his placid disposition and soft-spoken manner.

Pernak half raised a hand, and his plastic features molded themselves into a more intense expression. "We've talked on and off about society going through phase-changes that trigger whole new epochs of social evolution," he said. "Well, that's exactly what's happened down there. You can't extrapolate any of our rules into this culture. They don't apply. They don't work on Chiron."

Lechat didn't respond immediately. Eve Verritty elaborated. "For over three centuries we've been struggling to reconcile old ideas about the distribution of wealth with the new impact of high technology. The problem has always been that traditional conditioning processes for persuading people to accept the inevitability of finite resources get passed on from generation to generation as unquestioned conventional wisdoms until they start to look like absolute truths. Wealth was always something that had to be competed and fought for. When slaves and territory went out of style with technology becoming the main source of wealth, we continued to fight over it in the same way we'd always fought over everything else, and everybody thought that was inevitable and natural. They couldn't separate the old theories from the new facts." Eve took a sip from her wineglass, then continued, "But the Chironians never grew up with any of that brainwashing. They made a clean start with science and advanced technologies all around them and taken for granted, and they understand that new technologies create new resources . . . without limit."

Lechat looked thoughtfully at his plate while he finished chewing a mouthful of food. "You make them all sound like millionaires," he commented.

"That's exactly what they are," Pernak said. "In the material sense, anyway. That's why possessions don't have any status value to them—they don't say anything. That's why you won't find any absolute leaders down there either."

"How come?" Lechat asked, puzzled.

"Why do people follow leaders?" Pernak replied. "For collective strength. What do you need collective strength for? Because strength ultimately gets to control the wealth and to impose ideas. But why does a race of millionaires need leaders if it already has all the material wealth it needs, and isn't interested in imposing ideas on anyone because nobody ever taught it to? The Chironians don't. There isn't anything to scare them with. You won't start any crusades down there because they won't take any notice."

Lechat thought for a while as he continued to eat. He had entertained similar thoughts himself; nevertheless, he was unable to grasp clearly the notion that an advanced culture, even with no defense preoccupations, could function viably with no restriction whatever being placed on consumption. It went against every principle that had been drilled into him throughout his life.

Even as he thought that, Eve's words about brainwashing came back to him. Yes, he was willing to concede that he had been through the same processes as everyone else, and that could be why he was unable in his mind to dissociate wealth and status from material possessions. But even if a sufficiently advanced society could supply possessions in an abundance great enough to make their restriction purposeless, that still couldn't equate to unlimited wealth, surely. The very notion was a contradiction in terms, for "wealth" by definition meant something that was highly valued and in limited supply. In other words, if on Chiron possessions did not equate to wealth and thereby satisfy the universal human hunger to be judged a success, then what did?

"I can see your point to a degree," Pernak said eventually. "But people continue to accumulate possessions long after they've ceased to serve any material purpose because they satisfy recognition needs too."

"That's so true," Eve agreed.

Lechat looked puzzled. "That's my point—how do the Chironians satisfy them?"

"You've already said it," Eve told him. She studied the expression on his face for a few seconds and then smiled. "You can't see it yet, can you, Paul?"

Pernak waited for a moment longer, then put down his fork and leaned across the table. "On Chiron, wealth is *competence!*" he said.

"Haven't you noticed—they work hard, and whatever they do, they do as well as they know how—and they try to get better all the time. It doesn't matter so much *what* they do as long as it's good. And everybody appreciates it. That's their currency—*recognition*, as you said . . . recognition of competence." He shrugged and spread his hands. "And it makes a lot of sense. You just told us that's what everyone wants anyway. Well, Chironians pay it direct instead of indirectly through symbols. Why make life complicated?"

The suggestion was too extraordinary for Lechat to respond instantly. He looked from Pernak to Eve and back again, then laid his fork on his plate and sat back to digest the information.

"When did you see a shoddy piece of workmanship on Chiron . . . a door that didn't fit, or a motor that wouldn't start?" Eve asked him. "Have you ever come across anything like that anywhere there? It makes what we're used to look like junk. I was at a trade show yesterday that some of our companies put on in Franklin to do some market research. The Chironians thought it was a joke. You should have seen the kids down there—they thought our ideas of design and manufacturing were hilarious. Our guys had to give it up as a dead loss."

"That's how they get rich," Pernak said. "By being good at what they do and getting better. Who but a crazy would do anything and stay poor by choice?"

"You mean by reputation, or something like that?" Lechat asked, beginning to look intrigued.

"That's part of it," Pernak replied, nodding. "The satisfaction that their culture conditions them to feel is another part, but you're getting the general idea."

Lechat picked up his fork again. "I never looked at it in quite that way. It's an interesting thought." He began eating again, then stopped and looked up. "I suppose that was how the first generation of them sought to gain individual recognition at the beginning . . . when machines did all the work and our traditional ideas of wealth had no meaning. And it's become embedded in their basic thinking." He nodded slowly to himself and reflected further. "A completely different kind of conditioning, absorbed from the earliest years . . .

based on recognizing individual attributes. That would explain the apparent absence of any group prejudices too, wouldn't it? They've never had any reason to feel threatened by other groups."

"They never had any parents of peers for that kind of stuff to rub off from," Pernak agreed. "Classes, echelons, black, white, Soviet, Chinese . . . it's all the same to them. They don't care. It's what *you* are that matters."

"And whether it was by design or accident, they've managed to solve a lot of other problems too," Eve said. "Take crime for instance. Theft and greed are impossible, because how can you steal another man's competence? Oh, you could try and fake it, I suppose, but you wouldn't last long with people as discerning as Chironians. They can see through a charlatan as quickly as we can spot ourselves being shortchanged. In fact to them that's just what it is. They have their violent moments, sure, but nothing as bad as what's coming in from Africa on the beam right now, or what happened in 2021. But it never turns into a really big problem. There's no motivation for anyone to rally round a would-be Napoleon. He wouldn't have anything to offer that anybody needs."

After another short silence Lechat said, "It's a strange system of currency though, isn't it. I mean, it's not additive at all, or subject to any laws of arithmetic. You can pay what you owe and still not be any poorer yourself. It sounds—I don't know—impossible somehow."

"It's not subject to finite arithmetic," Pernak agreed. "But why does it have to be? Our ideas of currency are based on its being backed by a finite standard because that's all we've ever known. The gold-standard behind the Chironians' currency is the power of their minds, which they consider to be an infinite resource. Therefore they do their accounting with a calculus of infinities. You take something from infinity, and you've still got infinity left." He shrugged. "It's consistent. I know it sounds crazy to us, but it fits with the way they think."

"It certainly puts a new light on things," Lechat conceded. He sat back again, looked from one to the other, and spread his hands resignedly. "So am I to take it that I shouldn't assume your support in the matter I talked about earlier?"

"It's nothing personal, Paul. We think you're a great guy. . . ." Pernak frowned and sighed apologetically. "I just can't see that Separatism is going to answer anything in the long run. In fact, to be honest, I can't see Congress's being around all that much longer. On that planet down there, it's a dodo already."

"You could be right, but that's long-term," Lechat replied. "I'm more worried about what might happen in the shorter term. I need help to do something about it."

"Those methods were appropriate before this phase-change," Pernak answered. "They don't have any place now."

"What other way is there?" Lechat asked.

Pernak shrugged. "Just let the system die naturally."

"It might not want to die that easily," Lechat pointed out. "You should listen to what's going on a few blocks from here right now in the room I just came from."

"They won't stop anything, Paul," Pernak said. "They're up against the driving force of evolution. Canute had the same problem."

"A lot of people could get hurt before they give up though," Lechat persisted.

Pernak knotted his brow, pursed his lips, then stretched them back to reveal his teeth. "Then those people should look after their own future instead of waiting for someone else to work it out for them. That's the old way. They have to learn to think the Chironian way." After a second of hesitation he added, "That's what Eve and I are going to do."

"What do you mean?" Lechat asked, although in the same instant he thought he knew.

Pernak glanced at Eve for a moment. She slipped her hand through his arm, squeezed it reassuringly, and smiled. They both looked back at Lechat. "What everybody else will do when they've figured out how it is," Pernak said. He grinned, almost apologetically. "That's why we won't be able to help much, Paul. You see, we're leaving."

"I see . . ." Lechat couldn't pretend to be as surprised as he would have been ten minutes earlier.

Pernak tossed up his hands. "I've been to take a look at their university and what they do there. You wouldn't believe it. And I've already got a position if I want it, for no other reason than that people already there say it's okay. You get a house, for nothing . . . a good one. Or they'll build you one however you want it. How can you say no? We're going to become Chironians. And so will everybody else when they've gotten over the voyage. Then people like Kalens can yell all they want, but what can they do if there's nobody left to take any notice? It's as I said—you have to start thinking like Chironians."

"They've still got the Army . . . and a lot of nasty hardware up here," Lechat reminded him.

Pernak twisted his face through a few contortions, then sighed again. "I know. That crossed my mind too, but what is there to provoke any real trouble? There may be one or two flareups before it's all over, but this state of affairs can't last." He shook his head. "We're convinced this is the only way to go. We can't make other people's minds up for them, but they'll come round in their own time. Anything else would cause worse problems."

Lechat nodded reluctantly. "Well, it sounds pretty final, I guess."

Pernak spread his hands and nodded. "Yes. Sorry and all that kind of thing, Paul, but that's how it is."

Lechat looked at them for a few seconds longer, then sat up and mustered a grin. "Well, what can I say? Good luck to the pair of you. I hope everything works out."

"Thanks," Pernak acknowledged.

"I trust we'll all stay friends and keep in touch," Eve said.

"You'd better believe it," Lechat promised.

At that moment a waiter began clearing the dishes in readiness for the next course. "Have you heard the news from the surface?" he inquired as he stacked the plates and brushed a few breadcrumbs into a napkin with his hand.

"News?" Lechat looked up, puzzled. "When? We've been here for the last hour. There wasn't anything special then."

"It came in about fifteen minutes ago," the waiter said. He shook his head sadly. "Bad news. There's been a shooting down there . . . in Franklin somewhere. At least one dead—one of our soldiers, I think. It was at some place called The Two Moons."

◉ CHAPTER TWENTY ◉

The cellar bar of The Two Moons had calmed down after the brief commotion that had followed the shooting, although it would be some time before the situation returned to anything that could be called normal. Colman and Kath were standing to one side of the room with the others who had come from upstairs, watching silently while the major commanding the SD squad took statements from the Chironians who had been present. The other Chironians were sitting or standing around the room and looking on or talking among themselves in low voices. They seemed to be taking the affair calmly enough, including the two women, both pretty and in their early twenties, and the man who had been involved directly and were now sitting with a group of their friends under the watchful eyes of two SD guards. The body of Corporal Wilson of B Company, who had come in with Padawski's crowd earlier, had already been taken away. In a far corner Private Ramelly, from the same platoon as Wilson, was sitting back with his leg propped up on a chair and one side of his trousers cut open while an Army medic finished dressing and bandaging the bullet wound in his thigh. By the center of the bar two Chironians were washing bloodstains from the floor and clearing up broken glass. Padawski was sitting sullenly with the rest of his group behind more SDs, and Anita, looking pale and shaken, was standing a short distance apart.

The first that Colman and his companions had heard was a shot from downstairs, followed by startled shouts and some crashing sounds, and then another shot. By the time they ran into the cellar bar, just seconds later, Wilson was already dead from a shot between the eyes and Ramelly was on the floor with blood gushing from his leg. Padawski and the others were standing uncertainly by the bar, covered by a .38 automatic that one of the young Chironian women was holding. Several other weapons had appeared around the room. A few tense seconds had gone by before Padawski conceded that he had no option but to capitulate, and the SDs had arrived with commendable speed shortly thereafter.

Apparently some of Padawski's friends had the idea that the Chironian women were among the things that could be had for the taking on Chiron, and two of them had persisted in pressing lewd advances upon the two girls at the bar despite their being told repeatedly and in progressively less uncertain terms that the girls weren't interested. The soldiers, who had been drinking heavily, became angry and even more unpleasant, paying no attention to dour warnings from around the room. An argument developed, in the course of which Ramelly grabbed one of the women and handled her roughly. She produced a gun and shot him in the leg. There would probably have been no more to it than that if Wilson hadn't seized the gun and turned it on the Chironians who were about to intervene, at which point another Chironian had shot him dead from the back of the room.

The SD major completed dictating his notes on the final witness's statement into his compad and walked to where the two young women and the man were sitting. Their expressions as they looked up at him were not apprehensive or apologetic, but neither were they defiant. The deed was unfortunate but it had been necessary, the faces seemed to say, and there was nothing to feel guilty about. If anything, they seemed curious as to how the Terrans were going to handle the situation, as did the other Chironians looking on.

"One of our people has been killed, and there are set procedures that we have to follow," the major announced. "My orders require me to take you three back with us. It would make things a lot easier for everybody if you complied. I'm sorry, but I don't have any choice."

"Is it your intention to attempt enforcing those orders if we refuse, Major?" the Chironian who had killed Wilson asked. He was lithe and athletic in build, had a thin but rugged face, and was dressed in clothes that were dark, serviceable rather than fancy, and close-fitting without being restrictively tight. He reminded Colman of the bad guy in an ancient Western movie. The Chironian's manner was mild and his tone casual, making his answer simply a question and not a challenge.

The major met his eye firmly. "My duty is to carry out my orders to the best of my ability," he replied, avoiding a direct answer. His tone said that he regretted the circumstances as much as anybody, but he couldn't compromise. The display of tact seemed to do the trick. The Chironian held his eye for a moment longer, and then nodded. "Very well." Inwardly Colman breathed a sigh of relief. The women were evidently willing to allow the man to speak for them too. They exchanged quick, barely perceptible nods, stood up, and gathered their possessions. Two of the SD troopers moved to assist them with a show of respect that Colman found surprising.

The major hesitated for a second, and then said, "Ah . . . in view of the circumstances, it would be better if you permitted us to carry your guns back for you. Would you mind?"

"Are you telling us we're prisoners?" the Chironian man asked.

"I would prefer not to use that term," the major answered. "The legal ramifications are not for me to comment on. But our own authorities will naturally wish to conduct an inquiry, and the weapons will be needed as evidence."

"By *your* customs," the Chironian observed.

"It was one of *our* people," the major said.

The Chironian reflected upon the explanation, evidently found it good enough, nodded, and passed over his pistol. The girl who had wounded Ramelly followed suit. Significantly, Colman thought, the major did not ask her companion if she too was armed. As the guards began motioning Padawski and his group to their feet, the major marched over to where Colman and the others from D Company were standing with the Chironians who had been upstairs with them. He had already taken their names and established that they had not witnessed the incident firsthand. "You guys are free to go," he informed them. "If there's a hearing, you might be called in to testify. If so, the appropriate people *will* contact you."

"They know where to find us," Colman said. Kath's pocket communicator buzzed, and she took it out to answer. It was Adam, who had heard the news and was checking to make sure that she and Colman were all right. Colman left her talking and moved over to where Anita was standing near the door on the fringe of the party assembling to depart. "Why'd you ever get mixed up with that bunch?" he murmured. "Wise up when it's all over. Get out of it."

There was no repentance or remorse in her eyes when she looked at him. "It's none of your business anymore," she hissed. "How I choose to have fun is my affair and my life."

Colman snorted derisively. "You call that fun?"

"You know what I mean. They weren't doing anything. They'd just had a bit too much to drink. Those two bitches didn't have to do something like that."

"Maybe you should try looking at it their way," Colman said.

Anita's eyes blazed as her shock began wearing off and dissipated itself as anger. "Why should I? Bruce just got killed and Dan's got a hole in his leg, and you're telling me to see it *their* way? What kind of a man are you anyhow?" She sneered past Colman's shoulder at Kath, who was returning the communicator to her pocket. "I can see why. It didn't take *you* long, did it. Is she good?"

Colman ignored the remark. "Just think about it," he muttered. "For your own sake."

"I told you once already, it's none of your business anymore. Leave me alone. I don't want to talk to you. Just—go away and leave me alone."

Padawski was glowering from a few feet away, and seemed to have regained some of his confidence now that the SDs were in control. "You stay away from her, Goldilocks," he spat. "Stick with your nice, murdering friends. We won't forget you either." He turned his head back to glare at the whole room before turning for the door. "And that goes for all of you," he warned in a louder voice. "We won't forget. You'll see."

"On your way." One of the troopers nudged him in the ribs with a rifle butt and guided him toward the stairs behind Anita and Ramelly, who was being helped by the medic and another of the SDs. Colman watched until they had all left, then returned to the others. "Is she a friend of yours?" Kath inquired. "From a while back. But not anymore, I guess, by the look of it."

"She's a good-looking girl. What does she do?"

"A communications specialist at Brigade." Kath's eyebrows lifted approvingly. "Smart as well, eh?"

"She could do a lot better than waste herself with those bums. She's the kind that prefers the easy road . . . for as long as it lasts, anyhow."

"That's a shame," Kath said.

Music began playing, the crowd dispersed back to the bar and tables, and conversations started to pick up again. Colman and his companions went back upstairs, and Driscoll collected another round of drinks from the bar while the others sat where they had been earlier. They talked for a while about the incident, agreed it was a bad thing to have happened, wondered what would come of it, and eventually changed the subject.

"I guess you have to learn moderation in this place," Stanislau remarked, studying his half-emptied glass of dark, frothy Chironian beer. He shook his head slowly. "You know, this sounds crazy but sometimes I wish they would make us pay for it."

"I know exactly what you mean," Carson said. Driscoll nodded his mute assent also.

"I'm not so sure I agree," Swyley said, which meant that he did.

Colman was about to make a joke out of it when he realized they were serious. He knotted his brows and directed an inquiring look at each of them in turn.

"It's this whole business of not paying for anything," Stanislau said at last. "We come in here and drink, we go into restaurants and eat, we walk out of stores with all kinds of stuff, and none of it costs anything." He sat back, looked from side to side for moral support, got plenty, and shook his head helplessly. "It seemed too good to be true at first, but that soon wears off. It's not funny anymore, chief. It's getting to all of us."

"We feel we owe something, and we want to pay our way," Driscoll confirmed. "We don't want any free rides. But all we get are pieces of paper that aren't any good for anything here. What can you do?"

"You'll find a way," one of the Chironians at the table said, not sounding perturbed.

"Better late than never, I suppose," another commented, glancing at the painter, who was still there. The painter nodded but didn't reply.

"What does that mean?" Driscoll asked, looking at the Chironian who had spoken.

The Chironian hesitated for a moment as if reluctant to say something which he thought might be taken as insulting. Kath caught his eye and nodded reassuringly. "Well," the Chironian began, then paused again. "Most people here start to feel that way by the time they're about ten. I'm not trying to offend anyone—but that's the way it is."

Carson frowned and thought about the implications, then shook his head. "It's impossible," he said. "No system could work like that."

An intrigued and thoughtful look came over Swyley's face as he listened. He said nothing, which meant that he didn't agree.

✹ CHAPTER TWENTY-ONE ✹

Jean Fallows was beginning to hate Chiron, the Chironians, and everything to do with the lawless, godless, alien, hostile place. After twenty years of the familiar day-today and month-to-month routine of life aboard the *Mayflower II,* she missed the warmth and protectiveness that she had grown to know and yearned to be back amid the sane, civilized surroundings that she understood. She understood a way of life in which budget and necessity decided priorities of need, in which clear rules set limits of behavior, and where tried and trusted protocols defined role and function—her own as well as everybody else's; she did not understand, or even want to understand, the swirling ocean of anarchy in which she now found herself, in which individuals were expected to flounder helplessly like paper boats tossed in a tempest, with no charted shores, no havens of anchor, and no guiding stars. She had no place in it, and she desired no place in it. Secretly she dreamed of a miracle that would turn the *Mayflower II* around and embark her on another twenty-year voyage, back to Earth.

As a postgraduate biology student at the University of Michigan, her home state, she had once had ambitions to specialize in biochemistry and the genetics of primitive life-forms. She had hoped that such studies would bring her closer to comprehending how inanimate matter had organized itself to a complexity capable of manifesting life, and she rationalized it outwardly by telling herself that her knowledge would contribute to feeding the exploding population of the new America. And then she had met Bernard, whose youthful zeal and visions of the Reformation that would sweep the world had awakened her political awareness and carried her along with him into a whole new dimension of human relationships and motivations which until then she had hardly recognized as existing at all. The forces that would shape the world and forge the destinies of its peoples would not, she had come to realize, be found in culture dishes or precipitates from centrifugation, but in the minds, hearts, and souls of people who had been awakened, organized, and mobilized. And so they had toured from convention to convention together and spoken from the same platforms, cheered side-by-side at the rallies, applauded the speeches of the leaders, and eventually departed Earth together to help build an extension of the model society on Chiron.

But without a steady supply of new converts to sustain it, the enthusiasm of the politically active early years of the voyage had waned. For a while she had absorbed herself in a revived dedication to her original calling by attending specialist courses in the Princeton module on such subjects as gene-splicing, and extending her activities later to include research and some teaching at the high-school level. Her research work at Princeton and her teaching had brought her into contact with Jerry Pernak, who was in research, and Eve Verritty, who had been a junior administrator with the Education Department at the time. In fact it was Jean who had first introduced them to each other.

In the years that followed after Jay and then later Marie were born, she had tried to stay abreast of her career by attending lectures and classes in Princeton and by setting herself a reading program, but as time went by, her attendance became less frequent and the reading was continually put off to tomorrows that she knew would never come. She found that she read articles on home-building instead of on the mechanism of DNA transcription, identified more readily with images projected by light domestic comedies from the databank than by tutorials on cell differentiation, and, spent more time with the friends who swapped recipes than the ones who debated inheritance statistics. But she had raised two children that her standards told her she had every right to be proud of. She was entitled to rewards for the sacrifices she had made. And now Chiron was threatening to steal the rewards away.

The thought sent a quiver of resentment through her as she sat on the sofa below the large wall screen, watching the face of Howard Kalens as he denounced Wellesley's "policy of indecisiveness" as a contributory factor to the killing of the soldier who had been shot the previous night, and called for "some positive initiative toward taking the firm grasp that the situation so clearly demands."

"A boy of twenty-three," Kalens had said a few minutes previously. "Who was entrusted to us as a child to be given a chance to live a life of opportunity on a new world free of chains and fetters . . . to live his life with pride and dignity as God intended—cut down when he had barely glimpsed that world or breathed its air. Bruce Wilson did not die yesterday. His life ended when he was three years old."

Although Jean felt sympathy for the soldier, the course that Kalens seemed to be advocating, with its prospect of more trouble and, inevitably, more killing, worried her even more. Why did it always have to be like this? she asked herself. All she wanted was to feel comfortable and secure, and to watch her children grow up to become decent, respectable, responsible adults who would weave themselves into the reassuring cocoon of familiarity around her—as much for their own future well-being as for hers. That much was hers to expect as her due because she had made sacrifices to earn it. It threatened nobody. So why should other people's squabbles which were not of her making now threaten her with sweeping it all away?

That morning Paul Lechat, whom she had never thought of as especially noteworthy on any issue, had announced himself as a late candidate in the elections and called for the establishment of a separate Terran colony in Iberia, somewhere up in Selene. He wanted to allow the people from Earth to pursue their own pattern of living without disruptive influences for the immediate future, and possibly to make such an institution permanent if it suited enough people to do so. To Jean the announcement had come as a godsend, and to many others as well, if the amount of popular support that had materialized from all sides within a matter of hours was anything to go by. Why couldn't everybody see it that way? she wondered. It was so obvious. Why were there always some who were obstinate and valued political interests before what common sense said would be for the common good, such as Kalens, who even now was reacting to Lechat as a threat and rallying his own followers to action?

"Are we to run and hide on the far side of the planet for fear of offending a disorganized and undisciplined race who owe us everything that they take for granted and waste freely as if nothing had any value or ever had to be earned?" Kalens was asking from the screen. "Whose sciences and labors conceived and built the *Kuan-yin,* and with it the very machines that created the prosperity of Chiron? Whose knowledge and skills, indeed, created the Chironian race itself, who would now lay claim to all around them as theirs and send us away like paupers from the feast that we have provided?" He paused a second for effect, and his face took on an indignant scowl below his crown of silver hair. "I say no! I will not be driven away in such fashion. I will not even contemplate such an action. I say, publicly and without reservation, that any such suggestion can be described only as a surrender to moral cowardice that is beneath contempt. Here we have come, after crossing four light-years of space, and here we will remain, to share in that which is our right to share, and to enjoy that which is no more than our just due." A thunder of applause greeted the exhortation. Jean had heard enough and told Jeeves to turn off the screen.

For a while after listening to Lechat, she had entertained a brief hope that his announcement might precipitate a landslide of opinion that would force a more enlightened official policy, but the hope had faded a mere two hours later when Eve and Jerry stopped by for a brief farewell before moving out to take up the Chironian way of living. Apparently many people were doing the same thing, and there were even rumors of desertions from the Army. Jean had been unable to avoid feeling that Eve and Jerry were somehow deserting her too, but she had managed to keep a pleasant face and wish them well. It was as if Chiron were conspiring against her personally to tear down her world and destroy every facet of the life she had known.

The house around her was another part of it. She no longer saw it as the dream it had been on the day they moved down from the *Mayflower II*, but instead as another part of the same conspiracy—a cheap bribe to seduce her into selling her soul in the same way as a university research post and the lure of a free home had seduced Eve and Jerry. Chiron didn't want to let her be. It wanted her to be like it. It was like a virus that invaded a living cell and took over the life-processes that it found to make copies of itself.

She shivered at the thought and got up from the sofa to find Bernard. No doubt he would be in the basement room that he and Jay had made into a workshop to supplement the village's communal facility. Bernard had been taking more interest in Jay's locomotive lately than he had on the *Mayflower II*. Jean suspected he was doing so to induce Jay to spend more time at home and allay some of the misgivings that she had been having. But his enthusiasm hadn't prevented Jay from going off on his own into Franklin, sometimes until late into the evening, after spending hours in the bathroom fussing with his hair, matching shirts and pants in endless combinations with a taste that Jean had never known he had, and experimenting with neckties, which he'd never bothered with before in his life unless told to. Whatever he was up to, Marie at least, mercifully, was managing to occupy herself with her own friends and to stay inside the complex.

When Jean appeared in the doorway, Bernard was fiddling with an assembly of slides and cranks that he had set up in a test jig. She watched while he pushed a tiny rod which in turn caused all the other pieces to slide and turn in a smooth unison, though what any of them did or what the whole thing was for were mysteries to Jean. Bernard pulled the rod back again to return all the pieces to their original positions, then looked up and grinned. "I have to take my hat off to Army training," he said. "I'll say one thing for Steve Colman—he sure knows what he's doing. Our son has produced some first-class work here." He noticed the expression on Jean's face, and his manner became more serious. "Aw, try and snap out of it, hon. I know everything's a bit strange. What else can you expect after twenty years? You'll need time to get used to it. We all will."

"You don't mind, do you? Here . . . the way things are . . . it doesn't bother you. You're like Eve and Jerry." Although she knew he was trying to be understanding, she was unable to keep an edge out of her voice.

"Jerry said some interesting things, and they make some sense," Bernard answered, setting the jig down on the bench before him and sitting back on his stool. "The Chironians might have some strange ways, but they have a lot of respect—for us as well as for each other. That's not such a bad way for people to be. Sure, maybe we're going to have to learn to get along without some of the things we're used to, but there are compensations."

"Was it respect they showed that boy who was killed last night?" Jean asked bitterly. "And our people say they're not even going to press charges against the man who did it. What kind of a way is that to live? Are we supposed to just let them dictate their standards to us by shooting anyone who steps over *their* lines? Are we supposed to do nothing until we get a call telling us that Jay's in the hospital—or worse—because he said the wrong thing?"

Bernard sighed and forced his voice to remain reasonable. "Now, come on . . . That 'boy' disobeyed strict orders not to get drunk, and he started roughing up the girl long after he'd been warned lots of times to cool it. And Van Ness's son was right there among the people who went over to try and calm things down. Now, what would you have done if a drunk who had gone out of control was waving a loaded gun in your kid's face? What would anybody have done?"

"How do you know?" Jean challenged. "You weren't there. And that's not the way it sounded when Kalens was talking just now. And a lot of people seemed to agree with him."

"He's just playing on emotion, Jean. I had it on down here for a few minutes but couldn't stand it. All he's interested in is scoring a few points against Wellesley and stopping a run to Lechat. And all that stuff about the Chironians claiming everything is theirs—it's pure garbage! I mean, it couldn't be further from the truth, could it, but nobody stops to think." He frowned to himself for a moment. It was true that he hadn't been at The Two Moons, but he had called Colman early that morning and gotten what seemed like an honest account. But with Jean acting the way she was, he didn't want to mention that. "Anyhow, the facts about the shooting are on record," he said. "All you have to do is ask Jeeves."

Jean seemed to dismiss the subject from her mind. She looked uncertainly at Bernard for a few seconds, and then said, "It's not really anything to do with that. It's—oh, I can't put this any other way—it's you."

Bernard didn't seem as surprised as he might have been. "Want to spit it out?"

Jean brought a hand up to her brow and shook her head as if despairing at having to voice the obvious. "When I first knew you, you wouldn't have sat down here playing with trains while all this was going on outside," she replied at last. "Don't you understand? What's happening out there, right now, is *important*. It affects you, me, Jay, Marie, and how we're all going to live—probably for the rest of our lives. Twenty years ago you—both of us—we'd have *done* something. Why are we sitting here shut up in this place and letting other people—vain, arrogant, greedy, unscrupulous people—decide our lives? Why aren't we doing something? It's that. I can't stand it."

Bernard made no reply but let his eyebrows ask the question for him.

Jean raised her hands in an imploring gesture. "Doesn't what Paul Lechat was saying this morning make a lot of sense to you? Isn't it the only way? Well, he's going to need *help* to do it. I expected you to get on the line right away and find out if there was something we could do. But you hardly even talked about it. Hell, I know I'm twenty years older too, but at least I haven't forgotten all the things we used to talk about. We were going to help build a new world—our world, the way it ought to be. Well, we've arrived. The ride's over. Isn't it time we started thinking about earning the ticket?"

Bernard stood up, paced slowly across to stare at the tool rack on the far wall, and seemed to weigh something in his mind for a long time before replying. Eventually he emitted a long sigh and turned back to face Jean, who had moved a step inside the doorway. "We can still build it," he said. "But it doesn't quite work the way we thought then. Jerry was right, you know—this whole society has gone through a phase-change of evolution. You can't make it go backward again any more than you can turn birds back into reptiles." Bernard came a pace nearer. His voice took on a persuasive, encouraging note. "Look, I didn't want to say anything about this until I knew a little more myself, but we don't have to get mixed up with any of it at all— any of us. Kalens and the rest of them belong to everything we've left behind now. We don't need them anymore. Don't you see, it can't last?"

"What are you talking about, Bernard?"

"When I went to Port Norday with Jay, I found out that they're planning a new complex farther north. They're going to need engineers—fusion engineers. They practically told me I'd have no problem getting in there, to a top job maybe. Think of it—our own place just like we've always said, and no more crap from Merrick or any of them!" Bernard threw his hands high. "I could be *me* for the first time in my life . . . and so could you, all of us. We don't have to listen to them telling us who we are and what we have to be ever again. Doesn't that . . ." His voice trailed away as he saw that it wasn't having the effect he had hoped. Jean was backing away through the door, shaking her head in mute protest.

"It's getting to you too," she whispered tightly. "Just as it's already gotten to Eve and Jerry. Oh, how I hate this place! Can't you see what it's doing to us all?"

"But, hon, all I—"

Jean spun round and ran back to the elevator. Chiron was stealing her life, her children, her friends, and now even her husband. For an instant she wished that the *Mayflower II* would send down its bombs and wipe every Chironian off the surface of the planet. Then they would be able to begin again, cleanly and decently. Ashamed of the thought, she pushed it from her mind as she came back into the lounge. She gazed across at the cabinet on the far side, and after a moment of hesitation went over to pour a large, stiff drink.

◉ CHAPTER TWENTY-TWO ◉

"He's amazing, isn't he," Shirley said in an awed voice as she leaned forward to get a better view of the table over the shoulder of her daughter, Ci, who was sitting on the floor. "It must be a genetic mutation that makes sticky fingers or something."

"Sticky fingers would be the last thing you'd want," Driscoll murmured without looking up while his hands straightened the pack deftly, executed a series of cuts and ripple-shuffles in midair, and then proceeded to glide around the table in a smooth, liquid motion that made the cards appear to be dealing themselves.

"Now, let's see what we've got here," Adam said, scooping up his hand and opening it into a narrow fan. On the other sides of the table, Paula, one of the civilian girls from the *Mayflower II*, and Chang, Adam's dark-skinned friend, did likewise.

"There's no need to look," Driscoll told him nonchalantly. "You've got a pair of kings." Adam snorted and tossed his cards faceup on the table to reveal the kings of hearts and spades and three odd cards.

"What about me?" Ci asked, looking at Driscoll. She leaned to one side to let her mother see the hand she was holding.

Driscoll stared at her. "Three queens, and I could beat it," he said. Ci and Shirley exchanged baffled looks.

Paula was looking at him impishly. "Do you think you could beat mine?" she asked in a curious voice.

"Sure," Driscoll told her. His eyes twinkled just for an instant. "If you want to know how, I'd beat you with aces."

"Are you sure, Tony?" Paula asked. "You wouldn't want to bet on that, now, would you?" Paula turned her head to smile slyly at her friend, Terry, also from the *Mayflower II,* who was watching from behind.

Driscoll met her eyes calmly. "I'd risk it," he said. "Sure, if this was for real, I'd put money on it."

"How much?" Paula asked.

Driscoll shrugged. "What would you stake?"

"Twenty?"

"Sure, I'd cover that."

"Fifty?"

"I'm still with you."

"A hundred?"

"A hundred."

Paula slapped down four aces gleefully. "You *lose!* Hey, how about that? I just cleaned him out. See, I knew he had to be bluffing."

"Bluffing, hell." Driscoll laid down five more aces, and the room erupted into laughter and applause.

"Hey, you haven't asked me," Chang said. "I beat that."

"You do?" Driscoll looked surprised.

Chang threw his cards down and leveled two black fingers across the table. "A Smith and Wesson beats five aces." He grinned and stood up. "Everybody set for another drink?" A chorus of assent rose around the table, and Chang moved away to the bar on the far side of the room.

Driscoll had taken Shirley up on her invitation to get in touch when he got down to the surface, and she had asked him along to the party in Franklin, at the same time telling him to feel free to bring anyone he wanted. So Driscoll had invited Colman, Swyley, Maddock, and Stanislau, who among them had persuaded Sirocco to come too, and Sirocco had suggested bringing some of the girls from the *Mayflower II.* Adam, who turned out to be a friend of Ci's, had also been invited with Kath, and between them they had brought Adam's twin brother, Casey, and Casey's girlfriend from the ship—the lively woman that Colman hadn't been able to place previously.

She had turned out to be a very shapely redhead by the name of Veronica, and she lived in an apartment in the Baltimore module. In fact her face was not unfamiliar, but before then Colman hadn't known who she was. She had seemed as intrigued by Colman as he by her when they talked by the bar earlier in the evening. "Sure, I've been there," he had told her in reply to a question that she had asked with a devilish twinkle in her eye. "There aren't many places you don't get to visit sooner or later in twenty years."

"Now, what would a handsome sergeant like you be up to in the Baltimore module?"

"Why would anybody be interested?" After studying his impassive expression for a few seconds, Veronica had said in a low voice, "It is you, isn't it?"

"Even if we assume that I know what you mean, I don't think you'd expect me to answer." So now they both knew, and knew that the other knew. Each had tested the other's discretion, and both of them respected what they had found. Nothing more needed to be said.

With all public bars having been put off-limits to the *Mayflower II*'s soldiers after the shooting, the party couldn't have come at a better time, Colman reflected as he leaned against the bar and nursed his glass while gazing around the room. Swyley and Stanislau were behind him in a corner with a mixed group of Chironians and seemed interested in the planet's travel facilities; Sirocco was with another group in the center of the room discussing the war news with another group, and Maddock, looking slightly disheveled, was sprawled along a couch in an alcove on the far side with his arm draped around Wendy, another girl from the *Mayflower II*, who seemed to be asleep. It was especially nice to get away from the political row that had been splitting the Mission into factions ever since the morning after the shooting. Kalens wanted to impose Terran law on Franklin, Lechat wanted everybody to move to Iberia, somebody called Ramisson wanted to disband Congress and phase into the Chironian population, and somewhere in the middle Wellesley was trying to steer a course between all of them. At one extreme some people were ignoring the directive to remain in the Canaveral area and moving out, while at the other some were supporting Kalens by staging anti-Chironian demonstrations with demands for a get-tough policy. Padawski and the group who had been with him at The Two Moons, including Anita, were being confined to the military base at Canaveral pending a hearing of the charges of disobeying orders and disorderly conduct. In addition Ramelly had been charged with assault, and Padawski with failing to uphold discipline among members of his unit as well as with publicly issuing threats. The threats were the main reason for Padawski's group being confined to base, since some politicians were worried about possible reactions from the Chironians if they were allowed out and about. Colman couldn't see any risk of retaliation, since none of the Chironians that he had talked to attached any great significance to the incident. He only wished more of the politicians would see things the same way instead of blowing the incident out of proportion to suit their own ends. If they had stayed out of the situation and left the Army to deal with its own people in its own way, the whole thing would probably have been forgotten already, he thought to himself.

Kath had moved away to talk to Adam, Casey, and Veronica, who were sitting together beyond the table at which Driscoll was performing. Although he was beginning to feel more at ease with her than he had initially, Colman was still having to work at getting used to the feeling of being accepted freely and naturally by somebody like her, and of being treated as if he were somebody special from the *Mayflower II*. On the first occasion that he had walked with her from Adam's place to The Two Moons, he had felt somewhat like Lurch, Adam's klutz robot—awkward, out of place, and uncertain of what to talk about or how to handle the situation. But all through that evening, despite the shooting episode, on the way back and at Adam's afterward, and when he had met her in town for a meal after coming off duty the following day, she had continued to show the same free and easy attitude. Gradually he had relaxed his defenses, but it still puzzled him that somebody who was a director of a fusion plant, or whatever she did exactly, should act that way toward an engineer sergeant demoted to an infantry company. Why would she do something like that? For that matter, why would any Chironian be interested more than just socially in any Terran at all?

"Because she's seducing you," a voice murmured from behind him.

Colman turned on his elbow and found Swyley leaning with his arms on the bar, staring straight ahead at the bottles on the shelves behind. Colman raised his eyebrows. Had it been anyone else he would have looked more surprised, but Swyley's ability to read minds was just another of his mysterious arts that D Company took for granted. After a few seconds Swyley went on, "They're seducing all of us. That's how they're fighting the war."

Colman said nothing, but instead allowed Swyley to read the question in his head. Sure enough, Swyley explained, "They don't make bombs or organize armies. It's too messy, and too many of the wrong people get hurt. They go for the grass roots. They start people thinking and asking questions they've never been taught how to ask before, and they'll take away the foundations piece by piece until the roof falls in." He paused and continued staring at the wall. "You're an engineer, and she runs part of a fusion complex. If you want out, you've got a place to go. That's what she's telling you."

Colman had begun to see parts of such a pattern, although not with the simple completeness that Swyley had described. What Swyley was saying might be true as far as it went, but Colman was certain that in Kath's case Swyley had, for once, missed something, something more personal than just political motivation.

A hand descended on his arm and slid upward to tease the back of his neck. He turned round to find that Kath had come back. "You're starting a bachelors' party here," she said. "I have to break that up before the idea catches on."

Colman grinned. "Good thinking. We were starting to talk shop." He inclined his head to where Veronica was still talking animatedly between Kath's twin sons and evidently enjoying herself. "Somebody seems to be quite a hit over there."

"Isn't she a lot of fun," Kath agreed. "She's talking Casey into teaching her to be an architect. She could do it too. She's an intelligent woman. Have you known her long?"

Colman smiled to himself. "I've only seen her around. This may sound crazy, but I never really met her before tonight."

"After twenty years on the same ship? That's not possible, surely."

Colman shrugged. "Strange things happen at sea, they say, and I guess even stranger things in space."

"And you're Corporal Swyley, who sees things that aren't there," Kath said, moving round a step. "Your Captain Sirocco told me about your ability. I like him. He told me about the way you ruined the exercise up on the ship too. I thought it was wonderful."

"If you're going to lose anyway, you might as well win," Swyley replied. "If you win the wrong way, you lose, and if you lose either way, you lose. So why not enjoy it?"

"What happens if you win the right way?" Kath asked him.

"Then you lose out to the system. It's like playing against Driscoll—the system makes its own aces."

At that moment one of the Chironian girls from the group in the corner took Swyley lightly by the arm. "I thought you were getting some more drinks," she said. "We're all drying up over there. I'll give you a hand. Then you can come back and tell us more about the Mafia. The conversation was just getting interesting."

Colman's eyes widened in surprise. "Him? What in hell does he know about the Mafia?"

The girl gave Colman a funny look. "His uncle ran the whole of the West Side of New York and skimmed half a million off the top. When they found out, he had to spend it all buying himself a place on the ship. You didn't know?" For a second Colman could only gape at her. He'd known that Swyley had been brought on to the *Mayflower II* as a kid by an uncle who had died fifteen years into the voyage from a heart condition, but that was about all. "Hey, how come you never told us about that part?" he asked as the girl led Swyley away.

"You never asked me," Swyley answered over his shoulder.

He turned back, shaking his head despairingly, and looked at Kath again. Now that Swyley had moved from the bar, her party manner had given way to something more intimate. Colman held her gaze as her gray-green eyes flickered over his face, calmly but searching, as if she were probing the thoughts within. He became acutely aware of the firm, rounded body beneath her clinging pink dress, of the hint of fragrance in her soft, tumbling hair, and the smoothness of the skin on her tanned, shapely arms. Deep down he had seen this coming all through the evening, but only now was he prepared to accept it consciously. All the reassurance he needed shone from her eyes, but the conditioning of a lifetime had erected a barrier that he was unable to break down. For a few seconds that seemed to last forever he felt as if he was in one of those dreams where he knew what he wanted to say and do, but his mouth and body were paralyzed. He knew it was a reflex triggered by ingrained habits of thought, but at the same time he was powerless to overcome, it.

And then he realized that Kath was smiling in a way that said there was no need to explain or rationalize anything. Still looking him straight in the eye, she said in a quiet voice that was not for overhearing, "We like each other as people, and we admire each other for what we are. There isn't anything to feel hung up about on Chiron. People who feel like that usually make love, if that's what they want to do." She paused for a second. "Isn't that what you'd like to do?"

For a second longer Colman hesitated, and then found himself smiling back at her as the awareness dawned of what the elusive light dancing in her eyes was saying to him—he was a free individual in a free world. And suddenly the barrier crumbled away.

"Yes, it is," he replied. There was nothing more to say.

"I only live at Port Norday during the week," Kath said. "I've got a place in Franklin as well. It's not far from here at all."

"And I am on early duty tomorrow," Colman said.

He grinned again, and she smiled back impishly, "So why are we still here?" they asked together.

◎ CHAPTER TWENTY-THREE ◎

Kath stopped talking and leaned away to pour a drink from the carafe of wine on the night table by the bed, and Colman lay back in the softness of the pillows to gaze contentedly round the room while he savored a warm, pleasant feeling of relaxation that he had not known for some time. It was a cozy, cheerfully feminine room, with lots of coverlets and satiny drapes, fluffy rugs, pastel colors, and homey knickknacks arranged on the shelves and ledges. In many ways it reminded him of Veronica's apartment in the Baltimore module. On the wall opposite was a photograph of two laughing, roguish-looking boys of about twelve, who despite their years he recognized easily as Casey and Adam, and scattered about were more pictures which he assumed were of the rest of Kath's family. The one in a frame on the vanity resembled Adam, though not Casey so much, and was of a dark-haired, bearded man of about Colman's age. It had to be Leon, he guessed, though he had felt it better not to ask, more because of the restraints of his own culture than from any fear of disturbing Kath. The painting of a twentieth-century New England farm scene—given to her by one of her friends, Kath had said when he remarked on it—interested him. Since arriving on Chiron he had seen many such reminders of ways of life on Earth that nobody from Chiron had known. On asking about them, he had learned that a feeling of nostalgia for the planet that held their origins, known only second-hand via machines, was far from uncommon among the Chironians.

Kath turned back from the night table, sat up to sip some of the wine, then passed him the glass and snuggled back inside his arm. "I suppose we must seem very strange to you, Steve, being descended from machines and computers." She chuckled softly. "I bet there are lots of people on your ship who think we're really aliens. Do they think we walk like Lurch and talk in metallic, monotone voices?"

Colman grinned and drank from the glass. "Not quite that bad. But some of them do have pretty funny ideas—or did have, anyway. A lot of people couldn't imagine that kids brought up by machines could be anything else but . . . 'inhuman,' I guess you'd call it—cold, that kind of thing."

"It wasn't like that at all," she said. "Although, I suppose, I shouldn't really say too much since I've had nothing to compare it with. But it was"—she shrugged—"warm, friendly . . . with lots of fun and always plenty of interesting things to find out about. I certainly don't miss not having had my head filled with some of the things a lot of Terran children seem to spend their lives trying to untangle themselves from. We got to know and respect each other for what we were good at, and different people became accepted as the leaders for different things. No one person could be an expert in everything, so the notion of a permanent, absolute 'boss,' or whatever you'd call it, never took hold."

"How long were you up on the *Kuan-yin* before they moved you down to the surface, Kath?"

"I was very young. I'm not sure I can remember without checking the records. Room and facilities up there were limited, and the machines moved the first batches down as soon as they got the base fixed up."

"The ship's changed a lot since then though," Colman remarked. "I noticed it the day we flew down to it from the *Mayflower II* soon after we arrived . . . when Shirley and Ci met Tony Driscoll. The front end must be at least twice as big as it used to be."

"Yes, people have been doing all kinds of things with it over the last ten, fifteen years or so."

"What are all the changes around the back end?" Colman asked curiously. "It looks like a whole new drive system."

"It is. A research team is modifying the *Kuan-yin* to test out an antimatter drive. In fact the project is at quite an advanced stage. They're doing the same kind of thing back on Earth, aren't they?"

Colman's eyebrows arched in surprise. "True, but—wow! I had no idea that anything here was that advanced." Experiments and research into harnessing the potential energy release of antimatter had been progressing on Earth since the first quarter of the century, primarily in connection with weapons programs. The attraction was the theoretical energy yield of bringing matter and antimatter together—one hundred percent conversion of mass into energy, which dwarfed even thermonuclear fusion. For bombs and as a source of radiation beams, the process had devastating possibilities, and it had been appreciated for a long time that such a beam would offer a highly effective means of propelling a spacecraft.

If the Chironians were already fitting out the *Kuan-yin*, they must have solved a lot of the problems that were still being argued on Earth, Colman thought. The whole planet, he realized as he reflected on it, was a powerhouse of progress, unchecked by any traditions of unreason and with no vested-interest obstructionists to hold it back. If the pattern continued until Chiron became a fully populated world, it would effectively leave Earth back in the Stone Age within a century. "Have you actually flown it anywhere yet?" he asked, turning his head toward Kath. "The *Kuan-yin* . . . has it been anywhere since it arrived in orbit here?"

She nodded. "To both the moons, and we've sent missions to all of Alpha's other planets. But that was quite a while ago now. With the original drive. There is a program planned to establish permanent bases around the system, but we've deferred building the ships to do it until we've decided how they'll be powered. That's why the *Kuan-yin*'s being made into a test-bed. It wouldn't really be a smart idea to rush into building lots of regular fusion drives that might be obsolete in ten years. There's plenty to do on Chiron in the meantime, so there's no big hurry." She turned her face toward him and rubbed her cheek along his shoulder. "Anyhow, why are we talking about this? You told me I had to stop you from talking shop. Okay, I just did. Quit it."

Colman grinned and stroked her hair. "You're right. So what do you want to hear about?"

She wriggled closer and slid an arm across his chest. "Tell me about Earth. I've told you how I grew up. What was it like with you?"

Colman smiled ruefully. "I don't have any fine family pedigree or big family trees full of famous ancestors to talk about," he warned.

"I'm not interested in anything like that. I just want to hear about someone who lived there and came from there. Where did you come from?"

"A city called Chicago, originally. Heard of it?"

"Sure. It's on the lakes."

"That's right—Michigan. I think I was something of a not-very-welcome accident. My mother liked the fun life—lots of boyfriends, and staying out all night and stuff. I guess I was in the way a lot of the time."

"Was your father like that too?"

"I never found out who he was. For all I know, nobody else did either."

"Oh, I see."

Colman sighed. "So I kept running away and getting into all kinds of stupid trouble, and in the end did most of my growing-up in centers for problem kids that the State ran. Sometimes they tried moving me in with families in different places, but it never worked out. The last ones tried pretty hard. They adopted me legally, and that's how I got my name. Later we moved to Pennsylvania . . . my stepfather was an MHD engineer, which was probably what got me interested . . . but there was some trouble, and I wound up in the Army."

"Was that where you learned about engineering?" Kath asked.

"That came later—after I'd been on the ship for some time. At first I was with the infantry . . . saw some combat in Africa. I spent most of the voyage in the Engineer Corps though . . . up until about a year or two back."

"What made you sign up for the trip?"

Colman shrugged. "I don't know. I guess there didn't seem much risk of making any worse a mess of things than I had already."

Kath laughed and rolled back to stare up at the ceiling. "You're just like us, aren't you," she said. "You don't know where you came from either."

"That happened with a lot of people," Colman told her. "Things were so messed up after the war. . . . Does it matter?"

"I suppose not," Kath said. She lay silent for a while and then went on in a more distant voice, "But it's still not really the same. I mean, it must be wonderful to have actually been born there . . . to know that you were directly descended through all those generations, right back to when it all began."

"What?"

"Life! Earth life. You're a part of it. Isn't that an exciting feeling? It has to be."

"So are you," Colman insisted. "Chironian genes were dealt from the same deck as all the rest. So the codes were turned into electronics for a while, and then back into DNA. So what? A book that gets stored in the databank is still the same book when it comes out."

"Technically you're right," Kath agreed. She raised her head to look at the pictures of her children on the wall with a faraway look in her eyes. "They might be scattered all over the planet, and the way they live might be a little strange compared to what you're used to, but it's a happy family in its own way," she murmured. "But it's still not really the same. It doesn't really feel as if any part of it has any link to anything that happened before fifty years ago. Don't you think it's . . . oh, I don't know, kind of a shame somehow?"

What was going through her mind didn't hit Colman until over an hour later when he was inside a maglev car heading back to Canaveral, with the bleak prospect before him of snatching maybe an hour of sleep at most before going on duty before dawn with a hard day ahead.

Family?

Earth?

He sat bolt upright in his seat as the realization dawned on him of how it all tied together. Maybe Swyley did have it all figured out after all.

So *that* was why somebody from Chiron would want to get mixed up with a Terran!

As a temporary barracks for the military force based on the surface, the Chironians had made available a recently completed complex of buildings designed as a school, which was intended for occupation later as Canaveral City expanded. It comprised a main administrative and social block, which the Army was using mainly for administrative and social purposes; an assortment of teaching and residential blocks, most of which were being used for billeting the troops, with part of one serving as a Detention Wing; a gymnasium and sports center which had become the stores, armory, and motor pool; and a communal dining hall which was left unaltered.

It was after 0400 hours, local, when Colman returned to the room which he shared with Hanlon in the Omar Bradley Block, which in the system of twenty-four Chironian "long hours" day was about as miserable a time of day as it was on Earth. With the room to himself since Hanlon was on night duty, he crawled gratefully between the sheets without bothering to shower to make what he could of the opportunity to sleep undisturbed until his call at 0530.

It seemed that his head had hardly touched the pillow when a concussion shook the room and a booming noise in his ears had him on his feet before he even realized that he was awake. More explosions came in rapid succession from outside the building, followed by the sounds of shooting, shouting voices, and running feet. Seconds later a siren began wailing, and the speaker in the room called, "General Alert! General Alert! A breakout is being attempted from the Detention Wing. All officers and men report to General Alert stations."

What followed was a General Foul-up.

Colman found Sirocco in the Orderly Room, acting on his own initiative after receiving conflicting orders from Colonel Wesserman's staff. Sirocco ordered most of the D Company personnel to secure the block against intrusion and cordoned off the routes past it toward the outside. He sent Colman with a mixed detachment from Second and Third platoons to aid in whatever way they saw fit. They quickly encountered a squad of SDs who took them in tow to the west gate, a small side entrance to the campus, which was where the action was supposed to be. Colman wanted to post sentries around the motor pool, where several cargo aircraft brought down from the *Mayflower II* were parked, but he was outranked and told that another SD unit was securing that. Then all the lights went out.

Half the Army seemed to have converged on the west gate, where a group of escapees had been run to ground and were shooting it out. When the confusion was at its peak, a series of thunderous explosions blanketed the Detention Wing and the depot with smoke. When the smoke cleared, one of the transporters was gone. No one had been guarding the motor pool.

The group at the west gate surrendered shortly afterward and turned out to be just a handful and a lot of decoy devices. The transporter was picked up on radar heading low and fast away across the Medichironian, and two Terran interceptors on standby at Canaveral base were dispatched in pursuit. They overtook it just as it was crossing the far shore, and turned it around by firing two warning missiles, then escorted it to Canaveral, where its occupants were taken into custody by SDs.

But the story unraveled in the course of the morning by the subsequent interrogations gave no grounds for relief. Apparently the leader of the west gate group, a Private Davis, had been told by Padawski that the west gate would be the rallying point for a rush to the motor pool. Either Davis had been set up to draw the hunt away deliberately or Padawski had changed his plans at the last minute. Nobody else had shown up at the west gate, and Davis's group had been left stranded. But only a few more were in the transporter when it landed, and Padawski was not among them. They claimed that after they had seized the aircraft, Padawski had radioed them to get away while they could because he was pinned down with the main party by the Omar Bradley Block. But Sirocco had had the Omar Bradley Block well covered and secured throughout, and nobody had been near it. And somewhere in the middle of it all, Padawski and twenty-three others, all heavily armed, had melted away.

Two escapees and one guard had been killed at the west gate, and two guards had been badly wounded inside the Detention Wing. Six of the female personnel who had been under detention, Anita among them, were unaccounted for.

"It was one glorious fuck-up from start to finish," Sirocco declared, tugging at his moustache as he and Colman discussed the events late that evening. "Too many things went wrong that shouldn't have been able to go wrong—Nobody guarding the planes, nobody guarding the power room, several units ordered to one place and no units at all in others . . . And how did they get hold of the guns? I don't like it, Steve. I don't like it at all. There's a very funny smell to the whole business."

◉ CHAPTER TWENTY-FOUR ◉

Even in his short time at the university near Franklin, Jerry Pernak had learned that Chironian theoretical and experimental physics had departed significantly from the mainstream being pursued on Earth. The Chironian scientists had not so much advanced past their terrestrial counterparts; rather, as perhaps was not surprising in view of the absence on Chiron of traditional habits of thought or authorities whose venerable opinions could not be challenged until after they were dead, they had gone off in a totally unexpected direction. And some of the things they had stumbled across on their way had left Pernak astounded.

Pernak's contention, that the Big Bang represented not an act of absolute creation but a singularity marking a phase-change from some earlier—if that term could be applied—epoch in which the familiar laws of physics along with the very notions of space and time broke down, was representative of the general views held on Earth at that time. Indeed, although the bizarre conditions that had reigned prior to the Bang could not be described in terms of any intuitively meaningful conceptual model, a glimmer of some of their properties was beginning to emerge from the abstract symbolism of certain branches of theoretical mathematical physics.

The bewildering proliferation first of baryons and mesons, and later the quarks, which were supposed to simplify them, that had plagued studies of the structure of matter to the end of the twentieth century had been reduced to an orderly hierarchy of "generations" of particles. Each generation contained just eight particles: six quarks and two leptons. The first generation comprised the "up" and "down" quarks, each appearing in the three color-charge variants peculiar to the strong nuclear force to give six in all; the electron; and the electron-type neutrino. The second generation was made up of the "strange" and "charmed" quarks, each of them again appearing in three possible colors; the muon; and the muon-type neutrino. The third generation contained the "top" and "bottom" quarks; the tau; and the tau-type neutrino; and so it went on.

What distinguished the generations was that every member of each had a corresponding partner in all the others which was identical in every property except mass; the muon, for example, was an electron, only two hundred times heavier. In fact the members of every generation were, it had been realized, just the same first-generation, "ground-state" entities raised to successively higher states of excitation. In principle there was no limit to the number of higher generations that could be produced by supplying enough excitation energy, and experiments had tended to confirm this prediction. Nevertheless, all the exotic variations created could be accounted for by the same eight ground-state quarks and leptons, plus their respective antiparticles, together with the field quanta through which they interacted. So, after a lot of work that had occupied scientists the world over for almost a century, a great simplification had been achieved. But were quarks and leptons the end of the story?

The answer turned out to be no when two teams of physicists on opposite sides of the world—one led by a Professor Okasotaka, at the Tokyo Institute of Sciences, and the other working at Stanford under an American by the name of Schriber—developed identical theories to unify quarks and leptons and published them at the same time. It turned out that the sixteen entities and "anti-entities" of the ground-state generation could be explained by just two components which in themselves possessed surprisingly few innate properties: Each had a spin angular momentum of one-half unit, and one had an electrical charge of one-third while the other had none. The other properties which had been thought of as fundamental, such as quark color charge, quark "flavor," and even mass, to the astonishment of some, became seen instead as consequences of the ways in which combinations of these two basic components were *arranged,* much as a melody follows from an arrangement of notes but cannot be expressed as a property of a single note.

Thus there were two components, each of which had an "anticomponent." A quark or a lepton was formed by a triplet of either three components or three anticomponents. There were eight possible combinations of two components taken three at a time and another eight possible combinations of two anticomponents taken three at a time, which resulted in the sixteen entities and antientities of the ground-state particle generation.

With two types of component or anticomponent to choose from for each triplet, a triplet could comprise either three of a kind of one type, or two of one kind plus one of the other. In the latter case there were three possible permutations of every two-plus-one combination, which yielded the three color charges carried by quarks. The three-of-a-kind combinations could be arranged in only one way and corresponded to leptons, which was why leptons could not carry a color charge and did not react to the strong nuclear force.

Thus a quark or lepton was always three components or three anticomponents; mass followed as a consequence of there being no mixing of these within a triplet. Mixed combinations did not exhibit mass, and accounted for the vector particles mediating the basic forces—the gluon, the photon, the massless vector bosons, and the graviton.

Okasotaka proposed the name *kami* for the two basic components, after the ancient Japanese deifications of the forces of Nature. The Japanese gods had possessed two souls—one gentle, *nigi-mi-tama* and one violent, *ara-mi-tama*—and, accordingly, Okasotaka christened his two species of *kami* "nigions" and "araons," which a committee on international standards solemnly ratified and enshrined into the officially recognized nomenclature of physics. Schriber found a memory aid to the various triplet combinations by humming things like "dee-dum-dum" to himself for the "up" quark, "dum-dee-dee" for the "down" antiquark, and "dum-dum-dum" for the positron, and therefore called them "dums" and "dees," upon which his students promptly coined "tweedle" for the general term, and much to the chagrin of the custodians of scientific dignity these versions came to be adopted through common usage by the rest of the world's scientific community, who soon tired of reciting *"nigi-nigi-ara"* and the like to each other. The scientists were less receptive to Schriber's claim that Quan-dum Mechanics had at last been unified with Relativi-dee.

Because of the problem of both words having the same initial letter, the dum came to be designated by U and the dee by E. The dum carried a one-third charge, and the dee carried none. Two dums and a dee made the up quark, its three possible color charges being represented by the three possible permutations, UUE, UEU, and EUU. Similarly two dees and a dum yielded the down antiquark in its three possible colors as UEE, EUE, and EEU; in the same way two "antidums" and an "antidee" gave the up antiquark; and two antidees and an antidum, the down quark. Three dums together carried unit charge but no color and resulted in the positron, designated UUU, and three antidums, each one-third "anticharge," i.e., negative, made up the normal electron, UUU. Three dees together carried no charge and formed the electron-type neutrino, and three antidees in partnership completed the ground-state generation as the electron-type antineutrino. It followed that "antitweedles" didn't necessarily give an antiparticle, and tweedles didn't always make a particle. Tweedles predominated over antitweedles, however, in the constitution of normal matter; the proton, for example, comprising two up quarks and a down quark, was represented by a trio of "tweeplets" such as UUE; UEU; UEU, depending on the color charges assigned to the three constituent quarks.

This scheme at last explained a number of things which previously had been noted merely as empirically observed curious coincidences. It explained why quarks came in three colors: Each one-plus-two combination of dums and dees had three and only three possible permutations. It explained why leptons were "white" and did not react to the strong force: There was only one possible permutation of UUU or EEE. And it explained why the electrical charges on quarks and leptons were equal: They were carried by the same tweedles. Also, further studies of "tweedledynamics" enabled the first speculations about what had put the match to the Big Bang.

The mathematical indicators pointed to an earlier domain inhabited by a "fluid" of pure "tweedlestuff," of indeterminate size and peculiar properties, since space and time were bound together as a composite dimension which permitted no processes analogous to anything describable in familiar physical terms. There were grounds for supposing that if an expanding nodule of disentangled space and time were introduced arbitrarily through some mechanism— pictured by some people as a bubble appearing in soda water, although this wasn't really accurate—the reduced "pressure" inside the bubble would trigger the condensation of raw tweedlestuff out of "tweedlespace" as an explosion of tweedles and antitweedles, the tweedles preserving the "timelike" aspect, and the antitweedles the "antitimelike" aspect of the timeless domain from which they originated. Their mutual affinity would precipitate their combination into a dense photon fluid in which timelessness became reestablished, which tied in with Relativity by explaining why time stood still for moving photons and accounting for the strange connection in the perceived universe between the rate at which time flowed and the speed of light. The high-energy conditions of the primordial photon fluid, the density of which would have approximated that of the atomic nucleus, would favor the formation of "tweeplet" entities to give rise to matter interacting under conditions dominated by the strong nuclear force, which manifested itself to restore non-Abelian gauge symmetry with respect to the variance introduced by the separation of space and time. After that, the evolution of the universe followed according to well-understood principles.

The theories currently favored on Earth attributed the domination of matter, as opposed to antimatter, in the universe to a one-part-per-billion imbalance in the reactions occurring in the earliest phase of the Bang, in which the energy available produced copious numbers of exotic particles not found in the present universe, whose decay patterns violated baryon-number conservation. In the present universe they appeared rarely, only as transient "virtual particles" and were responsible for the almost immeasurable, but measured, 10^{31}-year mean lifetime of the proton.

It was believed virtual particles were virtual because the conditions of the present universe could not supply the energy necessary to sustain tweeplets. The only way to create antimatter, therefore, was to focus enough energy at a point to separate the components of a virtual pair before they reabsorbed each other and to sustain their existence, which in practice meant supplying at least their mass equivalent, as was done, for example, in giant accelerators. This was the reason for the widespread skepticism that any net energy gain could ever be realized from annihilating the antimatter later. At best it was felt to be an elaborate storage battery, and not a very efficient one at that; the power poured into the accelerator would be better applied directly to whatever the antimatter was wanted for.

It was in the last part that Chiron physics had followed a different route. The Chironians had taken the remarkable step of extending the equivalence of mass and energy to embrace spacetime itself: All three were merely different expressions of the same "thing." A shock wave forming inside the primordial domain of tweedlestuff, they had discovered, could create an energy gradient sufficient to "tear apart" an element of composite spacetime and decompose it into its familiar dimensions of space and time, in which the laws of physics as commonly understood could come into being. Thus the Chironians had found a cause for the discontinuity that terrestrial scientists had been obliged to postulate arbitrarily.

The subsequent expansion of space followed directly from the Chironian mass-energy-space equivalence relationship: The cooling photon fluid actually transformed into space as well as matter tweeplets, the ratio depending on the temperature and shifting from one favoring tweeplets to one favoring space as the universe cooled down. Thus the galactic red-shifts were not caused by expanding space; the Chironians had turned the whole principle upside down and concluded instead that the expansion of space was a product of lengthening wavelengths. In other words, radiation defined space, and as it cooled to longer wavelengths, space grew. Thus the

Chironians had completed the synthesis of tweedledynamics with General Relativity by relating the properties of space to the photon as well as the properties of time. The "islands" of matter tweeplets left behind from the cooling photon fluid remained dominated internally by the strong force while gravitation became the dominant influence in the macroscopic realm created outside, and in many ways they continued to behave as microcosms of the domain from which they had originated.

Even more remarkable was another prediction that followed from the Chironian symmetry relationships, which required the creation of an "antiuniverse" along with the universe, populated by antimatter and consisting of an extraordinary realm in which "antitime" ran backward and "antispace" contracted from an initial volume of zero. Universes, like particles, were created in pairs. And it was the duality of universes, each exhibiting a spacetime decomposed into two discrete dimensions, which gave rise to the two-way duality manifested by tweedles and anti-tweedles: Dums, dees, antidums, and antidees were simply spacelike, timelike, antispacelike, and antitimelike projections of the same fundamental entity existing in the timeless, spaceless domain of tweedlespace.

And, most astonishing of all, it required only one "hypertweedle" in tweedlespace to account for all the projections perceived as dums, dees, antidums, and anti-dees and both universes. A universe provided, in effect, a screen upon which the same projections were repeated over and over again as a consequence of the separation of the space and time dimensions of the screen itself, which of course was why every dum was the same as every other dum, and every dee the same as every other dee. It was as if a typewriter created paper as it typed on, leaving the planar inhabitants of the flat universe that it had brought into being to ponder why all the characters encountered serially in their own "flat-time" should have exactly the same form.

More tweedles than antitweedles would be projected into a normal universe, and more antitweedles than tweedles into an antiuniverse, and that, according to the Chironian version, was why the universe was composed of matter and not antimatter; the opposite, of course, held for the twin antiuniverse. The way to obtain antimatter, they therefore reasoned, would be to make a small part of the universe look like an antiuniverse so that tweedlespace could be "fooled" into projecting antitweedles instead of tweedles into it. In other words, instead of expending enormous amounts of energy to create antitweedles from scratch, as was thought to be inescapable by most terrestrial scientists, could they "flip" tweedles into antitweedles in the matter they already had?

To the astonishment of even themselves, they found that they could. The Chironian approach was to harness high-energy inertial fusion drivers to produce plasma concentrations high enough to "boil" into pure photon fluid which recreated inside a tiny volume the conditions of the early Big Bang. Within this region, space and time recoupled and contracted inward with the imploding core to simulate for an instant the bizarre, inverted conditions of an anti-universe, and in that instant a large portion of the tweedles liberated in the process transformed into antitweedles which, under the prevailing high-energy conditions, combined preferentially into antiquarks and antileptons rather than radiation. Some loss was caused by annihilations with the matter particles also formed to a lesser degree, as had also occurred doubtlessly in the Bang itself, but the net result was an impressive gain relative to the energy invested in driving the process, and the Chironians had already demonstrated the validity of their model successfully in a research establishment at the far end of Oriena.

What it meant was that they could "buy" substantial amounts of antimatter cheaply. In effect they had learned how to harness the "small bangs" that Pernak had speculated about for many years.

The theory opened up whole new realms, Pernak was beginning to appreciate as he sat back in his office to give his mind a rest from absorbing the information being presented on the wall screen opposite. What he was starting to glimpse hadn't just to do with the physics; it was the completely new philosophy of existence that came with the physical interpretation.

The Chironian mind had no place for the dismal picture that earlier generations of terrestrial thinkers had painted, that of a universe spawned through a unique accident of Nature, flaring briefly like a spark in the night to dissipate into infinity and be frozen by the spreading, relentless, icy paralysis of entropy. To the Chironian, the universe was but one atom of a possibly infinite Universe of sibling universes, every one of which coexisted at every point in space with the source-realm that had procreated its family with the profligacy of a summer stormcloud precipitating raindrops. Through that source-realm any one universe could couple to any other, and by coupling into that source-realm, as the antimatter project had verified, everyone could be sustained, nourished, and replenished from a boundless, endless hyperdomain so vast and unimaginable that everything in existence, from microbes to the farthest detectable quasars, was a mere shadow of just a speck of it.

Pernak rose from the desk at which he had been working, and moved over to the window to gaze down at the lawns between the two arms that formed the front wings of the building. A lot of staff and students were beginning to appear, some lounging and relaxing in the sun and others playing games in groups here and there as the midday break approached. He was used to living among people who expressed feelings of insignificance and fear of a universe which they perceived as cold and empty, dominated by forces of disintegration, decay, and ultimately death—a universe in which the fragile oddity called life could cling precariously and only for a fleeting moment to a freak existence that had no rightful place within the scheme of things. Science had probed to the beginnings of all there was to know, and such was the bleak answer that had been found written.

The Chironian, by contrast, saw a rich, bright, vibrant universe manifesting at every level of structure and scale of magnitude the same irresistible force of self-ordering, self-organizing evolution that had built atoms from plasma, molecules from atoms, then life itself, and from there produced the supreme phenomenon of mind and all that could be created by mind. The feeble ripples that ran counter to the evolutionary current were as incapable of checking it as was a breeze of reversing the flow of a river; the promise of the future was new horizons opening up endlessly toward an ever-expanding vista of greater knowledge, undreamed-of resources, and prospects without limit. Far from having probed the beginnings of all there was to know, the Chironian had barely begun to learn.

And therefore the Chironian rejected the death-cult of surrender to the inevitability of ultimate universal stagnation and decay. Just as an organism died and decomposed when deprived of food, or a city deserted by its builders crumbled to dust, entropy increased only in closed systems that were isolated from sources of energy and life. But the Chironian universe was no longer a closed system. Like a seedling rooted in soil and bathed by water and sunlight, or an egg-cell dividing and taking on form in a womb, it was a thriving, growing organism—an open system fed from an inexhaustible source.

And for such a system the universal law was not death, but life.

Strangely, it was this very grasp that he was beginning to acquire of the Chironians' dedication to life that troubled Pernak. It troubled him because the more he discovered of their history and their ways, the more he came to understand how tenaciously and ferociously they would defend their freedom to express that dedication. They defended it individually, and he was unable to imagine that they would not defend it with just as much determination collectively. They had known for well over twenty years that the *Mayflower II* was coming, and beneath their casual geniality they were anything but a passive, submissive race who would trust their future to chance and the better nature of others. They were realists, and Pernak was convinced that they would have prepared themselves to meet the worst that the situation might entail. Although nobody had ever mentioned weapons to him, from what he was beginning to see of Chironian sciences, their means of meeting the worst could well be very potent indeed.

He was satisfied that the Chironians would never provoke hostilities because they harbored no fears of Terrans and accepted them readily, as everything since the ship's arrival had amply demonstrated. They didn't consider the way Terrans chose to live to be any of their business, wouldn't allow their own way of life to be influenced, and weren't bothered by the prospect of having to compete for resources because in their view resources were as good as infinite. But he felt less reassured about the Terrans—at least some of them. Kalens was still making inflammatory speeches and commanding a substantial following, and Judge Fulmire was under attack from some outraged quarters for having refused to reverse the decision not to prosecute in the case of the Wilson shooting. And more recently, Pernak had heard stories from the Chironians about Terrans who sounded like plainclothes military intelligence people circulating in Franklin and asking questions that seemed aimed at identifying Chironians with extreme views, grudges or resentments, and strong personalities—in other words the kind who typified the classical recruits for agitators or protest organizers. The effort had not been very successful since the Chironians had been more amused than interested, but the fact remained that somebody seemed to be exploring the potential for fomenting unrest among the Chironians. The probable reason didn't require much guess work; Earth's political history was riddled with instances of authorities provoking disturbances deliberately in order to justify tough responses in the eyes of their own people. If some faction, and presumably a fairly powerful one, was indeed maneuvering to bring about a confrontation, and if what Pernak was beginning to glimpse of the Chironians was anything to go by, then that faction might well be in for some nasty surprises. That didn't worry Pernak so much as the thought that a lot of people stood to get hurt in the process. Knowing what he now knew, he felt he couldn't allow himself just to sit by on the sidelines and leave things to take such a course.

Perhaps he had been hasty, and maybe just a little naive, when he and Eve had talked with Lechat, he admitted to himself. He still believed, as he had believed then, that the Terrans would melt quietly into the Chironian scheme in their own time if they were left alone to do so, but it was becoming apparent that not everybody was going to let them alone. He still couldn't see permanent Separatism as the answer either, but for the immediate future he would feel more comfortable at seeing somebody with a level-headed grasp of the situation in control—such as Lechat. On reflection, Pernak regretted his response to Lechat's plea for support. But it was far from too late for him to be able to change that. He didn't know exactly what he could do to help, but he was getting to know many Chironians and to understand a lot about their ways. Surely that knowledge could be put to some useful purpose.

Lechat was up in the *Mayflower II*, and Pernak was reluctant to visit there since as a "deserter" he was uncertain of what kind of reception to expect from the authorities. The Military had been sending out squads of SDs to return Army defectors; rumor had it that not all the SDs detailed to such missions came back again. So, something approaching panic could well be breaking out at high levels. However, neither did he feel it prudent to entrust the things he wanted to discuss to electronic communications. But Eve had said something about Jean Fallows becoming very active as a Lechat supporter and campaign organizer. . . . That would be a good place to begin.

He nodded to himself. That was what he would do. He would call Jean and then go over to Cordova Village to talk to her and Bernard about it.

❂ CHAPTER TWENTY-FIVE ❂

Leighton Merrick formed his fingers into a fluted column to support the Gothic arch of his brows and stared down at the desk while he chose his words. "Ah, I've been looking over your record, Fallows," he said when he looked up. "It shows a consistent attention to detail that is very pronounced . . . everything thorough and complete, and properly documented. It's commendable, very commendable . . . the kind of thing we could do with more of in the Service."

"Thank you, sir." It was obviously a softener. Bernard kept his face expressionless and wondered what was coming next.

Merrick allowed his hands to drop down to his chest. "And how are you settling in? Is your family adjusting well?"

"Very smoothly, considering that it's been twenty years." Bernard permitted a faint smile. "Jean's finding some things a bit strange, but I'm sure she'll get over it."

"Good, very good. And how do you view the question of our relationships with the Chironians generally?"

"I find them a refreshingly honest and direct people. You know where you stand with them." Bernard gave a slight shrug. "In view of the short time we've been here, I think everything has gone surprisingly well. Certainly it could have been a lot worse."

"Hmm . . ." The reply didn't seem quite what Merrick hoped for. "Not quite everything, surely," he said. "What about the shooting of Corporal Wilson a week ago?"

"That was unfortunate," Bernard agreed. "But in my opinion, sir, he asked for it."

"That may be, but it's beside the point that I was trying to make," Merrick said. "Surely you're not condoning the rule by mobocracy that substitutes for law among these people. Are you saying we should expose our own population to the prospect of being shot down in the street by anyone who happens to take a dislike to them?"

Bernard sighed. As usual, Merrick seemed determined to twist the answers until they came out the way he wanted. "Of course not," Bernard replied. "But I think people are exaggerating the situation. That incident was not representative of what we should expect. The Chironians act as they're treated. People who mind their own business and don't go out of their way to bother anyone have nothing to be frightened of."

"So everyone becomes a law unto himself," Merrick concluded.

"No, the law is there, implicitly, and it applies to everyone, but you have to learn how to read it." Bernard frowned. That hadn't come out the way he had intended. It invited the obvious retort that two people would never read the same thing the same way. The difference was that the Chironians could make it work. "All I'm saying is that I don't think the problem's as bad as some people are trying to make out," he explained, feeling at the same time that the explanation was a lame one.

"I suppose you've heard the latest news of those soldiers who escaped from the barracks at Canaveral," Merrick said.

"Yes, but that situation can't last. If the Army doesn't get them soon, the Chironians will."

Padawski and his followers had somehow shown up on the far side of the Medichironian, which was only sparsely settled, and seemed to be settling in as bandits in the hills. What a bandit would hope to achieve on a world like Chiron was hard to see, but revenge against Chironians seemed to have a lot to do with it; two isolated homes had been invaded, ransacked, and looted, in the course of which five Chironians and one soldier had been killed. Three Chironians, including a fifteen-year-old girl, had been raped. The Army was scouring the area from the air and with search parties on foot, but so far without success—the renegades were well trained in the arts of concealment. Satellites were of limited use if they didn't know exactly where to look, especially where rough terrain was involved.

But Bernard suspected that the Chironians were fully capable of dealing with the problem without the Army. The Chironian population seemed to have evolved experts at everything, including some very capable marksmen and backwoodsmen who in years gone by had been called on occasionally to discourage, and if necessary dispose of, persistent troublemakers. Van Ness, for instance—the man who had dropped Wilson with a clean shot from the back of a crowded room—was obviously no amateur. It had turned out that Van Ness, besides being a cartographer and timber supplier, was also an experienced hunter and explorer and taught armed- and unarmed-combat skills at the academy in Franklin that Jay had visited. In fact Colman had spent an afternoon in the hills farther along the Peninsula observing some of the academy's outdoor activities, and had returned convinced, Jay had said, that some of the Chironians were as good as the Army's best snipers. But Merrick didn't seem inclined to pursue that side of the matter. "Nevertheless Chironians are getting killed," he said. "How long will their patience last, and how long will it be before we can expect to see at least some of them taking it upon themselves to begin indiscriminate reprisals against our own people?—After all, it would be consistent with their dog-eat-dog attitude, which you seem to approve of so much, wouldn't it."

"I never said anything of the kind. The whole point is that they are *not* indiscriminate. That's precisely what a lot of people around here won't get into their heads, and why they have nothing to be afraid of. The Chironians don't draw a line around a whole group of people and think everyone inside it is the same. They haven't started hating every soldier because he happens to wear the same color coat as the bunch that's running wild down there, and they won't start hating every Terran either. They don't think that way."

Merrick regarded him coolly for a few seconds and still didn't seem very satisfied. "Well, all I can say is that not everyone shares your enviable faith in human nature—myself included, I might add. The official policy conveyed to me from the Directorate, which it is your duty as well as mine to support irrespective of our own personal views, is that the possibility of violent reaction from the Chironians cannot be dismissed. Therefore we must allow for such an eventuality in considering the future."

Bernard spread his hands resignedly. "Very well, I can see the sense in being prepared. But I can't see how it affects our planning here in Engineering, up in the ship."

Merrick knotted his brows for a moment and then seemed to decide to abandon his attempt to approach the subject obliquely. "Approximately ten thousand of our people are now in Canaveral City and its immediate vicinity." He looked straight at Bernard. "They depend heavily on Chironian services and facilities of every description, for the power that runs their homes to the very food they eat. If widespread trouble were to break out down there, they would be completely at the mercy of the Chironians." He raised a hand to stifle any objection before Bernard could speak. "Clearly we cannot tolerate such a state of affairs. It has been decided therefore that, purely as a precautionary measure to protect our own people if the need should arise, we must be able to guarantee the continuity of essential services if circumstances should demand. Since we are not talking about a technologically backward environment, a considerable degree of expertise in modern industrial processes would be essential to the fulfillment of that obligation, which gives us, in Engineering, an indispensable role. I trust you see my point."

Bernard's eyes narrowed a fraction. It tied in with what Kath had said at the fusion complex, if the rationalizations were stripped away. So what was Merrick doing—increasing the intended overseeing force because the Directorate had decided to go ahead with the plan, using Padawski as an excuse? "I'm not sure that I do," he replied. "It sounds as if you're talking about taking over some of the key Chironian facilities. Wouldn't that only make any trouble worse?"

"I made no mention of taking over anything. I'm merely saying we should be sufficiently familiar with their operations to be able to guarantee services if we are required to. Now that we've had an opportunity to look at Port Norday and a few other installations, I am reasonably confident we could manage them. I didn't want to take up too much of everybody's time before, but since the whole thing now seems feasible I'd like you to have a look at what's at Norday. You should take Hoskins with you. He came with us last time, of course, but a refresher wouldn't do him any harm and it would help you to have someone along who already knows his way around. That was really what I wanted to talk to you about." Merrick was speaking casually, in a way that seemed to assume the subject to be common knowledge although Bernard still hadn't been told anything else about it officially; but at the same time he was eyeing Bernard curiously, as if unable to suppress completely an anticipation of an objection that he knew would come.

Bernard decided to play along to see what happened. "I'm sorry—how do you mean, last time? I must be missing something."

Merrick's eyebrows shot up in an expression of surprise that was just a little too hasty. "The last time we went to see the complex at Port Norday." Bernard stared blankly at him. Merrick seemed pained. "Don't tell me you didn't know. I went there with Walters and Hoskins a while ago. Didn't Walters tell you about it?"

"Nobody told me anything."

Merrick's pained expression deepened into a frown. "Tch, tch, that's inexcusable. How unfortunate. Let me see now—I can't remember exactly when it was, but you were on duty. That was why I couldn't include you at the time." That was an outright lie; Bernard had been there on his day off, with Jay. "But anyway, we can soon put that straight. You'll find the place fascinating. A woman runs most of the primary process—a remarkable lady—so I can promise you some interesting company as well as interesting surroundings. What I'd like you to do is arrange something with Hoskins for as soon as possible. I'm afraid I'll be tied up for the next couple of days."

Obviously something unusual was going on. Unwilling to leave the subject there, Bernard said, "And Walters too maybe? Perhaps he could use a refresher too."

Merrick drew a long breath, and his expression became grave. "Mmm . . . Walters. That brings me to the other thing I have to tell you," he said in a heavy voice. "Officer Walters is no longer with us. He and his family disappeared from Cordova Village two days ago and have not been heard of since. He failed to report for duty yesterday. We must assume that he has absconded." He shook his head sadly. "Disappointing, Fallows, most disappointing. I credited him with more character."

So that was it! Merrick's blue-eyed boy had let him down, and he needed a replacement. Merrick didn't give a damn about Bernard's qualities as an engineer; he was interested only in extricating himself from what was no doubt an embarrassing predicament. As Bernard thought back over the deviousness that he had listened to since he sat down, his memory of Kath's frankness and openness, even to a stranger, came back like a breath of fresh air. "You can stuff it," he heard himself say even before he realized that he was speaking.

"*What?*" Merrick sat up rigidly in his chair. "What did you say, Fallows?"

"I said you can stuff it." Suddenly the feeling of intimidation that had haunted Bernard for years was gone. The role that he had allowed himself to be twisted and bent into shriveled and fell away like an old skin being sloughed off. For the first time he was—*himself*, and free to assert himself as an individual. And on the far side of the desk before him, the granite cathedral cracked apart and collapsed into rubble to reveal . . . nothing inside. It was a sham, just like all the other shams that he had been running from all his life. He had just stopped running.

Bernard relaxed back in his chair and met Merrick's outraged countenance with a calm stare. "Nobody's going to shut that complex down, and you know it," he said. "Save the propaganda. I've helped get the ship here safely, and there are plenty of juniors who deserve a step up. I've done my job. I'm quitting."

"But you can't!" Merrick sputtered.

"I just did."

"You have a contractual agreement."

"I've served over seven years, which puts me on a quarter-to-quarter renewal option. Therefore I owe you a maximum of three months. Okay, I'm giving it. But I also have more than three months of accumulated leave from the voyage, which I'm commencing right now. You'll have that confirmed in writing within five minutes." He stood up and walked to the door. "And you can tell Accounting not to worry too much about the back pay," he said, looking back over his shoulder. "I won't be needing it."

Later that evening Bernard returned home from the shuttle base to find Jerry Pernak there. Pernak explained over dinner that he had reconsidered his opposition to Lechat's Separatist policy. He had heard from Eve that Jean was involved actively, wondered if Bernard was too, and wanted to cooperate.

Bernard couldn't see why Pernak had changed his mind. "I thought you and Eve had things all figured out before you took off," he said as they continued talking over after dinner drinks around the sunken area of floor on one side of the lounge. "Look what's happening—you've left, other people are leaving all over. You were right. Just leave the situation alone and let it straighten itself out."

"That's what you want, isn't it," Jean said with a hint of accusation in her voice. "You'd like us to be the way they are. But have you really thought about what that would mean? No standards, no order to anything, no morality . . . I mean, what kind of a way would that be for Jay and Marie to grow up?"

Jay and Marie were her latest weapons. Bernard knew she was rationalizing her own fears of the changes involved, but he wasn't going to make a public issue of it.

"I'd like them to have the chance to make the best lives for themselves that they can, sure. They've got that chance right here. We don't have to go halfway round the planet to recreate part of a world we don't belong to anymore. It couldn't last. That's all over now. You have to bring yourself to face up to it, hon."

"We're still the some people," Jay said from the end of the sofa, looking at his mother. "That's not going to change. If you're going to act dumb, you can do that anywhere." To Bernard's mild surprise Jay had shown a lively interest in the conversation all through dinner and had elected to sit in afterward. About time too, Bernard thought to himself.

Jean shook her head, still refusing to contemplate the prospect. "But why does it have to be over?" She looked imploringly at Bernard. "We were happy all those years in the ship, weren't we? We had our friends, like Jerry and Eve, we had the children. There was your job. Why should this planet take it all away from us? They don't have the right. We never wanted anything from them. It's—it's all wrong."

Bernard felt the color rising at the back of his neck. The pathos that she was trying to project was touching a raw nerve. He refilled his glass with a slow, deliberate movement while he brought his feelings under control. "What makes you so sure I found it all that wonderful?" he asked. "Aren't you assuming the same right to tell me what I ought to want?" He put the bottle down on the table with a thud and looked up. "Well, I didn't think it was so wonderful, and I don't want any more of it. Today I told Merrick to stuff his job up his ass."

"*You what?*" Jean gasped, horrified.

"I told him to stuff it. It's over. We can be us now. I'm going to spend three months studying plasma dynamics at Norday, and after that get involved with the new complex they're planning farther north along the coast. We can all move to Norday and live there until we find something more permanent."

Jean shook her head in protest. "But you can't . . . I won't go. I want to move to Iberia."

"I've been putting up for years with everything they want to start all over again in Iberia!" Bernard thundered suddenly, slamming down his glass. His face turned crimson. "I hated every minute of it. Who ever asked me if that was what I wanted? Nobody. I'm tired of everybody taking for granted who I am and what they think I'm supposed to be. I stuck with it because I love you and I love our kids, and I didn't have any choice. Well, now I have a choice, and this time *you* owe *me.* I say we're going to Norday, and goddamnit we're going to Norday!"   •

Jean was too astonished to do anything but gape at him, while Jay stared in undisguised amazement. Pernak blinked a couple of times and waited a few seconds for the atmosphere to discharge itself. "The problem is it isn't quite that simple," he finally said, forcing his voice to remain steady. "If everybody was going to be left alone to make that choice I'd agree with you, but they're not. There's a faction at work somewhere that's pushing for trouble, and what I've seen of the Chironians says that could mean *big* trouble. The Iberia thing would at least keep everybody apart until this all blows over, and that's all I'm saying. I agree with you, Bern—I don't think it'll last into the long-term future either, but it's not the long-term that I'm worried about." He glanced at Jean apologetically. "Sorry, but that's how I think it'll go."

Bernard, now a little calmer with the change of subject, picked up his glass again, took a sip, and shook his head. "Aren't you overreacting just a little bit, Jerry? Exactly what kind of trouble are you talking about? What have we seen?" He looked from side to side as if to invite support. "One idiot who should never have been allowed out of a cage got what he asked for. I'm sorry if that sounds like a callous way of putting it, but it's what I think. And that's all we've seen."

"Have you seen the news this evening?" Jean asked. "Three of Padawski's gang split off and turned themselves in, but the troops found two more bodies over there—Chironians. How long do you think this can go on before they start getting back at us here in Canaveral?"

Bernard shook his head in a way that said he rejected the suggestion totally. "They won't. They're not like that. They just don't think that way."

"But how can you be so sure?"

"I'm getting to know them."

"And I'm getting to know them better," Pernak told both of them. Something in his tone made them turn their heads toward him curiously. He spread his hands above his knees. "It's not exactly that kind of trouble I'm bothered about. But if this goes further than that . . . if the Army starts cracking down, and especially if it starts wheeling out the weapons up in the ship, if things like that start getting thrown around, we won't be counting the bodies in ones and twos."

Bernard looked at him uncertainly. "I'm not with you, Jerry. Why should it escalate to anything like that? The Chironians don't have anything in that league anyway."

"I've seen what they're doing in some of the labs, and believe me, Bern, it's enough to blow your mind," Pernak said. "Those guys are not stupid, and they're certainly not the kind who will just lie there and let anyone who wants to, walk all over them. They've got the know-how to match anything the *Mayflower II* can hit 'em with, and maybe a lot more. They've known for well over twenty years what to expect. Well, figure the rest out yourself."

Bernard stared at his glass for a few seconds, then shook his head again. "I can't buy it," he said. "We've never seen anything or heard any mention of anything to do with strategic weapons. Where are they supposed to be?"

"We've only seen Franklin," Pernak replied. "There's a whole planet out there."

"Ghosts in your head," Bernard said. "Come on, Jerry, you're a scientist. Where's your evidence? Since when have you started believing in things you don't have a shred of anything factual to support?"

"Gut-feel," Pernak told him. "The weapons have to exist. I tell you, I know how these people's minds work." Jay stood up and left the room quietly. Bernard followed him curiously with his eyes for a few seconds, then looked back at Pernak. "But it's a hell of a thin case for shipping everyone off to Iberia, isn't it? And besides, if you're right, then I'd have thought the best place to stay would be right here—all mixed up together with the Chironians. That way nobody's likely to start throwing any big bombs around, right?" He turned his head to grin briefly at Jean. "I think Jerry made my point."

Pernak remained unsmiling. "What about that ship sitting twenty thousand miles out in space?" he said.

Before Bernard could reply, Jay came back in carrying the landscape painting he had brought back from Franklin after his first expedition out exploring. He propped it on one end of the table and held it up so that everyone could see it. "Do you notice anything unusual about that?" he asked them.

Pernak and Jean looked at each other, puzzled. Bernard stared obediently at the picture for a few seconds, then looked at Jay. "It looks like a nicely done painting of mountains," he said. "Is this supposed to have something to do with what we're talking about?"

Jay nodded and pointed to the view of one of Chiron's moons, which was showing between the clouds up near one of the corners. "That's Remus," he said. "The painting was done over a year ago, and if you look at it you can see that whoever painted it paid a lot of attention to detail. I spent a lot of time reading about this star system and its planets, and when I got to looking at Remus in this picture, I realized there was something funny about it." Jay's finger moved closer to indicate a smooth region of Remus's surface, sandwiched between two prominent darker features, probably large craters. "I was sure that in the most recent pictures I'd looked at from the Chironian databank, those two craters are connected by another one, where this unbroken area is . . . a big one, several hundred miles across. When I checked, I found I was right—there's a huge crater right here, and it wasn't there a year ago."

Bernard frowned as the implication of what Jay was suggesting sank in. "Did you ask Jeeves about it?" he inquired.

"Yes, I did. Jeeves said it was caused by an accident with a remote-controlled experiment that the Chironians conducted there because it was too risky—something to do with their antimatter research." Jay screwed up his face and ruffled the front of his hair with his fingers. "But that's the kind of thing you'd expect somebody to say, isn't it . . . and Chironians don't make a lot of mistakes." He looked around the circle of appalled faces staring back at him. "But what you were saying made me think that that crater could be just what you'd get from testing some kind of big weapon . . ."

Bernard, Pernak, and Jean stared at the picture for a long time. Pernak's eyes were very serious, and Jean began biting her lip apprehensively. At last Bernard nodded and looked at the other two. "Okay, I'm with you," he told them. "Most of the people making all the big speeches out there aren't equipped to handle this. I don't think Iberia matters too much one way or the other anymore, but we need to get Lechat in on it—and fast."

❊ CHAPTER TWENTY-SIX ❊

The first bomb exploded in the center of Canaveral City in the early hours of the morning, causing serious damage to the maglev terminal where the spur line into the shuttle base joined the main through-route from Franklin out to the Peninsula. Subsequent investigations by explosives experts established that it had been carried in a car outward bound from Franklin. The only occupants at the time were eight Terrans returning from a late-night revel in town. They were killed instantly.

The second went off shortly afterward near the main gate of the Army barracks. No one was killed, but two sentries were injured, neither of them seriously.

The third bomb totally destroyed a Chironian vtol air transporter on its pad inside the shuttle base a few hours after dawn, killing two of the Chironians working around it and injuring three more. Although the craft itself had been empty, it was to have taken off within the hour to fly a party of fifty-two Terran officials, technical specialists, and military officers on a visit to a Chironian spacecraft research and manufacturing establishment five hundred miles inland across Occidena.

By midmorning Terran newscasters were interpreting the development as a Chironian backlash to the Padawski outrages and as a warning to the Terrans of what to expect if Kalens was elected to head the next administration after his latest public pledge to impose

Terran law on Franklin as a first step toward "restabilizing" the planet. Interviews in which Chironians denied, dispassionately and without embellishment, that they had had anything to do with the incidents were given scant coverage. Reactions among the Terrans were mixed. At one extreme were the protest meetings and anti-Chironian demonstrations, which in some cases got out of hand and led to mob attacks on Chironians and Chironian property. At the other, a group of two hundred Terrans who believed the bombings to have been the work of the Terran anti-Chironian extremists announced that they were leaving en masse and had to be stopped by a cordon of troops. Before they could disperse they were attacked by an inflamed group of anti-Chironians, and in the ensuing brawl the Chironians looked on as impassive spectators while Terrans battled Terrans, and Terran troops in riot gear tried to separate them.

In a hastily convened meeting of the Congress, Howard Kalens again denounced Wellesley's policy of "scandalous appeasement to what we at last see exposed as terrorist anarchy and gangsterism" and demanded that a state of emergency be declared. In a stormy debate Wellesley stood firm by his insistence that alarming though the events were, they did not constitute a general threat comparable to the in-flight hazards that the emergency proviso had been intended to cover; they did not warrant resorting to such an extreme. But Wellesley had to do something to satisfy the clamor from all sides for measures to protect the Terrans down on the surface.

Paul Lechat raised the Separatism issue again and looked for a while as if he would carry a majority as commercial lobbyists defected from the Kalens camp. But the timing of the moment was not in Lechat's favor, and Borftein torpedoed the motion fresh off the launching ramp with a scathing depiction of them all allowing themselves to be chased off across the planet like beggars from somebody's back door. Ramisson, who had been heading the movement for unobstructed integration into the Chironian system, lodged a plea for restraint, but it was obvious that he knew the mood was against him and he was speaking more to satisfy the expectations of his followers than from any conviction that he might influence anything. The assembly listened dutifully and took no notice.

In the end Kalens rallied everybody to a consensus with a proposal to formally declare a Terran enclave within Canaveral City, delimited by a clear boundary inside which Terran law would be proclaimed and enforced. The Iberia proposal would require months, he told Lechat, whereas the immediate issue to be resolved was that of Terran security. In any case, it could hardly be carried out without an electoral mandate. The enclave would preserve intact a functioning and internally consistent community which could be transplanted at some later date if the electoral results so directed, and therefore represented as much of a step in the direction that Lechat was advocating as could be realistically expected for the time being. Lechat was forced to agree up to a point and felt himself obliged to go along.

Kalens had evidently been working on the details for some time. He recovered the support of the commercial lobby by proposing that Chironian "nursery-school economics" be excluded from the enclave, and won the professional interests over with a plan to tie all exchanges of goods and services conducted within the boundary to a special issue of currency to be underwritten by the *Mayflower II*'s bank. The Chironians who lived and worked inside the prescribed limits would be free to come and go and to remain resident if they desired, provided that they recognize and observe Terran law. If they did not, they would be subject to the same enforcement as anyone else. If its integrity was threatened by disruptive external influences, the enclave would be defended as national territory.

Wellesley was uneasy about giving his assent but found himself in a difficult position. After backing down and conceding the state-of-emergency issue, Kalens came across as the voice of reasonable compromise, which Wellesley realized belatedly was probably exactly what Kalens had intended. Wellesley had no effective answer to a remark of Kalens's that if something weren't done about the desertions, Wellesley could well end his term of office with the dubious distinction of presiding over an empty ship; the desertions had been as much a thorn in Wellesley's side as anybody's.

That touched at what was really at the bottom of it all. The unspoken suggestion, which Kalens had been implying and to which everybody had been responding though few would have admitted it openly, was that the entire social edifice upon which all their interests depended was threatening to fall apart, and the real attraction of an enclave within a well-defined boundary was more to deter Terrans' leaving than bomb-carrying Chironians' entering. Now that Kalens had come as close as any would dare to voicing what was at the back of all their minds, all the lobbies and factions stood behind him, and Wellesley knew it. If Wellesley opposed, he stood to be voted out of office. So he concurred, and the resolution was passed all but unanimously.

Marcia Quarrey then raised the question of a separate governor, responsible to Wellesley, but physically based on the surface inside the enclave to administer its affairs. Perhaps the division of authority between the members of the Directorate sitting twenty thousand miles away in the ship had contributed to the difficulties experienced since planetfall, she suggested, and delegating it to one person who had the advantages of being on the spot would remedy a lot of defects. Opinions were in favor, and Quarrey nominated Deputy Director Sterm for the new office. Sterm, however, declined on the grounds that a large part of the job would involve policymaking connected with Terran-Chironian relationships, and since a Liaison Director existed to whom that responsibility was already entrusted, the sensible way to avoid possible conflicts was to unify the two functions. He therefore nominated Howard Kalens; Quarrey seconded, and the vote was carried by a wide margin.

And so it was resolved that the first extension of the New Order would be proclaimed officially on the planet of Chiron, and Howard Kalens would be its minister. He had gained the first toehold of his empire. "It's the beginning," he told Celia later that night. "Ten years from now it will have become the capital of a whole world. With a whole army behind me, what can a rabble of ruffians with handguns do to stop me now?"

That same night, on one side of the floodlit landing area in the military barracks at Canaveral, Colman was standing with a detachment from D Company, silently watching the approach of a

Chironian transporter that had taken off less than twenty minutes before from the far side of the Medichironian. Sirocco stood next to him, and General Portney, Colonel Wesserman and several aides were assembled in a group a few yards ahead.

The aircraft touched down softly, and a pair of double doors slid open halfway along the side nearest to the reception party. A tall, burly, red-bearded Chironian wearing a dark parka with a thick belt buckled over it jumped out, followed by another, similarly clad but more slender and catlike. More figures became visible inside when the cabin light came on. Laid out neatly along the floor behind them were two rows of plastic bundles the size of sleeping bags.

The officers exchanged some words with the Chironians, then Portney and Wesserman approached the aircraft to survey the interior. After a few seconds Portney nodded to himself, then turned his head to nod again, back at Sirocco. Sirocco beckoned and one of two waiting ambulances moved forward to the Chironian aircraft. Two soldiers opened its rear doors. Four others climbed inside the aircraft and began moving bodies. As each body bag was brought out, Sirocco turned the top back briefly while an aide compared the face to pictures on a compack screen and another checked dogtag numbers against a list he was holding, after which the corpse was transferred to the ambulance.

Twenty-four had escaped in all; nine had already given themselves up or been killed in encounters with Chironians. Anita had not been among them. Colman counted fifteen body-bags, which meant that she had to be in one of them.

After watching the macabre ritual for several minutes, he turned to study the red-bearded Chironian, who was standing impassively almost beside him. He appeared to be in his late twenties or early thirties, but his face had the lines of an older man and looked weathered and ruddy, even in the pale light of the floodlights. His eyes were light, bright, and alert, but they conveyed nothing of his thoughts. "How did it happen?" Colman murmured in a low voice, moving a pace nearer.

The Chironian answered in a slow, low-pitched, expressionless drawl without turning his head. "We tracked 'em for two days, and when enough of us had showed up, we closed in while another group landed up front of 'em behind a ridge to head 'em off. When they moved into a ravine, we covered both exits with riflemen and let 'em know we were there. Gave 'em every chance . . . said if they came on out quiet, all we'd do was turn 'em in." The Chironian inclined his head briefly and sighed. "Guess some people never learn when to quit."

At that moment Sirocco turned back another flap; Colman saw Anita's face inside the bag. It was white, like marble, and waxy. He swallowed and stared woodenly. The Chironian's eyes flickered briefly across his face. "Someone you knew?"

Colman nodded tightly. "A while back now, but . . ."

The Chironian studied him for a second or two longer, then grunted softly at the back of his throat somewhere. "We didn't do that," he said. "After we told 'em they were cooped up, some of 'em started shooting. Five of 'em tried making a break, holding a white shirt up to tell us they wanted out. We held back, but a couple of the others gunned 'em down from behind while they were running. She was one of those five." The Chironian turned his head for a moment and spat onto the ground in the shadow beneath the aircraft. "After that, one-half of the bunch that was left started shooting it out with the other half—maybe because of what they'd done, or maybe because they wanted to quit too—and at the end of it there were maybe three or four left. We hadn't done a thing. Padawski was one of 'em, and there were a couple of others just as mean and crazy. Didn't leave us with too much of a problem."

Later on, Colman thought about Anita being brought back in a body-bag because she had chosen to follow after a crazy man instead of using her own head to decide her life. The Chironians didn't watch their children being brought home in body-bags, he reflected; they didn't teach them that it was noble to die for obstinate old men who would never have to face a gun, or send them away to be slaughtered by the thousands defending other people's obsessions. The Chironians didn't fight that way.

That was why Colman had no doubt in his mind that the

Chironians had had nothing to do with the bombings. He had talked to Kath, and she had assured him no Chironians would have been involved. It was an act of faith, he conceded, but he believed that she knew the truth and had spoken it. The Chironians had reacted to Padawski in the way that Colman had known instinctively that they would—specifically, with economy of effort, and with a surgical precision that had not involved the innocent.

For that was how they fought. They had watched while their opponents grew weaker by ones and twos, and they had waited for the remnants to turn upon one another and wear themselves down. Then the Chironians had moved.

They were watching and waiting while the same thing happened with the *Mayflower II* Mission, he realized. When and how would they move? And, he wondered, when they did, which side would he be on?

PART THREE

PHOENIX

❁ CHAPTER TWENTY-SEVEN ❁

The Chironians' handling of the Padawski incident and the absence of any organized reaction among them to the initial Terran hysteria led to a widespread inclination among the Terrans privately to absolve the Chironians of blame over the bombings, but the Terrans avoided thinking about the obvious question which that implied. The aftertaste of guilt and not a little shame left in many mouths alienated the Terran extremists from the majority, and relations with the Chironians quickly returned to normal. Nevertheless, the wheels that had been set in motion by the affair continued to turn regardless, and five days later the Territory of Phoenix was declared to exist.

Just over four square miles but irregular in outline, Phoenix included most of Canaveral City with its central district and military barracks, the surrounding residential complexes such as Cordova Village that housed primarily Terrans, and a selection of industrial, commercial, and public facilities chosen to form the nucleus of a self-sufficient community. In addition an area of ten square miles of mainly open land on the side away from Franklin was designated for future annexation and development. Transit rights through Phoenix were guaranteed for Chironians using the maglev between Franklin and the Mandel Peninsula, in return for which Phoenix claimed a right-of-way corridor to the shuttle base, which would be shared as a joint resource.

Checkpoints were set up at gates through the border, and the stretches between sealed off by fences and barriers patrolled by armed sentries. Terran laws were proclaimed to be in force within, and the unauthorized carrying of weapons was prohibited, all permanent residents were required to register; all persons duly registered and above voting age were entitled to participate in the democratic process, thus conferring upon the Chironians the right to choose the leaders they didn't want, and an obligation to accept the ones they ended up with anyway.

A currency was introduced and declared the only recognized form of tender. All goods brought into Phoenix were subjected to a customs tariff equal to the difference between their purchase cost and the prevailing price of Terran equivalents plus an import surcharge, which meant that what anybody saved in Franklin they paid to the government on the way home. Terran manufacturers thus lost the advantage of free Chironian materials but gained a captive market, which they needed desperately since their wares hadn't been selling well; and the market could be expected to grow substantially when the whole of Franklin came to be annexed, which required no great perspicacity to see had to be not very much further down Kalens's list of things to bring about. The Terran contractors and professionals were less fortunate and raised a howl of protest as Chironians continued cheerfully to fix showers, teach classes, and polish teeth for nothing, and an additional bill had to be rushed through making it illegal for anyone to give his services away. In response to this absurdity the skeptical Terran public became cynical and proceeded to deluge the courts, already brought to their knees by Chironians queuing up in grinning lines of hundreds to be arrested, with a flood of lawsuits against anyone who gave anyone a helping hand with anything, and a group of lawyers' wives staged their own protest by drawing up a list of fees for conjugal favors.

Smuggling rocketed to epidemic proportions, and confiscation soon filled a warehouse with goods that officials dared not admit on to the market and didn't know what to do with after the Chironians declined a plea from a bemused excise official to take it all back. The Chironians outside Phoenix continued to satisfy every order or request for anything readily; Terran builders who had commenced work on a new residential complex were found to be using Chironian labor with no references appearing in their books; every business became convinced that its competitors were cheating, and before long every session of both houses of Congress had degenerated into a bedlam of accusations and counteraccusations of illegal profiteering, back-door dealing, scabbing, and every form of skullduggery imaginable.

Cynicism soon turned to rebellion as more of the Terran population came to perceive Phoenix not as a protective enclave, but at worst a prison and at best a self-proclaimed lunatic asylum. Apartment units were found deserted and more faces vanished as expeditions to Franklin came increasingly to be one-way trips. Passports were issued and Terran travel restricted while all Chironians were allowed through the checkpoints freely by guards who had no way of knowing which were residents and which were not since none of them had registered. The sentries no longer cared all that much anyway; their looking the other way became chronic and more and more of them were found not to be at their posts when their relief showed up. An order was posted assigning at least one SD to every guard detail. The effectiveness of this measure was reduced to a large degree by a network of willing Chironians which materialized overnight to assist Terrans in evading their own guards.

Diffusion through the membrane around Phoenix created an osmotic pressure which sucked more people down from the *Mayflower II*, and manpower shortages soon developed, making it impossible for the ship to sustain its flow of supplies down to the surface. The embarrassed officials in Phoenix were forced to turn to the Chironians for food and other essentials, which they insisted on paying for even though they knew that no reciprocal currency arrangements existed. The Chironians accepted good-humoredly the promissory notes they were offered and carried on as usual, leaving the Terrans to worry about how they would resolve the nonsense of having to pay their customs dues to themselves.

Nobody talked any more about annexing Franklin. Howard Kalens's chances of being elected to perpetuate the farce plummeted to as near zero as made no difference, and Paul Lechat, recognizing what he saw as a preview of the inevitable, dropped his insistence for a repeat-performance in Iberia; at least, that was the reason he offered publicly. Ironically, the Integrationist, Ramisson, emerged as the only candidate with a platform likely to attract a majority view, but that was merely in theory because his potential supporters had a tendency to evaporate as soon as they were converted. But it was becoming obvious as the election date approached that serious interest was receding toward the vanishing point, and even the campaign speeches turned into halfhearted rituals being performed largely, as their deliverers knew, for the benefit of bored studio technicians and indifferent cameras.

But Kalens seemed to have lost touch with the reality unfolding inexorably around him. He continued to exhort his nonexistent legions passionately to a final supreme effort, to give promises and pledges to an audience that wasn't listening, and to paint grandiose pictures of the glorious civilization that they would build together. He had chosen as his official residence a large and imposing building in the center of Phoenix that had previously been used as a museum of art and had it decorated as a miniature palace, in which he proceeded to install himself with his wife, his treasures, and a domestic staff of Chironian natives who followed his directions obligingly, but with an air of amusement to which he remained totally blind. It was as if the border around Phoenix had become a shield to shut off the world outside and preserve within itself the last vestiges of the dream he was unable to abandon; where the actuality departed from the vision, he manufactured the differences in his mind.

He still retained some staunch adherents, mainly among those who had nowhere else to turn and had drawn together for protection. Among them were a sizable segment of the commercial and financial fraternity who were unable to come to terms with an acceptance that their way of life was finished; the *Mayflower II*'s bishop, presiding over a flock of faithful who recoiled from abandoning themselves to the evil ways of Chiron; many from every sector of society whose natures would keep them hanging on to the end regardless. Above all there remained Borftein, who had nowhere else to attach a loyalty that his life had made compulsive. Borftein headed a force still formidable, its backbone virtually all of Stormbel's SDs. Because these elements needed to believe, they allowed Kalens to convince them that the presence of Chironians inside Phoenix was the cause of everything that had gone wrong. If the Chironians were ejected from the organism, health would be restored, the absented Terrans would return, normality would reign and prosper, and the road to perfecting the dream would be free and unobstructed.

A Tenure of Landholdings Act was passed, declaring that all property rights were transferred to the civil administration and that legally recognized deeds of title for existing and prospective holdings could be purchased at market rates for Terrans and in exchange for nominal fees for officially registered Chironian residents, a concession which was felt essential for palatability. Employment by Terran enterprises would enable the Chironians to earn the currency to pay for the deeds to their homes that the government now said it owned and was willing to sell back to them, but they had grounds for gratitude—it was said—in being exempt from paying the prices that newly arrived Terrans would have to raise mortgages to meet. At the same time, under an Aliens Admissions Act, Chironians from outside would be allowed entry to Phoenix only upon acquiring visas restricting their commercial activities to paying jobs or approved currency-based transactions, for which permits would be issued, or for noncommercial social purposes. Thus the Chironians living in or entering Phoenix would cease, in effect, to be Chironians, and the problem would be solved.

Violators of visa privileges would face permanent exclusion. Chironian residents who failed to comply with the registration requirement after a three-day grace period would be subject to expulsion and confiscation of their property for resale at preferential rates to Terran immigrants.

Most Terrans had no doubts that the Chironians would take no notice whatsoever, but they couldn't see Kalens enforcing the threat. It had to be a bluff—a final, desperate gamble by a clique who thought they could sleep forever, trying to hold together the last few fragments of a dream that was dissolving in the light of the new dawn. "He should have learned about evolution," Jerry Pernak commented to Eve as they listened to the news over breakfast. "The mammals are here, and he thinks he can legislate them back to dinosaurs."

Bernard Fallows leaned alongside the sliding glass door in the living room and stared out at the lawn behind the apartment while he wondered to himself when he would be free to begin his new career at Port Norday. He had broached the subject to Kath, as he now knew she had guessed he would, and she had told him simply that the people there who had met him were looking forward to working with him. But he had agreed with Pernak and Lechat that a nucleus of people capable of taking rational control of events would have to remain available until the last possibility of extreme threats to the Chironians went away, and that Ramisson's Integrationist platform, to which Lechat had now allied himself, needed support to allow the old order to extinguish itself via its own processes.

Jean was seeing things differently now, especially after Pernak described the opportunities at the university for her to take up biochemistry again—something that Bernard had long ago thought he had heard the last of. He turned his head to look into the room at where she was sitting on the sofa below the wall screen, introducing Marie to the mysteries of protein transcription—diagrams courtesy of Jeeves—and grinned to himself; she was becoming even more impatient than he was. Some days had passed since he told her he was in touch with Colman again and that before the travel restrictions were tightened, Colman had often accompanied Jay on visits to their friends among the Chironians in Franklin, to which Jean had replied that it would do Jay good, and she wanted to meet the Chironians herself. Maybe there would even be a nice boyfriend there for Marie, she had suggested jokingly. "A *nice* one," she had added in response to Bernard's astonished look. "Not one of those teenage Casanovas they've got running around. The line stays right there."

Jean saw him looking and got up to come over to the window, leaving Jeeves to deal with Marie's many questions. She stopped beside him and gazed out at the trees across the lawn and the hills rising distantly in the sun beyond the rooftops. "It's going to be such a beautiful world," she said. "I'm not sure I can stand much more of this waiting around. Surely it has to be as good as over."

Bernard looked out again and shook his head. "Not until that ship up there is disarmed somehow." After a pause he turned to face her again. "So it doesn't scare you anymore, huh?"

"I don't think it ever did. What I was afraid of was in my own head. None of it was out there." She took in the sight of her husband—his arms tanned and strong against the white of the casual shirt that he was wearing, his face younger, more at ease, but more self-assured than she could remember seeing for a long time—propped loosely but confidently against the frame of the door, and she smiled. "Kalens may have to hide himself away in a shell," she said. "I don't need mine anymore."

"So you're happy you can handle it," Bernard said.

"*We* can handle anything that comes," she told him.

◎ CHAPTER TWENTY-EIGHT ◎

Celia Kalens straightened the kimono-styled black-silk top over her gold lamé evening dress, then sat back while a white-jacketed steward cleared the dinner dishes from the table. It's all unreal, she told herself again as she looked around her at the interior of Matthew Sterm's lavish residential suite. Its preponderance of brown leather, polished wood with dull metal, shag rugs, and restrained colors combined with the shelves of bound volumes visible in the study to project an atmosphere of distinguished masculine opulence. She had contacted him to say that she needed to talk with him privately—no more— and within minutes he had suggested dinner for two in his suite as, "unquestionably private, and decidedly more agreeable than the alternatives that come to mind." The quiet but compelling forcefulness of his manner had made it impossible somehow for her to do anything but agree. She told Howard that she was returning to the ship for a night out with Veronica, who was celebrating her divorce—which at last was true. Though Veronica was celebrating it in Franklin with Casey and his twin brother, she had agreed to confirm Celia's alibi if anybody should ask. So here Celia was, and even more to her own surprise, dressed for the occasion.

Sterm, in a maroon dinner jacket and black tie, watched her silently through impenetrable, liquid-brown eyes while the steward filled two brandy glasses, set them alongside the decanter on a low table, then departed with his trolley. Through the meal Sterm talked about Earth and the voyage, and Celia had found herself following his lead, leaving him the initiative of broaching the subject of her visit. Finally, he stood, came around the table, and moved her chair back for her to rise. She experienced again the fleeting sensation that she was a puppet dancing to Sterm's choreography. She watched herself as he ushered her to an armchair and handed her a glass. Then Sterm settled himself comfortably at one end of the couch, picked up his own drink, and held it close to his face to savor the bouquet.

"To your approval, I trust," he said. Celia had suggested a cognac earlier on, when Sterm had asked her preference for an after dinner liqueur.

She took a sip. It was smooth, warm, and mellowing. "It's excellent," she replied.

"I keep a small stock reserved," Sterm informed her. "It is from Earth—the Grande Champagne region of the Charante. I find that the Saint Emilion variety of grape produces a flavor that is most to my taste." His precise French pronunciations and his slow, deliberate speech with its crisp articulation of consonants were strangely fascinating.

"The white makes the best brandies, I believe," Celia said. "And isn't the amount of limestone in the soil very important?"

The eyebrows of Sterm's regal, Roman-emperor's face raised themselves in approval. "I see the subject is not unfamiliar to you. My compliments. Regrettably, rareness of quality is not confined to grapes."

Celia smiled over her glass. "Thank you. It's rare to find such appreciation."

Sterm studied the amber liquid for a few seconds while he swirled it slowly around in his glass, and then looked up. "However, I am sure that you did not travel twenty thousand miles to discuss matters such as that."

Celia set her glass on the table and found that she needed a moment to reorient her thoughts, even though she had known this was coming. "I'm concerned over this latest threat to evict Chironians from Phoenix. It's not the bluff that many people think. Howard is serious."

Sterm did not appear surprised. "They have merely to comply with the law to avoid such consequences."

"Everyone knows they won't. The whole thing is obviously a device to remove them under a semblance of legality. It's a thinly disguised deportation order."

Sterm shrugged. "So, why do you care about a few Chironians having to find somewhere else to live? They have an entire planet, most of which is empty. They will hardly starve."

It wasn't quite the answer that Celia had been prepared for. She frowned for a second, then reached for her glass. "The reaction that it might provoke worries me. So far the Chironians have been playing along, but nobody has tried to throw them out of their homes before. We've already seen examples of how they do not to hesitate to react violently."

"That frightens you?"

"Shouldn't it?"

"Hardly. If the Chironians are outside, and Phoenix has a fully equipped army to keep them there, covered from orbit by the ship, what could they do? Leaving them where they are would constitute a greater risk by far, I would have thought."

"True, once they're separated," Celia agreed. "But how many more killings would we have to see before that was achieved?"

"And that bothers you?"

"Well—of course."

"Really?" Sterm's one word conveyed all the disbelief necessary; its undertone suggested that she reconsider whether she believed her answer either. "Come now, Celia, the realities of life are no strangers to either of us. We can be frank without fear of risking offense. The people live their lives and serve their purpose, and a few more or less will make no difference that matters. Now tell me again, who are you really worried about?"

Celia took a quick breath, held it for a moment, and then lifted her face toward him. "Very well. I've seen what happened to the corporal and to Padawski. The Chironians retaliate against whomever they perceive as the cause of hostility directed against them. If the evictions are enforced . . . well, it's not difficult to see who the next target would be, is it."

"You want me to prevail upon Howard to prevent his destroying himself."

"If you want to put it that way."

"What makes you imagine that I could?"

"You could talk to him. I know he listens to what you say. We've talked about things."

"I see." Sterm studied her face for what seemed like a long time. At last he asked in a strangely curious voice, "And if I did, what then, Celia?"

Celia was unable to reply. The answer lay behind a trapdoor in her mind that she had refused to open. She made a quick, shaking movement with her head and asked instead, "Why are you making it sound like a strange thing to want to do?"

"Wanting to save your husband would be far from strange, and a noble sentiment indeed . . . if it were true. But is it true?"

Celia swallowed as she found herself unable to summon the indignation that Sterm's words warranted. "What makes you think it isn't?" She avoided his eyes. "Why else would I be here?"

Sterm stared at her unblinkingly. "To save yourself."

"I find that insulting, and also unbecoming."

"Do you? Or is it that you are unable, yet, to accept it?"

Celia forced as much coldness into her voice as she could muster. "I don't like being told that I'm interested in protecting my own skin."

Sterm was unperturbed, as if he had been expecting such an answer. "I made no mention of your wanting to save yourself physically. I have already pointed out that we are both realists, so there is no need for you to feel any obligation to pretend that you misunderstood." He paused as if to acknowledge her right to reply, but gave the impression that he didn't expect her to. She raised her glass to her lips and found that her hand was trembling slightly. Sterm resumed. "The dream has crumbled away, hasn't it, Celia. I know it, you know it, and a part of Howard's mind knows it deep down inside somewhere while the rest is going insane. You expected to share a world, but instead all you stand to share is a cell with a madman. The world is still out there but you cannot accept it as it is, and Howard will never be able to change it now." Sterm extended a hand expressively. "And the future awaits you." He paused again, watched as Celia lowered her eyes, and nodded. "Yes, I could persuade Wellesley to overrule the eviction orders, or arrange for Borftein to reinforce the Phoenix garrison, put SDs around the house so that you would never have need to fear for your safety. But is that what you want me to do?"

Celia looked down at the glass in her hand and bit nervously at her lip. "I don't know," was all she could whisper. Sterm watched her impassively. In the end she shook her head. "No."

Sterm allowed a few seconds for her admission to settle. "Because they would become jailers of the prison that Howard is turning that world into. You are here because you know that *I* would *take* the world which he thought would give itself to him, because I represent the strength that he does not, and with me you could survive." Celia looked up again, but Sterm's eyes had taken on a faraway light. "Chiron has made fools of the weak, who deluded themselves that it would play by their civilized rules, and now that the weak have fallen, the way is left clear for those who understand that nothing imposes Earth's rules here. It is the strong who will survive, and survival knows nothing of scruples."

Celia's eyes widened as many things suddenly became clearer. "You . . ." Her voice caught somewhere at the back of her throat. "You knew this was going to happen—Howard, Phoenix . . . everything. You were manipulating all of them from the beginning, even Wellesley. You knew what would happen after the landing but you endorsed it."

Sterm looked back at her and smiled humorlessly. "Hardly what I would call manipulating. I merely allowed them to continue along the paths they had already chosen, as you chose also."

"But you saw where the paths led."

"They would never have listened if I had told them. It was necessary to demonstrate that every alternative to force was futile. Now they will understand, just as you have come to understand."

"How—how could you justify it?"

"To whom do I have to justify anything? Those rules belong to Earth. I make my own."

"To Congress, the people."

Sterm snorted. "I need neither. The same forces that will subdue Chiron will subdue the people also." His eyes flickered over Celia's body momentarily. "And they will submit because they, like you, have an instinct to survive."

Celia found herself staring into eyes that mirrored for a split second the calm, calculated ruthlessness that lay within, devoid of disguise or apology, or any hint that there should be any. A chill quivered down her spine. But she felt also the trapdoor in her mind straining as a need that lay imprisoned behind it, and which she was still not ready to face, responded. Sterm's eyes were challenging her to deny anything that he had said. She was unable to make even that gesture.

Howard had sought to possess, and she had refused to become a possession. Sterm sought not to possess but to dominate Chiron. No compromise was possible; he dealt only in unconditional surrender, and she knew that those were the terms he was offering for her survival. Perhaps she had known it even before she arrived.

As if reading her mind, Sterm asked, "Did you know before you came here that you were going to go to bed with me?" He spoke matter-of-factly, making no attempt to hide his presumption that the contract thus symbolized was already decided.

"I . . . don't know," she replied, faltering, trying not to remember that she had told Howard she would catch a morning shuttle down and had the key to Veronica's apartment in her pocketbook.

"Does he expect you tonight?" Sterm inquired curiously, although Celia couldn't avoid a feeling that he already knew the answer. She shook her head. "Where are you supposed to be?"

"With a friend in Baltimore," she told him, thus making her capitulation total. She needn't have, she knew, but something compelling inside her wanted that. She knew also that it was Sterm's way of forcing her to admit it to herself. The terms were now understood.

"Then there is no reason for us to allow unseemly haste to lower the quality of the evening," Sterm said, sitting forward and reaching with a leisurely movement of his hand for the decanter. "A little time ripens more than just fine cognac. Will you join me in a refill?"

"Of course," Celia whispered and passed him her glass.

◉ CHAPTER TWENTY-NINE ◉

"We'll take care of that." Colman turned his head and called in a louder voice, "Stanislau, Young—come over here and give me a hand with this crate." Rifles slung across their backs, Stanislau and Young stepped away from the squad standing on the sidewalk and helped Colman to heave the crate into the truck waiting to leave for the border checkpoint, while the Chironian who had been struggling to lift it with his teenage son watched. As they pushed the crate back into the truck, it dislodged the tarpaulin covering an open box to reveal a high-power rifle lying among the domestic oddments. The Chironian saw it and lifted his head to look at Colman curiously. Colman threw the tarp back over the box and turned away.

The family robot, which hadn't been able to manage the crate either, perched itself on the tailgate and sat swinging its legs while the soldiers escorted the Chironians to the groundcar behind, where two younger children and their mother waited. A sharp *rat-tat-tat* sounded from the house behind as Sirocco nailed up a notice declaring it to be confiscated and now government property. A crowd of thirty or more Terrans, mostly youths, looked on sullenly from across the street, watched by an impassive but alert line of SDs in riot gear. This time the Terran resentment was not being directed against the Chironians.

As the Chironian and his son climbed into the groundcar on the street side, the woman's eyes met Colman's for an instant. There was no malice in them. "I know," she said through the window. "You've got a job that you have to do for a little while longer. Don't worry about it. We can use the vacation. We'll be back." Colman managed the shadow of a grin. Seconds later the truck moved away, the robot sitting in the rear, and the groundcar followed, two wistful young faces pressed against the rear window.

Angry murmurs were heard from the Terran civilians. Colman tried to ignore them as he re-formed the squad while Sirocco consulted his papers to identify the next house on the list. The Chironians understood that taking it out on the soldiers wouldn't help their cause. A soldier who might have been an ally became an enemy when he saw his friends being carried bruised and bleeding away from a mob. Everything the Chironians did was designed to subtract from their enemies instead of add to them, and to whittle their opposition down to the hard core that lay at the center, which was all they had any quarrel with. He could see it; Sirocco could see it, and the men could see it. Why couldn't more of the Terrans see it too?

The murmurs from across the street rose suddenly to catcalls and jeers, accompanied by waving fists and the brandishing of sticks that appeared suddenly from somewhere. Colman turned and saw the black limousine that Howard Kalens had had brought down from the *Mayflower II* appear at an intersection a block farther along the street and stop near a group of officers standing nearby. Major Thorpe detached himself from the group and walked across. Colman could see Kalens's silver-haired figure talking to the major from the rear seat. Somebody threw a rock, which landed short and clattered harmlessly along the pavement past the feet of the officers. More followed, and several Terrans moved forward threateningly.

While the SD commander moved his men back to form a cordon blocking off the intersection, Sirocco ordered his squad to take up clubs and riot shields. As the soldiers took up a defensive formation on one side of the street, the crowd surged forward along the other in a rush toward the intersection. Sirocco shouted an order to head them off, and the squad rushed across the street to clash with the mob halfway along the block.

Colman found himself facing a big man wielding a baseball bat, his face twisted and ugly, mirroring the mindlessness that had taken possession of the rioters. The man swung the bat viciously but clumsily. Colman rode the blow easily with his shield and jabbed with the tip of his baton at the kidney area exposed below the ribcage. His assailant staggered back with a scream of pain. Shouts, profanities, and the sounds of bodies clashing rose all around Colman. Something hard bounced off his helmet. Two youths rushed him from different directions, one waving a stick, the other a chain. Colman jumped to the side to bring the two in line for a split second's cover, feinted with his baton, then sent the first cannoning into the second with a shove from his shield with the full weight of his shoulder behind it, and both rioters went down into a heap. Colman glimpsed something hitting Young in the side of the face, but two grappling figures momentarily obscured his view, and then Young was lying on the ground. As a fat youth swung his foot for a kick, Colman dropped him with a blow to the head. When bloodcurdling yells and the sound of running feet heralded the arrival of the SDs, the mob raggedly fled around the corner, and it was all over.

Young had a gash on his cheek that was more messy than deep and a huge bruise along his jaw to go with it, and four rioters were left behind with sore heads or other minor injuries. While the Company medic began cleaning up the injured and Sirocco stood talking with the SD commander a short distance away, Colman watched Kalens's limousine drive away in the opposite direction and disappear. That was how it had always been, he could see now. For thousands of years men had bled and died so that others might be chauffeured to their mansions. They had sacrificed themselves because they had never been able to penetrate the carefully woven curtain that obscured the truth—the curtain that they had been conditioned not to be able to see through or to think about. But the Chironians had never had the conditioning.

The inverted logic that had puzzled him had not been something peculiar to the military mind; it was just that the military mind was the only one he had ever really known. The inversions came from the whole insane system that the Military was just a part of—the system that fought wars to protect peace and enslaved nations by liberating them; that turned hatred and revenge into the will of an all-benevolent God and programmed its litanies into the minds of children; that burned and tortured its heretics while preaching forgiveness, and made a sin of love and a virtue of murder; and which brought lunatics to power by demanding requirements of office that no balanced mind could meet. A lot of things were becoming clearer now as the Chironians relentlessly pulled the curtain away.

For the curtain that was falling away was the backcloth of the stage upon which the dolls had danced. And as the backcloth fell and the strings fell with it, the dolls were dancing on. The dolls were dancing without the strings because there were no strings. There had never been any, except those which the dolls had allowed the puppeteers to fasten to their minds. But those strings had held up the puppeteers, not the dolls, for the puppeteers were falling while the dolls danced on.

Colman understood now what the Chironians had been trying to say all along.

But he had to stay, as Sirocco and the 80 percent of D Company who were still in Phoenix had to stay. After Swyley went, Driscoll went, and many of the others went, Sirocco had called the rest together and reminded them about the weapons in the *Mayflower II*. "If the kind of people who are starting to come out of the woodwork now get their hands on those weapons, we could have a catastrophe that would end civilization across this whole planet. You've all seen what's happening back on Earth. Well, the same mentalities are here too, and they're panicking. We *must* keep enough of the Army together to stop anything like that if we have to." And so they had stayed.

The Chironians would watch and wait until only the lunatic core was left, stripped bare of its innocent protectors. Eventually only two kinds would be left: There would be Chironians, and there would be Kalenses. And Colman no longer had any doubts as to which he would be.

In the D Company Orderly Room in the Omar Bradley barracks

block, Hanlon secured his ammunition belt, put on his helmet, and took his M32 from the rack. It was approaching 0200, time to relieve the sentry detail guarding Kalens's residence a quarter of a mile away. "Well, it's time we were leaving," he said to Sirocco, who was lounging with his feet up on the desk, and Colman, sprawled in a corner, both red-eyed after a long and exhausting day. "I'll try to shout quietly. I'd hate to be disturbing His Honor in his sleep."

Sirocco smiled tiredly. "You're excused from taking off your boots," he murmured.

"Are we still invited to the Fallowses tonight, Steve?" Hanlon asked, stopping at the door to look back at Colman.

Colman nodded. "I guess so. I'll probably be asleep when you come off duty. Better give me a call."

"I will indeed. See you later." Hanlon left, and they heard him forming up the relief guard outside.

"Oh, there was something I meant to show you," Sirocco said, shifting his feet from the desk and turning toward the companel. "It come in earlier this evening. Want a laugh?"

"What?" Colman asked him.

Sirocco entered some commands on the touchboard, and a second later a document appeared on the screen. Colman got up and came across to study it while Sirocco sat back out of the way. It was a communication from Leighton Merrick, the Assistant Deputy Director of Engineering in the *Mayflower II,* routed for comment via Headquarters and Brigade. It advised that, due to an unexpectedly high rate of promotions among junior technicians, Engineering was now able to give "due reconsideration" to the request for transfer filed by Staff Sergeant Colman. Would the Military please notify his current disposition? "Looks like they're running out of Indians," Sirocco remarked. "What do you want me to say?"

"What do you think?" Colman answered, and went back to his chair. Sirocco casually entered negative, and cut the display.

"So what will you do?" Sirocco inquired, propping his feet back on the desk. "Figured it out yet?"

"Oh, there's a lot of studying I've got listed—general engineering with a lot of MHD, then maybe I'll see if I can get into something at

Norday for a while. Later on I might move out to the new place they're talking about."

"Will Kath fix it up for you?"

Colman nodded. "To start with, anyhow. Then, I guess, it's a case of how well you make out. You know how things operate here." After a pause he asked, "How about you?"

Sirocco tweaked his moustache pensively. "It's a problem knowing where to start. You know the kind of thing I'd like—to get out and see the whole planet. The Barrier Range is as big as the Himalayas, there's Glace . . . a Grander Canyon out in Oriena . . . there's so much of it. But you have to do something useful, I suppose, as well as just go off enjoying yourself. But I think there's a lot of survey work waiting to be done yet. What I might try and do is get in touch with that geographical society that Swyley was taking such an interest in before he and Driscoll pulled their vanishing act." Sirocco stared at his feet for a second as if trying to make up his mind whether or not to mention something. "And then of course there's Shirley," he added nonchalantly.

"Shirley? . . . You mean Ci's mother?"

"Yes."

"What about her?"

Sirocco raised his eyebrows in what was obviously feigned surprise. "Oh, didn't I tell you? She wants me to move in. It's surprising how a lot of these Chironian women have a thing about Terrans to . . ." he frowned and scratched his nose while he searched for the right words ". . . assist with their future contribution to procreation." He looked up. "She wants my kids. How about that, Steve? Come on, I bet it's the same with Kath." Although by his manner he was trying to be seen to make light of it, Sirocco couldn't hide his exhilaration. Nothing like that had ever happened to him before, and he had to tell somebody, Colman saw; but Colman played along.

"You sly bastard!" he exclaimed. "How long has this been going on?" Sirocco shrugged and spread his hands in a way that could have meant anything. Then Colman grinned. "Well, what do you know? Anyhow—good luck."

Sirocco resumed twiddling his moustache. "Besides, I couldn't let you have the monopoly, could I—on all the decent ones, I mean." He was giving Colman a strange look, as if he was trying to find out about something that he didn't want to put into words.

"What are you getting at?" Colman asked him.

Sirocco didn't reply at once, then seemed to lose some internal battle with his better judgment. "Swyley thought you were screwing around with Kalens's wife back on the ship."

Colman kept a poker face. "What made him think that?"

Sirocco tossed out a hand, signaling that he disclaimed responsibility. "Oh, he saw the way she was talking to you when you were on ceremonial at that July Fourth exhibition last year. That was one thing. Do you remember that?"

Colman went through the motions of having to think back. "Yes . . . I think so. But I don't remember Swyley being around."

"Well, he must have been there somewhere, mustn't he?"

"I guess so. So what was the rest of it?"

Sirocco shrugged. "Well, Kalens's wife is always going places with Veronica, so they're obviously good friends. Swyley noticed something funny between you and Veronica at that party we went to at Shirley's, and that was the connection he figured out." Sirocco shrugged again. "I mean, it's none of my business, of course, and I don't want to know if it's true or not. . . ." He paused and looked at Colman hopefully for a second. "Is it?"

"Would you expect me to say so if it was?" Colman asked.

"I suppose not." Sirocco conceded, deflating with a disappointed sigh. After a second he looked up sharply again. "I'll do a deal with you though. Tell me after this is all over, okay?"

Colman grinned. "Okay, chief. I will." A short silence fell while they both thought about the same thing. "How long do you think it'll be?" Colman asked at last.

"Who can say?" Sirocco answered, picking up the more serious tone. "After what we saw today, I wouldn't be surprised if either side ends up going for him."

"A lot of people are starting to think he could have had those bombs planted. What do you think?"

James P. Hogan

Sirocco frowned and rubbed his nose. "I'm not convinced. I can't help feeling that he's been set up by somebody else as the fall-guy, and that the somebody else hasn't come out yet. I think the Chironians believe that too."

Colman nodded thoughtfully to himself and conceded the point. "Any ideas?"

Sirocco shrugged. "I'm pretty sure it can't be Wellesley. He's tried to play it straight, it's all sweeping him way out of his depth. Anyhow, what would he have to gain? All he wants to do is to be put out to pasture; he's only got a few days left. Ramisson obviously wouldn't be involved in something like that, and the same goes for Lechat. But as for the rest, if you ask me, they're all crazy. It could be any of them or all of them. But that's who the Chironians are really after."

"So it could take a while," Colman said.

"Maybe. Who knows? Let's just hope there aren't too many of them in the Army."

At that moment the emergency tone sounded shrilly from the companel. Sirocco jerked his legs off the desk, cut the alarm, and flipped on the screen. It was Hanlon, looking tense.

"It's happened," Hanlon told him. "Kalens is dead. We found him inside the house, shot six times. Whoever did it knew what they were doing."

"What about the sentries?" Sirocco asked curtly.

"Emmerson and Crealey were at the back. We found them unconscious in a ditch. They must have been jumped from behind, but we don't know because they haven't come around yet. They look as if they'll be okay though. The others didn't know a thing about it."

Colman was listening grimly. "What about his wife?" he muttered to Sirocco.

"How is Kalens's wife?" Sirocco asked Hanlon.

"She isn't here. We've checked with transportation, and she was booked onto a shuttle up to the ship earlier this evening. She must have left before it happened." Beside Sirocco, Colman breathed an audible sigh of relief.

"Well, that's something, anyway," Sirocco said. "Stay there, Bret, and don't let anyone touch anything. I'll get onto Brigade right away.

We'll have some more people over there in a few minutes." He returned to Colman. "Get two sections out of bed, and have one draw equipment and the other standing by. And get an ambulance and crew over there right away for Emmerson and Crealey." Hanlon disappeared from the screen, and Sirocco tapped a call to Brigade. "It looks as if the fall-guy has gone down, Steve," he murmured while Colman called the ambulance dispatcher on another panel. "Let's see who steps out from the wings now."

◉ CHAPTER THIRTY ◉

The strain that had been increasing since planetfall and the shock of the most recent news were showing on Wellesley's face when he rose to address a stunned meeting of the *Mayflower II*'s Congress later that morning. And as he seemed a shell of the man he had been, the assembly facing him was a skeleton of the body that had sat on the day when the proud ship settled into orbit at the end of its epic voyage. Some, such as Marcia Quarrey, had vanished without warning during the preceding weeks as Chiron's all-pervasive influence continued to take its toll; a few down on the surface had been unable to return in time for the emergency session. Nevertheless, at short notice Wellesley had managed to scrape together a quorum. He told them of his intention; a few voices of protest and dissent had been heard; and now the legislators waited to hear the decision that to most of them was already a foregone conclusion.

"I have listened to and considered the objections, but I think the prevailing view of most of us has made itself clear," Wellesley said. "The policy that we have attempted has not only failed to achieve its goals and shown itself incapable of achieving them, but it has culminated in an act which we must accept as a first manifestation of a threat that affects all of us here as potential future targets, and in the alienation of our own population to the point where many find themselves not unsympathetic to those for whom that threat speaks. Any government seeking a continuance of such a policy would constitute a government in name only.

"We are facing a crisis that jeopardizes the continued integrity of the entire Mission, and it has become evident to me that our difficulties stand only to be exacerbated by a continued division of authority. Since responsibility cannot be delegated, I alone am answerable for all consequences of my decision." He paused to look around the room, and then took a long breath. "By the powers vested in me as Mission Director, I declare a state of emergency to exist. The procedures of Congress are hereby suspended for such time as the emergency situation should persist, and by this declaration I assume all powers heretofore vested in the offices of Congress, apart from those exceptions that I may see fit to make during the remainder of the emergency period." After a short pause he added in a less formal tone, "And I ask the cooperation of all of you in making that period as short as possible."

Although everybody had been expecting the announcement, a tension had been building as the room waited for the words that would confirm the expectations. Now that the words had been said, the tension released itself in a ripple of murmurs accompanied by the rustle of papers, and the creaks of chairs as bodies unfolded into easier postures.

Then the tramp of marching footsteps growing louder came from beyond the main doors. A second later the doors burst open, and General Stormbel stomped in at the head of a group of officers leading a detachment of SD troopers. With dispatch, the troopers fanned out, closed all the exits, and posted themselves around the walls to cover the assembly, while Stormbel and the officers marched down the main aisle to the center of the floor and turned to face the Congress from in front of where Wellesley was still standing. Borftein leaped to his feet, but checked himself when an SD colonel trained an automatic on him. He sank into his seat, a dazed expression on his face.

Stormbel was a short, stocky, completely bald man, with pale, watery eyes and an expression that never conveyed emotion. A thin moustache pencil-lined his upper lip. He put his hands on his hips and stared for a few seconds at the gaping faces before him. "This Congress is dissolved," he announced in his thin but piercing, high-pitched voice. "The Mission is now under the direct command of the Military." He turned his head to Borftein. "You are relieved of command of both the regular and Special Duty forces. Those functions are now transferred to me."

"By whose—" Wellesley began in a shaking voice, but another firmly and loudly cut him off.

"By *my* authority." Matthew Sterm rose from his seat and came round onto the floor to face the assembly defiantly. "This prattling has continued for too long. I have no eloquent speeches to make. Enough time has been wasted on such futilities already. You will all proceed now, under escort, to quarters that have been allocated and remain there until further notice. We have business to attend to." He nodded at Stormbel, who motioned at the guards. "I would like Admiral Slessor to remain behind to discuss matters concerning the continued well-being of the ship."

As the guards started forward and the members continued to sit in paralyzed silence, Ramisson rose and walked haltingly to the center of the main aisle to face Sterm. "I will not submit to such intimidation," he said in a harsh whisper. "Remove your men from that door." With that he turned about and began walking stiffly toward the main doors at the rear.

Stormbel drew his automatic and leveled it at Ramisson's back. "You have one warning," he called out. Ramisson kept walking. Stormbel fired. Ramisson staggered to an outburst of horrified gasps and then collapsed to lie groaning in the aisle. Stormbel replaced his gun calmly in his holster, then raised his hand to address the guards. "Remove that man, and see to it that he receives medical attention." Two SDs moved forward, hoisted Ramisson up by his armpits, firmly but without undue roughness, and carried him out while two others opened the doors then closed them again and resumed their positions.

"Are there any more objectors?" Sterm inquired. Behind him Wellesley, white faced and haggard, slumped into his chair.

"Stop this now," Borftein advised grimly. "How much of the Army do you think will follow you?"

Stormbel gave him a contemptuous look. "How much of *your* Army is left?" he asked. "Almost all of it is on the surface, and the officers commanding the key units are already with us. Besides, *we* control the ship, which is the most important thing."

"For now," Sterm added. "The rest comes later."

Borftein licked his lips and thought frantically. As Stormbel was about to repeat the order to clear the room, Borftein looked at Sterm, closed his eyes for a moment, and then raised a hand and shook his head. Sterm looked at him questioningly. "I . . . I'm not sure I even know what's happened," Borftein said. "It's been too sudden. Just what do you think you're going to do?" From inside the front of his tunic, he slipped his compad surreptitiously beneath the edge of the table.

Sterm emitted a sigh of sorely tried patience. "I will endeavor to spell it out in simple terms," he replied. "This act of clowns has been . . ."

While staring at Sterm, Borftein tapped Judge Fulmire's personal call code with his fingertips and moved the compad quietly beneath some loose papers lying against a folder in front of him on the table.

Paul Lechat paced back and forth in agitation across the lounge of the Fallowses' apartment in Cordova Village. "I didn't think the Chironians would go that far," he said. "I thought they would react only against direct violence. Why couldn't they have just let everything die a natural death?"

"Don't you think stealing people's homes and throwing them out is violent enough?" Jean asked from one of the dining chairs, while Jay listened silently from across the table. "What were they supposed to do? They ignored the soldiers and settled it with the man responsible. He should have been expecting it."

Lechat shook his head. "It wasn't necessary. In a few more days Ramisson would have been elected, almost certainly. Then everything would have worked itself out smoothly and tidily. This action complicates everything again. Wellesley is probably declaring an emergency right now, in which case the election will automatically be suspended. It puts everything back weeks, maybe months."

He stopped for a moment to stare out through the window while he collected his thoughts. Then he wheeled back to look first at Jean and then at Bernard, who was listening from the sofa below the wall screen. "Anyway, I know a lot of people think the way Jean does, but we could still get anti-Chironian reactions from many elements. That's what worries me. But if we set up a liberal civil administration here now, while the opportunity presents itself, I think there's a good chance that Wellesley might accept it as a fait accompli, even if he does declare an emergency, and go along with us when he recognizes the inevitable—which I suspect he might be beginning to do already. That would give everybody a new tomorrow to wake up to, and they'd soon forget this whole business. But there isn't much time. That's why I skipped the meeting. Now you two can help, pretty much in the ways we've discussed. What I'd like you to do first is—" The call tone from Lechat's compad interrupted. He looked down instinctively at the breast pocket of his jacket. "Excuse me for a moment."

The others watched as he pulled the unit out, accepting the call with a flip of his thumb. Judge Fulmire peered from the miniature screen. "Are you alone, Paul?" Fulmire asked without preamble. His voice was clipped and terse.

"I'm with company, but they're safe. What—"

"Stay off the streets and keep out of sight," Fulmire said. "Sterm and Stormbel have pulled a coup. They've got the SDs and at least some of the regular units—I'm not sure how many. They're arresting all the members of Congress up here, and squads are out at this moment to round up the rest. I'm probably on the list too, so this will have to be quick. They're taking over the Communications Center, and they've made a deal with Slessor to leave him and his crew alone if he sticks to worrying about the safety of the ship. Get out of Phoenix if you can. I don't know if—" The picture and the voice cut out suddenly.

"Who was that?" Jean gasped, her eyes wide with disbelief.

"Judge Fulmire." Lechat frowned and tapped in a code to reconnect. The unit returned a "number unobtainable" mnemonic.

He rattled in another code to alert a communications operator. The same thing happened. "The regular net seems to have gone down," he said. "Even the standby channels."

"Oh, God . . ." Jean whispered. "They're going to bring out those bombs."

Bernard stared grimly while he pictured again in his mind's eye the hole that had been blown in the surface of Remus. "We've got to stop it," he breathed. "We've got to get a message up there somehow . . . to Sterm . . . telling him what he's up against. Thousands of people are still up there."

"He wouldn't believe us," Lechat said bleakly. "It sounds like the first bluff anyone would try."

Jean shook her head. "There must be something—the Chironians! He'd have to believe them. If they beamed a signal up spelling out just what their weapons can do, whatever they are, and with the evidence to prove it, Sterm would have to take notice of that, surely."

"But we don't even know which Chironians to talk to," Lechat pointed out.

Bernard fell silent for a few seconds. "Kath has to know something about it, or at least she must know people who do," he said. "After all, there aren't billions of people on Chiron. And Jerry said that she has a lot to do with the people working on the antimatter project at the university. Let's start with her."

Jean glanced at the screen and then looked at Bernard. "Should we try calling her through Jeeves . . . via the Chironian net? It shouldn't be affected, should it?"

"I'm not sure I'd trust any electronics," Lechat cautioned. "Could be risky," Bernard agreed after a second's reflection. "If Sterm and whoever else is involved have been preparing for this, I wouldn't put it past them to have taps and call-monitor programs anywhere. Someone will have to go there."

"Who," Jean asked.

"Well, Paul can't show his face outside. You heard what Fulmire said." Bernard replied. "So I guess I'll have to."

"But what about the border guards?" Jean looked alarmed. "We don't know who we can trust. Fulmire didn't know which side how much of the Army is on. There could be fighting out there at any minute. You don't know what you'll be walking into."

Bernard shrugged helplessly. "I know. It's a chance—but what else is there?"

A tense silence fell. Then Jay said, "I know at least one person in the Army who we can trust." The others looked at him in surprise.

Bernard snapped his fingers. "Of course, Colman! Why the hell didn't I think of that?"

"Who's Colman?" Lechat inquired.

"A family friend, in the Army," Jean said.

"Ye-es," Bernard said slowly, nodding to himself. "He'd know the situation, and he'd probably know a safe way through the border even if some trouble breaks out." He began nodding more strongly. "And we certainly know we can trust him."

"I could go and see if I can find him," Jay offered. "I don't think I'd attract much attention. Even if the SDs are out, they're not going to be looking for me."

Bernard looked at Lechat. Lechat frowned and seemed about to object. Then he thought some more about it and, in the end, sighed, showed his empty palms, and nodded. Bernard turned back to Jay. "Okay, see what you can do. If you do find him, ask him to get over here as soon as he can make it."

Jay jumped up and ran to a closet for a jacket. He looked at Jean as he pulled it on. "Yes, Mother, I'll be careful."

Jean forced a smile. "Just remember that," she said.

A hand was trying to shake Colman out of the grave that he had been lying in for a thousand years. "Sarge, wake up," the Voice of Judgment boomed from above, sounding uncannily like Stanislau. "Hanlon wants you over at the main gate."

"Wha—huh? . . . Who? . . ." Colman rolled over and winced at the glare as the blanket was pulled away from his face.

The Angel Stanislau descended from the radiance and assumed Earthly form beside the cot. "Hanlon's got someone over at the main gate who wants to talk to you. Says it's urgent."

Colman sat up and rubbed his eyes. "Why didn't he put a call through?"

"Regular comm channels are all down, to the ship . . . everywhere. They have been for over an hour," Stanislau said. "Emergency channels are restricted to priority military traffic." Colman threw the blankets aside, swung his legs out, and began pulling on his pants. "Strange things happening everywhere," Stanislau told him, handing him his boots. "Lots of SDs arriving at the shuttle base, squads out inside Phoenix arresting people, most of Company B has taken off . . . I don't know what it's all about."

"Is Sirocco around?" Colman moved over to the washbasin to rinse his face.

"In the Orderly Room. Hanlon got him up earlier. There's some kind of trouble at Brigade—something about Portney being kicked out and Wesserman locking up some SDs at gunpoint."

Colman wiped his face with a towel, tossed the towel to Stanislau, and snatched a shirt from a closet. "Do me a favor and straighten out this mess," he said. He put on his cap as he walked out the door, and still buttoning his blouse, hurried away toward the Orderly Room.

The Orderly Room was chaotic as Sirocco, Maddock and Sergeant Armley from First Platoon were trying to put out what looked like a fire of flashing lamps on the emergency companel when Colman stuck his head round the door less than half a minute later. "What the hell's going on?" he asked them.

"Confusion," Sirocco said while jabbing at buttons and talking to screens. "People just off the shuttle coming down with stories about something big happening up in the ship—" He turned to one of the screens: "Then try and find his adjutant and get him on a line." Then back to Colman: "I'm trying to find someone to confirm the rumors."

"Hanlon wants me at the gate for something," Colman said. "Talk to you in a few minutes."

"Okay. Get back here when you're through."

Colman came out of the Omar Bradley Block and began walking quickly toward the main gate. Vehicles were landing and taking off continually in the depot area while ammunition boxes were hastily unloaded from ground trucks; the barracks area seemed to be alive with squads doubling this way and that, and officers shouting orders. Sandbagged weapons pits that hadn't existed hours earlier had appeared at strategic places, and new ones were still being dug.

The guard had been doubled at the main gate. Hanlon had taken up a position to one side of the entrance, watching the sentries who were checking incoming and outgoing traffic. Jay Fallows was standing just outside, by the wall of the sentry post. Hanlon saw Colman approaching and sauntered across to meet him. "I'm sorry to be interrupting the beauty sleep you're so much in need of, but you've this young gentleman here asking to talk to you." Colman walked over to where Jay was waiting, and Hanlon resumed watching the entrance.

Jay began speaking earnestly and in a low voice. "My father asked me to find you. It's urgent. One of the people the SDs are looking for is at the house. Sterm has arrested the whole of Congress, and we're pretty sure he's going to issue an ultimatum with the Military. If they do, the Chironians will take out the whole ship. Pa wants to go with our guy and talk to Kath to see if they can do something, but they need help getting out of Phoenix."

Colman's face creased into a frown. "Take the ship out with what?"

"I don't know," Jay said. "It's a lot to go into now, but we're certain they've got the capability. It's really that urgent, Steve. When can you get over?"

"Oh, Christ . . ." Wearily, Colman brought a hand up to his brow. "Okay. Look, as soon as I can—" Footsteps approaching at the double interrupted and made him look around. It was Sergeant Armley, from the Orderly Room.

Armley stopped in front of Colman and beckoned Hanlon over. "Sirocco wants you both back right away," he said breathlessly. "I'll take over at the gate. There's trouble at the shuttle base. Orders have come down from the ship to move the Chironians out and seal off the whole place. Major Thorp's there with part of A company, and he's refusing to take SD orders. We've been ordered to send two platoons. Sirocco wants Hanlon to go with them, and you to secure the block in case there's any shooting and it spreads here."

Colman groaned to himself. Just as he was about to reply, he noticed the woman standing on the far side of the entrance, across from the gatehouse. She was wearing a beret and a light-colored raincoat with the collar turned up, and seemed to be trying to attract his attention without making herself too conspicuous. "Oh, Jesus—" He looked at the two. "Look, I need a few minutes. Jay, stay right there." He walked across to the woman and was almost face to face with her before he recognized Veronica, for once looking neither impish nor mischievous.

"I've just come down from the ship, Steve." She drew him close to the gatepost.

"Aren't the boarding gates being checked?" Colman murmured, surprised.

"Of course they are. It's all a mess up there."

"Then how—"

"I know Crayford and his wife. One of the crew got me through. That can wait. It's about Celia."

It wasn't a moment to be keeping up pretenses. Colman's frown deepened. "What about her? Is she okay?"

Veronica nodded her head quickly a couple of times. "She's not hurt or anything like that, but she's in a lot of trouble. She's gotten herself mixed up with Sterm, and she can't make a move without being watched. She could be in real danger, Steve. She has to get away from there."

Colman nodded but tossed up his hands. "Okay, but how can she?"

"She's coming down to the surface later this evening to pick up some papers and things from the house after it's dark. But she'll be under escort. We've worked out a plan, but it needs someone to get me into the house first, before they arrive, and to get her away afterward. Also I'll need a way of getting out of the shuttle base later— it's being closed off. You're the only person she'll trust. Can you get away inside the next hour, say?"

Colman looked away in a daze. Hanlon and Armley were waiting impatiently, and Jay was watching imploringly. He thought furiously. Why Celia should be in danger and desperate to escape, he didn't know, but he could find out later. If he said he had to get away for a few hours, Sirocco would cover for him, so that was okay. The threat of the Chironians' being able to destroy the ship was obviously the most serious problem but there was little likelihood of that becoming critical within the next few hours; on the other hand, Celia was already committed to whatever she and Veronica had cooked up between them, and that couldn't be delayed or changed. So Celia would have to come first. Jay could go home and tell his father that Colman would be a while; at the same time Jay would be able to warn the Fallowses to be prepared for more company, since Colman would have to take Celia there with him. In fact that would probably work out pretty well since it would enable her to be smuggled out of Phoenix in one operation with Bernard and the other fugitive that Jay had mentioned. Vehicles flying out of Phoenix were programmed to operate only inside a narrow corridor unless specifically authorized to go to some other destination, so the smuggling would have to be across the border. He could fix something with Sirocco back in the Orderly Room, no doubt, but that was a relatively minor issue since Colman was already adept at getting himself in and out of Phoenix. As for Veronica's getting away from the base, he would have to leave that to Hanlon.

"We can probably figure out a way to get you into the house, Veronica. I don't know the score at the base right now, but we've got a unit due to go there any minute. That means you'll have to trust some other guys too. Okay?"

"If you say so. Do I have a choice?"

"No." Colman turned his head and waved Hanlon over. "Bret, this is Veronica. Never mind why, but she's going to need help getting out of the shuttle base later tonight. What do you think?"

"We'll work out something. Where and when?" Hanlon said. Colman looked over at Veronica.

"A shuttle's lifting off from Bay Five at 2130," she said. "I'll be coming off it about thirty minutes before it leaves. All I need is to get over into Chironian territory. I can make it on my own from there."

"Where to?" Colman asked her.

"Casey's, I suppose," Veronica replied.

"Does Casey know?" Colman asked. Veronica shook her head. Colman thought for a few seconds. "I don't like the sound of what's going on around there," he said. "Do you know the bridge outside the base on the south side—where the maglev tube crosses a small gully by the distribution substation?"

"I think so. I can find it anyway."

"Make for the bridge and wait there," Colman told her. "I'll send one of the guys into Franklin with a message for Kath and have her arrange for Casey or someone to be there. SD patrols could be prowling around, or anything. Best not to risk it." Veronica nodded her assent.

"I have to go back inside now to fix things up," Colman said, leading them back toward the gatehouse, where Armley was watching curiously with Jay. "Mike," Colman said to him as they stopped by the door. "Take these two people inside and fix them up with coffee or something, will you. Jay, wait inside with Veronica. I have to get back in with Bret, but I'll be back in a few minutes. Don't worry. It'll be okay."

Ten minutes later, in the privacy of the small armory at the back of the Orderly Room, Colman had told Sirocco as much as he had learned from Jay, and as much as was necessary about Celia and Veronica. Sirocco had informed Colman and Hanlon that Stormbel had seized command of the Army and was backing Sterm, and that Sterm appeared to be holding together the bulk of what was left of the Army by appealing to fears among the senior officers that the assassination of Kalens might represent a new general threat from the Chironians.

"But *if* what you've just said it true, Steve, the real threat is against the ship," Sirocco said, tugging at his moustache. "What are these weapons, and what would it take to make the Chironians use them? I've got to have more information."

Colman could only shake his head. "I don't know. Neither did Jay. That's what Fallows and whoever this other guy is want to find out."

"We'll have to keep the unit intact in case there's a showdown,"

Sirocco murmured. "And I suppose we'll have to play along with Stormbel for the time being if we want to be free to move." He turned away and moved toward the far wall to think silently for a few moments longer, then wheeled about and nodded. "Okay. Bret, you have to leave for the base right away. Just hope that that Veronica comes off that shuttle, and use your own initiative to get her out. That's all you have to worry about. So, on your way." Hanlon nodded and disappeared back through the Orderly Room. "Steve," Sirocco said. "Pick anyone you want to send to Franklin, and we'll just have to leave the rest of that side of things to Kath. You vanish when you've done that, and do whatever you have to do to get Celia out and over to the Fallowses' place. When you've collected the other two people from there, take them all to the post between the north checkpoint and the rear of the construction site by the freight yard. Maddock's section will be manning that sector from midnight to 0400. They know how to distract the SDs, and I'll make sure they're expecting you." Colman nodded and turned to follow in the direction which Hanlon had gone. "Oh, and Steve," Sirocco called as a new thought struck him. Colman stopped at the door and looked back. "You say you know Fallows fairly well?"

"For a long time," Colman said.

"Don't leave them at the post," Sirocco said. "Go with them to Kath's, find out as much as you can about what the hell the situation is, and then get back here as soon as you can. That way, maybe we'll be able to figure out what needs to be done."

◉ CHAPTER THIRTY-ONE ◉

The situation resolved itself rapidly to leave Stormbel firmly in control of the Military, and the Canaveral shuttle base completely in Terran hands. Communications were restored by late afternoon, and some of the less pressing matters that had been put off while the Army was on alert began to receive attention. Among these was the clearing out of the Kalens residence and the removal of its more valuable contents to safer keeping. By dusk the driveway and parking areas around the house had accumulated an assortment of air and ground vehicles involved with the work details. Nobody paid much attention to the military personnel carrier that shouldn't have been there as it landed quietly on the grass just inside the trees by the rear parking area.

Inside, Stanislau shut down the flight-control systems, then walked into the passenger compartment without turning on the cabin lights to join Colman, Maddock, Fuller, and Carson, who were sitting with a large picture-crate propped between them, and a pile of cartons, tools, and packing materials around their feet. Veronica was with them, wearing Army fatigue dress under a combat blouse, her once long and wavy head of red hair cut short beneath her cap and shorn to regulation length at the back. Maddock climbed over the litter to open the door, and then climbed out with Carson and Fuller; Stanislau stayed inside to help in the unloading. Colman looked at

Veronica's face, shadowy in the subdued light coming from outside. "Feel okay?" he asked.

She nodded, then after a few seconds said, "Casey will have a fit."

Her attempt at humor was a good sign. Colman grinned and heaved himself from his seat. "Then let's go," he grunted.

When they were all outside, Carson and Maddock took the picture-crate, Stanislau a toolbox, Fuller assorted ropes and fasteners, and Colman some papers and inventory pads. Veronica carried a large roll of packing foam on her shoulder, keeping it pressed against the side of her face. Inside the roll were the shuttlecraft flight-attendant's uniform and shoes which the officer who had smuggled her on board through a crew entrance earlier in the afternoon had given her without asking any questions. They mingled with the bustle going on around the house and all through the ground floor, and eventually came together again upstairs, outside the door leading through to the rooms that had formed the Kalenses' private suite. Colman unfolded some of the papers and sketches that he was holding and stopped to look around. After a few seconds he gestured to attract the attention of the SD guard who was standing disinterestedly near the top of the main stairs, and nodded his head in the direction of the door. "Is that the way into the bedroom and private quarters?" he asked.

"It is, but nothing in there's to be touched until Mrs. Kalens has been back to get some stuff," the guard answered. "She should be on her way down just about now."

"That's okay," Colman said. "We just have to take some measurements." Without waiting for a reply he walked over to the door, opened it, poked his head in, called back to Stanislau, "This is it. Where's Johnson?" and went inside. Stanislau put down the toolbox and followed, then Colman came back out and squatted down to rummage inside it for something. Veronica appeared and went in with the packing roll, Stanislau came out, Colman went back in with a measure, and a few yards away along the corridor Carson and Maddock managed to get the picture-crate stuck across an awkward corner. While the SD was half watching them, Fuller came up the stairs to ask where Johnson was, Stanislau waved in the direction of the doorway, and Fuller went in while Colman came out. Carson dropped his end of the crate, Stanislau went in with a compad, Maddock started yelling at Carson, and Fuller came out.

In the bathroom through the far door of the bedroom behind the lounge, Veronica was already stripping off her fatigues and boots, which she then stowed beneath the towels in the linen closet. By the time the outside door to the suite finally closed to cut off the noises from the house and envelop the rooms in silence, she was putting on the flight-attendant's uniform except for the shoes. After that she used Celia's things to attend to her makeup.

Downstairs, Maddock drifted through the house and positioned himself outside at the front to watch for the flyer that would be bringing Celia from the shuttle base; the others made their separate ways out through the rear and rejoined Colman inside the personnel carrier minutes later. They settled themselves down to wait, and Fuller and Carson lit cigarettes. "Still think it'll go okay, Sarge?" Stanislau asked. "I could do a quick hair-job in there." He had brought the things with him, just in case.

Colman shook his head. "There shouldn't be any need. Celia's hair is a lot shorter. There'll be fewer people around later. It'll be okay . . . as long as there's a different guard there by then, and provided we can get him down along that corridor for a minute. And anyhow, they'll be expecting people to be going in there then."

"If you say so," Stanislau said.

"How long before the flyer shows up?" Carson asked.

Colman looked at his watch. "About half an hour if it's on schedule."

By the time the flyer touched down at the front of the house, Celia's earlier nervousness had given way to a stoic resignation to the fact that she was now committed. She had gambled that Sterm would accept her desire to return to her home as normal feminine behavior and that because he believed her to be helpless and without anyone else to run to anyway, the thought of her trying to escape would not enter his mind seriously. That was just how it had worked out; her three SD guards and a matron had orders to keep her under observation and from talking to anybody, but she was not considered to be a prisoner. Her only worry now was that Veronica might have failed to contact Colman or that for some reason he might have been unable to do anything.

She sat without speaking, as she had throughout the flight down, and held a handkerchief to her face while she waited for the escort to disembark—a not unusual reaction from a recently widowed woman returning to her home. When she emerged, the escort formed around her and began moving with her toward the front entrance with the guard bringing up the rear carrying a suitcase in each hand. Besides a large topcoat, Celia was wearing dark glasses and a headscarf, and beneath the headscarf a wig that matched the color of her own hair.

The party ascended the main staircase, at the top of which the two leading guards took up positions outside the door to the suite while the one with the suitcases accompanied Celia and the matron inside. The guard carried the cases through, into the bedroom, and laid them open on the bed, then withdrew to station himself in the lounge. While Celia began selecting and packing items from the drawers and closets, the matron went to the door at the back to look into the bathroom, swept her eyes round in a perfunctory check for windows or other exits, and then came away again to assume a blank-faced, postlike stance inside the lounge door, moving only when Celia went through to collect some papers and other items from the desk beyond. Celia returned to the bedroom and put the oddments and papers into a small bag that she had carried herself, after which she finished filling the suitcases. Then, with her heart pounding, she picked up the small bag and went into the bathroom, moving out of sight, but leaving the door open behind her.

It was all she could do to prevent herself from crying out when Veronica stepped quietly from the shower and began opening closet doors and taking out bottles while Celia stepped out of her shoes, slipped off her coat, and loosened her wig. There was no time for smiles or reassuring gestures. Veronica put Celia's shoes on her feet and the flight-attendant's shoes in Celia's bag; the wig went into place easily over her new haircut; the coat went over her uniform, and she tied the scarf over the wig while Celia took over the job of putting bottles, jars, brushes, and tubes into the bag to keep up the background noise. Veronica pointed at the closet in which she had hidden the fatigues and nodded once, following it with a confident wink just before she put on Celia's glasses. Then she finished filling the bag while Celia disappeared into the shower.

The matron didn't gave Veronica a second glance when she came out of the bathroom with Celia's bag on one hand and holding Celia's handkerchief to her face with the other. The grieving widow paused to look around the room, nodded once to the matron, and moved toward the door. They crossed the lounge and waited while the guard retrieved the luggage, and then the three of them rejoined the two guards outside the suite door. The party then reformed and began descending the stairs.

Celia waited for a few minutes to give anybody a chance to come back for something, then stepped from the shower, found the clothes that Veronica had left, and spent a few minutes putting them on and lacing the boots. Her hair was already tied high from wearing the wig, but she spent a while studying the cap in the mirror and making some adjustments before she considered herself passable. She was just walking back into the bedroom to wait when she heard the door on the far side of the lounge open, and immediately the suite was filled with the sounds of bodies moving around and voices calling to each other. A few seconds later Colman appeared in the doorway from the lounge. Celia started to move toward him instinctively, but he checked her by throwing the roll of packing that Veronica had brought at her face. "You're in the Army," he said gruffly as she caught it. "Move your ass."

It was the right thing to do. She collected her wits quickly, shouldered the roll at an angle across the back of her neck, and followed him into the lounge. Colman went ahead to stand peering through the doorway from one side while soldiers came and went in bewildering confusion and then he motioned her out suddenly. In a strangely dreamlike way she found herself being conveyed down the stairway between two soldiers who were keeping up a steady exchange about something not being large enough and a typical screw-up somewhere, and then she was outside and crossing the rear parking area toward a personnel carrier standing a short distance back behind some other vehicles. Suddenly, without really remembering getting in, she was sitting in the cabin. Figures materialized swiftly and silently from the darkness and jumped in after her. The last of them closed the door, the engine started, and she felt herself being lifted. Only then did she start shaking.

"Never say you don't get anything back for your taxes." Colman was sitting next to her, grinning faintly in the brief glow as one of the others lit a cigarette. But she had gone for so much of the day without speaking that she was unable to answer immediately. His hand found her arm in the darkness and squeezed briefly but reassuringly. "It'll be okay," he murmured. "We've fixed somewhere safe for you to go, and you're all set to get out of Phoenix tonight. I'll be coming with you into Franklin."

"What about Veronica?" she whispered.

"One of our units at the base is expecting her. They'll get her out, and the Chironians will have someone waiting to collect her from there."

Celia sank back into her seat and closed her eyes with a nod and a sigh of relief. One of the figures in the darkness wanted to know how come somebody called Stanislau knew how to fly something like this. Another voice replied that his father used to steal them from the government.

Colman stared at Celia for a few seconds longer. He still didn't know why Celia should have been so anxious to get away from Sterm or why she should have been in any danger. Life couldn't have been much fun with somebody like Howard, he could see, so the thought of her gravitating toward a strong, protective figure like Sterm wasn't so strange. And it didn't seem so unnatural that she should have stayed near Sterm after Howard was killed. In such circumstances it would have been normal to provide her with an escort down to the surface too, for her own security; but having her watched all the time and not allowing her contact with anybody made no sense. Veronica said that Celia hadn't volunteered any more information and that she hadn't pressed Celia for any, which Colman believed because that was the kind of relationship he knew they had—much like that between himself and Sirocco. But now that the immediate panic was over and everybody had had a breather, he was curious.

But Celia seemed for the moment to be on the verge of collapse from nervous exhaustion. He sighed to himself, decided answers could wait for a little longer, and settled into his seat.

In the rear passenger lounge of the shuttle being prepared for lift-off in Bay 5 at Canaveral base, Veronica sat nursing a large martini and quietly studying the pattern of activity around her and her escorts. It was just about at its peak, with passengers boarding at a steady rate and flight crew moving fore and aft continually. But most of the faces had not yet had time to register. The matron had evidently not considered it part of her duties to assist in packing or carrying anything, but had maintained her distance as a purely passive observer; there was no reason why she should change that role now.

Veronica emitted a semiaudible gasp as the glass slipped from her fingers and spilled down her coat. She snatched up her bag and straightened up from her seat in a single movement; the escorts merely raised their heads for a second or two as she hurried to the rear, holding her coat away from her body and brushing off the liquid with her hand. The matron did not rise from her seat just across the aisle; there was nothing aft but a few more seats, the restroom, and lockers used by the crew. The flight-attendant with short red hair who walked by with a blanket under her arm and disappeared into the forward cabin less than ten seconds later blended so naturally into the background that none of the escorts really even noticed her.

❀ CHAPTER THIRTY-TWO ❀

Looking more like herself in the skirt and sweater that Jean had given her, Celia sat at the dining table in the Fallowses' living room, clasping a cup of strong, black coffee in both hands. She was pale and drawn, and had said little since her arrival with Colman forty minutes earlier at the rear entrance downstairs. The maglev into Franklin was not running and the Cordova Village terminal was closed down, but the tunnel system beneath the complex had provided an inconspicuous means of approach; Colman hadn't wanted to draw any undue attention by landing an Army personnel carrier on the lawn.

"Starting to feel a little better?" Jean asked as she refilled Celia's cup. Celia nodded. "Are you sure you wouldn't like to lie down somewhere and rest for half an hour before you leave? It might do you a lot of good." Celia shook her head. Jean nodded resignedly and replaced the pot on the warmer before sitting down again between Celia and Marie.

Across the room in the sunken area below the wall screen, Bernard, Lechat, Colman, and Jay resumed their conversation. "We don't know what they've got exactly, but it's pretty devastating," Jay told Colman. "We figure they've already tested it. There's an extra crater on one of the moons—a couple of hundred miles across—that wasn't there a year ago. Imagine if whatever did that was to hit the ship."

"You think that's really a possibility?" Colman asked, looking concerned and doubtful at the same time.

"It's how the Chironians have been working all along," Lechat said. "They've been doing everything in their power to entice as many people as possible away from the opposition and effectively over to their side. Haven't they done it with us? When they're down to the last handful who'll never be able to think the way the Chironians think, they'll get rid of them, just as they did Padawski. That's how their society has always worked. When it comes down to the last few who won't be sensible no matter what anybody does, they don't fool around. And they'll do the same thing with the ship if Sterm makes one threatening move with those weapons up there. I'm convinced of it. The Chironians took out their insurance a long time ago. That would be typical of how they think too."

Colman frowned and shook his head with a sigh as he thought about it. "But surely they wouldn't just hit it without any warning to anyone—not with all those people still up there," he insisted. "Wouldn't they say something first . . . let Sterm know what he's up against?"

"I don't know," Bernard said dubiously. "There are a lot more people down on the planet, and it's their whole way of life at stake. Maybe they wouldn't. Who knows exactly how the Chironians think when all the chips are down? Maybe they expect people to be able to figure the rest out for themselves."

Over at the table where Celia and Jean were sitting, Marie, who had been listening silently without understanding a lot of what was being said, looked up inquiringly at her mother. Jean smiled and squeezed her hand reassuringly. "So what is it they've got?" Colman asked again. "Missiles wouldn't be any use to them, and they know it. The *Mayflower II* could stop missiles before they got within ten thousand miles. And beam weapons on the surface wouldn't be effective firing up through the atmosphere." He spread his hands imploringly. "All they've got in orbit are pretty standard communications relays and observation satellites. The moons are both out of range of beam projectors. So what else is there?"

"From what Jerry Pernak told us, it must have to do with

antimatter," Jay said. "The Chironians are into a whole new world of particle theory. That means they can produce lots of antimatter economically. With that they could make matter-antimatter annihilation bombs, super-intense radiation sources, guided antimatter beams, maybe . . . who knows? But it has to be something like that."

The mention of antimatter reminded Colman of something. He sat back on the sofa and cast his mind back as he tried to pinpoint what. It reminded him of something Kath had said. The others stopped talking and looked at him curiously. And then it came to him. He cocked his head to one side and looked at Bernard. "Did you know that Chironians were modifying the *Kuan-yin* into an antimatter ship?" he asked.

Bernard sat forward, his expression suddenly serious. "No, I didn't," he said. "Is that what they've been doing to it? How did . . ." His voice trailed away silently.

Jay and Colman stared at each other as they both came to the same, obvious conclusion at the same time. "That's it," Jay murmured.

Bernard's expression was grave and distant. "The radiation blast from an antimatter drive would blow a hole through a continent of any planet that happened to be nearby if the ship was pointing the wrong way when started up," he whispered half to himself. "It's been up there in orbit, right under our noses all the time. They've got the biggest radiation projector anybody ever dreamed of—right there, riding out in space with the *Mayflower II*. They put kids and comic robots on it, and we never even noticed it."

A long silence went by while they took it all in. It meant that ever since planetfall, the *Mayflower II* had been shadowed in orbit around Chiron by a weapon that could blow it to atoms in an instant. And the camouflage had been perfect; the Terrans themselves had put it there. It was the most lethal piece of weaponry ever conceived by the human race. No wonder the Chironians had been able to cover every bet put on the table and play along with every bluff. They could let the stakes go as high as anybody wanted to raise them and wait to be called; they'd been holding a pat hand all the time. Or was it the Smith and

Wesson that Chang had mentioned at Shirley's, perhaps not so jokingly?

"We might not be the only ones who've noticed there's an extra hole on Remus," Jay said at last. "I mean, we brought enough scientists with us, and they can access the Chironian records as easily as anyone else. The Chironians aren't exactly secretive about their physics."

"They could have," Bernard agreed. "But have they? It doesn't add up to the way Sterm's acting."

Jay shrugged. "Maybe he figures he's got a better than even chance of outshooting them. Maybe he's just crazy."

Lechat had digested the implications by now and appeared worried. "Maybe the Chironians have given a warning, but nobody realized it. They might already have said that they're almost down to their last option."

"How do you mean?" Colman asked.

Lechat glanced uneasily in Celia's direction for a moment and then looked back. "Howard Kalens," he said in a lower voice. "Couldn't that have been a final warning? Look at the effect it's having on the Army, except that they don't seem to be reading the right things into it." He looked at Jay. "I can't see that they've got it all figured out. They can't have."

Bernard sat back and drew a long breath. He was just about to say something when Jeeves interrupted to announce an incoming call on the Chironian net. It was Kath, calling from her place in Franklin. "I've heard from Casey," she said when Bernard accepted. "He's collected his package with Adam, and they're on their way home with it. I just thought you'd like to know."

Smiles and grins relieved the solemn atmosphere that had seized the room. From the direction of the table, Jean emitted an audible sigh of relief. Bernard grinned up at the screen. "Thanks," he said. "We're all glad to hear it. Talk to you again soon." Kath gave a quick smile and vanished from the screen.

"Veronica made it!" Jean exclaimed delightedly. "Steve, I don't know how you handled it all."

"It pays to have friends," Colman grunted.

"Congratulations, Steve," Bernard said, still smiling. "I wonder what those guards are doing right now."

"I'm very pleased," Lechat murmured. Jay grinned, and Marie smiled at what was evidently good news.

Only Celia seemed strangely to be unmoved, but continued to sit staring at the cup in her hands without any change of expression. Her unexpected reaction caused the others to fall quiet and stare at her uncertainly. Then Jean said in a hesitant voice, "You don't seem very excited, Celia. Is there something wrong?"

Celia didn't seem to hear. Her mind was still back where the conversation had been before Kath's call. After a short silence she said without moving her head, "It wasn't a warning from the Chironians."

The others exchanged puzzled looks. Jean shook her head and looked back at Celia. "I'm sorry, we're not with you. Why—"

"The Chironians didn't kill Howard," Celia said. "I did."

A silence descended like steel doors slamming down around the room. Those two simple words had extinguished all thoughts of the *Kuan-yin*'s weapons, and antimatter instantly. Every head turned disbelievingly to Celia as she sat staring ahead. Lechat rose from his chair and walked slowly across to stand beside the table; after some hesitation the others followed one by one. Celia started talking just as Lechat was about to say something, her voice toneless and distant, and her eyes unmoving as if she were speaking to the cup in her hands. "I couldn't have spent my life with a man who had closed his mind to reality. You can't know what it was like. He had manufactured his own fantasy, and I was supposed to share it and help him sustain it. It was impossible." She paused to gulp some of the coffee. "So, the thing with Sterm . . . happened . . . Howard learned about it . . ." Celia closed her eyes as if she were trying to shut out a memory that she was seeing again. "He lost control of himself completely . . . there was a fight, and . . ." She left the rest unsaid. After a few seconds she opened her eyes and stared blankly ahead again. "Maybe I wanted him to find out—provoked him to it. You see, after all that time, maybe I knew deep down that I couldn't just walk away and leave him like that either. What other way was there?" Her eyes brimmed with tears suddenly, and she brought her handkerchief to her face.

Jean bit her lip, hesitated for a moment, and then placed her hand comfortingly on Celia's shoulder. "You mustn't think like that," she urged. "You're trying to take all the guilt upon yourself and—"

Celia raised her head suddenly to look up at Lechat. "But I only shot him twice, not six times as the soldiers found. And the house hadn't been broken into when I left. Don't you see what that means?"

Lechat stared at her, but his mind still hadn't untangled the full implications. Beside him Colman's jaw clamped tight. "Somebody faked it to look like the Chironians did it," Colman grated.

Bernard's jaw dropped. "Sterm?" he gasped, then looked down at Celia. "You did tell him?"

Celia nodded. "That evening, as soon as I got up to the ship. I think I must have been hysterical or something. But . . . yes, I told him."

Lechat was nodding slowly to himself. "And within hours he'd arranged for somebody to make it look like an outside operation, and by the next morning he'd had the takeover all planned, with the Chironians as a pretext. Everything fits. But who would have done it?"

"SDs," Colman said at once. "It was a professional job."

"Would they accept a job like that?" Jean asked, sounding dubious.

Colman nodded. "Sure. They're selected and trained to obey orders and not ask questions. Some of them would shoot their own mothers if the right person said so. And Stormbel was in on it. It fits." He thought for a second longer, and then looked at Lechat and Bernard. "There were a lot of suspicious things about Padawski breaking out too. It couldn't have happened the way it did without inside help. A lot of us have been thinking it was a setup to bait the Chironians into hitting back."

Lechat's brows lifted and then creased into an even deeper frown. "And then there were those bombings . . ." He looked down at Celia. "Was Sterm behind those things too?"

"I don't know, but it wouldn't surprise me," Celia answered. "I just know the true story about Howard because . . . because . . ."

"Does anyone else know about Howard?" Colman asked. "Veronica, for instance?"

Celia shook her head. "Nobody until now."

Colman exhaled a long breath. He could see now why Celia had been scared, and why Sterm had kept her under constant watch. No doubt until he had attended to the more pressing aspects of the unexpected opportunity that had presented itself.

"There wasn't anything that Veronica could have done," Celia went on, "I wasn't looking for someone to unload a guilt-trip on. What I had to say was a lot bigger than that. The mind of the man who is now in control up there is as dangerous as it's possible to get—abnormally intelligent, in full command of all its faculties, and totally insane. Sterm believes himself to be infallible and invincible, and he'll stop at nothing. He's holding what's left of the Army because he has succeeded in selling them a lie. And I was the only person who could expose that lie. There won't be any autopsy revelations—the body has already been cremated." Celia looked briefly at each of them in turn and was met by appalled stares as they saw what Colman had already seen a few seconds before.

"Yes, I knew I was in danger, but that was secondary," Celia told them. "I still can expose the lie. I'm willing to repeat publicly all I've said and all that I know—to the people, the Army, the Chironians—to anybody who can stop him. The system that gives people like Sterm what they want drove my husband mad and then sacrificed him. There must be no more sacrifices. That was why I had to get away."

◉ CHAPTER THIRTY-THREE ◉

Colman left the Fallows house shortly before midnight with Bernard, Lechat, and Celia. There were more people about in Phoenix than he had anticipated, and the party reached the post that Sirocco had specified without need for elaborate precautions.

On their arrival, they learned from Maddock that there was little need for them to have bothered making the arrangements with Sirocco. Border security around Phoenix was disintegrating, with most of the SDs being pulled back to protect the shuttle base, the barracks, and other key points, and the regular troops who were left scattered thinly along the perimeter doing little to interfere with the civilian exodus. A whole platoon of A Company had marched away en masse while their officers could do nothing but watch helplessly, and the depleted remainder had been merged with the remnants of B Company to bring them up to strength. More SDs were disappearing too. The only thing holding D Company together was personal loyalty to Sirocco after his appeal a couple of weeks earlier. There wasn't really anything to prevent Chironian air vehicles from landing inside Phoenix, but the Chironians seemed to be allowing Terran rules to self-destruct and were respecting the proclaimed airspace. Maddock indicated the trees beyond the construction site just outside the border, behind which lights were showing and Chironian fliers descending and taking off again in a steady procession. "No need for you to walk very far," he told them. "I can call Kath and have her send a cab over. What's her number?"

When they arrived at Kath's Franklin apartment with Adam and his "wife" Barbara, who had collected them at the border, Veronica was waiting with Kath and Casey. Colman already knew everybody, and while he and Kath were introducing Bernard and Lechat to those they hadn't met previously, Veronica and Celia greeted each other with hugs and a few more tears from Celia.

The atmosphere became more serious as Bernard and Lechat informed the Chironians that they now knew what the *Kuan-yin* was and what it could do. "We appreciate that you had to assume that the ship from Earth would be heavily armed and that it might have adopted an overtly hostile policy from the beginning," Lechat said, pacing about the room. "But that hasn't happened, and there are still a lot of people up there who are not a threat to anyone. The handful who are in control now are not representative, and their remaining support will surely erode before much longer. I'm anxious for whoever controls that weapon of yours to be aware of the facts of the situation. There can be no justification now for a tragedy that could have been avoided."

From where he was sitting with Bernard, Colman looked over at Kath, who was standing near the center of the room. "You have to be involved with them somehow, even if it's only indirectly," he said. "You must know these people, even if you're not one of them yourself."

"What would you wish them to do?" Kath asked, implying that Colman was correct in at least one of his assumptions without giving any hint of which. She had reacted to the subject with calmness and composure, almost as if she had been expecting it, but there was a firmness in her expression that Colman had not seen on any previous occasion. Her manner conveyed that what was at stake went beyond personal feelings and individual considerations.

"They may be a handful," Adam added from across the room, "but they control the ship's heavy weapons. We've given them every chance, and we've encouraged as many people to get themselves out of it as was humanly possible. Our whole world is at stake. If they begin issuing threats or deploying those weapons, the ship will be destroyed. There can be no changing that decision. It was made a long time ago."

Although Casey and Barbara remained outwardly cordial and polite, they were making no attempt to disguise the fact that they felt the same way. Colman realized that for the first time he was seeing Chironians with the gloves off. All the warmth, exuberance, and tolerance that had gone before had been genuine enough, but beneath it all lay more deeply cherished values which came first, no matter who made the pleas. On that, there could be no concessions.

"That's true," Bernard agreed. "But the risk of Sterm trying anything with those weapons has to be greater if he thinks he can blackmail a defenseless planet. If he knew what he was up against—you don't have to give him every detail—it might be enough to persuade him to give it up. That's all we're asking. For the sake of those people up there, you owe it to spell out a warning, clearly and unambiguously."

"Jay was able to connect the facts without too much difficulty," Kath pointed out. "We didn't try to hide them. Haven't the scientists on the ship done the same?"

"I don't know," was all that Bernard could reply. "If they have, they haven't published it. But does it seem likely? Would Sterm be moving the way he is if they had? But you have nothing to lose by spelling it out to them. It has to be worth a try."

Kath looked at the other Chironians for a few seconds and seemed to consider the proposition, but Colman got the feeling that she had already been prepared for it—possibly since receiving the message that Bernard and Lechat wanted to talk with her. Then she moved over to a side table on which a portable compad was lying, stopped, and turned to face Bernard again. "It isn't a matter for me to decide," she said. "But the people concerned are waiting to talk to you." Bernard and Lechat exchanged puzzled looks. Kath seemed to hesitate for a second, and then looked at Lechat. "I'm afraid we have been taking an unpardonable liberty with you. You see, this was not entirely unexpected. The people you wish to speak with have been monitoring our discussion. I hope you are not too offended."

She touched a code into the compad, and at once the large screen at one end of the room came to life to reveal head-and-shoulder views of six people. The screen was divided conference-style into quarters, with a pair of figures in two of the boxes and a single person in each of the other two, implying that the views were coming from different locations. Kath noted the concerned look that flashed across Bernard's face. "It's all right," she told him. "The channels are quite secure."

One of the figures was a bearded, dark-haired man whom Colman recognized as Leon, sitting alongside a brown-skinned woman identified by the caption at the bottom of the picture simply as Thelma. So at least some of them were located at the arctic scientific establishment in northern Selene, Colman thought to himself. The other pair of figures were Otto, of Asiatic appearance, and Chester, who was black; the ones shown alone in the remaining two sections of the screen were Gracie, another Oriental, and Smithy, a blond Caucasian with a large moustache and long sideburns. From their ages they were all evidently Founders. Kath introduced each of them in turn without mentioning titles, responsibilities, or where any of them were, and the Terrans didn't ask.

Otto seemed to be the spokesman. He seemed anxious to reassure them. "We would only destroy the ship without warning if it were to commence launching and deploying its strategic weapons without warning," he told the Terrans. "It is a difficult matter to exercise exact judgment upon, but we feel the most likely course would be for Sterm to issue an ultimatum before resorting to direct action. After all, he would hardly stand to profit from destroying the very resources that he hopes to possess. Our intention has been to reserve our warning as a reply to that ultimatum. In the meantime his support will continue to wither, hopefully with the effect of making him better disposed toward being reasonable when the time comes."

"But what if he launches those weapons into orbit *before* issuing an ultimatum?" Bernard asked.

Leon nodded gravely from his section of the screen. "That is a risk," he agreed. "As Otto said, it is difficult to judge exactly. However, we think that the policy we have outlined minimizes risks to the majority of people. Nothing will eliminate the risks completely." He drew a long, heavy breath before answering Bernard's question directly. "But there can be no alteration of our resolution."

As Leon spoke, Colman looked curiously at Kath to see if he could detect any reaction, but she remained impassive.

Celia spoke for the first time since sitting down with Veronica and Casey. Until now she had not been fully aware of the reason for Bernard and Lechat's visit. "Either way a warning won't do any good," she said. "Whether you issue one now or later is academic. He would defy it. You don't know him. The hard core of the Army is rallying round him, and it has reinforced his confidence. He thinks he is unbeatable."

Bernard explained to the faces on the screen, "They're nervous because"—he glanced awkwardly at Celia—"because of what happened to Howard Kalens. Sterm is playing on that."

"That was unfortunate, but it was beyond our control," Leon said. "I hope you do not believe that we were responsible." Bernard shook his head.

After a long silence Otto looked up. "Then I'm afraid we can offer no more."

There seemed to be no more to say. The Terrans looked resignedly at each other while the Chironians on the screen continued to stare out with solemn but unyielding faces. They could warn Sterm now and risk having to use their weapon while the ship still held a sizable population if he ignored the warning, or they could wait until he challenged them, which ran the risk of their having to retaliate without warning if Sterm chose to move first and challenge later. Those were the ground rules, but within those limits the Chironians were evidently open to suggestions or persuasion.

Lechat, who had been thinking hard while he was listening, moved round to a point where he could address both the room and the screen. "Perhaps there is something else we can do," he said. Everybody looked at him curiously and waited. He raised his hands briefly. "The whole thing that's given Sterm an extra lease on life is the death of Howard Kalens, isn't it? Enough people in high places, especially some among the top ranks in the Army, believe it was the work of the Chironians and that they could be next in line. So they're clustering around Sterm for mutual preservation. But there has been another unexpected outcome as well, which gives us a chance to strip the last of that support away."

"What kind of outcome?" Thelma asked from beside Leon.

Lechat hesitated and looked uncertainly in Celia's direction. She returned an almost imperceptible nod. Lechat looked back at the screen. "Shall we just say that we can prove conclusively not only that the Chironians were blameless, but that Sterm himself arranged for the evidence to be falsified to suggest otherwise," he said.

"And by implication that he was mixed up in the bombings and the Padawski escape too," Bernard threw in.

The Chironians suddenly appeared intrigued. "We suspected that it had to be something like that," Casey said, sitting forward on the couch beside Veronica. "But how can you prove it?"

An awkward silence hung over the room. Then Celia said, "Because I killed him. The rest was faked after I left the house. Only Sterm knew about his death."

Murmurs of surprise came from the screen. In the living room, the Chironians were staring at Celia in amazement. Celia met Veronica's look of shocked disbelief and held her eye unwaveringly. Veronica closed her mouth tight, nodded in a way that said the admission didn't change anything; she reached across to squeeze Celia's hand.

Lechat didn't want to see Celia dragged through an ordeal again. He raised his arms to attract attention back to himself. "But don't you see what it means," he said. The voices on the screen and inside the room died away. "If that information was made public, it might be enough to cause Sterm's remaining supporters to turn on him—apart from the few who were in on the scam. Surely if that happened he'd have to see that it was all over. He's hanging on by the thread of a lie, and we possess proof of the truth that can cut that thread. That gives us an option to try before resorting to last, drastic measures. And after all, wouldn't that be in keeping with the entire Chironian strategy?"

Kath looked apprehensively at Celia. Celia nodded in answer to the unvoiced question. "Yes, that's the way I want it," she said. Kath nodded and accepted the situation at that.

"Exactly what are you asking us to do?" Otto asked from the screen.

Lechat tossed up his hands and began pacing again. "Anything to publicize what we've said . . . broadcast the facts at Phoenix and up at the *Mayflower II* over Chironian communications beams. At least some of the population would hear it . . . the word would soon be spread. . . . I don't know . . . whatever would bring word to the most people in the shortest time for greatest effect."

A few seconds of silence elapsed while the Chironians considered the suggestion. Their expressions seemed to say it couldn't do any harm, but it probably wouldn't change very much. "Is the case strong enough to turn the whole Army round in a moment?" Kath asked doubtfully at last "We have no proof about Padawski and the bombings. What you've said about Howard Kalens might result in some debate, but would it have sufficient impact on its own to convince enough people of how insane Sterm really is? Now, if we could *prove* all the incidents, all at the same time—"

"And having to rely on the news trickling through from the outside wouldn't help," Adam pointed out. "There have been so many rumors already. It would be more likely to just fizzle out."

"It's an idea," Bernard said, looking up at Lechat. "But it needs more of what Kath said—*impact.*"

"I agree, I agree," Lechat told them. "But we only know what we know, and we can only do what we can do. Surely doing so is not going to make things any worse. Will you try it?"

Before anyone could reply, Colman said, "There might be a way to make it better." Everyone looked at him. He swept his eyes around quickly. "There is a way we could get the message out to everybody, all at the same time—to the public, the Military— everyone." He looked around again. The others waited. "Through the Communications Center up in the ship," he said. "Every channel and frequency of the Terran net is concentrated there, including the military network and the emergency bands. We could broadcast from there on all of them simultaneously. You couldn't make much more impact than that." He sat back and looked around again to invite reactions.

Bernard was nodding but with evident reservations. "True," he agreed. "But it's up in the ship, not down here. And it must be strongly protected. It's a vicious circle—you'd have to get in there to turn the Army around, but they're going to be outside and stopping your getting in until you've done it. How can you break out of it?"

"And from what we've heard, their command structure is all a shambles anyway," Adam commented. "Could a penetration operation like that be organized now?"

Colman had been expecting something like that. "I know one unit of the Army that could do it," he said. "And they operate best when nobody's trying to organize them."

"Which one is that?" Leon asked from the screen, sounding dubious but also interested.

Colman grinned faintly and gestured across the room. "The same one that brought you Veronica and Celia."

A gleam of hope had come into Lechat's eyes. "Do you really think they might be able to pull something off?"

"If anyone could, they could," Veronica said from across the room. "That bunch could clean out Fort Knox without anyone knowing."

"She's right," Celia agreed simply.

Everybody looked at Colman again, this time with a new interest. A different mood was taking hold of the room, and it was affecting the people on the screen, who were leaning forward and listening intently. So far it was just an idea, but already it was beginning to hook all of them.

Bernard was rubbing his lip slowly as he thought about it. He caught Lechat's eye and appeared worried. "The message would have to go out live from there," he said slowly. "With active opposition around, you wouldn't want to go risking complications with remote links into it." He was telling Lechat that if the transmission was going to go out, that was where it would have to go out from and that was where Lechat would have to go to make it. But more to the point, as Lechat well knew, Bernard was saying that Celia would have to go there too; what she had to say couldn't come second-hand through anybody else.

Lechat pursed his lips for a second, and then nodded curtly. "I'll do it," he said simply. He averted his eyes for a moment longer, and then looked across at Celia. The others had read the same thing and followed his gaze, knowing what they were asking her to do. Colman could see the torment in her eyes as she looked back at Lechat. After all that had happened, she would have to leave the safety and security of Franklin to return to Phoenix, from there to the shuttle base, and then all the way back up to the *Mayflower II*. There was no other way.

Celia was already prepared for it. She nodded. Nothing remained to be said. The room had become very quiet.

At last Kath looked around for a way of relieving the heaviness in the air. "How will you get them up to the ship?" she asked Colman.

"I'll leave that to Sirocco," he replied. "He'll know more about the score at the base. We've had a unit there this evening, but they're probably back by now."

"How do you know he'll go along with it?" Barbara asked.

"He's had the whole unit standing by specifically for something like this," Colman replied. "He's waiting for news right now. That's why I'm here."

Celia had become very thoughtful in the last few seconds. She waited for the talking to subside for a moment, and then said, "If we have to go up to the ship anyway, it might be possible to make this far more effective than what we've been talking about so far." She paused, but nobody interrupted. "I know where the people who have been arrested are being held. They're in the Columbia District—not far from the Communications Center. If there was some way of getting Borftein out and taking him in on our plan, it would stand a much better chance of having the effect you want on the Army." Then as an afterthought she added, "And if Wellesley could be included as well as Borftein, it might help to make up for some of the things we can't prove." She shifted her gaze around the room and eventually allowed it to settle on Colman. "But I don't know if something like that would be possible."

"What do you think?" Bernard asked Colman after a short silence. "Could it be done?"

"I don't know. It depends on the situation. Maybe. That's something else we'll have to leave to Sirocco to decide."

Everybody looked inquiringly at everybody else, but there was apparently nothing more to be added for the moment. At last Colman rose to his feet. "Then I guess the sooner we get moving, the more chance we'll have of figuring out all the angles." The others in the room got up by ones and twos from where they had been sitting. Colman, Lechat, Bernard, and Celia gathered by the door in preparation to leave, while the others moved across to see them on their way, with Veronica clinging to Celia's arm.

"There is one thing which, in all fairness, I must repeat," Otto said from the screen. They turned and looked back at him. "We cannot alter our basic decision in any way. If Sterm becomes threatening, we will be forced to react. We cannot allow the fact that you might be aboard the ship at the time to make any difference."

Lechat nodded. "That was already understood," he replied grimly.

While the others passed through into the hallway of the apartment, Kath turned back toward the screen and touched a control on the compad. All of the views vanished except that of Leon, which expanded to fill the whole screen just as Thelma moved away out of the picture to leave him on his own. "We ought to commence evacuating the *Kuan-yin*," Kath said. "It looks as if it could be dangerous up there very soon."

"I had already come to that conclusion," Leon replied. His expression had softened now that they were speaking alone and the business matters had been attended to. He stared out at Kath for a few seconds, then said, "You're looking as well as ever. Are the children keeping fine too?"

"As ever," Kath told him and smiled. "And yours, Lurch?"

Leon grinned. "Mischievous, but they're fun." He paused for a moment. "He seems to be a good man. You should be very happy until whenever. I hope nothing happens to them. They are all brave people. I admire them."

"I hope so too," Kath said with feeling. "I ought to go now and see them off. Take care, Leon."

"You too." The image vanished from the screen.

Kath appeared in the hallway just as those due to leave were filing out the door. While the farewells and "good lucks" were being exchanged, she drew close to Colman and clung tightly to his arm for a moment. "Come back," she whispered.

He returned the squeeze reassuringly. "You'd better believe it."

"I wish I felt as confident as you sound. It seems risky."

"Not when you've got the best outfit that the Army ever produced on your side," he told her.

"Oh, is that what it is? I never realized. You never told me you were with a special unit."

"Classified information," Colman murmured. Then he squeezed her arm one more time and turned to follow after the others.

◈ CHAPTER THIRTY-FOUR ◈

Outside, dawn was creeping into the sky as Stanislau sat before a portable communications panel in one corner of the mess hall of the Omar Bradley Block, frowning at the mnemonics appearing on the screen and returning coded commands with intermittent movements of his fingers. Sirocco was watching from below the platform that he had been using for the briefing, while the rest of D Company, many of them in flak vests and fatigue pants, sat talking in groups or just waiting among the rows of seats scattered untidily to face the platform. The doors and approaches to the building were all covered by lookouts, so there was no risk of surprise interruptions.

Sirocco had devised a plan for getting the Company up to the ship and into the Communications Center, but it hinged on Stanislau's being able to alter the orders posted for the day, which were derived from schedules held in one of the military logistics computers. Lechat, who was standing nearby with Celia and Colman, had called for a test-run to make sure that Stanislau could do it, since if that part of the scheme didn't work none of the rest could. Sirocco had suspended the briefing to resolve the issue there and then.

Bernard was watching with interest over Stanislau's shoulder. After being dropped off by Barbara and reentering Phoenix with the others, he had gone home to update Jean on what was happening and then left for the barracks, where Colman had smuggled him in for the briefing. It was just as well that he had; the scheme that Sirocco finally evolved required some familiarity with the *Mayflower II*'s electrical systems, and while Colman had been prepared to have a crack at that part of it, Bernard was the obvious choice. So Bernard was going up to the *Mayflower II* too. He would explain everything to Jean later, he decided.

Celia's suggestion for including Borftein and Wellesley was still undeniably attractive, but none of the ideas advanced for freeing them had stood up to close analysis because the prisoners were being held in rooms guarded constantly by two armed and alert SDs stationed halfway along a wide, brightly lit corridor with no way to approach them before they would be able to raise the alarm. Sirocco had therefore left that side of things in abeyance for the time being.

Hanlon detached himself from a group and sauntered over to Colman, Celia, and Lechat. Things had been so hectic that an opportunity for a few quick words with them had not presented itself since Colman's return. "Well, I see there's no need to ask how things went on your side, Steve. I take it that Veronica's in safe hands now."

Colman nodded. "Her friends showed up, and she's in Franklin. It all went fine." He turned his head to Celia. "This is Bret. He got Veronica off the base."

Celia managed a smile. Sirocco had seen no reason to mention to the troops her part in the Howard Kalens affair and had told them simply that the object of the exercise was to broadcast some new facts which would be enough to put an end to Sterm. "I'm not sure what I'm supposed to say," she told Hanlon. "I'll never be able to thank you both enough. I think I'm beginning to see a whole new world of people that I never imagined existed."

"Ah, well, it's not over yet," Hanlon said. His eyes twinkled for a second as he remembered something else. "Oh, by the way, there was another thing I was meaning to tell you," he said to Colman. "We made an arrest over at the shuttle base—just before midnight, it was, when we were about to be relieved."

"Really? Who?" Colman asked.

"Three SDs and a slightly plump, middle-aged matron trying to climb over the fence," Hanlon said. "The woman was stuck on the top and making quite a fuss. Now, what do you imagine they could have been trying to run away from?"

"I have no idea," Colman said, grinning. Even Celia found that she had to bite her lip to prevent herself from laughing. "So what happened? Did you send them back up?"

Hanlon shook his head. "Ah, why be vindictive? We got her off and sent them all on their way. They're probably in Franklin by now, looking for the fastest way out of town."

At that moment Stanislau emitted a triumphant shout, and Bernard straightened up behind him to look across at Colman. "He's done it!" Bernard exclaimed. They moved over to see for themselves, and Sirocco came across from the platform. The rest of the mess hall quieted down. The screen in front of Stanislau was showing the day's duty roster for the entire infantry brigade.

"Is that just a copy file, or are you displaying the master schedule?" Lechat inquired.

"It's the master," Bernard said. "He's got overwrite privileges too. I just watched him try it."

"This looks like what we want, chief," Stanislau said to Sirocco, and pointed to one of the entries. Sirocco leaned closer to peer at the screen.

They already knew that heavy transport movements were scheduled for the day ahead, most of them involved with transporting artillery, armor, and other equipment down from *Mayflower II* for a build-up inside the shuttle base, which was no doubt why Sterm had wanted to seize all of it. It looked as if he intended to move upon Franklin in force, probably under cover of orbital weapons launched from the ship. With the coup in the *Mayflower II* now accomplished and the ship evidently considered secure, the SDs who had been concentrated there were being moved down to strengthen what was to become a fortified base for surface operations, and some regular units were being moved up to take over duties aloft. Stanislau had identified an order for C company to embark at 1800 hours that evening for transfer to the *Mayflower II,* which was just the kind of thing that Sirocco had been hoping for. Sirocco was willing to gamble that with a busy day ahead and lots to do, nobody would have time to question a late change in the orders.

"Let's see you overwrite it," Lechat said.

Stanislau touched in some commands, and immediately all references to C Company were replaced by references to D Company. Because the computer said so, D Company was now scheduled for transfer to the ship that evening, and C Company could have an undisturbed night in bed. Stanislau promptly reset the references to their original forms. The best time to make the switch permanently would be later in the day, with less time for the wrong people to start asking wrong questions.

Lechat nodded and seemed satisfied. "That gets us up there," he said. "Now what about getting into the Communications Center?"

Stanislau entered more commands. A different table of information appeared on the screen. "SD guard details and timetable for posts inside the Columbia District tonight," Stanislau said. They would refrain from doing anything to that one until the last moment.

"Good enough?" Sirocco asked, cocking an eyebrow at Lechat.

Lechat nodded. "It's amazing," he murmured.

"Well done, Stanislau," Sirocco said. "Let's hope that the repeat performance will be as good later today."

"You can count on it, sir," Stanislau said.

Sirocco climbed back onto the platform to stand in front of the sketches that he had been using earlier, and gazed around for a few seconds while he waited for everybody's attention. "Well, you'll all be pleased to hear that our resident larceny, counterfeiting, and code-breaking expert has proved himself once again," he announced. "Phases one and four appear to be feasible, as we discussed." To one side and below the platform, Stanislau turned with a broad, toothy grin and clasped his hands above his head to acknowledge the chorus of murmured applause and low whistles, rendered enthusiastically, but quietly enough not to attract undue attention to the block at that time of the morning.

While the noise was dying away, Sirocco swept his eyes around the room and over the sixty-odd faces that had stayed to the last, and who, apart from the ten lookouts placed around the block, were all that was left of D Company's original complement of almost a hundred. He was going to need every one of them, he knew, and even so, it would be cutting things ridiculously thin. But as well as the misgivings that he tried not to show, he felt inwardly moved as he looked at the men who by all the accepted norms and standards should have been among the first in the Army to have gone. But apart from the SD units, D Company's record was second to none. It was a tribute to him personally, expressed in the only common language that meant anything to the mixture of oddballs and misfits that fate had consigned to his charge. But Sirocco had always seen them not as misfits but as individuals, many of them talented in their own peculiar and in some cases bizarre ways, and had accepted them for what they were, which was all they had ever really wanted. But the term misfit was a relative one, he had come to realize. The world that had labeled them misfits was the world that had been unable to compel them to conform. Chiron was a world full of individualists who could never be compelled to conform and who asked only to be accepted for what they were or to be left alone. Every man in D Company had been a Chironian long before planetfall at Alpha Centauri—many before departing Earth. The highest form of currency that a Chironian could offer was respect, and these Chironians were paying it to him now, just by being there. Their respect meant more than medals, citations, or promotions, and Sirocco permitted himself a brief moment of pride. For he knew full well that, whatever the outcome of the operation ahead of them all, it would be the last time they would formally be assembled as D Company.

"Very well," he said. "Stanislau has had his encore. Now let's get back to business.

"First, let's recap the main points. The primary object is to get into the Communications Center and secure it while the transmission goes out; and after that to hold it and hope that enough of the Army reacts quickly enough to take the pressure off. Okay?" There were no questions, so Sirocco continued. "The big risk is that SD reinforcements will be brought up from the surface. If that happens, they'll have to dock at the Vandenberg bays, and that's why we've got

Armley's section there to stop them. What do you do if you can't hold them, Mike?" Sirocco asked, looking down at the front row.

"Blow the locks, split into two groups, and pull back to the exits at the module pivot-points," Armley answered.

"Right. The other—yes, question?"

"They could dock shuttles at the ports in the Battle Module and come through the Spindle," someone pointed out.

"Yes, I was about to come to that," Sirocco replied. He lifted his head a fraction to address the whole room again. "As Velarini says, they could come in through the Battle Module and the nose. The Battle Module is the main problem. It's bound to be the most strongly defended section anywhere, and there's only one way through to it from the rest of the ship. Therefore we assault it directly only if all else fails. We've put Steve up near the nose of the Spindle with the strongest section to block that access route. Steve's task is to stop any SDs getting out and, more important, to stop Sterm and his people from getting in if things go well and they realize they can't hold the rest of the ship. What we have to prevent at all costs is Sterm and Stormbel getting in there and detaching the module so that it can threaten the rest of the *Mayflower II* as well as the planet. Yes, Simmonds?"

"It could still detach, even without Sterm."

"That's a gamble we'll have to take," Sirocco said. "Sterm will hardly order them to fire on the rest of the ship if he's in it."

"Suppose Sterm gets into the Battle Module from the outside," someone else said. "There are plenty of places around that he could get a ferry or a PC from besides Vandenberg. He's only got to hop across a couple of miles. It wouldn't need a surface shuttle."

Sirocco hesitated for a moment, then nodded reluctantly. "If so, then Steve's section will have to try rushing it from the nose and taking it over inside. But that's only as a last resort, as I said." He looked across at Colman, who returned a heavy nod.

"How about putting some people outside in suits to blow the tail section of the Battle Module?" Carson suggested from the second row back.

"We're looking into that. It will depend on how many people

Steve can spare. Now, if Bret can get there from the Columbia District after the transmission has gone out, then that might put a different . . ." Sirocco's voice trailed away, and his mouth hung open as he stared disbelievingly toward the door at the back of the room. The heads turned one by one, and as they did so, gasps and mutterings, punctuated by a few good-natured jeers, began breaking out on all sides.

Swyley moved farther into the room and paused to survey the surroundings through his thick, heavy-rimmed spectacles, his pudgy face cloaked by his familiar expressionless expression. Driscoll was with him, and more were marching in behind them. Sirocco blinked and swallowed hard as they dispersed among the empty seats at the back and began sitting down. Harding, Baker, Faustzman, Vanderheim . . . Simpson, Westley, Johnson—all of them. They were all back. "We heard you could use some help, chief," Driscoll announced. "Couldn't leave it all to the amateurs." Ribald comments and hoots of derision greeted the remark.

Sirocco watched for a second longer, and then pulled himself together quickly. "Enjoy your vacation, Swyley?" he inquired with a note of forced sarcasm in his voice. "Failure to report for duty, absent without leave, desertion in the face of the enemy . . . the whole book, in fact. Well, consider yourselves reprimanded, and sit down. There's a lot to go over, and we're all going to need some rest today. The situation is that—" Sirocco stopped speaking and looked curiously at the figure that he hadn't noticed before—an unfamiliar face by the side of Swyley, who was still standing. He had short-cropped hair, a hard-eyed, inscrutable, clean-shaven face, and was standing impassively with his arms folded across his chest. "Who's this?" Sirocco said. "He's not from D Company."

"Ex-sergeant Malloy of the SDs," Swyley said. "He decided he'd had enough and quit over a month ago. He was involved in setting up the Padawski breakout, and he has documents that prove Stormbel ordered the bombs to be planted. He wants to go public." Swyley shrugged. "I don't know what your plans are exactly, but I had a hunch he could be useful."

The room responded with murmurs of amazement, but most of

those present didn't realize the significance. Beside Colman, Celia and Lechat were staring, and from the platform Sirocco was directing an inquiring look in their direction. Celia turned her head to look at Colman. "I don't believe this," she whispered. "Who is that corporal?"

"D Company's resident miracle worker," Colman answered, but his voice was distant as he fitted the new pieces into the picture in his head. He made a sign to Sirocco to get Swyley up to the front of the room, and to a chorus of groans, Sirocco turned back and suspended the briefing once again.

Five minutes later Swyley and Malloy had gone into conference in a corner with Celia and Lechat, and Colman stood apart with Sirocco and Hanlon, discussing tactical details. "We might have enough now to put a demolition squad outside to take out the Battle Module drive section like Carson suggested," Hanlon said. "Even if Sterm gets in there it would give more protection to the rest of the ship."

"I'll have to keep that option open until we see how things shape up," Colman said. "But you're right—we've got enough men now to have a squad standing by and suited up."

"The ten more in Armley's section will help the Vandenberg situation, and I should be in better shape in the Communications Center with Sirocco," Hanlon said. "So where does that leave us?"

"All set, except for springing Borftein and Wellesley," Colman said. "Now that we've got Malloy, those two would make the whole thing cast-iron." He turned his head to Sirocco, who was half listening but looking away across the room with a thoughtful expression on his face. "Had any more thoughts about that?" Colman asked.

"Mmm? . . ." Sirocco responded distantly.

"Borftein and Wellesley."

"I've been thinking about that . . ." Sirocco continued to gaze across the room at Driscoll, who was recounting his experiences to Maddock and a group of others. "He's pretty good, isn't he," Sirocco said, still half to himself.

It took a second for Colman to realize what Sirocco was talking about. "Yes . . . Why? What are you—"

"Come over for a second. I want to ask him something." Sirocco led Colman, and Hanlon followed. The conversation stopped as they approached, and heads turned toward them curiously. "Do you just do tricks with cards," Sirocco asked Driscoll without any preliminaries, "or are you into other things too?"

Driscoll looked at him in surprise. "Well, it depends on what you mean," he said cautiously. Then after a second he nodded. "But, yes— I can do other things too, a pretty diversified act, you might say."

Sirocco turned his head towards Hanlon. "Get a couple of pistol belts and sidearms from the Armory, Bret," he said. "Let's find out just how good this character really is. I think he might be able to help us solve our problem."

❁ CHAPTER THIRTY-FIVE ❁

General Kazimiera Stormbel did not make mistakes, and he was not accustomed to being held responsible for the mistakes of others; people under him tended to find out early on that they did not make mistakes. Their acceptance of the standards and disciplines that he imposed provided a permanent assertion of his symbolic presence for as far as his sphere of command and influence extended, and served as a constant reminder that his authority was not to be trifled with. Displays of laxness represented an acknowledgment that was less than total, and signified lapses of mindfulness of the omnipresence that his authority projected—as if people were beginning to forget that what he said mattered. Stormbel didn't like that. He didn't like people acting as if he didn't matter.

The bureaucrats who had mismanaged the sprawling politico-military machine that had come to dominate the North American continent had been unable or unwilling to recognize his worth and dedication while they heaped honors and favors on sons of spineless sycophants and generals' blue-eyed protégés groomed to the movie image at West Point, and he felt no compassion for them now as the laser link from Earth brought news of nuclear devastation across the length and breadth of Africa, and of titanic clashes between armies in Central Asia. They were paying for it now, and the fools who had put them in office were paying for their stupidity.

Wellesley and the Congress had tried to perpetuate the same injustices by eclipsing him with Borftein because he hadn't graduated from the right places or possessed the right family credentials. They had tried to fob him off with the command of what they had seen as a proficient but small and unimportant corps of specialists. They had all paid too. Now they all knew who he was and where they stood. He had no regrets about Ramisson's death; it underlined the lesson more forcefully than any words could have done. He was only sorry he hadn't made a cleaner sweep by shooting them all.

Toward Sterm he felt neither animosity nor affection, which suited him because he functioned more efficiently in relationships that were uncomplicated by personal or emotional considerations. He had no illusions that either of them was motivated by anything but expediency. Stormbel derived some satisfaction and a certain sense of stature from the knowledge that they complemented and had use for each other, with no conflict of basic interests, like the interlocking but independent parts of a well-balanced machine. Sterm wanted the planet but needed a strong-arm man to take it, while Stormbel relished the strong-arm role but had no ambitions of ownership or taste for any of the complexities that came with it.

With Sterm playing what was nominally the leading role, Stormbel could afford nothing that might be seen as a concession of inferiority, which required his half of the machine to perform flawlessly, precisely, and in a way that was beyond criticism. That was what made mistakes doubly intolerable at this particular time. But what made the whole thing completely baffling and all the more galling was that the escorts and their charge had not only checked in on time, but had actually boarded the return shuttle—having passed safely through all the riskier parts of the agenda—before vanishing without a trace. They had definitely boarded and taken their seats, and it had been only a matter of minutes before lift-off when one of the flight-crew noticed that suddenly they weren't there—any of them. The SD guards at the boarding gate had all known what Celia Kalens looked like, and they had been under special instructions to watch for her, but none of them had seen her when the escorts came out of the shuttle after somehow losing her; and shortly after that, the escorts had disappeared into the base and were never seen again. Nobody remembered seeing them around the base later; nobody had seen them at the perimeter; nobody had flown them out; and an intensive search carried on all through the night had failed to locate them anywhere. It was impossible, but it had happened.

Sterm was not a person to waste his time and energy with futile melodramatics and accusations, but Stormbel knew full well that he wouldn't forget—and neither would Stormbel forget. The Chironians were behind it, he was certain, just as they had been behind the subversion of the Army and even of some of Stormbel's own troopers. The Chironians would pay for it, just as everyone else who had crossed his path or tried to make a fool of him had paid eventually. They would pay the moment someone offered resistance when his troops moved into Franklin. His orders were quite explicit.

"The build-up at Canaveral is proceeding on schedule and will be completed before midnight," he informed Sterm at a midday staff meeting in the Columbia District's Government Center. "The greater part of Phoenix is being abandoned as we assumed would be unavoidable, but the key points are secure and the wastage among the regular units has been checked. Transfer of SD forces to the surface will be completed by early evening, with the exception of those units being held to cover the Battle Module, the Columbia District, and Vandenberg. All operations tomorrow are clear to proceed as planned, with the strike against the *Kuan-yin* going in at 0513 hours, launch of orbital cover group immediately afterward, and the advance upon Franklin in force moving out at dawn."

Sterm nodded slowly as he ticked off the points one by one in his mind, looking at Stormbel coolly, then turned to Gaulitz, one of the senior scientists, who was sitting with some advisers to one side of the room. "Let us be certain about the *Kuan-yin*," he said. "The success of the entire operation is at stake. You are quite sure?"

Gaulitz nodded emphatically. "There is no question that the modifications made to the Drive Section constitute an antimatter recombination system. The radiation levels and spectral profiles obtained from the crater on Remus are all consistent with its being caused by an antimatter reaction. The evidence of gamma-induced transmutations, the distribution of neutron-activated isotopes, the pattern of residual—"

Sterm held up a hand. "Yes, yes, we have been through all that."

Gaulitz nodded hastily and touched a control to bring a view of the *Kuan-yin* onto the room's main display screen. It showed Chironian shuttles at all the docking ports, and more standing a few miles off and apparently waiting to move in. "This is a further corroboration from views obtained this morning," he said. "All indications are that the Chironians have evacuated the vessel, which supports the contention of its being cleared for action."

Sterm studied the view in silence. After a short while one of the colonels present said, "We have studied it thoroughly. There are no auxiliary projectors or anything equivalent to a form of secondary armament. The only direction that it can fire in is sternward from the tail-dish. With eight missiles the odds of at least one getting through would be better than ninety-eight percent. With sixteen the chances of failure are about as near zero as you can get."

The *Kuan-yin*'s lower orbit put it out of synchronism with the *Mayflower II* and resulted in the two vessels being shielded from each other by Chiron's mass for a period of thirty-two minutes every three-and-a-quarter hours. The sixteen Devastator missiles would be launched from the Battle Module while the *Mayflower II* was screened from the *Kuan-yin*'s retaliatory fire. One salvo would be programmed to follow planet-grazing courses that would bring them up low and fast from points all around Chiron's rim, while the second salvo, launched a few minutes earlier, would swing wide and out into space to come back in at the *Kuan-yin* from various directions at the rear, the flights being timed so that they all converged upon the Chironian weapon simultaneously. A mass the size of the *Kuan-yin* could not maneuver rapidly, and the worst-case simulations run on the computers had shown an overwhelming margin in favor of the attack, whatever defensive tactics might be employed.

"The calculations and simulations have been verified?" Sterm said, looking at Gaulitz.

"Thoroughly and repeatedly. There is no risk that the *Mayflower II* might be exposed at any time," Gaulitz answered.

There were no more major points to discuss. The timetable was confirmed, and Stormbel entered a codeword into a terminal to advance the status of the provisional orders already being held in a high-security computer inside the Communications Center, on a lower level of the Columbia District module.

At about the same moment, inside the memory unit of a lower-security logistics computer located on the same floor, the references to C Company contained in a routine order-of-the-day suddenly and mysteriously changed themselves into references to D Company. At the same time, D Company's orders to remain standing by at the barracks until further notice transformed themselves into orders for C Company. Ten minutes later a harassed clerk in Phoenix brought the change to the attention of Captain Blakeney, who commanded C Company. Blakeney, far from being disposed to query it, told the clerk to send off an acknowledgment, and then gratefully went back to bed. Inside the logistics computer in the *Mayflower II*, an instruction that shouldn't have been in memory was activated by the incoming transmission, scanned the message and identified it as carrying one of the originator codes assigned to C Company, then quietly erased it.

◎ CHAPTER THIRTY-SIX ◎

Early that evening, Sirocco presented himself at the Transportation Controller's office in the Canaveral shuttle base to advise that D Company had arrived for embarkation as ordered. Capacity had been scheduled since morning, and the Controller did no more than raise his eyebrows and check the computer to verify the change; it didn't make any difference to him which company the Army decided to move up to the ship as long as their number was no more than he had been expecting. An hour later the company marched off the shuttle in smart order, and after clearing the docking-bay area in Vandenberg, dispersed inconspicuously to their various destinations around the *Mayflower II*. Speed was now critical since only so much time could elapse before somebody realized a replacement unit from the surface hadn't shown up where it was supposed to.

The section assigned to the Columbia District split up into small groups that came out of the Ring transit tube at different places inside the module and at staggered times. Colman, Hanlon, and Driscoll got off with Lechat, who was dressed to obscure his appearance since he was presumably still high on Sterm's wanted list. They rendezvoused with Carson and three others a few minutes later, then they headed via a roundabout route for the Francoise restaurant, which was situated on a public level immediately below the Government Center complex.

All entrances into the Center itself were guarded. Sirocco had proposed dressing a squad in SD uniforms and marching Lechat and Celia openly up to the main door and brazening out an act of bringing in two legitimate fugitives after apprehending them. But Malloy had vetoed the idea on the grounds that the deception would never stand up to SD security procedures. Then Lechat had suggested a less dramatic and less risky method. As a regular customer of the Franchise for many years, he was a close friend of the manager and had spent many late nights discussing politics with the staff until way after closing. They all knew Lechat, and he was sure he could rely on them. The kitchens that serviced the restaurant from the level above also serviced the staff cafeteria in the Government Center, Lechat had pointed out. There had to be service elevators, laundry chutes, garbage ducts—something that connected through from the rear of the Franchise.

The party arrived at the little-used connecting passage running behind the Franchise and its neighboring establishments, and the soldiers waited among the shadows of the surrounding entrances and stairways while Lechat tapped lightly on the rear door of the restaurant. After a few seconds the door opened and Lechat disappeared inside. Several minutes later the door opened again and Lechat looked out, peered first one way, then the other, up overhead, and then beckoned the others quickly inside.

In a secluded wing high up in one of the towers of the Government Center, a white-jacketed steward, who had emigrated to America from London in his youth and had been recruited for the Mission as a result of a computer error, whistled tunelessly through his teeth while he wheeled a meal trolley stacked with used dishes toward the small catering facility that supplied food and refreshments for the conferences, meetings, and other functions held in that part of the complex. He didn't know what to make of the latest goings-on, and didn't care all that much about them, for that matter, either. It was all the same to him. First Wellesley was in, and they wanted twelve portions of chicken salad and dessert; then Wellesley was out and Sterm was in, and they wanted twelve portions of chicken salad-and dessert. It didn't make any difference to him who—

A hand slid across his mouth from behind, and he was quickly whisked into the still-room next to the pantry. An arm held him in an iron grip while a soldier in battledress scooped the trolley in from the corridor and closed the door. There were more of them in there, with a civilian. They looked mean and in no mood for fooling around.

The hand over his mouth loosened a fraction after the door was closed. "Gawd! Wot's goin' on? Who—?" Somebody jabbed him in the ribs. He shut up.

"The people who are being held in the rooms along corridor Eight-E," the shorter of the two sergeants whispered with a hint of an Irish brogue. "You take their food in?" The steward gulped and nodded vigorously. "When is the evening meal due?"

"Abaht ten minutes," the steward said. "I'm supposed ter collect it next door any time nah." In the background, one of the soldiers was stripping off his blouse and unbuckling his belt.

"Start taking off the jacket and the vest," the Irish sergeant ordered. "And while you're doing it, you can tell us the routine."

Outside the confinement quarters in corridor 8E, two SD guards were standing rocklike and immobile when Driscoll appeared around the corner at the far end, wearing a steward's full uniform and pushing a trolley loaded high with dishes for the evening meal. Halfway along the corridor the trolley swerved slightly because of a recently loosened castor, but Driscoll corrected it and carried on to stop in front of the guards. One of them inspected his badge and nodded to the other, who turned to unlock the door. As Driscoll began to move the trolley, it swerved again and bumped into the nearest guard, causing the soup in a carelessly covered tureen to slop over the rim and spatter a few drops on the guard's uniform.

"Oh, Christ!" Driscoll began fussing with a napkin to clean it off, in the process managing to trail a corner of it through the soup and brush it against the hem of the second guard's jacket as he turned back from the door.

Driscoll moaned miserably and started dabbing it off, but was shoved away roughly. "Get off, you clumsy asshole," the guard growled. Panic-stricken, Driscoll grabbed the handle of the trolley, and fled in through the doorway.

Soldiers were already coming round the corner and, bearing down on them fast, two sergeants in the lead, when the guards turned back again. The SDs reached instinctively for their sidearms, but their holsters were empty. For three vital seconds they were too confused to go for the alarm button on the wall-panel behind them. Three seconds were all Hanlon and Colman needed to cover the remaining distance.

Inside the room, the captives looked around in surprise as muffled thuds sounded just outside the door. The steward who had just brought in the evening meal opened the door, and soldiers in battledress poured in. Wellesley gasped as he saw Lechat with them. "Paul!" he exclaimed. "Where have you been hiding? You're the only one they didn't pick up. What—"

Lechat cut him off with a wave of his hand. "Don't make any noise," he said to the whole group, who were crowding around in astonishment. "Everything is okay." He signaled Borftein over with another wave of his hand. Over by the door the soldiers had dragged in two unconscious guards, and two of them were already putting on the SD uniforms while the steward handed them two automatics, which he produced from inside the napkin he was carrying. "There isn't a lot of time," Lechat advised Wellesley and Borftein. "We have to get you downstairs and into the Communications Center. Now listen, and I'll give you a quick rundown on the situation . . ."

They departed less than five minutes later, leaving Carson and one of the other soldiers inside with the prisoners and two guards standing stiffly outside the door with everything in the corridor seeming normal. Hanlon took Wellesley, Borftein, and Lechat to a storeroom near the Communications Center where they could remain out of sight. Colman followed Driscoll to a machinery compartment on the lowermost level where an emergency bulkhead door, unguarded but sealed from the outside and protected by alarm circuits, led through to the motor room of an elevator bank in the civic offices adjoining the Government Center. Colman traced, checked, and neutralized the alarms. Then he double-checked what he had done, and nodded to Driscoll, who was waiting by the door; Driscoll opened the latches and swung the door outward while Colman held his breath. The alarms remained inactive. Sirocco was waiting on the other side with Bernard Fallows, who was wearing engineer's coveralls and carrying a toolbox.

"Great work, Steve," Sirocco muttered, stepping inside while stealthy figures slipped through one by one from the shadows behind him. "How did the Amazing Driscoll go over?"

"His best performance ever. Everything okay out there?"

"It seems to be. How about Borftein and Wellesley?" Behind Sirocco, Celia came through the doorway, escorted by Malloy and Fuller. Stanislau was behind, carrying a field compack.

Colman nodded. "Gone to the storeroom with Hanlon and Lechat. Everything was quiet upstairs when we left."

Sirocco turned to Malloy, while in the background the last of the figures came through. "Okay, you know where to go. Hanlon should be there now with the others." Malloy nodded. "We'll make a soldier out of you yet," Sirocco said to Celia. "You're doing fine. Almost there now." Celia returned a thin smile but said nothing. She moved away with the others toward the far side of the compartment. Meanwhile Stanislau had set up the compack and was already calling up codes onto the screen. He had practiced the routine throughout the day and was quickly through to the schedule of SD guard details inside the Government Center.

The next part was going to be the trickiest. The information obtained by Stanislau had confirmed that the outside entrances to the complex, which had already been bypassed, were the most strongly guarded, and the three inner access points to the Communications Center itself—the main foyer at the front, the rear lobby, and a side entrance used by the staff—were covered by less formidable, three-man security teams. The problem with these security teams lay not so much with the physical resistance they might offer, but with their ability to close the Communications Center's electrically operated, armored doors and raise the alarm at the first sign of anything suspicious, which would leave Sirocco's force shut outside with no hope of achieving their objective and facing the bleak prospect of either fighting it out or surrendering to the guard reinforcements that would show up within minutes. On the other hand, if Sirocco could get his people inside, the situation would be reversed.

Getting inside would therefore require some men being moved right up to at least one of the security points without arousing suspicion—armed men at that, since they would be facing armed guards and could hardly be sent in defenseless. Malloy had again discouraged ideas of attempting to impersonate SDs. The only alternative came from Armley—a bluff, backed up with information manufactured by Stanislau, to the effect that regular troops were being posted to guard duties inside the complex as well as SDs, and providing reliefs from D Company. Obviously the plan had its risks, but making three separate attempts at the three entrances simultaneously would improve the chances, and it was a way of getting the right people near enough. In the end, Sirocco agreed. Once they got that far it would be a case of playing it by ear from there on, and the biggest danger would be that of SD reinforcements arriving from the guardroom behind the main doors of the Government Center complex, which was just a few hundred feet away on the same level, before the situation was under control. That was the part that Bernard Fallows had come along to handle.

Stanislau stood back from the compack and announced that the changes were completed. Sirocco peered at the screen, checked the entries in the revised schedule that Stanislau had produced, and nodded. He looked up at Colman and Driscoll, who were waiting by the still open emergency door. "Okay, the last ball's rolling," he told them. "On your way. Good luck."

"You too," Colman said. He and Driscoll left for the forward section of the Spindle to join Swyley, who, if all was going well, would already be organizing the men drifting in from various parts of the ship to block off the Battle Module.

Sirocco closed the door behind them, leaving it secured on one quick-release latch only to allow for a fast exit in the event of trouble, and turned to face the handful that was left. "Let's go," he said.

They crossed the machinery compartment in the direction the

others had taken, passed through an instrumentation bay, and ascended two flights of steel stairs to reenter the Government Center proper behind offices that had been empty since the end of the voyage, using a bulkhead hatch that Colman and Driscoll had opened on their way down. There was no sign of the others who had gone ahead. Here the group split three ways.

Stanislau and two others, moving carefully and making use of cover since they were now in a part of the complex that was being used, headed for the storeroom near the front foyer of the Communications Center to join Hanlon's group, which by now should have been swollen by the arrival of Celia, Malloy, and Fuller; Sirocco took three more to where another group was assembling near the approaches to the rear lobby; and Bernard with his toolbox strolled away casually on his own toward the corridor that connected the Communications Center to the main entrance of the complex.

Fifteen minutes later, inside an office that opened onto a passageway to the rear lobby of the Communications Center, an indignant office manager and two terrified female clerks were sitting on the floor with their hands clasped on the top of their heads, under the watchful eye of one of the soldiers who had burst in suddenly brandishing rifles and assault cannon. "What do you think you're trying to do?" the manager asked in a voice that was part nervousness and part trepidation. "We don't want to get mixed up in any of this."

"Just shut up and keep still, and you won't," Sirocco murmured without moving his eye from the edge of the almost-closed door. "We're just passing through." After a short silence Sirocco tensed suddenly. "Here they come . . . just two of them with a sergeant," he whispered. "Get ready. There are two guys talking by the coffee dispenser. We'll have to grab them too. Faustzman, you take care of them." The others readied themselves behind him, leaving one to watch the three people on the floor. Outside in the passageway, the SD detail on its way to relieve the security guards at the rear lobby was almost abreast of the door.

"*Freeze!*" Sirocco stepped out in front of them with his automatic drawn and Stewart beside him holding a leveled assault cannon.

Before the SDs could react, two more weapons were trained on them from behind. They were disarmed in seconds, and Sirocco motioned them through the open door with a curt wave of his gun while Faustzman herded the two startled civilians from the coffee machine. Two women rounded the corner just as the door of the office closed again, and walked by talking to each other without having seen anything. Moments later Sirocco left the office again with two privates. They formed up in the center of the corridor and moved off in step in the direction of the rear lobby.

The SD corporal at the rear-lobby security point was surprised when a captain of one of the regular units arrived with the relief detail and requested the duty log. "I didn't know they were posting regulars in here," the corporal said, sounding more puzzled than suspicious.

Sirocco shrugged. "Don't ask me. I thought it was because a lot of SDs are shipping down to Canaveral. I just do what the orders say."

"When was it changed, Captain?"

"I don't know, Corporal. Recently, I guess."

"I better check those orders." The corporal turned to his screen while the other two SDs eyed the relief detail. After a few seconds the corporal raised his eyebrows. "You're right. Oh, well, I guess it's okay." The other two SDs relaxed a fraction. The corporal called up the duty log and signed his team off. "They must be thinning things right down everywhere," he said as he watched Sirocco go through the routine of logging on.

"Looks like it," Sirocco agreed. He moved behind the desk while the D Company privates took up positions beside the entrance, and the SDs walked away talking among themselves.

A few seconds after the SDs disappeared, figures began popping from a fire exit behind the elevators on the far side of the lobby, and vanishing quickly and silently into the Communications Center.

Meanwhile, the SD sergeant at the main foyer was being conscientious. "I don't care what the computers say, Hanlon. This doesn't sound right to me. I have to check it out." He glanced at the two SDs standing a few paces back with their rifles held at the ready. "Keep an eye on 'em while I call the OOB." Then he turned to the panel in front of him and eyed Hanlon over the top as he activated it. "Hold it right where you are, buddy." Hanlon tensed but there was nothing he could do. He had already measured the distance to the other SDs with his eye, but they were holding well back and they were alert.

Suddenly, from the outer entrance to the foyer behind Hanlon, a firm, authoritative voice ordered, "Stop that!" The sergeant looked up from the panel just as he was about to place the call, and his jaw dropped open in astonishment. Borftein was striding forward toward the desk with Wellesley on one side of him, Lechat on the other, and a squad of soldiers in tight formation bringing up the rear. Celia and Malloy were between them. The two SD guards glanced uncertainly at each other.

The SD sergeant half rose from his seat. "Sir, I didn't—I thought—"

Borftein halted and stood upright and erect before the desk. "Whatever you thought was mistaken. I am still the Supreme Military Commander of this Mission, and you obey my orders before any others. Stand aside."

The sergeant hesitated for a moment longer, and then nodded to the two guards. Borftein and his party marched through, and Hanlon began posting men to secure the entrance. Another section of B Company materialized from a stairwell to one side of the foyer and vanished into the Communications Center, taking with them a few bewildered secretaries and office workers that they had bumped into on the way.

But no Borftein was present to save the situation at the side entrance. "I don't know anything about it," the SD Officer of the Bay said from the screen in reply to the call the guard there had put through. "Those orders are incorrect. Detain those men." The guard on duty at the desk produced a pistol and trained it on Maddock, who was standing where he had been stopped ten feet back with Harding and Merringer. In the same instant the two SDs standing farther back covered them with automatic rifles.

"*Down!*" Maddock yelled, and all three hurled themselves

sideways to get out of the line of fire as a smoke grenade launched from around a corner some distance behind them exploded at the entrance. Fire from the entranceway raked the area as the B Company squad broke cover and rushed forward through the smoke, but the first of them was still twenty feet away when the steel door slammed down and alarms began sounding throughout the Government Center.

Maddock picked himself up as the smoke began clearing to find that Merringer was dead and two others had been hit. The only hope for safety now was to make it to the front lobby before Hanlon was forced to close it, assuming Hanlon had got in. "Go first with four men," he shouted at Harding. "Fire at any SDs who get in the way. They know we're here now." He turned to the others. "Grab those two and stick with me. You two, stay with Crosby and cover the rear. Okay, let's get the hell out."

But SDs were already pouring out of the guardroom behind the main doors of the Government Center and racing along the corridor toward the communications facility while civilians flattened themselves against the walls to get out of the way, and others who had been working late peered from their offices to see what was happening. The engineer in coveralls who had been working inconspicuously at an opened switchbox through an access panel in the floor closed a circuit, and a reinforced fire-door halfway along the corridor closed itself in the path of the oncoming SDs. The SD major leading the detachment stared numbly at it for a few seconds while his men came to a confused halt around him. "Back to the front stairs," he shouted. "Go up to Level Three, and come down on the other side."

On the other side of the fire-door, Bernard dropped his tools and ran back to the front lobby of the Communications Center, praying that the alarm hadn't been raised from there. Hanlon and Stanislau were waiting outside the entrance with a handful of the others. Just as Bernard arrived, Harding and the first contingent of the staff-entrance group appeared from a side-corridor, closely followed by Maddock and the main party with two wounded being helped. Hanlon speeded them all on through into the Communications

Center, and the security door crashed shut moments before heavy boots began sounding from the stairwell nearby.

Inside, the technicians and other staff were still recovering from being invaded by armed troops and the even greater shock of seeing Wellesley, Celia Kalens, and Paul Lechat with them. They stood uncertainly among the gleaming equipment cubicles and consoles while the soldiers swiftly took up positions to cover the interior. Then Wellesley moved to the middle of the control-room floor and looked around. "Who is in charge here?" he demanded. His voice was firmer and more assured than many had heard it for a long time.

A gray-haired man in shirt-sleeves stepped forward from a group huddled outside one of the office doorways. "I am," he said, "McPherson—Communications and Datacenter Manager." After a short pause he added, "At your disposal."

Wellesley acknowledged with a nod and gestured toward Lechat. "Speed is essential," Lechat said without preamble. "We require access to all channels on the civil, public service, military, and emergency networks immediately . . ."

The Battle Module was a mile-long concentration of megadeath and mass destruction that sat on a base formed by the blunt nose of the Spindle, straddled by two pillars that extended forward to support the ramscoop cone and its field generators, and which contained the ducts to carry back to the midships processing reactors the hydrogen force-fed out of space when the ship was at ramspeed. Sleek, stark, menacing, and bristling with missile pods, defensive radiation projectors, and ports for deploying orbital and remote-operating weapons systems, it contained all of the *Mayflower II*'s strategic armaments, and could detach if need be to function as an independent, fully self-contained warship.

The Battle Module was not intended to be part of the *Mayflower II*'s public domain, and restriction of access to it had been one of its primary design criteria. Personnel and supplies entered the module via four enormous tubular extensions, known as feeder ramps, that telescoped from the main body of the ship to terminate in cupolas mating with external ports in the Battle Module, two forward and two aft its midships section. One pair of feeder ramps extended backward and inward from spherical housings at the forward ends of the two ramscoop-support pillars, and the other pair extended forward and inward from the six-sided, forwardmost section of the Spindle, called, appropriately enough, the Hexagon. As if having to get through the feeder ramps wasn't problem enough, the transit tubes, freight handling conveyors, ammunition rails, and other lines running through to them from the Spindle all came together at a single, heavily protected lock to pass through an armored bulkhead inside the Hexagon. Aft of the bulkhead, the lock faced out over a three-hundred-foot-long, wedge-shaped support platform upon which the various lines and tubes converged through a vast antechamber amid a jungle of girder and structural supports, motor housings, hoisting machinery, ducts, pipes, conduits, maintenance ladders, and catwalks. There was no other way through or round the bulkhead. The only route forward from the Hexagon was through the lock.

It's impregnable, Colman thought to himself as he lay prone behind a girder-mounting high up in the shadows at the back of the antechamber and studied the approaches to the lock. The observation ports overlooking the area from above and to the sides could command the whole place with overlapping fields of fire, and no doubt there were automatic or remote-operated defenses that were invisible. True, there was plenty of cover for the first stages of an assault, but the final rush would be suicidal . . . and probably futile since the lock doors looked strong enough to stop anything short of a tactical missile. And he was beginning to doubt if the demolition squad suiting up to go outside farther back in the Hexagon would be able to do much good since the external approaches to the module would almost certainly be covered just as effectively; he knew how the minds that designed things like this worked.

"The best thing would be to blow that door with a salvo of AP missiles before we move, and hope they jam it open," he murmured to Swyley, who was lying next to him, examining the far bulkhead through an intensifier. "Then maybe drench the lock with incendiary and go in under smoke."

"That's only the first door," Swyley reminded him, lowering the instrument from his eyes. "There are two of them. Whatever we do to that one won't stop them from closing the second one."

"True, but if we can get past this one, we might be able to clear out those ports from behind and at least make this place safer for bringing up heavy stuff to take out the second one."

"And then what?" Swyley said. "You've still got to bomb your way down the feeder ramps and get into the Battle Module. Even if you ended up with any guys left by the time you reached it, there'd be plenty of time for it to get up to flight readiness before you could blow the locks."

"Got any better ideas?" For once Swyley didn't.

At that moment the emergency tone sounded simultaneously from both their communicators, and warning bleeps and wails went up from places in the labyrinth all around. They looked at each other for a second. The noise died away as Colman fished his unit from his breast pocket and held it in front where both of them could watch it, while Swyley deactivated his own. A few seconds later, the faces of Wellesley, Borftein, and Lechat appeared on the tiny screen. Colman closed his eyes for a moment and breathed a long, drawn-out sigh of relief. "They made it," he whispered. "They're all in there."

"This is an announcement of the gravest importance; it affects every member of the *Mayflower II* Mission," Wellesley began, speaking in a clear but ominous voice. "I am addressing you all in my full capacity as Director of this Mission. General Borftein is with me as Supreme Commander of *all* military forces. Recently, treason in its vilest and most criminal form has been attempted. That attempt has failed. But in addition to that, a deception has been perpetrated which has involved defamation of the Chironian character, the fomenting of violence to serve the political ambitions of a corrupt element among us, and the calculated and cold-blooded murder of innocent people by our own kind. I do not have to remind you . . ."

"That has to give us the rest of the ship and the surface," Swyley said. "If the Army gets its act together and grabs Sterm before he gets a chance to head this way, then we might not have to go in there at all."

Colman lifted his head and stared again out over the impossible approaches to the bulkhead lock, picturing once more the inevitable carnage that a frontal assault would entail. Who on either side would stand to gain anything that mattered to them? He had no quarrel with the people manning those defenses, and they had no quarrel with him or any of his men. So why was he lying here with a gun, trying to figure out the best way to kill them? Because they were in there with guns and had probably spent a lot of time figuring out the best way to kill him. None of them knew why they were doing it. It was simply that it had always been done.

On the screen of the communicator, the view closed in on Celia as she began speaking in a slightly quavery but determined voice. But Colman only half heard. He was trying to make himself think the way a Chironian would think.

◎ CHAPTER THIRTY-SEVEN ◎

Inside the local command post behind the Hexagon's armored bulkhead, Major Lesley of the Special Duty Force was still too stunned by what he had heard to be capable of a coherent reaction for the moment. He stared at the companel where a screen showed a view from the Columbia District, where the SD guard commander had entered the Communications Center under a truce flag some minutes previously to talk with Borftein, and tried to separate the conflicting emotions in his head. Captain Jarvis, Lesley's adjutant officer, and Lieutenant Chaurez watched in silence while around the command post the duty staff averted their eyes and occupied themselves with their own thoughts. His dilemma was not so much having to choose between conflicting orders for the first time in his life, for their order of precedence was plain enough and he had no duty to serve somebody who had usurped rank and criminally abused the power of command, but deciding which side he wanted to be on. Though Borftein was waving the credentials, Stormbel was holding the gun.

Jarvis scanned the screen on the far side of the post. "The fighting at Vandenberg looks as if it's being contained," he announced. "Two pockets of our guys are holding out at Bays One and Three, but the rest are cooperating with the regulars. The regulars have pretty well secured the whole module already, Stormbel won't be getting any help from the surface through there."

"What's the latest from the surface?" Chaurez inquired.

"Confused but quiet at the barracks," Jarvis told him. "A lot of shooting inside the base at Canaveral. Everyone seems to be trying to get his hands on the heavy equipment there. A shuttle's on fire in one of the launch bays."

Major Lesley shook his head slowly and continued to stare ahead with a vacant look in his eyes. "This shouldn't be happening," he murmured. "They're not the enemy. They shouldn't be fighting each other."

Jarvis and Chaurez glanced at each other. Then Jarvis looked away as a new report came up on one of the screens. "Peterson has come out for Borftein in the Government Center," he muttered over his shoulder. "I guess it's all over in the Columbia District. That has to give them the whole Ring."

"So they'll be coming for the Spindle next," Chaurez said. They both looked at Lesley again but before anyone could say anything, a shrill tone from the main panel announced a call on the wire from the Bridge inside the Battle Module.

Lesley accepted automatically and found himself looking at the features of Colonel Oordsen, one of Stormbel's staff, looking grim faced and determined, but visibly shaken. "Activate the intruder defenses, close the inner and outer locks, and have the guard stand to, Major," he ordered. "Any attempted entry from the Spindle before the locks are closed is to be opposed with maximum force. Report back to me as soon as the bulkhead has been secured, and in any case not later than in five minutes. Is that understood?"

At that moment a local alarm sounded inside the command post. Within seconds the sounds of men running to stations came from the passageways and stairs to the rear. One of the duty crew was already flipping switches to collect report summaries, and Chaurez got up to go to the outer observation room just as the Watch Officer appeared in the doorway from the other side. "There are troops approaching the lock," the Watch Officer announced. "Regulars—thirty or more of them."

Leaving Colonel Oordsen peering out of the screen, Lesley rose and walked through the door in the steel wall dividing the command post from the observation room and looked down through one of the ports at the approaches to the lock below. Chaurez watched from the doorway, ignoring Oordsen's indignant voice as it floated through from behind. "Major Lesley, you have not been dismissed. Come back at once. What in hell's going on there? What are those alarms? Lesley, do you hear me?"

But Lesley was not listening as he gazed down at the platform below, which fanned outward from the arc lights above the lock to become indistinct in the darkness of the antechamber. Figures were moving slowly from the shadows by the transit tubes and freight rails, spread thinly at the back, but closing up as they converged with the lines of the platform. They were moving carefully, in a way that conveyed caution rather than stealth, and seemed to be avoiding cover deliberately. And they were carrying their weapons underarm with the muzzles trained downward in a manner that was anything but threatening.

"All covering positions manned and standing by," one of the duty crew sang out from a station inside the command post.

"LCP's standing by and ready to fire," another voice reported.

"Intruder defenses primed and ready to activate."

"Lock at condition orange and ready to close."

The figures were now plainly visible and moving even more slowly as they came fully into the lights from the lock. They were regular infantry, Lesley could see. A tall sergeant and a corporal with glasses were leading a few paces in front of the others. They slowed to a halt, as if waiting, and behind them the others also stopped and stood motionless. Lesley's jaw tightened as he stared down through the observation port. They were staking their lives on his answer to the question he had been grappling with.

Jarvis appeared suddenly in the doorway beside Chaurez. "Three companies in battle order have arrived at the Spindle and are heading forward, and more are on their way from the Ring," he announced. "Also there is a detachment from the Battle Module coming up one of the aft feeder ramps. They must be coming back to close the lock."

Lesley looked at the two of them, but they said nothing. There was nothing more they could tell him. He could close the lock and commit himself to the protection of the Battle Module's armaments; alternatively, with the added strength of the regulars who had arrived below, he could hold the lock open against the SDs coming from the Battle Module until the rest of the Army arrived. It was time for him to decide his answer.

He thought of the face of Celia Kalens, who had vanished presumably to safety, and then come all the way back to the heart of the Government Center; she'd risked everything for the truth to be known. Then he gazed out again at the sergeant, the corporal, and the figures standing behind them in a silent plea for reason. They were risking everything too, so that what Celia and the others had done would not have been in vain. Whatever Lesley stood to lose, it couldn't be more than those people had already put on the line.

"Tell the men to stand down," he said quietly to Jarvis. "Deprime the intruder systems and revert the lock to condition green. Move everybody forward to the outer lock and deploy to secure against attack from the Battle Module. Chaurez, get those men down there inside. We're going to need all the help we can get." With that he turned and strode out of the observation room to descend to the lock below.

Jarvis and Chaurez caught each other's eye. After a moment, Jarvis breathed a sigh of relief. Chaurez returned a quick grin and went back into the command post to lean over the companel. "Lieutenant," Oordsen demanded angrily from the screen. "Where is Major Lesley? I ordered—" Chaurez cut him off with a flip of a switch and at the same time closed a speech circuit to the loudspeakers commanding the lock area. "Okay, you guys, we're standing down," he said into the microphone stem projecting from the panel. "Get in here as quick as you can. We've got trouble coming up a feeder ramp on the other side."

As Chaurez finished speaking, an indicator announced an incoming call from the Government Center. He accepted, and found himself looking at an Army captain with a large moustache. "Forward Security Command Post," Chaurez acknowledged.

"Sirocco, D Company commander, Second Infantry Brigade. Is your commanding officer there?"

"I'm sorry, sir. He just went down to the lock."

"What about his adjutant?" Sirocco asked.

"Gone forward to the outer lock."

Sirocco looked worried. "Look, there is a force on its way forward to occupy the nose. We want to avoid any senseless bloodshed. Those locks must be kept open. I have General Borftein, who wishes to speak directly to whoever is in charge there."

"I can speak for them," Chaurez said. "You can tell the general that the news is good."

Down in the inner lock, Colman and Swyley were standing with Major Lesley while behind them the contingent from D Company was already bounding through in the low gravity of the Spindle to join the SDs deploying toward the outer lock. "You took a hell of a chance, Sergeant," Lesley said.

"Fifty-fifty," Colman answered. "It would have been zero the other way."

"You think pretty smart."

"We're all having to learn how to do that."

Lesley held his eye for a second, then nodded. "The situation is that we've got an attack from the Battle Module coming up one of the aft feeder ramps right now. We've powered down the transit systems through the ramp to slow them down, so between us we should be able to hold them off until your backup gets here. How long should they take?" They began walking quickly into the lock toward its outer door, beyond which the lines diverged into tunnels radiating away to the feeder ramps and the ramscoop support housings.

"How far have they penetrated?" Colman asked.

"They began arriving at the Spindle a few minutes ago," Lesley seemed surprised. "How come you didn't know?"

"It's been kind of. . . an unorthodox operation."

Ahead of them, Jarvis had positioned soldiers to cover all of the tunnel mouths, with the strongest force concentrated around the outlet from the feeder ramp along which the SDs from the Battle Module were approaching, and he had retired to a sheltered observation platform from which he could direct operations with a clear view into the tunnel. Lesley, Colman, and Swyley moved behind a stanchion where Driscoll and a couple more from D Company were crouched with their weapons. A few seconds later the soldiers all around tensed expectantly.

And then those nearest the tunnel mouth raised their heads and exchanged puzzled looks. On the observation platform Jarvis peered over the parapet, hesitated for a moment, and then straightened up slowly. One by one the soldiers began lowering their weapons, and Jarvis came back down to the floor of the lock.

An SD major with a smoke-blackened face and one of his sleeves covered in blood emerged unsteadily from the tunnel mouth; immediately behind him were four more SDs looking disheveled and one of them also bloodstained around the head. Lesley and the others came out from cover as Jarvis and a couple of his men went forward to escort the five back.

Lesley and the major obviously knew each other. "Brad," Lesley said. "What in hell's happened? We were expecting a fight."

"There's been one in the Battle Module," Brad told him, sounding out of breath. "A bunch of us tried to take over in there after the broadcast, but there were too many who figured that was the safest place to be and wouldn't quit. It was all we could do to get out."

"How many of you are there?" Lesley asked.

"I'm not sure . . . maybe fifty. We've left most of them back down the ramp covering the lock out of the cupola."

"You mean the way's clear right down to the Battle Module?" Colman asked.

Brad nodded. "But Stormbel's people are in the cupola. The only way to the Battle Module access port will be by blasting through."

Lesley turned to Jarvis. "Power the tubes back up and get some more guys down there fast. Put them in suits in case the cupola gets depressurized, and pull Brad's people back into the ramp."

"We've got a section already suited up," Colman said. "Are those cars running?" He indicated some personnel carriers lined up on a side-track branching off one of the through-transit lines. Jarvis nodded. Colman turned to Swyley. "Get the section loaded up and move them on down the ramp." Swyley and Jarvis hurried away.

"The Army's on its way through the Spindle," Lesley said to Brad. "They should start arriving here any time now."

"Let's hope they don't waste any time," Brad replied. "Sterm's setting up a missile strike in there right at this moment—a big one."

Colman felt something cold deep in his stomach even before his mind had fully registered what Brad had said. "Sterm?" he repeated numbly. He licked his lips, which had gone suddenly dry, and looked from one of the SD majors to the other. "You mean he's already in there?"

Lesley nodded. "He's been there all evening. Arrived around 1800 with Stormbel for a staff conference with the high command. They're all in there . . ." He frowned at the expression on Colman's face. "Nobody knew?"

Colman shook his head slowly. There had been too much to think about in too little time. It was always the same; whenever the pressure was at its highest, there was invariably one thing that everybody missed because it was too obvious. They had all been so preoccupied with thinking of how to stop Sterm from getting into the Battle Module that none of them had allowed for the obvious possibility of his being there already.

"What's the target for the missile strike?" Colman asked hoarsely.

"I don't know," Brad replied. "I haven't been in on it at the top level. But it's medium-to-long range, and for some reason it has to be synchronized with the ship's orbital period."

Colman groaned. The target could only be the *Kuan-yin*. If the strike succeeded it would leave Sterm in sole command of the only strategic weapons left on the planet, and in a position to dictate any terms he chose; if it failed, then Sterm and his last few would take the whole of the *Mayflower II* with them when the *Kuan-yin* rose above Chiron's rim to retaliate. Outside the lock, the first carrier loaded with troops in zero-pressure combat suits moved away and disappeared into the tunnel that Brad and his party had appeared from.

"You look as if you might know something about it," Lesley said to Colman. "Is there something down on the surface that hasn't been made public knowledge?"

"No . . ." Colman shook his head distantly. "It's too much to go into right now. Look—"

An SD sergeant interrupted from behind Lesley. "They're here sir. Carriers coming through the lock." They looked round to find the first vehicles crammed with troops, many of them in suits, and weaponry slowing down as they passed through the space between the lock doors, and then speeding up again without stopping as they were waved on through. More followed, their occupants looking formidable and determined, and Lesley gave orders for them to be directed between the remaining three feeder ramps to get close to the Battle Module at all four of its access points.

Then Colman's communicator started bleeping. Bernard Fallows was calling from the Communications Center. "I guess you did it," he said. "But it's not over yet. We've found out where Sterm is."

"So have I," Colman said. "And it's worse than that. He's setting up a missile strike right now. The target has to be the *Kuan-yin.*"

Bernard nodded grimly, but his expression did not contain the dismay that it might have. Evidently he had been half-prepared for the news. "Borftein's been checking on that possibility," he said. "It'll be forty minutes before the *Kuan-yin* goes behind the rim. Sterm won't launch before then."

"Will the Chironians let him wait that long?" Colman asked. "Do they know he's in there and what it means?"

Bernard shook his head. "No. We're in touch with them, but Wellesley vetoed any mention of it." Colman nodded. He wouldn't have risked their deciding to fire first either. Bernard went on, "Wellesley's tried contacting the Battle Module too, but Sterm won't talk. We figure he'll keep the module attached until after the attack goes in—in other words if he doesn't pull it off and gets blasted, we all get blasted. The same thing applies if the Chironians decide to press the button. We have to assume he's on a forty-minute countdown. Hanlon and Armley are on their way there, and Sirocco left a few minutes ago. Borftein is sending through everybody he can scrape together. What are the chances?"

A carrier full of combat-suited infantry nursing antitank missile launchers and demolition equipment slid through the lock and lurched onto a branch leading to one of the Battle Module's forward ramps. "Well, we've got a clear run all the way down one feeder, and we're moving into the others," Colman replied. "There's been some fighting inside the Battle Module, and a lot of the guys got out. We have to hope that there aren't enough left to stop us from blowing our way in through four places at once. Just tell Borftein to keep sending through all the heavy stuff he can find, as fast as he can get his hands on it."

❂ CHAPTER THIRTY-EIGHT ❂

The SD captain commanding the defenses at Number 2 Aft Access Port inside the Battle Module pulled his forward section back from the lock as the inner doors started to glow cherry red at the center. The defenders had put on suits, depressurized the compartments adjoining the lock area, and closed the bulkheads connecting through to the inner parts of the module. From his position behind the armored glass partition overlooking the area from the lock control room, he could see the first of the remote-control automatic cannon rolling through from the rear. "Hurry up with those RCCs," he shouted into his helmet microphone. "Yellow section take up covering positions. Green and Red prepare to fall back to the longitudinal bulkhead locks."

"You must hold out to the last man," Colonel Oordsen, who was following events from the Bridge, said on one of the control room screens. "We're almost ready to detach the module."

"We will if we have to, sir," the captain assured him.

Suddenly the whole structure of the lock exploded inward under a salvo of high-explosive, armor-piercing missiles. Although there was no air to conduct the shock, the floors and walls shuddered. Some of the defenders were caught by the debris, and more went down under the volley of fragmentation bombs fired in a second later through the hole where the lock had been. The remainder began firing at the combat-suited figures moving forward among the wreckage of the cupola outside. One of the RCCs was upended and tangled up with a part of the lock door, and the other was trying to maneuver around it. "Red section, move to fallback positions," the captain yelled. "Covering—"

Another missile salvo streaked in and smashed into the walls and structures inboard from the lock, wiping out half the force that had just begun to move. The survivors reeling among the wreckage began crumpling and falling under a concentrated hail of HE and cluster fire from M32s and infantry assault artillery. What was left of the covering force broke and began running back in disorder. "Get everybody out! Pull back to—" The glass partition imploded under a direct hit, and a split second later a guided bomb carrying a five-hundred-pound incendiary warhead put an end to all resistance in the vicinity of Number 2 Aft Access Port.

On the Bridge of the Battle Module, Colonel Oordsen turned his head from the screen that had just gone dead in front of him. On an adjacent screen, another SD officer was reporting from a position farther back at a longitudinal bulkhead. "Negative at Number Two Aft," Oordsen said to Sterm, who was watching grim faced. "They'll be through there in a matter of minutes."

"How long before the *Kuan-yin* is eclipsed?" Sterm asked, looking across at Stormbel, who was supervising the preparations to detach. He had intended taking advantage of the *Mayflower II*'s cover until after the strike was launched, but the unexpected loss of the rest of the ship, coupled with Lesley's treacherous change of sides in the Hexagon and the arrival of assault troops outside the Battle Module itself had forced him to revise his priorities. There would be little point in destroying the *Kuan-yin* if he lost the Battle Module in the process.

"Eight minutes," Stormbel replied. "But its reaction dish is still aimed away from us. We are now ready to detach."

"You are certain that we could make the cover of Chiron safely?"

"The *Kuan-yin* will not be able to maneuver instantly," Stormbel answered. "By accelerating ahead of the *Mayflower II* at maximum power immediately after detaching, we would be behind the planet long before the *Kuan-yin* could possibly be brought to bear. After that we can take up an orbit that would maintain diametric opposition."

"Number One Forward Port has surrendered," Oordsen said tightly, taking in another report. "The firing has stopped there. Nickolson is leading his men out, including his reserve. We have no choice."

Sterm's eyes smoldered. "I want a full record kept of every officer who deserts," he reminded Stormbel. "The ones in the Government Center, the one in Vandenberg, Lesley in the Hexagon, that one there—all of them." His voice was calm but all the more menacing for its iciness. "They will answer for this when the time comes. General, detach the Battle Module immediately and proceed as planned."

Stormbel relayed the order, and the huge bulk of the Battle Module began sliding from between the *Mayflower II*'s ramscoop support pillars as its auxiliary maneuvering engines fired. The sound of twisted steel scraping across the outside of its hull reverberated throughout the module's stern section as one of the feeder ramps, none of which was retracted, first bent, and then crumpled. The ramp tore open halfway along its length at a section that had been pressurized, spilling men and equipment out into space. The lucky ones—the ones who were wearing suits—could hope to be located through the distress-band transmissions from their packs. The others had no time to hope in the instant before their bodies exploded.

"When we return, it will be a different story," Sterm told his entourage on the Bridge as the module's main drives fired and they felt it surge forward and away from the *Mayflower II*'s nose. "But first, we have to deal with our Chironian . . . friends. What is the report on the *Kuan-yin?*"

"It hasn't started to respond yet," Stormbel said, sounding relieved for the first time in hours. "Perhaps we took them by surprise after all." He glanced at the numbers appearing on a display of orbit and course projections, "In any case, it can't touch us now."

Sterm nodded slowly in satisfaction. "Excellent. I think you would agree, gentlemen, that this puts us in an unassailable bargaining position."

※　※　※

In the *Mayflower II*'s Communications Center, Borftein, Wellesley, and the others who had been coordinating activities all over the ship and down on the surface watched and listened tensely as pandemonium poured from the screens around them. Spacesuited figures were cartwheeling away from the mangled remains of one feeder ramp, and the exposed interiors of the cupolas at the ends of the others; all showed battle damage and one of them was partly blown away. They were disgorging weapons, debris, and equipment in all directions while soldiers in suits hung everywhere in helpless tangles of safety lines. "Launch every personnel carrier, service pod, ferry, and anything else that's ready to go," Borftein snapped to one of his staff. "Get them from Vandenberg or anywhere else you have to. I want every one of those men picked up. Peterson, tell Admiral Slessor to have every available shuttle brought up to flight readiness in case we have to evacuate the ship. And find out how many more we can get up here from Canaveral."

"Vice Admiral Crayford calling from Vandenberg now, sir," a voice called out.

"The Chironians on channel eight are requesting a report, sir."

"Major Lesley calling from the nose, sir."

"Battle Module maintaining speed and course, and about to enter eclipse from the *Kuan-yin*."

Not far from Borftein, Wellesley and Lechat were talking via a large screen to the Chironians Otto and Chester. Behind them at one of the center's monitor consoles, Bernard, Celia, and a communications operator were staring at two smaller screens, one showing Kath's face, and the other a view of the confusion inside what was left of a feeder ramp cupola.

On the second screen Hanlon, in a spacesuit blackened by scorch marks, was clinging in the foreground to the remains of a buckled metal structure sticking out into empty space, and hauling on a pair of intertwined lines with his free arm, while behind him other soldiers were pulling figures back into the shattered cupola and helping them climb to the entrance into the feeder ramp. "I think this might be the man himself now," Hanlon's voice said from the grille by the screen.

"Ah, yes . . . a little the worse for wear, but he'll be as good as new." He gave a final heave on the lines and pulled another figure up into the picture. Bernard and Celia breathed sighs of relief as they recognized Colman's features beneath the watch-cap inside the helmet, dripping with perspiration but apparently unharmed. Colman anchored himself to another part of the structure that Hanlon was on, unhitched his safety line and untangled it from the other one, and then helped Hanlon pull it in to produce another spacesuited figure, this time upside down and with a pudgy, woebegone face that was somehow managing to keep a thick pair of glasses wedged crookedly across its nose.

"Hanlon's got him," Bernard said to the screen that was showing Kath. "He looks as if he's all right. They've got Swyley too. He seems okay."

Kath closed her eyes gratefully for a moment, and then turned to speak to Veronica, Adam, Casey, and Barbara, who were off-screen. "They've found Steve. He's all right."

Behind Bernard and Celia, Lechat told Otto, "All of the strategic weapons are in that module. The remainder of this ship represents no threat whatsoever."

"We are aware of that," Otto said.

"We had to try," Wellesley insisted from beside Lechat. "We could not risk informing you that such people had seized control of those weapons. The decision was mine and nobody else's."

"I think I'd have done the same thing," Otto told him.

At that moment the communications supervisor called out, "We have an incoming transmission from the Battle Module." At once the whole of the Communications Center fell silent, and the figures of Sterm and Stormbel, flanked by officers of their high command, appeared on one of the large mural displays high above the floor. Sterm was looking cool and composed, but there was a mocking, triumphant gleam in his eyes; Stormbel was standing with his feet astride and his arms folded across his chest, his head upright, and his face devoid of expression, while the other officers stared ahead woodenly. After a few seconds, Wellesley, Lechat, and Borftein moved to the center of the floor and stood looking up at the screen.

Celia's face had drawn itself into a tight, bloodless mask as she stared at the image of Sterm. "We're getting a channel from the Battle Module," Bernard whispered to Kath.

"I know," Kath told him. "He's through to Otto and Chester as well via one of our relay satellites. It's a three-way hookup."

"A good try, Wellesley," Sterm said from the large screen. "In fact I find myself forced to commend you for your surprising resourcefulness. Unfortunately from your point of view, however, we now see it was in vain." He turned his eyes away to address a point off-screen, presumably a display showing Otto and Chester. "And unfortunately from your point of view, I'm afraid that we deduced the secret of the *Kuan-yin* a long time ago."

"Bernard," Kath said quietly from the console screen.

He turned his head back to look at her. "Yes?"

"Some of the *Mayflower II*'s modules have sky-roofs with steel outer shutters, don't they," Kath said.

Bernard frowned uncomprehendingly. "Yes . . . Why . . . What—"

Kath's voice remained low but took on a note of urgency. "Make sure all of them are closed. Do it now." Bernard shook his head, mystified, and started asking questions again. "Just do it," Kath said, cutting him off. "There might not be much time."

Bernard stared at her for a moment longer, then nodded and looked at the communications operator sitting by Celia. "Can you get Admiral Slessor on line here?" The operator nodded and sat forward to begin entering a code.

From the center of the floor Wellesley asked, "What do you want?"

"Good." Sterm nodded approvingly. "I detect a cooperative disposition." He turned his face toward the Chironians. "I take it that we are all beginning to understand one another."

"We're listening," Otto replied tonelessly.

"Perhaps it would be of benefit if I were to summarize the situation that now exists," Sterm suggested. "We command a complete strategic arsenal, the potency of which I do not have to spell out to you, and the only weapon capable of opposing us is now neutralized. Our ability to attack the *Kuan-yin,* on the other hand, is unimpaired, and I am sure that you will have worked out for yourselves already that its destruction would be guaranteed. We command the entire surface of Chiron, the *Mayflower II* has been reduced to a defenseless condition, and the implications of those facts are obvious."

Sterm allowed a few seconds for his words to sink in, and then made a slight tossing motion with his hands as if to convey to those watching him the hopelessness of their position. "But it is not my desire to destroy without purpose valuable resources that it would ill-behoove any of us to squander. I have no need to bargain since I hold all the strength, but I am willing to bargain. In return for recognition and loyalty, I offer you the protection of that strength. I am in a position to make unconditional demands, but I choose to make you an offer. So, you see, my terms are not ungenerous."

"Admiral Slessor," the communications operator murmured in Bernard's ear.

Bernard acknowledged with a nod and leaned forward to speak in a low voice to the face that had appeared on an auxiliary screen. "This is urgent, Admiral. Make sure that all the sky-roof outer shutters are closed immediately."

Slessor recognized Bernard as one of Merrick's former officers. "Why?" he asked, looking puzzled. "What are you doing there . . . Fallows, isn't it?"

"I'm not sure why, but it's important . . . from the Chironians."

Slessor's brow furrowed more deeply. He hesitated, thought for a moment, and then nodded. "Very well, I'll see it's done." He moved away from view.

"That's a strange offer," Otto said to Sterm. "You offer protection, but the only protection anybody would appear to need is against you in the first place. After all, you've just told us that you hold all the weapons. You seem to entertain a curious notion of logic."

For the first time a hint of anger flashed across Sterm's face. "I would advise you not to use this as an opportunity for demonstrating your cleverness," he warned. He allowed himself a moment to calm down. Then he resumed speaking more slowly. "Earth is tearing itself apart because it has failed to produce the strong leader who would crush"—Sterm raised a hand and closed his fist in front of his face—" the petty rivalries and jealousies which throughout history have frustrated any chance of expression of the full potential grandeur of collective unity and power. Earth has always been in turmoil because it has inherited a legacy of chaos of global proportions against which the efforts of even its most capable organizers have been of no avail. Is that the future that you would wish upon Chiron?

"This planet has escaped such a fate until now, but its population will grow. It has a chance to profit from what Earth has learned, and to plant the seeds of a strong, unified, and unshakable order now, before the diseases of disunity have had a chance to germinate and become virulent. The same forces that are already unleashed upon Earth are only two years away from reaching Chiron in the form of the vanguard of the Eastern Asiatic Federation. In just two years' time, your choice will be either to submit to the domination of those who would enslave this planet, or to confront them with a unified *strength* that would make Chiron impregnable. Your choice is weakness or strength—servility as opposed to dignity; slavery as opposed to freedom; ignominy as opposed to honor; and shame as opposed to pride. Weakness or strength. I offer the latter alternatives."

Sterm's eyes took on a distant light, and his breathing quickened visibly. "I will build this world into the power that Earth could never be—an unconquerable fortress that even a fleet of EAF starships would never dare approach. I will build for you the first-ever stellar empire here at Centauri, one people united under one leader . . . united in will, united in action, and united in purpose. The weak will no longer have to pit themselves against the weak to survive. The weak will be protected by the strength that will come from that unity, and by that same unity the strong who protect them will be invincible. That . . . is what I offer to share."

"Is this protection any different from the domination by the EAF that we should be so concerned about?" Chester asked.

Sterm looked displeased at the response. "Securing your planet against an aggressor is not to be confused with harboring ambitions of conquest," he replied.

Otto shook his head. "If Earth is tearing itself apart, it is because its people allowed themselves to believe the same self-fulfilling prophecies that you are asking us to accept, Mr. Sterm. But we reject them. We need no more protection from you against the people in the EAF starship than they need from their Sterms to protect them against us. We have no need of that kind of strength. Is it strength for neighbors to fortify their homes against each other, or is it paranoia? You must feel very insecure to wish to fortify an entire star system."

Sterm's mouth clamped into a grim, downturned line. "The EAF is committed to a dogma of conquest," he said. "They understand no language apart from force. You cannot hope to deal with them by any other means."

"On the contrary, Mr. Sterm, they understand the same language that people everywhere speak," Chester said. "We will deal with them in the same way that we have already dealt with you."

"And exactly what is that supposed to mean?" Sterm demanded.

Otto smiled humorlessly. "Take a look at the other lunatics around you," he suggested. "What happened to all the people? Where did your army go? They're all Chironians now. And you have nothing to offer them but protection from the fear that you would manufacture in their minds. But they have Chironian minds. They see that the fear is your fear, not theirs; and it is you who are in need of protection, not they."

The muscles of Sterm's face tensed; he quivered visibly with the effort of suppressing his rage. "I was willing to bargain," he grated. "Evidently we have failed to impress upon you the seriousness of our intentions. Very well, you leave me no further choice. Perhaps a demonstration will serve to convince you." He turned to Stormbel. "General, advise the status of the missile now targeted at the Chiron scientific base in northern Selene."

"Primed and ready for immediate launch," Stormbel replied in a monotone. "Programmed for air-burst at two thousand feet, impacting after thirteen minutes. Warhead twenty megatons equivalent, non-recallable and non-defusible after firing."

"Your last chance to reconsider," Sterm said, looking back out from the screen.

"We have nothing to reconsider," Otto replied calmly.

Sterm's face darkened, and his mouth twisted into an ugly grimace. His suave veneer seemed to peel away as his eyes widened, and for an instant, even from where he was sitting, Bernard found himself looking directly into the depths of a mind that was completely insane. He shivered involuntarily. Beside him Celia gripped his arm.

"General," Sterm ordered. "Launch the missile in sixty seconds."

Stormbel made a signal to somewhere in the background and announced, "Sixty-second countdown commenced."

"The countdown can be halted at any time," Sterm informed them.

Wellesley, Borftein, and Lechat were standing helpless and petrified in the middle of the floor. "He'll do it," Celia whispered, horrified, to Bernard.

Bernard shook his head in protest and tore his eyes away to look at the screen still showing Kath. "You can't let this happen," he implored. "Those are your own people up there in Selene. This will just be the first example. Then it'll get worse."

"We don't intend to let it happen," Kath said.

"But you are. What can you do to stop it?"

"You've already worked most of that out."

Bernard shook his head again. "I don't know what you mean. The *Kuan-yin* can't fire effectively. It's eclipsed from the Battle Module."

"It couldn't fire anyway," Kath replied. "It's modifications aren't completed yet. We've already told you that."

Bernard frowned at her in bemusement. Nothing was making any sense. "But—its antimatter drive . . . that's your weapon, isn't it?"

"We never said it was," Kath replied. "You assumed it. So did Sterm." Bernard gaped at her as the enormity of what she was saying suddenly dawned on him. Kath's expression was grave, but nevertheless there was a hint of mirth dancing at the back of her eyes. "We could hardly disguise our scientific work," she said. "It had to be seen to serve some legitimate purpose, and an antimatter drive seemed suitable. But the *Kuan-yin* project has been low down on our list of priorities."

Bernard's eyes widened incredulously. "But if the *Kuan-yin* isn't finished, then what made the crater in Remus?"

"Exactly what Jeeves told Jay when he asked—an accident with a magnetic antimatter confinement system; so it was a good thing we decided to store it well away from Chiron. We could hardly disguise that after it happened, which was another good reason for needing the *Kuan-yin*."

"We—we never believed that story," Bernard said weakly.

"Well, that was up to you. We told you."

Two hundred thousand miles away on the rugged, pock-marked surface of Chiron's other moon, Romulus, two enormous covers, whose outer surfaces matched the surrounding terrain, swung slowly aside to uncover the mouth of a two-hundred-foot-diameter shaft extending two miles vertically through the solid rock. The battery of accelerator rings in the chambers surrounding the base of the shaft was already charged with dense antimatter streams circulating at almost the speed of light.

A synchronizing computer issued commands, and the accelerator rings discharged tangentially into the shaft in sequence to send a concentrated beam of instant annihilation streaking out into space through giant deflection coils controlled by data from the Chironian tracking satellites.

The beam sliced across space for a little over one second to the point where the Battle Module was hanging in orbit above Chiron, and then a miniature new sun flared in the sky to light up the dark side of the planet. The flash of gamma rays ionized the upper atmosphere, and the sky above Chiron glowed in streaks that extended for thousands of miles. Sensitive radiation-monitoring instruments were burned out all over the outside of the *Mayflower II*, and because of the electrical upheaval, it was twelve hours before communications with the surface could be resumed.

◈ CHAPTER THIRTY-NINE ◈

Wellesley stood to deliver his final address from in front of the Mission Director's seat at the center of the raised dais facing out over the Congressional Hall of the *Mayflower II*'s Government Center. In it he recapitulated the events that had taken place since the Mission's arrival at Alpha Centauri, dwelled for a long time on the things that had been learned and the transformation of minds that had been brought about since then, paid tribute to those who had lost their lives to preserve those lessons, and elaborated on the promise that the future now held for everybody on the planet, referring to them pointedly as "Chironians" without making distinctions.

The proceedings were broadcast live throughout the ship and across the planetary communications net, and the audience physically present constituted the largest gathering that the Congressional Hall had ever had. All of the members who had been absent had returned for the occasion, and the only seats left vacant were those of the Deputy Mission Director, the Director of Liaison, the Commanding General Special Duty Force, and two others who had chosen to throw in their lot with Sterm. Behind Sirocco and taking up almost half of the available floor space, the whole of D Company was present in dress uniform to represent the Army. Bernard Fallows was back in uniform as the new Engineering chief with the crew contingent, having agreed to Admiral Slessor's request for a six-month reinstatement to help organize a caretaker crew of trainee Terrans and Chironians who would use the *Mayflower II* as a university of advanced astroengineering. Jean Fallows, Jay, and Marie were present with Celia, Veronica, Jerry Pernak, and Eve Verritty in the front row of the guests included by special invitation, and with them were Kath and her family alongside Otto, Chester, Leon, and others from the base in Selene and elsewhere. As if to underline and reecho Wellesley's acknowledgment of how the future would be, there was no segregation of Terrans and Chironians into groups; and there were many children from both worlds.

Wellesley concluded his formal speech and stood looking around the hall for a moment to allow a lighter mood to settle. In the last few days some of the color had returned to his face, his posture had become more upright and at ease, and his frame seemed to have shed a burden of years. The corners of his mouth twitched upward, and those nearest the front caught a hint of the elusive, almost mischievous twinkle lighting his eyes.

"And now I have one final task to perform," he said. He paused again, and the hall grew curious and attentive, sensing that something unexpected was about to take place. "May I remind the assembly that the declaration of a state of emergency has never been revoked, and that therefore, by the processes that we are still formally pledged to uphold, that emergency condition continues to remain in force, along with its attendant suspension of Congress and the vesting of all congressional authority in me." Puzzled expressions greeted his words, and a ripple of surprised murmurings ran around the hall. "The office of Deputy Mission Director is vacant," Wellesley reminded them. "Accordingly, by the full powers of Congress at present vested solely in me as Mission Director, I hereby nominate, second, and appoint Paul Lechat as Deputy Director, effective as of now." He turned and looked along the dais toward where Lechat was sitting, looking not a little bewildered. "Congratulations, Paul. And now would you kindly take your rightful place." He gestured at the empty chair next to him. Lechat rose up, moved along behind the intervening places, and sat down in the Deputy Director's seat, all the time shaking his head at the other members to convey that he was as confused about what Wellesley was doing as they were. Wellesley looked slowly around the hall one last time. "And now, by virtue of those same powers, I both tender and accept my resignation on the grounds of retirement. It has been an honor and a privilege to serve you all. Thank you." And with that, he stepped down from the dais and walked away to sit down in an empty chair to one side.

Lechat stared at the Director's seat next to him, and while he was still turning his head perplexedly from one side to the other, the first approving murmurs and ripples of applause began coming from among the members as one by one they realized what it meant. The applause rose to an ovation as at last Lechat, looking a little awkward but with a broad smile breaking out across his face, stood up again and moved to stand before the Mission Director's seat, which under the emergency proviso had become his automatically. Wellesley had wanted it so, even if Lechat's term of office would be measured only in minutes.

Lechat waited for the noise to die away and managed to bring his feelings under control sufficiently to muster a semblance of dignity appropriate to the moment. But simplicity and brevity were appropriate too. "I am honored and privileged by this appointment, and I will dedicate myself for the duration of my term to serving the best interests of our people to the best of my ability," he announced. "In accordance with that promise, my first official act is to restore the full powers of Congress as previously suspended, and my second is to declare the state of emergency ended as of this moment." Another round of applause, this time briefer than before, greeted the statement. "Next, I have two proposals to put to the vote of the assembly," Lechat said. "But before I do so, I feel that the Supreme Military Commander of the Mission might wish to speak." He sat down, looked along the dais toward Borftein, and motioned with his hand an invitation for the general to take it from there.

Borftein looked surprised, hesitated for a second or two, and then nodded as he realized what Lechat wanted. He rose slowly to his feet and paused to collect his words. "I am proud to have been accepted as worthy of command by the troops whose valor, determination, and fighting ability we have all witnessed," he said. "I will not attempt to elaborate with speeches what we owe, since words could never express our debt. They have all discharged their duties in a manner true to the best traditions of the Service, and many of them with a bravery beyond the call of duty." He paused, and his face became more solemn. "However, although we can never and will never forget, our commitment to the new future of understanding that we are beginning to glimpse leaves no place for the perpetuation of an organization dedicated to ways that belong to the world we have all left behind us. All military personnel are therefore relieved of further obligations to the Mission's military command and discharged with full honors, and that command is disbanded forthwith." The hall remained quiet while Borftein sat down. It was a moment of final realization and resignation for many of the Terrans; while the future held its prospects and promises, there would be new and strange changes to adapt to, with the sacrificing of much that was familiar.

Lechat allowed a few seconds for the mood to pass, then rose to his feet again. "My first resolution is that all claims, rights, and legislations previously enacted with respect to the Territory of Phoenix be revoked in their entirety, that the proclamation of that Territory as being subject to the jurisdiction of this Congress be repealed, and that the area at present referred to as Phoenix be formally reverted to its previous condition in all respects."

"I second the motion," a voice called out promptly.

"Those for?" Lechat invited. All of the members' hands went up. "Against?" There were no hands. "The resolution is passed," Lechat announced. Phoenix had officially become a part of Chiron once again.

Lechat slowly scanned the expectant faces. They all knew what was coming next. "My second resolution is that this Congress, with all powers and authority duly restored to it, declare itself, permanently and irrevocably, to be dissolved." The motion was passed unanimously.

The colonization of Chiron was over.

◎ EPILOGUE ◎

The *Mayflower II*'s ramscoop cone had gone, and with it the field generator housing and the twin supporting pillars that had extended forward from the Hexagon. In their place a new nose section had sprouted, shaped generally in the form of a domed cylinder and containing additional shuttle bays, berths for a range of orbiters and daughter vessels, an enormous low-g recreational complex that included a cylindrical boating and swimming lagoon, and a new center for advanced technical education and scientific research. The stern of the ship had undergone even vaster changes, its original fusion drive having been replaced by a scaled-up antimatter system developed from the prototype successfully tested on the *Kwan-yin*.

Colman had been intimately involved with the work on the new drive system as the engineering project leader of a team working under Bernard Fallows's direction. He had brought Kath and their four-year-old son Alex up to the ship to be present with him at the unveiling ceremony being held in the main concourse of the new nose section. Many of the faces from five years back were there too. Few of them had lost contact during that time, but it was rare for so many of them to be in the same place at the same time, except for their annual reunions. Most of D Company had assembled for the event—Sirocco, with Shirley and their twin daughters; Hanlon, who now instructed at the martial arts academy in Franklin, with Janet and their two children; Driscoll, who had taken a rest from his touring magic show, one of Chiron's major entertainment attractions; Stanislau, now a computer software expert; Swyley, who directed and produced movies, usually about the American underworld, along with a couple of the pretty girls who seemed to surround him wherever he went; . . . and there were others. Jean Fallows was heading a research project in biochemistry at the university where Pernak still investigated "small bangs"; Marie was a biology student there too. Jay, now twenty and with a young son, had built an old-fashioned railroad into Franklin—now a sizable and thriving city—which used full-scale steam locomotives and provided a sight-seeing attraction and historical curiosity that every visitor to the area had to ride on at least once. Veronica, a practicing architect, was there with Casey, Adam, and Barbara. Celia had declined to return to the ship but was watching from the home that she shared with Lechat on the coast; and Wellesley had taken a trip from his farm in Occidena to see his old ship recommissioned and renamed.

Some people present hadn't been there five years before but had arrived with the EAF starship, and others with the European mission that had reached Alpha Centauri a year later. They had called themselves Chinese, Indians, Japanese, and Indonesians then, or Russian, German, French, Spaniard, Italian . . . but now they were all simply Chironians. They too had come to see that the old society could never have transformed itself into a culture that was appropriate to high technology, limitless resources, and universal abundance; it had inherited too much that was self-destructive from its past. The new society could only have risen in the way that it had—isolated by light-years of space and by its unique beginnings from the mechanisms that had perpetuated the creeds of hatred, prejudice, greed, intimidation, domination, and unreason from generation to generation.

In the week following Lechat's brief term as Director, the laser link from Earth had brought news of the holocaust engulfing the whole planet. Then the signals had ceased, and for five years there had been nothing. No doubt many pockets of humanity had managed to survive, but mankind's first attempt to establish an advanced civilization had ended in failure . . . or almost in failure, for it had served its purpose; it had lifted humankind from its primitive, animal beginnings to a level where human, not animal, values could evolve, and it had hurled a seed of itself outward to take root, grow, and blossom at a distant star. And then it had died, as it had to.

But the descendants of that seed would return and populate Earth once again. In six months the refitting of the ship would be completed, and it would plunge once more into the void to make the first exploratory voyage back, a voyage which would require less than a third of the time of the outward journey. Lechat would be the Mission Director, Fallows the Chief of Engineering, and Adam would head one of the scientific teams. Colman would be returning too, as an Engineering officer; Kath would fulfill her dream of seeing Earth; and Alex would be about Jay's age by the time they returned to Chiron. Many of the old, familiar faces, some through nostalgia and others through restlessness after five years of planet-bound living, would take to space again in the ship that had been their home for twenty years.

Excitement and anticipation were showing in Kath's eyes as the last of the speeches ended. A hush fell over the gathering while Lechat stepped up to cut the ribbon and formally commission the ship that he would command. Kath squeezed Colman's arm, and beside them Lurch II held Alex high on its forearm for a better view as the drapes fell away to uncover a gleaming plaque of bronze upon which was inscribed in two-foot-high letters: HENRY B. CONGREVE—the new name of the ship that would bring Earth's children home.